A.C. DONAUBAUER
Rifts – Book 4

Rifts -
The Order: Book 4

A.C. Donaubauer

First published in as ebook in March 2017
Paperback
2nd edition

Copyright © 2019
     Astrid Donaubauer-Grobner
     Waltenhofengasse 3/3/3302
     1100 Vienna, Austria

The author online:
     www.ac-donaubauer.com
     www.facebook.com/acdonaubauer

Cover: Biserka Design

Editing: Jürgen Donaubauer
Proofreading: Philip Scott

Druck: CreateSpace, ein Unternehmen von Amazon.com
Februar 2019

ISBN 978-3-904142-08-3

For Heidi. Thanks for once again enriching my life.

Let's not wait for 15 years next time...

CHAPTER 1

An Unpleasant Arrival

Enric stood on deck watching the sun set. He marvelled at the colourfully painted layers of red, orange and yellow, the effects of light and shadow among the clouds and the reflections on the calm surface of the sea. Sunsets at home just didn't appear like this; he wondered why they were that much more spectacular here. Maybe he could find a book on that somewhere.

It had been a while since he had taken the time to watch a sunset. Sunrises, yes. He was an early riser and had for many years lived with bedroom windows angled in the right direction. But hardly ever sunsets. There was always work to do, though he had pretty much stopped working late since he had started living with Eryn. She was a good motivation for finishing on time, a reason to come home.

Right now she was asleep in their cabin. Pe'tala had observed her being physically sick several times and then sent her off to sleep with a little magic, cutting off her protests in mid-sentence. Eryn had been too surprised to raise any of her defences in time and had just sunk limply. At least he wouldn't be the one to pay for that later.

He had been worried about taking two pregnant women along on the long journey to Takhan, but so far everything had gone well enough.

Which was a relief as the start had not been too promising. While Junar had been more than willing to take a seat in the coach they had arranged, Eryn had not been thrilled about being expected to travel in it as well. She had tried to argue that fresh air would be beneficial for herself and the child, but Pe'tala had explained that several hours of riding in unfamiliar surroundings with a horse she didn't know was not a wise thing to undertake in her current condition. If she lost concentration and made a minor slip or if the horse was startled - which was quite a realistic chance with a mountain cat trotting nearby - she might fall and get hurt. He had listened to their discussion for a few minutes and then decided to intervene. He had offered Eryn two choices how to travel to Bonhet, neither of which contained the option of her being on the back of a horse: either awake or asleep.

1

She had flashed him an evil look and boarded the coach none too happily. Junar had been vexed about Eryn not wanting to ride in the coach with her and thus they had started the journey with three uneasy men, an unnerved healer and two grumpy, expectant women.

Vern had initially wanted to go in the coach as well as he had wanted to use the time for some reading, but had thought better of it when the two women started bickering. Enric hadn't blamed him. He wouldn't have endured this voluntarily for two days, either.

Junar had at one point started crying, something she was prone to lately, and Orrin had asked to delay their departure for some minutes so as to comfort her, while giving angry looks at Eryn at the same time.

That Eryn had found it necessary to point out to the others that this was exactly the reason why she didn't want to be stuck with the other woman in a small, enclosed space for two days had not exactly helped, either.

Vern had at one point given Enric a pleading look and asked whether sending Eryn to sleep was still open for discussion. Enric had told him that he was welcome to try that any time, as he himself was not willing to endure her wrath once she woke up again.

That had made Eryn angry at Vern. All of which led to a very disgruntled group departing the city.

They had stopped several times for Junar to get rid of parts of her breakfast again and had thereby needed around an hour longer than planned to reach their destination in the evening.

The second day had been easier as Junar had resorted to making do with a few slices of bread throughout the day to keep her stomach from rebelling too much. She had then devoured three helpings of the stew the publican in Bonhet had served in the evening to make up for her sparse fare during the day.

Eryn had been immensely surprised at how much Bonhet had changed since they last passed through during their first journey to Takhan about nine months ago. More people, more buildings and a general busyness that had not been there several months earlier.

Enric had taken a walk through the village with her, showing her the buildings he had constructed, giving her a tour through the shipyard and the tally house, strolling along the piers and jetties.

She had been pleased with how the workers had treated him: with respect but without the reflexive awe and admiration his rank inspired in most people back in the city of Anyueel. Not being constantly reminded of the importance and wealth of magicians had made country people act in a more down-to-earth manner when dealing with them. It probably also helped that their travelling clothes were not as elegant and showy as their usual attire. Wearing what they did, they looked functional and dusty after being on the road all day long instead of screaming *rich magician* to those who saw them.

They had boarded the ship after dinner as sleeping at the public house did not make sense since it would just cost them an entire night of travelling time. They could just as well employ the cabins on board to rest in.

Eryn had looked a little pale already before boarding the vessel. She obviously remembered well enough the last time she had been on a ship. Enric had explained to her that his was a larger vessel than last time, which meant that it was not as prone to the influence of lighter swell and would thus not rock as much.

It had taken Eryn less than an hour to vomit her dinner back up.

Amazingly enough, Junar did not seem to be suffering from any sea-sickness whatsoever - somewhat unexpected as her stomach had not been cooperative at all these last few months. Vern seemed to be immune to the rocking as well and spent most of his time drawing pictures of everything he saw, asking the crew members to show and explain things to him, as well as reading.

Orrin was another matter. His skin had taken on a slightly greenish tinge, but as neither Enric, Pe'tala, Vern nor Junar showed any sensitivity to the constant pitching of the ship, he was determined not the be the only one apart from Eryn showing weakness. When asked, he replied that everything was fine. Pe'tala and Vern had both offered to send him to sleep until they reached Takhan, but he had not wanted to hear any of that and kept insisting that all was well.

The wind was good, so they were expected to reach the city tomorrow in the late morning hours.

Enric turned when he saw Pe'tala climbing up from under deck. She nodded to him when she spotted him and stepped next to him, leaning against the railing.

"Eryn is still asleep. I will keep her that way until the morning when we have left the sea behind us and are on the river."

He nodded. "Thank you. I admit I am glad that you are the one doing this as it would have fuelled her anger at *me* otherwise."

She smiled. "This is one of the unpopular things healers are used to taking care of. Helping people does not always make them thank us."

"Not even other healers?"

She snorted. "*Especially* not other healers. Healers are the worst patients you can imagine. They think they know everything much better and do not need any help. And if they are willing to admit that a little aid would be a good idea, they try to tell you how to do it properly."

He chuckled. "Good thing healers don't need each other's help too often, then."

She nodded. "That is fortunate, indeed. We would otherwise have to increase the price for their treatment as they are particularly burdensome."

"Does this apply to you as well or are you more conscious of it all?"

Pe'tala grinned. "Of course it applies. I am worse than most. Can you imagine my having to admit to needing help in a field which I am known to be very proficient in? I pity any healer who has to deal with *me*."

Enric regarded her thoughtfully. "It is good to see you smile, Tala," he said softly. "I haven't seen that in a while. I can't help but get the impression that you are worried and restless. This is not your usual impatience with the world in general but something else. And you maintain your distance from Eryn, even though you keep watching her when you think nobody is noticing. What is the matter?"

She bit her lip and dropped her head. "It seems I need to be more careful around you. I am not used to people paying that much attention to their surroundings."

"Talk to me," he insisted. "It is something that has to do with Eryn, I am almost sure of it. Is everything alright with her and the child?" His voice had taken on a slightly concerned tone.

Shaking her head, she reached out for his hand and squeezed it when he took it. "No, Enric, I promise you that everything is alright with both of them. And let me tell you how very touched I am with the extent of both your and Lord Orrin's concern for your companions' wellbeing. It is not something I would have associated with warriors. It seems I fell prey to the common prejudice of fighters being no more than insensitive barbarians. I should have known better."

He exhaled in relief. "Good. Then what is it that you are fretting about?"

Pe'tala slid her hand back and turned away from him to look out into the darkness. "There is something Eryn will learn after we arrive in Takhan. It will be a surprise, and not a pleasant one, I suspect. Be prepared for her to be very distressed about the news she is about to receive."

"What news?" he insisted, frowning.

"It is not my place to tell you. I can see that you are worried now, but please do not push me. You will learn of it in less than one day. I promise."

Enric nodded slowly. "Alright, I respect your wishes. Just one more question, then I will leave it alone: does it have anything to do with her father?"

She looked up at him sharply. "You are a perilously sharp man, Enric. It would really be reassuring if you were wrong every now and again, you know."

He smiled without humour. "It is a burden at times. But I thank you for the warning. And thank you for taking care of her. I will try to catch some sleep now; it seems that I need to be well-rested and alert for tomorrow."

"Good night, Enric. Sleep well."

He climbed down the stairs and opened the first door to the right behind which Eryn slept peacefully, if not of her own free will. News about her father. And none she would appreciate. What a pity that her second arrival in Takhan might not be much more pleasant than her first.

4

* * *

Eryn slowly opened her eyes and stared up into two faces that looked down at her. Enric and Pe'tala. They took a step backwards when she slowly sat up. Memory returned to her and she shot Pe'tala an affronted look.

"You put me to sleep, just like that!"

Shrugging, the other woman leaned against the door. "I did so, yes. You were too proud to agree to it and I had no intention of letting your retching keep me awake all night. So I did us both a favour. No need to thank me."

"Yes, exactly. Thanking you was just what I had in mind..." she muttered and carefully got up from the platform bed to stretch.

"You'd better get dressed and wash yourself, my love," Enric put in. "We should arrive in Takhan in no more than two hours so you might want to eat something before that, too."

"Two hours? That means we have left the sea behind us," she said with relief.

He nodded. "That we have, yes. The last part of the journey should be fairly relaxed."

"How are the others doing so far?"

"Well enough. Orrin still refuses to admit that he was sea-sick, Junar is not doing any worse than usual, and Vern has by now drawn pictures of pretty much everything he has found on board, I think."

Eryn nodded and then looked at both of them in turn. "Look, why don't you go up on deck? It is a bit tight in here to wash and dress with the two of you standing in my way. Out with you."

They looked at each other, then Enric opened the door to let Pe'tala step out first.

When she was alone, Eryn took a seat on the bed again, breathing slowly. Only two more hours until she was back in Takhan again. Two more hours until she would encounter Malriel. The woman who had made sure Eryn got pregnant against her wishes. And the woman who had betrayed her companion twenty-nine years ago and had been careless enough to become pregnant by another man. A man Eryn didn't even know whether she wanted to know more about. All that counted was that she had taken away something that had been immensely precious to Eryn: the family she had found in House Vel'kim. She was still a member of their House, legally speaking. But with Ved'al not being her father, she had no claim of lineage to being part of the family.

The notion of Malriel made her heart increase its pace and she made herself close her eyes and breathe evenly to calm herself down again. Stress was not good, neither for her nor for the child.

When she emerged on deck several minutes later clad in the thinner garments she had purchased here during her first visit, she found Vern sitting on the stairs, drawing something.

"According to Enric you have already drawn everything there is on the ship. Are you starting all over again?" she quipped.

He looked up and grinned at her. "I don't have to, fortunately. Unlike at sea, there are landscapes around now, so I don't have to limit myself to the things on board."

"Have you had breakfast yet?"

He nodded. "Yes. Two hours ago. Not all of us like to sleep half the day away."

"I was put to sleep by a magician! It was not my fault!" she protested.

"Oh, I see - because under normal circumstances you like to get up as early as you can," he snorted and resumed his work.

"Why am I even talking to you?" she murmured and moved on to where Enric and Orrin were standing, looking out over the wide, rocky ridges. These were the foothills of mountains they had passed not long before. There was hardly any vegetation as the slow transition into desert had started already.

Orrin turned and nodded to her when she stepped next to them. He, too, had changed into lighter clothes. Junar had made them each a few sets to have something for their first few days in Takhan before they had a chance to see a local tailor. She had not adapted the style of their clothes, just the heaviness of the fabric, so he would still appear foreign in style, even if one did not look at the fair hair.

"Where is Junar?" she asked and looked around.

"Below deck," the warrior replied. "She woke only a few minutes ago and is getting herself ready." He studied her. "You look tense."

She set her face in a scowl. "I am not too thrilled at the prospect of seeing the Queen of Darkness again so soon."

Orrin frowned. "The what?"

"Queen of Darkness. Malriel," she explained.

"Charming," he murmured and shook his head at her.

"Why would I be? She isn't, either. I just hope she doesn't turn up at the port," she growled.

Enric thought that the chances for that were rather slim, but didn't put words to it. She was probably aware of it anyway.

Vern stepped next to them. "Can we repeat the thing with the greetings once again? I keep mixing it up."

Enric nodded and stretched out his hand to demonstrate. "Two men who greet each other formally link their fingers. The same goes for two women."

Vern linked his fingers with Enric's as instructed, then nodded. "Alright. And then there are the informal greetings. Men don't have any particular informal greeting but express fondness through whatever gesture they feel like performing, like squeezing a shoulder, slapping a back or whatever. Though with mixed sexes it's different, isn't it?"

Enric confirmed it. "Yes. When men and women greet each other formally, the man kisses the woman's hand like this." He took Eryn's left hand and pressed his lips against her knuckles. "Just make sure not to linger, or it might be taken as intrusive. Informal greetings between men and women consist in kissing both cheeks. The same goes for two women."

Vern nodded. "Thank you, Lord Enric."

He lifted both brows. "Pardon?"

The boy closed his eyes for a moment, then sighed. "Thank you... Enric."

Eryn grinned. "Ah yes, it seems you used the time I spent more or less hibernating to adapt to the custom of not using titles."

Enric sighed. "Yes, though it seems that this is quite a burden for our young friend here. He keeps flinching whenever I make him address me without it."

She looked at the boy. "Just remember that he is no longer in the Order and does thus not merit being addressed by it, anyway. He isn't your superior anymore, just a magician you happen to know."

He snorted. "Yes, sure. A magician in the case of which I have been taught to stay out of his way, not look him directly in the eye, address him without being asked and be very careful always to treat him with the respect he is due."

Enric looked taken aback. "That is what you were told?" He turned towards Orrin and raised an eyebrow at him.

"Don't look at me," the warrior shrugged. "I don't tell people not to look you in the eye or keep their mouth shut when they have something sensible to say, no matter how important you are. Must have been his teachers."

"Children are being told to keep out of my way and avoid eye contact with me?" he asked with a bewildered expression. That really was an unpleasant revelation. He shook his head in confusion. "Why?"

Orrin thought for a moment, then ventured, "There are stories about you beating up your fellow students and playing rather cruel tricks on them."

"I was younger than Vern back then!" he protested angrily. "The children that are being taught to cower in obedience before me were not even born at that time!"

"You were that kind of boy? Really?" Eryn frowned. "Why did I get a different impression from the stories I have been hearing until now? They painted a picture of a lazy, disrespectful, misunderstood boy with a tendency to express his frustration through *poetry*, not with fists. How is it possible that the destructive aspect of beating up other children got lost in there somewhere?"

He looked at her sheepishly. "It's all a matter of presentation, my love. I already had to work hard enough to make you like and accept me without your knowing about my dark past."

Orrin grinned. "Don't worry, Eryn, that was just for the first one or two years after he was brought to the Order. Let's call it acclimatisation problems, shall we?"

"Yes," Enric snorted. "After you got your hands on me, I had hardly any energy left to waste on my peers since you made me do so many extra training hours after class that I more or less fell into bed at the end of the day."

"That has worked well enough, hasn't it? You turned into an exceptional fighter and have learned to express your frustration with words instead of violence," the warrior smirked.

Enric looked at Vern. "Who told you to avert your eyes?"

The boy thought for a moment, then said, "My teacher in political strategy, Avlin."

"Avlin..." Enric mulled the name over, wondering why it did sound familiar, then he grimaced. "Ah..."

Orrin nodded. "Yes, him. You locked him inside a chest for several hours when you were boys. Twice."

Eryn shook her head at her companion. "So while I was training to be a healer at the age of... what? - thirteen, you were the scourge of your peers? And the most sensible thing they could think of was to teach you *more fighting*?" She sighed and looked at his former combat teacher. "Why not lock *him* up in a chest for a few hours as well to teach him a lesson?"

"I see we have very different approaches to raising children," the warrior said reproachfully. "Repaying a child in kind doesn't achieve much. Punishing him like that would only have made him angrier and wouldn't have solved the problem of his excess energy. Fighting requires discipline, so increasing the time he had to spend learning it served more than one purpose. It left him hardly any time or energy for torturing others and forced him to learn control and restraint."

Eryn nodded and smirked at Vern. "Well, you see it is safe enough to look him in the eye and address him without a title nowadays. It seems your father has tamed him for us."

"I don't really appreciate your phrasing it like that," her companion sighed. "Let us say he aided me in finding less destructive outlets for my energy and frustration, shall we?"

She nodded. "If that wording makes you happier, who am I to deny you?"

"A pity this approach has not worked on you, though," Orrin remarked. "Making you fight just *increased* your frustration."

"Yes," she growled. "And I had to have a child planted inside me finally to be permitted to halt this waste of time for at least a while."

"We could always have another one afterwards. That would make them spare you for even longer," Enric threw in casually.

"Hardly," she snapped at him. "Buying myself a few months without combat training will earn me another few *years* of a different kind of strain. Imagine if we get stuck with a troublemaker like Vern who teaches magical fighting to prisoners and defaces ancient city maps with drawings of naked women!"

"I thought I was too harmless to be bad?" the said troublemaker chuckled.

8

"I've changed my mind about that. You are now officially bad influence material. Just don't do anything I need to take responsibility for as the highest-ranking Order magician as long as we are in Takhan. And you had better get used to addressing Enric without a title. It will sound really strange otherwise," she warned him.

Pe'tala stepped next to them and pointed towards the horizon. "Look, there is my home city," she said with a touch of pride in her voice.

Vern cast a quick look at the view in front of him before he darted back to the stairs where he had left his drawing pad and pen. He started drawing frantically while the others just looked at the faraway silhouette of the grand city.

Enric noted Pe'tala's tense posture. She was also clearly not looking forward to their impending arrival.

*   *   *

They stood next to each other at the railing, watching the jetties drift past. This time they had been assigned a different one due to the size of their vessel.

A slow smile spread on Eryn's face when she spotted the small group of people that stood waiting on the landing stage. Valrad, Vran'el and Kilan. She was relieved to see Malriel was not among them and was pleased that there was no large party assembled that would have taken an eternity to greet, though she felt a small stab of disappointment at Ram'an not being there to welcome them.

She watched her travel companions and smiled at their wonder at seeing the foreign city for the first time, taking in the unusual sights around them.

When the ship had finally been secured by heavy ropes fore and aft, the gangplank was put in place to allow the passengers to disembark. She all but ran ahead and pulled both Vel'kim men at once into a stormy embrace, holding them pressed against her for several moments, before she stepped aside. She was not the only one who had to be eager to greet them.

Pe'tala approached them at a more moderate pace and smiled at her family. She first hugged her father, then her brother.

"Tala, my child," Valrad said tenderly and brushed a stray strand of hair behind her ear. "It is good to have you here again, even if it is only for a short while."

"It is good to be back," she smiled and leaned into his touch. "You would not believe how cold it is over there."

"I can when I look at how pale you have become," her father nodded. "Clearly not enough sunshine there."

"The Vel'kim girls back in the city," Vran'el grinned and winked at Eryn. "People here better hide in dark places."

Eryn then turned to Kilan and laughed when he pulled her close to kiss her cheeks. "Adapting to local customs, I see, Ambassador."

"I should, I am supposed to show my respect for my host country that way," he smirked.

Enric, Orrin, Junar and Vern had in the meantime reached them, and after Enric had greeted the three men affectionately, he introduced their travel companions.

"Orrin," Valrad mused and looked the fighter up and down. "The man who has made Eryn fight despite her repulsion to it."

The warrior nodded, the cool tone clearly not lost on him. "That would be me, yes," he replied slowly. "But I hope you will not reduce me to that alone."

Eryn swallowed and stepped next to Orrin, taking his arm to squeeze it reassuringly while looking at the man she had until recently considered her uncle.

"He has become a close friend since that time, Valrad. Somebody who has never failed me when I needed a place to go or a voice of reason to guide me." She grinned and gave Orrin a friendly shove. "Pretty much the father I never wanted."

She watched Valrad narrow his eyes at her last comment and wondered why this greeting was so uncharacteristically tense. She hurriedly turned from Orrin to his companion and introduced Junar, who was welcomed more warmly.

When Vern stepped forward, Valrad broke into a broad grin.

"And this must be Vern, the young man with not only the most incredible artistic talent but also an inclination to healing. I have seen the book you illustrated, and I cannot wait to introduce you to my colleagues. They were thrilled to hear that you would be among the party to come here."

Vern was clearly overwhelmed at the warm greeting that was so very different from the one his father had just received. It took him several moments to find his voice.

"Thank you, I am very glad I had the chance to visit here. And I am happy to meet you. I have heard a lot about you," he finally said and lifted his hand for the formal greeting.

Enric put a hand on his shoulder. "You usually wait for the other person to offer you his hand first if he or she is older or higher in status."

The boy swallowed and smiled nervously at the older man before him. "I'm sorry, it seems there are a few things I need to learn still."

Valrad laughed and linked their fingers. "No worries, my young friend. I will not take offence at minor things like that."

Eryn frowned when she saw Vran'el gaze over her shoulder and stiffen at the sight. She turned slowly, hoping against hope that she would not find herself face to face with Malriel.

No such luck.

The Head of House Aren came closer. Her face appeared confident enough, and yet there was a hint of caution in her moves. She reached Enric first and pulled him close to greet him with a kiss on each cheek.

10

"Enric, my dear. I am so very glad you are here. I truly appreciate what you are doing," she smiled.

He nodded at her once. "I am sure you do. Yet I want you to know that your methods do not meet with my approval," he said mildly. "But this is a discussion for another time."

Malriel's expression became slightly strained and she moved on to greet Orrin, Junar and Vern. Finally, she turned towards Eryn, who had gone stiff.

"Theá," the older woman said softly. "Welcome back to Takhan."

Eryn felt the rage shoot through her like a hot spear. The smile, the name she didn't want to be addressed with, this casualness despite the things she had done.

When Malriel stepped closer to kiss her cheeks, Eryn's reaction to this attempt at closeness was an automatic one. Her fist shot out and connected with the older woman's chin with a thud. Malriel's head was twisted violently to one side by the force of the impact and she staggered back several steps, the shock clear on her face.

"You black-hearted, untrustworthy, maleficent creature!" she shouted.

It had become quiet around them. Everybody within sight seemed to have frozen in mid-action to stare at the incredible scene of the mighty Head of House Aren being hit by what looked like a slightly younger version of herself.

Eryn felt a surge of pleasure, relief and dizziness at seeing Malriel out of her element for once. She was not in control of this situation.

"Oh dear," Vran'el sighed and looked up at Enric. "You ought to intervene, I would say."

The blond magician slowly shook his head and murmured, "No. Malriel had that one coming. I have no intention of aiding her. She deserved it well enough." And it was a nice way for Eryn to get rid of her anger instead of keeping it inside. That she could also apply her newly acquired skills in unarmed combat as a welcome side-benefit.

They watched Eryn approach her mother again. Malriel lifted her hands before her.

"Malth/á, this is not the right way to deal with our issues!"

"It works fine for me right now," Eryn hissed and kicked her hard in the stomach, sending her over the edge of the jetty and into the river with a loud splash.

She watched the water close over Malriel's head, then exhaled and turned to walk towards her rapt audience without looking back.

"I assume she can swim? Not that I intend to rescue her if she can't," she commented dryly.

Valrad had closed his eyes and slowly shook his head. "Not a good start," he murmured.

Vran'el nodded. "No, but not exactly unexpected, was it? Though I did not see that... physical aspect coming, I admit." He then turned to Kilan. "Would you accompany Orrin, Junar and young Vern to your residence, Kilan?"

"What about Eryn and Enric?" Junar asked, putting a protective arm around her friend's shoulders.

"They will come with us to our house. There is something we need to discuss," Valrad answered in his son's place. "I would very much like to invite all of you to spend your first evening in Takhan with us and have dinner with my family and me. I am sure I do not need to tell you that you are in capable hands with Kilan until then," he finished with an awkward smile.

They watched Malriel pull herself out of the water, her wet clothes clinging to her slim body as she climbed an iron ladder downstream of the ship, her long dark hair plastered against her head. When she was back on land, she closed her eyes and a moment later steam started to rise when she dried herself with magic. A minute later there was no more trace of her tumble into the river, and she walked back to them casting a warning look at her daughter.

Orrin gripped Eryn's upper arm and growled at her, "This is not responsible use of the things I taught you. Attacking somebody who has scruples about striking you back on account of your condition is not a very noble approach to the art of fighting."

She bared her teeth when she hissed back, "All I have to tell you is that this is of no consequence to me right now. None at all."

She saw Valrad frown at their exchange and freed her arm from Orrin's grip.

"Why are we to come with you? I would rather take a cool bath and sit down and relax for a while," she then asked, keeping Malriel in view in case another chance to give her a good kick presented itself.

"I will tell you when we are at home," Valrad spoke calmly and reached out for her hand. "It is nothing I would like to discuss in public."

"Is that vicious woman to come as well? If yes, you can count me out," she growled.

He sighed. "Yes, Malriel will accompany us. And no, you may not refuse to come." His tone contained an unmistakeable warning. "Enric, I would appreciate your help here."

Enric nodded slowly. It seemed they had just got the harmless part behind them and were now to face what Pe'tala had been dreading.

*　*　*

Eryn waited until Malriel had taken a seat on one of the cushions at the Vel'kim main room and then sat down at the furthest possible spot, glaring daggers at her. Enric glided onto the seat next to her and Valrad sank onto the cushion on her other side. Vran'el set down a tray with glasses, water and juice on the low table before them, then sat between his father and Malriel. Pe'tala had opted against joining the group and instead leaned against a wall close to the exit.

Enric raised a questioning brow at her. To escape, if necessary? She gave him a tired smile.

Valrad took Eryn's hand between his own two larger hands and waited until she had torn her glare away from Malriel to look at him instead before he addressed her.

"Eryn, my girl, Pe'tala has informed me that you are by now aware of the significance of your son's inherited illness."

"Yes," she swallowed and sent the woman opposite her another hate-filled look. "It means that Malriel of House Aren was not much more considerate in her companionship than in her other dealings. She was not only unfaithful but also careless enough to get herself pregnant from her affair, drunken encounter or whatever else it was."

Malriel opened her mouth to reply, but closed it again when Valrad gave her a look that made her reconsider.

Eryn frowned at that. "I don't really see why you are the one to talk to me about her misconduct. Delegating this duty to the brother of the man she did this to is low, even for her. But then I suppose I shouldn't be surprised at anything she does any longer."

"Eryn," Valrad said urgently, "please listen to me for a moment, will you? This is important. You are right. It was wrong of her to do this behind Ved'al's back, but she was not the only one to blame here."

She tried to pull away her hand, but the older man held on to it. "If you are about to tell me her bed-partner's name in order to make me spread my anger more evenly instead of making her alone be the one to bear it, I am very disappointed in you. I don't care who she took to bed. He is of no consequence to me."

Valrad closed his eyes and turned his head away for a moment.

The thought hit Enric like a fist in the stomach and he sucked in a sharp breath. His gaze shot to Pe'tala, who nodded at him once, guessing that he had figured it out.

Eryn turned to him when she felt shock and dread through the mind bond. "What?"

He just shook his head and quickly raised a mind shield to avoid distracting and worrying her.

"Eryn," Valrad then said, his face serious, his jaw clenched. "This is of considerable consequence to you. To all of us. *I* was the man she took to bed at the time when you were conceived."

She froze, staring at him uncomprehendingly. There were... words. She understood the meaning of every single one of them, but together they just made no sense at all.

"Pardon?" she enquired politely.

"The bone disease your son has inherited," he explained with a troubled expression, "has been passed on through our family for many generations now. Not all males inherit it, though - only one in four. Ved'al did not. But I did. And so has your son." He searched her face for a sign of comprehension, some emotion. "Eryn? Do you see what I am telling you? I am your father, and not only legally. You are of my blood, my daughter."

13

Her head sunk until her chin rested on her chest, her breathing becoming faster. "No. You are not. I refuse to believe that you did a thing like that to your own brother. Not *you*. You are the decent kind. You wouldn't."

She watched the pain on his face at her words and only then fully understood that he had spoken the truth. As the ache at realising this almost choked her, for a moment she felt that she couldn't breathe. Enric's arm around her shoulders pressed her against him and she felt his lips on her temple. It took her several moments to decipher that his voice formed actual words.

"I am so sorry, my love."

She sobbed quietly and buried her face in her hands.

After more than one minute she whispered, "Of all people! I see how *she* could have done this, but *you*?" Her voice rose in pitch. "He was your *brother*, damn you! How could you? And you played the role of the welcoming uncle so nicely when I first came here," she exclaimed, a tear running down her cheek. "A pity for you Malriel slipped me that fertility potion, or I would never have found out!"

Valrad's head snapped to Malriel and he stared at her. His voice boomed through the house, when he snarled, "You have done *what*?"

Malriel flinched as if he had hit her and just pressed her lips together, neither confirming nor denying it.

Enric looked at Pe'tala in surprise. "You didn't tell him?"

She shook her head. "No. It is not something to send via bird. One never knows who intercepts and reads those messages."

"I swear to you, Eryn, I had no idea of this. And neither did I suspect that I am your father. I only realised it when Pe'tala sent me the message about the results of her examination."

Eryn shook her head and rose. "I need to get out of here," she murmured and almost stumbled when she hastily climbed over the large cushions towards the stairs that lead to the exit. Valrad attempted to steady her, but she shied away from him. "Don't you touch me!" she snarled and ran towards the stairs.

Enric jumped up and tried to follow her, but Pe'tala blocked his way, shaking her head.

"No. Let me."

Conflicting emotions played across his face. When they heard the door downstairs being opened and thrown shut a moment later, Pe'tala grabbed his arms and added urgently, "Please?"

He finally nodded and forced himself to remain where he was.

"Vran'el?" she called out. "Bel's teahouse in half an hour."

When her brother nodded silently, she dashed off after Eryn.

* * *

She was blinded by the sudden bright sunlight and staggered for a moment before she shadowed her eyes with her hand and started running down the road that climbed from the street to the building.

When she reached the street that ran along one side of the Vel'kim land, she paused before she decided not to worry where she went as long as it would be away from here.

A hand on her shoulder made her cry out and whirl around, ready to throw a punch if it turned out to be Malriel or Valrad. But it was Pe'tala, her face grim and determined, who stood before her.

"Come," she just ordered and grabbed Eryn's upper arm to lead her in a direction that Eryn vaguely recalled leading towards the city centre.

"Let go of me," she ordered and tried to free her arm, but the younger woman held on to it and pulled her along.

"No. You stop that right now and come with me. I can hardly let you go running around alone in the city without a single slip of gold in your pocket and no more than rudimentary knowledge of the city layout. Who knows where you might end up."

Eryn laughed too loudly, her voice bitter when she said, "My concerned *little sister*, how very considerate of you to worry about me."

Pe'tala stopped and turned towards her, staring into her eyes and stepping closer until their noses were almost touching.

"You are damned right, you idiot! A month was a long time to carry the burden of this knowledge alone. I do worry and have done so since the moment I detected that disorder in your child. Or did you think it was a coincidence that I was standing next to the exit right now when you heard about this?" she said sternly. "Now stop being difficult until I get you to a place where we can talk. As you are quite a bit stronger than me, I need you to cooperate with me. Do you hear me?"

"Talk to *you*?"

"Yes, talk to *me*. Honestly, I am the person you *want* to talk to right now. Knowing Vran'el, he is very probably happy about the recent development, so having him around would just make you want to throttle him. It is no matter that you generally like him better than me. Enric would just hold you and listen to your wailing and then tell you how to analyse the situation in a way that makes it appear advantageous."

Eryn blinked and just stared at her.

"Are you coming now?"

Pe'tala waited for a moment, and when no reply came she resumed her brisk walk without letting go of the other woman's arm.

Eryn had no idea how long they had marched on before Pe'tala stopped next to a teahouse with white tents that protected the cushions on the ground from the sun.

"Sit," she commanded and lifted a hand to summon a server, instructing him to keep the tables around them empty to give them privacy and ordering a pot of tea, telling him to keep refilling it until ordered otherwise. Then she sank down next to Eryn, stretching out her legs and sighing wearily. "It seems coming to Takhan is never a very cheerful occasion for you, is it?"

Eryn exhaled and leaned back, closing her eyes. "No, I just want to hide somewhere dark..." Her voice trailed off. She opened her eyes again when she felt Pe'tala's hand on hers.

"Your hand is cold and your heart is beating much faster than our short walk here would warrant. You are in shock. I am going to do something about that as it is dangerous for you and the child. Do you hear me?" Her voice sounded calm but there was determination.

"Why do you keep asking me that?"

"Because confusion is a shock symptom. Relax now. Do not raise a barrier or anything, or I will grab the next magician I see passing along and make him help me overpower you just so I can smack you on the head."

Eryn slowly shook her head and felt pleasant warmth seeping into her skin as Pe'tala sent magic through her palm. "You do have a way with patients. No wonder they keep complaining about you."

Pe'tala opened her eyes again and smiled tiredly. "Nonsense. They complain, but in truth they are secretly delighted. They exchange horror stories about being treated by me when they meet. I am practically providing an additional public service by making sure there are conversation topics."

Eryn exhaled and noticed that she found thinking a lot easier. "What now? Do I pour out my grief and sorrow about the latest blow fate has dealt me, and you ease my pain with the balm of sisterly sympathy, or how does this work?"

"An interesting picture," the younger woman smiled weakly, "but not exactly in accordance with our preferences, is it? Let us instead try being angry together."

Eryn sighed and nodded. "Sure, why not? I can see why *you* would be angry."

"No," Pe'tala retorted sharply. "You cannot. Yet. But you might if you shut up for a minute and let me tell you bit about myself." She paused when the server brought them a metal pot with steaming hot tea and two glasses. The handles looked so delicate as if they might fall off any moment simply by being looked at the wrong way. When he had retreated again, she leaned forward to pour the tea for both of them and then leaned back with her glass in one hand to continue. "I was very young when my mother ran off with a trader. Four years old, to be precise. I know that her and father's companionship was not a particularly affectionate one, but I have never really forgiven her for leaving me behind like that. There are ways for a woman to separate from a man without giving up all contact with her children. In any event it seems we were no more than a burden to her - there was no space for us in her new life." She paused and stared into her glass for a short while before going on. "In this past month I have started wondering. I would never have pegged my father as the type to have an affair with a woman who is joined to another man.

16

Especially not his brother's companion, and not while he himself was bound to a woman. But learning of this... It has made me wonder if my mother had learned about this, too, and decided to leave because of it."

Eryn swallowed. So these were the thoughts that had plagued Pe'tala for the last month while she was stuck in a foreign country far away from her family and friends with nobody to talk to.

"I wish you had told me about this. That was a long time for you to be alone with it."

She shook her head. "No. It was not my place to share this with you. And I was angry at father and wanted him to see with his own eyes what pain his actions of so many years back would cause you." She looked up into Eryn's eyes. "It was a punishment for him. And Malriel. Though I have to mention that he asked me not to tell you about it. He never expected me to do his dirty work for him, as it were."

"Don't say anything nice about him now," Eryn grimaced.

Pe'tala smiled. "Alright, I will refrain from doing so for now. There are a few other reasons for me to be angry with him, so let us talk about those first. There was his choice of lover, for one thing. I mean, how could he ever be drawn to a woman like that?" She cast a disapproving face. "She is selfish, reckless and not exactly squeamish when it comes to the methods she employs. What kind of man would fall for those qualities? She is very pretty, I will admit. But I never thought that my father would find superficial qualities appealing enough to overlook what lies beneath. I would like to grant him the fact that he was young, but I find that very hard. Then I keep wondering how well I really knew my father. As you said before, doing this to his own brother is a cold, heartless thing. I never pictured him as that kind of person. And finally the absolutely ridiculous idea that a fully-trained healer cannot manage to avoid conceiving an unplanned child. Really now. How stupid can one be? This happens to teenagers who are either too caught up in the moment to think properly or have not understood how to prevent pregnancy, but not to a grown man. He had already made himself a name as a healer at that time, after all!"

Eryn waited for another reason she would have expected to be relevant here, but it had not been among those mentioned.

"And then there is *me*," she ventured.

Pe'tala rubbed her face and shook her head. "No, Eryn, you will probably not believe it, but you were not one of my reasons for being angry. You have not caused this any more than I have. And you know, after getting to know you better and leaving the mess with Ram'an behind me, I have decided that you are not *that* much of a nuisance. I was surprised at the work you did in your Kingdom and how you keep fighting and pestering the Order instead of just complying with what they wanted, leaning back to enjoy a life without worries at the side of your powerful and rich companion. And I will admit that your troubles with Malriel have made it a lot easier for me to forgive you for looking like her."

"How very generous of you," Eryn murmured.

"What can I say? I am known for that quality," she said, then became serious again. "I do not mind having you as my sister. I had fun in Anyueel, and you made it very easy for me to be accepted. Even though it took quite some determination from my side to stop Rolan from shying away from me due to my mighty and powerful family connections, namely you and Enric." She chuckled as she recalled the memory. "I swear to you, he was sweating blood when we were first invited to have dinner at your place."

Eryn smiled faintly at her recollection of the evening. "Yes, he did seem rather ill at ease."

They both emptied their cups and Pe'tala refilled them again.

"The time you have spent with Ved'al, your memories of him, this is something no unpleasant revelation can take away from you, you know," she then said. "He has been as much your father as... well, our father. He has raised you and made you the person you are today."

"I know," Eryn sighed. "Yet the thought that it has all been a lie... It may sound very cruel, but I am glad he never found out about this, that he did not live to see this day. How is a man to react when he learns that his only child is not his, but his brother's?" She stared at her cup, blankly.

They looked up when a figure stopped next to their table. Eryn's eyes narrowed when she recognised him after a few moments. Ram'an. He looked surprised to see them, but recovered quickly enough.

"Eryn. Pe'tala," he said slowly. "That is... unexpected."

Eryn didn't reply, but stared at him. He looked somehow transformed. Thinner, with more lines around his mouth and on his forehead. It seemed that his position as Head of House was not exactly one that afforded him a lot of time for himself. Or for sleeping.

"Ram'an," Pe'tala answered politely without rising. "At the risk of seeming unfriendly, would you mind leaving us for now? We are having a very personal conversation here and would appreciate our privacy. I am sure we will meet again soon. Either Malriel or my father will very likely host a welcome dinner."

He blinked and then nodded. "Of course. And yes, the invitations have already been sent out. I will see you in two days, then." Eryn noticed his quick glance at her belly before he turned away and walked towards a set of cushions at the other end of the teahouse. So he had obviously heard about her pregnancy. This was good.

"And there I was, thinking this day could not become any more unpleasant," she murmured, trying to ignore that he was still close enough for her to see him if she turned her head.

Pe'tala pointedly looked at the bracelet around her wrist. "I was under the impression that you parted as friends?"

Eryn nodded and played with the piece of jewellery. "That was what I had thought, too. But our correspondence was chilly at the beginning and ceased completely after a while." She shrugged. "Not a major concern of mine any longer after what I have heard so far today, though."

"Girls," Vran'el's voice said from behind them.

Pe'tala sighed and turned. "That was not half an hour, Vran."

He shrugged and squeezed between them. "No matter. I thought that annoying you by being early was preferable to my waiting at home, fretting." He raised a finger to signal the server to bring another cup. Then he looked at each of them in turn. "So. Tala, my sweetheart, I know that you must have known about it for a while. And Eryn, my dear, I see why this was not the most comforting start to your stay here. Though I have to say that I am very pleased that you both seem to have managed to get along well enough to be there for each other when there is trouble." He took Pe'tala's glass and emptied it. "And while at the moment this may seem like bad news and quite a shock..."

"Vran?" Pe'tala asked and after he had stopped, added, "Just shut it, will you?"

Eryn rolled her eyes. "You were right. Too cheerful by far. Terrible."

"What?" he asked in puzzlement.

"We are still in the throes of sharing with each other why we are angry at Valrad," Eryn explained.

"Angry at him?" His confusion increased. "Why ever would you be angry at him? What would that change?"

"Oh dear," Pe'tala sighed. "Can you just go off again? This conversation was a lot more meaningful before your arrival."

Vran'el accepted a glass from the server and shook his head. "Surely not! It seems to me like you are in desperate need of some positive influence here."

"Don't try to be positive with me right now," Eryn growled. "If you want to tell me something nice, say that nobody but us will ever get to hear of this latest family drama." She watched Vran'el's expression become studiously blank. "Vran'el? Why do I have the feeling that you are about to tell me something I will not appreciate hearing?"

He cleared his throat, then filled his glass with exaggerated care from the pot on the table, obviously to buy time.

"Vran'el!" she barked. "Stop playing around and talk to me! Who knows about this but us?"

"Nobody else so far," he said slowly. "But you surely remember that men born to the House of Vel'kim tend to be rather well known for their devotion and commitment to their offspring, do you not?"

She nodded and motioned for him to keep talking.

"Father plans to officially acknowledge you as his natural child in addition to being your legal parent at the next Senate meeting."

"*What*?" Eryn stared at him, her mouth agape. "You need to stop him! That won't look good for any of us!"

Vran'el looked at her with what she had come to know as his lawyer-expression: slightly indulgent with an air of solemn superiority. "I am afraid I cannot oblige you here. He would not take well to me interfering in this matter unbidden. And he is right, it is no more than correct and proper to take public responsibility for his actions."

"You have both gone mad!" she exclaimed. "I object to this!"

"You see, he is the Head of your House, so if he is determined to do this, your objections are rather useless, I am afraid," he shrugged.

"How about Malriel? I can't imagine her approving of a thing like that," Eryn asked urgently. "She can and will stop him, can't she?"

"No, sweetness, she will not even try," he sighed. "Aren women are a belligerent bunch, but they are not stupid, and avoid fighting whenever they know they cannot win. So now sit back and have another glass of tea; you are not able to change what is about to happen in two days. You are welcome to watch the revelation, though. Senate meetings are public most of the time, as you can surely remember."

"I don't want everyone to know this! Why is he so eager to share his shame with the world? What kind of man does a thing like that?" she moaned.

"Someone who does not consider being gifted with having another daughter a shame but rather a privilege, I would think," he said mildly. "A sentiment I share." He took Pe'tala's hand and squeezed it. "One sister has been a blessing so far, and having two is an even greater blessing." He attempted to take her hand as well, but she moved out of the way.

"Don't," she hissed, "just don't! You really don't see how I can be upset about this, do you? For you we are just a big, happy family where nothing much has changed, as I was adopted into your House anyway?"

"Eryn," he implored her, "we loved you before we knew about this, and we still do. You lost one father when you were still a child - why do you not see the miracle in unexpectedly finding another one and just accept it?"

"Because this situation is the result of infidelity, lying and betrayal! How would you react to finding out that Obal was not *your* daughter? Don't tell me you would approve of it as you daughter would be blessed with gaining another father!"

He raised an eyebrow. "That is hardly a valid comparison. I am still alive, after all. Of course I would not be happy about it. But Ved'al has been dead for so long, and without him there nobody is left to be hurt."

"It hurts *me*, damn you!" she hissed. "I just want some time to get used to this nightmare before it will be discussed by everyone." She forced herself to breathe and lean back again. "I have been looking forward to seeing you and your father again, I really have. That prospect was more or less the only pleasant thing about being compelled to come here again so soon. And now I feel like strangling you because you are so obstinate in your views. I wish I could hide from Valrad for the next month! My stomach churns at the mere thought of his having invited us to have dinner with you tonight!"

"Eryn, please," he tried again, "this is not supposed to be a burden to you. All he wants is the chance to be a father to you, too."

"I don't need a father," she snapped. "Is that so hard to understand? I had a father, and he is dead! What I need and what I appreciated very much last time I was here is a friend, an uncle, somebody I can trust! But this is not him any longer! How can I trust him ever again after discovering how he treated not only his brother, but his own companion, too?" She stood and glared at him. "I have no intention of serving as his big chance to repent for his bad deeds back then. I don't need him - I just want to be left in peace."

Her gaze fell on Ram'an who was observing her with interest from his distant corner of the large tent. Her eyes narrowed. This was as good a time as any. She fumbled with her bracelet until she had unfastened it and marched towards him, tossing it into his lap.

"Here! I don't want it anymore. It seems you and I have very different ideas about friendship. You have not held up your side, and I am sick of waiting for you to come to your senses. Let's stop pretending, shall we? Enric is eager enough to help your House back on its feet; you don't need me to carry your torch and demonstrate publicly how chummy our Houses are."

He blinked and began to rise, but stopped when she whirled and stomped off.

Vran'el also started to get to his feet and follow her, but Pe'tala sighed, holding on to his sleeve and pulling him back down. "Let her go. You just messed up all my efforts, and not just a little. What is more, I must say that I do not agree with some of the things you said. This is not an occasion of joy, but of great shock. And she has had no time to get used to it like the two of us have. Do try to be more considerate next time."

He stared at his sister. Being reprimanded for lack of sympathy by her was not something that occurred too often. It generally was the other way round. He lifted his hands and let them drop again helplessly.

"I just wanted to show her that she is welcome, that she has a home with us. That she is one of us," he said, looking perplexed. "It seems I made quite a mess of that."

"Considering that she has just jumped up and run off, you may safely assume that, yes," she remarked tartly.

"Where is that consideration you just reprimanded me about?" he growled.

She was about to reply to that, but shut her mouth when she saw Ram'an slowly walking towards them. He was looking down at the silver bracelet in his hand that Eryn had just thrown at him. He stopped in front of them, frowning.

"What is wrong?" he simply asked.

"I did not have the impression that you are on speaking terms, so I do not feel that you are entitled to an answer," Pe'tala replied coolly, but sighed when she saw the worry on his face. "Just make sure not to miss the next Senate meeting. That should answer your question sufficiently." She looked him up and down. "And you might want to get some sleep every now and then and reconsider your dietary habits. You look dreadful. That was some professional advice free from your friendly neighbourhood healer." Then she rose and dropped half a gold slip onto the table to pay for the tea. "If you will excuse me now, I need to make sure Eryn gets back to the ambassadorial residence unharmed, or Enric will skin my hide. Not being subjected to the restraint the Order puts on its magicians does not exactly make him *less* dangerous."

Ram'an watched her walk off, then he looked down at Vran'el, who did not look especially happy himself.

"You know," he said slowly, "seeing the two of them sitting together peacefully was not a sight I would have expected anytime soon. That your joining them could lead to some kind of escalation was the next shock. But having Eryn furious at me while Pe'tala treats me like a human being throws me completely off balance. I do not know what is going on at House Vel'kim, but I am determined to attend that Senate meeting in two days. Unless you feel like sharing?" he added casually.

Vran'el shook his head. "No. I cannot. You will have to wait like everybody else."

Ram'an nodded slowly. "Very well - I respect that of course. Should you change your mind, there is always a bottle of wine waiting to be shared at my place."

Vran'el smiled thinly. "You are shameless."

"And you are troubled, something I have not seen in a long time. Send me a message if there is anything I can do."

"Thank you. I appreciate the offer, even though I am not able to accept it for now." He rose. "A good day to you, Ram'an."

Ram'an watched the Vel'kim heir walking in the direction of his home. This was interesting. Pe'tala had gone after Eryn, but he did not. Whatever mess they were in seemed to be something major.

CHAPTER 2

Facing Valrad

Enric fought the urge to pace the main room at the ambassadorial residence and instead stood in front of one of the large windows and looked out. Unfortunately, he could not gain a view of the streets but of the green inner courtyard with its fruit trees and decorative shrubbery. It was a more pleasant scene than the dusty street, especially during the day, yet his concerns were hardly of an aesthetic nature at the moment.

He knew that Eryn was with Pe'tala and Vran'el, so there was no need for him to worry about her. Theoretically. She would be unlikely to get into any trouble, yet the thought of her being out there somewhere without him while she was so distressed was disturbing.

Kilan and Orrin were both sitting on the cushions on the floor at the centre of the room, watching him. He had imparted the news to all of them after his arrival less than half an hour ago, and Junar had immediately started worrying and had been about to storm off to start searching, through a city entirely unknown to her at the hottest time of the day, for Eryn. Vern had managed to convince her that Eryn was in good hands and then led her into her bedroom to get her to relax. Probably with a gentle prod of magic to ease her tension.

Enric watched his wrist and noted with relief when the symbols on it started getting darker. That meant she was approaching the residence. Finally.

Only minutes later he heard the door downstairs open and he rushed to the stairs to watch Eryn and Pe'tala come in. He reminded himself that seeming nervous and worried would not be helpful right now and waited for them at the top of the stairs instead of charging down as had been his first impulse.

When both women had reached him, he pulled his companion into a gentle embrace, kissed her on her temple and held her until she pulled herself free a short while later.

"Wine," she murmured. Enric looked at Pe'tala questioningly, and she nodded.

"One glass. No more," she accepted, then went to sit with the two men. "And something a little more potent for me, if you would be so good."

Kilan was about to get up, but she rolled her eyes. "Stay seated, Kilan. The great and mighty lord will surely manage to serve me a drink without your help. I have seen him do it before. He is rather good at it, considering that he is a rich barbarian who had no idea how to feed himself when he first came here."

Enric filled a glass for her and smiled to himself. That woman had a talent for dispersing tense situations by making fun of somebody. Or causing the same situations by doing so, however one wanted to see it.

He then pressed a glass of sweet wine into Eryn's hand and took her other hand to pull her towards the seating cushions with him. He felt a lot calmer now that she was beside him again.

"Has he informed you about the latest drama yet?" Pe'tala asked the men as she accepted the glass from Enric.

Orrin nodded and patted the spot beside him to make Eryn sit down. He put a strong arm around her shoulders and pulled her close to kiss her on the temple just like her companion had done before.

Pe'tala sighed. "You know, I strongly suspect that this is why my father has been somewhat stony to you, Orrin."

The warrior frowned. "Pardon?"

"That uncomplicated warmth between the two of you that looks a lot more like fatherly affection than normal friendship. You see, hospitality is in my culture an unwritten law, a way of life. The way he treated you today was a break with this, and I feel the need to make you understand why he behaved so."

"There is no need," Orrin assured her.

She took a copious gulp of the clear liquid and grimaced for a moment as it burned its way down her throat. "Oh, there is, believe me. A man of his standing is expected to be a role model. If those with the means to be hospitable do not demonstrate hospitality, then who can we expect to?"

"So what exactly is it you are saying?" the warrior enquired with a querulous expression. "That he is jealous of me?"

"Something like that I would suspect, yes," she agreed. "You see, in my House children are considered something of high value. Vel'kim men are in high demand as fathers, as they are very committed to their children, if not always so obviously to their companions," she added darkly. "The thought of a daughter who is not close to him - who even refuses to acknowledge him as her father - is no doubt an immense burden upon him. And seeing you with her, scolding her as if it was the most natural thing in the world, with her reacting to it like a stubborn daughter would, was very likely a little overpowering for him."

"So you are asking me to keep my distance to Eryn as long as your father is around?" he asked calmly with an even look.

"No, that is not what I am asking you. I would not dare proposing a stupid thing like that. I do not see why either of you would have to pretend you are less to each other than is the case because my father has unrealistic ideas of his long-lost daughter falling into his arms at a stroke."

Orrin relaxed visibly. "Good. I wouldn't have taken well to it."

Pe'tala chuckled. "Yes, that was the impression I had. I am not trained in fighting skills and I think you are quite a lot stronger than me. I am trying not to anger you if I can avoid it."

Kilan grinned. "Smart girl."

"I know," she grinned back.

"Such considerations did not exactly stop you from provoking Lord Tyront," Orrin pointed out.

"I told you, I only do it if I cannot avoid it. That day at the Council meeting there was no way to avoid it. I am a proponent of meeting stupidity with disapproval. How else are people to learn from their mistakes?" she shrugged.

Enric watched Eryn staring into her glass. She had not spoken a single word apart from ordering the drink. Pe'tala followed his gaze, then cleared her throat.

"Well, Eryn, I suppose you and I will have to get used to referring to each other as sisters without making it sound like a sendup or an insult. Though I can see why this would surely be hard for you. I am the younger, prettier and very probably more talented of us."

Eryn blinked and looked up at her. "One out of three. Not too bad for a start," she muttered. "But at least now you have a female role model to look up to. We might even manage to work together on a few of these character deficiencies that seem to have become stuck."

Enric gave Pe'tala a look of gratitude for teasing Eryn out of her lethargy. She winked back at him.

Vern entered the main room, carrying his cat.

"Ram'an has awoken," he pressed out between clenched teeth and with a grimace of pain due to the feline claws that had sunk into his shoulder. "He is not happy."

Kilan shook his head. "Another cat. At least this one is more compact in size, even though it does not exactly look like the cuddlesome sort."

"Ram'an is usually very well-behaved and mannerly," Vern pointed out indignantly and drew in a sharp breath when the cat strengthened its painful grip. "Now he is just disoriented and afraid."

"He isn't disoriented or afraid when he widdles on my shoes," Orrin growled.

"He hasn't done that in weeks!" Vern protested. Only then did he seem to notice the two women. "Oh, you are back." His gaze fell on the wine glass in Eryn's hand and he set down the protesting cat determinedly to walk over to her and pluck it from her grip.

"Are you quite mad? That is not good for your child!" He turned to Pe'tala. "And you just watched her instead of intervening!" he exclaimed reproachfully.

Eryn tunnelled her eyes into a stern look. "Give that back! Right now! Pe'tala permitted me one glass and I am in dire need of it. Don't make me get it from you. You would not like that."

Vern wordlessly gripped a carafe of water from the table and watered down the wine before handing it back to her.

"Nuisance," she murmured, but accepted the glass.

Vern sat down next to Pe'tala. "So, you two really are sisters. Not much of a surprise there, if you ask me. Mean temper, sarcastic..." He shut up when both women gave him evil glares.

They turned when they suddenly heard the cat hissing at something.

"Ah yes," Enric sighed and rose. "Urban has finally awoken. So this is where we see how those two will get along. Try not to move too much, it might startle them. I will stun Urban in case she decides that Ram'an is just the right size for a tidy snack."

The mountain cat slunk into the main room, complaining loudly and completely ignored the small red tom, which maintained its hissing and growling.

"Not too happy about being back in Takhan, your big cat, is she?" Kilan commented.

Enric shook his head. "It doesn't look like it, no. She probably remembers how hot it is here. Her natural habitat consists of shaded woods, after all. But at least she hasn't shown any ravenous inclinations when it comes to Vern's little friend. Yet."

Urban rounded the cushions twice, all the while caterwauling, before she stopped behind Pe'tala to sniff her hair.

"Yes, my girl," the women cooed and scratched the hairy cheek that was presented to her. "Yes, I am here, too. Do not worry, kitten, you can roam the gardens at the Vel'kim residence tonight. And in a week you will reign over those at the Aren residence."

"Kitten," Kilan murmured with a weary sideways glance. "Her shoulders are as high as my knees and she says *kitten*."

"You are as bad as my brother Vran'el," she sniggered. "His four-year-old daughter shows no fear while he walks on tiptoes when this cat is around."

"The dinner tonight," Eryn said calmly. "I would rather not go."

"Of course you will be going," Pe'tala threw in before Enric had a chance to answer. "An Aren never shows fear, and a Vel'kim never shirks an unpleasant duty. That does not leave much room for hiding. And especially not from my... *our* father. He may not always look the part, appearing friendly and harmless, but keep in mind that he still is one of the fifteen most powerful people in this country. If he feels that the only way of seeing you is having you move out of the ambassadorial residence and into his house, he can make that happen."

Eryn stared at her. "He wouldn't!"

"I would not count on that. He has not been unknown to resort to certain measures when he sees fit. He once punished me for disobedience by making sure that I was sent every single ailing infant under the age of two who was in need of a healer, for an entire month. After that I felt like sticking my head into a hole in the ground and never getting up again. I was fifteen at that time and my patience was not what it is nowadays."

"Yes, I see," Vern murmured. "Patience is definitely your most prominent virtue..." He flinched when she tugged his earlobe.

"No respect for your elders, my boy. And that despite growing up in that stuffy Order of yours."

He shrugged. "Eryn's bad influence, I am told."

"Nonsense. You are a little too old for that excuse. You are about to become a man, so you had better own up to being defiant and difficult. It is a more robust claim than saying that your character is the result of an older woman's influence. At least when it comes to girls." She looked at him thoughtfully. "You are interested in girls, are you not?"

He stared at her in shock. "What? Of course I am interested in girls! I am definitely not attracted to *boys*!" he exclaimed in horror.

She raised her brow at him. "You can calm down again now. I did not mean to imply anything of that kind, I was just asking. And you might want to be more careful with your reaction to that very question. My brother is attracted to men, and we are a lot more accepting of this kind of personal choice here than in your home land."

Vern froze. "Vran'el? To *men*?"

Enric exhaled audibly. "I see we should have dealt with this matter earlier to give you a chance to get used to the idea. Vern?" He waited until the boy had turned his head towards him. "I have come to regard Vran'el as a friend. He was a great help when we needed him and he is an intelligent and affectionate man. I would not take well to seeing you treat him with a lack of respect due to his personal and private preferences concerning his choice of partners. Have I made myself clear?"

Vern nodded slowly and swallowed. "Yes, L...Enric."

"Lenric?" Kilan chuckled. "It seems you are having difficulties omitting his title, young man."

"Doesn't seem to be the only kind of difficulty I am in right now," he sighed and watched his cat stalking the larger animal, clearly disgruntled at being ignored.

* * *

Eryn took a deep breath when Enric knocked at the door to the Vel'kim residence. The sun was setting and bathing the bright façade in a warm orange light. It only took a few moments until Valrad opened the door.

His eyes searched the party and his shoulders seemed to relax as soon as he had spotted Eryn. He had obviously been worried that she wouldn't come.

He smiled broadly and stepped aside to let his guests enter and jovially offered them a large bowl with cool, moist towels, asking them if Kilan had explained the custom to them when he had taken them to the ambassadorial residence. Junar confirmed that he had and gratefully accepted the humid cloth to wipe her forehead and throat.

When Valrad turned towards Eryn to offer her one next, his expression became concerned.

"Good evening, child," he said softly. "I was hoping that you would come despite your trying day."

"Yes, sure," she said calmly, wiping her own face without looking at him. She stilled when she felt his fingers at her chin to lift her face up to him.

"You look pale, my girl," he said after his eyes had searched her face. "Pe'tala told me that she had to heal away a shock reaction of yours today. You still do not look fully recovered. Would you mind if I had a look at you?"

Eryn forced herself not to shy away from his touch. "I would, actually. As you are the reason for my current mood I would rather not have you do anything that requires any physical closeness, if *you* don't mind."

Valrad pressed is lips together and let his hand sink from her face. "I understand that you have had hardly any time to come to terms with this new situation. I can wait."

He offered Enric, Orrin and Vern a towel each and then looked down at Urban, who had started sniffing his legs.

"My, my, your beast has grown quite a lot since I last saw her," he commented. "Vran'el will not be too thrilled at that."

When all of them had finished refreshing themselves, he preceded them up the stairs, conversing easily. "This is a typical outline for a Takhan residence," he explained to the newcomers. "The entrance area and store rooms are all downstairs, as it is cooler during the day. We take special care to insulate our walls to keep out as much heat as possible. The main room is on the first floor, a big central room that is the centre of family life and social gatherings. From the main room generally a number of corridors branch out that lead to bedrooms for family and guests, to the studies, library and sanitary rooms. The number of corridors and rooms depends on the wealth and preferences of the House. Ours is a bit more extensive than most, as my grandfather added an entire wing two generations ago. At that time it was still customary to have most of the family living under one roof. From the main room you can access the terrace. Due to its location on the first floor, it is generally elevated, so there are stairs to reach the gardens."

They reached the top of the stairs and Vern commented, "So this small table on the floor between the cushions is the only one?"

Valrad nodded. "It is indeed. The one at Kilan's place was especially made according to Ram'an's instructions for Eryn and Enric when they first came here. Though I am told that the current ambassador hardly uses it nowadays."

Enric nodded. "That's what he told me, too. He even is considering storing it somewhere."

Vran'el came in from the kitchen, carrying a large, steaming bowl. A grin spread on his face when he saw them, but quickly turned into an expression of shock.

"Your cat! Please tell me that she is fully grown at last?" His voice was on the edge of panic. Urban pricked her ears and then started trotting towards him, making him retreat a step.

"Stay where you are, you monster!" he commanded and closed his eyes, when she ignored his order and instead circled him twice to first sniff his legs and then rub her side affectionately against him.

Pe'tala laughed when she entered the room from the adjoining kitchen, taking the food bowl from his hands. "Give me that, you feeble excuse for a man, before you drop our dinner on the floor and we have to make do with cold fare. Better go back and get Eryn's dish."

Eryn blinked at the scene that had so many familiar elements, but seemed so strange in having them combined like this. Vran'el being afraid of Urban, Vern asking questions, Valrad taking the role of good-natured guide, Pe'tala's witty jibes. She had not seen Pe'tala and Vran'el together very often in the past, especially not in such a relaxed mood. Pe'tala had kept away from her home as long as Eryn had been here. She realised that they treated each other pretty much the way each of them treated her. Like a sibling. She pushed away the thought and looked in Valrad's direction. It seemed that she had just been addressed by him.

"I was asking what I can get you to drink, Eryn."

"Juice, thank you," she replied and followed Enric to the cushions to take a seat.

Orrin helped Junar sit down next to her.

"You know, this is very cosy and all," Junar sighed, "but sitting down and getting up is a bit of a challenge with my extra bulk."

Eryn smiled, determined not to spoil the evening for the others. "But at least it looks funny, if that is any consolation at all."

"It's not, and what's more I am looking forward to laughing at *you* in a few months," her friend retorted.

Vran'el returned from the kitchen with a smaller bowl and placed it at the centre of the table next to the larger one. Then he motioned for Enric to move aside so he could sit next to Eryn.

"Sweetness, I want to apologise for today. I seem to have managed to make a bad situation even worse for you. I am sorry. Will you forgive a fool who was too caught up in his own world to consider your feelings?"

She smiled when he leaned his forehead against hers. "I will. Provided that you have prepared a halfway decent meal for us, that is. I have been very concerned with eating lately, you know."

He laughed. "Then I have nothing to fear. You know how confident I am when it comes to cooking. I have been extra careful with spicing your dishes. I remember from Intrea's pregnancy that her stomach tended to get upset rather more easily than before."

When Vran'el leaned away from her again to fill her bowl, she saw Vern looking at her with a displeased frown. She lifted an eyebrow at him in question and sighed when he looked away hastily. She was not exactly in a mood to deal with his issues in addition to her own right now. This had to wait until later.

She leaned forward to use the water bowl to wash her hands and then pushed it towards Junar.

When all of them were ready to eat, Vran'el watched each of them pick up their bowls and waited until every last one of them had swallowed their first bite, just as a good host was supposed to do. Then he, too, started eating.

"What do you say, little sister? Did I promise too much?" he then enquired, sighing when she flinched at the term of address. "You better get used to that one quickly, Eryn. I have every intention of using it regularly."

Her smile looked a little strained when she replied, "I wouldn't want to steal Pe'tala's endearments, so why don't you stick with my name?"

Pe'tala huffed. "No need to worry on my account. He has started calling me *baby-sister*. Can you believe that? I had to become twenty-five years old to find out that I am not merely the younger of two, but the youngest of three, and the first thing that brute of a brother can think of is relegating me to *baby*."

"Why complain?" Vran'el smirked. "At least it finally matches your behaviour."

"Great," Eryn sighed, uneasy at their eerily natural acceptance of the fact that they had just like that acquired another family member. "How nice of you to treat your guests to a performance of the Vel'kim Siblings of Doom."

Pe'tala laughed at the term, and Vran'el grinned. "Vel'kim Siblings of doom. I like it. You do know that this includes yourself, do you not?"

"Children," Valrad reprimanded them, "do try to behave. We have guests and you are not affording them the best impression, I am afraid."

Enric smiled. "Don't worry, they have known Eryn for a while and are used to quite a lot."

Orrin nodded. "Yes. Not too long ago she was having breakfast in my bed, spreading bread crumbs all over it."

Enric watched Valrad's lips tightening slightly. It was the only external sign of his dismay at hearing another example of how close this man was to his daughter.

"Well, you just go and have breakfast in *her* bed as a revenge," Pe'tala shrugged.

"That is a bit difficult," he quipped. "Her bed happens to be my superior's bed as well."

Eryn smiled. "Bad luck, eh, Orrin?"

"You just wait. Your period of grace will be over in a few months and then you will be back in my hands for combat training," he retorted.

Pe'tala chewed thoughtfully, then said, "I have been thinking about taking combat lessons myself."

Several pairs of astonished eyes focused on her.

"What? I am the only magician who cannot use a sword in a place where everybody else can," she pointed out and grinned broadly when she added, "And I liked very much what Eryn did to the Queen of Darkness today. I enjoyed how she was kicked into the river. That was a work of performance art. It impressed me greatly."

"A work of art?" Valrad frowned disapprovingly. "I do not think that glorifying violence like that is an appropriate attitude for a healer, Tala. And I do not agree with your planning to learn it." His gaze rested on Eryn for only a short moment, clearly conveying the message that he was not at all happy that she had been made to do so and would be required to continue the training.

Orrin exchanged a knowing look with Enric and continued eating.

Pe'tala carefully put her empty bowl back on the table and said softly, "I am a grown woman, father. If I decide to acquire a skill that will help me to better adapt to the customs of the place I am staying at for now, then this is what I will do. No matter if you approve or not. I would ask Orrin if he is willing to teach me, though as you have not exactly been very friendly to him so far, I should henceforth refrain from doing so in your presence." Her tone had cooled down perceptibly towards the end.

Valrad closed his eyes for a moment. When he opened them again, his expression was calm and serene, as usual.

"Let us discuss this matter some other time, Tala," he said mildly. He turned towards Vern. "Would you care to accompany me to the clinic tomorrow, young man? There are a few people I would like to introduce you to, among them the man who asked you to do the artwork for his book."

Vern smiled and nodded eagerly. "That would be fabulous, yes!"

He then looked at Eryn. "And you, Eryn? Will you come as well? Iklan and Sarol have kept asking me when you will come by," he asked carefully.

Eryn shook her head. "Not tomorrow, no. There is a thing or two I would like to take care of tomorrow." Such as locking herself in a quiet place without seeing any of them. "I will drop by later. I know my way around, you know. But thank you for asking," she added politely. She could see in his eyes that this did not ease the sting of her telling him that she would go to the clinic soon enough, but not with *him*.

Vern carefully put down his bowl, his demeanour oddly awkward.

Enric looked at him, then had to hide a grin. He was waiting to be asked if he wanted another helping and wanted to avoid the appearance of doing just that.

Fortunately, Vran'el was a considerate host. "Can I offer you a refill, Vern?"

The boy pretended to consider the question, before nodding slowly. "That would be nice, thank you."

Vran'el filled the bowl once again and handed it to Vern, frowning slightly when the boy avoided eye contact with him.

When Vern had finished, Eryn straightened. Now that the dinner was over, she could move on the less pleasant matters. Well, *even* less pleasant, that is. The evening had not exactly gone swimmingly so far.

"I have learned about your intention to give an official statement at the Senate in two days," she addressed Valrad.

He visibly braced himself and nodded. "Yes?"

She cautioned herself to be careful. Phrasing it as a demand would hardly make him react favourably. It had to be a request.

"I do not feel comfortable with this. I would ask you to keep this knowledge private for now."

Valrad's eyes wandered over her face, then he slowly shook his head. "No, Eryn. I am afraid that this is not something I can do. I will make this matter public knowledge at the next Senate meeting. You will from then on be officially acknowledged not only as my legal, but also my natural daughter. It is the right thing to do."

Eryn exhaled. She had really hoped for him to comply with her request, so his words gave rise to anger and frustration. She caught Enric's warning look. He was obviously feeling it through the mind bond.

"Valrad," she said, using what she considered her most reasonable tone. "I appreciate your very responsible and honest approach in dealing with what has come about, though there are considerations that might cause harm to House Vel'kim."

"Such as?" he asked softly.

"Such as casting a bad light onto yourself as the current Head of House, on your brother of having been an unsuspecting, betrayed companion, and last but not least on me, being my own uncle's..." She stopped herself in time from saying what would definitely have caused offence.

"Your own uncle's *what*?" Valrad asked quietly, but his gaze had become sharp.

She stared into his brown eyes. Brown. Like Ved'al's. The brother he had so coldheartedly betrayed by having a physical relationship with his companion.

"Bastard," she said slowly, feeling dark satisfaction at the glint of danger in his eyes. "My own uncle's *bastard*. Is that what you want to tell the world, Valrad? That you were not only a terrible brother and an unfaithful companion, but also a careless healer who failed to prevent an unplanned pregnancy?" She saw Pe'tala closing her eyes for a moment, then open them again to glare at her. She did clearly not appreciate having her own words used to hurt her father like that.

"Watch your words, my girl," Valrad growled.

Eryn shot up from her seat, hands balled into fists. "I am not *your girl*! I don't need to listen to *you*!"

Valrad got up as well. "You are mistaken," he replied sternly. "I am your Head of House, something that alone puts me in a position to make you listen. And I am your father, no matter how displeased you are about that right now."

"You are *not* my father," she hissed. "Ved'al was my father! Your little tumble in the sheets with Malriel does not make any difference to *me*! I don't care about your guilt and misguided attempts to make things right again! If you want to do something good, keep your mouth shut about this instead of exposing us all to ridicule!"

"If being known to be my child is a matter of ridicule to you, then I am afraid you will have to learn to live with it," Valrad retorted angrily. His voice was calm, but the pulsating blood vessel at his throat betrayed the agitation within.

Enric and Pe'tala jumped up at the same time.

"Eryn and I will take a walk in the garden," Enric announced and pulled her with him, half dragging her out the terrace door and far enough away for them to be out of earshot.

He had wanted to reprimand her, but when she stood before him, breathing heavily, looking as if she was about to burst into tears, he just sighed in resignation and pulled her close.

She buried her face at his shoulder, breathing in his scent, feeling how being close to him comforted her, calmed her.

"I want to go home," she whispered.

"I know," he replied, silently cursing Malriel and the King for not being able to comply with her wish.

"I don't want to go back in there," she then said and looked up at him.

He sighed. "I am afraid we must. We can hardly leave now. This is awkward enough for Junar, Orrin and Vern as it is, even without our abandoning them on their first evening in a foreign country."

She nodded tiredly. "Very well. Then let's get this behind us. Let's not stay longer than necessary, shall we?"

He shook his head. "No, another hour, then we can leave without causing offence."

She laughed, her tone slightly hysterical when she retorted, "Yes, causing offence is definitely not what we want, is it?"

When they returned to the main room, Valrad and Vern were gone.

"Father has taken Vern to show him his library," Vran'el explained.

"Yes," Pe'tala added, "to give you both a few minutes to calm down again."

"I am calm," Eryn said coldly.

"Sure, I can see that," her sister remarked acidly. "Calmness radiates off you in gentle, soothing waves."

"Oh, shut up."

Enric made her sit down again and urged her to take a few sips from her juice.

"Vran'el?" she then asked.

"Yes, sweetness?" he asked carefully.

"I have a question pertaining to a legal matter."

"Alright. Let me hear it. Though I have to warn you: If you want me to assist you in having father locked up, I shall have to pass," he smiled, only half joking.

"Slipping somebody a pregnancy or fertility potion or however else you term it, it is illegal, isn't it?"

He nodded slowly. "Yes, it is."

"What is the general punishment for it?"

Exhaling slowly, he looked at her doubtfully. "For once, being made to cover the expenses of the upbringing of the child if it was somebody other than your companion, who would have to do that anyway. Then an additional payment for damages to the mother of the unplanned child is usually decreed as well."

"Only monetary punishment?" Eryn frowned. "She could afford that well enough. And Enric is rich enough, whatever she would have to pay would not make any difference to us. How about some personal limitations like being locked up, being put under a curfew or having her magic blocked for a period of time?"

"Eryn," Vran'el sighed, "there is hardly any chance for you to have her convicted. You would need to prove that she did it. This is impossible after this much time has passed."

She shook her head. "Alright, then the accusation will simply serve to damage her reputation. Even if I do not manage to get her convicted, people will know well enough that she did it. They will probably think twice before entrusting her with business decisions in the future. My determination not to have children was known well enough, after all. And my getting pregnant shortly after her leaving Anyueel is a fairly good pointer of guilt."

She turned her head when she heard Enric's voice.

"No."

"No? It's not obvious?" she frowned in confusion.

"No, you will not do this. You will not accuse Malriel of having planted a child inside you," he clarified.

She blinked. "Why not?" Then she glared at him. "Don't tell me you are protecting your House?"

"Not that." His expression was serious. "Not my House, but my son. I don't want him to grow up with the impression that he has been forced upon us by his own grandmother." He looked into her eyes and she could see the determination in them. "You may still not be too happy about this, but I am. And I will not have him thinking that he was anything else but a gift, a blessing. This is not open for discussion."

"I agree, sweetness," Vran'el added quietly. "He is right. Making your son grow up surrounded by this is not worth taking revenge on Malriel for. Not in that manner. Find another way to make her pay."

She looked over at Junar, who had laid a hand on her belly protectively. Her expression was pleading. So, she, too, was on Enric's side.

Orrin sighed. "The child comes first, Eryn. Has to. Really, you would regret doing this."

Eryn rubbed her face with both palms and sunk back into the cushions, defeated. "Any other suggestions how to get back at her?"

Junar smiled. "How about kicking her into the river once more? Or something that gets her not only wet but filthy? A dung heap or something?"

Eryn stared at her for a moment, then grinned. "Nice start, but not distasteful enough. Though I would go for a pit with venomous, stinging creatures within." Then she turned serious again and looked at Pe'tala.

"How do I get Valrad off my back?"

Pe'tala looked at her indulgently. "You do not. He will wear you down. One reason why Vel'kim men are good fathers, is their determination in combination with their patience. He will give you some time to come to terms with this state of affairs and give you a chance to come to him. If you do not, he will come for you."

Eryn stared at her. "So I am, what - trapped? Are you telling me there is no way out?"

"There is, sister: giving in and letting him be a father to you. He will accept nothing less."

She gulped and shook her head. "I don't care what he accepts. I will not be bullied into anything by him." She shot Pe'tala and Vran'el a sceptical look. "Why are you so accepting of this? Why aren't you angry? Why aren't you on *my* side?"

"We are, sweetness," Vran'el said sadly. "Unfortunately, *you* are not."

Eryn ground her teeth and looked at Pe'tala. "Alright, he is sentimental and not clear in the head. What about you? Why this willingness to accept me as your sister when you were about to tear the house apart when your father adopted me back then, when you still thought I was merely your cousin?"

Pe'tala shrugged. "Well, what can I say? Maybe I have unconsciously always wanted a sister, who knows? And maybe, just maybe, I think that after your dealings with the Queen of Darkness you deserve an actual parent, one who cares for *you* first instead of his own interests. Have I mentioned that I do like that term very much? It describes her so very accurately."

Eryn shook her head. "So not a single one of you is prepared to respect my wishes here? Really?"

Vran'el's eyes narrowed. "You are not withdrawing from us as well, are you?"

She looked at him. This was the lawyer speaking, she noticed, not the cousin or brother.

"No, of course not," she smiled, feeling her heart break a little at the thought that she would from now on have to keep him, too, at a certain distance.

He kept studying her. "Do not do this, Eryn," he implored her, his gaze piercing. "This is not a feud."

She looked away. No, it wasn't. But it would be *diplomacy*, the art of making things appear differently in order to keep everyone sufficiently deceived to avoid a war.

"Of course not, Vran," she murmured, "What a thought."

Her gaze fell on Junar, and the quiet understanding in her friend's eyes made her look away again. It made pretending so much harder.

CHAPTER 3

Settling a Debt

Enric checked once again the shipping papers for the goods they had arrived with on the ship to make sure the lists contained everything he had ordered. So far the only thing that had gone missing was a bale of purple silk cloth.

Kilan had offered him his study for the morning as there was a matter Enric wanted to take care of. One that required some privacy, as it was rather delicate.

He had learned about the short encounter between Eryn, Pe'tala and Ram'an at the teahouse the day before and Eryn's spontaneous decision to throw his bracelet back at him. A harsh gesture, and probably none he was very pleased about, Enric mused.

Ram'an was the visitor he was expecting any moment now. Enric had sent him a short message yesterday afternoon and had received a confirmation for the meeting today little later. The residence was quiet at the moment, considering how well-inhabited it currently was. Junar and Orrin were at a tailor's shop, Vern was at the clinic with Valrad and Kilan had decided to meet with somebody at a teahouse. The only one at the residence apart from himself was Eryn.

After the trying day she'd had, Eryn's night had not been exactly restful, either. She had lain awake for hours and spent the little time after she drifted off into a fitful sleep tossing and turning. Only in the early hours when the day announced itself had she finally collapsed into something that resembled unconsciousness more than sleep.

He heard the knocking and quickly moved towards the entrance door to admit Ram'an. He didn't want to wake Eryn and have her unexpectedly face his visitor only moments after getting up. He had briefly considered meeting at the Arbil residence instead, but discarded the idea again as he didn't want Eryn to be alone for the present.

After he had opened the door, it took him a moment to recognise the man he had invited. Ram'an looked different, and not to his advantage. He had lost weight and there were lines showing on his face that had not been there a few months ago. So it seemed his father's death and the strain of taking over the House had taken their toll.

"Ram'an," he nodded and stretched out his hand for the formal greeting. "Thank you for coming. Please come in."

"Enric," the other man nodded. "Your message was rather terse, but I assumed that you would not ask to meet me barely after arriving here if it were not important."

Enric handed his guest a moist towel and waited until he had wiped his face and hands before going ahead of him up the stairs.

When Ram'an had entered the study, he closed the door and motioned for the other man to sit.

"What can I offer you to drink, Ram'an?"

"Water will be fine, thank you."

Enric poured them each a glass and placed one before his visitor before taking a seat behind Kilan's desk.

"Before we get to the reason why you have asked me to come, let me congratulate you on the child you are expecting. I admit I was a bit surprised that you have managed to change her mind about having children that swiftly." His gaze became slightly leery. "I am assuming that you were able to change her mind?"

"As opposed to forcing her to become pregnant?" Enric enquired candidly.

"I admit that thought has crossed my mind, yes," Ram'an admitted calmly.

"I have not sunk that low, no."

"Does this mean that she wanted to have children?" the lawyer asked again.

Enric pursed his lips. Evasive answers were clearly not going to wash with a man of the law. At least not with this one.

"Saying that would probably be going a little too far," he said carefully.

"It would?" Ram'an narrowed his eyes at him. "Are you telling me that she did not want to have this child, but that you are not the one who is responsible for its conception?" He thought for a moment, then stiffened and drew in a breath. "Malriel."

"I would like to point out that I have not put words to any such allegation," Enric stated impassively.

"Of course not. Tell me why I am here."

Enric pushed the shipping papers towards him.

Ram'an looked down and frowned at the list that ran to different kinds of wine, fabrics, spices, herbs, wood and ore.

"I am afraid I do not quite follow you."

"A debt between us that has not yet been settled. I am herewith changing this."

He watched understanding and then shock appear on the other man's face. "A shipload of goods... Oh no. You are not serious, are you?"

"I am. A load of my produce in exchange for an embrace," Enric nodded and raised both brows when the list was shoved back at him.

"I told you, I did not expect you to comply with that condition. I just wanted to see how desperate you really were back then and was hoping to make you appear like a miser. I did not count on your honouring that condition." He got to his feet and turned towards the door. "And neither will I take those goods from you. I do not charge a man a king's ransom for supporting the woman he loves. Good bye to you, Enric. I will see you at the Senate tomorrow, I assume," he said coolly.

"Ram'an, please wait," Enric sighed.

The dark-haired man breathed out patiently and turned back with some reluctance.

"We both know that you are currently not in a position to refuse a load of goods that will fetch a very good price. I was permitted to bring them here over and above the already fulfilled trade quota between our countries, as the wares are not meant to generate profit for me. I couldn't sell them here even if I wished. It would be breaking the conditions of getting them here. So you either accept them or I can as well give them away on the streets."

"I cannot take them. Your gesture might be a noble one, but for me to accept it would be shameful," Ram'an said quietly. "You are right, there is not much I have left at the moment, my House stands on the brink of ruin. But what I do still have is my pride. I will find another way of getting back on course."

Enric sighed. Pride. Of course. That was hardly a great surprise. He himself would very probably have reacted the same way.

"Then let me make you an offer instead. You will accept the goods from me and consider them as a loan that enables you to meet your current payment obligations." He gave a thin smile, then added what he knew would make agreement easier for the man opposite him. "I am not doing this out of pure goodness of my heart. I am about to take over House Aren for a time, and House Vel'kim is for now the only ally I can be sure of retaining. Helping your House recover will surely earn me your goodwill. And for House Aren - a strong ally is a lot more useful than a weak one. Let's get you back on your feet for our mutual benefit, shall we?"

Ram'an stared at him, clearly torn. Enric waited patiently for him to nod in agreement.

"Good. Then you will pay me back when you can afford to. Take your time, though. As I told you, my interests are not of a monetary nature with you."

"I will prepare a formal agreement so as to have the conditions of our deal in written form," the Head of House Arbil sighed. "I will send a messenger when I am done to have you approve of the content."

"Don't bother. As I was willing to give the goods to you for free, I will be satisfied with whatever terms you see as appropriate."

"Then I suppose the only thing that is left for me to do is to thank you."

Enric shook his head. "There is no need for that. I think we have established that I am not doing this for entirely charitable reasons."

Ram'an finally managed a smile. "Of course not. I simply forgot for a moment that you are a hard, no-nonsense business man without consideration for anything other than his own advantage."

"Don't make the mistake of thinking I am relenting because I am not kicking you while you are down," Enric replied mildly. "I have my pride, too."

"I would not make such a mistake. Eryn would not have accepted a weak man."

Good, Enric thought. He had been wondering how to broach that subject.

"About Eryn. I assume you are not harbouring any more hopes about winning her for yourself now that we are not only joined in a third level bond, but are also about to have a child together."

Ram'an glared at him. "No. I am no fool. I know when I am beaten."

"Splendid. Then I can safely ask you to set things straight with her again. After yesterday she could do with another friend here."

"Yesterday, yes..." Ram'an nodded slowly. "Quite a mess, is it not? A sensitive matter for House Vel'kim that causes them considerable solicitude. I imagine that Eryn is not happy about this entire setup. Especially not as it will all be revealed to the Senate tomorrow."

Enric narrowed his eyes. "You are aware of this?"

"Of course. That kind of news is hard to keep secret in a city like that."

Both men regarded each other for a few moments, before Enric slowly shook his head. "Just a minute; I think you are trying to trick me into telling you about it! Pe'tala told me that you saw them yesterday at the teahouse. Clever."

"Not clever enough, it seems," Ram'an sighed. "So I will have to wait until tomorrow, after all. Can you at least tell me if is something bad? The three of them did seem rather agitated yesterday at the teahouse."

Enric grimaced. "The trouble is that depending on who you ask, the answer to that is either yes or no."

Ram'an opened the study door and stepped out into the corridor that led to the main room. "Alright, then I will wait patiently until the Senate meeting."

Enric felt a surge of annoyance and panic through the mind bond. That had to mean that Eryn had got up and heard Ram'an's voice. He

40

had not told her that he had asked the Head of House Arbil to come here today, and from what he could perceive she was not pleased.

He slowly walked towards the main room, giving her enough time to retreat if she wished so.

When the corridor opened into the main room, he was surprised to see her sitting calmly on the cushions, holding a glass of tea in her hand. Her external appearance did not betray any of the commotion he detected inside her. He was impressed.

She pretended to notice them only now and put her tea aside on the low table before her before she rose with a polite smile. Enric thought how much more elegant she looked rising from the cushions than a few months ago. He wondered if she had secretly been practising.

"Ram'an," she nodded and walked towards him, stretching out her hand to greet him formally.

His guest looked slightly puzzled, but recovered quickly and smiled at her, taking her hand in his to kiss it.

"Eryn. I am glad to see that you are in a better mood today," he said with a casual smile.

She nodded. "The pregnancy, you know. It does make me prone to even more extreme mood swings than before. At least that is what I have been told," she replied lightly.

Enric watched her closely. She kept Ram'an at a distance with cool politeness and meaningless chitchat. Unusual. This was not her preferred way of showing disapproval, if a hardly less effective one judging by Ram'an's uneasy frown.

"Then having you around will be an even greater adventure than before, my dear," he smiled and winked at her.

She ignored the familiar gesture completely and appeared thoughtful for a moment before she replied, "I certainly don't hope so. I try to spare people around me as well as I am able. If you would excuse me now, Ram'an, I need to get myself ready for an appointment. It was nice to see you."

"Yes," he said, slightly confused, "it was. I look forward to seeing you tomorrow. I am sure we will meet at the Senate before we do at the dinner."

Her smile was cool. "Certainly." Thus she turned and walked back to the table to pick up her tea before retreating to the corridor that led to their bedroom.

Ram'an stared after her, then slowly turned to look at Enric. "She has either become a lot better at pretending than she used to be, or she has somehow managed to turn her anger at me from yesterday into indifference inside one single day." He shook his head. "I very much hope it is the first one. The other option would truly disturb me."

Enric nodded. He knew well enough that she was everything else but impassive, but maybe thinking so would motivate Ram'an to make every effort to mend his dealings with her. He accompanied his guest downstairs to the door to see him off and then returned to their bedroom.

He leaned against the doorframe and folded his arms, watching her stand in front of the window with her tea and staring out into the small garden unseeingly.

"That was interesting. Your little performance impressed and unsettled Ram'an quite a lot. Had it not been for the mind bond, even I might have fallen for it," he commented.

She turned and sighed, the cool façade having slipped. "I have decided that I cannot keep snarling and spitting poison at all the people I am upset with right now. There are too many of them around, and all of them happen to be Heads of Houses."

He chuckled. "Yes, you do have a propensity for taking a dislike to important people. So your new approach consists of cool and aloof politeness? I admit it was effective enough right now, but I wonder if this is the right way for *you*. It seems out of character." Disconcertingly so, he added to himself. It felt wrong and he wondered how hurt she truly had to be to be able to keep the impulses that had made encounters with her stimulating if not exactly hazard-free, locked up within.

She took a sip from her glass and perched herself on the low windowsill. "I remember a conversation with Malriel the evening before her departure, when she must have slipped me the potion. I told her that I have no more intention of hating her, as this only means hurting myself, and that I would work towards being indifferent to her. She said that this was even worse than hate, and I am beginning to think that she is right. Not worse, mind you, that is just her point of view. I think it is more final, more powerful. And it will give me peace."

He swallowed. "And you intend to use this new strategy on Valrad and Ram'an as well as with her?"

"I do, yes," she confirmed. "Maybe it is time to say goodbye to the legendary Aren temper. It is nothing more than a burden, a character flaw." She walked towards him and leaned her forehead against his shoulder, smiling when his arms encircled her. "Time to grow up."

She didn't see his concerned expression. This felt wrong, as if she had decided to stop being herself.

"A pity," he murmured, "It was what first fascinated me about you. I would miss it very much."

She chuckled. "Then I will treat you to a private performance every now and then when you have the impression that your life is about to become too dull or peaceful."

"I will hold you to that," he remarked airily and wondered how well she would really be able to follow her resolution. He hoped not to the degree she had demonstrated only minutes ago.

* * *

Vern stormed into the main room and let himself collapse onto the cushions right next to Eryn. He had just returned from his visit at the clinic. An extended one, as he had left in the morning and now the sun was about to set.

"You seem to be walking on air," she commented when he grinned broadly at her and couldn't help but smile back. "I assume you had a satisfying day?"

"It was incredible," he sighed, clearly tired but blissed out. "The building is so big! So many healers! And they were happy to meet *me* of all people! Can you imagine that? They have all seen the book I gave to Ram'an back then, and they told me what extraordinary work it was. Then they asked me questions about healing back home in Anyueel and gave me a tour of the entire clinic! They have so many different areas of expertise here, I don't even remember all of them! I even met the Head of the clinic, but I forgot his name. He said it would be his pleasure to let me work and learn here for the duration of my stay! Can you believe that? I am going to work there!"

Eryn smiled her wide approval at him.

"What is this commotion about?" Orrin asked when he entered the room. "Junar is having a lie-down, so you had better lower your volume."

"Sorry, father," Vern grimaced. "I got carried away."

The warrior smiled and came closer to join them. "I assume you had a successful day with Valrad?"

The boy's face brightened again and he resumed rhapsodising. "Absolutely! I swear to you, they treated me like a king! They have a huge library there and they said I could go there and use it as often as I wanted. And they have something like a pub directly at the clinic where all people who work there can eat for free if they have this little silver badge. They call it a cantina, I think. The pub, not the badge. And they were asking about you, Eryn," he went on. "Especially one rather unfriendly healer, the one without magic."

"Sarol," she added with a grin.

"Yes, right, him. And another one, rather young but very important. An expert on head-things, I think."

"Iklan probably?"

He thought for a moment, then nodded. "Yes, that does sound familiar. They wanted to know when you would be dropping by and why you didn't come today and how you are doing and..."

"Vern? Don't forget to take a breath every now and then," she chuckled.

"Pe'tala was there, too," he went on after drawing a deep breath. "The unfriendly healer was happy to see her, I think, but he didn't want to admit it. Ram'an's cousin, the healer who wanted the drawings, was there as well. I showed him my pictures and I swear to you, he was completely speechless for almost a minute! He then showed the pictures around and they were immensely impressed and kept saying that they had never before seen anything like it!"

Eryn laughed. "Good thing you have ears, my lad, or your grin would circle your whole head and make the top half fall off." His good mood was contagious.

"They think I am brilliant and a genius!" he giggled lightheadedly.

She ruffled his hair. "You are, Vern. And it seems you have come to the right place to have people appreciate that."

"That they have! And your fa... Valrad," he corrected himself hastily, "had to send people away and promise them that he would take me to them some other time because they all were pushing to talk to me! Did you know that he is very important there? He used to be in charge of the place but stepped back voluntarily to concentrate more on leading his House and working with patients again."

"Yes, I heard about that," Eryn remarked dryly. "I was here once before, remember?"

"Yes, that's right. Of course," he nodded, shaking his head at himself. "You know what? They offered me a place with their trainee healers for classes!" He fumbled for a sheet of paper. "This is a list of the topics the second years are going through in the next ten days, and I can just go there and listen to what they are being taught! How amazing is that?"

"Pretty amazing," she nodded. "I swear to you, if you manage to get certified as a healer here before me, I will throttle you. And you can't even defend yourself because there is no hitting the pregnant lady," she sighed.

He jumped up. "That reminds me!" He dashed downstairs and came back a few moments later with a heavy book under one arm. "This Sarol guy sent this along for you. He said now that you are back and have time at your hands you might as well do something useful with it. He wants you to read this. It is about non-magical diagnosis, I think."

Eryn grabbed the book eagerly. "Thank you! That is great; it means he wants me to start preparing for the last missing exam!" It would give her something to do here, finally!

"He is really rude, you know," the boy pointed out. "I wonder why everybody puts up with it, even your... Valrad."

She swallowed her annoyance at his repeated lapse. "Because he is really, really, *really* good at what he is doing. He has revolutionised non-magical healing, has turned it into a real discipline that is now acknowledged to such a degree that even magician healers have to learn something about it," she explained. "He is a genius, too." She looked up from the book and into his inquisitive face. "And just like you, he is entitled to his peculiarities because of it. If he is unfriendly to you, it means that he likes you. If he doesn't like you, he doesn't even bother noticing you."

That made him think. "I see." Then he grinned. "That probably means he likes me. He snapped at me twice!"

She giggled. "Sure proof."

"You look dusty, sweaty and exhausted," Orrin cut in. "I think you should take a bath and make yourself presentable for dinner. Enric is in the kitchen preparing it right now, so it will soon be ready. Off you go."

Vern obeyed reluctantly and shuffled off.

"How are you doing, my girl?" he asked when they were alone. "You still don't look like yourself, though I can see that Vern's enthusiasm just now has perked you up."

"I am well enough, Orrin. Thank you for asking," she smiled. "I am just tired. I didn't sleep very well or for long last night. Maybe I will ask Vern to give me little magical push this time. I want to be well rested tomorrow for that damn Senate meeting." Her expression had become dark.

"Are you sure you want to go there? I didn't have the impression that you will be able to stop him from announcing his news to the Senate."

She shook her head. "No, I won't. I am aware of that. But there is a thing or two I want to say there as well."

"There is?" he frowned.

"Yes." She looked up in relief when Kilan entered the main room. "Where have you been all day long? I thought you just wanted to meet somebody for tea?"

"Initially, I did. But then I ended up at his house answering a lot of questions about the newcomers that are staying at my place."

She grinned. "That's what you get for harbouring guests. Next time you ought to think twice before agreeing to that."

"I could hardly let you poor castaway travellers sleep on the street, could I?" he smirked. "Imagine the political consequences if one of your two monsters had snacked on a Takhan citizen."

"Then let me congratulate you on your providence. I had thought that your hospitality had something to do with the fact that Orrin and I happen to be your superiors and you didn't dare refuse our request on that account. But I was obviously mistaken."

Kilan took a fresh glass and poured himself a glass of dark fruit juice. "At least you realised your mistake. Enric is cooking dinner, I assume?"

"He is, yes," she confirmed. "How about your own cooking skills? Have you improved them in these last months here?"

He nodded. "There was no other way. They laugh at adults who cannot cook a proper meal. Ask me how much fun it is to prepare formal dinners for thirty or forty people all alone. I spend almost all day long in the kitchen. In addition to going hunting first, of course." His smiled then. "But at least this will not be a problem tomorrow as I have quite a number of helpers here."

"Tomorrow?" she frowned. "But tomorrow is the welcome... Oh no. No! Please not."

"No what?" Orrin enquired.

"The bloody welcome dinner," she sighed. "It is going to be held here at the ambassadorial residence, isn't it?"

The ambassador nodded. "Yes. Both Malriel and Valrad requested such." He shot her a meaningful look. "Very likely because they wanted to make sure *you* have no other choice but to attend since it is at the place you are staying at."

She moaned. "But that means that I have to stay until the very end! Come on, why didn't you refuse?"

He looked at her indulgently. "Refuse a polite request from two powerful Heads of Houses? Is that a serious question?"

"I am not going to help you cook!"

"That is just as well, after your reaction just now I would be worried about your poisoning the lot of them," he snorted. "But as I still have the three men here in addition to Vran'el, who has offered his help, we will manage somehow without you."

Her face soured and she sighed. All these people here at this place with no chance to leave early. It was not even possible for her to claim indisposition in order to have an early night. There were just too many healers around to take care of whatever ailment she used as a pretext. And they would of course work out quickly enough that it was an excuse and probably even expose her to the others. Who would ever have thought that staying in a city with so many well-trained, knowledgeable healers could turn out to be such a nuisance?

CHAPTER 4

The Announcement

Eryn felt her palms start sweating when she turned the corner and saw the Senate hall appear before her. The last time she had been there, several months ago, was when she'd had to face the vote that had decided the outcome of the trial Malriel had subjected her to. The decision had been in her favour, but the day had nevertheless also brought the unpleasant revelation that Enric had been adopted into House Aren in exchange for Malriel choosing not to harm House Vel'kim.

Malriel might not have managed to get Eryn held in Takhan for two years back then, but she had only little later achieved something equally remarkable: compelling Enric, and without fail his companion, to return to Takhan for a time span that was yet to be determined despite their resistance.

Returning to that very building, knowing that another dreadful thing was to happen in connection with that same woman was not easy. And yet she had to be present and to endure it, maybe even get them to suffer for it.

She concentrated on slowing her breathing and thereby relaxing her body when all impulses were to tense. She wanted to keep her composure in there - she needed to. She had treated the senators and the triarchy to occasional proofs of her temper in the past, but today this was out of the question. No more Aren temper; it would just remind people of her connection to that vile woman, even more than their resemblance did already.

Enric walked a step behind her. He had considered offering her to return to the ambassadorial residence or go anywhere else in the city instead of the Senate hall, but he knew she couldn't stay away from it, no matter how painful it would turn out to be for her. Neither would he, in her place, have opted out. She seemed serene enough - if one didn't know her well enough to read the tiny, less obvious signs in her body language. The slightly lifted chin, the tighter than usual lips, the tense set of her shoulders hinted at some inner turmoil.

Vern, Orrin, Junar and Kilan were with them, and none of them had uttered a single word since they had left for the Senate hall.

They had reached the stairs that led up to one of the three large entrance portals with the high double doors, and Eryn started climbing them without any discernible hesitation.

When they entered the hall, most of the senators were present already and conversing among themselves in hushed tones. Malriel was talking to Legara of House Finran, one of her allies, who had been very open in her support for House Aren during the trial. Valrad conversed with Uvel of House Tokmar, the father of his son's lover Neval. He looked up when the group of fair-haired people with one dark-haired woman among them entered the building.

Their gazes locked for a long moment, before Eryn broke the contact and let her eyes wander over the rows of occupied and empty seats. She found Ram'an easily enough and forced herself to nod at him once politely before her attention was drawn on the first row to the very woman who was once again to blame for what was about to happen.

Malriel did not seem outwardly ill at ease, yet her usual arrogant stance was not as pronounced today. So she, too, was dreading what was to come. The thought somehow lifted Eryn's spirits a tiny bit. Malicious glee was a helpful emotion at times, she mused, even if not a particularly attractive one.

Vran'el walked towards them, smiling unhappily.

"Have a seat here in the back. The last two rows are available for visitors to the meeting. Word has not yet got out concerning the impending revelation," he murmured, "so at least this is going to be over quickly as no large crowd is attending today."

He hastily returned to his seat next to his father's when three figures entered the hall and marched towards the podium at the centre of the semicircle the seats formed.

"Are these the triarchs?" Vern whispered.

Enric nodded and explained quietly, "They are, yes. Their seats are on the podium. The meeting starts when they arrive and ends when they declare it over. The woman is Torke'na, the man to her left Abrak and the other one is Golir. I stayed at his home during the trial, as it looks like he is virtually the only magician around who is stronger than me."

It became quiet immediately after the three triarchs had taken their seats.

The woman, Torke'na, sat between her two colleagues and cleared her throat.

"Senators, welcome to today's meeting. Let us not lose time unnecessarily but start with the first matter at hand: Malriel's impending departure. Enric of House Aren, I see that you are present. Good."

Enric stood, towering over the seated senators.

"I am, yes."

"You are about to take over the responsibility of a House, Enric," the triarch spoke. "We wish to convey our thanks for your willingness to take this upon yourself. As you have not had the chance to spend a lot of time here yet, the position will no doubt be a challenge for you. We expect you to uphold the values of your House and this Senate, of which you will soon be a member, and in turn offer you our support should you require it. The responsibilities of your new position will include ensuring the wellbeing and also financial security of the family as well as participating in the political process in your capacity as senator. Are you willing to accept this role for the duration of Malriel's absence with all it entails?"

Enric nodded. "I am, yes."

"Very well." She then turned towards Malriel. "One week is not a long time to prepare a man from another country for such a role."

Malriel smiled confidently. "Enric is an unusually intelligent and capable man. I have no doubts whatsoever that he will take on his responsibilities wonderfully. I will give him all the information I can during the last few days I am still here, and I am certain he will manage to sort out the rest himself quickly."

"The members of your House will have to take the oath with him. Have they agreed to that?"

She nodded. "They have, yes."

"You are aware, of course, that they must give their oaths voluntarily? I would expect that this might be an issue for some members of your House, considering both Enric's origins and the circumstances of how he came to be your heir," Torke'na pointed out.

"I have managed to convince them that this solution is preferable to all other options."

The triarch raised her brow. "I imagine you have, yes..." It seemed as if she was not entirely convinced of the voluntary nature which the members of House Aren had agreed to that. "This is settled, then. Let us move on to the next point. Valrad, you have asked for permission to address the Senate today by giving an announcement you wish to make. The floor is yours."

Eryn held her breath when the Head of House Vel'kim rose from his seat and stepped forward into the centre of the semi-circle to look at his colleagues.

"I thank you for hearing me today, dear fellow senators, dear members of the triarchy. I wish to share something with you today, a fact with which I have only recently become acquainted myself and which has unfortunately resulted in quite some discord in my family. I stand here before you because I want to assume responsibility for my actions several decades ago. Looking back, I know that they were shameful, but when I look at the outcome," his gaze fell on Eryn, "I cannot bring myself to regret it the way I know I should."

It had become hushed within the Senate hall; he had his colleagues' rapt attention on him. They were waiting for him to go on, some of them were even leaning forward in eager anticipation of a scandalous morsel of news to be revealed.

"I had an affair with Malriel of House Aren almost thirty years ago," he announced loudly, his chin lifted defiantly. "At that time she was joined with my brother Ved'al. And I with my companion Genfra." He paused when the senators started murmuring.

Malriel sat still as a statue, clearly waiting for the last bit of incriminating information to be revealed, getting it all over with.

"The reason I am telling you this," Valrad went on and the murmuring died down again, "is that it has turned out that there are unexpected but by no means unwelcome consequences. Eryn, or Maltheá, as many of you know her as, is *my* daughter and not my brother's. I have come here today to acknowledge my daughter before all of you officially. What has been mine under law from a few months ago is now also mine in blood. I herewith make an application for the respective genealogical documents in our archives to be adapted accordingly. I will take care of doing the same with the medical information in the clinic archives."

Eryn felt heat flushing her cheeks at the many pairs of eyes that had swivelled towards her and stared. Ram'an's expression was glum and sympathetic and she quickly looked away from him. The other senators' faces displayed a range of different expressions: simple surprise, pity, shock, disapproval, incredulity and dark delight.

She forced herself to make eye contact with every single one of them, showing them that she didn't care, whatever they thought.

When the murmuring was about to start again, Golir addressed Valrad from the top of the triarchy's podium and the noise died down immediately.

"What led you to discover this circumstance? What evidence do you have to support the assumption that you are Maltheá's father?"

"If you permit, I would ask my daughter Pe'tala to answer that question. She was the one to find the evidence."

The triarch nodded and a moment later Pe'tala got to her feet from a seat at the other side of the Senate hall. Eryn had not even noticed that she was present.

The young healer walked towards her father, who stepped away to give her space.

"Pe'tala," Golir nodded. "Can you confirm your father's claim? And if yes, give the Senate your reasons."

She turned towards the assembled senators and her gaze rested on Eryn for only a short moment before she looked away again.

"Senators, I hereby confirm my father's claim that Maltheá of House Vel'kim, who was until today considered Ved'al's daughter, is instead of Valrad's blood. As most of you are aware, Maltheá is currently expecting a child, a male. As is customary, I performed the usual examination as to inherited diseases and congenital malformations. In the course of this I came across a bone disease that is passed on through both the maternal and paternal lines, but only emerges in male offspring. While it is passed on by females without any external symptom, this does not apply in the case of men. If they inherit it, it shows. Ved'al did not have this disease and thus he cannot have passed it on to Maltheá and consequently her son. Enric of House Aren does not have the disease either, so his son cannot have received it that way." She paused. "Valrad *has* inherited the disease."

Eryn saw several frowns and a few nods. Pe'tala had explained the complicated rule of inheritance in a fairly understandable way, but most people probably had not much contact with such matters and were a little overwhelmed. Those few that were able to follow Pe'tala's explanation without any problem were very likely healers themselves.

Golir thought for a moment, then asked, "How many families currently pass on this disease as far as you are aware? House Vel'kim has always prided itself on keeping track of these matters."

"Two," she answered immediately and added with a sideways glance, "Unless Malriel's love life was very... enriched in variety at the time of Maltheá's conception, I would assume that Valrad was the one to father her daughter."

That earned her a chuckle or two from her audience.

"Thank you for your statement, Pe'tala," Golir dismissed her and then turned to Malriel. "Malriel, do you confirm that you had intercourse with Valrad at the time of Maltheá's conception?"

She nodded once.

"Did you have intercourse with any other men apart from your companion at this time?"

She flashed him an annoyed look, but kept her mouth shut in favour of shaking her head.

Eryn's thoughts raced. The only evidence they had was her son's disease, but that had been healed away, hadn't it? So the only thing that supported Valrad's claim was Pe'tala's statement. A statement she was no longer able to prove...

"This seems to conclude that matter. Valrad, the triarchy herewith acknowledges..."

"Wait!" Eryn rose from her seat hastily. "I wish to ask for permission to speak."

Golir nodded slowly. "Granted. Would you like to step before the Senate?"

She shook her head. "That will not be necessary." She lifted her head. "I challenge the allegation made by Valrad." She focused her stare on Golir, but saw from the corner of her eyes how once again all faces twisted towards her. "There is no evidence to support the assertion that I am his daughter, as far as *I* am aware."

"You do not acknowledge the evidence of your son's inherited bone disease?" Golir asked mildly.

She smiled thinly and raised her chin defiantly. "There is no bone disease," she stated calmly.

Pe'tala jumped up from her seat and exclaimed with a murderous look at her, "Because I healed it away!"

Enric next to her closed his eyes for a moment, before he murmured lowly, "Eryn, don't. Please."

She ignored him and instead turned her head to look at Pe'tala coolly. "Did you?"

The younger woman narrowed her eyes. "You are *not* publicly declaring me a liar, are you?"

The noise level rose when Eryn failed to reply and simply looked straight ahead at Golir, waiting for him to decide how to proceed.

He exhaled wearily. "I see. Is there any other evidence to support your claim, Valrad?"

Valrad shook his head. "No. Nor is there any need for any other."

"Not for you, but Maltheá has raised a valid objection. I can think of only one way to settle this matter," he mused and his gaze wandered back to Pe'tala.

She cursed and got up from her seat again. "Alright, I will undertake it!" she huffed and stomped back to the place in front of the podium, all the while muttering under her breath.

Golir nodded and rose from his seat to step down from the podium. Only when he took the hand she offered him Eryn realised what was about to happen. Pe'tala had just agreed to subject herself to a truth block, or lie filter, as they called it here. Damn!

"The bone disease you claim to have found in Maltheá's child, was it genuinely present?" the triarch asked calmly while keeping his palm pressed against hers.

"Yes," she replied clearly and for all to hear.

"And is to your knowledge the explanation of Valrad being her natural father the only likely one, assuming that Malriel had no more than two carnal partners at the time?"

"Yes," she answered again without hesitation.

"Can you exclude the chance of Ved'al having fathered her with absolute certainty?" he insisted.

52

"In accordance with my knowledge, which reflects the current status of knowledge in this area to a high degree, I can exclude that chance, yes," she confirmed confidently.

Golir nodded with satisfaction and let go of her hand again. "Thank you." Then he turned back to the Senate. "She has spoken the truth. Of the healers present, do any of you find a logical fault in the argumentation presented as evidence for Malthreá being the natural daughter of Valrad of House Vel'kim?"

A few senators shook their heads.

"Then I consider this matter concluded. Valrad, the genealogical information will be adapted accordingly. The Senate acknowledges you as the natural father of Malthreá of House Vel'kim."

Valrad's relieved sigh was audible throughout the Senate hall.

Eryn felt all the energy draining from her limbs at her defeat, but forced herself to remain upright.

"There is one more thing I would like to ask," she said and again all eyes were on her. "I am no expert in your laws, but I assume that there normally are consequences if people break a third level commitment bond?"

Golir nodded slowly. "Depending on the circumstances, this is possible, yes," he replied carefully.

"The circumstances being how influential the culprits are?" she asked boldly.

That did not sit well with the present senators.

"Not good," she heard Enric say quietly. "You are not making any friends right now by accusing them of being lenient with the rich and powerful."

"I apologise for that," she added quickly. "It was disrespectful and I have caused offence by letting my emotions get the better of me."

"It was indeed disrespectful," Golir confirmed with a hard look, "but it is good to see that you realised your error. Let me inform you as to the true circumstances I was referring to. The breaking of a third level bond is a matter between private parties and does not lead to automatic intervention of a higher authority. If such intervention is desired, there needs to be a claimant, a wronged party who is seeking punishment or compensation. Betrayed companions would qualify for that description, for example. As neither person involved is currently in a companionship, there can be nobody to raise such a request."

"There is me," Eryn said slowly.

"You wish to charge both your parents with breaching a third level commitment bond? Do I understand you correctly?" Golir frowned, taken aback.

She nodded, and he considered her for a few moments before he said, "I do not see how you qualify for the term *wronged party*, Malthreá. Your circumstances have not changed, you are not subject to any financial disadvantage, you are still a member of your father's House, and there are no political alliances at stake as a consequence of this new information."

"This is true," she retorted calmly, "but I consider my own personal disadvantages due to being the result of an illegitimate affair as by no means any less aggravating than any financial consequences might have been. And the reputation of the man I do still consider my father, despite your decree, has suffered as well."

"Ved'al's reputation, Maltheá, has suffered far greater damage through his own actions than through his brother's and companion's," Abrak pointed out.

"So you are saying that I am not entitled to seek retribution for them?" Eryn enquired.

"What kind of retribution is it you are seeking for them?" Golir asked patiently.

She thought for a moment. "What is the most serious sentence you have here?"

"The one for treason," he replied mildly.

"So be it, then I take that. Twice."

A wave of indignation was caused among the senators by that statement.

"Maltheá," Malriel's voice rang through the high hall, "you are aware that the sentence for treason is *death*, are you not?"

Eryn pursed her lips and then nodded slowly before looking back at Golir. "I see. In this case, I elect to have it applied once only."

"Maltheá!" the Head of House Aren hissed again. "You would never have me killed!"

Eryn rolled her eyes and amended, "Alright, alright, lifelong incarceration for Malriel, then."

Malriel threw her hands up into the air, the resentment and anger clear on her face.

Golir shook his head at her. "This is a rather more severe punishment than we consider appropriate for mere infidelity, Maltheá. And also highly inconvenient in this case as we are to send Malriel on a very important mission to secure the peace of our country. I trust that you see that incarceration would make that rather difficult," he commented tartly. "I have to deny your request for retribution. The true victim here, if you care to use that term, is Ved'al, and he is no longer among us so mercifully will never learn of it. Thus no compensation of any kind, in the form of a fine or imprisonment, is justified here." He sighed. "This is not an easy situation for you, I understand that well. Coming to terms with it is not something the Senate can help you with. This is what your family will do, despite your unflattering attempts at refusing their efforts at including you. You may consider yourself lucky that members of House Vel'kim tend to be more forgiving than others."

Eryn swallowed and nodded once. "Yes. Lucky. Of course." She felt how the anger came closer and closer to the surface. "Would it be considered as another show of disrespect if I leave the meeting prematurely? I do feel an urgent need for fresh air."

"No," Golir replied. "It would not. You may leave."

She carefully pushed back the chair, when she would have preferred kicking it out of the way, and walked towards the high doors with a controlled pace instead of storming out. She closed her eyes for a moment when she was standing outside in the bright sunlight.

That had not been at all pleasant, but there was one victory she could be proud of: keeping herself in check. She had not once become emotional, not counting her disrespectful remark which she had immediately afterwards apologised for.

She slowly started walking back to the ambassadorial residence. It would take little more than a few hours until most people in the city would have heard about the revelation in the Senate. It meant every single one of the guests tonight would be aware of it. She wondered if this was considered a polite topic for conversation around here. And why not, indeed? Valrad was obviously pleased enough about having another daughter. *He* would probably not mind talking about it.

She heard hasty steps behind her and walked on without turning. They were not heavy enough to be Enric's or Orrin's and too light and dynamic to be Junar's of late.

"That was not very flattering," Pe'tala complained when she had drawn level. "Though I will admit I had expected worse. You took it well enough, considering your Aren deficiencies, that is."

Eryn turned to her. "Seriously? You follow me to insult me after what just happened? Go away and leave me in peace!" Her voice became louder towards the end.

Pe'tala looked at her, then nodded. "Good. I was a little worried about that frosty, controlled routine in there."

"Did you just provoke me to make sure of... what exactly?"

"I was just checking if the anger and frustration are still simmering underneath or if you have already managed to bury them deep enough to be dangerous to your health." She shrugged. "It is good to see that a little provocation gets them to reappear. I think you should see Iklan about this. He is very good with unresolved issues. I am sure he would agree to working with you."

Eryn frowned in confusion. "What are you talking about? What would I be doing with Iklan?"

"He can help you master your anger and whatever else is seething inside you."

"I can master my anger well enough, thank you very much," Eryn growled. "And I explicitly remember sending you away."

"You did. And I forgive you for it. Now come."

"Come where? I am not going to your residence, just so you know!"

"I had no intention of suggesting that. I am not stupid, whatever other deficiencies you may see in me. But neither will we return to the ambassadorial residence. Too much commotion there, the preparations for the dinner tonight have started already, which do not make it exactly a very relaxing place right now. We will visit House Feral. Intrea and Obal will be very pleased at seeing us. Well, Intrea will. Obal still does not care for you much, I think. We can tell them about how Erbál is doing and sit in their garden. They have a very nice, shadowy one." Without waiting for a reply, she took Eryn's hand and pulled her into a different direction. "And they do not yet know about what was announced at the Senate today, so there will be no awkward conversations for now."

Eryn sighed and gave in. That last argument was a winner.

*   *   *

A servant opened the door of the Feral residence, nodded when he recognised Pe'tala and stepped aside to let them both enter. After they had put aside the moist towels, they followed the man up the stairs into a spacious main room with an array of colourful carpets and tapestries on the walls.

Intrea was sitting on the cushions with something that looked like a drawing pad on her lap, looking up in surprise when they emerged.

"Tala! Eryn!" she exclaimed and jumped up, dropping her paper and pen to the floor. She pulled Pe'tala into a fierce hug and then kissed Eryn on both cheeks. "That is a sight I would not have thought possible! The two of you here together in the same room, voluntarily!"

Eryn remembered that this was where Pe'tala had stayed back when she had been put under Ram'an's supervision at the Vel'kim residence.

"Yes, things have changed a little," Pe'tala smiled. "Where is that niece of mine?"

"Out in the garden, playing with one of the servants." She nodded at the paper on the floor. "It gives me a little time for indulging myself in my old pastime."

"We have brought the genius from Anyueel with us, the smart young man who made the illustrations in Ram'an's book," Pe'tala told her. "You can exchange views on drawing."

Intrea grimaced. "I am afraid my efforts cannot compete with what I have seen of his work. I would be ashamed to show him anything I have drawn."

"Don't be," Eryn shook her head. "He has never before had the chance of talking to somebody who had any inclination or talent for drawing. I know that he would be delighted to."

"Then maybe I will reconsider," their hostess smiled. "Say, you have not by any chance just come from the Senate hall, have you?" she then enquired curiously.

"Why do you want to know that?" Pe'tala asked evasively.

"Because Vran has been keeping something from me. I have been pestering him for at least two weeks now and he keeps telling me to wait for the Senate meeting today." She looked at both of them in turn. "I strongly suspect that it must have to do something with either or both of you, as the Senate meeting was timed for shortly after your arrival here. Come on, ladies, out with it!"

Eryn looked glum. "I had hoped to leave that behind me for a few hours, you know."

Intrea gave her a pitiful look. "Oh, please - come on! All the senators and whoever else was at the meeting knows, and I do not. I have been waiting to hear of this for so long now!"

"Tell her," Pe'tala sighed. "She will not let it lie otherwise. Honestly, she will just continue pleading and end up embarrassing herself."

"You tell her. I don't want to."

"Very well," the younger woman sighed. "Then let us sit down and have something to drink first. Intrea, you are neglecting your duties as a hostess. If my throat is dry, I cannot talk of the news."

Intrea dashed off towards what was very probably the kitchen and returned only few moments later with two carafes, one filled with water, the other with dark yellow juice.

"Tala, you know where the glasses are," she instructed and put down her load on the low table amidst the cushions.

Pe'tala joined them a moment later, putting three glasses on the table before them and taking her time carefully pouring each of them a drink.

"You are doing this on purpose," Intrea accused her. "Hurry, or Obal will be here any moment."

"Eryn is my father's daughter," Pe'tala said simply.

"What do you mean, his daughter? Of course she is, he has adopted her. We are not talking of...?"

"Her being his love child from a night of sin between him and Malriel? Exactly that."

"Did you have to put it like that?" Eryn sighed.

Her sister shrugged. "If you did not like the way I phrased it, you should probably have done it yourself." She turned back to Intrea. "Father announced it at the Senate today, acknowledging his illegitimate child."

"Vel'kim style," Intrea nodded and then looked at Eryn. "You do not look happy about it."

"I am not."

"She is not," Pe'tala confirmed. "She first tried to challenge the evidence which meant I had to agree to repeating my medical findings under the influence of a lie filter," she explained with a withering glare at Eryn. "Then she tried getting her own parents convicted for breaking a third level bond. Her first choice of punishment was a *death sentence*."

Intrea stared at her. "That does seem a little harsh," she said slowly.

"I didn't know that we were talking about a death sentence," Eryn sighed. "Golir just said something about a severe punishment for treason, and that sounded fine to me."

"You amended that by saying you only wanted it for Malriel," Pe'tala pointed out. "You knew what you were talking about then."

"I never said that," Eryn protested. "I just said I would take only one instead of for two, and Malriel just assumed that I meant her."

"Which you did. You looked at her."

"So what? I amended that one, too, didn't I?"

"Yes, to lifelong incarceration," Pe'tala huffed.

"Which they didn't grant, either. So what exactly are you complaining about?"

"Your unhealthy attitude towards your parents in particular and your family in general. Not only did you publicly reject Malriel and father, but also by implication me, by making me appear unreliable with your contesting my statement."

Eryn groaned. "You thwarted that attempt well enough, so take it easy, will you?"

"Girls, shut up! Both of you," Intrea cut in. "You are giving me a headache with your bickering."

"You asked for it," Pe'tala shrugged.

"I did, yes. Now I am asking you to shut up and give me a little time to take in the news." She shook her head. "Malriel and Valrad. Who would have thought it?" She looked at Eryn. "When did you hear about it? You still seem shaken. Not today at the meeting, did you?"

"No, they told me two days ago on the day of our arrival here. Last time I came here I got to know about Malriel, and this time I got a new father as well to complete the set. How jolly," she jibed.

"I see that this is not easy for you," Intrea said sympathetically. "Though as fathers go, Valrad is definitely not the worst you could have ended up with. Vel'kim men are known to be very dedicated fathers, believe me, I know."

"Eryn does not let him get close."

Intrea grimaced. "That is not going to be easy. Especially not with you expecting his grandchild."

Eryn swallowed her remark about her pregnancy obviously being common knowledge here already. This was her brother's companion, after all. Of course she would know.

"Have you thought of a name so far?"

She indicated that she had not, grateful that they had changed the topic. "It seems there are quite a few things to consider when picking one."

Pe'tala nodded. "The first letter needs to be a V. Very important Vel'kim rule for males. We abandoned it for girls, fortunately."

"It's not quite as easy. Enric insists on following the Aren rules as well. For boys that means that the name needs to contain a syllable of the father's name."

A slow smile spread across Pe'tala's face. "Dear me, and there is not a single possible name that comes to mind, sister?"

Eryn gave her a considered look. "Can you stop calling me that? This is kind of a raw issue for me presently, you know?"

"No," the younger one said simply. "Do you want to hear about my epiphany now or not?"

"Why not? Just consider that it needs to sound halfway appealing as well. That was Enric's own condition."

"No problem there. What do I get if I deliver you an idea that not only meets with all the requirements you just mentioned but will also enable you to exact a little bit of revenge and at the same time publicly declare your stance?" Pe'tala smiled.

"I will refrain from publicly accusing you of lying from now on."

"No. You do that again, and I will slap you around for it. I would do so right now, but expectant women do have a certain status here. Also, as I am also a healer who should know better, they would punish me extra heavily. No. Make me another offer. A good one for a change."

"You know what? I have changed my mind. This child will be a girl. Her name will be Maltala, a nice combination of her evil grandmother and her annoying aunt," Eryn snapped.

"Alright," Pe'tala rolled her eyes. "Let us say you just owe me a favour if you use it. Are you ready for it?"

"As ready as I will ever be," she replied with an impatient sigh.

"I am rather proud of it, you know. So you better make sure to praise it adequately. My proposal for your son's name is *Vedric*."

Eryn had been prepared to make a slicing remark, but instead stared at Pe'tala with her mouth open.

"I knew you would like it!" Pe'tala exclaimed triumphantly.

"It's brilliant," Eryn whispered. "It has everything!"

"It is slightly sinister," Intrea commented with a frown. "You would tell people that you still consider Ved'al your true father."

"That is why she likes it," Pe'tala nodded.

"You could take *Valric* instead," Vran'el's companion suggested. "Less controversial."

Eryn snorted. "No. I love it. This is it. This will be his name!"

"You think that your companion will agree? He might find it a little... undiplomatic," Intrea ventured. "It will annoy your parents, after all. Each of whom happens to be a Head of House, incidentally."

She smiled. "How very fortunate for me, then, that it is the mother who picks the name."

"Also where you come from?" Intrea asked.

"No," Pe'tala grinned. "But he is so worried about her right now that he will indulge her. I am confident."

"Tala!" A dark-haired streak shot from the terrace door towards the seating cushions and all but jumped into her aunt's arms.

"Greetings, Obal! I see you are still as rampant and unruly as you were when I left here. I approve very much of it. Do not change one bit, do you hear me?"

Obal giggled and grabbed a random glass from the table, holding it with both hands and emptying it with greedy glugs. Then her eyes found Eryn. She frowned and looked around the room, before she asked in confusion, "Where is Enric? And Urban?"

"Enric is meeting with a few very important people today at a big place in the city," she explained, trying not to be offended at the show of indifference.

"The Senate," the girl nodded wisely.

Eryn blinked and turned to Intrea. "You know, whenever I try to simplify my language in a way that I see as appropriate for a girl her age, I end up appearing as uneducated."

Intrea smiled. "Her father and both her grandfathers are senators, Eryn. Of course she is familiar with this particular word. Try explaining to her why cleaning up after herself is a good thing, and she will demonstrate complete bewilderment that suggests that she does not even speak our language," she added dryly.

Obal's eyes wandered to Eryn's abdomen. "You have a baby in there," she stated matter-of-factly.

"I do, yes."

"Why?"

Eryn gave Intrea an intense look. "Would you like me to elaborate on that and see how advanced she really is for her age? I promise, that information will come in handy sooner or later."

"I think you are misunderstanding her question, sister. Obal knows well enough how it got in there. What she wants to know is the reason why you want to have a child," Pe'tala smirked.

"She knows?" Eryn stared at both women.

"Underdeveloped barbarians," the healer sighed and rolled her eyes. "Yes, she knows. I heard the stories you tell your children when they ask where babies come from. I was horrified."

Intrea leaned forward eagerly. "Tell me!"

"One story goes that you go to a magician and he more or less conjures it into the woman's belly. Another one I heard was that the King is responsible for bestowing them as a favour," Pe'tala laughed.

"Busy man, your King," Intrea hooted and wiped a tear away from the corner of one eye. "Good thing he is still young enough to have the stamina for providing the whole country with children!"

Eryn shook her head. "Are you done with ridiculing my home country?"

"No, there is one more," Pe'tala shook her head. "One child told me that they bought her little brother at the baker's shop."

"Hilarious!" Intrea tittered. "I wonder what else that baker sold. That storeroom must be quite an eye-opener..."

"I know how it is done," Obal stated. "A man puts it in there when he feels the need."

"The need?" Eryn asked weakly.

"The need to procreate," the girl nodded solemnly.

"Oh dear."

"Look at her," Pe'tala sniggered, "her ears are all red! She is embarrassed talking about it to a five year-old-girl. Some healer you are!"

They paused when the heard the entrance door open and close.

"Grandfather!" Obal crowed and jumped up and down. And indeed, a few moments later Enkil, Head of House Feral entered and raised his brow at the unexpected guests.

"Ladies," he nodded and kissed his granddaughter, his daughter and Pe'tala on the forehead. Then he kissed Eryn's hand.

"How are you doing, Malth... Eryn?" he asked carefully. "I had the impression that you were rather agitated when you left. It pleases me to see that you deem my home a place fit for regaining your spirits," he smiled. "Especially as you came here with your sister. It seems you have learned to appreciate each other in Anyueel."

"I pitied her," Pe'tala shrugged. "I was the only civilised person there in that backward country, after all."

Eryn snorted. "Hardly. There is still Erbál."

That made both Intrea and Enkil smile. "How is my boy doing? He wrote that he finds adapting to your customs fairly easy, even though he needs to be very careful with what he says. It seems there are quite a few restrictions concerning conversation topics."

She nodded. "Yes, compared to your country that is definitely true. Though he manages it admirably."

"I hear Sanaf has not proved as... capable of adapting?" Enkil asked, the ghost of a smile playing around his lips.

"Yes, one could say that," Eryn admitted.

"Which is why you decided to recommend Erbál for the position instead, I assume," Intrea winked at her. "That was quite a favour you did him and House Feral, you know."

Eryn smiled. "Yes, he told me. It seems you somehow *by accident* voted for the wrong side during the trial."

That obviously made Enkil slightly uneasy and he cleared his throat, grateful at the diversion when Obal demanded his attention.

"Very diplomatic," Pe'tala next to her murmured. "Good thing they are in your debt and are therefore more or less obliged to like you."

"I liked her already before that," Intrea shrugged and then rose to ask her father, "I shall leave with you the choice of entertaining our guests or cooking lunch, whichever you prefer."

Enkil very obviously avoided looking at Eryn before saying, "I will cook."

"Good," his daughter grinned, seeing right through him. "Make enough for all of us."

"Of course," he sighed and walked towards the kitchen, his granddaughter clinging to his leg and enjoying herself immensely at being dragged along.

"I embarrassed him," Eryn grimaced.

"That is alright," Intrea grinned. "It will help him to remember which side he is on next time."

"I do not intend to repeat that experience, so from my point of view there will not be a next time," she replied.

Pe'tala snorted. "Considering your propensity for getting yourself into trouble that is a very bold thing to claim."

"When are you supposed to be leaving again?" Eryn growled at her.

"In five days, sister. Five more days of fun and intimacy," Pe'tala quipped. "Is this not great?"

"Yes," she sighed with little enthusiasm. "Just great."

CHAPTER 5

The Welcome Dinner

Eryn quickly slipped into the dress Enric had laid out on the bed for her. She had to hurry - the guests were due to arrive in about half an hour and this was a culture where being too early was considered a virtue while being fashionably late was unpardonable. That meant that a few people would be uncomfortably over-punctual while she was not supposed to take more time for making herself pretty. So she had probably no more than ten or fifteen minutes left.

Pe'tala and she had spent the afternoon at House Feral, and as it had been a surprisingly pleasant one, considering Enkil's initial awkwardness; she had returned quite a bit later than she should have and now had to hasten.

"That looks like a battle, and one you are about to lose," a male voice came from the doorway. Vran'el.

Eryn rolled her eyes without turning around and cursed when two of the shoulder straps kept intertwining and refused to be pushed into place. "Don't just stand there and watch me struggle, help me!" She grimaced when she looked at herself in the mirror. "I look like the victim of a robbery, all tangled and rumpled."

"More like you have just returned from a tumble in the sheets," he joshed and stepped closer. "Let me assist you."

She felt his warm hands on her shoulder when he turned her towards him. He looked immaculate, as usual. She let her arms sink and felt how the fabric around her body slipped into place after he had pulled here and there and made it cling the way the tailor, in this case Junar, had intended it to.

"It looks a lot better like that," Vran'el chuckled. "And now sit. We do not have much time to do your hair and face."

63

"Skip the face," she instructed. "Just do the hair in a way it covers most of the face. That way both are taken care of."

"Really," he sighed exhaustedly. "You are a piece of work. Stop fidgeting. I brought some of Intrea's hair tools with me, so this time I do not have to make do with kitchen implements."

"Eryn, what am I supposed to..." Vern's voice trailed off when he came into her bedroom and saw Vran'el stand behind her and brush her hair. "Oh. I apologise," he said stiffly. "I wasn't aware that you have a visitor."

"She does not," Vran'el said simply. "I am not a visitor, I am her brother."

She saw the boy's jaw clench at that. For some reason he didn't seem to like Vran'el, and she wondered if it was because of his inclination towards men. He had not exactly reacted very favourably to that piece of information the first time.

When she had been here last time she had got to know that quite a number of men felt uncomfortable when being close to a man with Vran'el's tastes. They often confused his friendliness with sexual attraction and were appalled, inevitably asking themselves what about them had not seemed manly enough so that they were seen to be open for that kind of attention. Vran'el, being who he was, knew this well enough and used it to entertain himself. He had tried it on Enric, flirting with him, but had soon realised that the barbaric foreigner was confident enough not to mind. It had been the beginning of a friendship.

"You are both men who enter a lady's bedroom uninvited," she sighed. "What do you need, Vern?"

"It's nothing, really. I will figure it out..."

"Vern?" she growled. "Out with it."

He looked at Vran'el for a moment and away again, probably embarrassed at whatever had led him here. "I just wanted to ask if you could tell me how to tie this odd-looking belt here."

Vran'el chuckled. "That is not a belt, my lad. It is a sash. Take a seat. I will help you put it on as soon as I am done with Eryn. Give me ten minutes."

Vern quickly shook his head. "No, that won't be necessary. Really. I will sort this out somehow. No problem at all."

Both of them watched him with a puzzled expression when he retreated hastily and all but fled out of the bedroom.

"You know," Vran'el said slowly, "you may call me overly sensitive, but I do have the feeling that he is not very fond of me."

Eryn shared that feeling, but didn't want to admit it. "He is just trying to adapt to a foreign place. It is the first time he has left the Kingdom, after all."

"Whatever you say, sweetness," he sighed, clearly not convinced. "I heard from Pe'tala that you spent the afternoon with my daughter."

"Yes. I think we are about to become friends. I learned a lot from her today. She enjoys lecturing me. Scholar material if ever I saw it."

"That is my girl, yes," he smiled proudly. "She has recently discovered her fascination for all kinds of animals. Your monstrous cat might have triggered that. Where is the creature, by the way? I assume you will not keep her around with the guests here? Some of them might be a bit nervous if they sit down and find themselves facing a predator. On eye level."

"How very considerate of you to take the *other* people's discomfort into account," she sniggered.

"What can I say? That I am not a healer like most of my family does not mean that I do not care for my fellow human beings. Now look down. Further. Now keep your head like that."

Enric smiled when he entered the bedroom. The picture that presented itself to him a peaceful, intimate one. Her older brother doing her hair with skilled, experienced moves, Eryn as relaxed as was possible for her in a situation like that. He had heard part of their conversation while walking along the corridor towards them.

"That monstrous cat will be put to sleep for tonight," he told them.

Vran'el clucked his tongue disapprovingly when she lifted her head to smile at her companion.

"I told you to keep your head down, did I not?" he scolded her.

She obeyed and asked, "Vern had trouble with his sash. Did he manage somehow?"

"Yes, I helped him."

"How about the others? Are they all fixed up and ready for the fun to start?"

"They are, yes," Enric confirmed. "Junar sent me here to see if you need help with the dress, but I see you worked out all the straps on your own."

"Not quite," Vran'el said teasingly, then stepped in front of her to look at his work. "We can leave it like that. Now the face. We will just do a little with the eyes, there is no time for the rest." He sat on the bed and pulled her towards him, chair and all. "Now close your eyes and keep them closed. If you open them while I work you will either ruin my efforts or end up with things inside your eye that are not supposed to go there."

"You know," she said, keeping her eyes closed obediently, "there is a saying about beauty having its cost."

"What of it?"

"I decided that I am not really willing to pay it. From now on I will go to these occasions being ugly."

"You would not look ugly, sweetness, but sloppy. Ugly is difficult to change unless you are willing to pay the horrendous prices the cosmetic healers ask, but sloppy is just a lack of effort. That would cast an unfavourable light on our House. You might not be too keen on pleasing father right now, but there are others as well. House Vel'kim has currently eighty-six members, after all. Eighty-seven after your son is born."

She opened her eyes in astonishment and made him curse.

"Eryn! Your attention span is truly disturbing, it is hardly more than Obal can manage! How do you manage to heal people? Close your eyes and keep them shut! I have to take a minor corrective measure now thanks to your inability to follow a simple instruction like keeping your eyes closed." He sighed. "Not that we are pressed for time or anything..."

"Eighty-six members?" she repeated his words. "Why have I never met any of them before? They are all cousins or what?"

"Most of them live on the estates we own and make sure they run the way they are supposed to. Others do have regular jobs. Quite a few of them are healers, of course. I am sure you have met a few of them at the clinic already without being aware that they belong to our House. The number of members is fairly stable, as the men's offspring do normally join other Houses."

"This is pretty much an average size for a House here," Enric explained to her. From the direction of his voice she could hear that he was still standing somewhere close to the doorway. "Aren is a bit bigger, they have currently more than one hundred members."

"Still collecting every piece of information you can find," Vran'el smiled. "I bet it is absolutely impossible to run out of conversation topics with you. Eryn, you may open your eyes now. We are done."

They heard voices coming from the main room.

"Just in time," Enric nodded and took her hand to pull her up from her chair. "Come. Let's be social."

She plastered a smile on her face, which didn't reach her eyes. An entire evening with Malriel, Valrad and Ram'an around her. That would very probably lead to more than one temptation to be *un*social.

No, she reminded herself. Restraint, control and collected politeness. These would be her weapons of choice.

* * *

Enric put his empty bowl on the table before him and leaned back. Eryn sat exactly opposite him. She had asked Vran'el and Junar to sit next to her on either side to keep any of the three unwanted guests from getting too close. It had worked fairly well. Wherever Junar was, Orrin was not far away either, though Valrad had taken a seat right next to his son on her other side. The advantage was that despite being closer to her father than she would prefer, she did not have him in her immediate field of vision, which made attempts at conversation with her more difficult for him. Malriel sat closer to Enric, and Ram'an had placed himself strategically close enough to be able to talk to her and far enough away to have her in his field of vision. In a circle that contained about forty people and considering that Eryn was trying to avoid him that had been quite an accomplishment.

The drinks before the dinner had been taken standing, as was customary in both their countries, as it allowed people to mingle and chat as they pleased. Eryn had constantly been on the move from one

66

group to the next, keeping an eye on the three and excusing herself with a smile to hurry on to somebody else whenever one of them came too close for her liking. It had at times felt like an odd kind of dance.

Kilan was keeping an eye on his guests' eating progress, refilled bowls and carried out his hosting duties surprisingly smoothly and methodically. It seemed as if he had had ample opportunity to practice in the few months since his appointment as ambassador.

Vern had just finished his third serving and leaned back contentedly. He had taken a seat between Valrad and Ram'an.

Enric got up together with Kilan to take care of the used dishes when all guests had finished. Now came the difficult part. There was no more obligation to avoid potentially tricky topics as there had been during their meal.

Eryn, too, realised this and quickly stood up to help the two men with the tableware, but Vran'el swiftly grabbed her arm and tugged her back down on her cushion.

"No, sweetness," he shook his head. "An expectant woman does not get up to carry dishes when it is not necessary. It would not only put Kilan and Enric in a bad light, but also all the other guests who are aware of your pregnancy and watching you instead of doing it for you."

She nodded reluctantly and sank back. Pity. It would have been a welcome opportunity to get out of this room for a minute or two. Or find reasons to linger in the kitchen even longer. Like a glass of juice that had accidentally been spilled intentionally and needed to be wiped up. Very carefully, of course. And being careful required time. The more careful one was, the more time one had to take. Pregnant women were expected to be *very* careful in this country...

She turned to Junar next to her. "How was your trip to the tailor yesterday? I forgot to ask."

Orrin next to her sighed heavily. "I had no idea that talking to another person in what is theoretically the same language could take so much time, cause so many misunderstandings and require so much patience."

"Which of them was difficult? Your tailor or this one here?" she grinned.

"Both, in combination with each other, I would say. Junar wanted to save time and wrote down my measurements for them to work with. It turned out that our units at home do not correspond to what they use here. So they first calculated around to figure out the conversion factor, but gave up soon and measured me all over again. So Junar now has my measurements in both systems. Then she wanted to give them instructions how to cut my tunics and somehow managed to offend them by suggesting cutting the fabric closer to the edge than is considered honourable here, for some reason." He raised his eyes to the ceiling and took a sip from his water glass. "We finally agreed to have my tunics cut in the same style as Enric's only in my size. I knew it made sense to use the same tailor. That probably saved us another hour of explaining, gesturing, pointing and discussing."

Junar between them looked sullen, her arms folded. "This was so frustrating! They have different names for everything here! I feel as though I have to start learning my profession anew here before I am able to place a single stitch! I can't even go and buy myself supplies as I have no idea what I am looking for!"

"You could just as well spend the time until the birth learning the words you need," Eryn pointed out. "It will keep you busy without having to run around too much. I can try to get you books on tailoring, if you like. Or get a tailor to spend a few days with you and fill you in. With the money we leave here to have new clothes made I dare say this should not be that much of a problem."

Orrin gave her a grateful look when Junar nodded slowly. "I suppose we could do that, yes."

When Enric and Kilan returned, they each brought several bottles of the dark, heavy wine that currently sold so well here in Takhan.

Eryn eyed the bottles and sighed.

"Vexed about not being able to drink the wine, sweetness?" Vran'el enquired sympathetically.

"It's my favourite," she nodded. "I really miss it. And watching others drinking it while I can't doesn't make it any easier."

"I remember Intrea's impatience when she had to stop riding her horse. She is quite an able hunter, as you surely remember. So no more riding and hunting for quite some time made her really irritable, believe you me. The first thing she did when she was able to sit up straight again without any pain was to push Obal into my arms and swing herself onto the next horse."

"That is not true!" Intrea's indignant voice came from somewhere close to Malriel. "I had hardly finished giving birth before you snatched her away and took her with you wherever you went. You clung to that girl from the minute they showed her to you. Me having pushed her on you is a preposterous thing to say, my dear. I was struggling to have her to myself every now and then. Luckily you had to give her back to me when she was hungry."

"Vel'kim fathers," Uvel of House Tokmar chuckled and winked at Vran'el. Then he looked at Eryn. "It will be interesting to see how our latest Vel'kim mother will do."

"We might already be gone by the time I give birth," she smiled. She hoped.

"That would be a great pity," Legara, Malriel's friend, said. "I am sure all of us would very much like to take a look at Malriel's first grandchild."

"It would not be the only opportunity for you to do so," Eryn replied mildly. "We would come to visit every now and again. Our son has family here, after all."

"Regular visits will be essential," another Head of House agreed. "He will be the next heir to House Vel'kim, after all. The better he gets to know his own House, the easier it will be for him to take over the responsibilities from his uncle Vran'el one day."

Vran'el chuckled. "You are planning very far ahead, Anfer. My nephew does not even have a name yet."

Pe'tala's amused voice cut in. "You are mistaken, brother. She has picked one only today."

Enric raised both eyebrows in surprise. She had?

"It seems this is also news for the child's father," Ram'an remarked, which earned him a few good-natured laughs.

"Well?" Vran'el urged her, "What is it to be?"

Eryn swallowed and beamed Pe'tala an unhappy look. "I would rather not say it here and now, Vran."

"Nonsense," he huffed. "Why would you not?"

She looked at Enric, who was smiling at her.

"I admit I, too, am curious."

So there was no way out. Maybe it was better to get it behind her now.

She drew in a breath, held it for a moment and then announced, "His name will be Vedric."

Enric's eyes widened only a fraction at the surprise. It had become quiet at the table. She didn't dare look at Malriel or Valrad.

"Vedric of House Vel'kim," Ram'an's voice said thoughtfully into the silence after a while, as if testing the sound of the name. "A name that not only takes into account the naming traditions of both his parents' Houses but also pays tribute to the man who raised Eryn and taught her healing. A gesture of respect. A good choice, Eryn. I approve."

Eryn felt the tension around them easing almost immediately. Ram'an had just given the other guests an alternative to being shocked and unsure of how to react. Now they could take the easy way out and agree with him. And it had eased the sting for Malriel and Valrad, as there was now another possible motive behind the choice besides the obvious one of demonstrating to them her attachment to the man they had both wronged.

"Indeed," Intrea nodded. "And considering that he will grow up at the other side of the ocean, we can consider ourselves lucky she has chosen a name that we can even pronounce without problems." That remark was followed by relieved laughter.

"Enric, what are your thoughts? Do you approve as well?" Pe'tala asked. There was a malicious glint in her eyes.

He nodded and looked at Eryn. "I do, yes. Vedric. I like it." He smiled. "Not that you have left me much of a choice to disagree here without losing face, mind you," he added with a lopsided grin.

"Well, if you had disagreed, she just could have refused to go back to Anyueel before the child was born. As long as she is here, it is the mother's choice what a child's name is, after all," Legara pointed out with a shrug.

"We generally prefer a more... cooperative approach," Enric replied gently.

Do we? Since when? Eryn's raised eyebrow conveyed the questions as clearly as words would have.

"That does not seem to be the impression your companion has, Enric," Uvel chuckled.

"Cooperation is not normally the spirit those of Aren blood are noted for," Amgil of House Roal smiled. This was the House Sarol belonged to, Eryn remembered, the one both Vel'kim and Aren were at enmity with, as it were. That statement coming from this particular Head of House was a clear provocation.

"I prefer to be known for assertiveness rather than fraud," Malriel replied coolly. That did shut him up and caused a couple of guests to look in different directions or pick up napkins to hide their grins.

Pe'tala got up and walked in the direction of the sanitary room.

"Vern," a man in his early forties said, "I am Belkim, Head of House Turbar. My House is what many would consider the authority in everything connected with fine arts. We have in the past produced quite a few admired artists, yet I have to admit that I have not yet seen your equal when it comes to drawing. I wonder if you would be interested in spending an afternoon at the Turbar residence? There are quite a number of my family who would very much like to meet you."

Vern's expression slowly morphed from staggered into delighted. "I would be honoured!"

Valrad smiled. "So it seems the healers now have to compete with the artists for your attention, Vern. You will have to take care and make enough time for both, or we will sooner or later start arguing over you."

"Then I had better reserve a time slot for myself, as long as neither group manages to monopolise him completely," Ram'an cut in. "Vern, I would be very interesting in testing you. I do not know if you are familiar with our custom of testing young people as to their talent and inclination?"

"I know that you did it with Eryn, yes," the boy nodded.

"Yes, exactly," he smiled and looked at her for a moment before returning his attention to his conversation partner. "Back then she also asked me what category I would tend to see you in, and I have to say that judging from the little I knew of you then I was at a loss. I still am. Would you agree to this? It will only take about two hours of your time and we could then sit down over a glass of tea and discuss the results, as they are analysed at House Arbil."

He grinned. "That would be fabulous! I would love to try this!"

"Excellent. The results are usually delivered to the Head of House, but I will give them to you personally since you are not a member of any."

Pe'tala returned from the sanitary room, scowling. "There is a puddle of a rather distinct, yellowish nature right in front of your sanitary room, I am afraid."

Vern groaned and rolled his eyes. "That was Ram'an. I will clean it up right away."

All guests fell silent and stared first at the boy, then their gazes pivoted to a very shocked Head of House Arbil.

"I do beg your pardon," he remarked with barely contained indignation, "but I feel the need to point out that this allegation is a rather outrageous one. I am certainly not responsible for *anything* of the kind."

Eryn felt the violent urge to break out in giggles and managed to hold it in. For about three seconds. Her eyes met with Enric's, who had a broad grin on his face, and it simply burst out. Junar next to her smiled, but clearly had more sympathy with both Ram'an and the boy, who both looked shocked and a little embarrassed at Eryn's open amusement.

"What?" Vern exclaimed, his face blushing crimson. "No! That was not what I meant! I mean..." His voice seemed to deny cooperation with the realisation of what he had just said.

Enric came to his aid. "He was talking about his cat. He brought his pet here and it seems that the animal is not too cheerful about being here. He tends to communicate his discontent through his bodily functions. A very effective, yet hardly appealing way."

Ram'an blinked once, then nodded and looked at Vern, even managing a smile. "I see. You named your cat after me? Was that before or after his propensity to micturating in random places was known to you?"

"Before," the boy blurted out, still horrified at the social faux pas he had made. "I swear to you, it was meant as a compliment!"

"Then I shall take it as such," he replied solemnly and winked at Eryn, who was by now wiping away tears of laughter. She looked away, taking a sip of water. She was annoyed at his attempts at being friendly to her now that she had given him a piece of her mind and hurled his bracelet back at him. It was a bit late for that.

Vern exhaled in relief and then got up to take care of the puddle his cat had made.

"So now you have two cats with you?" Uvel asked.

"Yes," Enric replied, "Though Vern's cat is a lot smaller than ours, although it is a lot more vicious. We don't see it often around here, it tends to either hide or stalk Urban. The boy pretty much seems to be the only person it likes."

"Is this a common practise, to have animals living with you in the rooms of houses in your Kingdom?" Koral, Head of House Partém enquired.

"Not usually, no," Orrin replied. "Eryn brought that beast along for Vern to practise healing on it. The cat looked quite different when she brought it in - a lifeless little bundle of red fur on her shoulder, half an

71

ear missing, various appalling infections fighting for dominance inside it, from what my son told me. Vern was supposed to release it again, but the cat found a warm place inside with regular meals more appealing than fighting for some meagre scraps on the streets."

"Understandable," Vran'el nodded. "It is how we got stuck with Pe'tala. Ow!" he exclaimed when a small but weighty decorative cushion struck him full in the face.

"Nice aim, Tala," Intrea sniggered. "Vran, that was well-deserved," she reprimanded her companion.

"They never really grow up when they are together, do they?" Enkil, Intrea's father smiled.

"I need to keep my combative spirits alive," Vran'el shrugged. "A companion, a daughter and two sisters – how is a man to stand his ground, I ask you?" he added in mock desperation.

Eryn felt the change in the atmosphere almost physically. It was as if the people present had just waited for an opening for that particular topic, a hint that those involved would accept talking about it. And mentioning *two* sisters had been exactly that hint. She braced herself, reminding herself to keep her anger under control and appear resigned to the new situation. Cheerfulness would not be very credible after her attempt at thwarting the acknowledgement at the Senate today, so the required acting skills would not need to be too elaborate. She could deal with this.

"That was quite a surprise you sprang on us today, Valrad," Tanif, the Head of House Landred remarked. Apart from Ram'an he was the youngest person to hold this position. "A noble gesture."

"Not completely unselfish," Valrad smiled. "Who would hesitate to claim a daughter like Eryn as his?"

Eryn made herself smile briefly at the compliment, wishing she could shove it back into his mouth. She saw Malriel watching her, probably waiting for a less reserved reaction. Well, she wouldn't get one. Not today.

"Indeed," Uvel agreed and looked at Pe'tala. "How do you like suddenly having a big sister?"

She shrugged. "I had a lot of time to get used to her and fortunately she has turned out to be less of a nuisance than I feared. And she took the burden of providing an heir for the House off my shoulders," she smiled.

"Fine," Eryn retorted, "That means that you can now take your hands off my Head of Administration."

"Hardly," she chuckled unperturbed. "Annoying *you* was a side-benefit from the beginning."

"So you did find yourself a little something to pass the time in Anyueel?" Tanif asked, smiling knowingly.

"Not merely passing time," Eryn shook her head. "They are cohabitating from what I saw. I strongly suspect that he is the reason why she has decided to stay in Anyueel for now."

72

Valrad frowned. "You are not thinking of relocating there for the sake of this man, are you?"

"That is a little early to say, father," Pe'tala sighed. "But as I will have a chance to try him out, so to speak, until Eryn and Enric return there, I will probably have made a decision by then."

"I do not approve of the prospect of having both you and your sister so far away from here," her father stated plainly. "If you are attached to him, you may as well bring him here."

"He has an important position at the clinic, father. I am surely not going to ask him to give that up. He is doing a very competent job from what I have seen. Eryn would have my scalp for luring him here!"

"I would, yes," she confirmed. "I am glad this is self-evident and I didn't need to put words to it."

"Not that you would have hesitated to do so," Pe'tala grinned.

"No. I have learned that directness is the only way to get your attention, if not your compliance."

"Good to see that you have found a man that keeps you company for now, baby sister," Vran'el smiled. "Though I, too, would have preferred somebody who would not keep you away from here. I expect you to bring him over and let me have a look at him. I need to determine if he is good enough for you."

"Baby sister?" Intrea grimaced.

Pe'tala gave him a dark look. "Yes. He has taken to addressing me like that to distinguish between his two younger sisters. Charming, is it not? It makes me want to kick him each time he says it."

"I share that sentiment," Eryn murmured. "One of these days we will ambush you in a dark street."

"I can certainly deal with two feeble women," he snorted.

"Hardly," she smiled. "I am stronger than you and unlike you I am trained in the art of hand-to-hand combat. And you are not supposed to hit me back as long as your nephew is growing in my womb."

He thought for a moment, then nodded reluctantly. "I see your point. Any chance that you can delay your ambush until after the birth?"

"Why would I give up such a strong advantage?"

"Why indeed," he sighed.

"You are lucky one is leaving again soon," Kilan grinned. "The two of them seem like a lot to take on for one man."

"Tell *me*," Enric murmured. "They behaved like children for several weeks until they managed to agree to some kind of truce. I can't tell you how glad I am that this child is going to be a boy. I could really do with some backup, especially if Tala is to stay in Anyueel."

"Says the man who forces me to have *family dinners*!" Pe'tala reminded him. "If you want peace and quiet, stop throwing your weight around to make me spend time with you, Order Lord!"

"A desperate attempt to provide some civilised framework for you to train your underdeveloped manners," he retorted with a sneer.

"And I am no longer an *Order Lord*, so if you feel like challenging me this is your chance."

She shrugged haughtily. "No, I will not. I would not want to make you look bad here in front of all these people. You are supposed to be a person of respect, taking over a House."

"Too kind of you," he nodded.

"What can I say? You are a nuisance, but family is family."

"Like another brother you never wanted?" he grinned.

"Sure. Vran'el got another sister, and I do not like to be outdone. If you are the best to be had, I will make do with that somehow."

"Your family is growing rather rapidly at the moment, Valrad," Intrea laughed.

Eryn felt herself relax. This banter kept their guests entertained enough to refrain from asking any inconvenient questions at the moment. So far Malriel, Valrad and Ram'an had behaved themselves as well and not tried to use the situation to make her join in conversation with them. Maybe this evening would turn out as a lot less tedious than she had feared.

"Eryn, I am teaching a group of second-year healers tomorrow," Valrad ventured. "I think it would be nice for them to learn something about the herbs that are native in your country. I can pick you up tomorrow morning after breakfast."

Or maybe the tedious part was only about to start.

"I would rather not," she said carefully, "I am without my books and illustrations and would worry about mixing things up."

Vern, who had just returned from cleaning up the damp spot, frowned at her. "You? Mixing *herbs* up? I saw you lecture the herb gatherers in the middle of the wilderness without any books or notes!"

She narrowed her eyes at him, willing him to shut up. Or drop to the floor unconsciously. Whatever would make him stop talking.

"You just ruined a perfectly good subterfuge," Pe'tala shook her head at him. "Now she has to tell him openly that she has no intention of spending time with him. How very undiplomatic of you, Vern."

Vran'el rolled his eyes. "Yes, *you* are definitely the right person to speak about diplomacy, Tala," he admonished her.

Valrad's expression was calm; he didn't show any sign of disappointment. But it wouldn't have mattered if he had. Asking her like that in front of the other guests was surely no way to make her comply. She didn't care what they thought. She turned to her right side and talked to Junar and Orrin instead.

CHAPTER 6

Settling in

Eryn returned from the clinic with another two books under her arm, letting them drop on the seating cushions beside her when she leaned back in Kilan's main room. She had finished the first one given her by Sarol, and in his usual way of accepting accomplishments as due and proper and nothing that required any praise, he had taken the book back without a comment and instead pushed two more at her. He had informed her that he had set the date for her final exam, the last one that was missing for her healer certification in Takhan, for three weeks' time. Eryn had asked him if he didn't think that this might be a little too short for her to prepare for a subject she had next to no experience in and hardly any knowledge of, but he had just stared at her and replied that three weeks was plenty of time if one didn't waste it.

Their first full week in Takhan was virtually over, and it had been a busy one for every single one of them. Enric had spent his days at the Aren residence with Malriel, going over the particulars of the House and what needed to be done to keep it running. And where to find the information he might require - who to ask, where to look. He had taken to keeping a notebook with him at all times and after a few days, half of its pages were filled with writing and it was bulging with little notes he had affixed between the pages. Malriel had also started assembling the fifty most significant members of her House to have them swear the second level commitment oath to her interim replacement. This meant about half the House was now bound to him by magic. The rest - children, older people or adults in positions that were not directly related to the family's various businesses - did not have to take the oath. This would be too much effort considering Malriel was expected to return to the position in a few months.

Vern had been invited to so many gatherings, lectures, dinners and locations where either healing or art was practiced that Eryn had hardly seen him. He had kept sending messages whereby he excused himself from meals since he had once more been invited to dine at someone's residence or at a guest house. Valrad stayed with him at the clinic until he had managed to find his way around the place and Intrea had kept him company when he had dived into the world of art. Vern had soon been accepted into both circles as, despite his occasional confusion about how to react in certain situations, he was bright and willing to learn. And swift to apologise for whatever inappropriate behaviour he might inadvertently have shown.

Orrin had spent quite some time with the three members of the triarchy, talking to them about the potential threat their northern neighbour posed and what measures would theoretically be required to prepare the city of Takhan for defending itself.

Junar had spent her time taking walks through the local markets with Kilan, who was more than willing to show her where which various supplies could be purchased. Their walks had never been very long, as Junar was in her seventh month and avoided being on her feet for too long. She also kept visiting the tailor's shop they had ordered their clothes from, and thanks to Vran'el's friendly request they were more than willing to respond to all her questions, demonstrate their techniques to her as well as inform her where to get the best price for different haberdashery items.

Considering that they were all living under the same roof, they had spent curiously little time together since their arrival.

Neither had Eryn herself been idle. She had met Sarol at the clinic several times and visited those healers she had met a few months ago. They were all eager to hear about how things were going at her own clinic in Anyueel and she kept retelling the story about a new Head of Healing being appointed, of the changes Pe'tala had implemented and how more and more patients from remote places came to the city as the news of the new services had spread.

She had run into Vern and Valrad a few times and had been very careful to treat the latter with the respect he was due as a high-ranking healer in front of his colleagues. But respect and politeness was as much as he got. There was no affection and warmth when she talked to him, no genuine joy in her smile when she saw him.

He had once more asked her to spend a day with him treating patients, in the way they had done a few months ago, but she had declined politely, claiming that she preferred to use the time for preparing for her exam with Sarol. At least that really was a valid argument.

Ram'an, too, had tried to get in touch with her. He had sent her a message, asking her to have tea or lunch with him whenever it suited her. Him too she had refused politely, informing him that her current workload did not allow much time for social interaction.

They had met again at a dinner at House Partém, where he enquired when she foresaw having more time at her disposal. She had told him that this was hard to specify, since after obtaining her certification she intended to work at the clinic. At her proposal that she would contact him when she had more time at her hands, he had just lifted an eyebrow at her and shaken his head almost imperceptibly. He had been as aware as Eryn herself that she had no intention whatsoever of doing anything of that nature.

She was annoyed at his attempts to meet her as though nothing had transpired between them. He had been the one to push her away, after all - and none too subtly after first assuring her that he wanted to be friends. She had accepted his token of friendship, then she had accepted his change of heart, and now it was on him to accept her reaction to it. It was as basic as that.

The people she had actually enjoyed spending time with were Pe'tala, Vran'el and Intrea, not counting her friends from the Kingdom. Pe'tala and Intrea smiled at her occasionally rather frustrated comments at the situation between her and Valrad, but Vran'el was not as willing to tolerate them and kept starting discussions every time to convince her that them being actual siblings was a beautiful thing and nothing to kick against. She had started swallowing certain statements when he was around.

The thought that Pe'tala was to leave again for Anyueel in only two days saddened her a little. Of course it was great that the clinic would have her back as none of the healers there were trained to an extent that enabled them to deal with difficult cases. And yet Pe'tala had unexpectedly turned out to be a kindred spirit in these last weeks, especially in the past few days since she had learned about Malriel's affair with Valrad. She was reassuring, particularly as she found talking to Vran'el not as uncomplicated as it once was.

Strange, she thought. Never in her dreams had she thought that talking to Valrad and Vran'el could ever be anything but pleasant.

There was one event she was looking forward to, though: Malriel's impending departure tomorrow. Only one day longer and she would be gone. For quite a spell. One person fewer to avoid in the city. She had been invited to a farewell dinner at the Aren residence tonight and she was of course supposed to attend with Enric. The last occasion for the next months to be in the same room with her. That was acceptable; it was a sacrifice Eryn was willing to make in exchange for seeing the back of her.

The last dinner they had been at together, the welcome dinner at the ambassadorial residence, had been surprisingly harmonious. Strangely prosaic even, considering the private topics that had been discussed in the presence of all the mighty Heads of Houses. Vran'el had later explained to her that even though not all Houses got along very well with each other, they had still known one another for decades. And the higher up one went in society, the fewer people could be found there. The Heads of Houses were at the pinnacle, and this elite circle was not exactly a large one. Very similar to a family that did not always appreciate each other, but made it work out of a sense of duty.

She had known better than to point out that she understood that concept well enough. He wouldn't have reacted favourably to that.

Malriel's departure would make moving in to the Aren residence necessary as Enric would from tomorrow evening onwards officially be the Head of the House. That thought was not a particularly cheering one. Malriel's place with all her private belongings, the house she had spent all her life in. And the place Eryn's earliest memories were connected with after they had been made accessible by removing the mind block Ved'al had placed in her head.

And there was one other matter she needed to take care of: talking to Vern about his behaviour towards Vran'el. What she had at first judged to be awkwardness at the unfamiliar concept of two men being openly in a relationship had turned into subtle rejection. It was nothing like unfriendly remarks or jibes, but the refusal to accept any favours, information or help from Vran'el, avoid his presence whenever possible and making a point of treating everyone around him with friendliness and openness as opposed to the tense politeness Vran'el received.

Vran'el had noticed it, naturally, but had not commented on it. He normally enjoyed putting narrow-minded or prejudiced people in their place, but had refrained from doing so for now for Eryn's sake, that she knew. It did, however, make it her responsibility to do something to remedy it.

And she would. As soon as Vern returned. He could use the dinner tonight as a first chance to demonstrate his newly adapted attitude towards Vran'el.

She listened to the sound of the entrance door downstairs opening and shutting again. It couldn't be Enric, he had taken his clothes for the dinner with him and would change then and there instead of returning here for that purpose and then setting off again. He had commissioned Kilan and Orrin to make sure to bring her with them when they came. Where was the trust?

Orrin and Vern strolled into the room, both looking exhausted. They had yet to become accustomed to the heat here.

"Is it too much to ask for a bit of a breeze every now and then?" Vern complained and poured himself a glass of water, taking the carafe with him to the seating cushions. "Just a light zephyr would do! The air is standing thick in the streets. At least the houses here are built with heavy walls that keep the heat out a little."

"Not only that," Eryn explained, "they also have employed a few tricks with the local architecture to keep the buildings cool. It's all about having openings of the right size and in the right places to ensure air circulation. And the bright façades, of course. They reflect a good part of the sunlight. That's all I remember. If you want to more about that, ask Enric. I bet you everything I own that he has read at least one book on the heat-reducing characteristics of western city architecture."

Orrin gulped down a glass and then turned to walk to the sanitary room. "The two of you should not get too comfortable. We are to leave here in little more than one and a half hours, and we all have to bathe. Has Junar returned?"

Eryn nodded. "Yes. She fell asleep over what looked like a tunic and some sewing things I have never seen before. I think she is suffering under the heat. We need to make her carry a pouch of water with her whenever she goes outside."

He nodded curtly. "I will make sure she does." Then he was gone.

Good. That gave her the chance to have that little chat with his son.

"Vern?"

He opened his eyes, sweat drying on his forehead. "Huh?"

"There is something I need to talk to you about. I have to tell you that I am not exactly happy about how things are going between you and Vran'el."

Vern groaned. "No, not that again! Not you, too!"

She frowned at him. "What do you mean, not me too? Did Vran'el say something?"

"No, but that scary sister of yours treated me to a tirade that left me speechless. Not to mention trembling slightly."

"She did?" How very convenient. "What did she say?"

"She told me in her uniquely friendly way to stop behaving like a complete git towards your brother because she knows that this is not how I usually am." He looked pained. "She intends to watch me closely at the dinner tonight, and if I don't loosen up my behaviour towards him she has threatened me with a few things that do sound rather painful, at least those I was able to understand. I think one included a golden belt and a horse bridle or something of the sort," he concluded with a frown.

She smiled. "Good. That saves me the trouble of talking you into submission myself. Though I wouldn't have issued any painful threats. Not yet."

He sighed in defeat and nodded. "I suppose I now have two pairs of watchful eyes on me tonight?"

"You suppose right, my lad. Better be convincing." She regarded him thoughtfully for a moment. "Can I ask you something? Why don't you like Vran'el? When I imagined the two of you together, I was convinced that you would get on well with one another without any problem."

"Pe'tala had a theory." He looked at her sheepishly. "She thinks I am jealous."

"Jealous?" Of Vran'el? "So you don't mind about his..."

"About his liking men? No," he slowly shook his head. "Not really. I mean, it was a bit of a surprise at the beginning, I'll admit. And also that everybody else seems to know and accept it. Not to mention his companion and his daughter. But basically he is not harming anybody, so I have no right to be prejudiced against him."

She smiled, suddenly relieved. He was not narrow-minded - well, not much - but instead jealous.

"Why would you be jealous of him?"

Vern looked away. "I don't know. Well, he kind of turned into your brother from one day to the next. And he treats you like one. I mean, it doesn't feel right from where I am standing. I have known you for a lot longer than him!"

Eryn took his hand and laid it against her cheek. "Idiot," she said softly.

"Don't, I am sweaty..."

"I don't mind. Your father just told us to take a bath, so I will wash it off soon enough anyway. Vern, you don't have to worry about Vran'el. You are the first real friend I ever dared have in my life. And you have proved it more than once in the past. I will never forget that, no matter how many unexpected siblings are yet to turn up."

He nodded. "That's pretty much what Pe'tala said. She also told me not to worry as this also happens to older people who really should know better. She thinks *your* father is jealous of *my* father because he is close to you. Do you think she is right?"

"I don't know. I don't know Valrad that well, but it might be an explanation for his behaviour. I have never seen him that distant with anyone before."

"Will that turn out to be a problem? I mean, Valrad is very important, isn't he? But treating father badly would make *you* angry and he probably wants to avoid that. Well, *angrier*." He looked to the floor. "You know, he has been very kind to me and helped me a lot these last few days."

"You are not trying what I think you are trying? Don't."

"He is a good person, that's what everybody says about him..."

"Vern," she warned him, "shut up. I will not react well to any attempts at reconciliation. Not from his side and not from yours."

Orrin returned from the sanitary room, looking fresh and clean with damp hair and clothes that sported the same mix of local cut with unadorned fabrics as Enric's.

"Neat," she nodded appreciatively. "That was very speedy. How did you manage to get yourself tolerably clean in only a few minutes?"

"Women," he sighed. "Getting into the water, using soap to scrub oneself clean, rinsing the soap off and drying is a matter of minutes. Go on, you are next. No dawdling."

She rose with a chortle. "Save your fathering for that daughter of yours. It's too late for me, anyway. I am a lost cause."

"And yet people keep competing for the job," Vern muttered, then shrank under her irate gaze.

"You," Orrin pointed at his son, "No provoking the expectant lady. And you," he looked at her, "go wash yourself. I won't hear the end of it if I don't manage to get you there in time."

She gave the boy a last devastating look, then walked off to get herself ready.

"Now, lad," she heard Orrin saying sternly, "before we leave, we need to talk about your behaviour towards Vran'el."

She laughed when she heard Vern's desperate moan.

"Come on! Seriously? Not you, too!"

*　*　*

Eryn stood amongst the crowd that had assembled to bid goodbye to Malriel at the square in front of the Senate hall, the great heroine who was about to sally forth to serve her country so selflessly.

Two servants were tying sacks on to a magnificent large horse, being careful to balance its load evenly.

"Say," Vran'el's voice said from behind, "the two of you did not happen to have a little talk with young Vern, did you?" It was a casual enquiry, but one that left no doubt that he knew the answer to it already.

"What?" Pe'tala snorted derisively, "Little sister and baby sister are supposed to protect a big, strong chap like yourself from a sixteen-year-old boy? Do not be ridiculous, Vran."

Eryn hid a smile and looked at him. "What makes you ask a thing like that, pray tell?"

"His completely changed behaviour yesterday evening at the dinner and his fearful glances in your directions. And the satisfied smiles you kept giving him whenever he said something pleasant to me. I feel a bit emasculated by that, to be honest," he frowned. "Stop mothering me. I would have talked to him soon enough. My acceptance limit had not yet been reached."

"But ours had been, so stop being difficult," Pe'tala growled and watched Malriel come towards them. "And now shut up. The Queen of Darkness is drawing near."

Eryn straightened. She could and would not let herself be angered, provoked or otherwise goaded, she promised herself. She would meet that woman with detached indifference.

"Walk with me to my horse, Theá, would you?" Malriel said calmly when she had reached them.

Eryn nodded briskly and moved forward. When they were out of the crowd's earshot, Malriel spoke.

"I am pleased you have come to say goodbye to me. If things go very wrong indeed, this might as well be the last time we ever see each other."

"I have come to make sure you are leaving. I am sorry if this destroys your illusions," Eryn replied evenly. "And make no mistake about perishing there. This is surely not the last time we shall meet."

"So reluctant to face the thought that you might be losing me for a second time, my girl?" Malriel smiled bleakly, the sarcasm uppermost in her voice.

"I lost you a second time when you accused me of having killed my own father," Eryn replied. "Your coming back here alive is the key to

81

me being able to return to my home. If you expire on me up north, Enric is stuck as Head of your House. This is not going to happen. If you do anything stupid and make them kill you, I will travel up there and drag your sorry carcass back here to bury it in your garden just so that I can spit on your grave every morning after I get up."

Malriel blinked, taken aback by these harsh words being delivered in a tone so oddly free of emotion. She nodded slowly.

"A pity that we once again separate like this, on unfriendly terms." Her eyes wandered down to her daughter's abdomen. "I wish you the best with your pregnancy and the birth of my grandson, Theá. I very much look forward to holding him in my arms in a few months," she said softly and made to reach out.

Eryn took a step back to avoid the contact. "Don't. Let's part without pretence. It is not the friendliest way, but at least it's honest. We can be honest with each other, if nothing else. Goodbye, Malriel. I wish you success for your people's sake."

With this she turned and walked away, ignoring the unexpected stab of regret.

* * *

"What does a wrinkle above the base of the nose signify?" Vern asked, the heavy book on his lap.

"A reduced level of activity in that gland I reactivated and thereby got Junar pregnant," Eryn replied wearily. He had been asking her questions about the symptoms in the book for the last hour. "Let's take a break. My head doesn't want to cooperate anymore."

"Ten minutes," the boy granted her graciously. "You need to be fit in two days and we still have one more book to go through."

"I know," she yawned. Only two more days until Sarol put her through his paces. She had pretty much managed to go through all the material he had told her to learn - but with that man, being well-prepared might still turn out to be inadequate. He was not one to acknowledge half-accomplishments.

She had asked him carefully about the chance of her repeating the exam if she somehow failed, but he had merely stared at her in the way he had whenever he was confronted with a concept that didn't fit his view of the world. She had then talked to other healers, enquiring about the portion that usually failed his examinations. The answer had not been very encouraging: on average six out of every ten people failed the first time. Yet that meant that there was indeed a second time, which was at least a small comfort.

It was a shame that Pe'tala had left for Anyueel two and a half weeks ago. She would surely have been immensely helpful for the preparation, having passed the exam herself only a few years ago.

Valrad, too, had offered her his assistance, but she had declined politely, rather willing to fail at her first attempt than accepting his help.

He had in these last three weeks left her fairly much undisturbed, sending an occasional invitation for dinner at his home, asking her how she was doing when he happened to meet her somewhere. They had never been together on their own, always in the presence of others, fortunately. So he had made no attempts to talk about personal things, not particularly happy with her aloofness, but accepting it.

When Eryn had accompanied her sister to the ship, Pe'tala had told her to give up her stubborn resolve to keep Valrad at a distance, as no matter how resilient to his attempts she proved, he would outlast her. She had no chance against his determination. She had repeated her warning that their father would wait a little longer, but then he would take steps to force Eryn to deal with him and their changed relationship. She had predicted that he would probably not do anything until her exam was over, but following that...

Eryn closed her eyes to clear her mind of those thoughts. They were an unwelcome distraction from the things she was meant to be concentrating on right now.

Vern had dedicated the entire afternoon to testing her in order to disclose the areas that she needed to have a closer look at. So far they had identified two.

She appreciated his efforts, especially as he had started attending lectures at the clinic, regularly meeting with artists, and had even been introduced to a few young people his own age from the right Houses, who took him out occasionally. One of them was the second nephew of Malriel, another one a distant cousin to Intrea. It really seemed like above a certain level they were all related to each other here somehow. No wonder they found it necessary to keep track of the inherited illnesses, she thought with dismay. That was the result of child-bearing criteria that focused on magical abilities and political advantages. But as long as there were healers available to take care of any unwanted consequences there was no real need for the Houses to rethink their approach to hanging on to their power.

Malriel had managed to profit from her involvement with Enric twofold. She had not only got fresh blood into her House, but also managed to include him in this whole network of power. And that when Eryn had hoped to free herself of it by renouncing her House. But instead her actions had opened the door for Malriel to sink her hooks into Enric. Regrettably.

It had seemed like Enric hadn't minded about that very much back then, but it had recently turned out to be a convenient string for Malriel to pull him across to Takhan, even though he preferred not have to come.

"You know," Vern spoke into her gloomy thoughts, "I have to admit that I prefer staying at the Aren residence to our prior accommodation." When she scowled, he amended, "I know that you don't like spending time here very much, because it reminds you of Malriel, but as regards luxury and comfort, it is so superior to almost all the other places I have seen so far. The gardens are amazing, especially in a hot and dry place like this, everything here is so modern..."

"Yes," she interrupted him acidly, "because they tend to blow up parts of their residence at regular intervals and need to rebuild them. So this is hardly a proof of an open mindset but merely a matter of necessity."

"The reason why they did it hardly makes a difference if staying here is comfortable, does it?" he pointed out with a shrug.

It didn't, she had to admit. But hearing something positive about anything connected to House Aren triggered a reflexive response from her that consisted of countering with the negative.

"What are your plans for tonight?" she then asked. "Will you be having dinner here with us for a change or have you been invited somewhere?"

"I have been invited," he replied apologetically. "But I can spare you another two hours before I need to get myself ready."

"You know what?" She stretched. "I can do the rest on my own. You should relax a little before you go out. I suppose you are not going to return too early tonight, and you still don't lie down at noon."

"On your own?" he frowned. "Testing yourself doesn't sound very efficient."

"I will ask Enric or Orrin to spare me half an hour and help me if need be. Go and enjoy yourself or have a nap; you don't take enough time for yourself at the moment."

"But your exam..."

"Will be fine. I will go through the other book before dinner. I think I need a longer break now, I tire more easily."

He smiled. "I imagine you do. Do you know that your bump has started showing?"

"Lad, if you have noticed that, don't you think that I have had to adapt my clothes to my increased girth already?"

He grinned. "Well, if you say it like that... Good thing you can still slip into Junar's slacks from a few months ago."

She snorted. "Hardly. When she was my size we were still at home and it was cold outside. Now we are in a country with a hot climate. If I wore her clothes, I would just melt away. They are too thick. And Junar did not have many slacks, she is the dress-wearing kind of girl."

"Both valid arguments, I admit," he nodded generously.

"Thank you so much," she replied dryly. "Now go and do something unproductive. But bring me something to eat first. Fruit would be good."

He nodded and got up. "Not much else here to feed to you between meals anyway, as you keep rejecting the baked things people keep bringing here for you to try."

"I am not trying to be difficult; the things they make here are just too sweet for my taste right now. They do everything on a grander scale here when it comes to cooking and baking: everything here is either spicier, sweeter, more fatty or harder to chew than at home."

"I like it. I think our food at home is comparably boring. I'll get you your fruit." He walked to the kitchen and returned with a bowl filled with bite-sized pieces.

"You are the best, my lad," she smiled.

"I know," he grinned immodestly. "There are a few pieces of sweet pastry left. The ones Vran'el brought by yesterday. As you don't seem to like them, can I have them?"

"They are all yours." She watched him return to the kitchen and when he passed her a minute later, he was holding a plate full of pastries to take it with him to his room. If there had been any justice in the world, he should be about three times his size with the quantities of food he gobbled down. But no, he retained his lanky look. If he reduced his intake of food to that of normal person he would probably just vanish. He had acquired a good tan in these last few weeks and had taken to wearing local fashion. He had started getting along with Vran'el, was attending regular lectures in healing, keeping in contact with various artists and spending the rest of his time, evenings especially, with people the same age as himself. All in all he was adapting extremely well.

Junar had started making contact with other pregnant women who were at her stage and more or less on the verge of giving birth, and was spending quite a lot of time at the clinic to familiarise herself with the procedures that were common here when delivering a baby. She had learned about how to breathe properly in order to deal with the pain and had attended information evenings where first-time mothers were shown how to handle an infant without causing it harm.

Enric was so busy with gaining an insight into the ways of the House for which he was now responsible that she hardly saw him more than two hours each day before they went to bed. At least he made sure to always have dinner with her, even if they had not been invited anywhere.

All in all they had settled down at the Aren residence and found a rhythm to their lives that worked. Vern was not around much; Enric spend almost all his time in Malriel's study; Junar was busy with her birthing preparations and catching up on the sleep she didn't manage to find at night lately; Orrin was working on training schedules and the like, and she herself spent her days with studying for her forthcoming exam. Basically every single one of them had some kind of routine that did not overlap much with the others that lived under the same roof. It was odd, somehow. Back home it had been the other way round: they lived at different locations but their work and training obligations kept them in constant contact.

Iklan had asked her to share with him any insights she might have regarding the mind bond. It was an almost entirely unexplored area and he was very keen to learn more about it, especially as she and Enric had made significant progress in understanding it in a short time. She had asked him for a little patience and promised him to get back to him after she had sat her exam with Sarol. At least she wouldn't get bored anytime soon once she wasn't filling her days with study any longer.

She sighed and picked up the one book she had yet go through. When she was in the middle of repeating what changes of the skin in temperature, texture and colour could mean, Orrin appeared at the top of the stairs. She hadn't even heard the entrance door.

"You don't look so happy," she commented and patted on the cushions next to her. "Come, sit and share your tribulation with me."

He snorted and grabbed a fresh glass before walking over to her.

"Share my tribulation with you? Are you that desperate for a break from your studies?"

"I am done with studying, I am just revising a few things to make sure they are still up there when I need them." She tapped her forehead with her index finger. "But so far it looks good. I feel prepared enough for the exam and can even afford to relax tomorrow. So you are not interrupting anything critical if you talk to poor, lonesome me for a while," she smiled.

He looked down at her and frowned. "Lonesome... I guess we have all been rather busy lately."

"That was just a joke, Orrin," she laughed, but couldn't help feeling a certain surprise that there had been at least a grain of truth in it nonetheless. She realised that she had not talked to anybody about how Valrad's insistence at reconciliation, Ram'an's attempts to spend time with her and how much her efforts at being calm, collected and cool during every public occasion she met them had exhausted her. Vran'el was not a good conversation partner; he was on his father's side. Telling him that this was a strain on her nerves would just make him repeat that it was in her power to put an end to it and sit down to have a long, friendly talk with their father.

"Was it?" He sighed and sank down beside her.

"Absolutely," she lied and filled his glass with water from the carafe on the low table before her. "Talk to me. Is the triarchy not cooperating with your suggestions on how to transform Takhan into a city fit for armed retaliation?"

"The triarchy is not the problem. They are happy enough with letting me plan what defensive skills should be taught. The trouble is the people who are supposed to be learning it. There are major discussions about who is to be forced into learning combat skills. I presented my ideas at the last Senate meeting, and the first thing the senators started arguing about was why their Houses and the professions connected with it should be exempted from it." He shook his head tiredly. "Enric volunteered five of the members of House Aren, though I suspect they are not exactly doing it voluntarily but are being egged on by him."

"How about Valrad?" she asked.

"The King of Healers in this city, if not this country?" he quipped. "What do *you* think? That he hasn't taken to me didn't exactly help, either. And of course this did not make a very good impression on the others. I am associated with Enric and yourself, after all, and if he as a friend doesn't support the idea, who can be expected to?"

"I am sorry," she said.

"No, you are not," he retorted. "You think healers shouldn't be made to train in combat skills at all, so don't pretend you have changed your mind about that just because we happen to be in another country right now."

"That doesn't mean that I do not appreciate what you are trying to do here. Or that his not wanting healers to be made to train in combat skills doesn't mean that he should be against teaching it to those who are willing to learn. Learn voluntarily, mind you," she emphasised. Maybe she needed to talk to Enric about making people do it just because they happened to born into the House he was currently leading.

"As if I was in a position to compel anybody," he sighed. "And judging from the lack of enthusiasm in the Senate I suppose there won't be too many people prepared to give it a try."

"You could ask Enric to help you arrange a public demonstration. You could have a show fight or something like that," she suggested.

"No, not really. Showing them something they need years to accomplish would only discourage them even further. I dare say the best way is to make the senators see that they would ultimately profit from being able to defend their city. Takhan is the most densely populated spot in this country, so if the city falls, there is nothing much left to conquer. The four other smaller cities are not nearly as significant."

"How about the other Houses allied with House Aren? No help from them, either?"

"Eryn, we are still strangers here. People who look strange compared to what they are used to, who behave differently at times and may or may not be trusted. Enric is respected to a certain degree, but mostly due to the things he did as an ambassador several months ago, not because of his experience in his current position. For all they know he might make a huge mess of it, and being allied to him could turn out to be a problem. Everybody is being very careful around him at the moment. They first want to see how he manages his new task. Three weeks have not been nearly enough time for them to see about that. And until they have decided that he is doing a good job and being associated with him is useful, my job will be very hard indeed." He smiled at her. "But this is not your problem. You had better make sure not to embarrass us by failing that exam with that magician-detesting healer."

"Thank you so much for that little push," she rolled her eyes. "As if I needed any more pressure right now."

"You will do fine," he promised her and squeezed her hand. "How are you faring yourself? How is that son of yours behaving so far? Any kicking yet?"

She smiled and laid a hand on her belly. "It is a bit early for that. There will likely be another three or four weeks until that starts. So far he is too small to misbehave."

"That will change soon enough, no matter if he takes after you or Enric," he smiled, then became serious again. "How about that situation with your father? You have not yet talked to him yet, have you? You keep avoiding him."

"I have talked to him. There were dinners, if you remember. As we move in the same circles, there is no avoiding him."

"That is not what I mean, and you know it," he reminded her. "What will you do about that? You can't keep him at a distance all the time. You are going to be working in the same building soon enough. And he is your son's grandfather. He will want to see the boy occasionally. That child is going to be the heir of his House, after all."

"Orrin," she wailed, "leave me be! I have other problems right now. Like this very important exam with a man who is not too fond of magicians, if you remember?"

"So you will take care of this after your exam? In addition there is Ram'an. Another situation that requires solving."

"I don't promise that I take care of it after the exam, but I might be more willing to listen to you talking about it than I am now."

"Why am I even bothering?" he sighed and shook his head.

"I don't know," she shrugged. "But you might as well ponder that question somewhere else as I am supposed to go through that book here one last time. I fully intend to have a very relaxing, quiet day tomorrow so I can face Sarol with a calm and collected brain the day after."

"Yes," Orrin nodded, "calmness and collectedness seem to be your most prominent characteristics lately."

"Are you hinting at how I have been treating Valrad and Ram'an?" she asked suspiciously. "I thought we agreed on putting that topic aside for now."

He rose. "As you wish. I will take a stroll in the garden now that the worst of the heat is over. I really miss my study," he sighed. "My bedroom is taken up by my sleeping companion and I am kicked out of that room here because you need to learn."

"Poor Orrin," she cooed. "If you promise to keep your mouth shut you may as well stay here."

"Thank you, too kind," he growled and turned towards the terrace door to find a spot where he could sit in peace for a while without having to bother with what either of the two pregnant women in the house demanded of him.

88

CHAPTER 7

An Idea

"So, tomorrow is the big day," Vran'el smiled while they were strolling through the streets. It was late morning. Neither of them was an early riser if it was something they could avoid.

"It is indeed," Eryn confirmed and stopped at a fountain to dip her hands in and let the water cool her skin for a minute.

"Nervous?"

"A little," she admitted. "I suppose it will become worse in the evening."

"Most healers really dread Sarol's exam," he explained. "Some of them start trembling so hard they need to be soothed magically before they go in. He has the highest failure rate of any exams."

She sent him a considered look. "Thank you so much for pointing that out one day before I am due to face him. That is very considerate of you. Tell me that Pe'tala failed the first time."

He shook his head. "No, sweetness, I am afraid I cannot. She mastered it at the first time. She did very well at all her exams. Had to. There was still the matter with her suitor to overcome, the one she has plagued with images of birds that followed him around. She had to prove that she was an able healer, and good exam marks were one important step in that direction."

"So she will mock me if I fail," Eryn sighed and took a sip from her water pouch.

"That she will," Vran'el confirmed unperturbed. "But do not worry too much. Father told me that Tala was pretty demanding when she tested you back then. She certainly seems to have made it uncommonly difficult for you, going into very much detail. And yet you passed."

"I take it he has read the transcript Pe'tala handed in for confirmation that I passed?"

"Yes. Though he was not among those to verify that little detail. One might imply that if one of his daughters tests the other he might be a tiny bit biased in your favour. So he just had a look at the papers after the assessors were through with them."

"He can look at them just like that?"

He chuckled. "Of course he can. He is very important, you know. The only reason he is not in charge of the clinic any longer is because he does not want to be."

Which was a stroke of good luck for her, she thought.

They walked on and Eryn spotted another fountain not far off.

"You really have a lot of those standing around," she remarked.

"We do, yes. Considering how warm it is here, offering fresh, cool and clean water fit for drinking is vital to the people here. The basins have different colours. This one ahead of us is green, which means that you may cool your feet in it, but you are not supposed to drink from it. The red ones are for drinking, the blue ones for washing your face and hands. And the yellow basins are shallow enough for children to jump in and play and splash around without risk of drowning."

"Neat." She thought for a moment. "Which colour was the one I washed my hands in just now?"

"Yellow. So you did not violate any conventions," he promised. "I would have warned you otherwise. I cannot let you stumble into more trouble after you barely managed to escape the one from last time a few months ago."

"That was hardly my fault!" she protested.

"It was not, I grant you that," he nodded.

They stopped when a group of children aged between six and seven ran across the street.

"What are they doing?" she asked.

"Playing," he smiled. "All but one of them hide within a designated area. The one left behind has to wait for a while and then starts looking for them. The last one to be found is the seeker in the next round."

"Really?" She laughed out, delighted. "That is almost exactly what we played when I was a child back home in the Old Kingdom. Funny, how little the games children play differ."

"Hiding and seeking are two very basic pursuits, or were back in the times before there were cities. I imagine there are probably not many countries where children do *not* play that particular game in some variation." He smiled when the group of children split up and they disappeared into different alleys. "You know, sometimes I am a little envious when I watch them. It was a fun game, but it is frowned upon when adults want to play it. A pity. I bet many of us still feel that urge to play every now and then." He grinned. "But unless somebody comes up with a very good excuse for running around in the city and hiding from each other, I imagine that will not happen anytime soon." He stopped and turned when he realised that Eryn was no longer walking beside him.

She stared at him, her thoughts racing. Hiding and seeking. Or a variation thereof. Like... attacking and defending... or sneaking in and being detected. Was it possible? But why not? Even if the idea seemed novel and unusual, if it came from one of the visitors from across the sea, they might be willing to play along...

"Eryn? Is everything alright?" Vran'el's expression was alarmed and he had grabbed her arm.

"Yes, perfectly alright! You just gave me an idea, though I have not yet considered whether it is a stupid or a brilliant one. That is for somebody else to decide. Come!" She took his sleeve and pulled him with her.

"Come where?" he asked, clearly confused.

"To find Orrin. I need to tell him about this."

"About what?"

"Hiding and seeking," she said impatiently, dragging him along.

"If your children play it as well, he knows about this, trust me. I mean, he has a son, after all."

"I will explain this, just come."

"Do you even know where Orrin is right now?" he asked, obviously not taken with that plan of hers he couldn't fully comprehend.

"Either at the Aren residence or at the Senate, I would think. But in case he is not home, he will surely have left a note where he can be found. He wants to be available if Junar needs him, after all."

"This sounds insane. Why are you dragging me along?" he grumbled.

"Because. Now stop being difficult and come."

He gave in and followed her to the Aren residence. They had only been walking for about twenty minutes at a leisurely pace so they were not too far away from it.

"Orrin?" she shouted when she had ushered Vran'el in.

"What about my moist towel?" he asked with a pout. "Just because you are excited you cannot forego the common rules of hospitality. And letting your guests refresh themselves is among them."

She rolled her eyes impatiently. "Being a nuisance again, are you? Just turn around and take one from that bowl! And you keep emphasising that we are siblings now, which would imply that you are not exactly a guest where I am at home, which means that you can bloody well grab your own towel. Orrin!" she shouted once again.

Enric appeared at the top of the stairs and looked down to them.

"He is with Junar in their bedroom. She wanted to take a nap, which is now probably over thanks to your gentle way of enquiring about Orrin's whereabouts," he said mildly. "Hello, Vran. That was a rather short walk or have I lost track of time?"

"No, you have not," he sighed. "She seems to have had some kind of epiphany which must be shared with Orrin instantly."

"You have?" Enric asked and looked at his companion who had in the meantime climbed the stairs and was standing next to him.

"There is a good chance of that, yes," she nodded and looked towards the corridor that lead to Orrin's and Junar's bedroom when she heard the sound of footsteps coming closer.

"Orrin!" she exclaimed when he appeared suddenly in the main room with a none-too-happy expression.

"You woke Junar up," he said accusingly.

"Never mind that now," Eryn waved him off and took his hands. "I might have a solution for your problem."

"My problem?" he frowned. "A weary and exhausted pregnant companion who can't sleep at night? I am told sending her off to sleep magically is not advisable. It would also affect the child and hinder its development if done too often."

"Not that! The combat training nobody wants to do – I have an idea how to get people interested in it! You are wrong, it's not the senators you need to convince. They are very likely as sluggish and unwilling to accept new ideas as is our Magic Council. You need to address the people who are supposed to learn it directly, and I might have an idea how to do that."

His interest was clearly awakened now. "How?" he just asked.

"Hide and seek!"

"Pardon me?" He eyed her suspiciously. "Have you been out in the sun for too long?"

She ignored his comment and went on, "The children's game, where most of them hide themselves and one goes looking for them. We saw a group of children playing just that in the streets a few minutes ago, just like at home. Vran'el said that sometimes he envies them because adults are not supposed to play it any longer and would just be thought a little odd if they did!" She looked at him expectantly, but he just stared back at her blankly.

"A game of hide and seek for adults," she heard Enric's thoughtful voice behind her when he came closer. "One that not only consists of hiding, but also fleeing and fighting back, by any chance?" he ventured.

"Exactly!" she beamed, happy that he understood what she was aiming at. "There could be two teams, invaders and defenders. The invaders need to reach a certain point, such as the Senate hall, in order successfully to occupy the city, and the defenders need to avoid just that by finding and capturing them before they reach that point."

"The capturing could be done with weak magical strikes," Enric mused, clearly intrigued by the idea. "There would have to be rules as to shielding and attacking and so on. They could put their knowledge of the streets to good use. Of course the defenders have to lose the game, or there will be no point in showing them that learning defensive battle skills would make sense."

"I am not yet sure if this is complete nonsense or simply brilliant," Orrin frowned.

Eryn laughed. "I was hoping for you to tell me that. Though Enric seems to be rather taken with it."

"Orrin, Vern and you would need to be on the side of the invaders," Enric went on with his eyes unfocussed as if talking to himself. "I as Head of House will have to be among the defenders. Otherwise it would not be good for the reputation I am trying to build here. Seeing me as a defender of their city will earn me extra points..."

She shook her head at him. "A politician, through and through."

Enric looked up, focus returning to his eyes. "Eryn." He kissed her forehead. "You truly are amazing, an explorer through and through. Orrin? We need to sit down and devise rules for that game. Come." There was a gleam in his eyes and he walked back towards his study.

"From the looks of it Enric is clearly among those who miss playing games," the warrior murmured, and followed the younger man.

Vran'el chuckled. "That went well, sweetness. I am curious what they will come up with. And if it will work out the way you hope."

She turned to him. "Would you play along?"

"Me? Definitely. And as I am already aware which side is meant to win, I will definitely join the invaders," he grinned and ruffled her hair, "and fight side by side with my little sister to conquer the city together with the barbarians from across the sea."

"Opportunist," she sighed, but couldn't help smiling at the image of them roaming the streets of Takhan, hiding in nooks, glancing around corners and running from one place of cover to the next to reach their destination.

"That is not a very respectful way to talk to your big brother," he scolded her. "If you do not behave I will sacrifice you to the enemy so I can be among the victorious survivors."

"Charming," she sniffed. "That is the kind of brother every girl dreams of. Now I remember why I don't show you the respect you so unreasonably seem to think you deserve."

He laughed and rubbed his hands together. "I hope they get on with their planning, I want to do this before you grow too big to participate."

She nodded, sharing that sentiment.

* * *

Eryn closed the door of the room she had just had the exam in behind her and released a breath that seemed to have been held for hours. Vern was waiting for her in the corridor, and got up from the floor.

"And? How did it go?" he asked eagerly, his brow high, his eyes wide.

"I am not so sure," she said exhaustedly. Where was all the energy that had been there only a minute ago? Probably gone as soon as the tension of being tested was over.

"But you must have some feeling about whether it was good or not? How many of the questions did you manage to answer?" he insisted, clearly a bit worried now.

"I don't know exactly," she sighed helplessly.

"How can you *not* know that?" he complained.

"Look, I am not saying this to annoy you, or because I am unduly modest, but because I have no idea what the main questions were. He asked so many, and I think several of them were just to see how detailed my knowledge was. I don't know how he rates those, if they are as important as the main questions or not. If yes, I am in trouble. If not, I might have a chance."

"So they didn't tell you if you did well or not? Or at least if you have passed?"

"No, nothing. They told me to wait in front of the door until they have decided on that."

"Did they say how long that will take?"

"A few minutes," she replied.

"How many of them are in there?"

"Three. So I hope the discussion does not take them too long."

He snorted. "As if three people couldn't discuss things for a long time. Ask my father. Some of the Council meetings consisted of nothing more than discussions between two or three people and the rest of them either about to fall asleep or stare at the ceiling."

"I need something to eat," she declared and started off towards the canteen.

"No!" Vern exclaimed in panic. "They told you to wait here, you can't just run off like that!"

"I am hungry and expecting a baby, I assume they will forgive me if I am gone for a few minutes," she pointed out.

"Or they won't and become so angry that they change their mind and say you failed. If they even wanted to let you pass beforehand, that is," he amended. "Wait here. I will get you something to eat. Anything in particular or just some fruit?"

"No fruit right now, I need something a bit more substantial. Check if they have any..." She stopped and froze when the door behind her opened and Sarol stuck out his head.

"We have reached a decision. Come in."

She gulped, cast Vern a slightly panicked look and followed the healer back inside the room she had just come out of.

The three men before her sat at their table and looked up at her with unreadable expressions.

Not good, she decided instantly. If she had passed, they would probably be smiling.

At that moment two of them broke into wide smiles and stood up. Sarol was the only one whose expression didn't change, but he, too, got up again as if reluctantly complying with what his colleagues seemed consider appropriate.

"Eryn, congratulations. You have passed your last exam and are herewith a fully certified healer in accordance with the standards of the city of Takhan."

She felt her knees becoming soft from relief at Sarol's words and again released the breath she had been holding.

He held up a silver pin, just like the one every fully trained healer at the clinic and everywhere in the Western Territories wore. It was in the form of a small silver hand with rays radiating from it, the symbol of healing in these parts.

"This identifies you as a fully trained healer and will grant you access and free sustenance at every healing place in the country. It also enables you to treat and advise patients without the presence of another healer. You are from here on one of us. Welcome to the noble profession!"

She lifted a slightly trembling hand to accept the needle and stared at it for a few seconds before pinning it to her tunic directly above her heart, where it was supposed to go. She had once worn Valrad's insignia for an hour at the canteen to get free food there, dreaming of the day when she would have her own. That day was today.

"Any ceremonious words you would like to get rid of?" Sarol asked, clearly hoping that she wouldn't.

She laughed and shook her head. "Not really. The only thing that is of interest to me right now is whether I can start working here tomorrow."

She frowned when Sarol swallowed and exchanged a look with his colleagues.

"Basically, yes. Though as you have not been trained here in Takhan like all other healers, the provision of being allowed to treat patients unsupervised will be on hold for a while. We do not really have an insight into your practical abilities, so for the next weeks you will work together with an experienced healer from the clinic."

"Alright," she shrugged, "I am fine with that. So I suppose I just come here tomorrow morning and meet my supervisor and work with him."

The three of them nodded, obviously relieved at something. Probably that she had accepted the limitation without complaints.

When she walked out of the room, Vern's eyes dropped to her insignia immediately.

"You did it!" he howled and threw his arms around her neck.

"Your joy is understandable, young man, but do try to remember that this is a place where ill and injured people come to be treated, if you can," Sarol said with a sour expression and walked past them. "Now come, it is time for lunch. You will eat with me." And on he went without waiting for a reply or checking if they were following.

"What an old grouch," Vern mumbled.

"I heard that," Sarol called back without turning, several paces ahead of them.

"Damn," the boy whispered.

"And no cursing! A bit more respect for the healing profession, young man! I very much look forward to taking the exam with *you* one day," the healer said in a tone that held promises of unspoken terrors.

Eryn grimaced sympathetically when Vern's face became white under his tan.

"That hearing of his is quite something, eh? Come, let's hurry. He doesn't like to be kept waiting. You can try to make him like you while we are eating."

Vern nodded feebly and followed on as she increased her pace.

* * *

Eryn opened the door and admitted Kilan.

"It's about time!" she chided him while reaching out for the bowl with the towels. "I am starving!"

"When are you ever not these days?" he said under his breath.

"That was extremely ungallant," she glowered at him.

"But not exactly wrong, is it?" he smiled.

"Which does not make it any less ungallant," she countered. "Now stop insulting me and up you go. First you make an expectant woman wait for you, then you insult her for being hungry because of it. You are aware that a woman with child is held in very high esteem here, aren't you? How about adapting to that little custom?"

"You make that very hard," he retorted. "But I promise I will work on it. I will start practising with Junar, I think." He speedily climbed the stairs when she began to roll up and throw another small, moist towel at him.

"Did you tease the pregnant lady?" Enric asked him when he entered the main room. "We do try to avoid that here, you know."

"In your situation that is probably a useful survival strategy. You do have an above average number of them around," Kilan nodded.

"Yes," Eryn growled behind him, "and you have been invited to celebrate my great success tonight, so don't make me hurt you. You can't hit me back. I am with child."

"Convenient excuse these days," the ambassador shrugged.

"Convenient?" she huffed. "Why don't *you* try healing away an upset stomach every few minutes whenever you eat something you should have avoided and fighting with clothes that are getting less comfortable each time you put them on?"

"Kilan?"

"Yes, Enric?"

"Shut up and sit down. No teasing the pregnant lady. That has become an important rule of this house."

"Sorry," he mumbled and went over to where Junar was sitting to kiss her on both cheeks. "How is everything going with you? You can't have a lot of time to wait."

"One month," she sighed. "And I am looking forward to getting my body back. Not that I don't like to share, but after the birth there will be a father and a big brother to do some of the carrying around."

Kilan grimaced. "And the heat is not really so handy for you, either, I suppose."

"Talk to me about the heat," she moaned. "If I could, I would spend the whole day in a bathtub with cold water. The water takes off some of the weight, at least."

"Well, it's only one more month. Four short weeks. They will speed by quickly enough," he promised.

"What do you know?" Eryn murmured and looked up when Enric and Orrin entered the main room, carrying a large, steaming bowl and several smaller ones. "Finally!" she exclaimed.

Vern followed with an arm full of glasses and a carafe of water.

When they had all washed and dried their hands, Enric served out the food.

"Meat-free tonight?" Junar asked.

"Yes," Enric nodded, "we haven't been on a hunting trip in these last few days. And it doesn't hurt to leave it off every now and then."

When they had all started eating, the host, too, picked up his bowl.

"How are your plans for the invasion game coming along?" Eryn enquired. "Any progress on the rules you started pondering yesterday?"

Orrin nodded. "Not only have we determined a complete set of rules, but also asked the members of the triarchy for a meeting to introduce the idea to them and see if they are likely to permit it. It requires a good deal of organising as some areas in the city need to be prepared for it. We were thinking of starting at nightfall. Fewer people around on the streets. They are either having dinner somewhere or are at the music houses at that time."

"That was quick," she said appreciatively. "I am curious what the triarchy will say. But as they are in favour of training people, they are hardly likely to disagree, are they?"

"We don't really expect them to, no."

"Tell us about that exam of yours. Your passing it is the reason we are sitting together here, after all," Kilan remarked. "Though I am a bit surprised Vran'el isn't here as well."

"He would have told his father, and then either both would have come or Valrad would have been angry for not being invited. I don't care about that a lot, but apparently Enric cannot afford to be as casual as me when it comes to upsetting another Head of House. Thus we decided to keep the natives away for one evening and concentrate on our fellow countrymen and women," Eryn explained.

"Fine for me," Kilan shrugged. "Now tell us about the exam. Is it as scary and hard as people keep saying?"

"It might be if you are not prepared well enough. Sarol tends to consider this a personal insult. But as I spent several weeks learning almost day and night, I was able to pass. Not easily or with extraordinary results, but that was never really an objective of mine." She leaned forward so he could get a better look at her new insignia. "Behold, my new item of jewellery."

"This is the first piece of jewellery I have ever seen her enthusiastic about," Enric grinned.

"Lovely," the ambassador nodded. "I suppose you will now want to work at the clinic?"

"That is the plan, yes," Eryn confirmed. "Though they are not fully convinced of my practical abilities despite giving me the pin. They want to watch me work for a time before they unleash me on patients unsupervised. That means I will be working with an established healer over the next few weeks."

"You seem fairly relaxed about that," Vern commented.

She shrugged. "I am. I know that my skills in treating patients are up to their standard, so I don't expect any difficulties there. I would be surprised if they really insisted on watching me for several weeks. I dare say they will probably need a few days to convince themselves of what I can accomplish. It's not as if I am really a beginner. I have been treating people for these last fifteen years, after all." Then she grinned. "Vern managed to annoy Sarol after I passed the exam. First he expressed his joy at my success too loudly for Sarol's taste, then his subsequent mumbling about his being an old grouch was too loud to go unnoticed. Vern was very quiet when we had lunch together afterwards."

"He said he was looking forward to testing me," the boy said grimly. "I bet he won't grant *me* a pass the first time."

"He didn't *grant* me a pass, either," Eryn retorted haughtily, "I earned it. It is a triumph fully deserved and justified." She set her empty bowl aside.

"Would you like another helping?" Enric enquired.

"No, thank you," she declined. "Not at the moment. I imagine I will fetch myself another bowl in an hour or two."

When all of them had finished eating, Kilan cleared his throat. "There is one little matter I am afraid I need to address, even though this is meant to be a happy occasion." He looked at Eryn apologetically. "I received a messaging bird from Lord Tyront today. It seems he has been waiting to hear from you for a while and is not overly pleased about your ignoring his messages to report to him."

She looked chastened. "He contacted you to get me to write to him? Really?" Oh dear, that meant that he was getting truly impatient.

"Well, he doesn't have a lot of other choices, does he? Enric is no longer in the Order, so he can't make you write, technically. Me he can contact directly at the embassy and even though I can't order you to do your reports, I can at least pass on *his* orders."

"Alright," she grimaced. "I will write to him tomorrow. I promise."

"Good. The notion of delivering his threats to you on a regular basis is not very appealing," Kilan sighed.

"I'll make sure she takes care of this," Orrin promised. "I won't let her go to sleep before I see her report."

"You are not even supposed to see what I am writing to Tyront," Eryn said critically. "High-ranking Order business."

The warrior raised one eyebrow at her. "I don't see what you could have to report that is too confidential for me to know. He doesn't want you to write him because he is afraid of missing anything important. I write to him regularly, after all, so he is well-informed. He wants you to remember who you are subordinated to. And refusing to write him conveys the impression that this is exactly what is happening."

"I already said that I will write him tomorrow, so leave me be for tonight," she grunted. "I don't want to brag, but I am here to be feted tonight."

Enric nodded. "Indeed, you are." He rose. "If you will excuse me for a moment." He walked towards the kitchen and returned little later with a tray that was covered with a white cloth. After placing it on the low table before his companion, he motioned for her to remove the cover.

She did and sucked in a surprised breath. "Bread buns!" she then exclaimed, staring greedily at the repast before her. "How did you manage that?"

He smiled at her reaction, glad that the surprise had worked out.

"I had Tyront obtain the recipe and send it via bird. I went to two different bakery shops here and had them experiment for a week until one of them came up with a result that pretty much resembles what we know from home."

She bit her lip. "And they are all mine?" she whispered.

"Well, yes. Though I suppose you might want to share them with the rest of us as you will hardly manage to eat them all before they go stale."

"There are only fifteen pieces," she said slowly. "If I have to share them with you, they will be gone very quickly."

Enric nodded solemnly. "I see your dilemma. Good thing, then, that I brought two trays. One to share, the rest for you."

She took his hand between hers and pressed a kiss on it. "Thank you so much! I am going to keep you. Really."

He shook his head. "At least your needs are not complicated. If I had known that a few bread buns would bind you to me eternally, I would have supplied you with them sooner."

"I already bound myself to you quite tightly with that third level bond, if you remember," she snorted. "Which reminds me, I have promised Iklan to talk to him about the mind bond and how we are dealing with it. I think it makes sense if you come as well. You are the one who does most of the shielding, after all. Now that I am no longer supposed to be mugging up for that exam, I need to return to dealing with the world outside."

"Good. That means you have energies available to take care of that little issue with Valrad. And Ram'an, while you are at it," he said lightly.

"Don't," she just hissed and sent him an angry look. She had no intention of going anywhere near either of them.

He nodded once. This was not the best setting to discuss this, anyway. The trouble was that she was not only excluding her own father from celebrating what he, too, had to consider a very desirable accomplishment on her side, but also Vran'el, and that was really worrying. Unfortunately, there was no talking to her about this topic, she just jumped up to leave the room, snapped at him or ignored him completely every time he tried.

Valrad usually waited for him after the Senate meetings in order to talk to him and enquire about how Eryn was doing, how the baby was coming along and if she wasn't overdoing it. He was worried about his daughter who simply couldn't forgive him the affair he had had with Malriel. She still clung to memories of Ved'al and was nowhere close to ready to accepting another man as her father.

From what he gathered she didn't talk to anybody else about the situation, either. Junar was not to be burdened unnecessarily, Vern was hardly ever around, Orrin was busy with his companion and his challenging task in Takhan, Vran'el was of the opinion that she should give up her childish resistance and he himself only seemed to hit bedrock every time he tried to breach the subject. He didn't even pressure her to give in, just to do something about the current state of her relationship with Valrad that would make staying in the city easier for her. It wasn't as if she could completely avoid her father for the months ahead.

He looked up when Orrin grabbed his arm.

"Sorry, what?"

"Lost in thought? I was asking if we are to serve the wine now or wait?"

Wine sounded good to him right now. "Let's serve it now. I could really do with a glass."

CHAPTER 8

The Supervisor

Eryn yawned on her way from the Aren residence to the clinic. She had risen early today, eager to start her first day as a healer at the clinic. The silver insignia gleamed at her collar and she was munching on another one of the bread buns Enric had acquired for her.

Thinking of him, she felt slightly guilty about the way she had reacted yesterday evening when he had suggested taking care of the situation with Valrad after presenting her with her favourite bread. But then tackling her over the issue with Valrad while she had been trying to enjoy herself had not been a smart move on his side.

She pushed the thought aside for now. The clinic had come into view and she stopped to polish off her breakfast. It wouldn't make a good impression if she walked in there chewing. After making sure that no crumbs were clinging to her lips, tunic or fingers, she walked on, a pleasant anticipation lending a swing to her step.

She entered the by now familiar waiting area for patients and asked a young man behind the registration desk where she was expected. He smiled at her, congratulated her on passing the exam the day before and sent her along the corridor to a treatment room. Her supervisor was already there and waiting for her, he informed her.

Eryn nodded her thanks and followed his directions to one of the doors that bore the sign of a treatment room, stopping briefly in front of it before entering. She hadn't really given much thought as to whom they might have chosen as her supervisor, but even if it was somebody tediously picky she would only have to get through a few weeks with him or her at the most.

101

She knocked three times and didn't wait for an invitation but entered.

"Good morning, I am..."

The healer inside looked up from his papers and they stared at each other.

She really, really, *really* should have seen that coming, she thought, numbness spilling into her brain. Pe'tala had warned her that he would try something as soon as the exam was over.

"Good morning, Eryn. Come in," Valrad said calmly and slowly got up from his chair.

She swallowed hard. "No."

"Do close the door while we are discussing this, will you?"

"There is nothing to discuss," she said tersely. A moment later she felt a gust of wind when he lifted his hand and the door handle slipped out of her grip when the door pushed itself shut.

"I admit I am glad to see a crack in that cool façade you have taken to displaying in my presence lately," he spoke. "Indifference is a cruel thing - it negates all emotional involvement. Anger at least shows some kind of emotion, being an admission that something is in need of resolution."

She breathed in and out to calm herself, then forced herself to meet his gaze. "I have no wish to resolve anything with *you* right now."

"Then you are going to find the next few weeks - over the course of which we perform our work together - very trying, I suggest."

"I demand a different supervisor," she said stiffly.

His smile was calculated. "You are not exactly in a position to make any demands. Our granting you an exam date outside the regular schedule and providing accelerated handling of all administration involved were gestures of goodwill that people here agreed to in order satisfy *me*. Your making demands would not be received very well, believe me."

"A request, then," she growled. "I will make an official request to be granted another supervisor."

"Quite useless," he said sternly. "The reason why you are being subjected to supervision at all is because I requested it. If you demand a different healer, I will make sure that it is treated with the utmost care and consideration possible. *Months* may go by before a different solution would even be considered."

She felt her shoulders dropping. "Trying to intimidate me, Valrad? Is that how low you have sunk?" She turned to open the door, but froze when she heard his words.

"If you leave now, working at the clinic will not be open to you any longer," he warned her. "Think carefully if opposing me is worth invoking that. I will leave you alone for a few minutes while I get myself something to drink. Come to a decision. There can be no discussion. If you are still here when I return, I shall consider these terms accepted."

She hastily stepped out of the way when he walked towards the door to avoid touching him. A moment later she was alone in the scrubbed, white-walled treatment room.

She shook her head in disbelief, leaning her forehead against the wall and closing her eyes for a moment. Two options, neither of them appealing. Either she walked out of here, showing him that he couldn't treat her like an uncooperative wretch and then paying the price for it, or she accepted. The price of not being allowed to work here, was she willing to pay it? Was her pride worth such a penalty?

The other option was seeing him every day, working with him side-by-side, suppressing her fury. Could she do that? Was it worth being welcome here as a healer? They had told her that the insignia would grant her access to all healing places in the Western Territories, enabling her to work anywhere. It seemed that this did not apply for the one place where her Head of House was all but in charge.

Images of herself spending her days at the Aren residence, wandering aimlessly through Malriel's corridors, looking for ways to keep herself occupied came up. She knew without doubt that she would regret dearly walking out of here. And yet it was so very tempting. Just to make a point.

But making a point here and now was not worth bearing the consequences for however long she was stuck in Takhan. Severing her connections with the clinic would also not be a bright thing to do in the long run when she considered her own healing centre back in Anyueel.

She breathed out and opened her eyes again. There was only one choice for her. She would stay and endure working with Valrad. That cool façade she had cultivated; he would be getting to see a lot more of it, she thought with grim determination, and straightened. If he thought that being made to spend time with him would alter her opinion of what he had done, how he had treated his own brother, he would soon work out that getting through to her was not as easy as that.

She turned when the door opened again and Valrad came in. She could see the relief on his face when he spotted her.

"I am glad you decided to stay, my girl," he smiled.

"Let us lay down a few rules for the time I am being made to work with you," she said coldly. "I will treat you with the respect and politeness your position here at the clinic and in my House entitles you to. I will do my work to the best of my knowledge, skill and ability. You will in turn refrain from referring to me as *my girl*, *my daughter* or any other endearment that comes to your mind. I will not take my meals together with you or spend any time with you outside this treatment room unless it is required in order to do my work. Have I made myself clear?"

"Perfectly," he replied gently. "Yet as I pointed out to you before, you are not in any position to make demands or set rules here. I will continue to refer to you in whatever way I see fit. Also, we will take some of our meals together, as this is part of the respect you yourself pointed out I am entitled to be shown. Seeing you sitting alone somewhere instead of with me while having lunch will have people wondering and will not cast me in a good light. It would furthermore turn out to your own disadvantage, as being seen to oppose me will make people very careful around you. Most of them will try to avoid making it seem as if they sided with you against me."

How could she have failed to notice that iron resolve the first time she had been here? Enric had warned her that a Head of House could hardly remain in power by being amiable all the time, but it had never really fitted her picture of him. Until now.

"Now come." He put down his steaming mug on the desk against one wall and opened the door again. "Let me show you our system for filing and updating patient documents. Now that you are certified you have access to all this information."

She reminded herself to keep her frustration and ire at being outmanoeuvred like that from showing and followed him out into the corridor. That was going to be a long day indeed.

*   *   *

Enric kept listening for the sound of the entrance door. He knew that she had stopped working at the clinic more than two hours ago and that walking back here usually took her no more than fifteen minutes. That she was not yet back very likely meant that she had felt the need to be alone for a while.

Lately she preferred seclusion to spending time with anybody else. He had a fairly clear idea what the reason for that might be, yet he would have preferred for her to come to him and seek solace by talking to him instead of choosing isolation.

He had decided to go looking for her in the teahouses she had frequented when feeling the need to get out of the house while learning for her exam, when he heard the entrance door close and recognised her steps as she climbed the stairs. Finally.

She did not come to his study, but instead paced towards the terrace door and out to the garden, he noted with a frown. He got up from the chair and looked out the window, watching her strolling towards one of the larger trees. It was still quite warm outside, and she chose a spot that afforded her some shade for sitting under.

He decided to join her and see if he could encourage her to talk to him. For some reason there had been little time for that lately. Leading House Aren had turned out to be rather a challenge considering that he was used to holding a position of power. But somehow the dynamics here seemed to work differently. His instructions were not always carried out as promptly and diligently as he might have wished, and he was yet to work out how to deal with that without alienating the people that were, legally speaking, his family.

104

"You don't look happy, my love," he stated when he had reached her and bent down to kiss her before sinking down on the grass next to her.

"I am not," she confirmed without looking at him.

"This does not happen to have anything to do with meeting your supervisor today?" he ventured.

She looked up sharply. "Don't tell me you knew about this and failed to mention it! I would not take that well right now," she warned him with narrowed eyes.

"I didn't," he promised. "But I had a feeling that Valrad would use this opportunity for his own purpose. It's what I would have done in his place."

"You might have warned me," she scowled.

"I could have been wrong," he shrugged. "And I wouldn't have told you, even if I had known. It might have stopped you from showing up there today. I think this is a good chance for you to finally mend relations with your father."

She shook her head at him, her expression disappointed. "Stop this. I don't like you constantly pressuring me about this. I am sick of people pushing me to do something about it. I don't want to! Is this so hard to understand? Just leave me alone with this from now on. I don't want to hear another word about it from anyone. Neither will I mention it again. Just don't ask me how my day was when I come home from the clinic, alright?"

He held on to her hand when she rose. "Eryn, I am sorry. Sit with me for a while, will you? I was worried when you didn't return here after work."

"No, I just want to be alone. Let go of me. Please."

He did.

She looked at him. "Do you know why I didn't return here after I was done at the clinic? Because I had a feeling that talking to you about this wouldn't be pleasant. I needed time for myself and just stayed at the next available teahouse for a time, where nobody bothered me. But as you told me that you have somebody shadow me at all times, you probably knew about that already."

Well, she was not wrong, there was somebody following her around. But the agent had not yet reported back for today.

He watched her walking back towards the house and disappear through the terrace door. He regretted joining her. Or rather opening his mouth at all. Was she more sensitive lately than before due to her pregnancy? Or was he less considerate than usual? Or both? He rubbed his face.

Vran'el had told him that Eryn avoided talking to him as well. He, too, was worried about that. She still sent messages to Pe'tala by message bird, though it was hard to tell if she was sharing her thoughts with her faraway sister at all.

He considered going through her things, looking for the letters Pe'tala sent back. They would surely provide some insight. He decided against it almost immediately. Eryn would not react well to such a breach of trust if she found out. Neither would he in her place.

He watched the light breeze that had come up gently stroking the blossoms of the tree Malriel had manipulated into holding more than one species. A faint sensation of the sweet smell its varied blossoms exuded wafted towards him, making him breathe deeply through his nose.

It was a pity that nobody seemed to be able to get through to Eryn right now. His thoughts wandered to Ram'an. He had managed to make her volunteer information more often than once in the past, shamelessly using skills on her that came with his being a trained lawyer. But unfortunately she was not on speaking terms with him, either.

He sighed. How bad did things really have to be if he was now wishing for Ram'an to be closer to her again?

* * *

Eryn forced herself to close the entrance door gently behind her instead of throwing it shut, aiming to avoid waking Junar. This was usually the time for her second afternoon nap these days. She quickly fingered her trouser pocket to make sure that she had enough gold with her to pay for a pot of tea, then strode off quickly, turning the next corner to be out of sight of the Aren residence.

She didn't want Enric to come after her. He would either make her come back or insist on accompanying her. Neither option was very appealing right now. A nice tent, something to drink to soothe her nerves, a little peace and quiet with nobody to bother her about the things she had no desire to talk about.

She felt sweat forming on her forehead. It was still warm enough outside for a march like this to be arduous. She had no particular teahouse in mind, just one that was not situated along one of the larger streets. She didn't want to bump into anybody she knew.

After turning into a street at random, she turned another corner and found a little way off a tent that looked small enough not to be one of the preferred meeting places for the rich and important. She decided to give it a try, wondering wearily if with her luck right now it would turn out to be exclusive and an insider's haunt for members of the Houses.

She found an unoccupied island of cushions at the end furthest away from the passers-by and sat with her back to them to maintain the utmost anonymity possible. She had not spent that much time in Takhan, but her face was well known due to her being not only the former heiress of House Aren, but also a public sensation first because her own mother had accused her of having caused Ved'al's death and lately because the Head of House Vel'kim had publicly announced that he was her natural father.

A server stopped next to her and she saw a quick glint of recognition in his eyes. At least he didn't say anything apart from asking her what she wanted to drink. She took the golden slip out of her pocket and asked how many pots of tea that would buy her. The server smiled and informed her that with this she could have about twenty pots.

She nodded in relief and ordered one pot for starters. She had no idea how long she would sit here, but knowing that she wouldn't run out of something to drink was a comfort.

Leaning back, she stared up at the sky, noting how the quality of the light started changing slowly to announce the nearing evening. The light breeze she had felt back at the house outside in the garden had not found its way here between the buildings.

This solitude felt good, she decided. It was a different kind than the one she lately felt in the presence of those close to her. More honest. Even Enric's presence was a strain at the moment, too many expectations from him. Vern, too, was not exactly happy about all of this, because Valrad had taken over the role of his mentor and they kept spending time together.

She wilted at the thought of returning home later, of sleeping in one bed with her companion and hoping he wouldn't talk to her or touch her. Even being held by him felt like an unreasonable demand lately; she found herself enduring instead of enjoying it. That was probably the most frightening thing about this whole mess: slowly feeling herself drifting apart from him.

She wished she still had some preparations to do. Having passed the exam yesterday had suddenly left her with free afternoons and evenings she didn't really have any use for. Would she spend them brooding while hiding from the world in teahouses?

A stab of homesickness made her swallow. Sitting in her own study at home with a cup of tea and something to nibble on, the cat at her feet, familiar books around her at the walls... She would even prefer dealing with the King instead of Valrad right now.

She wondered how things at the clinic in Anyueel were going, whether Lord Poron, Rolan and Pe'tala were managing to work together. Pe'tala had written to her, and so had Lord Poron, informing her that everything was running smoothly. Which was good, she assured herself, pushing aside the narcissistic thought that things were not supposed to run that smoothly without her. Where would that leave her, after all? Being easy to replace was not pleasant to ponder, even though Pe'tala was of course a skilled professional in her field despite her youth. Being raised in a healing House obviously had that added benefit.

Healing House. House Vel'kim. Valrad. She pushed aside the wandering thought angrily, returning to her clinic. Plia. She, too, had written, telling Eryn how much she missed her and that the house was so very empty without them. Another stab of longing went through her. She wondered how Plia's plants on the roof were growing, if she still spent so much time up there in her new glass house.

She closed her eyes, imagining that she was sitting on a bench at the river back in Anyueel, as she had the day before they had left for Takhan. Enric had joined her and sat with her for a short while. That had been before that void between them had emerged and started growing. She had felt dread about returning to Takhan back then, yet looking back, that time seemed oddly blissful and free of worry. It was strange how looking back changed things.

* * *

She woke with a start and sat bolt upright. It was night and she was still at the teahouse. Things slowly swam into focus. Somebody had covered her with a blanket against the cool night air and she drew in a sharp breath when she saw the man sitting on the cushions opposite her, a book on his lap and his slightly curious gaze resting on her.

Ram'an. Oh no.

"Eryn," he smiled. "Welcome back among the living."

She swallowed her impulsive reaction at airing her dismay at finding him here like this and instead took a sip from the now cold remnants in her half-full cup.

"Ram'an," she nodded politely. "What bestows upon me the honour of your unexpected company?"

That made him chuckle. "Still determined to play it cool? I admit you are getting better at it. Though I do not think this is particularly healthy, mind you." He leaned forward and poured her another cup of tea. This one was still steaming hot. "I came along and found you sleeping. As it was getting colder and I do not think it advisable for a woman to sleep alone in public, I decided to sit with you for a while and make sure you did not freeze."

To guard her sleep, she thought and kept herself from huffing. "How long did I sleep?"

"I am not sure, but I have been sitting with you these last two hours. It seems you were rather exhausted," he commented and put his book aside.

Two hours alone with him, and she had not even realised it. She pushed aside the blanket and lifted her hands up to her hair to push the few strands that had escaped the braid behind her ears.

"I thank you for your gallantry. Now I had better leave. I imagine Enric will be worrying where I am."

"No need for that. I have sent him a message that you are at a teahouse with me and that I will personally ensure you get back to the Aren residence safely."

"That is very generous of you," she replied stiffly, "but I am by no means unable to find my way back alone. And as I am not only trained in what Orrin likes to call the art of fighting, but also strong enough to defend myself magically if need be, there will hardly be any danger I couldn't manage to deal with."

"So loath to spend even a few minutes with me, Eryn?" he asked softly. "Sit with me for a little longer, will you? I would like to talk to you and you have so far evaded all my attempts to do so."

"That is because I have no wish to talk to you and feel no need to resolve anything between us," she remarked, equally calmly, proud that she had managed to speak the words without spitting them at him in the way she would have preferred to. She stood. "I thank you very much for your considerateness in sitting here with me, though I would prefer it if you woke me next time in case you find me in a similar situation ever again," she said formally.

He sighed and nodded. "As you wish."

She dropped a slip of gold onto the low table and looked at him when he chuckled.

"No, my dear, the tea was on me. And this would have been a little too much anyway, as you seem determined to rush off without waiting for the change." He got up as well. "Come. Let us get you home since you cannot be prevailed upon to talk to me. There will be other occasions, when you are less tense due to the unpleasant surprise of finding yourself working with your father."

She closed her eyes for a moment. "That seems to be common knowledge already."

"I like to keep myself well-informed," he shrugged. "From what I heard you are subjecting him to the same icy politeness that I have to deal with."

"Would you prefer me to abuse you and storm away every time I see you?" she asked.

He thought for a moment, then nodded. "I think I would, actually. It would be more authentic. I told you before that I do not want any diplomacy between us, that I prefer honest disagreement."

She looked him in the eye. "That is unfortunate for you, Ram'an. Diplomacy is all I have to offer right now." She stepped aside when he attempted to take her arm. "I was being serious when I told you that I do not need you to escort me back. I appreciate your willingness, but I would prefer to walk alone. I thank you very much for respecting that."

He grimaced. "As much as I would like to oblige you in this, I am afraid there is no choice as I have given my promise to Enric to bring you back safely. In the unlikely event that you happen to stumble into some kind of trouble on your way back or get lost, that would seriously endanger the frail alliance I am trying to keep alive with House Aren, considering that your companion is the current Head of the House. How will he ever trust me in business matters if I do not even manage to keep a promise as simple as accompanying you back home? You would hardly wish to endanger my House's chances of recovery, would you? I cannot afford to anger House Aren right now. And I myself have no wish to. So I would be eternally indebted to you if you took it upon yourself to endure my presence a little longer so that I can keep my House from perishing due to stirring Enric's wrath."

Eryn made herself force a smile at his theatrics. It seemed there was no way out of it. "Of course. I would not want to have your House's demise sitting on my conscience because I insisted on walking alone."

"That is very considerate of you," he bowed with a smirk and lifted his arm for her to take it. "Is offering you my arm too bold? How eager are you to appear polite and detached, I wonder?"

"Not that eager," she said calmly and started walking.

"Eryn?" she heard him behind her, but ignored him. "That is the wrong direction, unless you are secretly planning a detour to spend more time with me. I have no objection to that, mind you."

She stopped and cursed silently, schooling her features back into a neutral expression before turning back to him.

"Lead on, then," she instructed with a tense smile.

They walked next to each other silently for a while, before Ram'an ventured, "You may not be willing to talk to me, but this should not stop you from listening when I do. I would like to apologise…"

"Please, don't," she stopped him with a hand lifted. "I do not want to hear it. There is nothing to apologise for. I forgive you whatever you think you did wrong and thus you may put to rest this need to set things right."

"What a wretched thing to say to me," he murmured. "I am aware that my behaviour, the way my messages must have seemed to you…"

"I mean it," she pressed out between clenched teeth. "You either stop this right now, or I will shake you off and continue back home alone. I can do it, trust me. You surely remember that special shield of mine, don't you? I can block an entire opening into an alley with it and leave you behind."

She saw his jaw muscles working at her words and waited for him to reach a decision. After a few moments he nodded reluctantly.

"Have it your way. I will accommodate you this time. Let me assure you, though, that I will not let this situation remain the way it is now. This is not acceptable, and I do not appreciate your refusal even to listen to me."

"That is your problem, I am afraid. I do not see any need to change things between us. I deem the situation between us appropriate, considering our history. Any closeness or even friendship would seem unnatural and strange, allowing for the circumstances." She walked on without waiting for him to reply.

He ran a few steps to catch up with her and walked next to her silently until they had reached the Aren residence.

"Good night, Ram'an," she said politely. "Thank you for taking the trouble to see me home. I will let Enric know that you kept your promise."

He quickly took her hand and pressed it against his lips in the formal greeting, lingering a little longer than was polite, holding on to it when she tried to pull it back.

"Good night, Eryn. It was nice being with you, even though you spent most of the time asleep," he smiled. "Next time I will not make avoiding talking or even listening to me that easy for you. And believe me, there will be a next time."

She pushed open the door when he released her hand and closed it behind her a moment later, letting out a long breath while she leaned against the door from the inside. There was light up in the main room. Of course; Enric wouldn't have retired before her return. She closed her eyes. What an unpleasant day. But that meant that tomorrow couldn't be any worse.

"Ram'an didn't want to come in for a glass of wine?" she heard Enric's voice from above.

She looked up at him. "No."

"I assume that means you didn't offer him it."

"Correct. Don't tell me you expected me to?" she asked with a raised brow.

"Hospitality is quite important here, as you know," he sighed, then decided to let the topic go. "Eryn, I think you and I need to sit down and talk."

Her eyes narrowed. "No. I think I need to go to bed. I just fell asleep at a teahouse. And if anybody else feels the need to talk to me I will seriously start practising how to knock myself out."

She climbed the stairs and walked past him towards the corridor at the end of which their bedroom was situated. A dark, quiet place to just lie down and forget the world for a few hours, escape into blissful sleep... Strange, how her ideas of luxury had changed.

CHAPTER 9

Health Check

Eryn nodded when Valrad informed her that there would be two more patients for today before she was free to leave, then lifted the two files for her to see before handing her the first one. So far he had been present at every single treatment she had carried out.

They had been working together for about one week now, and it had been less distasteful than she had feared. He had twice tried to talk to her about interpersonal issues, but she had signalled clearly but politely to him that she had no intention of working on a family reunion. He kept complementing her on her work, which she could live with. It even pleased her, as it was - whatever their personal difficulties - praise from an older, more experienced healer for a younger colleague.

They had taken lunch together twice so far, once also including Sarol and Vern and once with Iklan, who had asked her once more about a meeting to talk about the mind bond. She had promised him to visit at an early opportunity as she first needed to ask Enric when he was free to accompany her.

A young girl of no more than twelve years came in and coughed several times.

"Oh dear," Eryn smiled, "that does sound like we should have a look at you."

The girl nodded and lifted her hand for the healer to take, clearly not a stranger to magical treatments. She had not even brought a parent to accompany her inside.

Eryn closed her eyes and focused her attention on the delicate chest. The lungs were slightly inflamed, but the girl had come early enough for it to be halted before any more serious symptoms could arise. It took only a few minutes to heal away the inflammation.

"Drink a lot of water and eat vegetables and fruit, not too many sweets for now. Also try not to run around too much and go to bed early. Your body needs to recover from the healing. Do you hear me?"

The girl nodded obediently, then giggled.

"What's funny?" Eryn smiled.

"The way you talk," she replied.

"Really?" The healer frowned in mock confusion. "That is rather strange, you know. I always thought that everybody else around here talks in a funny way. But you know what?" She cleared her throat and then went on, imitating the local accent with its rolling rs and prolonged vowels, "I have been working on sounding like people here. What do you think? Could I pass for a Takhan woman?"

The girl laughed and nodded enthusiastically. "You sound like my great-aunt!"

"How old is your great-aunt?"

"Seventy-two," the girl answered.

"Then that was not a great compliment, I think," Eryn sighed, returning to her usual way of speaking. "Off you go, my dear. And don't forget what I told you. What are you supposed to do?"

"Drink water, eat fruit and no running," the girl recited.

"Close enough," Eryn said.

"You are not so bad with children, you know," Valrad smiled. "Or have you discovered this new ability as a reaction to the one you are expecting?"

She shrugged. "Probably. Or maybe Obal is the only child in this country who doesn't take to me."

"She likes you well enough," he chuckled. "She is just a little jealous of you because Vran'el is so fond of you. And she is fascinated by Enric, who is yours as well."

Eryn stretched and nodded at the file he was still holding in his hand. "This is the last one for today?"

"It is, yes," he said slowly. "I think you can manage this one alone. It is no more than a standard health check. You know how to carry them out; we have done three of them together this week. If you do not remember what it entails, this is no problem. There is a checklist in the first drawer of my desk, where you need to write down the results. Just go through it item by item."

"My first patient to be treated without supervision? My word, I am getting somewhere it would seem." She straightened her posture. "As you keep mentioning how satisfied you are with my work, I was thinking that maybe a few weeks appear a little long..."

"No," Valrad interrupted her indulgently and shook his head. "There is no way for you to shorten the assigned period you are supposed to work under me."

She breathed a sigh and nodded in defeat. Of course not. Supervision was not really the main purpose of this, after all.

"So be it. Then let's take care of this last patient." She reached out for the file and Valrad placed it in her hand.

"I will be at the canteen and having a cup of something sweet. Do come there before you leave."

She nodded and watched him depart, the file on her lap. Before the door clicked shut, she heard the healer say, "She is free now, you may go in."

Her gaze fell on the name on the file and she stifled a groan. Ram'an, Head of House Arbil. Damn! It was hardly a coincidence that Valrad had chosen this exact time to have a nice drink. And hadn't he seemed a bit edgy when he had handed her the file?

A moment later the door pushed open and in he came, a broad smile on his face.

"Eryn." He came closer and took her hand to kiss it. "A good day to you. I heard I am your last patient for today, so we can take all the time we need. Is this not convenient?"

Her smile showed too many teeth when she replied, "Yes, most convenient. But let me assure you that I will not take up more of your valuable time than absolutely necessary. I am aware that you are an important man and undoubtedly have a full schedule."

"True enough, but for one's health one should take enough time, I always say."

She just lifted an eyebrow at this obvious lie. Judging from how much he had changed, he had not been taking nearly enough time for his health lately. Opening his file, she looked at the date of his last health check.

"You are three months early," she pointed out. "You are supposed to do this every year. Though I do have the feeling that you will not accept my offer to make another appointment for you in three months."

"You are absolutely right," he nodded. "I am determined to be checked over today. I have been having a rather stressful time of late and I was told it has left its mark. Interestingly enough, the only one who dared pointing it out to me was your sister. One has to hand it to her, she is not afraid of saying what is on her mind." He took a seat when she nodded at a chair opposite her. "This is one of the things I have always admired about you, too. Until recently, that is."

She ignored the last comment and reminded herself that he was to be treated like any other patient.

Leaning back, she looked him up and down and switched into professional mode.

"Pe'tala is right, your external appearance has changed from a few months ago," she stated calmly. "Your face is more lined, which indicates insufficient hydration and nutrients, too little sleep and not enough exercise. Furthermore, you have lost slightly more weight than you had to spare."

"Yes," he confessed, "my recent eating habits do leave a lot to be desired, I have to admit. My brother is currently residing at one of our

114

estates to test out a new watering system, and I do not like to cook just for myself." He leaned forward with a roguish smile. "If you would care to join me every now and then, I am sure my nutrition would improve quite quickly. I would make sure to prepare healthy meals. We would both profit from that." He nodded at her belly. "What do you say?"

She exhaled, determined not to react to his little game. "That is very kind of you to offer, but taking a personal interest in your dietary habits is a little more service than the clinic offers." She pulled open the desk drawer Valrad had indicated and pulled out a sheet with a list of information to be completed.

"How many hours do you currently sleep?"

"About five, I would say."

"That is too little. How much did you sleep before that stressful time you mentioned?"

"Around seven."

"Better. Try to return to that length of time. The lack of sleep does obviously not agree with you. How regularly do you eat?"

He thought for a moment. "I try to eat at least once a day, though I had a time when I forgot even that."

She blinked and forced herself not to look up at him. His voice sounded strained. He had very likely referred to the time after his father's death.

"But I have regained some of the weight I have lost, so I am halfway back to normal already," he said in a lighter tone.

Halfway back? That meant he had been even thinner?

"How much alcohol or other intoxicating substances do you consume?"

"I drink about one or two glasses of wine a day now. I have reduced it. Not too long ago it was a bottle a day."

She closed her eyes for a moment. Too much alcohol, too little food and not enough sleep.

She looked up at him when she heard his amused voice.

"Have I managed to pierce that sober front of yours, my dear Eryn? Good. Although compassion is not what I want from you; you might remember how little I appreciate pity. But it shows me that you are not completely indifferent to me, which is a relief."

Eryn raised an eyebrow at him, then consulted her list again, determined not let him get to her.

"How often do you have to go to the toilet?" she asked, wondering why asking him this question seemed so much stranger than when it came to other patients. Probably because this was a lot more than she had ever intended to learn about him.

"Defecate or urinate?" he asked.

"Both."

"The first about every second day, the second several times a day."

"Any pain or other discomfort when doing so?"

115

"None whatsoever I am happy to state."

"Any other problems, symptoms, pain?"

"I have the feeling that I am a little more restless than I used to be. And I have regular headaches, though I heal them away of course."

"Can I have a look at your heart? There might be indicators for high blood pressure as a reaction to the changes in your life." She lifted her hand for him to take. He did so immediately, taking it between both of his.

"One hand is sufficient," she said softly while closing her eyes.

"I know," he said, the smile clearly audible in his voice.

She focused on his chest, observing the rate of his heart and the flow of the blood.

"Slightly higher than it should be for a man your age," she said and opened her eyes to make a mark on her list. Then she returned her attention to him. "I will now have a look at your head. That entails your brain, eyes, ears, sinuses, mouth and teeth and your throat."

"Look at whatever strikes your fancy, my dear. I am all yours," he grinned.

She ignored him once again, took his hand and started examining the areas she had just listed. After several minutes she opened her eyes again and bent over her sheet to fill in the information.

"Everything looks fine in there," she told him when she was finished writing. "Now your inner organs. The heart I have already seen, now I'll look at the rest. This will take a little while. If you prefer to lie down, just let me know."

He shook his head. "Sitting will be fine. I can undress if this makes things any easier."

She stared at him. "Why would you undressing make a magical examination easier? Do you have any injuries, moles or rashes I need to see?"

Ram'an seemed to ponder the question, then grinned suggestively. "I might. There is only one way to be sure, is there not?"

Cool, calm, collected, she repeated the three magical words that had helped her through the last few weeks.

"Ram'an," she said sternly, "if you continue to treat this examination as a jolly distraction, I will ask one of my colleagues to take over. One of my *male* colleagues."

"I do not discriminate between male and female healers," he smiled, "my charm works on both."

She got to her feet and began walking to the door, but he quickly reached out for her hand and pulled it to his lips with an apologetic expression.

"Forgive me, my dear Eryn. Do not leave. Please. I will behave myself."

Sighing, she nodded and returned to her seat. "So, you are quite sure you do not want to lie down?"

116

"Yes." He took her hand in his and waited for her to start.

She closed her eyes once again, feeling how his fingers started caressing hers.

"Stop that, please. It distracts me," she murmured.

"Of course."

She focused her attention on his organs.

"Your heart is beating too fast, we need to do something here," she said quietly.

He chuckled. "It is not normally that overactive, I assure you. This is mostly on account of being close to you and touching you."

Eryn slowly opened her eyes and shook her head. "You know, I don't think you should be doing this with me. Really. I think it will be easier for you to work with another healer."

"Afraid, Theá?" he smiled. "You do know that I am just joshing with you a little, do you not? I fully acknowledge that you are not available anymore, that you are his. But if it keeps you from doing your work, I will stop. I promise."

"You promised to behave once before, and yet you keep teasing me."

He shook his head. "I was not. I still do react to you. This should not worry you, though. See it as a compliment. It surely is no danger to you."

She exhaled. "Let's get this behind us, then. You just be quiet and only speak when asked, alright?"

"As you wish," he nodded and took her hand again. "Do your thing."

She closed her eyes again, and this time she managed to get through with the examination of all his organs without any interruptions or disturbances.

"Your intestines might need a little help. Try to eat more raw vegetables for a time. And drink more water." She lifted her fingers to his face and touched his forehead and cheeks. "Your skin feels dry, but the water should help here, too. You have acquired a few more lines around the eyes and the mouth. Prematurely. Would you like me to take care of that?"

He laughed. "Lady Eryn really is offering me a free cosmetic correction? I imagine some of your rich lady clients at home would faint from the shock."

"Take it or leave it," she replied in an offhand way.

"Well, if you are offering it, I will certainly accept your generosity."

She closed her eyes once again, put her hand on his forehead and corrected the superficial wrinkles with little effort.

"That means we are finished," she then said.

"Are we?" he smiled. "I seem to recall a certain question your colleagues usually ask me. Is it possible that you are embarrassed to do so?"

She swallowed and pretended to consult the list. He leaned over and pointed to an empty line on the upper half of the paper.

"Of course not," she retorted mildly. "Just a minor oversight, I assure you." She cleared her throat. "Do you have any problems as regards your ability to have an... erection?" She saw him grinning and lifted her index finger, warning him with narrowed eyes, "If you are about to suggest that this can only be worked through with my help, I shall kick you out of here. Literally. With my shoe against your backside. I mean it!"

He sighed. "Alright, let us do it the grown-up way then. No, I have no problems whatsoever in that area. Quite the opposite. I would rather need something to dampen his enthusiasm every now and then. Any suggestions from a healing point of view?"

"This is not the grown-up way," she growled. "We are finished. Finally. Out with you. Now!"

"Wait!" He lifted both hands, palms facing away from him, as she reached behind her to grab the first heavy object she managed to reach. A mug. He jumped up hastily and opened the door, hiding behind it and only poking his head in.

"Have lunch with me tomorrow," he suggested. "I will cook something healthy and nutritious. It is your responsibility as my healer to make sure I adhere to your instructions."

"No!" she shouted and hurled the mug at him, watching it burst into a thousand fragments when it hit the door he had closed quickly to escape the missile.

She closed her eyes and buried her face in her hands. So much for cool, calm and collected. This was the first time since she had arrived in the city that her restraint had failed her. It was simply not up to his skills of provocation.

Her shoulders started shaking and she burst out laughing, covering her mouth, surprised at her own reaction. What a bloody nuisance that man was!

* * *

Junar sat in the main room on the cushions and was obviously staring a piece of fruit into submission.

Eryn grinned. "Greed against a full stomach. Which one is winning?"

"Greed. What else?" the seamstress sighed and plopped the sweet piece into her mouth. It had never really had a chance. "You look... different. Did you have a good day at the clinic?"

"I am not sure if it was a good day. Let's call it a strange one. And what do you mean, I look different?"

Junar thought for a moment. "You are not frowning, for once. And you smiled. I haven't seen that in a while."

"I smile regularly," Eryn protested.

"No, not really," the other woman shook her head. "It is this false smile, the one you have been using a lot recently, which keeps people at a distance. When you just came in, there was a genuine one. Tell me about that strange day of yours. Whatever has put you in a good mood must be worth telling." She patted the cushion next to her.

Eryn complied good-naturedly. It would probably be enjoyable to relate it to her.

"I just had a very interesting conversation with Ram'an about his bowel movements and sexual prowess."

"You had *what*?" Junar exclaimed. "You don't even greet him properly if you can avoid it!"

"He came to have his annual health check today. Valrad scheduled him as my last patient and for the first time left the room while I was treating somebody."

The other woman looked serious. "Was that very unpleasant? But then it seems to have lifted your spirits, so the answer is probably *No*."

Eryn snorted. "It was unpleasant enough at times, trust me. He certainly had a lot of fun in there. I wasn't as enthusiastic and tried to refer him to another healer. Twice. He kept making inappropriate remarks and unsuitable offers and inviting me to take meals with him."

"And your new strategy of freezing out unwanted people with indifference didn't work on him?"

"No," she sighed. "He made me throw my mug at him. I spent a long time afterwards cleaning the bits up. But it was worth it. It was liberating."

"Of course it was," Junar smiled and squeezed her friend's hand. "You keep locking up your real self inside you. Giving it a chance to lash out every now and again is necessary to avoid going insane, I think. I hope you have learned something from this," she added sternly.

"That I need to destroy random pieces of pottery to be happy?"

"Idiot," Junar sighed, but there was no real heat in it.

"Where are the boys?" Eryn enquired to change the topic.

"In Enric's study, if you mean Enric and Orrin. They received a message from the triarchy today. Their little game was approved. Or yours, from what I have heard. They are discussing the details. I have no idea where Vern is. Probably dazzling the art world with his talent," she added with a proud smile.

"Do you mind if I leave you alone and join the men? I want to make sure they know that I am going to participate in their little thing. I came up with the idea, after all. I should be permitted to join in, don't you think?"

Junar grinned. "Absolutely. Just make sure they have it soon, or you will have become too round to roam the streets."

Eryn nodded, remembering that Vran'el had said something like that, too. She then glanced at the empty fruit bowl. "Do you need more of that while I am still here?"

"No, I shouldn't. I swear to you, my stomach has shrunk to the size of my fist. I eat something, then I am full after a few bites, yet a few minutes later I am hungry again."

"That is because your daughter is applying pressure on your organs to squeeze out some space for herself," the healer explained.

Junar waved her off. "Oh, leave me alone with your healer-talk! Go and annoy your companion. And mine. I lack the energy to do it myself."

Eryn stood and walked towards the corridor that lead to Malriel's study. She heard agitated discussions going on through the door and knocked briefly before entering without waiting for permission.

Enric smiled when he saw her and stepped towards her to plant an enthusiastic kiss on her mouth.

"Hello, you. The triarchy granted that idea of yours," he explained.

She nodded. "I know, Junar told me just now. I am here to tell you that there is no way you can keep me from joining in the fun."

Orrin laughed. "We had no intention of attempting a thing like that. We need you there, in fact."

"You do?" she asked in surprise. "Because only my unparalleled battle strategy skills will help make this a success?"

"You may think I am being funny, but compared to the people here, your skills are far advanced," Enric pointed out.

"Can I be an invader?" she pleaded.

Her companion nodded solemnly. "Absolutely. I had a feeling that you wouldn't mind being on opposite sides from me."

"Who else will be playing?" she asked.

"Vern and Kilan. Though Kilan doesn't know anything about it yet. But you as his superior can order him in case he thinks he is able to refuse," Enric smiled. "Myself, of course. And Orrin."

"Vran'el also volunteered," Eryn added. "That probably means we can also count in Neval and Intrea. How many people do we need for it to work?"

"For the area the triarchy has granted us, sixty people would be good. That would make fifteen pairs on each side," Orrin explained.

"Pairs?" she enquired. "Is that one of the rules you have made up?"

"It is, yes," the warrior confirmed and handed her a sheet of paper. "These here are the others. What do you think?"

Golden belts to reduce the available magical strength to a certain level to avoid stronger magicians having an unfair advantage. Groups of two to fight together against opponents. When one member of a pair is down, the remaining one can unite with another single fighter to form a new team. Shielding and attacking is allowed without limitation.

"Can I use my special barrier?"

Both men shook their heads, and Enric replied, "No. That would be an unfair advantage. And as it requires the use of a good deal of magic, the belt would block that anyway."

"And you will be among the defenders, I expect?" she addressed her companion. "You mentioned something like that when we first talked about that. Political considerations. That probably means that Kilan as ambassador should also be seen to be defending the city instead of trying to conquer it, I assume."

"Exactly," Enric confirmed. "But Orrin and Vern will be on your side. That makes three of you against two of us. That should enable you to win. Each of you will pair up with a local, which will combine strategic skills with knowledge of the city layout."

She nodded. That did sound reasonable. "Can I pick my partner? I think Vran'el would be rather upset otherwise."

"Of course," Enric smiled. He was glad to see that she intended to do this with her brother. Having a bit of fun together would surely do them good. Though he would have preferred pairing her up with a healer, just in case.

"Excellent!" She rubbed her hands together. "When will it take place? Any chance to have it soon enough for me to be still halfway agile and able to see my toes while standing upright?"

"One week from now," Orrin nodded. "Unless your son is an exceptionally quick developer, that should not be a problem."

"He has so far adhered to the rates expected, so if he manages to grow that much in one week, I know for sure that he is doing it just to spite me," she sniffed. "And I would make him pay for that when he is old enough to be embarrassed."

"Loving words from an expectant mother," Orrin murmured.

"What can I say? They come from the heart," she smiled. "Now you need to excuse me. I feel the urge for a bread bun. Or three. Do we still have some?"

"The servants are under orders to never let the supply run down," Enric assured her. "A survival strategy."

"Well done," she nodded graciously. "I shall remember this fondly when I am aiming shots at you in one week." Thus she turned and went off towards the kitchen.

Orrin pursed his lips. "She is in a much better mood today. I wonder why."

"Ram'an had an appointment for an examination with her today. It seems he has managed to cheer her up."

The warrior regarded the younger man thoughtfully. "He has been able to accomplish that while none of us were lately? Is that good?"

Enric sighed. "Probably not. But then right now I take what I get. If he is the one to get through to her right now, then I intend to make use of it."

"And have him watched closely, I assume?"

"That goes without saying."

CHAPTER 10

Ram'an's Approach

Enric knocked at the door of the Arbil residence and waited. He had been all but summoned here, which was unusual since Ram'an had no authority over him and was furthermore not really the demanding type. His House currently very much depended on the benevolence of its allies. Yet the message had not been a particularly friendly one.

It was chiefly curiosity that had brought Enric here. He had considered sending a sharp message back, but only briefly. If Ram'an did something that was not only out of character for a man with a generally more studied and diplomatic approach, but could also be considered unwise when it came to the business relationship their Houses currently had, it probably was worth listening to. Though he had an idea what this might be about.

Working with Ram'an had been pleasant and unproblematic so far. He had turned out to be a reliable business partner who did not promise more than he could or wanted to deliver and who honoured the agreements he made. That was something Enric had come to value in the years since he had taken to running his own businesses.

Considering the timing of this particular invitation, it very likely was about Eryn. Two days had now passed since Ram'an's appointment with her at the clinic. She had mentioned it briefly, but not given Enric any details. He was careful not to pressure her and instead met with Vran'el who had been more than happy to share the few things he knew from his father.

Ram'an had requested an earlier health check and had needed several attempts to make Valrad relent to let him have it with Eryn. And alone. Valrad had been reluctant to more or less bluffing her into

122

treating her former suitor, but Ram'an had pointed out that essentially forcing her to work with her father against her will was definitely more of a strain to her than spending half an hour with *him*. Valrad finally had agreed under the condition that if she refused to do the health check with Ram'an, that she would not be coerced, cajoled or otherwise pressured to carry it out. It was on him to keep her in that treatment room with him. Without making use of his superior magical powers to make her stay.

When her father had returned to the treatment room, she had been cleaning up fragments from what had once been a mug before she threw it against the door, judging from the dent left at head height. So Ram'an had triggered a reaction - managed to make her leave her shell of aloofness and restraint for a brief moment. Enric remembered her mood that day after she returned from the clinic. She had shown spirit and energy, insisting on being made to join their game.

The door opened and Ram'an nodded to him, lifting his hand for the formal greeting before admitting his guest.

"Thank you for coming. I admit I was not sure how you would react to the way I phrased the message," Ram'an began and added with a thin smile, "But then pushing a person to see where the limits are has turned out to be an effective way of getting to know people better."

"Or make them your enemies," Enric replied civilly.

"I think the two of us being able to have a reasonable conversation and even do business with each other after everything that has happened is quite an accomplishment. I do not think that a short message, however harsh it might appear to you, would make you my enemy. Come on," he said when Enric had finished using the moist towel to refresh himself, "let us talk in my study."

So he wanted to give this a formal touch, Enric mused, and followed him up the stairs and into the spacious, traditionally furnished room Ram'an used for working in.

"May I offer you something to drink?"

"Not at the moment, thank you."

"Then do take a seat, please." The host rounded his desk to sit in his chair. "After getting to know you a little I assume you will appreciate it if I get to the point right away. I want to talk about Eryn."

Enric nodded. "I assumed as much."

"Of course. You surely heard about my seeing her at the clinic?"

"I did, yes. It seems she threw a breakable object after you."

Ram'an smiled. "She did, yes." His expression changed and he became serious again. "And that was an event I am proud of. She has for more than a month been remote and unreceptive to me and from what I have heard also to Valrad. This is uncharacteristic for a woman with that much Aren temper within her. In the short time I have known her she has always expressed her dismay or anger openly and without restraint, even if she had to suffer the consequences afterwards."

"Maybe she changed her ways," Enric suggested gently, knowing fully well that it was not the entire truth.

The lawyer lifted his brow at him. "If I thought that you really believed that, I would be even more worried than I already am. No, the temper is still there, she just does not let it out. And this is not good for her. I had to provoke her quite a lot to trigger that reaction two days ago." He waited for a moment to see if Enric wanted to comment on that and went on when he didn't. "She is seen sitting at teahouses, always alone, brooding. She likes to choose remote ones where meeting people she knows is less likely. And she keeps changing her location; she hardly ever goes to the same twice in a row."

"And yet you seem to stumble across her again and again. What a coincidence," Enric remarked with a pointed look.

"House Arbil owns quite a number of teahouses in the city, both small ones and fancier establishments. When I first saw her sitting and trying to hide from the world, I started making enquiries. And I talked to people at the clinic. From what I have understood she never spends more time than absolutely necessary with her father, appearing resigned when he somehow manages to make her have lunch with him. She has not entered the Vel'kim residence voluntarily in a considerable time, and according to my sources her contact with Vran'el has also suffered a lot."

"Very thorough, these sources of yours," Enric remarked.

Ram'an shrugged. "One tries to keep track of things. Like the fact you have not been seen out together with Eryn in a good while. Is it possible that she is withdrawing from you, too?" His gaze had become sharper.

"That is none of your business, I would suggest," the blond magician retorted.

"One could probably choose to see it that way, yes," the lawyer nodded.

"But not you, obviously," Enric sighed. "Or I wouldn't be here, would I?"

"Obviously. Despite the... er, tension between us I do consider her a friend." He opened a drawer and pulled out the silver bracelet he had given Eryn at the day of their Third Level Commitment and that she had thrown back at him on the day of her arrival after she had heard about Malriel's and Valrad's affair. He held it in one hand and regarded it thoughtfully. "I am determined to make her wear this again."

"Good luck there," Enric smirked. "Making her toss mugs after you might not be the way to accomplish that, though."

Ram'an lifted an eyebrow. "It is a precise first step in that direction," he contradicted. "I have managed to get her out from behind that wall of detachment she has built around herself, if only for a moment. But you are aware of that, are you not? Otherwise you would have demanded of me to stay away from her, I suppose." He returned the bracelet to the desk drawer and then leaned back. "I have talked to my cousin - the healer who is working with Vern on that book about birth and maternity - about Eryn. He thinks she might be suffering from a subdued state of mind that comes with being overwhelmed by some situation. In her case it might be the result of several episodes." He used his fingers to list them. "Her becoming pregnant against her wishes; being compelled to come here again so soon; discovering that the man she had thought of as her father was merely her uncle; being made to work with Valrad now he wants to attempt reconciliation with her. Also, probably a certain neglect on her companion's side of the relationship, but I can only speculate about that."

Enric's gaze became threatening. *"Neglect on her companion's side of the relationship?"*

Ram'an sighed. "Do not be angry at me for putting words to a general theory."

"It did not sound like you were recounting a general theory, but making a very specific insinuation from where I stand," he growled.

"So you are absolutely sure that she gets all the attention and support she needs from you, are you?" Ram'an asked airily. "Despite the challenge leading House Aren presents to you?"

No, Enric had to admit to himself, he was anything but sure of that. In fact, he felt helpless in dealing with this. He thought making Eryn face the difficulties with her father would then lead to everything being in order again, but instead his attempts had pushed her further away from him. Now she even avoided being alone with him if she could. And how did Ram'an know about the problems at House Aren?

"I shall take your silence and the expression that goes with it as an answer in the negative," Ram'an remarked.

"You are mistaken," Enric lied coolly, "everything is fine between us."

"Is it indeed? When did you last have sexual intercourse, if I may ask?"

He closed his eyes for a moment, forcing himself not behave in any socially unacceptable way. He could afford losing control no more now than back when he was here as an ambassador. That the answer was not exactly an encouraging one did not help at all.

"You may not," he said calmly, managing to keep his voice level. "You are not supposed to take any interest in that as you have assured me that you have no intention of pursuing her any longer. I will not answer what is frankly an outrageous personal question."

Ram'an sighed, then rubbed his eyes. "Ah yes, the prudery of your people... I forgot about it for a moment. Imagine that." Then he regarded Enric with a knowing smile. "Or is this just an excuse so you do not have to admit that I am right? You did seem to adapt to our customs fairly well when you first came here, I seem to recall."

Enric exhaled and flashed the other man an impatient look. "Why am I here, Ram'an?"

"You are here because you hope that I can help you with your little dilemma with Eryn, I would imagine," the dark-haired man smiled.

"I meant: What do you want? I know exactly why *I* have chosen to respond to your less than friendly invitation."

"I want you to understand that something must be done; you cannot let this go on. The longer you do, the harder it will be for her to find her way out of this. These unresolved issues will not just wither away once your son is born. She will then have even fewer resources available to deal with them."

"Interesting words from a man who embodies one of these unresolved issues," Enric gave back cuttingly.

"Oh, indeed. This is why I intend to do something about things. She has now acquired her qualification which means I will not hold back much any longer. I have heard about that game you and Lord Orrin..."

"Orrin," Enric interjected. "We don't use the title here."

"The game you and *Orrin*, then, are planning. I would like to join in. Preferably in a team with Eryn."

"You are more than welcome to join. But firstly, Eryn will be playing on the side of the invaders, and this might not be too attractive an option for a Head of House; and secondly, she has already chosen Vran'el as her game partner."

Ram'an shrugged. "Being an invader does not pose any problem for me. Unlike you, I am in no need of proving my loyalty to my fellow senators. People do not question my commitment to my country, rather my House's abilities to pay its bills," he added bitterly.

"That is why you have called for me? To have me team you up with her for the game?" Enric enquired.

"That and to see if you are aware of the problem."

"I see."

"I am still wondering about that, but so far you have been more reasonable than I might have hoped. You do not want to admit your trouble to me, which is to a certain degree understandable, considering our history together. Yet you have clearly realised the role I can play in helping her, even if you do not like to put words to that, either."

"Don't I, now," Enric commented dryly.

"Yes. Otherwise, as I mentioned before, you would surely have warned me to stay away from her and stop annoying her. Yet you have not. And I doubt that you intend to for now."

"I dare say that should convince you that I am *aware of the problem*, as you phrased it. What now?"

"Now I want you to help me create situations where I will be able to spend time with her without her being in the position simply to run away. Such as a dinner at your house where you will have invited me, meetings at music houses and so on. Public enough for her to feel she

126

needs to be polite but not crowded enough so she will be able to hide behind others," Ram'an explained.

Enric nodded slowly. "I can facilitate that. To a certain degree, anyway. If I start dragging her out every evening she will soon go on strike." He regarded the other man thoughtfully. "Why are you doing this?"

The lawyer gave him a considered look. "I think you know that well enough, do you not?"

"I know that you still care for her, but seeing her, and subsequently me, suffering might just as well be compensation for your injured pride."

"It would be if I were the kind of man to find watching others suffer a pleasant thing," he pointed out coldly. Then he smiled without humour. "And there is always the possibility of your facing an untimely demise. In this case it would surely be useful for me if she remembers me with fondness."

"Perfectly charming," Enric growled and rose. "If I were to take that last statement serious, I would have to reconsider doing business with you. And start watching my every step."

"Instead of watching only your companion's every step by sending observers after her?"

"I had better start sending observers after *you* as well," Enric snapped, disconcerted by the turn the conversation had taken.

"Feel free," Ram'an shrugged and grinned, clearly delighted that he had managed to unsettle the man who was known for his nerves of steel, especially after stepping between Eryn, Malriel and Malriel's mother Malhora during their last stay in the Western Territories.

"Tomorrow evening. Dinner at the music house where I made you dance with me that time," Enric said offhandedly and walked towards the door, catching a glimpse at Ram'an's displeased expression at being reminded of that little incident. It was a small triumph and a rather petty one, and yet he had depended on those a lot lately.

* * *

Eryn dragged her feet, but Enric held on to her hand, making her walk along with him.

"Come on, my love," he sighed. "We haven't been out together in quite some time. You spent weeks buried under your books, and I was locked away in that study. I want to go out, meet people, have a meal I didn't have to cook, dance with you."

"You know, your attempts at cheering me up are laudable, but I had a long day and I would really prefer to just sit down at home, put my feet up and be lazy," she moaned.

"You can sit down, put your feet on my lap and be lazy at the music house," he promised.

"Then what is the sense in going there if I will just do the same there I would rather be doing at home?"

"Being among people again."

"We have people at home to be among! An entire family, to be precise! You remember? The ones you thought we should have move in with us? Huge, expectant woman; a growing, lanky lad who eats a lot; plus a grumpy guy in his early fifties with a scar down one side of his face?"

"Just do me the favour and spend an evening out with me, will you? I have been looking forward to dancing with you again."

"We danced in Anyueel. More than once."

"I am not talking about ballroom dancing, but about the kind they do here. The relaxed, enjoyable kind. I distinctly remember that you liked that. Vran'el will be there, too." And Ram'an, but that was hardly an argument to encourage her to come along more willingly.

They reached the building and heard the stirrings of lively conversation from inside. The large windows were still covered, as the sun had not yet subsided enough to enjoy the evening air otherwise. Enric pulled aside a colourful curtain for her to enter and her stomach commenced grumbling audibly at the smell of the combined dishes that hung in the air.

"I suppose that means I ought to make sure to get you fed quickly," he smirked.

She nodded her head in the direction of where Neval was now standing, waving to them to come to the table he and two others were sitting at. One was Vran'el, of course. The other...

She froze when she recognised him.

"What is Ram'an doing here?" she asked quietly, her fingers gripping the seam of her tunic tightly.

"He is as entitled to spending an evening out as we are," he replied carefully. "And our three Houses are officially allied, so sitting together at the same table is nothing unusual. Quite the opposite. It doesn't hurt to be seen to get along."

"This is either a political plot or you are trying to make me forgive him," she muttered, low enough not to be overheard by the other guests, as Enric took her hand to tug her along with him. "I appreciate neither. Especially as each of those options means that you deliberately withheld the little detail that he would be here from me."

"I trust that you will be on your best behaviour," he retorted. "It's pretty much the only thing I can be sure of with you lately." He regretted the words instantly. He had not meant for them to come out like that. It showed how his own level of frustration kept rising. While she had her behaviour under uncharacteristically iron control, his own seemed to slip more and more often.

"I am sorry, my love," he sighed and lifted her hand to kiss it. "I know none of this is easy for you. I am trying to help you, but I am at a loss as to how."

"Don't try to help me," she said coolly. "I am neither a victim, nor a child. I can deal with my problems alone. I would rather have you respecting the way I have chosen to handle these matters."

Which was to run away if possible and hide behind icy politeness if it wasn't, he thought but knew better than to put words to it.

When they reached the table, all three men were standing and Vran'el stepped towards her first, pulling her into an embrace and kissing her on the cheeks.

"Good evening, sweetness! It is high time to have a little fun, for all of us I would think. I have taken the liberty of ordering for the both of you already. Tonight they offer a dish I have cooked for you once before. You liked it, or at least pretended to," he added with a wink. "Of course I will insist on you telling me afterwards how much better my choice was."

Eryn smiled. "Of course. I wouldn't dare not to." Then she turned to Neval. "Hello. It has been a while."

He nodded. "Indeed. Too long, my dear." He took both her hands, kissed her on both cheeks and then held her at arms' length, still holding on to her fingers. "Let me have a look at you." His eyes wandered down her body and stopped at her belly. "Well, well, it has finally started to show. Only a little, but there clearly is a bump. Is everything alright in there?"

"Yes, everything is fine. Thank you for asking."

She braced herself and turned to Ram'an, who was watching her with that quietly amused expression he had at times.

"Good evening, Ram'an," she said politely.

"Good evening, my dear Eryn," he smiled and took her hand to kiss it. "How is your mood tonight? Do I need to be careful around the tableware?"

"I apologise for my extreme reaction the last time," she said stiffly. "I promise you that this will not happen again."

"Do not worry about that. I did not mind too much," he assured her.

"Getting a lot of crockery thrown after you, then?" Neval enquired mischievously.

Ram'an shrugged. "I have had my share, I will admit."

Eryn remembered Vran'el's words about Ram'an having a way with the ladies and believed him instantly.

Neval turned towards her and Enric. "I am so glad you have arrived. I have been sitting with the two of them for about fifteen minutes, and the only topic they seem to be able to come up with is lawyering," he complained.

"I do not think this term actually exists, darling," Vran'el chuckled.

"Well, consider it established now," Neval threw back. "I define it as the lack of stimulating conversation topics due to being studied in the law and thereby having no other area of interest to fall back on, consequently being helpless to do anything other than bore to death any non-lawyers who happen to be stuck with you."

"Nice," Vran'el nodded. "Though I fear that the definition is rather too long to make it into any of the reference books. And it is not a vice only lawyers fall prey to. I have grown up in a House of healers. We might as well establish the term of *healering* while we are at it."

"We could probably find terms like this for every single group of professions," Enric smiled.

"No," Neval shook his head. "Lawyers and healers are more prone to talking about their work in lengthy terms and without any consideration for other people present than other skilled practitioners. Honestly! I am involved with a lawyer and his family consists mostly of healers. I know what I am talking about. Whenever I was left alone with Pe'tala and Valrad, I felt like the dimmest person in this country, unable to understand every second word they said."

"You know that you have just managed to insult three out of four people at your table, don't you?" Eryn pointed out with a raised eyebrow.

Neval grimaced. "Sorry for that. I would look for another insult for Enric, but I am a little wary about that as his reputation is rather frightful."

Enric sighed in mock regret. "The story of my life - feared instead of loved."

"Not feared, my friend," Vran'el assured him and patted his shoulder, "but respected and admired. And I dare say that has helped you in conducting your various businesses more than once."

"True enough," he admitted with a grin.

"Also, I would imagine your height is not exactly a disadvantage, either," Neval threw in. "Or those piercing blue eyes."

Vran'el cocked his brow. "Do I need to worry about you discovering your fancy for the tall, blue-eyed, exotic type?"

"Not more than *I* have to, I would think," he grinned back.

"It seems you have made quite an impression on the male population of Takhan," Ram'an remarked.

"So it would seem. Though obviously not thanks to my unique individual characteristics but merely to those that are common at my place of origin. Being blond and tall seem to be my main attractions," Enric sighed.

"Do not forget blue-eyed," Vran'el sniggered.

"I suggest it is the matter of being exotic by the standards of the place one currently resides," Ram'an stated. "When I was in Anyueel, people showed quite an interest in me there, too."

"Not merely," Enric shook his head. "I remember that Sanaf was a lot less popular at home."

"Which is why they called him back here again," Vran'el nodded. "So being exotic is clearly not all there is."

"Sanaf was being sent back here because his behaviour was inadequate and intolerable," Eryn pointed out with a sour expression, remembering how he had talked about her fainting problem in the bedroom openly at a Royal dinner. She still felt an echo of the embarrassment. "He managed to alienate quite a number of important people within a short time."

"You included, little sister. You were the one who got rid of him in favour of Erbál, after all. By the way, Sanaf arrived here in Takhan last week. From what I hear he has not been seen out much, probably staying in, licking his wounds."

"What makes you think that I was the one responsible for that?" she asked uncomfortably. So much for inconspicuously pulling strings in the background.

"Oh, please!" Neval rolled his eyes. "The only reason he was chosen for this position despite his lack of personal qualities and training was that he is a member of the right House to please *you* and Enric. House Finran is the only family both of your Houses are allied with right now, apart from Arbil, that is. So if he was called back, it must be because he had *failed* to please you. And one hears gossip, of course," he added as an afterthought.

"You hear gossip from Anyueel here?" she asked incredulously.

"But of course we do!" Vran'el cried out. "Tala writes to me, if you remember. She knows how much we like choice little morsels of information here. She told me that you seemed to be getting along with Erbál exceptionally well from the start. And about your little game with Malriel and how you made her depart a week early by starting to cry in front of the rich and powerful." He smiled at his lover. "I remember reading that letter to Neval and we imagined you squeezing out tears to make Malriel look bad. We could not stop laughing for ages."

"Pe'tala really supplies you with chitchat such as that?" She shook her head. "I wouldn't have thought her the type. What else has she told you?"

"About your attempts at convincing your Council that ended with your having to clean out horse stables for a few days. And about Enric inviting Pe'tala and her new lover to family dinners. Then about Enric and Orrin having been publicly punished for something by your Order's leader, but she could not tell me what exactly," he listed, then leaned forward and looked at Enric expectantly. "What were you punished for?"

Enric cleared his throat. "That is not exactly a topic for a semi-public discussion like this."

"Does that mean you will tell me about it some other time?"

"No."

Vran'el groaned in frustration. "A secret! And I do so *not* appreciate them!"

"Because you are way too nosy, my dear," Neval chuckled.

"As are *you*!" the lawyer shot back and turned back to Enric. "I will not let go of this, mind you. I will find out about this one way or another."

"He throttled the King," a quiet voice supplied. Four astonished pairs of eyes turned towards Ram'an, two of them because of the absurdity of the claim, the other two in surprise that he possessed this scrap of information.

"What?" Vran'el exclaimed.

"Quiet!" Eryn hissed at her brother, then turned to the other lawyer, who was now the centre of attention. "How do *you* know about this?"

"I like to keep myself well-informed, my dear," Ram'an shrugged.

"Why did he throttle the King?" Neval whispered, his eyes wide.

"Because he had taken liberties with Eryn when he locked her in with him, seemingly to test her progress in the fighting disciplines Orrin was training her in."

"How can you possibly have heard about this?" Eryn stared at him, slightly panicky. If this information had found its way even to this faraway place, who else knew? "And who else has?" She looked at Enric, who did not look too thrilled either, judging from his tensed jaw and narrowed eyes.

"Do not worry, my dear. This is not common knowledge. I have managed to secure a very comprehensive source of information in your city," he explained calmly.

"Well, with telling those two gossips here it will soon be known to all," she growled, wondering who could have told him. Servants? How would they have learned about it? Erbál? She would have a little chat with him to find out. Well, a written conversation.

"They will not pass it on," Ram'an assured her. "Your brother might not appreciate secrets, but only if they are kept *from* him. He likes keeping them from others well enough. Knowledge is an advantage one does not share with others just at the drop of a hat."

"True," Vran'el admitted, then turned towards Eryn. "So, what liberties did he take with you?"

She looked concerned. "Do we really have to talk about this now?"

"Just this one question, then I will let go of the topic for now," he promised.

Sighing, she nodded, seeing from his expression and the eager posture that he would not let go if she didn't answer him. "He kissed me."

She saw anger flare up in his eyes. "Kissed you? I assume we are talking about the invasive type of kiss here? That one that a woman in love with and joined to another man would very likely not expect or wish to have?"

"I thought we were done after this one question?" she reminded him.

"It is part of the first question," he insisted.

"Yes, the invasive, unwanted, non-compliant kind of kiss that a woman in my position would not wish for. And now we really are finished with that topic," she stated with finality. She could see that he wanted to say more, that the information was not sitting well with him. But he held back and nodded.

"Have it your way. At some other time I am going to ask you why he did it, but not now. But let me say one last thing: It gives me great pleasure to see that Enric dared to stand up to that King of yours, willing to bear the consequences. I know that many a man would have shied away from something like that."

Eryn sighed in relief when their food arrived. She started eating greedily after washing her hands in the bowl on the table, not even taking time to dry them first.

"Hungry, are you?" Neval noted. "Enric, you need to feed this woman regularly. Aren temper, pregnancy and hunger are a combination that is not exactly healthy for bystanders."

"Not to worry, Neval," Ram'an smiled and looked at her. "That temper is currently locked away rather securely. She is determined not to show any vulnerability."

Eryn swallowed her mouthful and deadpanned, "It may be I have reserved that privilege of opening myself up for people important to me. That might place *you* out of danger, but not Neval."

"That wounds me deeply, Theá," Ram'an sighed and placed a hand over his heart. "But at least I may rest safe in the knowledge that your ready wit has not suffered any impairment so far."

"I would very much thank you for not calling me by that name," she gave back sharply. "I remember having asked you that many times before now. It seems your memory suffered damage where my wit has not."

He nodded solemnly and picked up his own bowl to start eating. "Forgetful me, indeed. The trouble is that I cannot help but find *Eryn* a rather... plain name for you."

"Fit for the country healer's daughter that I am."

"Hardly, my dear. You are the daughter of two of the most illustrious people in that country of ours, both Heads of Houses. We do not have that very often, as they are not supposed to join due to obvious reasons of succession. Your origins are a little more noteworthy than a mere country healer's daughter, dear lady."

Eryn put aside the bowl, which she had emptied in record time, and forced herself not to lash out at him. Somehow she had the feeling he was doing this deliberately. She would not accommodate him.

"Are you trying to provoke her, Arbil?" Vran'el enquired suspiciously.

He shrugged. "To what avail would that be, pray tell? She does not lower herself to show her dismay to the likes of me anymore, as it seems."

Eryn exhaled and turned to her brother. "Arbil?"

"Yes, sweetness. If you address a Head of House with his House's name, it is a way to show your annoyance or disrespect. In another context it may be considered friendly teasing, dependent upon what terms you are on with the person." He lifted a warning finger. "Do not consider addressing father that way. He would not take it well from you."

She lifted an eyebrow. "And why would I care about that?"

"Well, the argument of being nice to your family is obviously wasted on you. Let me point out then, that he is your superior for as long as you are working at the clinic."

She took a sip from her glass and washed down her acidic reply together with the water. As if she would need such a reminder. Somehow it seemed that she kept ending up in situations where the wrong people were in charge of her. Enric in the Order, and now Valrad at the clinic.

Ram'an cleared his throat to get Eryn's attention. "By the way, I have tested your young friend."

Enric suppressed a chuckle when he saw the spark of interest that she tried to hide by being nonchalant and seemingly bored. "Yes, I heard about it. It seems you had to test him twice because something went wrong the first time. I assume you have results now?"

"It did not actually go wrong, I was just perplexed by the outcome and could not assign his profile to any known combination of categories. I considered that there might have been some mistake in carrying out the test, but the results did not vary when we repeated it," he explained.

She looked confused. "What does that mean? That he is an oddity?"

"You could say that, yes. There are people who fit more than one category, but having a tendency towards more than two is practically unheard of. Young Vern fits *four* of them, and I am not even sure if the test is in its current design able to assess *all* his facets. I have asked two of my cousins to look at his results and consider adapting the testing methods. And maybe even establish a new category for Vern. He has incredibly versatile abilities. I have never seen anyone like that."

Eryn felt pride rising inside her and mellow her a little. These people here who thought themselves so bright and advanced in comparison with the Old Kingdom had come across a boy who turned their perception of ability upside down.

"Does he know about this yet?"

Ram'an shook his head. "Not yet. I have not had an opportunity to talk to him about it."

Enric smiled. "I would hazard a guess that he will be very smug about that. What categories does he fit?"

"Healer, artist, leader and scholar. I have already talked to Orrin about characteristics that are considered useful for becoming a warrior. This might be another category to include in the future. We will probably even divide it into a few sub-categories such as fighter, strategist and analyst or something along those lines."

"So it seems your contact with our country has already started causing a few changes here as well," Enric noted with obvious satisfaction. It was good to see that not only back home things had started to change, that people here across the sea also found a few features of their new friends worth considering.

Neval was the last to put aside his empty bowl upon which the first notes of a song rang out.

"That is a very nice, slow and easy magical song," Vran'el smiled and nodded at Enric. "It should be doable even for two barbarians with hardly any training in civilised dancing like yourselves."

"Perfectly charming," Enric muttered, but turned to his companion. "What do you say, my love? Will you grant a barbarian such as I the honour of this dance?"

She nodded and held his hand, letting herself be lifted up from the cushions, then following him to the dance floor. As soon as they had passed through the shield put around the dancing area, she felt the effects of the magical music, though not as strongly as a few others she had danced to in the past. Vran'el had been right. It was nice and easy.

Enric's arms found their way to her waist and they followed the slow melody, their limbs moving more or less of their own accord due to the musical instructions that probably went right through their ears to the part of their brain that was responsible for magical abilities. She would have to ask Iklan about that one of these days.

"Will he be staying at our table all evening?" she asked.

"It's more like we are staying at *his* table, to be exact. There is no regular table for the members of House Aren or Vel'kim at this place; we are his guests, so to speak," he replied, bracing himself for her reply.

"His guests. I see," she spoke, the fury not overt, but clearly visible beneath a thin skin. "I assume you just forgot to mention that little detail when you made me prepare for an evening out."

"We need to make and maintain contacts, Eryn. And Ram'an is one of them, whether we like it or not."

"I don't have the impression that you are very averse to it, so don't make it sound like this is some kind of sacrifice for you," she said evenly. "You *wanted* to meet him here. Why couldn't you have just left me at home?"

"Because it is a while since we have been out together, and this is a nice opportunity to meet people and maintain important business contacts," he explained. He could see that she didn't believe him, knowing fully well that he had brought her here to make her face Ram'an in a setting that would not allow her merely to excuse herself.

"If you keep trying to push me in his way to make me reconcile with him, I will not go out with you anymore," she threatened while the music made her legs follow the gentle steps of the dance.

Enric nodded once to indicate that he had understood. At least she had had a halfway normal conversation with Ram'an about Vern's test results. But then this was hardly worth alienating her even more from himself.

"I am sorry, my love," he said quietly.

"You should be. Stop urging me towards Valrad or Ram'an. I mean it."

"What am I supposed to do, then? Watch you withdraw from the people around you even further?"

"I am not withdrawing from people around me," she protested.

"Of course you are!" he growled back at her, now angry himself. "You don't greet me when you come home; you pretend to be asleep when I come to bed, tense when I want to touch you; and you wait until I have started working before you get out of bed in the morning. Do you think I haven't noticed?"

She swallowed hard. There was no denying it, he was right. And no, she was not aware that he had realised she was trying to stay out of his way lately.

"We will get up together in the morning from now," he declared, twirling her once. "Have breakfast together. We will go out in the evening more frequently. If you feel the need to be alone for a while every now and then, fine. If this continues to be a daily occurrence, I will not go along with it any more. If you do not return home after the clinic and there was no note in which you tell me where you can be found, I will come looking for you."

"That is absolutely no..." she started, but was interrupted harshly.

"There is no space for discussion about this. This time *I* mean it."

She gulped back the words she had wanted to throw at him and they finished the dance in silence before he took her hand to lead her back to their table.

The three men watched them approaching, their expressions clearly conveying that they had been watching if not listening to the awkward exchange on the dance floor.

"It seems an easy dance is not the right thing for either of you right now," Vran'el declared dryly. "It obviously leaves you too much energy to think. Come, sweetness, the next one you will dance with me. It is a non-magical one, which means you have to concentrate on what you are doing."

She scowled. "Vran, I really don't..."

"I insist," he said simply and pulled her along with him back on the dance floor.

Vran'el was right, she had to admit. Being forced to focus on the steps made pondering unpleasant truths as good as impossible. And somehow that was a relief. A few minutes of fun, even though not entirely without exertion, were a welcome distraction from the troubled dance with Enric before.

The next two dances she was allowed to sit and recover, Enric pointedly putting an arm around her shoulders, warning her with a glance to stay where she was instead of casually slipping out from under it.

Neval was the next one to ask her to dance. Another non-magical one, as he, too, was of the opinion that true proficiency in dancing could hardly be reached when magic made everything easier. When she pointed out that becoming proficient was not really an ambition of hers, he just got a mocking look in his eyes and walked off towards the dance floor, confident that she would follow him. Which she did, of course.

Once the next magical song started, Enric pulled her to her feet once again. She felt her jaw clenching with resistance, but followed him without objection.

It was a slow and heavy dance, laced slightly with melancholy. He pressed her against him and kissed her on her temple.

"I love you," he said quietly.

She released the breath she had not realised she was holding. Quite a large part of the tension she felt drained from her muscles.

"I know. Or I would already have kicked you out that door," she murmured. She smiled when she felt him chuckle.

"Then I am glad that I escaped that fate. It just wouldn't look good for me, as I am currently trying to establish the reputation of somebody not to be trifled with." He lifted her chin with his index finger and kissed her lightly on the mouth. "If I free you from the strain of this evening prematurely, will you promise to be awake when I slip into bed with you tonight?"

"Just awake or…"

"I admit I am hoping for some *or*," he nodded.

She smiled despite herself. "Are you trying to bribe me into sleeping with you?"

"Oh, absolutely. This should give you an idea of how desperate I am."

She thought for a moment, then pursed her lips. "Why don't you throw in a backrub and we'll call it a deal?"

"Done."

When they returned to their table little later, he announced, "Gentlemen, my companion is rather worn out owing to her condition. I am going to take her home now."

Ram'an got to his feet quickly.

"In this case I would like to take this last chance to ask you for a dance, my dear." He looked around. "I hope you will not deny me this when you have granted one to everyone else at our table."

Enric squeezed her hand. "I won't push you if you would rather not," he murmured into her ear.

Eryn smiled politely and looked Ram'an straight in the eyes when she said, "Don't be ridiculous. Why wouldn't I? It doesn't bother me at all."

She would dance with him alright, just to show him and her companion that making her meet him would not change anything. She could deal with him like with anybody else she had no particular regard for: cool, calm and collected.

"I am glad to hear it," the lawyer smiled and took her hand. "The next one is another magical dance, a slow one. That means you do not have to concentrate on the steps."

Which would enable her to have a conversation with him while dancing, she thought in dismay, but followed him without showing any displeasure.

"It seems you were able to work on your little disagreement with Enric during your last dance," he pointed out once they had started dancing. "When a man suddenly tells his party without any prior indicators that he needs to take his companion home, this does lend itself to certain deductions."

She managed to keep her expression blank. What an absurd thing to talk about between the two of them.

"I am sure I have no idea what you mean."

"Of course not," he smiled, innocent as a new-born babe. "I admire that great strength of will you keep proving, my dear Theá. I can sense that being held by me right now annoys you, but you are getting through it with that new, commendable restraint that seems to be working so well for you lately."

"And yet you keep trying to make me lose it," she remarked with a thin smile. "Does it constitute a challenge for you, I wonder?"

"Less of a challenge than a matter of concern. I admit that your treating me with indifference does not sit well with me. It is so much more reassuring if you throw things after me than wall me out with this coldness. It shows me that there is something left, that there is still enough regard for me buried somewhere within you that makes you angry at me."

"Which is why you keep trying to provoke me."

"Exactly. An angry reaction is better than a frosty one. But what I really want from you is a little of your time and an open ear for talking about my reasons for treating you the way I have."

"That is a pity," she replied with mock regret, "Because I have no intention whatsoever in obliging you with that."

"That means I will continue to provoke you on purpose," he warned her. "One day you will either explode and make a building collapse in the fine Aren tradition we all know, or you will simply give in to get me away from shadowing you. I would be fine with either option, mind you. Even if you do not want to listen to me, being known to have caused an Aren woman to lose her temper will do wonders for my currently rather compromised reputation."

"Don't call me an Aren woman," she admonished him more out of habit than with any real heat.

He shrugged. "I could tell you that I am sorry, but it would be a lie. By the way, I am very much looking forward to the new game in a few days. I hear that you will be on the invaders' side, trying to conquer the city that has been the source of so much strife for you lately. Me as well. So we will be fighting side by side, more or less."

"What a coincidence," she said with a dash of irony.

"None whatsoever, I assure you," he grinned. "I first had to find out on which side you will be playing, then found to my chagrin that you had already chosen a partner and then signed up for the same side. You see, there was some effort involved."

She smiled. "I suppose you had better make sure you don't have me on your rear flank. A stray bolt of mine might hit you."

"You would not do anything like that," he said confidently. "Enric and Orrin need the invaders to win this game, do they not? I strongly suspect that this is a little trick to get the reluctant people of Takhan to let themselves be taught the fighting skills we neglected to hone over more than two centuries."

"And you think your participation is instrumental in achieving this?" she asked sweetly.

"It might be. Are you willing to take that risk?"

Eryn sighed in relief when the last notes of the music faded. "Thank you so much for that dance, Ram'an," she smiled insincerely. "But now you do have to excuse me. I shall wish you a pleasant remainder of the evening."

"Good night, Theá. I will see you, at the latest, at the game."

She nodded, thinking that this would rather be the earliest than the latest occasion she would meet him again if she had any hand in it.

CHAPTER 11

The Game

Eryn stretched and yawned while perched on cushions in the Aren residence's main room. Enric looked up from his book and smiled. She looked relaxed, which was not something he had beheld too often during these few weeks since their arrival in Takhan. She had her feet in his lap and he had one hand on them, the other hand holding the book on the varied uses of magic shields.

"Did you know that they know how to use colours for shielding?" he asked.

She shook her head. "No. To what purpose?"

"The natural colour of a magical barrier is a very pale blue, as you know. If the nature of the shield is changed slightly, it reflects light differently and thus changes our perception of the colour. It works by almost the same principle as altering hair colour by magic, but here it is not the underlying item being perceived differently, instead the shield itself. Orrin was playing around with this and has managed to come up with a very handy use for this for our game tomorrow."

She sat up straighter and leaned forward, intrigued. "He has? How?"

"The colour of the shield of each participant will change with the number of hits they have taken. So when you look at somebody from the opposite team, you will see how many more hits will be required to put them out of the game."

A slow smile spread across her lips. "That means if somebody needs only one more hit it is better to concentrate on that person instead of pursuing somebody who can take another two."

"Exactly," he confirmed, satisfied how she had at once come up with a strategy to make use of this new information. He wondered if

140

she would thank him for pointing out to her that her fighting and strategy lessons had obviously had quite an effect. Probably not.

"So, what are the colours you will use tomorrow?"

"No, you will learn about this with everybody else. No unfair advantages on any side," he said, shaking his head.

They both listened when the entrance door opened and closed rather more energetically than usual. A few moments later a flustered looking Vern appeared in the doorway.

"You are back early, my lad," Eryn noticed. "I thought you were playing around with your new artist friends today?"

The boy looked unhappy and let himself plump down onto the cushions next to her, grabbing her water glass and emptying it with greedy gulps before refilling it from the carafe on the table and pressing it into her hand.

"Here, drink."

Enric smiled at the caring gesture, knowing that she had not yet fully adapted to the higher intake of liquids that was required in this climate. She obeyed and took a few sips before handing him the half-full glass back.

"What's the matter, Vern?" she asked again.

He drank down the water and sighed. "I am confused. Unsure. Annoyed. I had a conversation with the man who is fairly much considered the top authority on the visual arts here in Takhan. He told me that I have great potential, but that I am far away from making real use of it."

Eryn lifted both brows. "Really? What does he consider your current work to be? Doodles?"

"He says I am doing no more than copying reality. That a real artist creates from what is inside him, not what their surroundings dictate. He might make use of external influences, but as no more than inspiration, not as a model to be replicated." He looked down at the empty glass in his hands. "I don't really know what to make of this. He showed me pieces that he considers great works of art. Sculptures where one hardly recognises what they are supposed to be depicting, and paintings that I thought looked strangely malformed and more like random eruptions of colour than any actual effort at representing something." He sighed and looked up helplessly. "That is just not the kind of art I see myself doing. My passion is looking at things and putting them on paper the way I see them. I like it when people can see what I was thinking of when I draw something - without standing together and discussing if the bit at the bottom left corner is supposed to represent a traumatic event from my childhood or a piece of fruit I decided to include on the spur of the moment."

"Look at that," she marvelled. "I had no idea that being an artist was so complicated. So he does not consider your work as actual art, or what exactly are you telling me?"

"That's what it seems like, yes," he growled. "Though he graciously grants me that I might yet turn into an artist if I put my heart into it.

He says my work is sober, impersonal and heartless. He told me to express what is inside me, and I have no idea how to do that. I thought that I was doing that already." He rose tiredly. "If you will excuse me now, I will sit outside in the garden for a bit and wait for inspiration to tumble over me so I can unleash the artistic talent I am obviously keeping locked within."

Enric smiled sympathetically once he had left them. "It seems our young friend is facing something of a crisis of meaning at the moment."

She nodded slowly. "Obviously. I don't like this. Who is that man to pronounce on what art is and what it isn't?"

"The leading authority in these parts, as it seems," Enric pointed out. "Though who knows? Vern might actually discover a whole new side of his talent by being made to question his previous efforts. Such a challenge might do him good."

"He looked disheartened. I don't feel good about it."

Yes, he thought, that was not a pleasant thing to watch in somebody close, was it now?

*   *   *

Eryn stood together with about one hundred others in front of the stairs leading to the Senate hall and looked up at the two blond magicians, who waited for silence to settle before addressing the crowd. About sixty of those around her, she knew, would participate in the game, the others were simply curious onlookers. Vran'el and Vern stood next to her, Intrea and Neval not far away either. For now the two teams were intermingled; one could not yet distinguish who would be fighting on which side.

"Good afternoon to all of you," Enric's voice boomed out. She suspected that he was using a little magic to make it carry further. "I am very happy that so many of you have decided to join our little game today. The procedure will be as follows. I will first of all give you an introduction to the rules, then you will be split up into your teams and each will join your team leader. That will be myself for the defenders and Orrin for the invaders. We have allotted two hours for putting on the manacles and for preliminary coordination of your efforts before we start. Now the rules." He lifted a hand with two broad golden manacles. "Each of you will be wearing a pair of those. They work the same way as the golden belts you use here. Your magical abilities will be reduced to a base level to give every participant the same chance. They furthermore serve to identify you as a member of either team. The golden ones are for the defenders, while the invaders will wear silver-coloured manacles. This should enable you to identify who to attack and who to assist." He let his arm sink again. "Each participant can take two hits, with the third hit knocking you out of the game. You may shield yourself, but consider that a single shield can only withstand *one* bolt. Two people shooting at you will penetrate your protection and strike you."

"Will that count for one or two hits?" a voice from the crowd asked.

"For two," Enric replied. "If they strike you at the same time, that is. If one shot removes your shield and then the second one strikes you, it counts as only one hit. Figuring out how to coordinate this will give you a considerable advantage. We have done a good deal of work on the manacles and now they will give you information about your opponents and your allies. A player who has not been hit at all will sport a green shield. A bright blue shield signifies one hit, and somebody with two hits can be recognised by a red barrier. This might help you to decide who to concentrate on. Shielding is not subject to any limitation which means you may shield as much as you like."

"Only for myself or others as well?" Intrea called out.

"Preferably your allies as well, if the occasion calls for it. As most of you know already, teams consist of a pair of players. You are supposed to protect yourself and your teammate from your enemies."

"What if my teammate is taken out?" another player asked.

"Then you will continue on alone and see if another player from your side has the same problem. In this case you may form a new team of two and continue."

"But that is not compulsory, is it?"

"No, it isn't. You may just as easily continue alone if this seems advisable to you. Just consider that four eyes can see more than two and somebody watching your back may turn out to be invaluable," Enric explained. "The point to be secured in order to win the game is the Senate building," he went on, and lifted his arm to indicate the building behind him. "If at least one invader manages to reach the top of the stairs, the invaders have successfully captured the city. If the defenders succeed in preventing this for two hours, they shall be adjudged the winners. Any more questions?"

"What about those who have suffered three hits?" another voice asked.

"Their manacles will turn black and they will not have any magic at their disposal until they have left the designated playing area. Which they are expected to do at once. The level of magic in the game will not be high enough to cause any harm to an unshielded person, but it is still not a pleasant sensation to be hit by a weak bolt."

"How do we see where the arena of play ends?" Neval wanted to know.

"Orrin and I will show you on a city map after you have been divided. It is part of the preparation." Enric looked around to see if anybody else required any further detail, then nodded. "Alright, then let us get on with it. All of you who have been assigned to play on the side of the defenders, step to my right side. The invaders assemble around Orrin. We will take you to the location where the final meeting will take place." He smiled at the men and women around him. "I wish you good look. May the better team win."

"Is there a prize for the winners?" Kilan asked.

"Yes, my friend. The losers will throw a lavish dinner for the winners. If my team wins, it will take place at the Aren residence. If Orrin takes the city, we will hold it at the ambassadorial residence with you as the host."

That earned him several laughs.

Kilan sighed theatrically. "Why do I get to cook if you lead us into peril, I wonder?"

"Because I am a Head of House and only wish to host a dinner when it is in celebration of my victory," he grinned.

"What about my awe-inspiring position of ambassador?" Kilan called back.

"Not as impressive as Head of House, I am afraid," Enric smirked.

After the laughter had died down, those participating in the game went to their assigned team leaders and soon two groups of thirty were facing each other. Eryn saw a few bewildered expressions when she didn't join Enric's team.

"Good," Enric nodded. "Have a last look at your opponents and remember their faces. If they somehow manage to hide their manacles from you, knowing whether you are supposed to be hitting or protecting them would be extremely helpful. Orrin?"

"Yes?"

"The best of luck to you. You will need it."

"Same to you. I look forward to that dinner. I am confident that I will not be the one cooking it."

"Keep dreaming, old man," Enric tossed back with a lopsided grin, winking at his companion before he turned away to lead his group to the room where he would plot with them to decide how to go about defending the place.

* * *

Orrin waited until all of the twenty-nine other players were assembled in the room at their starting point, then cleared his throat to have their attention. He stepped towards a large map that illustrated the streets of the city and put his index finger to the point they were currently at.

"Listen here, everyone," his voice boomed through the room. "We are right here and we need to end up there." His other hand indicated the Senate building at the city centre. "The trick is to get there without all of us being taken out. The red lines here mark the part of the city that the game will be limited to. You see that this extends to about one sixth of the city. The edges of the playing field are protected by a magical shield that you will not be able to pass through as long as you are wearing the manacles. As soon as you have been hit three times, the manacles will turn black and allow you to pass, which you should do as quickly as possible. You will be almost completely without protection as then your entire magic is blocked – otherwise you wouldn't be able to pass the shield. Theoretically none of the players of the other side is then supposed to attack you when they see the colour of your manacles, but there might be stray bolts flying around. You in turn are also meant to let people with black manacles pass unhindered. If I hear of anyone of you doing otherwise, I will have a nice long talk about fairness with you."

Eryn hid a smile. He was treating this bunch of foreign magicians almost like a class of his juvenile fighting trainees at home. Funnily enough, they didn't act much differently, whispering to each other when he wasn't looking, falling silent immediately when he turned in their direction and exchanging tell-tale looks.

"Basically, it will suffice if only one of us makes it to the top of the stairs," he went on, "but I would not like to cut it that close. We have a very good chance of winning this game. Most of you were born and raised here, which means that you have helpful understanding of the city layout. The three of us from the Old Kingdom - Eryn, my son Vern and myself - will depend on that knowledge and will in turn make use of the tactical skills we were trained in. There are three of us against two of them. As soon as you see Enric approaching, get out of his way. His own tactical skills are excellent, and it is unlikely that he will fall for any plots or traps you might have set. If you still want to try, count on being taken out. This does not apply to Kilan. He has never had much interest in tactics and will not pose that much of a threat. I will try and keep Enric occupied so he is no danger to the rest of you." He looked around the room. "How many fast runners do we have here? Raise your hands."

Eryn watched as Neval and seven others raised their hands.

"Very good. That is more than I had hoped. Half of you will lead enemy teams away from the route I want to clear, the other four will aim to climb the stairs to the top of our destination. Mind, though, that quite a few of them will be waiting there to prevent just that happening. You will have to shield yourself and preferably your partners." He walked towards a table with thirty pairs of manacles. "All of them have already been enchanted with the characteristics needed for the game. The only thing that remains to be done is for me to adapt them to your individual magical strength to lower it to an equal level. This will take no more than one minute per person. After that we will go through the rules of the game once again, form pairs, discuss the strategy we are going to use and equip you with a water pouch each." He pointed at Vran'el. "You. As Eryn's partner you will take special care that she does not get hurt, overexert herself or is befallen by any other harm. If she is out of breath, you will rest and stay with her, if she needs more water, you will give her your pouch. If you are not ready to do this, I will find her a partner who is."

Vran'el gave him a dark look. "I *will* take care of her, do not worry. You are aware that it is my *sister* we are talking about here, are you not? I would not let any harm come to her simply to win a *game*, warrior!"

Orrin nodded. "No need to huff. I just wanted to be sure she is in good hands."

"Boys?" Eryn cut in, hands on her hips. "I would thank you for not pretending that I am not even present. I will take care of myself. I have not joined to be a burden others have to look after! Now let's get on with this. There are teams to form, manacles to distribute, rules to repeat and a strategy to discuss, if I remember correctly. Go on, don't waste time here! This game is hardly going to be won by standing around and glaring at each other." She walked briskly to the table, picked up a pair of manacles and eased them on to her wrists.

Orrin looked down at them and sighed. "I remember promising never to put any of those on you again," he said quietly.

She remembered that day as well. It had been after the King had kissed her.

"Yes, I know. But I knew I would have to wear them when I signed up for the game. Don't worry; this is completely different. I can deal with it."

He nodded once and sealed the seams shut, lessening her magical powers to a fraction of what she normally had at her disposal.

* * *

Enric listened to Iklan's answer to one of the questions he had asked his players and nodded appreciatively.

"Good. What happens if you face a greater number?" he then asked the group.

"They will be able to penetrate our shields if they manage to hit us," a woman in her late thirties offered.

"Exactly. What will be your course of action then?"

"Taking cover, preferably behind a house wall," she answered. "And then trying to outrun them, unless the situation is in our favour and we can easily keep them busy without exposing ourselves to strikes too much."

"Well done," Enric nodded, satisfied with the answer. "If you have the chance to engage a superior number without danger to yourselves, use it. When facing several opponents, which ones will you concentrate on?" he continued.

"The one with the red shield," Intrea answered this time. "Always take out the easiest target first. Then the one with the blue shield and when nothing else is left, attack the ones that are still glowing green."

"What will you do if you spot Orrin?"

"Run and hide," a man in his early twenties piped up.

"What else, if possible?"

146

"Try to lure him towards our mighty and knowledgeable leader," Kilan smiled and pointed to a spot on the map. "Which means right here, where you will try to stay and block the way, as this is a very likely path for them to take."

"Well done, Ambassador," Enric grinned. "We will yet make a fighter out of you." He turned back to the group. "What is your main objective when facing a superior number of opponents?"

"Inflict as much damage as possible on them before they take us out of the game," said a man Enric dimly remembered as a member of House Sarol, the one at enmity with his own House.

"Correct," he acknowledged. "Now turn towards your partner, link your arms and check if your manacles are sealed and properly enchanted. Try to push your partner backwards with the aid of magic, not using your physical strength. It should not be possible, as you should be equally strong in that way." He watched them carry out his order, aided where help was needed and then pointed to the table with the water pouches. "Now take one each and fasten it to your belt in a way that will keep it in place when you have to run or jump."

Enric observed his troops and smiled. It was predestined that they would lose, but that didn't have to mean that he would make winning easy for Orrin. There were little victories to be gained, after all. Such as eliminating his old teacher from play. And maybe even Ram'an, if things went exceptionally well.

*   *   *

The sun had almost set and the evening air was already noticeably cooler. Good. That would make running a lot less of a strain. The twilight made the buildings around them stand above a sea of shadows.

Eryn took a deep breath and smiled at Vran'el, who had taken her hand in his, and smiled back. Vern and Ram'an were standing next to them.

"Then let's conquer that city of yours, shall we?" she said lightly and nodded towards the street Orrin had assigned to them.

"By all means, little sister," her brother grinned. "Let us give them a taste of the Vel'kim Siblings of Doom. Or at least of the two that are presently here."

"Be careful, you hear?" Vern told her with a worried frown. "Better take a hit than do anything that might hurt the baby."

Eryn pinched his cheek. "I am insulted you think you have to remind me of a priority like that, my young friend. Better take care of yourself. Don't let those cocky foreigners take you out without giving back more than they deal out, you hear me?"

"I am standing right next to you, being one of those cocky foreigners. Though technically speaking *you* are the foreigners here right now," Ram'an said a touch reproachfully.

147

"I know. Doesn't make the lot of you any less cocky, looking down on us barbarians," she smiled sweetly and turned to walk off with Vran'el when Orrin gave the starting signal, ducking into a side street to their left.

"How long until we come upon the first defenders?" Eryn whispered. Orrin had instructed them to be careful with their conversations, keeping them as infrequent and quiet as possible.

"About ten minutes, I would say," he replied and nevertheless took a quick glance around the corner before venturing out into the open street to run to the entrance of the next alley. Eryn followed him, assiduously avoiding any tell-tale noises.

"We are quite close to the edge of the playing area," Vran'el whispered in the semi-darkness. "We need to be aware of that and avoid being pushed into a dead end with that shield they put there. If more than one pair manages to trap us there, we are done for."

She nodded and followed him when he moved on. She caught an occasional glimpse of another team moving along the alleys to their right, but couldn't identify them at the distance and in that light.

They kept on moving stealthily through the deserted streets, sometimes looking up to catch sight of a head that observed them curiously from a window. The area approved for the game had been put under a three-hour curfew, leaving it open to the inhabitants either to stay indoors or leave their homes for that period. It seemed a few of them had chosen to stay and watch what was happening. They had been warned about flying bolts of magic, even though they would be too weak to do any more damage than the unpleasant experience of being thrown backwards a few steps.

They both froze when a few minutes later the sounds of first bolts hitting shields sounded to their right. Vran'el instinctively moved towards the commotion, but Eryn grabbed his sleeve and shook her head determinedly.

"This is a distraction we can use to move on. With a little luck, the other defenders in that area will be drawn to the noise just like you. Come on, that way," she insisted and pulled him along the alley they had intended to follow.

Vran'el crouched when they reached the next corner and took an appraised look around it, quickly pulling his head back and lifting two fingers to indicate that there was a single pair of opponents in the street.

"How far away?" she mouthed silently.

"A few paces," he returned, equally without a sound.

"Shields active?" she enquired.

He nodded.

"Green?"

Another nod.

Her thoughts raced when she considered their options. If they attacked the unsuspecting pair, this would no doubt draw attention from other teams, both on their side and the others'. They would then depend on their allies arriving first. That was too risky for her taste. She took Vran'el's sleeve and pulled him a few steps back with her, guiding him into a nook that would hide them and let the other two pass unless they decided to slip into that very alley. In this case they still had the option of attacking them first.

"If they come here," she whispered, her lips against Vran'el's ear, "we both shoot at the left one, the one closer to us, first. At the same time, so that our hits count for two."

He nodded to confirm and she grabbed his arm and felt his tense muscles under her fingers while being pressed close to him so they could both fit inside the small alcove.

They both held their breaths when they heard two pairs of quiet steps passing not too far away. She heard the two whispering something, but it was too low for her to make out actual words. They waited another minute, then stepped out of their hiding place again.

"Now we need to start watching behind us as well," she breathed. "That is the disadvantage of letting them pass. But that also means that they still don't know that we are here, which gives us the advantage of surprise if we are able to make use of it." She looked around and regarded the open street in front of them with dismay. "Is there another way we can take? This is way too exposed, no cover at all."

"Not on this side of the street," Vran'el grimaced. "I am afraid we need to cross it at least. I can go first, and you come after me if it is safe," he stated and began to move forward. Eryn quickly grabbed his shoulders and shook her head emphatically. "No separating. Alone you are an easy target, even for a single team." She pointed to an alley on the opposite side of the street. "These are no more than ten paces. We don't need more than two or three seconds for this. Come on."

Without waiting for his consent, she grabbed his hand and tugged him with her as she began to bolt across the street. A high squeal escaped her mouth when a bolt of magic almost brushed her ducked head. Only Vran'el's momentum saved her from her own impulse to stop right in the middle of the street, instead propelling her forward into the relative cover of the alley they had been aiming for. This time he was the one who held on to her hand to pull her along.

"Run!" he hissed and jerked her forward towards the next side road, turning a sharp corner into the next small lane to their right and moving on with unaltered speed until they had veered into the next alley. There he pressed her against the wall, covering her mouth with his hand to muffle her heavy panting.

They heard two sets of footsteps rapidly coming closer.

"The left one," Vran'el whispered quickly, and a moment later two figures passed their alley without looking left or right.

Eryn quickly lifted her palm, raised a shield and together with her partner let lose a bolt. It hit its mark and the green shield of the runner turned red instantly. His partner, a woman in Eryn's age, turned quickly at the sound of the impacts and stood frozen instead of diving for the next cover. Vran'el's bolt hit her a moment before Eryn's, and thus her shield only changed to blue after she staggered back a few steps before raising a new one. Meanwhile the first one had recovered enough to remember that he was supposed to avoid being hit and attempted to run towards his partner, but Eryn's bolt caused his red shield to collapse entirely, and Vran'el's subsequent one turned the manacles around his wrists black.

The woman stared at them for a second longer, then turned in a flash to run, barely making it around the next corner before Vran'el's next missile hit the spot where she had stood a moment before.

Eryn forced herself to hold down the triumphant laugh that wanted out, but would only serve to broadcast their location to their opponents.

"Yes!" she hissed instead with a fist hitting the air above her. "One out!"

"And one escaped, knowing our location," Vran'el said, dampening her enthusiasm immediately. They watched the magician before them sighing and regarding the black shackles with dismay.

"You know," he said with a displeased look at them, "I would not have thought that I would be among the first to leave the game. I guess pursuit is not exactly as safe as I thought." Then he strolled off towards the nearest edge of the playing field.

Eryn shrugged. "Well, that means we had better leave the spot before she comes back with a few friends."

"A sensible suggestion, sweetness," Vran'el agreed.

"Do you remember where we are supposed to proceed?"

He nodded. "Yes, of course. We have just made a slight detour, but nothing that requires retracing our steps. We just need to turn left again at the next halfway safe position and then right and we are back on track."

She grabbed his arm to silence him and listened intently. "Do you hear that? Is it possible that she has found another team so quickly?"

Vran'el stared at her. "That would be rotten luck if ever there was one."

They heard careful footfalls approaching them, clearly more than two players this time.

"Quickly - there is that uneven wall over there," Vran'el urged her. "Climb up to that low roof! It will not fool them for long, but it will give us one unexpected shot. Go!"

She turned, frantically looking for the wall he had indicated and instantly started feeling her way up the gaps between the stones that conveniently afforded enough space for her feet to find a hold. She felt a gentle push from below and pulled herself up over the low edge of the roof, shifting over to one side to make space. Barely a moment after Vran'el had flattened himself next to her, they saw three figures turn into the alley below them, the woman from before being one of them. The other two were men, one not much older than Vern and a healer she remembered from the clinic.

"On her, now!" Vran'el hissed and both of them released a bolt towards the woman. All three of them looked around them in panic to see where the missiles came from, but only when the woman's shield had collapsed and her manacles had turned black, she jabbed her index finger at their location causing the siblings to duck hastily.

"She is basically out of the game, so how can she still reveal our location?" Eryn complained and drew in a sharp breath when a bolt hit the wall only slightly to her right side. "That was close! What now? They have both still green shields, we are barely covered and can't run without exposing ourselves, and they are drawing nearer!"

"We have taken out two already without suffering a single hit! We can do this!" Vran'el insisted. "We took out the most vulnerable one of them already and lowered their superior number to be equal. Do not despair, sweetness. We will beat them, even though we will very likely be hit once or twice in the process due to our disadvantageous position up here."

Eryn exhaled slowly, forcing herself to relax. Stress was not an aid right now; it blocked the ability to think clearly.

"Alright," she said after a moment, sounding calmer than before. "I jump up quickly and draw their bolts. At the same time I will let loose one bolt at the younger one. You shoot at him, too. If we are lucky - or their timing is bad - I will be able to dodge one bolt, so that I will get only one strike. Ready? Now!"

Jumping up, she waited until Vran'el had raised his palm and aimed, then they both released their attacks, Eryn letting herself drop back to the floor, her shield shimmering bright blue.

She drew in her head when another shot hit the stones next to her. "Did we manage it?"

He nodded. "One hit left for the young one, still three for the older man. Let us do this again, this time *I* shall get up. We must hit the other one this time, or we will waste a shot. Now!"

It worked just as well the second time, Vran'el took no more than one hit and the older man's shield was reduced to red.

They looked at each other and grinned like maniacs, jumping up quickly when they heard the sound of hastily retreating steps.

"The older one!" Eryn instructed and two bolts flew after him, one hitting his shield slightly earlier than the second one which took him out completely. The younger man had turned around to watch his partner falling under enemy fire without looking where he was going. He stumbled over a stone and fell, landing face first in the dust.

Eryn immediately released another bolt and Vran'el followed suit, removing him, too, from the game.

"Oh dear," she chuckled. "That was almost too good to be true. First they panic and run, then the second one stumbles while he is still within reach."

"Come on," Vran'el urged her and climbed down the wall again, waiting below to catch her in case she lost her foothold. "The noise might have drawn more unwanted attention. I suggest we find a fairly protected spot and gather our strength for a few minutes."

She lifted a brow. "Not on my account, I hope? I am fine to go on."

"Are you sure? These were a few quite eventful minutes right now. Do not overexert yourself! I would never hear the end of it, neither from Orrin, nor from father."

"I am sure, yes. Lead the way."

*   *   *

Intrea looked at her partner and sighed. "You know, being in a team with you is not really a great challenge, dear. We just take those poor sods out one after the other, they do not even know what has hit them most of the time."

Enric chuckled and peeked around the corner, watching two invaders running away from the scene of the street battle they had barely made it out of with their shields red. Four others were grumbling and slouching off with black manacles.

"You want more of a challenge, Intrea?" he smiled. "I can oblige you there. Come. Let's go look for Orrin. He won't make it half as easy for us."

"Good. It will look as though I was nothing more than your accessory if I end this game with a green shield, you know," she sighed.

"I promise that I shall hit you with a bolt in case your shield is still showing that embarrassing colour by the end of the game," he announced solemnly.

"Trust you to find an easy and even more shameful solution for it..."

"Well, then let's have Orrin take a few shots at you. I am confident that he won't miss every time."

She nodded and followed him when he made sure that the street ahead of them was free of attackers and quickly crossed to the other side, listening for any footsteps or other noises that indicated approaching players. But they only heard faraway bolts hitting distant house walls and shields.

"Orrin is very probably roving about the main street that leads to the Senate building from the south. What is the safest route there? Preferably one where we are exposed as little as possible."

Intrea nodded to her right. "Come this way."

Enric let her take the lead and noted with satisfaction that she had observed him well and took the same precautions whenever they needed to turn a corner or venture out in the open for a few moments. He liked working with fast learners. That made him think of Eryn and he wondered how she was doing. He had caught the occasional rush of triumph over the mind bond, and in between she had once been somewhat worried. He had little doubt that she was still in the game. With Vran'el she was in good hands, that he knew. Her brother knew the street layout well and he was a hunter. That meant he had knowledge of stealth and how to move surreptitiously. And Eryn seemed to be at her best when she was cornered. He was confident that the two of them would not present easy targets.

He looked up when he felt Intrea's grip on his forearm.

Her voice sounded excited when she whispered, "Look what we have over there!"

Enric followed her gaze and grinned. Two well-known figures had just passed an opening to their right.

"Would going on the hunt for a pair of Vel'kims be an acceptable alternative to Orrin?" he asked lightly.

She sniggered. "Oh, it would be, really. And who says we cannot do both? Let us just start with the two of them, shall we?"

He nodded. "Confident. I like that in a woman."

"I noticed. Or you would not have ended up with an Aren woman." She started moving again. "Come on. Let us take out our companions!"

"You are aware that we will never hear the end of it if we really do?"

Intrea rolled her eyes. "Come on, I cannot believe that a man with your reputation is afraid of shooting a friendly bolt or two at the woman he has won so manfully."

He sighed. He could hardly ignore such a challenge. He motioned for her to follow the alley they were in, thus moving parallel to Eryn and Vran'el.

"A little quicker. If we overtake them, we can wait at the next junction and then surprise them with a few bolts. If we time it well, we should be able to take out one of them. Both already have blue shields."

She nodded and increased her pace slightly. They ducked at the next corner and then had to wait only for a few moments until, two buildings to their right, two figures moved very deliberately in the dark.

"Now!" Enric commanded and two bolts were released from their hands, though not exactly at the same time, so if they hit something it would count as only one strike. Not enough to take either of them out.

They watched the trajectory of their bolts and a moment later the first one hit Vran'el's shield, removing it so that the second attack reduced his colour to red. Both he and Eryn ducked quickly behind a low wall.

"Pity," Intrea called out. "I was hoping to get rid of you completely!"

"Intrea?" Vran'el's voice sounded from the other side. "Of course it is you! You really would attack your loving companion and father of your only child? That does seem a little heartless, you know? But then

I suppose it was only a matter of time until we find each other on different sides in a street fight. You are a very antagonistic woman, after all!"

"Says the man who is attempting to conquer my home city!" she called back and hastily jerked back her head when Eryn shot a bolt at her.

"Enric? Is that you with Intrea?" Eryn called out. "There is this sensation of amusement in my head that is clearly not mine."

"Well done, my love," he replied.

"So you are really hunting your companions together? That is very queer, if you do not mind me saying so!" Vran'el growled.

"Do not be such a hypocrite, Vran! You knew well enough that there was a good chance that we could face each other like that when we signed up for different sides!" Intrea shouted back.

She sniggered when another bolt was thrown her way, this time by her companion.

"You may just come out with your arms behind your back and then we might show you leniency," she called out.

"Oh, good," they heard Vran'el snort. "As if expecting leniency from the likes of you is a mistake I am likely to make any time soon."

They heard several impacts of bolts on shields and a curse from the other side of the building. Enric leaned forward slightly so that he could maybe catch a glimpse of what exactly was going on. He saw Vran'el rising from his crouching position, his manacles black. A moment later he saw a man running towards where he knew Eryn was cowering, grabbing her hand and pulling her with him, closely followed by a pair he recognised as defenders.

Ram'an. So he had finally managed to be in a team with Eryn. He felt her annoyance through the mind bond and wondered if the bolt that had taken out Vran'el had been *friendly* or enemy fire.

*   *   *

Eryn gulped and increased her speed a little further when another bolt came dangerously close to striking her shield. Ram'an pulled her into a maze of narrow alleys, turning corners so quickly that she soon lost what little orientation she had so far been able to hold on to.

Their pursuer's steps became fainter and Ram'an pushed her into an alcove, squeezing in next to her and whispering into her ear, "Quiet now. They have been able to follow us because they had the sounds of our footsteps to guide them. Lower your shield, the glow is a giveaway."

She nodded and listened intently for the sounds of approaching people, hyperaware of the arms that encircled her. She tried to push them away, but he tightened them further, shaking his head when she tried to complain. Grinding her teeth she remained motionless in his unwanted embrace, keeping her attention focused on the sounds around her. The dusk had made way for the night in the meantime and it was almost completely dark around them with only the stars giving off a little light.

The nights were brighter here than at home, she mused. Probably because there were no clouds to cover the sky.

After a few minutes of standing awkwardly and avoiding making any noise, Ram'an relaxed noticeably and removed his arms.

"This is a good opportunity to take a sip of water," he advised her and unhooked the pouch from her belt without waiting for her consent. He weighed in his hand. "It is still full, you need to drink more, especially in your condition."

She took it from his hand and took a few gulps to shut him up. She had no intention of starting an argument here in the dark alley with him. And it was not as if he were wrong.

"I take it you lost Vern to the defenders?" she whispered.

"Yes. Classical scholarly attitude: a lot of knowledge that would be helpful in winning this game, but not much stamina when it comes to outrunning those who can prevent him from using it. Does he get bullied a lot by his peers back in Anyueel?"

She shook her head. "No. Scary father."

"I see. That is why his speed is so uncharacteristically sluggish for a smart lad," he chuckled.

She stepped out of the alcove, carefully checking her surroundings, then turned to him. "I will thank you for getting me out of the trouble you first got me *into* by leading them my way. Good luck," she added and turned to walk away.

His hand on her wrist stopped her before she had taken her first step. "Wait! What do you mean, *good luck*? You lost your partner, I lost mine. We are a team now. Neither of us has any chance to take out other players working on our own."

She swallowed. In a team with *him* of all people? Keeping her face neutral, she suppressed the groan that wanted to come out.

"There are things single players can do apart from removing players from the game," she pointed out. "Being a distraction, leading teams away from others, engaging them from a strategically advantageous position..."

"Eryn," he said patiently. "All the things you just listed can be accomplished more easily by two than one, with the added benefit that we can take people out of the game. Come, join me." He changed his grip from her wrist to her hand and pulled her along. He stopped and looked at her, when she didn't budge. "Really? You would rather risk losing the game than continue with *me*? Do not be stubborn, Theá. You will surely not want to miss seeing people shooting at me. You can use me to seek cover behind me, after all."

"That is very considerate of you, but..."

"You are pregnant and I will not let you run around in a city you do not know very well on your own and in the dark," he insisted sternly. "What if you are to stumble, fall on your belly or hit your head somewhere then pass out?"

That silenced her. There was nothing much to say when he put it like that.

"Funny, how people think I am helpless without a big strong man to protect me nowadays," she grumbled, but let herself be pulled along with him.

"Not only nowadays, my dear," he corrected her. "You have always had a tendency to get yourself into trouble from what I have heard."

She briefly considered reducing his blue shield to red with a bolt just to see the annoyance on his face, but decided against it. He was right. She could use him as cover if push came to shove, after all.

* * *

Enric smiled grimly when they turned the next corner and saw three invaders battling five defenders. Orrin was shooting bolts along with two rather scared looking young women whose shields had both already been reduced to red. With the superior numbers they were facing, it was just a matter of time until they were taken out. Retreat was not something open, the barrier that delimited the play arena was shimmering visibly at Orrin's back.

The warrior briefly turned his head and cursed when he spotted Enric and Intrea. That made three against seven, one of them a very well-trained warrior. Not good.

"He seems to be a little too occupied to be much of a challenge," Intrea pointed out, disappointment audible in her voice.

Enric laughed. "You just made a very dangerous mistake, dear: never underestimate *that* man, especially not when he is backed into a corner. Come on, let's join the fun. You may yet cast off that green shield you dislike so much."

"Yes, right," she snorted, but followed him to another corner that got them closer to Orrin. "This is not much of a challenge, either," she complained. "Seven against three!"

A moment later she was knocked back on her heels and stared at the red glow that surrounded her.

"What was that?" she exclaimed.

"That was you not taking proper cover and underestimating Orrin," Enric grinned smugly. "He sees a weakness - he exploits it. I hope red is more to your liking than green, because the only other colour that is now available is black."

"Very amusing," she growled and crouched behind him, making sure that no part of her body was sticking out and providing a target for another attack.

"I warned you," he shrugged and took in the arrangement of his team members around Orrin. "Their placement is not ideal," he murmured. "They are virtually all in front of him instead of encircling him. His has only a very limited chance to take cover, and he uses that in the best possible way. If they continue like this, he can keep us all at bay for who knows how long and then make it easier for the others to get to the Senate building. Come along, we should approach from another flank where he won't be able to hide from us that well."

He squeezed past her and then turned left to round the building to enter an alley that would get them closer to Orrin and his two helpers. Intrea rubbed her hands and tiptoed after him, clearly eager for some action.

The sounds of bolts hitting shields grew louder again, and when they took a quick peak outside the alley, two bolts struck Enric's shield in quick succession, turning it blue.

Intrea whistled through her teeth appreciatively. "He really is that good, is he?"

"The best," Enric sighed. "We didn't make him Head of the Warriors for nothing."

"Next time I want to be on *his* team," she grinned.

"Thank you for that vote of confidence," he grumbled.

"Not that you are not a very impressive fighter yourself," she added quickly, "But he seems to be even more astounding."

"Can you save your admiration for the enemy until after the game has played out?"

"Sorry," she grimaced. "What now?"

"I am thinking about sacrificing you to distract him," Enric said with a twinkle of mischief in his voice.

"You would not dare!" she hissed.

"Don't provoke me," he replied, then returned his attention to the problem they faced. "He has taken one hit already, and the other two players are red. That means they are the ones we need to knock out first. Once he is alone, he will be in a purely defensive position without a chance to inflict any harm. On the count of three, we will both aim a bolt at the one on his right-hand side, taking her out of the game. Are you ready?"

She nodded.

"One, two, THREE!"

Both looked around the corner, raised their palms and sent off two bright magical strikes. While Enric pulled back immediately after releasing his attack, Intrea didn't, but waited to see if they would hit their target. That was a grave error. At the very moment she was about to clap her hands in triumph, her own shield faltered and disappeared, her manacles turning black.

Enric leaned against the house wall at his back and sighed at her. "We do NOT wait and watch, but take cover again immediately."

"He is amazing!" she whispered, watching the black shackles in awe.

"Obviously. Now get out of here. You can walk out there; your black manacles should protect you from any attacks. The barrier is behind Orrin - just step through it. I don't think the game will go on for too long now. Half of the time is over, and I would guess more than half of the teams have been taken out so far."

She nodded and straightened up, carefully stepping out into the street, sending another admiring look in Orrin's direction before stepping through the barrier. Enric saw that she didn't walk away, but stayed to watch how this scene would end.

It was six against two now, and Orrin had managed to shift his position slightly to be better protected from the side where Enric was hiding.

Enric shook his head when he saw Intrea jumping and clapping her hands, when Orrin and the young woman next to him managed to take out another defender. That woman clearly needed to develop some proper team identity, he thought. But at least she recognised and appreciated unparalleled skill properly when she came across it. That was a point in her favour, at least.

He returned to the fight before him. Five against two. He couldn't do much alone from where he was positioned now. Without a partner to coordinate attacks with, his bolts would merely manage to remove a shield, and then he had to be lucky enough to have one of the others hit within two seconds before it was raised again. Not a very promising prospect, especially as Orrin was well covered. He decided to make his way over to the other five attackers, bringing two of them with him, then returning to where he now stood.

When he reached the corner around which they were hiding, he frowned. Only three were left. Kilan and Iklan, the healer, were among them.

"Did he take out another *two* of you?" Enric asked.

Kilan grimaced. "He did. That man is a nightmare! I wish I had been more attentive during his lessons twenty years ago! You lost a hit, too. Was that him?" He nodded towards the place where Orrin and his partner were hiding.

"Yes. He took out Intrea. Full health," he sighed.

"We were seven against three, and now we are four against two!" Iklan exclaimed in frustration. "How does he do it? And he is still blue!"

Enric looked at the colours of the shields around him. He himself was blue, Kilan as well, Iklan was down to red, and so was the fourth person, a woman in her late thirties who was clearly at a loss what to do next.

"The two of them need to coordinate their hits very well if they want to take out Kilan or myself with one attack. Only if they hit us at the same time will they succeed in that, instead of simply reducing us to red. With the two of you," he nodded at Iklan and the woman, "they need to be less careful. Hitting you consecutively will be enough."

"Does that mean you want to use me as bait because my chances of survival are the best, apart from yours?" Kilan asked suspiciously.

Enric grinned. "And there you go saying you weren't paying attention to his lessons, old friend. I am a firm believer in the idea that there is no problem that can't be solved by sacrificing a minion."

"Should there ever be a next time, I will be on Orrin's team," the ambassador said grumpily. "I resent being referred to as *minion*."

Another one lost, Enric sighed to himself, wearily. That people had to react so testily to being sacrificed...

"What am I to do, then? Sprint across the alley to draw their fire and then you shoot at them in turn?"

Iklan smiled. "Sounds fine to me."

Kilan gave him a sideways glance. "Where is that compassion healers are supposed to display, I ask you?"

"Out of place in a situation like that, I would think," the healer replied good-naturedly and patted the ambassador on the back. "It has been a privilege fighting at your side. Now you go and be a good target."

"That is what I get for defending that city. Really now," Kilan muttered and took a few calming breaths before taking a run-up and dashing across the street. He almost made it to the other side, before two well-timed, well-aimed bolts turned his manacles to black.

Three bolts shot from the defenders towards the invader's cover, and Orrin was only a moment too slow to avoid the attack completely.

Three versus two, Enric mused.

"We hit him once! He is red now!" Iklan cheered.

"Yes," Kilan called from the other side of the street and prodded the black shackles discontentedly, "brilliant accomplishment. Never mind my being out of the game, taking two hits for you only scoring a single one in return. From where I stand, you just wasted me!"

"Take it like a man, Kilan," Enric teased him as the ambassador strode towards the barrier, grinning when his friend turned to send him a dark look before leaving the play arena.

"Not bad, Orrin," Enric then called out. "You impressed my team members."

"I will accept your capitulation anytime," the warrior replied.

"There are still three of us against two of you."

"We were three against seven before. Considering that, we still outnumber you," Orrin shouted back.

"He has a point there," Iklan nodded seriously. "We could just walk away."

Enric looked at him with a cocked brow. "Really? Walk away from a powerful opponent who is trapped in a dead-end street? If we don't take him out now, there won't be another chance in the game for it, honestly. We want him gone."

"He will take us with him," the woman pointed out sullenly.

"The outcome of the game is more important than the ambitions of a single player," Enric explained, feeling slightly insincere in doing so, as the intended outcome of the game had been planned long before. And it would not be in their favour.

"Very well, then," she said. "What do we do? The same thing once again? I run and get hit, you take out Orrin?"

Enric shook his head. "That won't work a second time. It only worked the first because he could afford to lose a hit and at the same time take out somebody with a blue shield."

"How about waiting them out?" Iklan suggested. "Can we just trap him here without doing anything?"

"Not good," Enric shook his head. "If it takes three of us to keep two of them busy, this is not a ratio in our favour. We will do the following: You two stay here and keep shooting bolts at their cover as quickly as you can. I will approach them and try to flush them out from their hiding place for you to attack. There is one thing I would ask of you, namely not to hit *me* in the process."

Both of them nodded eagerly. A plan that did not involve their venturing out in the open, but Enric. That did sound good.

"Ready?" Enric asked and waited for them to nod and start shooting before he moved out, edging forward slowly, crouching to make himself less of a target for his own people. This was one of the disadvantages of being unusually tall, he mused. There was more surface to serve as a target in situations like this.

He kept his palm raised and readied as he approached their hiding place. He quickly jumped to one side, narrowly avoiding two bolts coming from behind him and another fired by Orrin.

He heard two other strikes hitting shields behind him and quickly let loose a bolt at the warrior in front of him before he was able to duck back. The exchange had happened so quickly, he had no idea who had been hit and who was still in the game. His own shield was still shimmering blue, so he had obviously come out of it unscathed.

He tensed when two heads emerged from cover only a few paces away from him. He had no chance to jump behind a protective structure quickly enough to avoid any direct bolts being shot at him, but he instantly realised that this would not be a problem. Orrin had no more shield, and the manacles on his arms where black. The same applied to the woman next to him. He grinned broadly, and turned towards his own people only to see that they, too, had both been taken out of the game.

"Three against seven," Enric sighed and shook his head. "This doesn't even feel like a real victory."

Orrin smiled and turned to walk towards the barrier. "Good. It wasn't one, if you consider the odds."

"At least I have got rid of *you*."

The warrior grunted. "You have, my friend, but at what cost?"

Enric got back on his feet and turned to see if he could find another way to make more trouble for the invaders without endangering their victory too much.

*　*　*

Ram'an held on to her hand as they moved stealthily along another alley that led towards the city centre and the prized Senate building.

She almost walked into him when he halted abruptly. At the other side of the alley there were three defenders, who had already spotted them.

"Run!" Ram'an commanded and pulled her along into a sprint in a different direction that would make sure they were not in a direct fire line. As before, he again turned several corners to stay out of their pursuers' sight, but these were more adept at tracking them than those before. He cursed when they turned into another alley and suddenly found themselves facing the barrier that limited the arena of play.

He looked around and up, then quickly pushed Eryn against a wall.

"Climb, and quickly. Go!"

As with Vran'el previously, she made her way up the wall by touch, realising soon that this wall was somewhat higher than the other one. She panted once she reached the top shaking her fingers to get the circulation flowing again. Ram'an landed beside her only a few moments later, also breathing hard.

They both remained lying on the roof, keeping their heads down to remain out of sight.

"They will determine soon enough where we went," Ram'an whispered almost inaudibly. "They will either turn around or try to come after us. Either option is fine for us, actually." He lifted his head slightly to better hear what was going on underneath them.

There was a discussion of some kind going on, though they could not make out the words themselves.

"Can't we take out at least one now?" Eryn suggested. "They are directly underneath us, no cover in the way."

"They might be trying to provoke us into doing just that and then take out one of us," he considered and shook his head. "Too risky."

They heard the sound of a shoe on stone and Ram'an grinned widely. "They are climbing up. Excellent. Get ready. The first one to emerge we will hit, both of us at the same time if we can. Two of them were blue, one red, so none of them would remain in the game if hit the right way."

Eryn waited tensely, her heart beating rapidly. Several seconds later she saw a dark head emerging above the edge of the roof.

"Now!" she called out and both of them released a bolt, hitting the blue shield and making it disappear. The player groaned.

"I told you we should have turned around!" he complained to the other two below.

Ram'an and Eryn quickly darted forward, seeing one of the remaining two players clinging to the wall and looking up at them in dismay. He had no opportunity to shoot at them without losing his tentative grip and falling.

They took him out with another pair of well-timed bolts. That left only one, the one with the red shield, who had been watching his two comrades fall, then turned to run before two more bolts were thrown after him, both missing. A moment later he disappeared around a corner.

Ram'an grinned broadly and she could see his white teeth in the darkness. "We make a pretty good team, my dear Theá." Before she could reply, he urged her, "Now please drink something. We will take a short rest before going on." He turned away from her to look over the rooves around them. "You see, there are two routes open to us now. We could stay on the rooves, which is not likely to be a place where our opponents would look for us. On the other hand we would be detectable more easily against the night sky that way. What do you say?"

He waited for her to consider his words.

"How far apart are the rooves? How dangerous is stepping from one to the next? I am not the most confident person in my footing under the best of circumstances, and great heights in combination with darkness will surely be a disadvantage."

He nodded. "Then we will return to the streets." He stretched out his hand and pointed towards a tall building not far away. "You see? This is the Senate hall. We are not far away from it now. I wonder if you and I could make it up the stairs without being taken out."

Eryn squeezed the last drops of water out of her pouch and pushed away Ram'an's when he offered it to her. "Why should we have to take the stairs?" she pondered. "I mean, the condition for winning is not *climbing* the stairs, but reaching their top, isn't it? We could just as well come from any other side, couldn't we?"

He stared at her for a few moments, then nodded slowly. "Indeed, you are right."

"Is the rear side of the building even climbable? I have no intention of braving a slick, vertical wall."

"It should be, yes," he said thoughtfully. "The building is rather old, so there are a lot of uneven stones with a few small crevices and gaps that should provide footholds. The building is a lot broader at its base than at the top, so we just need to get from one floor to the next." She could see the gleam in his eyes even in the dark. "Come on, let us give it a try!"

Before she could reply, he had scrambled back to his feet and was pulling her up as well.

"How do I get back down to the street?" she asked. "Climbing down is a lot harder than up," she pointed out. "And don't even consider asking me to jump," she warned.

"Then I may offer you the conventional way, my dear, which consists of taking the route through the inside of the house."

"The inside? So, breaking into somebody else's living space?" she frowned, taken aback.

"If need be, yes. We are invaders, aiming to conquer and rule this city, after all," he grinned and went to a wooden trapdoor, knocking on it a few times. "But to take your delicate approach to trespass into consideration, we will first see if we can be granted access voluntarily."

And indeed, a few moments later they heard a commotion underneath them and the door lifted, a bearded man in his early sixties looking up at them.

"What are you doing up here?" he asked with a frown. "Are you not supposed to be down there?"

"We are, yes," Ram'an nodded. "Can I prevail upon you to let us get down there through your house? The lady I am with is with child and should not climb down walls in the dark."

"Which has obviously not stopped you from making her climb *up* walls in the dark," the man concluded, but he made space for them to climb down a ladder attached to the trapdoor.

"Thank you so much," Eryn smiled at the man and followed Ram'an down and then through a cosy main room out and back onto the street.

They quickly disappeared into the next available narrow alley, aiming once more for the Senate building.

"How many have you taken out?" Eryn asked him quietly.

"Three. You?"

"Four, plus the two we just got rid of from the roof top. That makes minus nine. Not bad. Assuming that the others have taken out a few themselves, they are surely down to about one third at least. Knowing Orrin, he has probably taken out ten on his own," she reflected. "I wonder if Enric is still in the game."

"We will probably find out soon enough. Now, there are two more open streets for us to cross until we reach the square where the Senate hall sits. The first one is just ahead of us." He took a quick peek around the corner, then pulled back his head hastily. "Your question about Enric still being in the game, I can answer it in the affirmative."

She swallowed. "Around the corner?" she mouthed.

He nodded. "Take him out?"

Grimacing she swayed her head. "Difficult."

"Would you like to?" he asked again, grinning.

She thought for a moment, then sighed and nodded. Taking *him* out would be the real victory as the ending of the game was predetermined in any case.

"How?"

Ram'an thought for a few moments, then looked at her. "A small distraction. Just go along with what I do. When I tell you, shoot at him."

"Wait!" she whispered, "More information!"

"No time, he is approaching quickly," Ram'an whispered sternly and pulled her out with him into the street. "Come on, Eryn!" he said loudly, pulling her close towards him, circling her with his arms. "Do not tell me you never wanted to know what it would be like to kiss me! Just one kiss, and I will never again bother you, I promise!"

Eryn rolled her eyes, wondering if Enric would really fall for a clumsy thing like that.

"Hey!" she heard him call out angrily from a few paces to their left. He did, obviously. Well, in this case he didn't deserve any better.

"Now!" Ram'an commanded and they yanked up their arms to send a bolt each at the tall magician, who realised a moment too late that he had been fooled.

Both bolts struck him full on and he staggered back a few steps until he collided with a wall and slid down to the floor, looking spent.

Eryn and Ram'an walked towards him, each with their separate reasons for grinning.

"Look at that! Well, Aren, it seems we felled you like a tall tree. I think this was a very good example of the advantageous coordination of simultaneous bolts you mentioned at the beginning, was it not?" Ram'an sneered. "I shall see you at the Senate hall, when you acknowledge our victory." Thus he took Eryn's hand and pulled her with him. She looked back at Enric, worried that he might be hurt, but he just winked at her and got back to his feet, looking in obvious annoyance at the manacles that had turned black.

They reached the rear of the Senate building in a matter of minutes and Eryn nodded slowly. The wall did look climbable enough, even considering her swollen belly and clumsiness in the dark.

Ram'an ran his fingers over the uneven stones and motioned for her to step next to him when he had found a route he thought she could follow up to the next floor.

"You start here. This is big enough for your foot. Then you grab this stone, placing your other foot here, then push yourself up. The next hold is that slightly darker stone up slightly to the right and then that gap a little to the left. Do you see? From there you should easily be able to reach the first roof. Do not use your arms to pull yourself up, but instead push with your legs. This takes a lot less strength and energy. I will wait here until you are up there safely. This way I can catch you in case you fall. Are you ready?"

She nodded and did as he had instructed.

"No pulling up with your arms! Use your legs!" he reminded her when she seemed to be struggling.

She exhaled in relief when she reached the first roof, crouching low in case there were members of the other team around.

Ram'an was beside her only a minute later.

"You are good at this. Why?" she asked.

He shrugged. "As opposed to Vern I did not have a scary father and as a boy was chased around a lot by others. Climbing turned out to be a very handy skill in losing pursuers."

They scaled the next wall the same way and the one after that until there was only one final floor to conquer. One last time he told her which stones and gaps to place her hands and feet on, then smiled. "This game will be over in a few minutes. I had great fun doing this with you, Theá. Remember this when I next ask you to have tea with me, will you?"

She blinked, surprised that he had chosen this moment to bring up her reluctance to spend time with him. Without answering, she turned to the wall to brave the last hurdle that stood in the way of victory.

When Ram'an was standing next to her, they rounded the top floor that contained the Senate's meeting hall to get to the front entrance and with that the top of the stairs.

After turning the last corner, they both stopped in surprise as a figure emerged, ducking under a bolt that seared after him from below. He reached the top of the stairs completely out of breath, his shield shimmering red. He sank down on the top stair, yanked both hands up into the air and let lose an inarticulate cry of triumph. He had just won the game for the invaders.

Ram'an sighed and stared at the man. "Pity. We were only a few seconds too slow to claim the honour of winning the game ourselves. But this is not a bad turnout either."

"Why?" she frowned.

"Because," he smiled, "this man here is your second cousin. He is a member of House Aren. Your companion has been defeated by a member of his own House. I do cherish the irony of it all. It is even better than having his companion defeat him. It will give people here a sense of accomplishment."

Eryn thought for a moment, then nodded. He was right. Having a native win the game was preferable to having her as a foreigner doing so. It made it a Takhan victory.

*   *   *

The man glanced up at the two figures that emerged behind him, then his expression relaxed when he recognised their silver manacles.

"What are you doing up here?" he then asked.

"We were also trying to win, but you beat us," Ram'an said and took a seat at one side.

Eryn sat down at his other side. "Hello. I just learned that we are cousins. Well done braving the stairs, cousin. What's your name?"

"Derbel," he replied. "Nice to meet you officially, Maltheá who likes to be called Eryn. I have seen you around."

They looked down at the square in front of the building, where quite a lot was going on. Numerous torches and lamps were lit, returning that part of the city to what it normally looked like at this time. The players on both sides - both active ones with shields still glowing in red and even a few blue ones, as well as those taken out - came walking from different directions, talking animatedly to each other and pointing up to the top of the stairs where the three figures sat together, watching the goings on from above.

"How do you like your new Head of House?" Eryn suddenly asked, catching her cousin unaware.

"He is doing well. Thank you for asking," he replied politely.

"Eryn," Ram'an chuckled and shook his head. "What kind of answer did you expect now? He does not know you, and it is your companion you are talking about. If Derbel was not happy with the situation, you would probably be the last one he would tell."

She shrugged. "I suppose. I just wanted to know if he is more or less of a pain than Malriel."

That made Derbel smile. "That would depend on how you look at it. He is less fearsome, but we are still in the process of adapting to his style of leadership."

That did not sound too promising, she thought, and wondered if Enric was aware that at least a few members of his House were less comfortable with the change.

She narrowed her eyes when a figure approached from one side.

"Is that Golir from the triarchy?"

Ram'an nodded. "Yes. A high honour. I suppose he has come to officially deliver the city to us and negotiate the terms of capitulation," he teased.

She saw Enric approaching from the other side of the square and meet the triarch in front of the stairs, exchanging the formal greeting. She couldn't understand what they were saying, she was too far away for that. Orrin joined them a few moments later, smiling and probably accepting congratulations on winning the game.

"This is great," Derbel said, his breathing slowly returning to normal. "I like the view from up here. It is like being no more than a casual observer instead of being in the middle of this whole commotion."

Eryn nodded. "I know what you mean. After roaming the streets, attacking, being attacked, fleeing, hiding and finally climbing up here, I would rather lean back and have a cool drink up here instead of going down there."

"We could just stay here," her cousin suggested without much hope.

At that moment the triarch and both leaders of the teams looked up at them and Enric lifted his arm to motion them to come down.

"No such luck," Eryn sighed and got to her feet slowly. "Would you like us to carry you down on our shoulders in honour of the great victory you achieved?" she offered with a broad grin.

"The day I let myself be carried on the shoulders of a pregnant woman is not going to be a particularly triumphant one," he laughed and started walking down himself.

"He is right, it would diminish his glory considerably," Ram'an agreed and descended the stairs as well.

Eryn sighed and followed them. It had been pleasant, she had to say, even though teaming up with Ram'an was not exactly her idea of a fun game. Taking out Enric had been terrific, though, she had to admit.

She watched the many faces on the square turning towards them as they walked down the stairs, and among the members of the invading team spontaneous applause broke out. She joined in, and so did Ram'an. Derbel stood there, looking more than just a little embarrassed at the sudden attention he received.

Eryn felt a mischievous impulse rising and decided that this was just the right occasion to indulge herself. She stopped a few steps before she would have been on the same level with all the others and cleared her throat before changing the air streams so that her words would carry further.

"Greetings, citizens of Takhan!" she exclaimed. "Your city has been taken, but this does not have to change life as you know it. If you pay your tributes and worship us the way we deserve, we will refrain from maltreating and humiliating you! We will be compassionate rulers, providing you do not oppose us, leading you into a new era of progress and peace!"

"That is a great relief," Golir remarked dryly, "I do so appreciate a smooth change of sovereignty without humiliation and maltreatment."

Several laughs erupted at that.

Eryn nodded graciously. "We aim to please our new subjects."

Enric reached out and took her hand to pull her down next to him. "Does having me as the father of your child afford me any extra privileges under this new regime?"

"That will depend on your conduct, subject," she replied loftily. "But as long as I live under what we have for now to consider your roof, I will grant you certain exemptions."

"Glad to hear it," he nodded. "Very generous of you. Clemency is a very attractive trait in a usurper."

"Yes, isn't it? You will start showing us your appreciation by cooking that dinner you promised not long ago."

"By all means. I wouldn't dream of trying to dodge that." Then he turned to her cousin. "Derbel, well done. You will be our guest of honour tomorrow evening. It obviously takes an Aren to defeat one."

Eryn rolled her eyes at that. "So glad to see that you take pride in your new House."

"I assume I can remove the shield around your play arena now?" Golir asked.

"Of course," Enric nodded and waited until the triarch had removed the barrier, before lifting his wrists. "And the manacles, if you would be so kind."

He then removed Orrin's shackles and announced, "You may now come to either me or Orrin to have your manacles removed. We will not discriminate between invaders or defenders, so do not bother with that." He turned back to Eryn to remove hers first, then Derbel's. "You two can help, it will be faster that way."

"Splendid," she sighed and touched Ram'an's manacles when he lifted them towards her to open them. "So much for enjoying my new status as supreme ruler," she grumbled. "Being made to do actual *work*."

"Wouldn't I be the supreme ruler as the leader of the invaders?" Orrin cut in.

Eryn snorted. "Hardly! We can't have a foreign barbarian ruling Takhan, can we?"

"You are a foreign barbarian as well," he pointed out.

"True enough," she acknowledged. "But I don't look so different, so I might get by with assuming the position of grand ruling mistress."

Golir watched their exchange with a doubtful look, then said slowly, "Why do you not leave the ruling of the city to the triarchy until you have thought through who of you is to take over that task?"

"A sensible proposal!" Eryn agreed immediately. "I like it. We herewith charge you with running the place to your best understanding and abilities."

Enric shook his head at her. "A little light-headed, aren't you? It is probably time to get you to bed."

Eryn smiled when she saw Vran'el approaching. "Hey you!"

"Sweetness," he smiled at her. "Well done." Then his gaze wandered to Ram'an and his eyes narrowed.

"Do you want me to remove your manacles or do you want Neval to do it tomorrow?" she grinned.

Her brother lifted his wrists to her to remove the restraints and nodded in appreciation. He turned to leave again, then stopped and turned back.

"Father does not know that you participated in this game. He will have discovered it by tomorrow, and I have to warn you that he will not be pleased. Just prepare for it when you meet him at the clinic, will you?"

Eryn frowned and nodded. "Not that he has any right to object, mind you."

Vran'el smiled without humour. "Sweetness, I am afraid you and he have completely different perceptions concerning what rights he does or does not have. He is under the impression that he is your father, while you continue to deny it. It seems you are about to face a situation in which this will turn out to be a massive hurdle."

Eryn felt how her spirits had been dampened by the prospect of facing a displeased Valrad the next morning. Dealing with his emotions would make keeping herself calm and collected so much more arduous.

CHAPTER 12

Therapy

Eryn covered her face with her pillow when Enric opened the curtains. He had ordered them as they were not customary in these parts, yet the sun tended to rise so damn early that they made at least another hour of sleep possible.

"Time to get up, my love," he announced, much too awake for her taste.

"I don't want to," she moaned. "I will stay at home today. Say that I am ill, will you?"

"Hardly a plausible excuse for a healer, I would say. And it would likely have Valrad storming over here to see what is wrong with you instead of saving you from his presence. Which is what I assume this is about?"

"I have no idea what you are talking about," she insisted stubbornly.

"So this has nothing to do with Vran'el's parting remarks about Valrad and what he will have to say about your participation in the game?"

She sighed and pushed the pillow off her face. "Maybe. Not that I care what he has to say about anything, mind you. It is just that his being in a bad mood will make working with him even more tiresome than I already find it."

Enric nodded slowly. He was on the verge of telling her to open up more, to let her father see what was going on in her mind, but he

169

knew well enough that this would just make her angry at him, so he kept his mouth sealed.

"Breakfast?" he asked instead. "Sounds like you need all the energy you can get for today."

She nodded and pushed aside her blanket to get out of bed.

"Any bread buns left?"

"A fresh load was delivered just this morning."

He grinned at her relieved expression and watched her bend over a chest and pull out a tunic and pair of trousers, appreciating the view. He remembered the evening before, when she had teased the triarch, displaying her usual inconsiderate approach to authority. It had been a glimpse of herself again. Unfortunately, her troubles seemed to have caught up with her already. He worried a bit about Valrad and what he might find necessary to tell her. She would not react well to him assuming a role she did not grant him, but that he thought he was entitled to. And neither would she appreciate being told what she should have refrained from doing.

She did not like it when her superiors in the Order tried to do so, and neither would she welcome it from a man she held a significant grudge against.

He also wondered how permitting her to participate in the game would change his own relationship with the Head of House Vel'kim. Valrad would probably have to say a few words to him, too. It would certainly not hurt to prepare for that and consider how to handle the situation in a way that would not compromise the relationship between their Houses.

He longingly thought back to the business relationships he maintained back home, where personal connections were considered a hindrance and were therefore avoided as much as was possible. He would have welcomed that luxury a lot here.

Eryn slipped into her clothes and walked out of their bedroom towards the main room, where the servants had prepared their breakfast consisting of a large bowl of different fruits.

Orrin was already seated there, nodding at her as she entered.

"Good morning, you."

"Same to you," she replied and plumped down on the cushion next to him. "Is that companion of yours still asleep?"

"Yes. Like most nights, she has hardly closed an eye and then dropped from exhaustion in the early morning hours. It is time for that child to be delivered, if you ask me."

"She still has one whole month to go," Eryn corrected him. "It is not good for a child to be born too early. So both of you will just have to stick it out until then."

"I am very much looking forward to throwing those words back at you in a few months," he sighed, putting his empty fruit bowl aside.

"Don't," she advised him with a lopsided grin. "I promise I won't react well to it."

"Well, at least you gave me a fair warning," he nodded and stood. "I'll be off, then. The triarchs have invited me and Enric for a meeting to discuss the outcome of the game yesterday." He looked up when Enric entered the main room. "Ready to leave?"

Enric nodded. "I am, yes." He walked over to where Eryn was sitting and bent down to kiss her forehead. "Goodbye, my love. I shall see you in the afternoon. Let me know how your day with Valrad went once you are back."

She acquiesced reluctantly. "I will."

*   *   *

Eryn closed the door to their usual treatment room and immediately sensed that the mood in the room was altered. Valrad was bent over a patient file and ignored her for the first few moments after she had entered. When he finally acknowledged her presence, he leaned back and regarded her unsmilingly.

"Sit," he commanded.

Well, she thought, at least they would deal with it right away. She folded her arms.

"I would rather stand, if you don't mind."

"I do mind."

She pressed her lips together, wondering how she could avoid opposing him openly without making him think that she would comply with being treated that way. Tricky. She walked over to a desk against the opposite side of the wall from where he sat and took a seat there.

"I am sitting," she said calmly, bracing herself.

"I have learned about your joining that game your companion and Orrin arranged."

"I did," she confirmed and folded her arms. "What of it?" She watched his jaw muscles tensing.

"I do not approve."

"A little late for all that, isn't it?" she said lightly, and flinched when his fist pounded the surface of the table in front of him.

"Be still!" he thundered and glared at her. "In your condition this was an immensely foolish thing to do! Do you have any idea of the many things that could have gone wrong? Climbing roofs, running and jumping around are not activities that are recommended for expectant women! You are a healer, why did you fail to realise this? Why did you put my grandchild in such danger?"

She stared at him, taking in the anger he radiated.

"Firstly, I am, as you have pointed out, a healer," she said calmly. "That means I assessed the risk and decided that is was not great enough to forego participating in the game. Secondly, I am in a position to heal away whatever damage might have occurred in the course of the game. And thirdly, this is hardly a matter that concerns *you* to such a degree, as it is *my* child we are talking about here. I am in charge of it and responsible for protecting it."

"Hardly a matter that concerns me to such a degree," he repeated her words slowly. He rose from his chair and walked over to her, startling her when he grabbed both her shoulders. "I realise that the recent changes in your life are not easy for you to adjust to, but there is only so much foolishness you are entitled to because of it," he hissed. "I am your Head of House and your father, meaning I am entitled to raising binding objections when you are doing something I do not consider advisable," he pointed out, staring straight into her eyes.

Eryn took a calming breath and exhaled slowly. "My Head of House you may be, Valrad, but this does not entitle you to influence or object to personal decisions that are none of your business."

"I am your father, too," he repeated when she failed to comment on this.

"No," she said with the utmost composure she could master, "you are not. You are one of many men who had an affair with Malriel. Which is your business entirely. I grant you that, and you will in turn allow me to live my life as I see fit without uninvited interference. If I require your medical advice with regard to my pregnancy, I will ask you for it. As long as I refrain from doing that, I will thank you for not forcing it upon me."

Valrad closed his eyes for a moment as if to force himself to maintain his composure. When he opened them again, there was determination in them. He removed his hands from her shoulders and stepped back.

"Eryn, I have been observing your refusal to cope with these new truths long enough now. And your aloofness towards me. This is neither healthy, nor am I willing to put up with it any longer. Such an attitude is beneficial neither for yourself, nor for your family or your relationship. I wish to enforce an obligation for you to see Iklan twice a week until he considers you fit to handle this situation in a more positive way."

She thought about his words for a few moments, then shrugged. "I already meet Iklan more often than that since I have started working here. We have lunch together regularly at the canteen," she pointed out.

Valrad stared at her for several seconds, then blinked. "Is it possible that you failed to understand what I have just told you? *Seeing him* means that you need to go to his treatment room, sit with him for one hour and work with him on the issues that burden you."

"What?" She blinked in utter incomprehension. "Treatment room? What for? I am perfectly healthy! I check myself regularly, and both the child and I are well. What are you talking about? And what makes you think that you can compel me to undergo any kind of treatment? Even in that assumed father-role that you seem to delight in right now you would have no right to force a thing like that on me!"

"Maybe not as your father," he said coldly, "but as your superior this is well within my rights if I consider your current state of mind one which is unfit to treat patients unsupervised. I have already cleared this with the Head of the Clinic. Your first appointment with Iklan is today after your shift ends. I would advise you to keep that appointment. Otherwise you might be stripped of your insignia."

She gasped and stared at him open-mouthed. Her hand flew up to the silver pin above her heart, grabbing it possessively.

"You wouldn't!" she hissed.

He raised an eyebrow at her. "Do not make me prove to you that my threats are to be taken seriously, my dear girl. If you doubt my determination, talk to your brother and see what he has to say about my enforcing unpleasant measures."

Eryn felt the hairs on her arms standing up and suddenly felt cold, despite the warm room. She shook her head slowly in disbelief, rubbing her upper arms with her palms.

"Why?" she asked weakly and closed her eyes. "Why can't you just let me be?"

She heard him exhale.

"Because I cannot watch you bury that pain inside you any longer instead of dealing with it," he said softly. "You are hurting yourself. A great deal. You withdraw from the people close to you and spend more and more time alone. This is a dangerous development - one I do not wish to witness any longer. You need help, and if you are not willing to accept it voluntarily, I will order you to. This is the responsibility which family has, Eryn. We look out for each other, no matter whether you chose to regard me as your uncle or father right now."

"If I refuse," she said slowly, opening her eyes and staring at the floor, "you will take away my qualification? Don't you think that will cause me even more pain?"

"I know it will. This is why I hope that avoiding it proves to be a strong motivation for you to work with Iklan in order to hang on to what you have put so much effort into achieving," he nodded.

"And coercing me is your path to improving our family bonds? Really?" She looked up at him incredulously.

"Yes," he replied mildly. "That is indeed what I am counting on."

Eryn looked into the brown eyes that resembled his brother's - her father's - so much.

"I hate you," she told him deliberately, feeling dark joy at the stab of pain she saw for a quick moment.

"I know. But this is not a new problem arising from my sending you to Iklan, but the very source of what induced me to arrange for it." He turned and walked the few steps to his desk, picking up a patient file and handing it to her. "Now take a few minutes to compose yourself before I call in the first patient."

She clung to the file as if it were a lifebelt that kept her floating above in the air of reality instead sinking of in the deep water of this absurd dream she felt she had wallowed into. Forcing herself to breath regularly, she opened the cover, staring at the first page unseeingly for several moments before first letters and then words started to cohere in front of her eyes.

She needed to push this aside for now, she implored herself. Losing her calm right now would only prove to Valrad and his completely wrong assessment that she was in urgent need of some kind of treatment.

* * *

Eryn paced along the clinic's corridor, her face a stolid mask. Valrad was directly behind her. He obviously didn't trust her to keep her appointment with Iklan and wanted to make sure she really did go there. She ignored him and climbed the stairs up to the floor where the healer's treatment room was situated.

He was one of only very few healers in the clinic who had a room for themselves, moreover even with an assistant who sat in an anteroom to see who was permitted to enter. She remembered the young woman from her first visit here several months ago.

"Ah, Eryn," she smiled. "You are right on time. Just go in. Iklan is expecting you. Valrad," she nodded.

Eryn sighed and turned left to the adjoining door, opening it without knocking, walking in and closing it in Valrad's face.

Iklan looked up from his desk and smiled. "Good day to you, Eryn. Valrad does not want to come in for a moment?"

"No," she just said.

The healer nodded slowly. "I see." He rose from his chair and stepped towards her to kiss her hand. "Then let us take a seat and talk about what is going to happen, shall we?"

Eryn remained standing and folded her arms. "From what I gathered you are intending to heal away my disdain for the man who likes to call himself my father," she said accusingly. "Or try to do so. I wonder if your skill can match up to the depth of my aversion."

Iklan looked at her, taken aback. "Heal away your...?" He shook his head in disgust. "Even if I could, I would never just make emotions disappear! They are an expression of fulfilled and unfulfilled needs and wants; removing them like that would be careless and a violation of the healing principles! It would be like numbing the pain of a wound just to remove the discomfort instead of healing it." He raised his brow at her immediate look of relief. "But this is surely not what Valrad told you I would be doing with you, did he? He knows better than that."

Eryn sighed and let herself drop onto the cushions on his floor. "No, he didn't, you are right. This was an assumption I made when he told me that I have to find a more constructive way to deal with my unresolved issues."

She watched him sit down at her left side, not too far away to make it impersonal, though not close enough to give her the impression of being crowded out.

"Healing away an ailment is not the only way to deal with it," he explained calmly. "Sometimes it just has to heal on its own with a gentle push in the right direction."

"Apart from the fact that I do not consider myself to be *ailing*, I assume you mean as with illnesses, when you do not heal them away completely but instead just aid with the right nutrition and herbal remedies to make the body strong enough to overcome it on its own and be less susceptible to future infection?"

He considered that for a moment, then said, "I have never considered it that way, but I suppose you could compare it with that, yes. Only that I will not work with herbs or anything, but with words." He smiled at her doubtful look. "I can see that you are not familiar with the concept of healing through words?"

"You mean like singing a magical song? I heard that magical music can be used to promote healing…"

He shook his head. "No, Eryn, nothing like that. There is no magic involved in this, none at all. We will *talk*."

Eryn wondered if maybe he was suffering from the heat because he had spent too much time outside over noon without any protection from the sun.

"You are going to heal me by talking to me?" she asked slowly. That sounded crazed.

"Not exactly. I am going to help you heal yourself, but you will be the one talking to me, mostly. The idea is that you assist me to help you to help yourself."

She stared at him. That sounded even more crackpot. "I am expected to do most of the talking, which equals *work* in this case. And they *pay* you for that?" she asked carefully.

She blinked when he broke out in laughter.

"Imagine, yes, they do," he nodded.

"I am a tiny bit sceptical of it all, to be completely honest with you."

He nodded. "Yes, I have gathered that much. And thank you for phrasing it so very diplomatically. I am very well aware that you are not here voluntarily, that your father coerced you into it. I advised him against doing it that way, but he said he saw no other method of getting you to come to me. It is easy for him, of course. He thinks he has performed his duty by having you treated. My problem is now that I have a very reluctant patient who does not want to work with me at all. This makes things somewhat more difficult than with willing patients."

"I am not your *patient*," she contradicted. "Especially as I don't consider what you do here to be actual *treatment*."

"Alright, then let us find another name for our relationship, shall we? Lawyers like to use the term *client*. As opposed to a customer, a client is entitled to absolute confidentiality, exactly the way a patient would be. Would you be more comfortable with that?"

She thought for a moment, then nodded reluctantly. "Alright, client then. Let me get this straight, just to make sure I didn't misunderstand anything here. I shall come to you twice a week for one hour and talk to you, which according to you is a treatment that will enable me to deal with my unresolved issues. This will go on until you consider me healed."

He nodded. "One could summarise it that way, even though I do detect a touch of resentment in the way you phrased that."

She ignored his remark and asked instead, "What happens if I don't turn up next time?"

"Then I am bound to report this to the Head of the Clinic and to the healer who recommended the treatment, namely Valrad. I dare say the latter informed you of the measures he intends to take if you refuse to cooperate."

Taking away her insignia, she remembered only too well.

"Excellent. Now that we have clarified the general conditions, let's get on with it, shall we?" she proposed with exaggerated enthusiasm. "How do we go about this?"

"I would say you tell me about the things that are currently on your mind," he suggested.

She nodded. "Alright, I can do that. Only yesterday I received a letter from Anyueel. It was from Vyril, Lord Tyront's companion. Lord Tyront is the leader of the Order, but I think that is fairly much common knowledge here already. Anyway, his companion works with me, or rather for me, as I pay her to run the orphanage in the city. She wrote that things are going very well, that the construction work is finished and the teaching plans and feeding arrangements so far are working out well. She has begun to contact craftspeople all over the city to see if they are willing to take on orphans as trainees and apprentices once they are old enough. We both think that raising children in a healthy environment is one thing, but enabling them to learn a profession that makes it possible to sustain themselves afterwards is just as essential..." She stopped when Iklan lifted a hand.

"Eryn, when I told you to talk about what is on your mind, I was rather thinking of more personal things, for example how you feel about discovering that Valrad is your father, about finding yourself pregnant despite your well-known determination not to have children. Matters of that sort."

She looked at him, her expression disconcerted. "But these are very personal topics," she pointed out.

He gave a sigh and then said, "You know, this is the idea of the kind of treatment I do: to deal with personal things that are a burden and need to be resolved."

Eryn frowned and let her eyes wander over his expensive looking furniture and the many books that took up one entire wall. Talking about the two issues he had just mentioned was clearly not going to be the way ahead. They were none of his business.

"Well, there is one thing I might have where a little assistance would be helpful," she then said. "Vran'el keeps calling me *little sister*. I do find that annoying and I have tried telling him not to call me that, but he just seems to like it even better when I object. Then I tried ignoring it in the hope he would get bored with teasing me with it, but he keeps using the term. I would like it if you could talk to him about that."

She saw Iklan exhale slowly, thinking how he looked like his patience was on trial. "I am afraid this is not quite in accordance with my role. My task is not to go and solve your issues with other people. It seems I did not express myself adequately when explaining that."

"Then at least tell me what to tell him," she demanded.

"That, neither, is anything I am doing."

"What exactly is it what you *are* doing, then?" she asked in frustration. "It is obviously neither solving my problems, nor telling me how I can do it myself!"

"I cannot present you with cut and dried solutions, as they would be *my* solutions."

"But your solution is surely better than no solution at all!" she protested.

"That is the question. A solution suitable for *me* does not necessarily mean it is the best way for *you*. The ideal solution is the one *you* come up with yourself."

"If I were able to do that, we wouldn't be talking about the problem!" she exclaimed, completely lost where this was supposed to go.

"This is where I come in: I will ask you the right questions that are intended to lead you to the solution that comes from within yourself and is a satisfactory course of action which you can commit to and are willing to bear the consequences of."

"The solution needs to come from within me?" she asked, puzzled. "Why would I need you to find out something I already know?"

"Because we are not always aware that we are able to access that solution. Negative feelings, blocks and other hindrances may keep us from doing so. The right questions may lead you there."

"Why do I need you for that? I can talk to my friends, they can ask me *questions*."

"Two reasons: Firstly, your father has sent you to me because he says that you do not talk to anybody about your problems - neither your companion nor your friends. That entirely rules out *their* asking you questions. And secondly, only properly posed questions will bring the desired effect." He rose to grab two glasses and a carafe of water, placing them on the low table next to them. "What we can talk about, though, is why being addressed with *little sister* annoys you. It might have to do something with why you flinch every time I mention your father."

177

Did she really? Probably. There was a stab of anger every time she heard Valrad referred to as such.

"I don't think I feel comfortable talking to you about this. You told me I am entitled to confidentiality as your client, but I know very well that this does not apply when it comes to discussing cases among colleagues. And I know that Valrad is going to ask you how things are progressing with me. I dare say you will not defy your own superior by not answering or by lying to him."

"It is true," he admitted, "that your situation is quite a bit more involved than ones my other patients find themselves in. I normally refuse to treat family members of my colleagues to avoid just such a dilemma you mentioned, especially when it comes to my superiors. For this reason I have agreed with Valrad that he may enquire about general progress, but no particulars. The topics we are talking about are not for him to know. I hope you consent to this. If you do not feel that your confidentiality is safe with me, we may as well stop right here."

"Well, if you put it like that…" she threw in immediately.

"Wait. It just means that we have to find another healer to work with you, not that you are free to halt the treatment, of course."

She leaned back, sighing disappointedly. "Then let's go through with this, by all means. I don't want to talk about Valrad, Malriel or the baby. Everything else is permitted."

Iklan lifted an eyebrow at her. "That you want to avoid all those topics causing you discomfort is not a good starter for resolution, you know."

"These are personal topics, and I don't know you well enough to talk about them."

He nodded. "A valid argument, and one I respect. We can work on those topics when you have got to know me better, then. Tell me about how you are adapting to life in Takhan, then."

She nodded in relief. That was a harmless enough topic where she could tell as much or little as she felt comfortable with.

*　*　*

Enric and Orrin stood in Malriel's study and stared down at the box that had been placed on the desk. It was full with messages that had been delivered while they had been at their meeting with the triarchs.

"That is a lot to go through," Orrin noted and began to turn and walk out of the room.

Enric quickly grabbed his shoulder to stop him. "Well spotted, Orrin. Thus I appreciate your generous offer to help me go through them."

"I don't remember making any such offer," he growled.

"You didn't?" Enric said in mock confusion. "Then I will generously overlook that lapse and pretend that you have."

"You are not my superior anymore. I don't have to do this. Theoretically," the warrior added cautiously.

"True," Enric nodded. "And yet you and your family are staying under my roof, profiting from my hospitality. A very comfortable and luxurious roof too, I might add."

"Yes, I just remembered that bit," Orrin sighed and grabbed a chair to sit down in front of the stack of messages to pick up the first one, then open it impatiently.

Enric smiled and took a seat at the other side of the desk, reaching into the box and taking out a bunch of messages.

They spent the next hour reading, before Enric got up to go to the kitchen to refill the water carafe.

"I would never have expected quite such a reaction to that game," Orrin remarked upon his return. "Most of the participants were thrilled with it, no matter whether they were on the winning or the losing side. They are urging you to arrange for another one, and soon. The ones not so happy are determined to have another game, as well, but have told you what they think needs to be changed in the rules. Then there are messages from people who did not participate and want to do so next time, some demands to include non-magicians in the game – however that is supposed to work out." He looked up at Enric. "I think we accomplished our objectives with it and then some. A major part of them wants to be trained in magical fighting to increase their chances of staying in the game longer." He leaned back and chuckled. "Incredible. And Eryn came up with the idea that would require people to queue for the chance to be trained in fighting. How strange is that, I ask you? I was extremely pleased with her own performance in the game, by the way," he added. "She eliminated mighty Lord Enric, after all."

Enric nodded. "Though not all on her own, mind you. But of us foreigners she was the only one to remain in the game until the end, even finding herself at the top of the stairs to the Senate hall. Not what I would have expected, not at all." He lifted several of the opened messages. "You made quite an impression on the locals, by the way. The tale of that little skirmish of ours where you took out a group more than twice the size than what you had on your side has spread wide and far. I, too, have many requests for training, explicitly asking for *you*." He shook his head. "Not that I have any time or inclination to do any combat training sessions, but I'll admit that this does vex me a little."

"I might reserve an hour or two per week for some extra training for you, if you want," Orrin smirked. "As a courtesy to my considerate host."

"Too kind," Enric smiled insincerely.

"What is the next step now? Are we going to plan another game or should we first have them trained?"

Enric pursed his lips while he was mulling that question. "I think we should set a date for another game. It should motivate people to put more effort into their training, if they see a chance to make use of their new skills in the not too distant future. How much time do you need to train them in fighting and strategy? Would four months be realistic?"

"Depends on what I am supposed to teach them. They are quite advanced in shielding here, though not really for combat purposes. But that is a minor thing to show them. They also know the basics of shooting magical bolts, which leaves the matter of training them to actually hit the targets they aim at. And what will probably take most of the time is *strategy*. They have hardly any clue about that, apart from those who go hunting regularly, that is. A few of those did rather well in the game."

"The trouble is that you are only one man, and this limits the number of people you can train effectively. I am afraid the demand for your services will after yesterday be higher than what you can manage. This means we have to select people and inevitably annoy those not selected."

Orrin nodded slowly. "True enough. Though I suppose I could pick a few of the quicker and more talented learners and concentrate on training them well in a very short period over several hours a day. An intensive programme, as it were. They could then help train the others."

"A sensible approach, let's make it so." He looked into the box. There were still about fifty messages left to go through. "I think we can handle those in the next hour, then I should join Kilan and his numerous helpers at the embassy to prepare that dinner."

The warrior grinned. "Absolutely. We can't have it look like the great leader is trying to shirk the menial tasks, can we?"

Enric looked up when Eryn appeared in the doorway. She did not seem happy.

"On the other hand, why don't I leave you to deal with the rest of the messages alone and take a nice walk in the garden with my lovely companion?"

"Yes, why don't you?" Orrin said in a complaining voice, but turned back to the box obediently. "At least *I* don't have to do any cooking and serving tonight," he mumbled.

Enric kissed her on her forehead and took her hand to lead her out into the garden to a nicely shaded spot under a tree. He had asked her in the morning to tell him about how her day with Valrad had gone, and judging from what he could see this was not going to be a very happy account.

"How did it go?" he asked carefully.

"Not good," she grumbled. "He told me that he was angry because I participated in that game despite my advanced pregnancy, and when I told him that this was none of his business, he put pressure on me."

"Pressure? How? And to do what?"

"I have to see Iklan twice a week for some kind of strange talking treatment or he will take my insignia away and thereby stop me from working at the clinic."

He frowned. "Strange talking treatment? What do you mean by that?"

"I am supposed to see Iklan and talk to him about my problems."

Enric lifted his brow. "Talking about problems is not a totally unknown way to deal with them, but not exactly what I would have thought of as a treatment routine. Why do you need a healer for that?"

"Exactly!" she exclaimed and threw her hands up. "He doesn't do any healing at all! There is not even magic involved! He just listens and asks me questions. *I* do all the talking and he gets paid for that. I wonder if I should offer something like that back home; it sounds like money earned without having to exert yourself."

"Which is exactly your ambition in life," he couldn't help but state, grinning broadly.

She had to smile at that. "Well, that is a drawback, yes. But people at home would never go for anything like that, would they? I mean, the idea seems to be to encourage me to talk and talk until I finally manage to stumble upon the solution that was obviously inside me all along!"

"An interesting approach," he noted cautiously, determined not to support her negative attitude while at the same time signalling that he understood her dismay.

"Yes," she snorted, "the same way a badly tuned instrument is *interesting*, but hardly appealing. I distrust this imaginary healing principle. You are the Head of a powerful House, aren't you? Surely you can get me out of this?"

He sighed, sad that he had to deny her request. She hardly ever came to him with a problem, and now he had to reject her plea.

"Sorry, my love, I am afraid that is nothing I can do. I have next to no influence at the clinic, it is a Vel'kim domain. And even if I had, it would not at all improve the relationship between our Houses. I would be interfering with internal Vel'kim matters. Or healers' matters, if one wants to look at it from that angle. I can only lose here and inflict damage in the process." He took both her hands in his. "How important is working at the clinic for you, truly? You know that you don't have to go there, you are free to do whatever you like here. No restraints. You could go through all the libraries you can find in the city, learn a new craft, study their laws, do whatever you feel like. If you feel that being treated like that by your... by Valrad is not something you want to endure any longer, you don't have to. If you can continue without working at the clinic, that is," he concluded with his initial question.

She dropped her head and her shoulders sank. "It *is* important for me, very much so. I wish it wasn't."

"Then I am afraid there is nothing more you can do than follow the requirements that will enable you to continue working there," he said softly. He was pleased with her answer. Healing was still the one thing she was willing to put effort into, something that made sense and was worth fighting for. Seeing her abandon it would have troubled him a lot. And who was to know - there might still be a chance that this unusual treatment method they used here would work.

CHAPTER 13

Vern's Frustration

Enric felt content, which had become a rare and thus treasured state of mind lately. He sat under a tree in the Aren gardens, his arm around Eryn, both of them reading from their books. He had started informing himself about the care and nurture of new-borns, she about magical music.

The sun had lost some if its strength already and was nearing the horizon, but would still afford them enough light to read on for a while. He glanced at their wrists, both of them dark with their commitment symbols at this nearness.

When his thoughts would stay on the text no longer and started wandering, he closed the book and let it sink onto his lap, fondly remembering the evening before when Kilan and the defenders had hosted a large dinner for sixty at the ambassadorial residence.

It had been a merry occasion with lively conversation that had solely focussed on the game. Battle stories of brave deeds, risky manoeuvres, confusion, violent exchanges, narrow escapes and newly discovered places to hide had been exchanged. The story of how Orrin had defeated six players almost single-handedly had been a great favourite. Intrea had secured herself a place next to the fighter during the dinner, showering him with her admiration, praising his fighting prowess and pestering him until he finally promised her to be her partner during the next game. The question whether there would actually be another one had not even been asked seriously. It had just been treated as the most natural thing in the world that a marvellous event like that could not remain a one-time occurrence.

Vran'el had muttered into Enric's ear that he suspected that Intrea was taking a bit of a shine to Orrin and that he hoped she would behave herself and manage to keep her hands off him, considering how he was about to become a father again in only a few weeks. When she had had several glasses of wine and kept touching Orrin a bit more frequently than was appropriate, Vran'el had taken her aside to have a little chat with her and then made sure that she no longer sat next to the warrior.

They both looked towards the terrace door when angry footsteps became audible from the main room. A moment later Vern stormed out, looking wild and upset, focussing his gaze on them when he spotted them and marching towards them determinedly.

"I will not ever again have anybody refer to me as an artist!" he thundered. "This term is from now on an insult to me!" He stomped his foot. "I am so furious, I wish I could hit something!"

Enric smiled and rose. "Come here."

"Not you!" the boy exclaimed in horror. "Preferably something that doesn't strike me back a lot harder!"

"I won't," he promised. "You hit, I shall just dodge and absorb. Don't be shy, it will help you get rid of that destructive energy. It's not healthy to keep it bottled inside."

Vern was clearly in two minds about that offer. If there was a target that could stand being hit, it was the tall, trained fighter in front of him. Yet that very man was not only quite a bit too important to be used as a target for angry energy just like that, but even a casual, accidental hit by him would probably cause multiple fractures.

"How afraid of me are you, now? Still too much to hit me even if I don't fight back?" Enric smiled.

Eryn grinned when this remark made Vern straighten and aim a punch at her companion's chin, missing when the fighter ducked away.

Enric then caught several blows with his palms, dodged a few others and let himself be hit three times, very probably to aid the boy's self-confidence.

After about twenty minutes Vern sank down onto the grass, exhausted from the exercise while Enric was not even breathing any faster.

"Thank you. I really needed that," the boy sighed and let himself fall back so that he was lying on the grass, staring up at the sky.

"That's the impression I had, yes," Enric remarked dryly. "And now talk."

"I told you about that one artist, the great and much admired Elwoi, if you remember."

"I don't recall the name, but that's the one who told you that you are in no danger making use of your considerable potential anytime soon, isn't he?" Eryn ventured.

"The very same, yes," Vern sighed. "I had another discussion with him today, and in front of his devoted admirers, too. I told him that I have taken some time to think about what he told me, about having to depict what is going on inside me to express my inner self. I asked

184

him if he didn't think that my choice of models would reflect that to a certain degree, or the way I chose to draw them. I said that the things I draw when I am upset are a lot different from my drawings when I am relaxed or happy. He started going on at me that I hadn't understood anything he had been trying to get me to understand. He said that I don't take my art seriously enough, that the mere fact that I chose to continue my training as a healer instead of focusing all my attention on art shows that clearly enough."

Eryn sat up straight, her body tense. "Wait, what? Don't tell me he wants you to stop following healing? Tell me where I can find this what's-his-name and I will have a brief and very persuasive - painful - chat with him!"

"No, you won't," Enric stated calmly and put an arm around her shoulder to make her lean back again. "This conflict is for Vern to handle; you can't wade in and solve his problems for him. This is part of growing up. And even if he decides to give up healing in favour of drawing, there is nothing you can do against it, only accept it. Though judging from his mood I don't see much danger of that right now," he ended wryly and nodded at Vern to continue.

"Yes, that's exactly what Elwoi told me. He says I need to decide between healing and drawing, that I will excel in neither discipline if I cannot decide to follow one, put all my time and efforts into improving it. He didn't leave me in much doubt about which one he considered the worthier one, though. Instead of detailing in pictures how the human body works I am supposed to work on expressing myself, drawing something that inspires my fantasy - like an abstract concept, love or whatever else," Vern grumbled, some of the anger seeping back into his voice. He sat up abruptly and glared at the world around him. "Love! I will give him bloody love!" he shouted. His eyes suddenly focussed on Eryn, looking at her for a few moments, then his head shook slightly. "You are useless right now, too sombre." Then he looked at Enric. "You."

"Me?" His voice was half surprised, half amused. Taking a few swings at his former and future superior had clearly lifted his confidence quite a lot.

"Yes. You are crazy about her, aren't you?"

"That is a valid statement, yes," Enric nodded slowly, curious where this would go.

"Good. Then concentrate on that and give me your hand. Think of whatever it is about her gives you a warm and fuzzy feeling," he commanded and waited for Enric to recover from his tone and finally nod before he raised his hand for the boy to take.

He felt a warm surge of magic passing from Vern's fingers into his own palm and spreading throughout his body. This was not a healer's exploratory, focused magical impulse when he was attempting to detect an injury or illness, but like an enveloping wave that did not concentrate on anything in particular, but instead everything in general. After no more than a minute, the boy opened his eyes again, a determined glint in them, and jumped up to storm away without another word.

Eryn slowly shook her head. "That was strange. Even for him. Do you want to hazard a guess what he is up to?"

"Judging from his exclamation of *give him bloody love* I would suspect that he is about to draw something. Though I wonder if his current state of mind is one that makes concentrating on that very emotion possible without distorting into something less appealing."

"Should we go after him and check that he doesn't do anything stupid?" she then asked.

He chuckled. "Follow an artist full of nervous energy? No, thank you. He is a sensible lad, I trust that he is not going to do any harm to himself or others. Let's just sit here and enjoy the evening, shall we? It's Orrin's turn to cook tonight."

Eryn nodded reluctantly and leaned back against him. "I know. You are right." Then she grinned. "Never in a million years would I have thought that I would live to witness Orrin cooking a meal for me. Maybe we can send the servants off tomorrow and have him clean the place, too?"

"That might be going a bit too far, my love. But let me know if you want to try that. I'd love to watch."

* * *

Junar yawned and stretched out as much as her very round belly permitted her to. "I think it's time for me to retire. I can hardly keep my eyes open any longer." She looked towards the corridor where Vern's room was. "How long has he been in there? He hasn't even eaten anything! That is unheard of!"

"More than six hours," Enric said. Eryn could hear that he, too, was slightly worried.

Orrin stood and pulled his companion to her feet. "When I went in there about three hours ago, his room was a muddle of paint and paper and he just grunted something at me I didn't understand. It did not sound human."

"Paint?" Eryn frowned. "I didn't know that he painted?"

"The artists made him try it and thus he went and bought supplies," his father explained.

Their heads turned as one when they heard a shuffling from Vern's room and little later they looked at an exhausted, paint-smeared, tousle-haired creature that resembled something from a child's nightmare.

"Is there some food left?" he croaked.

"I think it is trying to communicate," Eryn whispered. "That almost sounded like actual words!"

Vern's bleary gaze focussed on her and he shook his head slightly. "Idiot," he murmured.

"Now I recognise him," she grinned. "Of course there is food left. If you don't eat with us, there are usually enough leftovers to feed a medium-sized family. It's in the kitchen, large bowl."

He nodded and trotted with new-found vigour towards the place that held the promise of nourishment.

"Should we go and...?" Junar ventured.

"We really shouldn't..." Eryn grimaced.

"And we won't," Orrin cut in sharply. "Though..."

Enric rolled his eyes and a moment later a barrier shimmered in the doorway to the corridor that lead to Vern's room.

"Spoilsport," Eryn grumbled.

Vern returned with the large bowl in his arm. He had obviously not bothered with any cutlery and ate directly with fingers from the serving bowl. He blinked when he spotted the shield that barred the way to his room.

"What is going on here?"

"I was valiantly holding back that horde that was about to storm your room to see the piece you have been working on these last few hours and that you were about to show to us *before* you sat down to stuff yourself," Enric explained with a smile that was not exactly friendly.

Vern swallowed the bite he still had in his mouth and put down the large bowl on the table with a heavy sigh, giving it a last longing look before he moved back to where he had just spent several hours. The shield flickered away a moment before his forehead would have touched it.

"At least we wouldn't have stopped the poor boy from eating," Junar jibed.

"No, you would have barged into an adolescent boy's room without permission or giving notice. A dangerous thing to do, you know. But if you don't mind my words, you will find out about that soon enough," Enric retorted.

They waited impatiently for Vern to reappear and looked expectantly at the canvas he held before him with its back to his audience.

"Well?" Orrin prompted him.

"If I show it to you, will you let me eat in peace?" the boy pleaded.

"Yes," they promised in unison.

Vern then turned towards a convenient wall, leaned the picture against it and all but bolted towards the bowl on the table, hugging it close to him as if afraid that somebody would make another attempt to separate him from his delayed dinner.

Eryn blinked and slowly walked closer to the picture. It was... colourful. That was the first impression. Unusually so, considering that his drawings had mostly been black or shades of grey in the past with only occasional spots of colour, such as his illustrations for the herb gatherers' book.

The longer she looked at it, the clearer the structure, the logic behind it, became. What looked like a countless assortment of different sized branches and twigs radiated in all directions from the centre of the picture.

"What is this?" Junar whispered in awe.

"The system of blood vessels in the human body," Eryn said quietly.

"Really?" the seamstress asked, surprised. "That's what they look like? A bit more colourful than I would have imagined."

"No," Eryn objected, "not exactly like that, this is more like a..." She broke off, lacking the words.

"A stylised depiction," Vern's voice sounded from the cushions. His words were hardly comprehensible due to his stuffed mouth.

"Yes, that," Eryn nodded. "He's captured the nature of the thing without adhering to every little detail, turning to into something of his own." She frowned at areas that seemed too organised in their colour distribution to be no more than an artist's ballistic approach to splashing colour on an available background. She turned to the boy. "These are areas of activity, aren't they?"

"I thought you wanted to let me eat!" he complained, but rose from the cushions without putting aside the bowl. He walked over to them.

"This is what you saw when you took Enric's hand, isn't it?" Eryn marvelled, crouching in front of the picture to trace the lines with her fingers without touching the still damp paint. "Activity in the brain, a lot of it the chest and the lower abdomen," she said quietly. "Light activity in the arms... none in the legs. Remarkable." She got up again and looked at Vern with a reverent expression. "You know, my lad, that you are very likely the only person in this or indeed our own country who could have created a piece like that? It is incredible!"

"I don't pretend to understand everything I can see, but this is clearly a work of immense skill and perception," Enric chimed in.

"It's beautiful," Junar nodded, wiping a tear away. "You are so talented!"

Orrin merely nodded. He wasn't the type to offer praise when it would just have consisted in repeating what others had stated already.

"What are you going to do with it?" Eryn asked.

"I will take it to Elwoi and throw it at his feet. Then I will probably set it on fire. I don't know," Vern shrugged before shoving another load into his mouth.

Four dismayed faces stared at him.

"What?" he exclaimed with a full mouth.

"You will do no such thing, you twit!" Eryn said sharply. "You may show it to him, then you should bring it back here!"

"But that would be a grand gesture!" he protested.

"Find another one!" She shook her head and sent him a glare. "Set it on fire! I must be dreaming!" she muttered under her breath, disgusted by such an outrageous idea. "You just lost all rights of ownership to this creation. It is *mine* now, and if you let any harm come to it I am going to skin you alive," she threatened.

"Did you just steal my painting?" Vern enquired, frowning.

"You were about to *burn* it! So, yes! You may borrow it, though, to show it to that snotty artist with his limited view of the world," she added graciously.

"That's how quickly one is dispossessed around here," the boy murmured, but didn't object any further.

"What do you care? It's not like you wanted to keep it. I do. When are you planning to see that man? I am coming with you, just to see the look on his face," Eryn announced.

"Tomorrow afternoon, after my lectures at the clinic."

"Splendid. You can pick me up after my shift and we will go to him together. Don't forget to bring the painting along with you in the morning. I expect we will be able to leave it either in my treatment room or your classroom for a few hours without anything befalling it." She rubbed her hands and walked off towards her own bedroom. "Bloody artists," they heard her intoning.

Vern swallowed his current mouthful, then turned towards Enric.

"About that afternoon..." he started, his face an apologetic scowl.

"What about it?" Enric enquired mildly.

"My behaviour might have appeared a little less appropriate than might have been customary."

"You are forgiven. Consider the confiscation of your painting by my companion sufficient compensation for making me experience your artistic short fuse."

Vern nodded, clearly relieved and returned to once again sit down on the cushions and finally eat in peace.

* * *

Eryn flinched when one corner of the canvas scraped a wall as Vern carelessly turned from his corridor into the main room.

"Give me that, you barbarian!" she snarled and snatched the painting out of his hands, meticulously examining the part that had made contact with the wall and released her breath with relief when no damage was visible. "I will carry that. You are not treating my property with the respect it deserves."

"Yes, right," the boy sighed and rolled his eyes. "Are you ready? I am due at the clinic in less than half an hour."

"So am I," she nodded and skipped down the stairs to the entrance door.

They walked along the bright, sunny streets, watching the goings on of people strolling purposefully towards their workplaces, servants doing the shopping for their employers and a few lucky ones that had time and leisure to sit outside under a teahouse tent.

When they entered the clinic, Dikea, a healer for urgent treatment whom Eryn had first met when Valrad introduced her during her first stay in Takhan, was about to hurry past them, but stopped when she caught sight of them.

"Good morning, the two of you. What do you have here? A little something to make our place here seem a bit friendlier?"

She stepped in front of Eryn and motioned for her to turn the canvas around so she could have a look at the picture. Eryn obeyed and grinned at the gasp the sight provoked.

"Incredible!" Dikea whispered and looked up at Vern. "You created that?"

Vern just nodded.

"This is... the blood system of the human body!" she exclaimed. "What are the orange and yellow areas? They signify something, I am sure, do they not?"

"Activity level when the body is subjected to the emotion of love," Vern explained in a low voice directed to his shirt front as if embarrassed.

"How remarkable!"

"You'd better get rid of that acquisitive look in your eyes. It's *mine*," Eryn pointed out.

"You bought it? Damn!"

"No, I dispossessed him. Much cheaper," she grinned.

"Can I buy it from you?" Dikea whispered, her eyes never leaving the painting.

"No chance whatsoever," Eryn shook her head.

"Belnar, Urbel!" Dikea then shouted, and a few moments later two unnerved-looking male healers stuck their heads out of their treatment rooms.

"I already said I do not like it when you... what is that?" the first one, a man in his late thirties, started to complain until his eyes fell on the canvas. The rest of his body followed his head out into the corridor and he came closer with narrowed eyes.

"Intriguing," he said slowly.

The second healer, a man of Eryn's age, approached as well, both eyebrows lifted in wonderment.

"It really is," he agreed and nodded. He then looked at Vern. "Are you selling it?"

"No," Eryn answered. "It's mine."

"Will *you* sell it, then?" he repeated his question to Eryn.

"No. It is going to continue being mine."

"You use that word an awful lot," Vern snorted. "Mine, mine, mine. Like a child defending her plaything!"

"Well, as other children keep gathering and trying to snatch it away from me, I feel I need to make a point," she shrugged. "Out of my way now - I am due for my shift in a few minutes, and I dare say that the excuse that I was waylaid by you lot will not quite cut it." She pushed through and walked quickly towards the treatment room

Valrad usually used, turning the picture towards her so that it was protected from curious looks and people wouldn't stop her on her way.

"Meet me in the canteen after your lectures," she called to Vern over her shoulder.

Valrad turned away from the cupboard he was restocking and greeted her. Their interaction had not exactly become any warmer since he had pressed her to attend that first appointment with Iklan only two days ago. Eryn had started a policy of only speaking to him when absolutely necessary while before she had at least adhered to basic rules of politeness.

Without acknowledging him, she propped the painting against a cupboard and went to Valrad's desk to pick up the patient file on top of the heap to one side, opening it and reading through the last few treatments this person had received at the clinic.

Valrad had in the meantime picked up the painting and turned it around so he could look at it. She heard him sucking in a surprised breath.

"Incredible! I do not really have to ask who painted this," he said and stared at the picture. His expression became fascinated as his eyes traced numerous lines branching out from the depiction of a heart in the centre of the humanoid maze of intertwining lines. After about three minutes of thorough scrutiny, he looked up at Eryn. "Why do you have it with you? If he wants to sell it, I am willing to offer him a very good price for this. Preferably before too many of my colleagues have had a look at it."

She ignored him and went to open the door to indicate to the first patient that he could come in.

"Really, Eryn?" her father sighed. "How long do you want to go on like this? You cannot ignore me forever."

No, she thought, and smiled when a young woman in her mid-twenties with a swollen belly came in, but she could try to.

*　*　*

After three hours Valrad eased himself away from the wall he had been leaning against with folded arms. "This is enough. We cannot go on like this. We will not get any work done this way. After every patient there is at least one healer waiting at our door wanting to have a look at that picture and make an offer to buy it. I will get on with healing while you take it outside so they can gape at it as much as they wish. Otherwise we will never get through with this heap." He patted the stack of patient files that had indeed not shrunk very much since they had started in the morning. They lost several minutes after every patient when another healer slipped in to take a look at the masterpiece everybody kept talking about.

Eryn wordlessly got up from her chair and walked over to the painting to pick it up and do as she had been told.

191

"Eryn?"

She stopped dead. Unfortunately she could not afford to ignore his instructions as he was still her superior. She waited with her back to him.

"We will have lunch together at the canteen. Meet me there."

She nodded once curtly to indicate that she had understood the command and then left the treatment room, hearing his troubled sigh. When she stepped out into the corridor, she blinked. At least ten healers were leaning against the wall, all turning in her direction as she appeared outside, their eyes immediately dropping to the canvas in her hands.

"What is going on here? A party nobody told me about?" she asked testily.

"We are here to see if Dikea has exaggerated," one healer said and nodded at the picture.

"Seriously? Don't you have any work to be getting on with?" she huffed.

"I have more than enough work to do," a woman in her late fifties snapped and nodded at her. "Now turn that around so that I can go back to it again."

Eryn looked around the corridor and shook her head. "Not here. You are blocking the patients' way to and from the treatment rooms." She determinedly moved forwards until she had reached the room where the patient files were stored and opened the door. That looked roomy enough, she decided, and walked in to prop the painting against a shelf filled with files before stepping back again to let the healers gaze at it.

She smiled when she heard several low whistles, impressed comments and amazed exclamations. It seemed Vern's angry showpiece had made quite an impression on the local healing world.

"Dikea said it is yours," one healer turned towards Eryn. "Is that true?"

"It is, yes," she confirmed, waiting for the inevitable offer that would undoubtedly be made any moment.

And surely enough, it came hardly three seconds later. "One hundred gold slips for it."

"One hundred and twenty," another voice closer to the door piped in.

"Two hundred!" another added.

Eryn, speaking calmly but firmly, lifted both arms. "Stop right there, I am not going to sell it!"

"Three hundred!"

"Not even for a *thousand* gold slips! Now give up and go back to your work!" she implored them. Three hundred gold slips! Vern's eyes would probably fall out if he heard about that. And he had wanted to burn the painting! So much for his usual common sense.

"Where is the boy presently, by the way?" one healer asked nonchalantly.

Eryn shook her head. They would surely not storm the teaching room to beleaguer him, would they? But then they had offered up to three hundred gold slips for a painting of his.

"He is attending the lectures the second-year healer trainees are having," she told them, hoping that this would finally help her get rid of them. She would just leave dealing with them to Vern. He was the reason they were acting like this, after all. She pushed aside the thought that maybe the fact that she had suggested bringing the painting here so that they wouldn't have to return to the Aren residence later to pick it up had also had something to do with that.

Once they had all left, she closed the door, and was about to lean against it when it opened again almost immediately followed by another three healers who insisted on taking a look at what was currently the premier conversation topic in the building.

Eryn stifled a groan and stepped aside, sitting down on the floor and preparing herself to refuse the next offers that would be given.

*   *   *

Vern lifted his arm and waved to her when he saw her come in the canteen. He was seated at a table with Valrad. How convenient, considering that the latter had ordered her to have lunch with him today.

Almost all eyes in the large room immediately focussed on the canvas in her hands and she flashed hostile looks at the healers, daring them to annoy her with their unwanted offers while she was wanting nothing more than a quiet and peaceful meal. Well, as quiet a meal with Vern or as peaceful a meal with Valrad could be.

She sat down next to Vern, lodging the painting against the cushions between her and Valrad, employing it as a handy barrier.

"You won't believe what happened today!" the boy burst out and pushed the food they had already ordered for Eryn towards her.

"Let me guess," she smiled. "A steady stream of healers kept interrupting your lecture to pester you about this painting of yours. Am I right?"

"How do you know that?" he asked in annoyance, clearly peeved about not being able to puzzle her.

"Because that's where I sent them after they kept getting on my nerves. Imagine - they kept offering me unimaginable amounts of money for it!" she laughed. "One went up to three hundred gold slips – can you believe that?"

Vern giggled. "If you call that unimaginable, wait until you hear what they offered me!"

She raised both brows. "More than three hundred?"

"They went up to five hundred!" he whispered and watched with pleasure when her eyes widened. "And that even though I kept telling them that it was no longer in my possession! And you know what is most hilarious? That last offer came from the Head of the clinic – he

193

was called to stop the healers from constantly interrupting the lecture, but used the chance to bid for the picture himself! How unbelievable is that?"

"Utterly!" she exclaimed. "Whatever the artists may think about you, the healers clearly are in thrall to your talent, dear lad."

Vern sighed. "Yes. It seems it is quite clear which crowd I will be sticking with."

"Don't be sad to get rid of those artists, Vern," she said and leaned towards him to press her lips to his forehead comfortingly. "If they don't appreciate you, they don't deserve any better. And the way it looks right now you might get rich and famous enough by selling your work to the healers. What a stroke of luck that most seem to be too rich for their own good and willing to pay extravagant prices, eh?"

That reminded him of something else. "When I told them that this painting was not for sale, they starting bidding on whatever I would do next! Can you imagine a thing like that? Several of them were willing to pay in advance – for something I haven't even painted yet!"

"It seems that you have managed very accurately to meet the preferences of a specific group of people with your style of artistically interpreting the human body," Valrad smiled. "Non-healers might still be intrigued by what they see, but healers can in addition to that also understand it intellectually. I have to admit that I would be willing to pay handsomely for this picture as well. Whatever induced you to create it?"

Vern looked at him sheepishly. "Anger and defiance, I seem to remember."

"That is not entirely unexpected," the healer nodded understandingly. "Works radiating great energy almost always require energy to create them. Energy, that emotions can provide. Though the nature of the picture is not necessarily one I would have associated with *those* emotions. It seems to depict something entirely different, if I am not very much mistaken?"

The boy nodded. "It is what I saw in Enric's body when I asked him to think of Eryn."

"Love, then," Valrad nodded and smiled at Eryn. "I can see why you do not want to part with it. One could call it a visual proof of his deep affection for you."

She blinked and looked away. This was a delicately delightful way of phrasing it, and she was irritated that he was the one to find such appealing words for it. She didn't want to be touched by anything that he said.

"Why did you bring the picture here?" he then asked the boy, obviously well aware that Eryn was unlikely to answer any question addressed to her.

"I want to show it to Elwoi and tell him that my kind of art is not what *he* thinks I need to do. I wanted to throw the painting at his feet and set fire to it, but Eryn says I'm not allowed," he ended with an exasperated snort.

"Set it on fire?" Valrad's expression showed pure horror and he stared first at the boy, then at the canvas next to him. "Of course you cannot! It would be a despicable act!" he then exclaimed, his eyes wide at the thought of destroying a work like that. "She is absolutely right in not permitting you!" He leaned back, shaking his head, muttering, "Setting it on fire – incredible!" Then he leaned forward again. "Are you going to paint another one in the near future? Have you accepted any of the advance bids on your future work yet?"

"No, I couldn't do that," Vern protested. "I mean, I don't even know if I will ever again be able to paint something like that! As I told you, it was the result of anger and defiance. What if these emotions never again occur?"

Eryn snorted. "You are almost seventeen, I can honestly tell you that there will be more than one occasion for you to be really, really angry."

"What if next time my anger doesn't trigger a particular urge to *paint* anything, but so do nothing more than smash things against walls?" he argued.

"Then you will find a way to sell that to those healers as another masterpiece," she grinned broadly.

"Very amusing," Vern growled. "I am having a serious creative crisis, and you are poking fun at me! That is the reason why having artists around to talk about these things would have been good – they know what I am going through and can tell me what to do."

"Can't you just remain friends with one or two of them instead of subjecting yourself to this Elwoi character?"

Valrad shook his head. "That is not a practicable approach, I am afraid. Elwoi commands immense authority and would impose sanctions on any artist who supported or even merely kept loose contact with somebody he did not approve of."

Eryn swallowed her last mouthful and set her empty bowl aside. "I am so sorry, my lad. What a nuisance that this is obviously not mainly about living your gifts, but subordinating yourself to somebody who thinks he can tell you what standards you need to hold to instead of being yourself. You know, they think they are so much more advanced here compared to us, but in some areas I am really wondering."

That made him smile. "Well, we are also subordinated to others when it comes to healing here."

"But that is in order to maintain quality standards and protect life and health, not to cater to the craving for power of one single person," she objected and flashed Valrad a quick critical look. "Well, in most cases."

Her father lifted an eyebrow at her. "You are not suggesting that I am misusing my influence here in any way, are you?"

Eryn raised her chin and was about to give him an answer he would not at all appreciate, but Vern quickly got to his feet and pulled her up with him.

"Of course she wouldn't *dream* of saying such a disrespectful thing as that," he assured the high-ranking healer. Clutching the painting with his free hand, he all but dragged her after him. "I am afraid we really need to leave now. There are things we need to take care of, like turning a certain influential artist into a mortal enemy and things like that. Goodbye, Valrad."

"Goodbye, children," the healer said and watched the two of them leaving, Eryn whispering sharp words at Vern.

"I sometimes feel like *I* am the adult of the two of us, you know," Vern complained once they had left the building. "You have been freezing people out lately, with the few occasions when you decide to be yourself happening in the most unsuitable situations possible. What would you have gained by opposing him in a large room full of his colleagues, I ask you?"

She remained silent, knowing fully well that he was completely and utterly right. That didn't make it any better.

"No smart riposte to that?" Vern snapped.

"No," she grumbled. "Just that this doesn't happen when *you* are not around."

"So it's *my* fault now?" he cried out indignantly.

"I didn't say that, did I?"

"Funny, that's exactly what it sounded like to *me*."

"Stop harassing me, and hand me that picture before you smash it against another inconvenient wall or decide to burn it!"

He rolled his eyes, but pressed the canvas into her hands before starting to walk towards the artists' academy.

"Do you even know if he will be there at this time of day?"

"Yes, I am fairly confident. He usually delights his underlings with his wisdom this time of day."

"Then we are interrupting a lecture, speech or something of that kind?" she murmured. "Brilliant. Why attack him privately if we can do it in front of a lot of people?"

"That is a strong thing to say for you," Vern huffed. "Which of us constantly provokes Lord Tyront in front of the Magic Council, I ask?"

"I'll have you know that I also provoke him when we are *not* in a Council meeting!"

"That is hardly the point, is it?"

"Save your anger for the artists, don't waste it all on me," she sighed.

"There is enough here for all of you, don't you worry," he snapped and walked on more briskly, forcing Eryn to run a few steps to catch up with him.

"Don't exhaust the expectant lady," she instructed.

"In your case we need a rule that protects *me* from being exhausted by you," he sighed, but slowed down again so she didn't have to struggle.

They continued in silence for a while, Eryn looking around curiously. She had not really taken in this part of the city before. It looked older, but not because it was dilapidated or poorly maintained, but rather as if people had fought against modernisation in favour of keeping old structures and styles alive.

"How many artists are there?" she then asked.

"Quite a few. But not all of them visual ones. Of those there are painters, sculptors and architects, though the last are considered outsiders, as it were."

"Because they are doing something practical?"

"More or less. They need extra knowledge apart from the characteristics of their materials, which means they need to do a lot of calculations and stuff like that, which makes them more craftspeople then artists."

"What other artists are there? You said *visual* artists. What does the rest do? Make music?"

"There is that, yes. And the literary arts, of course."

"Such as writing poems, I suppose?"

"Not only, but also, yes. Poems, song lyrics, beautifully phrased speeches for special occasions, stories and so on," he explained.

She nodded. "I remember that I was told about people who write commitment oaths for money, but that this is frowned upon. I guess I know now which people you might turn to for that. This is it?" she asked when they stopped in front of a richly ornamented building with numerous columns, niches, colours and sculptures integrated into the façade. "I does kind of scream *artist*, I must say."

He just nodded and his expression became grim when he marched on towards the middle one of three large entrance portals.

"Three? Seriously?" Eryn murmured and followed him in.

Vern had obviously been here a few times already, because he didn't need any time for orientation, but seemed to know exactly where he wanted to go. Two flights of stairs and three corridors later they stood in front of another large door as big as the entrance portals. The artists clearly liked big and imposing structures.

Vern took a deep breath, then pushed open the double doors without knocking. Eryn wondered briefly if this would be considered as impolite here as it would be at home, but one glimpse of the shocked faces of the audience comprising about fifty people gave her a good idea that it was. Definitely.

She saw a tall thin man, with a long dark beard that was showing some white, clad in dark red clothes which looked much too warm for this climate on a platform. Elwoi, very probably.

When he had recovered from the jarring surprise of having been interrupted so rudely, his eyes narrowed and he started talking with a high-pitched voice with an expression like he had just bitten into a sour fruit, "Young Vern, I do not know how things are in that place where you are from, but in these parts..."

"Forgive me my rude behaviour, Elwoi," Vern sneered, "but as you have never tired of pointing out to me the barbaric nature of my

197

home country in the past, this can hardly come as much of a surprise for you, can it?"

"If this is the way how you intend to reciprocate our generous readiness to open our doors for you, you may just as well turn around and..."

"Don't worry about that," Vern interrupted him once again, adding a little magic to his voice to make it sound more impressive. "After today I have no intention ever again to defile your sacred halls with my presence."

Eryn noted how the audience's gaze snapped from one speaker to the other in rapt attention. Seeing their mighty chief artist being goaded this way by an adolescent boy was obviously not an everyday occurrence.

"I have come here to inform you that I consider your demand to decide between healing and art inappropriate, and that I have no intention of letting you force me into anything of the sort. The only thing you may be able to prevent is my having any more contact with that elite institution of yours, but that's all. You can't stop me from being an artist any more than you can keep me from healing."

He turned towards Eryn and stretched out his hand for her to give him his painting. She did so, though somewhat reluctantly. She still didn't trust him completely that he would leave it intact. His fingers closed around the edges and he lifted it high over his head for all of them to see.

"This is what comes out of me when I paint *Love*!" he shouted. "It is a combination of what I see and know, and I have no intention of apologising for it or changing my way of expressing myself to make you feel that you have succeeded in pressing me into one of your moulds! If there is the choice between being with the healers or being with you, then there is no real choice! The healers appreciate my art, they ask me for illustrations, want to work with me *because of* it and not *despite* it! You want me to give up what is as much a part of me as my art is, and you have no right to demand that! You simply don't! And do you know what? The healers offered me as much as five hundred golden slips for this painting here! I have no idea how much you usually ask for your work, but for me this is a lot of gold and shows me that I am appreciated by them." He let his arms with the painting sink, seeming oddly small now that he had rid himself of all the angry words, as if they had made him seem more imposing. "I bid goodbye to you. May you find satisfaction in serving yourself instead of the arts and getting rid of those who refuse."

With this he turned and walked out again, leaving the large hall in utter silence. Only when they had passed the huge portal, did Elwoi seem to have found his voice again.

"You will not storm in here and..."

Vern didn't even slow down as he pushed the painting into Eryn's hands and lifted both arms, without turning, and by using magic closed the heavy door with a massive thud.

She followed him out into the open in silence, not sure whether he wanted to talk right now. They stopped in front of the building, and they boy turned to her, his expression unsure.

"What did you think of that?"

She blinked, then grinned broadly. "I think that was absolutely, totally and infinitely brilliant!" She laughed. "Did you see their faces? And especially the grand master's? First it was white as snow, then it turned scarlet!"

Now Vern, too, was giggling. "I thought for a moment that his eyes would fall out the way they were bulging."

"Yes," Eryn nodded emphatically, "like a fish!"

"And now?" the boy asked. "I don't want to return home. Let's do something!"

"How much money do you have with you, my lad?"

"Three gold slips," he replied.

"Splendid. That means we can celebrate properly in a teahouse. You will have something grownup to drink while I should stick to something that doesn't harm my passenger," she grinned and rubbed her belly.

CHAPTER 14

Unexpected Consequences

Eryn nodded to Iklan's assistant with a dour expression and was told to go right in. The second of her meetings with him, today she had arrived not a minute earlier than absolutely necessary. It had been another tedious day of working with Valrad, avoiding any exchange that was not essential for their work. But at least the memory of Vern's dealings with Elwoi the day before and their subsequent three hours at the teahouse had brightened her up.

"Good afternoon, Eryn," the healer greeted her jovially as she entered his office. She walked over to his comfortable seating arrangement. "What can I offer you to drink?"

"Whatever you are having," she answered and little later accepted a tall glass of dark yellow juice.

"How are you today?" he asked once they were both seated.

"Very good. Exceptionally good actually," she smiled enthusiastically. "I was thinking a lot about what you told me last time. So many things have become clearer. I have a clear path in front of me that will help me to leave the issues with my family behind me finally. I know now what I must do."

Iklan looked at her in surprise. "Do you now? I would be very interested in hearing about this path if you would care to tell me."

She nodded. "Of course. It is fairly simple, and yet realising it was a revelation! I need to open up more, stop being frosty towards those people who love me. And I have to talk to Valrad, clear up this whole knot of misunderstanding, listen to what he has to say, tell him how I feel about all of it."

"That is quite impressive progress you have made in only a few days, I must admit," the healer smiled encouragingly. "It is so very considerable and unusual after only one appointment that I cannot help but wonder if it is not a little too good to be true, in fact. You would not mind repeating what you just told me under the influence of a lie filter, would you? Just to maintain my professional integrity when I go to your father and tell him that you are not in need of my counselling any longer, you see."

Eryn gave him a look of being hurt. "So little trust in me, Iklan? Yet you are asking me to entrust you with my most personal secrets and worries. Is trust not something that needs to play in both directions? Where is *your* trust in *me*, I ask you?"

He gave her a gentle smile. "Nice try, Eryn, but you are not the first... client wanting to convince me prematurely that my services are no longer required. Let me ask you again now: How are you doing?"

"I am fine, thank you. And yourself? How is the talking treatment business going? You do look a bit tired, you know."

"Well, thank you for your enquiry, but we are not here to talk about *me*." He took a sip from his glass before he continued, "I remember your telling me that you have no intention of talking to me about Valrad, Malriel or your child. I was wondering if you would be willing to talk about Ram'an instead."

No, no, no! She, too, picked up her glass to gain a little time to remind herself to be calm, cool and collected.

"Ram'an. Head of House Arbil, you mean?"

"The very same," Iklan smiled indulgently. "So?"

"Sure, no problem there. Let's talk about him. I hear he is working hard to get his House back into the game. Did you know that he is quite an able climber?"

"I was not referring to gossip when I suggested this topic," the healer sighed. "I want you to tell me how you are getting along with him."

"Very well indeed, considering our troubles in the past. We can meet and converse like civilised people. An impressive accomplishment that speaks of great maturity on either side, if you ask me. And he and Enric also get along well. Enric does quite a lot of business with his House, both as a representative of House Aren and in his own capacity as a business man."

"Another attempt at encouraging you to speak of your feelings well dodged," he sighed. "Moving on to your companion's dealings with him was an especially elegant strategy to push the focus away from yourself. But let me tell you that it is common knowledge that matters between you and Ram'an are not quite as uncomplicated as you would have me believe. He is seen inviting you to meals and tea repeatedly, but you keep refusing him with a smile."

"Common knowledge? As in *gossip*? Iklan, I am shocked!" she cried out in gleeful indignation. "I thought you were averse to unreliable sources of information like that!"

He rubbed his face and sighed. "You are determined to make this especially difficult for me, are you not? But let me assure you that you cannot make me give up this way. This will serve to prolong the time we spend together, nothing more." He smiled at her dismayed expression at that. "Have I just found some way to urge you cooperate, Eryn? By pointing out that this will free you from having to come to me sooner?"

She shrugged. "Oh, but why? This is a very appealing room, with comfortable seating, and you serve very good juice. Why would I want to cease coming here for a nice little chat every now and then?" she said lightly.

"As you wish. We may as well devote the entire length of time you intend to spend in Takhan to this. I am sure your father will not mind. Ah yes," he smiled broadly. "There was that flinch again. Tell me, dear, why does my calling him your *father* make you react like this?"

"Because it may just as well be true as not," she replied and folded her arms.

"How may I understand that? That you have chosen not to accept him as such?"

"Rather that I am convinced that this might just as well have been a mistake. Pe'tala could be wrong, a minor error which is understandable. She is human, and humans make mistakes, after all," she added generously.

"Do they now?" Iklan remarked mildly. "I wonder how your sister would react to a statement like that. How very interesting. When I call her your *sister*, you do not show any physical reaction, even though it is a result of the same circumstances that make Valrad your father. You see? You flinched again. You try to suppress it, but there are small signals if one knows what to look for and waits for them."

"Stop observing me like that! I don't like it," she rasped.

"A matter of habit, I am afraid. And a very useful one in my profession, as you might imagine. Sometimes people's bodies communicate so much more honestly than their voices, you see. But let us return to what you were saying. You think Valrad being recognised as your natural father might have been a misconception?"

"Yes. I was told in my childhood more often than once how much I resemble my father in intelligence, and that I have his nose. Valrad's nose looks completely different."

Iklan leaned back and looked at her for several moments. "You are trying to build your own reality here to escape from one you are not willing to accept. This is one way of dealing with pain - refusing to believe that the circumstances that caused it do not really exist. Unfortunately, it is not a healthy way to go through life. If you look at this carefully without pushing away the things you do not want to see, you will see that from a healing point of view your arguments are not valid. Pe'tala might be human, but she is an exceptional healer, especially considering her youth. This was her way of dealing with the troubles she had when she was younger, striving for excellence to prove something to herself and the people around her. As for your resemblance to Ved'al, intelligence is to a certain degree determined by the way we are raised, namely if growth and development are permitted and promoted, not merely a matter of inheritance. As for your nose, you are surely aware that the laws of inheritance do not apply only to the generation immediately preceding, are you not?"

"I don't want to hear this," she said curtly and looked out the window.

"Of course not. My words are a threat to that cage of ignored facts and wishful thinking you have built around yourself. You are fleeing from the truth instead of dealing with it. I remember your companion's commitment oath. He mentioned something about your propensity for fleeing, did he not?"

"That was something completely different!" she protested.

"Was it?" he smiled. "If you say so, my dear Eryn."

"Don't patronise me!" she snapped back.

Iklan sighed heavily. "It is true what they say, you know. Healers truly are the worst patients there are."

"Firstly, I remember we agreed on my not being your *patient*, and secondly I find that your pointing out to me that I am difficult is hardly professional, is it?"

"You are right of course. *Client*, not patient, in your case. As regards your second objection, I do not see that our relationship fits the usual characteristics. You *want* to be difficult, and I am merely giving you feedback that you are succeeding in that. That is hardly an insult to you, but a compliment, is it not?"

It was, she had to admit. She was frustrated by being made to come here as a condition for being allowed to continue working here, and she didn't see why she should be the only one to suffer for it.

"Tell me what it feels like for you when you hear Valrad being referred to as your father," he returned to the topic at hand.

She groaned. "Can we return to talking about Ram'an? I think I am willing to now."

Iklan smiled broadly. "By all means. Whatever you wish."

* * *

Eryn stepped outside the clinic and sighed, blinking against the sunlight.

"Hey there," Vern's voice came from behind her where he was leaning against the wall in the shade. "Are you done for today?"

"Hello, my lad. Why are you still here? Didn't you finish about two hours ago?"

He shrugged. "I did, yes, but I was waylaid by several healers who were eager to talk to me about my painting. I was hiding behind doors and ducking into alcoves finally to be able to make it out of here in the end. I knew that your chat with Iklan had to end around now, so I decided to wait for you. There is something I wanted to ask you."

"Go on, then."

"I have noticed people whispering and murmuring a lot, and when I came closer, they stopped immediately. Do you know what's going on? What's more, they kept giving me funny looks."

Eryn nodded slowly. "I know what you mean. A few of the healers gave me strange smiles and several of the patients stared at me in a knowing way; I had the impression that they wanted to say something, but didn't dare."

"Pity you are not on speaking terms with Valrad," the boy sighed. "He might have been able to tell you what was going on. Though you could have asked Iklan, couldn't you?"

She sighed. Yes, that she could have indeed. But she was in no mood to return to him to do so.

"Let's go home. I feel the need for a cold bath and something sweet to eat - preferably a bread bun. Or two."

Vern nodded and set in motion towards the Aren residence.

"You see?" he whispered. "People are looking at us out here, too!"

She looked around and saw that he was right. Curious glances followed them, some seemed disparaging, others approving. What was going on here? This was surely not some delayed reaction to his hair colour, was it? Vern was not the first nor the only blond visitor from the Kingdom around, and they were surely used to seeing Kilan around by now.

They both breathed a sigh of relief when they reached the residence, escaping into the cool, shadowy building and closing the door behind them quickly to beat the heat. They wiped the sweat off their faces and necks with cool, damp towels and then climbed the stairs up into the main room.

They both blinked in surprise when they saw Enric sitting on the cushions, a book on his lap. At this time of day he was usually locked up in his study instead of enjoying a leisurely early afternoon with a book.

"The healers are home, good," he smiled. "Sit with me for a while, if you would."

His voice sounded serious, despite the friendly face.

"Are we in trouble or something?" Eryn asked suspiciously, her words mirroring the concern on Vern's face.

"Not from my side, no," he said slowly.

Both of them exchanged a wary look and then walked over to him, taking a seat next to each other facing him.

Enric raised one eyebrow at them. "I am not about to chastise you like naughty children, so there is no need to keep maximum distance to me. Come here, my love, and let me greet you at least." He lifted a hand to pull her next to him, which she cautiously took.

He kissed her lightly on the lips, long enough to show her his appreciation at having her close, but brief enough to avoid making Vern feel awkward.

"I don't know if you are aware, but your stand against Elwoi at the artists' academy yesterday has made quite an impression on the local art world," Enric said to the boy.

"What?" Vern asked dumbfounded, blinking.

"I take that as meaning you weren't," Enric commented crisply.

"What kind of impression? Good or bad?" Eryn asked curiously.

"That depends on who you are talking to, I would say. It seems they have all but split into two camps: those for Elwoi and those against him. It seems our young friend here has inadvertently kindled an uprising."

"Me?" Vern exclaimed horrified. "But... but I just told him that I don't want to deal with his academy any longer! I never asked anybody to fight or oppose him! Honestly!"

Eryn nodded. "He is right; he wasn't trying to start a rebellion or anything. I was there. He just showed them the picture and proclaimed that he was over and done with them, that he would rather stick with the healers than that narrow-minded mob."

"I am not saying that this is what he intended, mind you," Enric explained calmly, "But it seems like there has been significant resentment simmering under the surface of this honourable institution for a while, and Vern's scene yesterday obviously triggered a hefty reaction. From what I heard, several artists - especially younger ones that feel that they had to discard ideas and techniques that were not to Elwoi's liking - have decided to leave the academy and found their own institution."

"Why?" Vern shook his head, his eyes wide. "I mean, I don't understand all this!"

"Your reputation preceded you here, Vern," Enric elaborated. "Your name was already well known here when we first came, thanks to the book you gave to Ram'an. Both the circle of healers and artists had seen your work and were looking forward to seeing more of it. Your talent was undisputed. The healers see the great benefit an artistic healer presents to them through the advantage accurate and skilful illustrations by somebody who actually *understands* what they are drawing. You know what to look for, what to focus on. The combination of magician, healer and artist is a sensation for them, as you have no doubt experienced already. The artists, however, face the dilemma of having to include what they see as a *craftsperson* into their elite circle of people who like to break loose from the coarse reality you are intertwined with so tightly."

"Why did they invite me, then?" the boy complained.

"Because of your talent. They did not have much choice. Rejecting you at the outset would have looked very bad, both to the artists themselves, who mostly like to think that talent is what really matters, and to the outside world. They would have had a lot of explaining to do without having any actual reasons that are socially acceptable. The ambition merely to preserve a status for selfish reasons and thus reject new ideas and innovation is frowned upon here in general, and this would have been their only argument." Then Enric smiled and shook his head. "The fact that the healers were incredibly excited about the picture you brought to the clinic yesterday did not exactly help smooth the waves, either. The story that you were offered five hundred gold slips for it spread like wildfire. This is vastly more than an artist usually gets for a painting here, and many artists have started wondering if being associated with Elwoi isn't more of a burden than an advantage. And finally but no less importantly many of them have come to admire you personally and objected to the way you were treated." He smiled when Vern gulped, clearly ill at ease. His face had drained of colour. "Don't worry. This isn't your fault as such. You managed to inspire quite a few people, and not only through your art, but by our brave actions. That is quite an accomplishment for somebody your age, standing firm in his beliefs and being willing to bear untoward consequences that might arise from them."

"How do you know about all this?" Eryn asked in astonishment. "I mean, we were there only yesterday, and you have just analysed the history and politics of the art world based on what Vern did!"

"The artists' academy has quite a few members, my love. Several of them belong to House Aren. In fact, almost all Houses have visual artists among them, so this bit of news has spread wide and fast. People have started questioning if the academy's interests really are promoting the arts as such. Seeing an exceptional artist such as Vern being treated that way suggests otherwise and has caused a lot of non-artists to think."

"What will happen now?" Vern whispered. "I singlehandedly destroyed a place of art! After only one and a half months here! I will probably lay waste to the entire city if I should stay here much longer!"

Enric chuckled. "Hardly. I can't tell you for sure what will happen, but there are a limited number of options. If Elwoi is smart, he will reconsider his approach to restraining artists this way. This would very likely save his position and avoid an open revolt among those who follow him and those who decided to leave the academy. He would lose some of his influence, but from what I can see there is no way around that anyway."

"What if he is not smart?" Vern enquired with a scowl.

"Then he will try to hold on to his reign at all costs, claiming that the principles of art must not be corrupted by those few who never understood the spirit of it and are essentially dispensable anyway," Enric shrugged. "This will very likely lead to either open squabbling, pitched battles or whatever else artists like to do to each other, or in a second academy-like institution being established, constantly challenging the status of the first in the years to come, competing for the most talented artists, the richest collectors and sponsors."

The boy covered his face with his fingers. "I didn't want that, I swear! I have just started a mutiny!" he moaned.

Eryn nodded. "Looks like it, dear lad. Though my gut feeling says that that is not necessarily a bad thing. You couldn't have triggered something like that without the right preconditions being in place already." She remembered a conversation like that she had had with Ram'an several months before, when he had used exactly that reasoning to explain to her why she might have played some role in her father's death, but not been the cause of it. It had helped her back then, and she could see that it made Vern think, too.

"Would you excuse me and Vern for a moment, my love? There is a little business matter I would like to take care of."

She frowned. "Business matter? Between you and *Vern*?"

"Yes." He stood without offering her any further explanation and looked at the boy, who looked equally puzzled but got up from his seat as well. "It will not take long, I promise."

Enric walked towards his study and closed the door after Vern had entered.

"This is about your picture," Enric started. "I have received quite a few messages so far today, most of them from healers imploring me to persuade Eryn to give up the painting and sell it to them."

Vern blinked in surprise. "Really? This is absolutely crackpot, people here are just nuts! At home nobody even looks twice at what I am doing, and here they just won't back off!"

"That rather makes me wonder which people are the crackpots - the ones here who appreciate your work or those at home paying no heed to it," Enric remarked dryly and went to his desk to pick up a small, sturdy-looking wooden chest about as long as his forearm. "Here, this is for you. Careful, it is heavy."

Vern frowned, clearly perplex. "What's in there?"

"Five hundred gold slips in payment for the painting."

Enric quickly grabbed the chest to keep it from falling when all tension drained out of Vern's hands.

"I don't understand... I mean, I gave it to her!"

"No, she *took* it from you; you just didn't care enough to claim it back. But now that we have seen what it is worth on the open market, this is no longer acceptable. This is the price the highest bidder offered," he pointed out and held the chest in one hand while he fished in his pocket with the other, producing a single gold slip. "And this makes five hundred and one. I have officially out-bidden him and thereby purchased your work wholly and correctly."

"You don't have to do this, really!" Vern insisted and took a step backwards to increase the distance between himself and the offending chest.

"I do. And you should work on your attitude towards accepting payment for your art."

"But not from *you*! And not that much!"

Enric shook his head and looked pained. "However is it possible that you managed to negotiate prices and conditions with the apothecaries, my boy? Right now my belief in your business acumen

207

is not exactly unshaken. Now take that chest and get out of here," he ordered sternly. Since being together with Eryn, he thought, he seemed to be doing nothing but pushing money towards people who didn't want it: firstly and repeatedly to his companion, then to Ram'an with the shipload of goods, and now to Vern.

Vern blinked at the tone and obeyed almost automatically, enforcing his arms with a little extra strength and taking the heavy box with him, carrying it through the main room and to his bedroom.

Eryn eyed him with mild curiosity, when Enric returned to sit with her. "I assume that heavy burden Vern was just getting to his room was about - oh, let me see - five hundred and one gold slips?"

He grinned. "You have come to know me quite well, my love. He was resisting me - can you believe that? That must be your influence. Spending time with you must have led the poor boy to believe that money truly is something tainted. I assume nonetheless that you approve of what I did?"

She nodded. "I do, yes. I admit I had a rather queasy feeling after hearing how much they were willing to pay for it, and I had more or less stolen it from him. You salved my conscience, more or less."

"Only more or less?"

"Yes. Now I owe *you* five hundred and one gold slips," she clarified.

"Allow me to present it as a gift to you," he laughed and put an arm around her waist.

She thought for a moment, then nodded. "I feel generous today, so yes, I'll accept that. I permit you the privilege of spending an indecent amount of money for something that serves no other purpose than being looked at."

"I am glad to see that you have discovered the joy of buying nice things."

She sighed. "That is your influence. I am drifting off into a sea of decadence and degeneracy."

Enric threw his head back and let loose a deep and dark laugh. "Excellent! My sinister plan finally worked!"

Eryn looked at him for a few moments, then got up. "Seriously? And *you* are going to raise a child? I shudder at the thought."

"What?" he called after her when she sauntered off into the kitchen, no doubt to snaffle another bread bun.

CHAPTER 15

Politics

"How was your second appointment with Iklan, by the way?" Enric enquired as they sat side by side with their breakfast bowls on the terrace steps, looking out over the lush Aren gardens.

She shrugged and swallowed a piece of fruit. "Tiresome. Again. He wanted me to talk about Ram'an."

"So, did you?"

"Not at first, but then he forced me."

He raised both brows. "He did? How was he able to do that and how long will it take me to learn?"

"Most amusing," she said. "He kept pestering me about Valrad and why I don't like it when people refer to him as my father, until I gave in and accepted talking about Ram'an as the lesser of the evils," she sighed.

"And?"

"And what? You are not asking me to reveal to you the particulars of what is being said in the very confidential healer–client relationship I have with Iklan, are you?"

Enric sucked in a sharp breath and his eyes widened in mock horror. "I wouldn't dream of it! Ever! Unless you feel the urge to share, that is..." he added casually.

"You are nosey," she accused him.

"True," he admitted unashamed.

"I simply told him that I am sick of Ram'an's mood swings, that I find his behaviour unsettling and cannot rely on him to know what he wants. This is why I hold my distance from him. That's it."

"That's it? Really?" he asked mildly. "No regret involved from your side?"

"None," she stated.

"Good for you," Enric nodded, not believing a word of it.

"Exactly. No need to try and make me search through my feelings or some such." She shivered. "I don't think I want to get to know myself as well as he is trying to make me."

"Scary, I know," he grinned. "I know what you are going through."

She narrowed her eyes. "In getting to know yourself or me?"

"I imagine this is one of the questions a man should answer tactfully when talking to an expectant woman, isn't it?"

"Idiot," she growled and rose.

"Wait. I shall walk you to the clinic. There is a Senate meeting today, and we have almost the same route."

"Any particular topic or just the same stuffy procedures?"

"There are two things, actually, that might make things rather interesting. The Senate will discuss the matter of the artists today."

Eryn frowned. "The Senate? Really? Why?"

"Because the artists are supported through public funding to a certain degree. If the academy is about to break apart, that is something to be dealt with."

"You can't force them back together if they don't want it, can you?"

"No, I don't think so. Membership of the academy has always been optional."

She sighed in relief. Apart from the fact that those on Vern's side had to be the good ones - which left the current academy on the side of wickedness - she also had a soft spot for rebels for some reason.

"And the second topic?"

"Combat training. Orrin has spent the time since the game assessing the volunteers for the most promising candidates, whom he can then train to help him teach the others. He has finally got a list with six people he wants to work with."

"How does that affect the Senate?" she asked. "As long as they want to be trained voluntarily..." Her eyes narrowed. "No. Surely not. Don't tell me you are trying to do something about that voluntary part."

He breathed heavily, wishing he had kept his mouth shut. Of course she wouldn't endorse his proposal, considering that she was currently fighting the system of compulsory warrior training back home and attempting to get herself and the other healers and other unwilling non-warriors exempted from it.

"Very well, I won't tell you."

She shot him an angry look, determined to have a word with Vran'el about it all. He was a senator for a healing House, he would surely know how to put a stop to this. He was about to learn about Enric's plans in the course of the forthcoming meeting. She wondered if such an attempt would finally induce Vran'el to be on a different side to her companion.

* * *

Eryn waved when she saw Vran'el in the entrance area of the clinic, her smile turning into a look of apprehension when she saw his expression. He did not look at all happy.

She walked towards him, bidding goodbye to the healer she had been made to work with today since Valrad had been at the Senate meeting. Judging from Vran'el's look, it had not been a very amiable one.

He had sent her a message in the course of the morning, asking her to go to a teahouse with him after she was done working.

"Let me guess," she ventured without any greeting, "Enric's little idea about compulsory combat training does not sit well with you."

"It does not really, no," he nodded, his features set determinedly. He looked unusually serious and she wondered if this was how people knew him when they had to deal with him in a work-related context. The lawyer - solemn, tight-lipped, critical. His usual jovial leisure time attitude was probably a way of compensating for that then, she realised.

He took her arm to lead her outside into the early afternoon sun, turning left towards what she knew to be his second-favourite teahouse. His number one was too far away from the clinic to walk there comfortably at this time of day.

They arrived at their destination a little later and Eryn sighed in relief when she sank down on a shady island of cushions.

"Fruit juice," she said when Vran'el opened his mouth to ask her. He then nodded once and lifted a finger to summon a server and order their drinks.

"If he were not that much taller and stronger than me, I swear to you I would choke the life from him!" he snarled without any preamble.

She nodded. "Tell *me*. I am trying to get healers exempted from compulsory combat training back at home, and he is trying to establish the same damn system here."

"Father is just as angry, especially as he is extremely averse to your being made to train in the discipline against your will. He was glaring daggers at your companion during the whole meeting." He raised his brow at her. "You could have warned me that he would be proposing something like that today. You obviously knew about it."

"I only heard of it today before I left for work, and sending you a message at the stage would hardly have made a lot of sense as you would be learning of it a little later anyway. How did the other senators react? Tell me they threw things at him, laughed or otherwise demonstrated their blatant disapproval."

"Hard to tell. There was a lot of muttering, of course, but not the outrage I would have wished for, unfortunately. I know of two Houses that will very likely vote against it with us, but it is hard to tell with the others. Especially as I am not sure how strictly some of the Houses take their alliance with House Aren now that Malriel is gone. I have no idea how many contacts Enric has made here, whether the old alliances are still intact, or if he has forged some new ones. In his case this would not even surprise me very much."

"What are you going to do now? Hope that enough of them will vote against it?" she enquired impatiently.

"No," he shook his head vehemently, "I am going to promote the vote against, and I may need your assistance for this." He leaned forward and took both her hands in his. "The question is whether this will throw a shadow over your relationship with Enric, sweetness. I will not have you suffering for this."

She smiled. "No, really, this will not make much of a difference."

"Are you completely, totally, absolutely sure of this?"

"Let me put it like this: our relationship has managed to survive my trying to get out of the Order ever since I was made to join it, repeatedly ignoring commands and him getting adopted by Malriel. I am *very* confident that supporting my House over a proposal I am known to oppose vehemently will not drive a wedge between us." She squeezed his hands. "But I thank you for your concern, Vran."

He smiled, looking relieved. "Good. I admit that is good news. Having somebody at my disposal who has experienced that system and can tell people that it is not as great as Enric wants us to think will surely be helpful."

"How does this work, now? Should we walk from door to door and try to sell our idea of voting against Enric?"

"More or less. Though in case of Roal we may spare that effort, they will not vote in favour of anything an Aren proposes. House Tokmar is the one Elwoi belongs to, and as Enric will vote in favour of a new academy, he will in turn lose their vote. I am confident of Anfer's support, that would be House Ulverd. That makes four, counting our House."

"Which means another three Houses need to be convinced," Eryn concluded.

"Exactly. I will take a nice bottle of expensive wine to House Ordel tonight and try to see where they stand. They are traditionally allied with House Aren, but I may be able to convince them otherwise. There is not much hope with House Finran, though."

Eryn frowned, then bit her lip when she remembered why. "That is Sanaf's House, isn't it? And after I caused him to be sent back here, they will not support my House. That is so short-sighted! Why do grown people play stupid games like that instead of concentrating on how to best serve their country? Really now! It's like dealing with children!"

"Human nature, sweetness," Vran'el shrugged. "No House can really afford to have many others against it or it will soon find itself standing alone." He paused, then took a deep breath before saying carefully, "I am really trying to spare you the politics, but there is the chance that I will have to send you to House Arbil to talk to Ram'an."

Eryn almost chocked on her fruit juice. When she had finished coughing, she glared at him. "You want to do *what*?"

"I cannot tell for sure yet, but if I do not manage to convince enough Houses, I will have to approach House Arbil, and I am positive that your going there would have quite a different impact to my turning up."

"Come on!" she wailed. "Send me to any other House! I will tell them colourful stories of my suffering under the merciless fist of Orrin, I will invent stories of cruel torture, dungeon cells, whatever you want, but don't make me go to Ram'an!"

"Firstly, Orrin has become something of an icon, so your trying to make him look bad would not reflect well on our cause here," he pointed out. "And secondly, the said cause should be more important than your personal pride! Did you not just tell me that grown people should concentrate on serving their country instead of playing stupid games?"

"That's very well for you to say, but this isn't even my country, and you are not the one to be sent to a man you would rather avoid!" she protested.

"But nevertheless a man who is still susceptible to your charms and has been trying to make up with you for quite a while now." He smiled sternly. "He even took me out during the game so he could be in a team with you."

Eryn stared at him. "What? Surely not!"

"Believe me; I remember exactly where that bolt came from, and it was not from any of his pursuers. That is a small affair, where one day a happy opportunity for revenge will present itself. But not now. Do not worry for now, sweetness. If I can avoid it, you will not have to go to him - but prepare yourself in case I do not manage to get all the votes I need. Alright?"

She let her head fall back and groaned. "Alright, then! But you had better make sure to be as convincing as you can with the other Houses! Promise?"

"I promise solemnly," he nodded. "Would you like a first level commitment on that?" he offered and raised his palm.

"No, don't bother. Let's just say you owe me a huge favour if you cannot manage to save me from going there, shall we?"

He rolled his eyes. "Alright, agreed; one huge favour it is. Being a lawyer I am very aware of the danger that agreeing to an unspecific promise like this entails, but I am just assuming that you will not make me suffer too much since I am your beloved brother."

She smiled without humour. "Yes, *brother*, you go on believing that."

*   *   *

Eryn was cursing under her breath all the way from the Aren residence to Ram'an's spacious abode. Vran'el's message had come after dinner. It had written of good and bad news, the good news being that he had secured all but one of the necessary votes against Enric, with the bad news that he had tried all other Houses except Arbil.

She had told Enric that Vran'el had sent for her, figuring that it was not exactly a lie. She had not bothered with dressing up or anything, as that would just send the wrong signal.

Around the next corner the building came into view and she halted to go through the things Vran'el had written that she could offer him on behalf of House Vel'kim. She pulled his message out of her pocket to check if she had confused anything and then marched on, determined to get the obligation behind her as quickly as possible, at the same time wondering how successful she could really be with such an attitude. If this did not work, this was entirely Vran'el's fault, she decided.

She walked up the broad approach path to the entrance and knocked four times, half hoping that nobody would be there to answer the door. But all too soon there were steps audible and the door was opened by the very man she had spent avoiding six entire weeks only to end up alone at his residence with him. How ironic.

He lifted both eyebrows at the sight of her, taking a sip from the wine glass in his hand and letting his gaze wander over her.

"Unexpected, but not unwelcome. Do come in, my dear Eryn," he said politely, stepping aside to let her enter. She nodded, glad that he opted not to give any physical greeting. He handed her a moist towel, even though it was dark outside already and cool enough that wiping away perspiration was not really necessary now.

When she had replaced the towel, he proceeded her up the stairs, through the main room and out onto the terrace. She followed him, not seeing anybody else around. She had heard that he was living with his brother and wondered if the man was away tonight.

The garden looked almost the same as she remembered it from the first time she had been here, when he had cooked dinner for her, or rather together with her.

Tonight there were plenty of glowing lanterns hanging from trees, the dim light creating a cosy atmosphere. They swung lightly in the soft breeze and she pulled her thin vest more tightly around her shoulders.

He was leaning against a wall behind her, holding his wine glass, observing her with curious eyes while she let her gaze wander over the garden.

"What brings you to me at this late hour, Eryn? It must be quite important if you come to my house voluntarily and alone, I imagine," he remarked pointedly.

"I need your support. It is about Enric's proposal in the Senate," she said quickly before her courage could drain away. He was right. Coming here had not been easy, and his being aware of this was probably not going to be exactly helpful.

Ram'an raised his brow and drained the last of his wine. "You want me to support your companion?" he said with mild amusement.

She smiled without humour. "I am not here to ask you to support him. I want you to vote against his proposal."

That made him smile. "You want me to support you in rejecting Enric's motion?"

"I do. House Vel'kim does not agree with his course of action. We have managed to convince five of the Houses so far. But somehow I have the feeling that you are aware of this."

He smiled. "So you come to me as a last resort. The final missing vote."

"Yes," she forced herself to admit. "If you are going to decline, just say so right now. I would like if we could avoid playing games or any attempts at you humiliating me. It will save time."

He slowly placed his empty glass on a small side table and folded his arms. "What is House Vel'kim offering for my support?"

"The pleasure of seeing me oppose Enric publicly?" she ventured.

His smile was thin. "What makes you think I care that much for you to offer my vote so cheaply?"

She exhaled slowly. That had put her in her place alright. "We are willing to share the quota of wine from the east with you."

Ram'an pursed his lips. "Half?"

"A quarter. For one year."

He nodded. "Very well. Something else?"

"The use of our premises in the north for the next generation over the summer months."

He considered for a moment, then shook his head. "We have a similar arrangement with House Partém already."

"A ten percent share in our berry harvest for the next five seasons."

"No, our own bushes carry enough fruit."

She sighed. "Is there anything that we could offer that would interest you?"

Now he smiled. "Yes, there is a little something I have been after for quite a while now. Though it is nothing House Vel'kim can grant me, but *you*."

She stiffened. "Go on."

He watched her closely when he spoke his next words. "I still want that one voluntary kiss."

"What?" she exclaimed, "Have you taken leave of your senses? I don't know how much of that wine you have had tonight, but obviously more than you can handle!"

He laughed, and she felt the heat of her anger increasing at his next words. "I cannot tell you how very relieved I am to see that my request has managed to provoke you enough to be yourself again, at least for a short while."

"I should have known that coming here and trying to talk to you like a grown-up person is futile," she snapped and walked towards the terrace door. "Good night, *Arbil*."

She barely managed to stop before she bumped into the shield that blocked the way back into the house.

"Not so fast, Theá," he purred. "I have been trying to get you to spend time with me, I am not just letting you leave here again after barely more than five minutes."

"Let. Me. Out."

"You are outside already, if you forgive me for being a stickler for detail. It is the lawyer thing, I am afraid," he smirked.

"In, then!" she pressed out from between clenched teeth.

"No, let us stay out here for a bit, I find it quite agreeable. A touch romantic, even, with the lanterns, would you not agree?" he asked conversationally as if they were just having a leisurely talk about the weather.

"Remove that shield, or I will..."

"Yes?" he asked interestedly.

Instead of an answer she lifted her palm and shot a bolt at him, one that would send him to his knees, maybe even knock him out. He swiftly raised another barrier in front of him, blocking her attack easily.

"Look at that," he marvelled, "There it is, all that temper I have been missing lately. Apart from the shattered mug at the hospital, that is."

She bored a hateful glare into him and turned to walk around the house instead of through it, but was stopped by another barrier only a few steps later.

Panic. It emerged without warning and became more powerful by the second. She forced herself to breathe evenly to keep it at bay. Turning around to him, she made herself walk back, grab the front of his tunic and pull his face close. "Let me leave. Now. Or I swear to you..."

"But you have not yet accomplished what you came for, have you?" he smiled and leaned forward slightly so that their noses were touching.

She released him and all but sprung back, unsteady on her feet. His hand grabbed her wrist quickly to keep her from falling and pulled her towards him and back into balance.

Her panic reached the next level and she sobbed and shoved hard against his chest to push him away, a tear running down her cheek.

"Theá," he said soothingly, his expression no longer amused and teasing, but serious, and worried. "I am sorry. I admit I enjoyed provoking you, but I never meant to make you cry. Come here." He pulled her close, wrapping his arms around her and pressing her against his warm chest.

She tried to breathe the agitation away, calling herself a fool for showing him a weakness like that, cursing her volatile emotional state. Instead of soothing her, being close to him made the tears flow even more freely. She could smell his soap, feel his lips on her temple, the gentle moves of him swaying her comfortingly. Unbidden pictures of them together on the cushions of a teahouse, talking about meat-free nutrition, emerged. Then others where he had showed her how to use a shield to change her hair colour, how to imbue medicine with magic and even one where they were children in this very garden where he had been reciting for her the names of plants he had learned especially for her. The pain of things that could have been - a valuable friendship she would have treasured if he hadn't become so frigid after they had parted a few months ago - choked her and she sobbed more violently, feeling her body shake against his steady one.

He didn't speak, just held her close with his cheek pressed against her temple and one hand stroking her back, and let her cry.

She buried her face in his shoulder, no longer concerned with seeming weak and pathetic. It was too late for avoiding that now, anyway. His embrace tightened a little, and his hand moved from her back up to her hair, petting the back of her head.

After a while her sobbing died down and he held on to her until she lifted her head and stepped back, avoiding looking at him.

"I want to say sorry for that," she said stiffly. "It was inappropriate."

"No, Theá," he shook his head, his voice soft. "No more escaping behind that wall of icy detachment. There is a lot of pain, and I know that I am the cause of some of it. I think you are ready to listen to me now. You owe it to me, and to yourself. Come, sit with me." He took her hand and pulled her along with him to the steps that led from the terrace down into the garden, sinking down on one of them. "Sit," he commanded when she didn't follow his example, holding on to her hand.

She looked down at him with a frown, unsure what to do.

"Why do you never make it easy for me, I wonder?" he sighed and gave her hand a slow, but determined pull until she was sitting beside him. "Now let us have that long overdue talk, my dear girl." He wiped a drying tear away from her cheek with his thumb before he started, "I sometimes think back to when I was made to give you away at the day of your commitment ceremony here in this very garden." His tone had become sombre. "I thought my world would end and my heart burst from the agony. He chose his revenge well."

"Ram'an, we don't..."

"No, please. I would like you to hear this," he said insistently and took her other hand when she fumbled to rise again. "The only thing more painful than watching you commit to Enric was the thought of not having you in my life at all. This is why I gave you the bracelet, the token of my House's friendship, and my own. I had the need to bind you to me somehow, be it even in such a trivial way. Then you went away, and the void inside me seemed to expand. When the pain became almost unbearable, I started drinking too much. But after a while, even that did not help with dulling the pain completely. In one of my more lucid moments I decided that cutting off an aching limb was less painful than suffering the ache. I decided to break off the contact with you, to purge you from my life as best I could by pushing you away until you retreated. To give myself a chance to forget you."

She kept silent, feeling more tears burning behind her lids but managing to keep them in.

"But unfortunately that did not stop me from thinking of you. And then I had not counted on your returning here so soon and for such a long period, becoming present in my life again." He smiled. "Seeing you at that teahouse together with Pe'tala and Vran'el on the day of your arrival was like you had never really gone. Suddenly you were back, and I realised that spending time with you is a lot less painful than not. My decision to discard the friendship you accepted after everything we had been through haunted me." He played with her fingers. "It was a terrible mistake I have been trying to compensate for ever since you returned here. Can you forgive a damn fool, my dear Theá, and ease his aching heart a little?"

She looked into his warm brown eyes that returned her gaze unblinkingly, waiting for her reply.

Exhaling slowly, she gave a nod, feeling immediately as if a crushing load had been lifted from her. Breathing was a little easier suddenly, the burden on her shoulders weighing a little less heavily than before.

A broad smile turned the corners of his lips upwards and he lifted both her hands to kiss them.

"Thank you." He then reached into his pocket and pulled out something thin and silver. The bracelet she had thrown back at him when she had seen him again six weeks ago.

He lifted a questioning brow at her. "May I?"

She nodded again, lifting her wrist for him to fasten it on. Had he kept it with him all that time in case a convenient opportunity for returning it to her presented itself? Nonetheless, it felt good having it back again. She had become used to wearing it those few months, missed it after it was gone. She looked up at him when she felt the metal slightly warm against her skin.

"Did you just...?"

"Strengthen the metal with a little magic to make taking it off a lot harder? Dear me, would I ever do that?" he grinned.

She looked up at the sky, amazed at how very different this visit was from what she had expected.

Turning to him, she smiled lopsidedly. "I assume now that we are friends again you will vote with my House against that appalling idea Enric came up with?"

He pursed his lips. "That, my dear Theá, depends on whether you are going to agree to the little condition I mentioned before."

"Ram'an," she groaned and covered her face. "How can you say a thing like that? I am carrying another man's child!"

He frowned as if he didn't understand the argument. "Yes, I am aware that you are with child. But why would I mind about that? Your pregnancy becomes you extremely fittingly, you are even more gorgeous than before - radiant, even."

She stared at him for a few moments, then blinked and laid a hand on her slightly swollen belly self-consciously. It surprised her how good it felt to hear the compliment.

"You really think that? I feel bloated and clumsy."

He leaned closer, again taking both her hands in his. "Do not tell me that companion of yours does not compliment you on how immensely beautiful you are right now? How your skin glows, your eyes shine?"

"I..." She exhaled. "We don't see each other very much at the moment. There is a lot he has to take care of at House Aren. And the Senate. And I am working at the clinic..."

Ram'an pursed his lips and his gaze was intense, slightly angry even. "So that yellow-haired idiot is neglecting you."

She shook her head and started to speak, "No, it's just that..." His index finger on her lips stopped her.

"Why do you not grant me that kiss I asked for, and we pay him back for it at the next Senate meeting by thwarting his plans?"

He had told her that she was beautiful, radiant. She had not heard that in quite some time. Enric was attentive, affectionate, but compliments had been rare lately. And she really missed them, especially now.

And she needed Ram'an's vote.

Why did it seem so much more acceptable to let him kiss her now than the last time she had been in the Western Territories? Maybe because it was still somehow flattering that he had not lost his interest in her completely.

"Alright," she heard herself saying and felt her heartbeat quicken uneasily. It didn't feel exactly correct, but not as wrong as it was supposed to be, either.

A broad smile grew on Ram'an's face and he gently lifted her chin with his index finger.

"What, now?" she swallowed and leaned back in surprise.

"Of course *now*," he chuckled. "I do not want to give you time to change your mind later."

He took her hands and pulled her closer. "Do not be nervous, Theá. I will not cross any lines. A kiss, nothing more. No magic, no touching of inappropriate areas, and you decide when to end it."

She breathed out slowly and nodded. That did sound reasonable.

He laid both her hands on his chest as if to make it easier for her to push him away and put his arms around her before he lowered his lips onto hers. He kept his touch light as if to give her time to change her mind and retreat. When she didn't after a few seconds, he opened her mouth and their tongues met in a slow dance.

She was surprised at how pleasant it felt. It was non-threatening, soft, friendly. He tasted nicely of sweet wine and his lips were smooth and gentle. There was no feeling of repulsion as she had feared, but also no waves of lust or need, no pull. Just a warm feeling in her stomach, the joy of being appreciated as a woman. There was no demand in his caresses, he did not take more than she was willing to give.

He clearly knew what he was doing, no clumsiness, but instead subtle skill.

When she leaned back slightly to end the kiss, he stopped immediately and slowly pulled her into a hug instead, stroking her back, leaning his cheek against hers. It felt oddly friendly, as if he was comforting her.

When he released her again, he looked down at her thoughtfully. "Are you alright?"

"Yes," she nodded slowly. It had been too friendly to raise sexual tension, but still a kiss which mere friends would not exchange just like that.

"That was nice," she admitted and searched for something else to say in that strange situation.

He smiled and shook his head slightly. "That sounds very surprised. I am insulted." Then he added with a wink, "There is more where that came from. As a gentleman, I feel I need to offer that I will be at your disposal any time."

She grinned despite herself. "Very considerate of you, thank you. So I have your vote, Head of House Arbil?"

"You do, Eryn of House Vel'kim," he replied formally with a slight bow. "Granted and paid for. Come back if you need more favours," he added with a lazy grin.

*　*　*

Eryn stepped out into the street in front of the Arbil property and jumped when she heard a voice saying her name softly.

"You startled me," she complained when Enric stepped towards her.

"I am sorry, I didn't mean to." Reaching her, he frowned when he turned her face towards one of the many street lanterns. "You have been crying." It was no question, but a simple statement of not quite such a simple truth.

"I have, yes. Why are you here?"

"I felt anger, frustration, panic and finally desperation through the mind bond and hurried over to the Vel'kim residence," he explained a tad reproachfully and watched her flinch. "Imagine my surprise when I learned that you were not with Vran'el as I had been led to believe. He told me where you had gone. I was about to storm in, when your feelings became less intense and finally even positive." He lifted her hand and looked down at the silver bracelet with the Arbil crest on it. "I assume this means that things between the two of you are taken care of?"

She nodded, swallowing.

He lifted a brow. "Why do I detect a slight feeling of guilt in you, my love?"

It was impossible to tell him about the kiss. Not now. Probably never. It had felt harmless only a few minutes ago, but standing before him like that, feeling his warm hand holding hers, it had suddenly started transforming into something else: betrayal.

She had agreed to something she had had no right to offer, something only the very man before her was entitled to. Why ever had she done a thing like that? Where had these thoughts, these feelings of guilt been when she needed them, only a short time ago? Why was her brain so infuriatingly sluggish and why were her emotions so incredibly powerful all of a sudden, when she had managed to keep them sealed away for several weeks? Were they somehow trying to make up for lost time or had she entered a kind of brain-numbing stage in her pregnancy now? But blaming it on being an expectant mother was too easy, too cowardly, wasn't it?

She didn't feel particularly brave right now, either. Not brave enough to tell him. It would hurt him, something she didn't want. And what could she say? That she had let herself be kissed by a man who had tried to take her away from her companion not too long ago and who had admitted to her that he was still in love with her so she could assist Vran'el in foiling his, Enric's, plans for compulsory combat training?

Too much thinking, too few resources available for it right now.

Pushing that landslide of thoughts away, she simply slung her arms around Enric's waist.

"You know that I love you, don't you?" she intoned against his shoulder.

His arms encompassed her immediately, pressing her close. This felt right. Her body fitting against his like this was the place it was supposed to be. She wondered if it had always been like that or if they had adapted to each other.

"I do, yes," he sighed. "But judging from that turmoil inside you I am not sure if this statement was not just a distraction from answering my question about why you are feeling guilty. In fact, after asking you, the feeling seemed to have grown."

Stupid, idiotic mind-bond, she cursed silently. That she kept neglecting to shield her emotions so only the really strong ones could be detected by him didn't help, either.

"Why did you come here tonight? Why would you avoid him for so long only to come to him..." His voice trailed off when one possible explanation occurred to him. "Vran'el sent you here," he said slowly. "To persuade Ram'an to vote against my proposal at the Senate.

That's why he was so cool and distant when he opened the door and told me where you are!"

She nodded and looked down. Why had they ever thought they could keep an attempt like that from him? Especially if she and her damn mind-bond were involved, she considered.

He sighed. "Then I suppose I know now what to attribute your guilty conscience to: plotting against me."

She blinked. That was convenient. Did not contradicting him count as lying? Probably. Omission was a kind of lie, wasn't it? Lying without words...

Maybe she could make amends by sharing one morsel of information with him. "Ram'an's vote was the last one he needed to be sure your proposal will be rejected by the Senate," she informed him.

He shrugged, obviously unperturbed. "That doesn't really matter."

She stared up at him. "It does not?"

"No," he shook his head. "I am not counting on the senators agreeing to a thing like that. The change would be too radical. But it is a nice way to get them used to the idea of combat training and any subsequent discussions. My real objective is making them agree to unbroken funding of training for combat for the one hundred magicians who volunteer for it."

Eryn closed her eyes for a moment. No. This was just cruel. It meant she had let herself be kissed for what a lenient observer might have called a *noble cause* only to find out that it didn't matter anyway. The plan they had been so eager to thwart had not even been one he had wanted to push forward with. Damn!

"You look annoyed," he commented.

"That happens when I am confronted with my own stupidity," she murmured.

"What was that?"

"Never mind," she sighed. "Let's go home. I need a bed. Not only that - a bread bun."

*　*　*

Enric's unblinking expression revealed his lack of enthusiasm as Ram'an was led into his office. "I don't have much time. What do you want?"

"I know," his visitor replied in a voice unruffled and showing no offence at the harsh welcome. "This is why I am here."

"Pardon me? I fail to understand that statement."

Unasked, Ram'an took a seat and leaned back. "I am here because you clearly are not taking enough time for certain things. You are neglecting your companion."

Enric stiffened. "I don't see how this is any of your..."

"Shut up and listen," Ram'an snapped, the irritation clear in his eyes. "I have given up my claims on Theá, and one consideration was

222

seeing that you two have a genuine connection. But I did not give her up, only to observe your neglect of her."

Staring at his visitor, Enric exhaled. This was a bizarre situation. But telling him again that it was none of his business didn't seem right when the warning was about taking better care of Eryn.

"You did not give up your claim on her voluntarily because you were reasonable, but because you had no other choice. Let us not fool ourselves on that account. Now, what gives you the impression that I am neglecting her?" he asked calmly.

"That she permitted me to kiss her yesterday evening, something I have never been able to make her agree to before. And I hope you appreciate my coming here to tell you this and risking another punch in the face. Think well before you let your fists speak."

Enric desperately fought the anger, the wrath that was rising quickly. Anger at Ram'an, which was not exactly being dampened by the circumstance when it seemed as though Eryn had welcomed the man's attentions. And that Enric was being told that it was his own neglect that had made her agree to it.

"Go on," he pressed out between clenched teeth.

"Good. I am glad to see that we are able to continue this conversation without resorting to violence for now," Ram'an nodded, but kept his eyes on Enric's tense hands. "She came to me to ask me for a favour, and I told her I would grant it in exchange for a kiss. It was only when I told her how beautiful she is that she agreed. It seems you do not give her the feeling of being attractive now that she is carrying your child. I do not know what the custom is in your country with regard to this, but here we treat a pregnant woman like the goddess she is. We esteem the bounty she gives to us by worshipping the very ground she walks on." He flashed Enric a hard look. "It is normally next to impossible to make a mother-to-be agree to allow herself to be kissed by another man, because in this stage of her life she does not lack admiration from her companion or feel the need to seek it somewhere else. But not with Eryn. This makes me very angry. She deserves better than that."

Enric fought to retain control, to hang on to the thoughts that he needed to continue this conversation instead of only seeing before him the picture of Ram'an with Eryn in his arms, kissing her.

"I can see how this troubles you greatly," Ram'an said with a slightly smug smile. "Good. It should do. But let me ease your conscience at least a little so you may return quicker to thinking coherently: it was not a passionate kiss, I kept it friendly, like an intimate embrace. I am not the sort of man to prey on vulnerable women, whatever else you may think of me. Eryn herself was immensely surprised at how much she had needed to be held - so that even being held by a man she had until yesterday been avoiding as best she could was welcome."

Enric closed his eyes. A sense of humiliation made him swallow. Shame at his own failure and that he needed the man opposite to point it out to him. His thoughts returned to Ram'an's description of the kiss. *Friendly* he had called it. How *friendly* could a kiss be when it involved another man's tongue tasting the inside of his companion's mouth? He breathed in and out a few times to keep himself from bestowing upon his visitor a *friendly* punch to the jaw.

"I will be checking on her regularly," Ram'an went on. "This will keep you on your toes, I hope. There is one thing to be sure of - if she needs attention and closeness, she will find it with me should you fail again. I would be delighted to raise your son as my own," he added factually.

"Let's not plan that far ahead," Enric said, aware that he was being provoked and feeling determined to remain above it.

Ram'an smiled. "As you wish. It is in your hands to prevent any of it."

"Why are you telling me all this? I wouldn't have thought of you as being interested in preserving my companionship with Eryn but rather delighting in every rupture it shows."

"A question I was pondering for quite some time last night, believe me. And there is a conclusion I have reached. Seeing her unhappiness - no, that is not right, let us say, *discontent* - in her relationship with you has not satisfied me in the way I would have expected. Perhaps the nature of my feelings for her has started to change. Do not get me wrong; I will probably always love her. But it might one day be the love of a friend." He then got to his feet. "Now I need to get going. I will see you in two hours at the Senate. There is your proposal to discuss, if I remember correctly. And one more thing: leading a House is a strain, that I know very well. But if you learn to delegate some of the tasks you will see that you have enough time to devote both to your House and your companion. I had to learn the hard way that one person is not enough to take care of everything. Nor should they be. The members of every House need to know that they are needed and that their contributions are important. I have heard that some members of House Aren are discontented with your authoritative style of leadership. They are used to a more cooperative approach. This is a *family* you are leading, not the Order. They have a stake in this, even more than you do, because they were born into it. You are a foreigner who has taken over their House and who is too strict and unapproachable. But this is all the unbidden advice you shall hear from me today."

There was a knock at the door and Eryn stepped in. She froze when she saw the two men standing together.

"Ah, there you are," Ram'an smiled broadly and stepped towards her to cup her cheeks in his palms and kiss her forehead as if this had always been their usual way of greeting each other. He turned back to Enric. "I have taken the liberty of asking your servant to call for her." Focussing his attention on Eryn, he took her hands. "Theá, my dear, I have informed your companion about yesterday evening and the kiss

I made you agree to. I warned him to take better care of you and that I will check that he does."

"You have *what*?" she whispered in disbelief. Her stomach clenched and she felt suddenly cold despite the warmth.

"Do not worry, he seems to have taken it well enough, considering that I am still standing upright. I am pushing my luck even further and take you out for lunch tomorrow. No," he shook his head when he saw she was about to object, "I will not accept you declining my invitation. I will be at the clinic at noon to pick you up." He kissed her forehead again and left, closing the door behind him.

They stood for what felt like an eternity and stared at each other in silence. He had in the past not reacted well whenever anybody had touched her, but this was the first time she had permitted it to happen willingly. She gulped and tried to gauge his mood. He stood rigid like a statue and she felt fear slowly creep up inside her.

Then he started moving around his desk, slowly, and stopped in front of her, looking down at her with a frown. Being angry at her would be wrong, he decided and brushed aside his annoyance.

"I never thought I would see the day when *he* would warn me to treat you better. And neither did I think that he would be justified in doing so." He took her hand and lifted it to his lips. "I have been neglecting you. My ambition at playing this political game here well has made me lose sight of what *you* need."

"I am sorry," she whispered.

He sighed and shook his head. "Don't be. I dare say he wouldn't have given up trying to kiss you at least once until one day you gave in. I am relieved he didn't achieve it through force. And I am even more than astonished that he came here to inform me and use it as a warning. An effective one, I might add." He bent down to kiss her lips. "You are a sight to behold, my love. Every morning I wake up next to you, I thank my lucky stars for blessing me with you and the miracle you bestow on me. Do remind me to tell you this more often, will you?"

She swallowed and blinked to hold back the moisture that threatened to make her eyes swim. Stupid supersensitive emotions. Nodding, she leaned her head against his shoulder. Relief almost made her knees buckle under her.

"And now I want to know what the true reason for your letting him kiss you was." His voice was calm and he stepped back to make her look up at him. "I don't think that me neglecting you alone is a valid reason for you to run around and seek such attention elsewhere. I dare say I have made my objections to other men kissing you more than clear. What did he say to make you agree to it?"

She shook her head. "Nothing much. It's ridiculous, really."

"Why don't you let me be the judge of that?"

Eryn swallowed and grimaced. "He warned me against assuming that he still cared for me. That hit me hard. I mean, I don't want him to care for me the way he used to or still does, but the thought of his not liking me at all was painful in some way."

"You still feel guilty," he sighed. "About him waiting in vain for the girl they promised to him when he was a boy."

She nodded. "Yes, I think I do. I know it's not rational, not my fault. That I am not to blame, neither for that stupid custom here nor for my father taking me away. But still..."

"So letting him kiss you..."

"... was like the proof that he still liked me," she finished his sentence sheepishly.

Enric cupped her cheek. "He does. Very much so, in fact. More than I appreciate, I have to admit. But he does seem to have found a way to deal with his feelings that allows him to look out for you, even though he has given up his claims on you. He wants to be your friend. And he knows that this will only work with my approval. That is why he told me."

"And do you approve?" she asked carefully.

He smiled. "I would hardly have let him coerce you into having lunch with him tomorrow in my presence if I didn't. But it is a measured approval. If he kisses you again, I *will* hurt him. Dreadfully."

"You say he has given up his claims on me. Then why did he want to kiss me at all?"

"To satisfy his curiosity for once, I would think. And probably to see if he could make you do it. You are vulnerable right now, not only through your troubles with him and Valrad but also due to your generally instable emotional state thanks to your pregnancy. I assume he came to a similar conclusion overnight. He attributed his success not to his own doing but to *my* failure, otherwise he would probably not have come here to upbraid me for it."

She tilted her head and looked at him. "The way you put it makes everybody else but me to blame for the kiss."

Enric raised one brow. "I wouldn't go that far. I don't appreciate your permitting other men to kiss you, whatever reasons you think may justify it. In the future I hope you will keep that in mind or you will find me putting restrictions on your freedom to move around. I am sure you will perceive those as neither pleasant nor reasonable."

She nodded silently. This was not a good time to contradict him. The threat was not to her liking, and she knew that it was not an idle one. But she had no intention of letting Ram'an or anybody else kiss her again, so why object? And considering that Enric had handled this situation with admirable restraint, she had no wish to oppose him. It would send the wrong message.

"Good. And that guilt I noticed yesterday was obviously more well-founded than I had thought," he said dryly and lifted her chin to kiss her. "Would you like to come to the Senate and watch my proposal being rejected?"

She smiled, relieved that the mood had become lighter again. "Would I? What a question! I hardly ever witness any of your plans being foiled, and I will just block out the knowledge that you didn't even want this one to succeed."

"Little victories, eh?" he smirked.

"They are hard enough to come by, so I am taking each one I can. Especially against you."

He shook his head. "I wonder if we will one day be on the same side so that *my* victories will at the same time be *yours*."

She rose to her toes to kiss his cheek, "Oh, but how tedious would that be, now, Darling?"

CHAPTER 16

Breakthrough

Eryn took a sip from the tea she had let go cold to make it more palatable during the hottest time of the day. Vern was perched on the cushions next to her with Ram'an sitting opposite her.

The latter had, as promised the day before in Enric's study, turned up at the clinic to pick her up for lunch. Vern had been standing with her, listening to a discussion between her and Dikea about splinting fractured bones properly, so Ram'an had extended his invitation to lunch to include Vern as well.

Eryn was glad that he had. She felt a bit awkward in Ram'an's presence after the kiss two days ago followed by their short and very strange meeting yesterday, and Vern was a nice buffer between them.

"Now then, Vern," Ram'an smirked at the boy. "You have turned out to be quite a disruptive element within the local art community. I have two second cousins who were present when you all but stormed the grand hall at the academy with this impressive picture everybody is still talking about. I wonder if I might have a look at it some time?"

"You need to talk to Eryn about that. She is keeping it in her bedroom."

"A place I am not likely to be permitted within in the foreseeable future," the lawyer quipped in mock desperation.

"I wasn't aware that you were still trying," Vern tossed back with uncharacteristic sauciness.

Ram'an looked at him in surprise, then chuckled. "I am not. I accept when I have lost. Have the artists contacted you yet, by the way?"

The boy shook his head. "No. Why would they?"

228

"The Senate's decision on their cause was rather promising, and I would have expected them to try and win you over as a member to their cause."

Eryn leaned forward, interested. "What decision?"

"The artists who have split have asked the Senate for permission to found their own academy," he explained. "At the same time Elwoi has asked us to bar any attempt to do precisely that."

"Well?" Vern enquired curiously. "What was the outcome?"

"The Senate decided that the arts as such would be served best if diverse development is encouraged, which means we decided against the ban Elwoi requested and instead voted in favour of the second academy. The triarchy has added a little amendment to that, though. They want to have the two sides at the table first in order to discuss whether there is not an amiable solution possible that would benefit both sides."

Eryn snorted. "Nice try. I dare say such a solution is not very likely though, is it? Why would the rebellious artists agree to subjecting themselves to Elwoi when they can have their own academy?" Then she sighed. "Of course - founding a new institution requires money, doesn't it? Money they very likely don't have readily available."

"Money is a point certainly," Ram'an agreed, "yet Elwoi is the one worrying about it. There are public funds which support the academy, and having another one would mean that he would lose half of the subsidy he currently enjoys. That means that he will try to prevent another academy being founded. Furthermore, several of the artists wanting to split from the old academy originate in the Houses, meaning there is a chance of some extra money from wealthy sponsors."

She nodded slowly, taking in this new information. "So you think this is going to happen? There will be a second institution for artists?"

"It looks like it, yes," the lawyer smiled. "I would be very surprised if Elwoi managed to hold on to the wayward artists."

"And where does House Arbil stand on this?" Eryn asked lightly.

Ram'an looked at Vern and smiled. "On the side of the rebels, of course. How could we ever support such an old-fashioned teaching model that keeps artists from finding themselves?"

"I take it that your two cousins are not supporters of Elwoi either?" she asked with a quiet smile.

"They are not, no," he admitted. "But several of the Houses allied with my House are, so it was not an entirely unproblematic course to choose. But House Aren, too, had to emancipate itself from certain ties to act in accordance with the more enlightened values it now represents."

Eryn blinked. "That sounded very diplomatic. Am I to assume that Enric broke an alliance or two?"

"To be frank, he did. Legara of House Finran approached him before the vote. You probably remember her? She is Malriel's cousin and friend. She was the one asking a few inconvenient questions at your trial back then."

She nodded with a wrinkled nose. "I remember her well enough, yes."

"She told Enric that Malriel would not have approved of a schism in the academy and that she hoped he was aware what his duties were, namely representing Malriel's point of view when it came to the vote."

"Oh my," she chuckled. "I dare say he didn't take this very well. He really does not like to be told what to do."

"He was... polite about it. He thanked her and told her that he had a very clear idea about his duties and then voted against Elwoi. I imagine Legara is looking forward to having Malriel back in power rather sooner than later, if you ask me."

It was not only Legara, Eryn added silently. She herself didn't want Enric to become too accustomed to his new position of power, either.

"Enric told me that House Aren has a few artists, too. Do you know where they stand? On the same side as their Head of House or is he about to act in opposition to his own people, as well?"

"He is fortunate here," Ram'an explained, "because he has both the conservative *and* the more progressive artists in House Aren, so he has not alienated all of them. Though there is no decision he could have reached which would satisfy them all, either. But considering his connection with Vern, hardly anybody should be surprised at his vote for the rebels. Not even Legara."

"Don't say that!" Vern moaned. "I don't want to be the reason behind this whole split between the artists! Why couldn't they find some other time to do this?"

"What is the trouble, my young friend?" Ram'an smiled. "You do not value the role you played in their seemingly long overdue endeavour to fight for their beliefs?"

"No! I don't, not at all!"

"And why is that, if I may ask? One would think that this is a great achievement you can be proud of, being an inspiration to so many," the lawyer asked.

"It sounds strange, but I feel as though I have to be grateful to him, and that I have caused him so much trouble doesn't really make it any easier to bear," the boy explained, crestfallen.

Eryn's eyes bulged. "Grateful? To Elwoi? Are you joking? What for? For disrespecting and insulting you?"

"Without him I wouldn't have ended up painting this picture! He challenged me in a way that made me so angry and enabled me to discover a new artistic side in myself! I have found a new way of expressing myself thanks to him. I feel like I owe him something, and I don't feel comfortable doing so. And causing all this trouble for him is like increasing that indebtedness."

She was about to tell him that this was complete nonsense, but stopped as Ram'an leaned forward.

"Vern, there is one aspect in a person's behaviour that you need to consider apart from the outcome: the intention behind it. A favourable result is sometimes the outcome when people take actions aimed at harming you. They are no more than a coincidence at times and hardly a reason for being grateful to the person behind the actions. We do distinguish between intent and outcome from a legal point of view here. A person who has caused harm without intention by - let us say, carelessly causing an accident - is punished a lot more lightly than somebody who *wanted* to do harm."

"So you are saying I don't owe Elwoi any gratitude because what he really wanted was to subdue me instead of helping me develop?" Vern mused.

"I am, yes," Ram'an agreed. "And I dare say that not many other artists would have been able to harness that situation the way you did. Most would have bowed to his demands and chosen one discipline or another. You had the resources, the courage and the talent to overcome an obstacle, smash that barrier he was trying to raise and instead turn it into a chance for you to grow."

Eryn nodded appreciatively. "I agree with what he says. Well put, lawyer."

"Thank you so much, *healer*," he retorted.

Vern thought for a few moments, sipping his tea. "I think I can work with that, yes," he then decided. "The idea that I don't owe him anything is an appealing one, I'll admit."

"Then I would recommend you hold on to it. I suggest not even Elwoi himself would come up with the idea that he is the one to have helped you along in this regard," Ram'an advised.

"Thank you," the boy nodded earnestly. "That was a great help. I feel a lot better - relieved. It's useful to have the two of you liking each other again. Nicer lunches than at the clinic with Eryn trying to avoid looking at Valrad."

"I never *stopped* liking her," Ram'an smiled.

"You definitely had a funny way of showing it," Eryn said.

"Children... be nice to each other," Vern sighed.

She chuckled. "Of course, wise and mighty Vern, starter of revolutions, current sensation of the art and healing world, venerated..."

"You know what? Now that I think of it, have a go at each other again. Why should I have to serve as your target just to keep the peace between the two of you?"

"To preserve that fragile understanding between the honourable Head of House Arbil and myself?" she ventured.

"A fragile understanding wouldn't make it very long, anyway," he grinned.

"This is a valid point," Ram'an nodded.

"You know what? I think I will go home now. I don't really feel that my pregnancy privileges are recognised sufficiently here." She began to get up but stopped at Ram'an's next words.

"I had this teahouse here stock the bakery product you currently seem to be so fond of. Bread buns you call them, I think."

She pursed her lips, then sank back down to the cushions behind her. "But then maybe after careful consideration, staying here is not that much of an imposition..."

"Good. I was confident that you would come to that conclusion," he smiled and lifted a finger to summon a server and have him fetch the promised treats.

"Buying a pregnant woman with food is mean, by the way," she growled, but her eyes focused on the entrance of the building through which the server had just disappeared.

"Why?" Vern shrugged. "Enric has been doing it for a while, and since he is the only one at the residence having sex at the moment, it clearly is a successful approach."

Eryn's head snapped back to him, her mouth agape. "What?" she stammered, her cheeks flushing red from embarrassment.

"Well, it had been a bit quiet around your bedroom for a while, but lately the bribe seems to be working again," he said.

"What do you mean, *more quiet*? Don't tell me you can *overhear* us?" she hissed, shocked.

"You tend to leave your window open when you go to bed, and so do I. They both face into the garden," he explained. "Don't worry - I don't think father and Junar are able to hear you, you are not *loud* as such. Well, not usually."

Eryn closed her eyes, breathing slowly and consciously to get a grip on her unease. He had very quickly adapted to the open manner of the locals when it came to talking about sex, she had to give him that.

"I suppose I am the only one here to find this conversation topic quite inappropriate?" she mumbled.

Ram'an nodded, smiling. "You are. I find it highly entertaining. It seems sharing a house with others, with all its little ups and downs, is something you have yet to get used to."

"That is not true! We have Plia living in our House at home..." she started, but trailed off. Had the girl, too, been able to hear them at night? The thought was mortifying. They might have traumatised her for the rest of her life! But then their doors were sturdy and it was usually too chilly to leave the windows open at night. And they didn't face the same direction, anyway.

"Are you wondering if you have been treating your house guest to any unexpected acoustic entertainment, dear Theá?" Ram'an said with a teasing grin.

Vern laughed. "Just try to remember whether she avoided looking at you in those mornings afterwards."

"Idiots, both of you!" she cursed them. "I am starting doubt whether putting up with you is worth any number of bread buns!"

Just when she was about to rise again, this time in anger, the server arrived with a plate that held several pieces of the desired article and she sighed. "Bad timing, really. Just a quick one, then, perhaps…"

"Amazing," Ram'an marvelled and watched her take a hearty bite. "I have never seen any bakery product that has quite that effect. Neither is there any magical protection against it." He lifted a bun and inspected it curiously. "A magnificent weapon. I will make sure to have them available wherever I meet you in the months ahead."

"You unscrupulous wretch," she said softly between bites.

$$*\quad*\quad*$$

"Good day to you, Eryn," Iklan smiled and motioned for her to sit. "Fruit juice again is it?"

She nodded. "Yes, that will be quite acceptable, thank you."

"How are you doing today?" he asked while he prepared their drinks.

"I am doing fine, thank you for asking. And yourself?"

"Likewise. How is that son of yours behaving inside you? How far along are you now?"

"The fifth month. He has started moving very noticeably recently. I feel his kicks every now and then," she smiled, laying a hand upon her belly. "Unfortunately, he seems to be an early riser, like his father. He likes to kick in the mornings."

"Yes, it is amazing the things we get passed on from our fathers, is it not?" he said and sat down, handing her the juice in a tall glass.

"And we are back to the topic you are always urging me to talk about," she sighed. "Very elegant."

"By no means, I assure you. May I congratulate you on your reconciliation with Ram'an of House Arbil?"

"How do you know about that?" she asked, suspiciously.

"You were seen yesterday at a teahouse with him and young Vern."

"I see that gossip is no less favoured as a way of passing time here than back home," she said and rolled her eyes.

"A human trait, I am afraid," he smiled. "Exchange of information keeps the social structure interlocked."

"Sure it does - especially for those who provide the material, eh?"

"Not necessarily, I will admit. But just consider that you are doing a good deed for the rest of us. You are known to care for things like that. And it is in accordance with your House's values, too, so be content to serve both ideals," he grinned.

"I am not sure I approve of your being paid to make fun of me," she snapped.

"I would not dare. Teasing an Aren woman is a dangerous thing to do, after all. And I am very attached to my office. It would be a shame to have it collapse around me," he shrugged.

"Most amusing," she muttered.

"You have not contradicted my assessment of your relationship with Ram'an, so I take it I was correct."

"Yes, we have made up with each other again." She lifted her wrist for him to see the silver bracelet. "And he used the opportunity to make it plainly visible to everyone."

"And you object to that? You have been so careful in appearing polite and correct in your public dealings with him, so many will just think the rumours about the two of you not getting along all that time were wrong."

"No, I suppose I don't mind. It reduces the people I am keen to avoid by half, after all," she added dryly.

Iklan leaned forward. "Now *you* were the one to return to that topic. I feel the need to point this out before I go on."

"You are terribly stubborn, you know," she sighed. "Out with whatever wisdom you want to impart to me, then."

"I would like to talk to you about safety."

She frowned. "Safety? Like locking the door before going to bed - or what do you mean?"

"No, not that kind of safety. I mean the inner one that gives you stability and makes you feel secure about yourself."

She folded her arms. "What about it, then?"

"Uncovering a massive secret such as the one you were confronted with upon your arrival here has a great impact on a person. It is a trauma, something that needs to be dealt with. One way of doing so is seeking to talk about it."

"Which I clearly have not done. So I am what, damaged? Because I chose to go back to my life without letting it be affected by that disturbing new fact?"

"True; you have avoided dealing with it and instead chosen to suppress it. That, too, is a normal human reaction. In your case, though, it has been going on for quite a lot longer than is natural or healthy. It is time for you to deal with it soon to avoid unpleasant long-term consequences. But let us return to the matter of safety. The human perception of it depends very much on the knowledge of who and what we are, where we come from and who we can trust. The revelation of a great secret can lead to a disturbance in one or more of these and thus change how secure we feel about ourselves. Or how we have perceived ourselves until that point."

"So I am lost in uncertainty, unable to recall who I thought I was, blundering about in darkness, hoping to find myself again?" she said, doubting. "Not exactly the image *I* have of myself, I have to say."

He studied her. "That is another topic - our own perception of ourselves and how others see us - but not one I would like to venture into right now. Let me ask you a question, and I challenge you first to think about it genuinely and then answer me honestly. If you are brave enough."

She nodded. "Go on." Clever, she thought. Phrasing it as a challenge made refusal almost impossible.

"Who were you before you first came to Takhan?"

As instructed, she pondered the question. "A healer. Enric's companion. An Order magician. An orphan. A subject of King Folrin."

Iklan nodded, satisfied. "Good. Some of these have remained unchanged while others have not. A healer you still are, though the testing has revealed that your true strength lies not primarily in that one area, but is more generally applicable. Enric's companion... that is another interesting one, as coming here has acquainted you with two facts: that you were originally intended for somebody else and that your non-magical commitment to Enric was not that powerful here as back in your country. An Order magician you have never ceased to be. The topic of which country you belong to was also challenged, as belonging to a powerful House has called that into question for you. And then last but not least the most powerful change: your status as an orphan. Meeting Malriel was the first shock, but you dealt with it well. That you discovered your family on the Vel'kim side was very helpful in handling the situation, I imagine. Valrad and Vran'el were very supportive and fond of you right from the start, even though Pe'tala was obviously more of a challenge to deal with."

Eryn blinked. That had been a lot. She stared at the healer for a while, then gulped. "So what you are saying is that my whole identity was put in question by coming here back then?"

He pursed his lips. "That is a valid possibility, yes. What do *you* say? You came here with the knowledge that Malriel was dead and that Ved'al was your father. In the course of a little over half a year you discovered that your mother is very much alive and your uncle is your natural father. Your perception of yourself was changed a second time within mere months. That is an immense burden to handle."

"And you are telling me that I am not doing that very well, I am sure," she deadpanned.

"It is neither my place nor my wish to judge you, Eryn, rather to assist you. You remember what I told you about what influences our perception of safety?"

She thought for a moment. "Where we come from and who we are."

"And who we can trust," Iklan added. "Yes. The trouble is that the things you have learned changed all three of those. First you thought you were an orphan, which influenced your picture of where you came from and part of what you are. This you are no longer. As regards whom you can trust... You did trust Valrad, safe in the knowledge that he was your uncle, and that you could rely on him to love you and support you. This trust has now gone, both for him and for *yourself*. Correct me if I am wrong, but you have probably started asking yourself what and who else you have trusted which might not be exactly how they appear. The nagging question whether those close to you really are what they seem."

Eryn's breathing had become more rapid, her heartbeat hammering in her throat. One hand had come to lie on her belly, the other one was gripping the juice glass.

"Stop," she whispered. "No more of this."

Iklan leaned forward, looking straight into her eyes, "The question, whether you can trust yourself and your own judgement any further, when it led you to believe in all these falsehoods."

"I said STOP!" she screamed and jumped up, squeezing the glass hard enough to make it shatter into numerous fragments that spiked into her palm and then dropped to the floor, wet with the remainder of the juice and traces of blood. She walked towards the door, careful to concentrate on pushing away the burning sensation of the juice in her wounds and avoid stumbling.

Iklan rose, too, frowning with concern. "Eryn! Wait! Come back! I promise I will let go of this for now! Eryn!" he called after her one last time once she had fled through the door.

Eryn felt a strong grip on her arm and tried to push free, but Iklan was holding on to her. "No, I cannot let you run off like this."

She averted her face, tears running down her cheeks. She wouldn't go back in there with him, nor could he force her.

"I will take you home. No," he shook his head when she attempted to push away his hand, "I will not let you run around on your own out there in your current state of mind. Come on," he instructed and pulled her along.

*   *   *

Enric looked up and dropped the pen onto the message he was currently writing, staining it in the middle of the page, making it illegible. A surge of desperation, a certain forlornness had assaulted him out of nowhere, making him breathe out slowly and raise a shield to block out her emotions. When the sensation had ebbed mostly away, he stood. She had her third appointment with Iklan right now, that he knew. He didn't care whatever great results Iklan had been expecting from whatever torment he was obviously subjecting her to. He would get her out there.

The entrance door opened just as he was descending the stairs, and Orrin walked in. He stopped and frowned at Enric's grim expression.

"What happened?"

"Eryn," Enric said simply and pushed past him through the open door. Orrin turned without a word and followed him back out, pulling the door shut behind him.

After no more than a few minutes of brisk, silent walking, the warrior lifted his arm to point towards two figures who were moving in their direction.

Enric saw Iklan with his arm around Eryn's waist and her hand in his as if he wanted to keep her from bolting from him. He increased his pace even further until he had reached them, then he pulled her into his arms, relieved when she didn't push him away but merely rested her forehead against his shoulder. She looked drained and miserable.

His cold gaze wandered over to Iklan. He forced himself to speak calmly. The healer, too, looked worried. And he had been on his way to take her home. That was considerate of him.

"What is going on here?"

"I am afraid I pushed her a little too far today. Making up with Ram'an seems to have weakened those steely defences quite a lot. She is obviously not as able simply to lock away the pain as effectively as she used to do," Iklan explained. "That is not a bad thing as such," he continued, "as it is a sign that we can start the actual work now, that the healing can begin. Yet I would have wished to breach her barrier of sarcasm and detachment a little more gently. She needs a certain time to recover now. And somebody around she can trust and who will not make any demands or otherwise exert pressure."

Enric nodded and was about to lead her away, when she stiffened and then turned her head towards Iklan. "Don't tell Valrad about this."

The healer sighed with regret. "Eryn, dear, trust me when I tell you that he knows already. This still is *his* clinic, no matter who sits in his old study now. When something happens, he learns about it, especially when it concerns his daughter being in tears when she is being led through the corridors."

She stared at him in dismay, then turned away towards where Enric and Orrin had come from, not even bothering to curse.

"Eryn?"

She quietened but didn't look back at the healer.

"I would like you to come to me when you feel you are ready to return to your tasks. Alright?" Iklan said softly.

"Is that a recommendation or a command?" she asked flatly.

He sighed. "A command, I am afraid. I do not think that you would heed a mere recommendation."

Enric nodded at the healer once, then turned to get his companion out of the heat and into more calming surroundings. Orrin followed them back, his jaw tense.

When they arrived at the Aren residence, Enric pushed those strands of her hair that had escaped her braid behind her ears. "Would you like to lie down for a bit, my love?"

"No." She shook her head, then, taking him by surprise, said, "I need to talk."

"Of course, we can..." he started but stopped when she indicated negatively.

"No, Enric. Not to you." Her gaze focused on Orrin. "To him."

He could see her flinch at the stab of his hurt she received through the mind bond before he was able to shield. She immediately took one of his hands between both of hers and held it against her cheek.

"No, please, don't feel rejected now," she pleaded. "You are too close for this, I need somebody with a degree of distance."

He exhaled slowly. Good. At least it wasn't because she didn't trust him enough. Then he nodded.

"Alright, my love." He leaned forward and kissed her on the forehead. "I am glad you are finally willing to do any talking at all, no matter who it is with."

There was a flash of annoyance at that statement. "And this is the reason why I didn't want *you* to be the one I would talk to right now. This is exactly the kind of expectation Iklan was talking about avoiding."

He blinked, surprised when he realised that she was right. Had he been putting pressure on her in the past through remarks like that without intending to or even noticing the expectation he was creating?

Pulling his hand back, he rubbed his face. "You are right. I am so very sorry. I suppose it really is better for you to talk to Orrin," he admitted with a sigh. "Why don't you go out into the garden, find a shadowy spot and I will bring you both something to drink and make sure you are not disturbed?"

She nodded with a relieved smile and then turned to Orrin, who took her hand and climbed the stairs with her.

He hadn't spoken a single word since they had met on the street and waited until she was seated in the shade under one of the larger trees before he commanded, "Talk."

"What's with that pressure I am not to be exposed to?" she smiled weakly.

"Doesn't count with me," he snorted. "That's my usual tone with you. It would just unsettle you if I demonstrated unexpected compassion right now. You would hardly want to talk to me, of all people, if this was what you needed right now."

He wasn't exactly wrong there, she had to admit. She didn't want sympathy at the moment, but somebody she could trust in and who had common sense without any objective of trying to heal her as instructed by the man who still seemed to be the unofficial Head of the Clinic.

Out of the corner of her eye, she saw Enric stepping out into the garden with a tray containing two carafes of water and glasses. He scanned the garden until he had found where they were sitting, then walked casually towards them, putting the tray between them on the grass and returning to the house without uttering a word.

When she could no longer see Enric, she turned back to Orrin.

"Iklan said a few things today that really got to me." She sighed. "Things I had not been aware of and that still exert such power over me."

Orrin raised his brow and waited for her to go on.

"Iklan told me today how the truths we believe in shape who and what we are. Or who we think we are." She played with a blade of grass, watching it flex and twist under her fingers. "There have not been many truths in my life, and the ones I had before were rather simple. Before I was taken to Anyueel there were three simple ones: Ved'al was my father, who loved me unconditionally and the only person in my life I could safely trust. The second truth was that my mother was dead. And the last one was that I had to keep my magical abilities a secret at all costs or something terrible would happen to me." She smiled wistfully. "After I came to your city, it took me many months to realise that the consequences of having my magic revealed had not been *that* dreadful."

The warrior smiled at that, but made no comment.

"Then there was Enric. Virtually from the start he was a person I considered my greatest enemy, and then it turned out that I had allowed him take me to bed on the Freedom Night. I felt like the greatest fool in the world. I mean, how stupid does a woman have to be to unknowingly have sex with the one man she would rather kill herself than let herself be touched by? And then he turned out to be a human being instead of the monster I had pictured him as. Another truth evaporated."

"An unpleasant one, though," he murmured.

"Yes, but still one of several construed facts which my view of the world and myself was based on. Then there was the big bad Order. I am still not too thrilled about many of its aspects, but that does not make them bad people simply because they have a view of the world that is almost completely limited to one of conflict and combat. Yet there was a place for healing in it, and for me. My father was wrong. I still feel uncomfortable with that thought, and I suppose it is what makes me oppose Tyront so often. Perhaps I still want to prove my father right about the Order so I don't have to face the fact that he was wrong. My memory of him is all I have; I don't want to be forced to question the things I know about him. And yet so many things around me that keep happening only leave me with no choice other than to do that." She paused to fill the two glasses with water, handing one to Orrin and taking a few sips from her own before she went on.

"First hearing that he had lied about Malriel, then being told about the things he did before he fled from here... And finally the greatest shock of them all: that he was not even my natural father. You know, coming here for the first time also held a few pleasant truths. Apart from discovering that my mother is a power-hungry, stone-hearted Queen of Darkness, I found a family. An uncle and a cousin who welcomed me into their family as if I had never left. And now that, too, has evaporated." She wiped away a tear and was grateful that Orrin didn't follow any protective instincts to offer her comfort right now. It was not at all what she needed at the moment.

"The worst is probably that I have started to wonder about why Ved'al took me away with him from here in the first place. What if he was already aware that I was not his? It could have been he just wanted to take revenge on Malriel and his brother? Perhaps he didn't take me because he loved me so much, but because it was the most convenient way for him to inflict suffering on both of them." She pulled her knees close and wrapped her arms around them, but realised that with her distended belly that position was not as comfortable as it used to be.

"What difference would that make?" Orrin shrugged.

She stared at him. "What kind of a question is that? It would make a considerable difference!" she exclaimed.

"Did you even once in your life have the feeling that he didn't love you the way a father was supposed to?" he asked.

She thought for a moment, then shook her head. "No, I didn't. The opposite is the case. I was always sure that I was the most important thing in his life."

"There you go. Even if he had been aware that he was not your natural father, he still had it in him to care for another man's daughter as though she were his own. That would show a great deal of generosity, too." He leaned forward, his gaze intent. "Vern's mother didn't manage to love her own son enough to stick around and be there for him, so if Ved'al had it in him to love you the way he did despite knowing that he was not your true father, you should be grateful instead of doubting his regard for you."

Eryn swallowed, suddenly feeling small. He was right, she realised. Ved'al *had* loved her; this was not just a role he had played for many years. Children were intuitive when it came to matters like that, they were not easy to fool in that regard as there were still in closer contact with their instincts and not afraid to listen to them, unlike adults - who often disregarded facts when they couldn't explain them rationally.

"I'll give you that," she nodded. "But having one truth after the other vanish like the dew before my eyes makes me wonder if trusting anybody or anything is a smart move anymore. I have not exactly shown great judgement in seeing through untruthfulness, lies, deception and other dirty tricks. Who knows what else that is wrong I believe in right now? For all I know, you might be a criminal, cajoling impoverished old widows to part with their savings or breaking into houses at night to steal valuable items!"

Orrin grimaced, taken aback. "I take offence at that! At least at the cajoling of widows. Breaking into houses at least requires a degree of skill when it comes to dexterity and stealth," he said.

That made her smile. "Alright - no widows, then. But you know what I mean, I am sure. The feeling of not being able to trust even myself anymore is just... harrowing."

"Well, nobody can be sure the whole time whether their judgement is right, you see," he sighed. "But then there are a few people around you about whom your judgement has turned out to be correct, aren't there? Apart from myself and the criminal career you suspect me of, there is Vern, Junar and Plia, for a start. And so far Vyril I think and her work for the orphanage have not disappointed, either. Then there are several of the Council members you identified as unpleasant and stupid immediately – and were right. Every wrong judgement we make is a chance to learn for the next time, not a cause to doubt our decision-making entirely."

She sighed and shook her head at him. "Why does everything you say seem so logical and correct that I don't know how to contradict you?"

"Because I am wise and cannot falter," he smiled. "Try to remember that at all times."

"Cannot falter, Orrin? Really?" she laughed. "At least you don't suffer from any false modesty."

"Why would I? Omniscience makes that unnecessary."

"Prove it, oh all-knowing Orrin. What secrets do you know?"

He gave her a quiet smile. "How about the matter of my son having smuggled candles to you when you were still a prisoner to enable you to light that cell of yours?"

She gaped at him. "How...?"

"I take your astonishment as valid proof of my omniscience, thank you so much," he nodded, clearly satisfied with himself.

"Why didn't you stop him, then?" she asked in confusion.

"It made you like him, mellowed you a bit. And that in turn made you like *me* a bit more, as it was unlikely that an adorable, caring boy like him could have such a dreadful father. Vern and I have always had a good relationship, so the fact that he likes me no doubt influenced your own attitude towards me."

"You really are devious! I just had no idea how much!" she exclaimed.

"You see?" Orrin smirked. "You did appraise *me* correctly. There is still hope for you, after all. Do you want more wise words from me on how to deal with Valrad?"

She rolled her eyes. "Spare me. I feel the urge to eat something."

"Funny, a lot of conversations with you tend to end with that statement these days."

"Says the man with a companion who is about to give birth any day now," she jibed.

He stood up and pulled her to her feet. "Come, let's get you fed. It will keep you from talking at least for a short time."

CHAPTER 17

The New Academy

Enric raised both eyebrows when the servant who had just knocked at his study door announced that Valrad, Head of House Vel'kim was here to see him. He asked for his visitor to be sent in. Eryn was at the clinic, which was where he would have expected Valrad as well.

"Enric," Valrad smiled when he entered and held both the younger man's shoulders to pat them with hearty affection. Despite the jovial gesture he radiated a certain nervousness.

"Valrad," Enric smiled and offered him a seat and something to drink. "What brings you to me at this time of day, when I would have thought you were treating the ill and needy?" he asked lightly.

"What do you think, my young friend, has led me here?"

"If I had to take a guess I would say it concerns Eryn's rather distressed departure from the clinic with Iklan yesterday."

"And that guess would be absolutely correct," the healer nodded with a tired smile. "I admit I did not expect her to come to work today. I have left her to assist a colleague of mine for now so I could have a word with you alone."

"So she doesn't know you are here?" Enric asked.

"No. And I would like it if you refrained from mentioning it to her," he sighed. "She has not taken well to my having an interest in any aspect of her life so far, so I fancy you will save us both some trouble by not telling her of my visit."

"So be it."

"Thank you. I have come to talk to you about how she is doing. Iklan does not share any information with me, of course. There is the convention of confidentiality between healer and patient, thought I

242

admit that I would very much like to disregard this for now. But I am supposed to be a role model, and it would not only look very bad if I did, but also reduce to nothing my chances of making up with Eryn once she had learned of it."

"So you have come to me to ask me to share personal information with you?" Enric frowned. "I am afraid I have to tell you that I will not betray her trust like this, either."

"I am aware of this, Enric, and I would never ask it of you. If you agreed to a request like that you would not be the man I would wish for my daughter," Valrad stated calmly. "What I have come to ask you is about how she is doing. If somebody was around yesterday to take good care of her. And how my grandson is developing."

"She is doing better than a few weeks ago. The reconciliation with Ram'an helped - it was good that he was so persistent." Even though he could just as well have done without that damn kiss, he thought. "Orrin and I were both here yesterday, so she was not alone." He smiled, his expression softening. "And your grandson is doing fine. Healthy and strong. He has started kicking his mother only recently."

Valrad smiled with unmistakable pride. "That is so good to hear." Then he closed his eyes for a moment, hiding the pain within behind his eyelids. "It is hard to be with her over several hours a day without being able to chat to her about such things. There is so much I would like to say to her, to explain. But every time I attempt it she turns away or leaves the room. I keep waiting for Iklan to perform some miracle and make her hate me just a little less - enough for her to at least sit with me and listen, if not talk, to me." He paused and opened his eyes again. "I had the impression that things between you and Eryn were a bit strained for a time."

How quickly certain knowledge spread, Enric thought cynically. He wondered if this was thanks to gossip or spies.

"We have had to weather troublesome times, but we are in good shape now. Honestly."

The healer nodded in relief. "That is excellent to hear. She needs people around her whom she can trust and love unconditionally. I was worried that her relationship with you had suffered from these strains, too."

"Nothing permanent," Enric assured him.

"Good, good." Then Valrad's gaze became serious. "There is one additional thing I wish to address. It concerns that war game you and Orrin organised before."

Ah yes, Enric thought, that topic at last.

"Eryn told me that you disapproved of her participating in it."

"I did and still do. It was dangerous and I am surprised that you permitted it. I would have expected you to insist on her staying out of it for her own good."

"I was considering it," Enric replied. "But it had been her idea originally and it was the first thing she had shown any enthusiasm for in a long time, so I decided against stopping her. She was not happy about discovering her pregnancy at first, but she has adapted to it very well and would not cause harm to the child. Also, her brother was looking after her. Well, until Ram'an got rid of him. But he, too, would not have put her in harm's way." He looked out of the window. "This baby is very likely my only chance of having any children, Valrad. Cruel as it may sound considering the circumstances under which she became pregnant, I am lucky to be in this position and I wouldn't risk my son's life had I thought it could have been dangerous. Eryn is an experienced healer, and every single player in that game had basic healing skills in case she had needed help. In addition to which there is the mind bond, allowing me to learn about any trouble almost instantly. Eryn was sure that the game was not dangerous, and I trusted her in that. She may at times be a little careless when it comes to taking care of herself, but I have never seen her put anybody else in danger." Aside from that little fracas at the inn when she had shared a room with Plia, he remembered grimly, but decided to leave it unmentioned. He was trying to make a point here, after all.

Valrad leaned back. "Forgive me for bringing your judgement into question, Enric. I can see that you have given it all quite a lot of thought. I did not mean to offend you."

"You haven't. I can understand how you are concerned about her wellbeing and frustrated that she doesn't let you contribute to it. But I am confident that this is just a matter of time. She will in due course learn how to deal with her relationship to you."

"Thank you. Even after raising two children, suddenly finding out that I had another grown daughter was a challenge. I was not happy about the things that happened to her in Anyueel from an *uncle's* point of view, but now that I have taken the view of a father on them, they weigh even more heavily. It would have been my responsibility to protect her from all of this all along."

"I have been protecting her almost from the moment she set foot in our city," Enric told him. "And so has Orrin. Despite the fact that she is quite a troublemaker, she has a talent for making people around her want to protect her. Well, at least those who don't want to throttle her." Bad choice of words, he decided immediately. Again he had to think of the man at the inn who had tried to do just that.

"Her prison warders protected her?" Valrad raised a brow. "That is a little hard to believe, if you do not mind me putting that so bluntly."

"She was important from the moment her true hair colour was uncovered, and even more so after her magical abilities were revealed. We were very eager not to let any harm come to her." He briefly considered telling her father about how she had dropped her shield at the testing of her magical strength and almost got herself killed, but decided against it. He would probably not focus on the fact that Enric had saved her life but on the one that she had been desperate enough to try and end it.

"You still make her undergo combat training against her will, do you not?"

"Not since we found out about the child. But, yes - she will have to resume training afterwards."

"I object to this very strongly," Valrad said pointedly, folding his arms.

Enric sighed. "I can't really do anything here. I am currently not even a member of the Order as long as I have House Aren to take care of. But Eryn is working on that herself. She has been pestering the Magic Council with exempting healers from combat training, and after her return she will join that very Council. I would be surprised if they don't give in one day, be it just to shut her up."

"And you would support that cause?" Valrad asked suspiciously. "Vote in her favour, if you have the custom of deciding such matters by vote, that is?"

"Absolutely. You forget that I have to live with her," he chuckled. "You know the reputation of the legendary Aren temper better than I do."

That made the healer smile. "Indeed I do. Though I assume that you had more first-hand experience with it than me. But I am glad to see that this training will probably not be an issue in the remote future. I expect that she will wear them down if it is possible."

Enric nodded. "So do I."

Valrad got to his feet. "I thank you for seeing me, Enric. You have put my mind at ease regarding certain issues. By the way, House Vel'kim will support the new academy of artists by donating an old building we have not been using for rather a while. It is located not too far from the city centre, is rather spacious and should provide for a very nice location for them. I would like it if you could mention this small detail to Eryn if the conversation should run in that direction."

Enric nodded. "I will. Considering that the city's current sensation is staying under our roof, I dare say this will come up for discussion sooner rather than later."

The healer turned towards the door, then hesitated. "About that matter with the compulsory combat training you put to a vote in the Senate..."

"Yes?"

"I hope you understand why House Vel'kim had to take a stance against this."

Enric smiled. "Your House supporting it would have shocked me to no end."

"I just wanted to make sure that our being on different sides on the matter of fighting is not going to endanger our Houses' connection from your point of view. And even if it does, I hope you will remember that Eryn's wellbeing is still a concern we share."

"Don't worry about that, Valrad. I come from a place where mixing private and business dealings is frowned upon. I can distinguish between following your House's values and personal disregard."

"That is good to hear, my friend. Good bye to you."

Enric watched the Head of House Vel'kim walking out and leaned back thoughtfully. So her father had decided to take on a more active role in making sure Eryn's interests were safeguarded. To a certain degree that was his right, but it might as well turn out to be a hindrance, especially considering that the child Eryn was carrying under heart was the next but one in line for inheriting the position of Head of House Vel'kim. He would very probably be eager to be involved in raising the boy. Perfect. He could very well imagine Eryn's reaction to that.

* * *

"A message from Anyueel," Enric announced and dropped the small paper roll on her lap. "It's addressed to you. Royal seal."

She took a deep breath and picked it up to unroll it. He watched her eyes darting along the lines, then how she exhaled disappointedly and crumpled it.

"Would you care to fill me in?" he prompted her.

"Just a dismissive reply to a little request I sent to the King. I asked him to release me from the Order for the time being as I have started involving myself politically by assisting Vran'el in drumming up votes for the Senate. I wrote that I am considering taking my brother's seat in the Senate for a time, and that this would surely be just the same conflict of interests as in your case."

He raised both eyebrows in surprise. Her together in the Senate for House Vel'kim with her father? Voluntarily?

"You are really thinking about becoming politically active? You? Seriously?" he asked.

She shook her head. "Not really. But I thought it would make an effective argument."

"I take it he was not too enthusiastic about your request?"

She grunted. "That is putting it mildly. The very first word instead of a greeting is *No*. Then he writes that I am to stay out of their Senate by royal order and that my leaving the Order is not open to me now and will never be as far as he is concerned."

Enric shook his head at her and smiled indulgently. "Now, what did you expect? An honourable discharge with his best wishes for the future? You are his best chance of getting us both back home within a reasonable time."

"I reckoned it was worth a try," she shrugged and tickled the large brown cat which was stretched out lazily on the cushion beside her.

"Well, at least you keep him entertained. I fancy he enjoys hearing from you."

"Good," she sighed. "I wouldn't want him to be at a loose end, would I? Who knows what ideas he might come up with."

"I had lunch with Kilan today. He sends his regards and was very carefully pointing out that Tyront and the King keep mentioning your rather inconsistent intervals of reporting to them."

"So he asked you to make me mend my ways?"

"No, he is much too realistic to make a request like that. I think he just wanted a sympathetic ear to share his grief."

The entrance door downstairs closed zestfully and a moment later Vern came in, bristling with excitement.

"The new academy has officially been founded!" the boy exclaimed.

"What? So fast?" Eryn marvelled. "I thought Elwoi wanted to sit down with the artists to try and keep them with him?"

"He tried, but they more or less laughed him out the door when he came with his suggestions," Vern snorted. "He said he was willing to let them have more of a say in what they wanted to do, permit them to try out new things – to a certain reasonable extent, as he phrased it."

"Let me guess," Eryn grimaced. "He intended himself as the one to decide what extent is reasonable?"

"You hit the mark. They told him that they would rather take half of the subsidy the Senate grants the arts and do with it what *they* saw as reasonable. Their new leader swore never again to subject himself and his followers to Elwoi's narrow-minded approach to art. And then they founded the new academy the very same day."

"Sounds to me as if they knew before the meeting that there would be no agreement," Eryn grinned.

"That is a very reasonable suggestion," Enric smiled. It was an excellent opportunity to have Valrad's generosity mentioned, and better to have Vern do it. Less likely to arouse suspicion. "Have they taken care of the organisational matters yet?"

Vern nodded. "Not all of them, but they covered the basics, I think. Vran'el and Ram'an were there to hand over the documents."

Eryn's ears pricked up. "What documents? And why them?"

The boy chuckled. "What, you don't know?"

"Don't I know *what*?" Eryn enquired.

"House Vel'kim has made a very generous contribution to the new academy in the form of a building they can use. Vran'el was there officially to hand over the deeds, and Ram'an offered his services as legal advisor for free since he cannot really afford to help them out with gold at the moment."

She swallowed. Damn him. So Valrad had done something nice for the people that supported and valued Vern. Good for them. That didn't mean she had to like him for it, though, did it? Who knew what political advantages he might be expecting in return. He had probably just wanted to reinforce his alliance with the other Houses which supported the new academy as well. Who was to say that it was a selfless gesture?

She thought about Iklan's words about forming her own reality around facts she didn't appreciate and cursed him for the influence he'd had on her after only three meetings.

"That was... generous," she made herself say.

Vern lifted an eyebrow at her. "Dear me, that must have been painful!"

She flashed him a cool look. "I have no idea what you are talking about." Then she got up. "If you would excuse me now."

Enric watched her walking towards their bedroom, then looked at Vern.

"Sorry," the boy murmured. "One should think I would have learned something."

"Yes, really," Enric remarked without pity. "So now you must go after her and get her in a better mood again. I have no intention of paying for your lack of sensitivity. Should you consider pointing out that I am currently not your superior and thus theoretically not in a position to issue you with any orders, let me give you the same reason for cooperating that worked so well with your father: The nights are chilly here, especially when one has to sleep outside on the street."

Vern rose grumpily, muttering something about subjecting underage magicians to unreasonable duress and slipped away to where Eryn had disappeared only moments before.

"What?" she growled when she heard the knock at her door.

"It's me," she heard Vern's muffled voice. "Can I come in? Please? Enric will kick me out the house if you don't talk to me. And if you remember from the expedition, I am not good with sleeping outside. Pleeeeease?"

She couldn't help but smile at that. "Come in then, soft, pampered city boy."

He opened the door and entered wearing an expression of profound relief. "Thank you. I have really got used to staying in this fancy place here, you know."

"It is unlikely that he would really have kicked you out on account of not coming after me," she sighed.

"I am not going to take your word for that and risk angering mighty Lord Enric. There is a reason people keep out of his way at home, you know."

"Man up, my lad," she sighed.

"I would rather first live long enough to fully *grow* up, if it's all the same to you," he retorted and flopped down on the bed next to her. "Can I ask you something?"

"What if I were to say no?"

"I would still ask you. It's a polite phrase you are supposed to answer with an offer for me to share whatever is on my mind with you. We really need to make you attend some lady-training. Basic courtesies and stuff like that."

She rolled her eyes. "Of course you may ask me whatever you feel you need to get rid of, my friend!" she trilled in a forced, high-pitched voice.

"Yes, very good. That leaves the matter of authenticity to be taken care of, but for now I will accept whatever I can get. I was asked to teach at the new academy."

Eryn sat up. "You were? But this is fabulous news! Why do you look so unhappy about this? It's a great proof of their admiration, I would think."

"It is yes," he sighed and gave her a pained look. "But I remember a certain teaching experience I had not too long ago where things went completely wrong. I mean, I almost made the healers run off when I took over training them in your absence! What if the same thing happens with the artists? They just fled from one place, they don't have many more choices now!"

She laughed at that. "Come on, they won't just run away from you! I think you have learned from your mistakes, haven't you? I remember that the healers said that you were too demanding, that you expected as much of them as of yourself. Which is rather a lot, considering that you are a bloody genius. Just take this into account with your next class."

"Help me," he pleaded. "Tell me how teaching works. What do I have to bear in mind? I mean, I am younger than every single one of the artists. How do I even make them listen to me?"

"Forget your age, my lad. They invited to you teach them because you have proven your skills beyond any doubt, so I would say they are more than willing to listen to you. About teaching as such... I am not an expert myself, I have to admit. I was just clumsily trying to pass on what my father has imparted to me. But it's not as if you don't have anybody else you can ask. Your father has been training fighters for more than two decades, and Ram'an teaches lawyers. Why not go and ask them? There is so much expertise around you, so make use of it."

Vern looked at her thoughtfully. "You know what? You are right! But I would still like to hear what you think is important. The healers like being taught by you, so you have obviously done it right, even if only by accident instead of design."

"Thank you very much for putting it like that," she said but took a few moments to consider the question. "I have found it helpful to avoid giving too much information at once, to let them try it themselves, if possible. Hearing it is one thing, doing it yourself is what makes you really understand it. I have no idea if this applies to art as well. What exactly is it you are teaching them, in any case?"

"Drawing. It seems their training has so far only focused on creative techniques, but not on what Elwoi would call *copying reality*. But a number of them are very keen on learning just that."

"How can a society pass on knowledge without representing objects properly?" she wondered.

"Well, explanatory pictures have only been made by craftspeople so far. And that's why their quality was not always exactly brilliant. I don't mean to disparage craftspeople," he added hastily. "It's just that usually their strengths are not in drawing, but in the skill their craft requires."

"When are you supposed to be starting your lessons? Is there a lot of construction work to be done at their building?"

"Hardly any. They are already moving into one part of the building. I was asked to start in a few days. Is there any chance that you could come to my first lesson? I would feel a lot less nervous with you there. And if you as a non-artist can understand what I am telling them, it probably means that I am getting it right."

She nodded, touched by the request. "Sure, just tell me when exactly to be in which place and I will let them know at the clinic that I shall not be working that day."

Vern hugged her for a short moment, the relief plain on his face. "Thank you so much! Really, I value that a lot! Now I will wait for father to come home and ask him to share his wisdom with me." He rolled his eyes. "Oh dear, will he be pleased about that opportunity!" He jumped up and sent her another pleading look. "Could you just come out for a moment and casually pass your fearsome companion - maybe give him a smile to let him see that I changed your mood back from annoyed to amiable?"

Eryn smiled. "Alright, you big coward, I will. Though I promise he won't kick you out onto the street to fend for yourself. I wouldn't allow him. And even in that hugely unlikely case, Ram'an or Vran'el would take you in."

"I am trying to provide for my future here, Eryn," he sighed. "In a few months he is going to be my superior again, and I would like him to look upon me with kindness."

Shaking her head, she rose. "So you are not cowardly, but rather sneaky? I wonder if that is much better. But who am I to judge?"

"Yes, exactly," he snorted and opened the door for her, dodging the pillow that came flying at him.

CHAPTER 18

A First Approach

Eryn took a deep breath and knocked at Iklan's door. His assistant had told her that this was a good time for her to try, as he usually saved that time slot for his administrative work.

"Come," she heard his voice from behind the closed door and pushed down the handle to enter.

He smiled when he beheld her. "Ah, Eryn. Do come in. I had been expecting you yesterday already when I heard that you were back at work." The reproof was very mild, but it was clear.

She closed the door behind her and walked to the seating cushions. "I know. I was not really up to seeing you yesterday. I needed a little more time to think things over."

"And, did you?" he asked kindly, rising from his chair to walk over to her. "Think, I mean."

"I did, yes." She looked up at him. "I have decided that I need to tell Valrad a few things."

Both Iklan's eyebrows rose at that statement. "I see," he said slowly, carefully hiding his enthusiasm about that unexpected development.

"I don't want to do it alone, though. And I don't even know if it is a good idea. Or whether things will be worse afterwards than they are now."

"You have made a good decision to talk to him. I would refrain from interfering, of course. Unless you express a wish for my assistance, that is. And you may ask me to leave the two of you alone at any point. Is that acceptable to you as far as the circumstances are concerned?"

251

She blinked. That was a little more specific than she was willing to commit to at that moment. But then she could always change her mind, couldn't she?

"That sounds fine, yes," she nodded slowly. "Then I suppose you will let me know what would be a good time for you, and we should see if Valrad is available at..."

Iklan smiled and walked to the door. "Oh no, dear Eryn, too many complicated layers."

She became terror-stricken and sucked in her breath when she heard him talking to his assistant. "Just run down and see if Valrad is available right now, will you? Tell him his daughter would like to speak to him."

"What? Right now?" she exclaimed when he returned and closed the door.

"Sure, why ever not? You might as well do it now. Why procrastinate?" he shrugged.

"I haven't prepared what I wanted to say to him!" she protested, her voice breaking slightly.

"Do not worry, Eryn. I am confident that the right words will come to you. I do not have the impression that you are usually at a loss for them."

"You still might have asked me first!" she moaned, seriously considering whether escaping before Valrad turned up was feasible.

"Forgive me," Iklan said in a conciliatory manner that did not exactly convince her.

She narrowed her eyes at him. "You did that on purpose! So I would have no chance at all to change my mind!" she accused him.

He lifted his brow in mock surprise. "Do not tell me you intended to leave that possibility open for yourself? It would imply a certain lack of security."

"Of course I lack security!" she wailed. "This is why I am here, or isn't it?"

"A very valuable insight," he nodded. "And I am confident that talking to Valrad will be a very helpful step in regaining some of it." He turned when a knock at the open door sounded. "Ah, Valrad! Very good of you to come over so quickly. Please shut the door behind you, this is something that requires privacy."

Eryn breathed in and out several times. It had been unexpectedly swift.

"Of course." Valrad did as requested and then nodded to his colleague. "Iklan." Then he turned to Eryn. "Do you mind if I sit with you, my dear girl?"

Eryn swallowed a remark about *my dear girl* and motioned for him to take a seat on the cushions. He did, careful not to get too close to make her feel crowded out. Iklan had retreated behind his desk, removing himself from their immediate field of vision.

"You wanted to see me, Eryn?" Valrad asked softly, his gaze intense.

"I... yes. There is something I want you to hear. And maybe we can then move on to a less painful way of relating to each other," she replied stiffly.

"I would very much like that." He leaned back and waited for her to go on.

Eryn looked at him for a while, studying his features. She hadn't really looked at him for quite a while now, always eager to avoid his gaze and ignore him. He looked the same as before, when she was here, maybe a little more ill at ease than she knew him. But then why should the revelation of the true nature of their kinship have changed his appearance, she asked herself. Perhaps, for some foolish reason, because so much had changed inside her that she had expected this change to be mirrored in his appearance.

"I am angry at you," she started, feeling her heartbeat quickening. "You are not the man I thought you to be. I trusted you, and you turned out to be untrustworthy. That hurts. A lot. And I am angry at myself. For misjudging you, for trusting you. It has made me doubt the people I am close to. And doubt myself. That hurts even more. I was on the verge of pushing away those I love because I was wondering whether getting hurt isn't too great a price to pay for trusting people."

She saw him swallow, and the muscles in his jaw becoming tense, but he remained silent, though with a visible effort.

"I want you to understand," she went on, "that I had a father. The best one I could have wished for in fact. I have seen a lot of loveless men who saw a child, and a daughter especially, as no more than a nuisance. But not my father. He was kind to me, taught and protected me. He made me feel cherished. I feel as though I am now expected to replace him with you, more or less from one week to another. Like I am supposed to rejoice now that I can so conveniently cast aside one father to gladly accept a richer, more influential one. I don't need another father. I don't want one."

"What is it you want, Eryn?" Valrad asked gently. "Name it and I will provide it if I can."

"I want back what we had before. I want my uncle back. I want to be allowed to think of my father as being your brother, not you." Her voice was trembling slightly.

There was regret in his eyes when he sighed and leaned back. "Not that, Eryn. I cannot give you that. I can never go back to being your uncle, it would be wrong. I am sorry, my child." He shook his head with a heavy sigh. "I know that Ved'al was the only father you had ever known. And I am eternally grateful to him that he raised you the way he did, turning you into the confident and capable woman you are today. And yet it was a role that should have been mine. Always." He leaned forward again, gently laying one hand on hers. "Your wellbeing is my responsibility now, and returning to being merely your uncle is not the reality of it, Eryn. Being a fatherly friend is not acceptable when in truth I am your father. I could not bear it."

Eryn pulled her fingers away from under his and turned away. "That is unfortunate. It seems our wishes are contradictory. There is not much of a compromise possible here, it seems." Her voice had returned to being stiff and cool.

"I do not expect you to just push Ved'al's memory aside like that," Valrad assured her. "It would make me sad even if you were able to. It would mean that your bond with him was not a particularly strong one. I also understand that you have lived almost half of your life without a father, and that accepting somebody else in Ved'al's place is not a minor issue. But it is one you and I can accomplish in time. I love you, Eryn. And I am proud to call you mine. Will you let me tell you a story, my girl? Of three young people who did so very well in making each other as miserable as possible?"

She shook her head vehemently and got up with difficulty. "I can't. I am sorry. I just... can't. Not now." She had an urgent need to get out of here, escape into the open with no walls around her and fresher air.

Valrad nodded disappointedly, but managed a smile. "Another time, then. I see that you are not yet ready to hear it." He stood as well, holding on to her hand as she was trying to leave. "Eryn," he said urgently, "let us not part like that. Please do not run from me."

She halted without looking at him, waiting for him to say what he wanted. His fingers around hers were warm.

"I would like to tell you that I am glad you chose to talk to me today. I would like to release you from all and any supervision in connection with your work here at the clinic from this moment on. You are a healer with full rights and duties now."

Her head snapped to him, her eyes wide with surprise. "I am?"

"Yes." He glanced at Iklan. "I will also no longer oblige you to see Iklan if you do not wish to. I think you would still profit from his help, but I will leave that decision to you. There will not be any consequences from my side if you decide against it."

She blinked, not sure if she had heard him correctly. Had he just released her from both measures he himself had established to make her cooperate?

"Why?" was the only thing she could think of uttering.

"Because I see that you have steered some changes in the right direction already, my girl. And I fear that having me continue to push you will do more harm than good to our relationship." He smiled. "There is too much Aren in you. Will you have dinner at my place tomorrow? With Enric and your friends?"

She thought for a moment before answering. It would be rather ungrateful to reject his invitation now that he had accommodated her like that. She nodded and found that accepting it was less of a burden than she would have envisaged. His gesture had obviously affected her the way he must have hoped.

"Thank you." He lifted her hand to touch his cheek for a short moment before releasing it again. His smile had become a lot more supple.

She nodded at him once and walked out, unsure of what to make of the conversation she had just had. It had not really changed what she had hoped, namely making Valrad see that there was little chance of her accepting him as a father and all that entailed. Yet it had clearly improved her circumstances at the clinic. That had to count for something.

* * *

Enric watched her carefully, trying to discern any sign of anger or resignation, but she seemed relaxed, even somewhat still surprised. The latter sentiment he shared. She had more or less voluntarily talked to her father, been freed from his conditions for working at the clinic and had even agreed to have dinner with him at his place. He didn't remember receiving any particularly strong emotions through the bond while she had been in Iklan's office, so it had obviously been a liberating if a not entirely pleasant conversation.

He reminded himself not to make any inconsiderate remarks about it being high time for her to take care of this matter and similar. It was the kind of pressure she had resented in the past.

"I am looking forward to going there," he said casually. "I have the impression that Urban finds the Vel'kim gardens more attractive than ours. They are more extensive, after all."

"Not only that. Valrad grows a few herbs there that she is very fond of and either rolls around in or gnaws the tops off them," she explained. "I need to check which ones she likes, then perhaps I can ask Plia to see if she can raise them at home and plant them in our garden."

He had called the Aren gardens *ours*, she thought. He obviously felt very much at home at the Aren residence already. She wondered if that was going to be problematic when it came to leaving here again. Maybe the King's and Tyront's concerns about him not returning were not as unfounded as she had assumed.

"The Senate has received a message from Malriel," he said into her reflections, observing her tense reaction, how she tried to play down her interest with a nonchalant shrug.

"So she is still alive and kicking."

"Evidence would suggest that, yes," he remarked, hiding his amusement well.

"And? What does she write? Are we at war with them already or does her warm and welcoming personality appeal to them for some odd reason?"

"It was only a short message - you know the limitations of what one of those birds can carry. She says the negotiations have not yet started, that they are taking a long time for preparations and first insisted on getting to know her better to see if she could be trusted."

"I could have saved them the time and effort," Eryn huffed. "She can't be trusted. Absolutely and definitely not. It was risky enough to send her there, if you ask me. Unless..." Her eyes narrowed. "Is it possible that the Western Territories *want* a war?"

Enric sighed. "Your trust in your mother is not exactly overwhelming."

She looked at her rounded belly pointedly, then back at him with a raised brow. "You don't say."

"No, they don't want a war. They don't even know how to fight one. Who would you have sent in her place, just for argument's sake?"

"I don't know. Anybody with a less belligerent attitude, I think. Some diplomat."

"Malriel can be pleasant enough when she puts her mind to it. You have seen her at more than one social occasion. Think back to how quickly she had Anyueel's rich and important wrapped around her little finger."

"That may work with people who consider her a novelty and appreciate her exotic way of talking. And it's not as though they weren't more than happy to side with her after I annoyed several of them previously. Up in that northern country she won't have any of these advantages."

He smiled. "And yet she is an experienced negotiator, politician and businesswoman - even if she did not exactly blanket herself in glory in her dealings with you. Sending a Head of House furthermore signals that this is considered a matter of importance. What is more, of the Heads I have met, she is clearly one of the more remarkable ones. That she is attractive as well and knows how to use it might also have been a consideration in her favour," he added.

Eryn sent him a dark look. "I don't appreciate your pointing out that last bit. Not at all."

"Not jealous, are you?" He leaned forward eagerly and grinned widely.

"Listen, you don't want me jealous," she said, her tone prickly, and folded her arms. "And what sane man would exchange his spouse for an older version of her, anyway?" A version that was theoretically older, but didn't look it, her unbidden thoughts added. A more suave, elegant, cunning and experienced version of herself. And one that presently didn't have a rounded belly, a little extra on the hips and constant cravings for baked sweet buns that would make her even rounder.

"No sane man would ever exchange you, my love, no matter who you were pitched against," he smiled and leaned forward to kiss her, holding on to her arm when she turned away. "No, don't sulk. I admit it does me good to have you worried about losing me for once. Usually *I* am the one being haunted by that possibility."

"Always eager to accommodate you," she murmured and let him brush her lips.

"There is something else she wrote. She said to convey her love to her daughter and hoped that her grandson is doing well."

"Has she been doing any additional adoptions lately?" Eryn asked sweetly. "I don't recall a daughter - just a son, unless I am very much mistaken."

He hadn't really expected her to react with any enthusiasm to that, but he wondered if it was truly aversion that had spoken or if she really was worried and compensating for it that way. He hoped it was the second. It would mean that there was still hope for the two women to reconcile with each other one day. She had so far made up with Ram'an and had taken a promising step towards the same with her father. Who was to say that this wasn't also going to be possible with Malriel?

"Will you see Iklan again?" he changed the topic. "In his professional capacity, I mean. I expect you will meet him as a colleague occasionally."

She shrugged. "I don't know. Not for now. I'll admit he was helpful to a certain degree. But our appointments were not exactly soporific. I don't mind not meeting him for a while. By the way, he wants to talk to us both about our mind bond. He hasn't brought it up again since my exam, but that surely had something to do with the fact that I suddenly ended up as his patie... er, client."

"Then you'd better agree a date and time with him. Just take my Senate meeting appointments into consideration. Afternoon is generally easier for me."

She nodded. "I will." Then she leaned back and glanced up at the ceiling. "Why do you think he has freed me of both?"

It took him a moment to follow her mental leap back to their initial topic. "You wouldn't have in his place?"

"I don't know. It seems a bit risky for him, though. I could just as well have used this opportunity to have nothing to do with him anymore. He could have freed me from working with him and still oblige me to go on seeing Iklan. It would still have been a gesture of goodwill."

Enric nodded. "True. But he would still have been forcing you into doing something you didn't want. And he obviously seems to view your progress as satisfying enough for him to assume that you can handle the rest without coercion. Freeing you from either Iklan or himself would have been a halfway gesture. In my dealings with him I didn't get the impression that he is a man for half measures. A bit like Orrin. If he considers something right, he takes care of it. Simple and straightforward."

"Yes, a man with principles," she muttered. "Pity he didn't have them back when he impregnated his brother's companion."

"Has he told you anything about that? The circumstances?"

"He wanted to," she sighed. "But I didn't want to hear it. One day maybe. But not right now."

They looked up when Junar paddled in, looking tired and hot. Enric quickly got up to help her sit, gently letting her sink down onto the cushions next to Eryn.

"You look exhausted," he remarked sympathetically and pressed a glass of cool water into her hand.

"I can't sleep, I can't walk anywhere for more than a few minutes, I can't see my feet anymore. I can't do anything," she sighed unhappily. "It's time for that child to be out. I mean it." Another heart-breaking sigh followed. "I can't even sleep lying on my front any longer. That is my favourite sleeping position, always has been. But I haven't been doing a lot of sleeping lately, so that probably doesn't matter. At night she kicks like mad and during the day it's too hot really to sleep for more than minutes at a time when I am too exhausted to keep my eyes open." She looked up at Enric. "And now I have turned into a whiner!" she added.

"No worries, Junar," he smiled and squeezed her hand. "You have been doing very well, we are all proud of you. You are entitled to a bit of whining."

"Every additional week your daughter stays inside will allow her to grow stronger and healthier," Eryn stated, without much compassion. "Which means you should rather be wishing to hold her in there for as long as you are able."

Both their heads turned towards her, looking at her. Enric clearly not thrilled with her lack of sympathy, Junar just annoyed.

"Says the woman whose greatest inconvenience so far has been a craving for bakery products," she complained. "Stop your healer talk or I will throw something at you! I don't think the rules for how to treat expectant mothers apply in my case. I am the more pregnant!"

"Well, if your daughter is on schedule, she should be due in about one week," Enric cut in. "You can manage one more week, surely, Junar. Just take the opportunity to make all of us around you jump at your smallest wish for a few more days," he smiled. "These pregnancy privileges tend to disappear when the pregnancy is over, you know."

She smiled impishly. "If you are suggesting it... I would very much like one of Eryn's bread buns if that greedy woman has left anything of today's delivery."

"I don't have to leave any of them to any of you. They are *mine*!" Eryn huffed.

Enric rose quickly to feed them. One of them at least would soon be free of hauling that burden around in the hot climate. He briefly wondered if that would really be much of an improvement, but pushed the thought aside quickly. It was a bit too late for that now, anyway. *He* had been the one to insist on their moving in here, after all.

* * *

Eryn swallowed when they walked up the hill to where the Vel'kim residence made a peaceful yet imposing picture with the glowing sunset behind. They had walked here at a leisurely pace to make sure Junar wasn't overwhelmed by the exercise. She had emptied an entire pouch of water on the way here and had a few minutes ago mentioned that a bathroom would be handy fairly soon.

"Everything alright?" Enric asked her softly and squeezed her hand.

Eryn nodded uneasily and even managed a valiant smile. "Perfectly."

"Good. I wouldn't want you to bolt on the first occasion. Your expression reminds me a touch of what I saw at our first commitment ceremony," he said, only half-jokingly.

"I agreed to come here, remember? I can do this," she promised, smiling when Urban trotted ahead and around the house to enter through the terrace door. "I hope she doesn't startle whoever is preparing the food. That might cause an unnecessary delay."

He nodded. "In case of Vran'el that is likely enough, yes. He is still skittish around her."

She raised an eyebrow at him. "I thought this term was only used for horses?"

"Watch the way he sidles about to keep his distance to the cat. It does indeed remind me of a nervous horse," he shrugged.

They were still several paces away from the entrance door when it was opened by Vran'el.

"Your cat just scared ten years off my life, thank you very much!" he complained. "There are more gentle ways to announce your arrival, you know?"

Eryn shrugged. "Why bother? This seems to work well enough. Is that your daughter I hear squealing in the background? I am sure she will protect you from the big bad cat if you ask nicely."

He rolled his eyes and looked at Junar, who was breathing heavily after the short climb. "Come, Junar, you look exhausted. Is there anything I can do for you to make you happy?"

She nodded enthusiastically and her voice had taken on a slightly urgent tone. "You can, yes. I really, really, really need to use your bathroom."

"That *does* sound urgent. Let me guide you to the nearest one, dear Junar," Vran'el said gallantly and took the arm Orrin had just released to lead her away.

Enric reached behind him to hand them moist towels and then preceded them up the stairs into the main room, where Vran'el's daughter was trying to get her hands on the mountain cat. Urban made sure to stay out of her reach and moved quickly every time the girl came too close.

"Obal, you need to be more gentle with that cat. She does not like your energetic handling of her. Come and sit here before she bites off

259

your head," Intrea instructed and patted the cushions next to her. She smiled when she spotted the other visitors. "There you are! I am trying to save your pet from Obal's greedy, sticky hands," she sighed and rose to kiss each of them on the cheeks.

Obal had lifted her head and grinned widely when she spotted Enric, turning away from the cat and running to him with raised arms for him to catch and lift her.

"Good to see that she is still more into me than Urban," Enric grinned and placed her on his hip.

The girl was about to raise her hand to his hair when she stopped and stared at Orrin and Vern.

"And there goes her fascination with you on account of being bright-haired," Eryn laughed and took a seat on the cushions on the floor.

Valrad entered through the kitchen door and smiled widely.

"Good evening everybody," he beamed at the sight of them. "The food will be ready any minute now. Please take a seat and let me know what I can get you to drink. Ram'an will be the last one to arrive, and he should be here any moment now."

Enric took a seat next to his companion, shifting the girl so that she came to sit on his lap.

"He has invited Ram'an as well?" Eryn whispered to him. "Why?"

"To give you the feeling that you are among friends and help you relax, I would assume," he murmured. "Do you object? I thought you and Ram'an were getting along now?"

"We are. It just surprised me, that's all."

Intrea sank down on the cushions next to Eryn, joining the low conversation. "Valrad has always liked Ram'an, though of course the story with Pe'tala and then his attempt to bind you to him strained his regard somewhat in the past. But now both his daughters are more or less settled with other men, and Ram'an seems to have helped you to overcome your phase of seclusion from the people around you. That has relieved the tension quite a bit," she explained.

"I recall no such phase," Eryn said stiffly, miffed that it had been so obvious even for people who were not that close to her. But then maybe Vran'el had talked to her about it.

"Of course not," Intrea smiled with a wink and then nodded at her daughter, who was still holding on to Enric's arm but had taken to studying Vern. "It seems her fascination for you has shifted towards a younger man. She really does have a thing for blond men."

"That's how quickly one is replaced these days," Enric sighed.

"Right enough," Eryn nodded. "And don't you forget it."

"This doesn't apply to *you*," he grumbled. "You don't get to replace me."

Junar and Vran'el entered the main room, the seamstress with a relieved expression on her face. When they heard a knock at the entrance door, Vran'el led her to Orrin.

"May I return your lovely companion to you, Orrin? This should be Ram'an."

A few moments later they indeed heard Ram'an's voice from downstairs. When both men returned, Ram'an greeted first the women, then the men before taking a seat next to Intrea.

When Vran'el and Valrad then brought in two steaming bowls, one larger, one smaller, Eryn was the first to lean forward to wash her hands, eager to commence eating.

"Hungry, sweetness?" her brother grinned and placed the smaller bowl and a heap of tableware in front of her.

"Don't tease the expectant woman," she growled. "Rather feed her."

"Them," Junar chimed in. "Feed *them*. There is more than one of us who needs to eat for two."

Valrad laughed and started filling bowls, serving the two mothers-to-be first.

"My brother sends his regards to all of you," Intrea told them. "He says it is pretty uneventful in Anyueel since Eryn left. He asked me for the latest gossip about her."

"Asking about gossip? That is hardly befitting his noble and important rank as ambassador, is it?" Eryn asked between bites.

"Just as much as much as talking with a half-full mouth is for you, you high-born barbarian," Junar grinned.

"You are seriously calling *me* a barbarian?" Eryn spluttered. "You are one yourself - you were even born in the Kingdom, while I got there when I was Obal's age."

"I am not talking about where you grew up, but about your table manners," the seamstress shot back.

"There is not much gossip about me currently, is there?" Eryn turned back to Intrea.

"A thing or two. That you took your own companion out of the game, for example – with Ram'an. And how you are dealing with your new family situation. Or failing to."

Eryn ground her teeth. "Failing to? I am here tonight, am I not? That should indicate that I am adapting to the circumstances."

Vran'el shrugged. "It is a start. Spending an evening at your House after so many weeks is a first sign, but not the end of the line, sweetness."

Enric shook his head almost imperceptibly to indicate to the other man to avoid exhorting her.

"I would think that Vern's accidental kindling of that revolution would also make for nice gossip," he suggested, to steer the topic away from his companion.

"Definitely," Intrea nodded eagerly. "I can hardly believe that all this is really happening." She turned to the boy. "I am very much looking forward to your first drawing class in three days. I have registered for it and can hardly wait! I have ordered Vran'el to take care of his daughter for that time."

Vern grimaced. "Don't expect too much. My last teaching experience was not an entirely pleasant one." He turned to Ram'an. "I have been wanting to ask you for a few tips in regard to that. Eryn told me not to give them too much information at once and let them try out things themselves to see if they understood it. Father says that pairing stronger with weaker students is a good way to make them teach each other, in case the teacher's approach does not always appeal to them."

Ram'an chewed thoughtfully, then swallowed and nodded. "I have no experience when it comes to teaching art, but with the laws quite a few techniques are possible. Do not lecture them too much in one go, but let them contribute something as well. Sometimes they know quite a lot already. Being allowed to show that pushes their confidence. Do not give them all the information without making them work for it. Let them work things out themselves; it stays in their heads longer that way. Let them discuss without interrupting them and see what they come up with. Of course you need to tell them afterwards which of their solutions was the correct one."

Vern nodded, leaning forward attentively. "Let them work things out; alright, I've got that. Make them discuss and try out things. Anything else?"

The lawyer shrugged. "Only the obvious, such as starting with simple stuff and progressing to more challenging areas. Or checking on their progress regularly and encouraging them to ask questions if something is unclear. From what I have heard, Elwoi is not a teacher to welcome questions or even react favourably to them. That is a great pity in my opinion since questions are a very efficient way to learn. Try to encourage your students to ask you, and show appreciation for their questions. Do not patronise them - it is not an attitude that is generally received very favourably, especially considering your age. But be prepared to be authoritative if necessary. If somebody asks a question, for example, and others laugh about it, put a stop to that immediately. It does not provide for a constructive learning and working environment. If a student criticises you, do not see it as a personal insult but a chance to understand more. As long as you admit to gaps in your own knowledge without letting it embarrass you, it cannot be used as a weapon against you."

Eryn smiled appreciatively. There were quite a few helpful suggestions she might use for herself in her healing training sessions when she was back in Anyueel.

Obal, who was still sitting on Enric's lap, fed him with bits from her own bowl.

"Don't get used to that," Eryn warned him. "You are soon going to be the one doing the feeding."

He shrugged. "We might hire your niece for that. She is doing a very good job."

"Speaking of my grandson," Valrad spoke and put aside his empty bowl. "How is he doing? Was everything alright at your last routine check?"

Eryn blinked in confusion. "He is fine, yes. I check regularly on him."

The healer frowned. "But you are going to the routine checks, are you not? Mothers, even when they are magicians and even healers, are not supposed to undertake the checks themselves."

"Well..."

Valrad exhaled slowly, sending her a reproachful look. "When did Pe'tala last have a look at you? A proper one?"

"Not that long ago, it was before we left for Takhan."

"That was almost two months ago! Come here," he instructed before he stood up and stretched out his hand. "You are supposed to do this every month!"

"What, here? Now? No! And how am I supposed to know about how you do things here? I told you, I check on the baby regularly, and I am not exactly a beginner, you know!" she protested.

"I see," Valrad nodded, his arms now akimbo. "Then I suppose you have not only checked the child's vital functions but also if everything is in order with the umbilical cord and placenta?"

"Eryn," she heard Enric's voice next to her. It had a slightly warning undertone. "Don't oppose him on principle on this. I will not put up with carelessness in this. Now get up and let him have a look at you."

She turned to him with an annoyed expression. "When did you become the judge of which procedures are to be carried out concerning healing?"

"Since my child started growing inside you," he replied and then turned to Valrad. "Will this take long?"

"No, only two minutes if everything is in order."

"I can do this tomorrow at the clinic!" she objected. "This has hardly to be done now!"

"Or you can do it right now and save yourself the humiliation of having me accompanying you to the clinic tomorrow to make sure you take care of this," Enric smiled with narrowed eyes.

"You are angry," Obal whispered, her eyes wide.

"Not at you," he clarified, his expression softening. "I just have to be a little strict with your aunt so she takes good care of the baby inside her."

"She does not take good care of him now?" the girl exclaimed, clearly shocked at such neglect.

"Oh, perfect," Eryn mumbled and climbed to her feet with an effort, "rile her up against me, why don't you?"

She stepped over three pairs of legs until she was standing in front of Valrad. "Let's get this done, if it really is necessary."

He nodded and pointed to a cushion between him and Ram'an. "Have a seat." He held her hand to make sitting down easier for her and then followed suit. The others around them fell silent and watched when the healer put his hand on her rounded belly.

He looked up at her and smiled broadly when there was a slight movement under his palm. "Your son just kicked me."

"Yes," she sneered, "I can relate to that well enough."

She heard a snigger from Vran'el's direction, satisfied with the lack of amusement on Valrad's face before he closed his eyes to concentrate on the examination. True to his word he was done after a short while and nodded.

"Everything is perfect. I hope you will attend to this regularly from now on. I will make sure to enquire." Then he turned to Junar. "And you, my dear lady? When did you last have a healer take a look at your daughter?"

"Last week," she replied obediently and then patted Vern's hand. "Not counting my very eager personal healer. He checks on me every single day."

Eryn rolled her eyes and considered briefly if she wanted to return to her seat next to Enric, but decided that it wasn't worth the effort of getting up again as she was not particularly pleased with him right now.

"I hear the date set for the next game is in about two months," Intrea enquired casually, then winked at Orrin. "I hope you still remember that you promised to pair up with me the next time, Orrin."

The warrior grinned broadly and nodded. "I wouldn't dare forget it. You were very insistent at that dinner."

Eryn saw Junar frowning slightly at that exchange, probably wondering if she should worry about another woman being so eager to roam the streets with her companion.

"A pity that you will not be in any shape to participate in that game," Ram'an sighed and looked at Eryn. "I found you very useful last time."

Enric looked up when Vran'el stood and took the seat next to him which Eryn had given up.

"I have a score to settle with him," Vran'el murmured, low enough for only Enric to hear. "I want to pair up with you. I do not care on which side I am, I just want to be on the one where I can hunt him. He is going to be made to pay for kicking me out of the game last time so he could steal my partner."

Enric smiled with a certain relish. There was the little matter of Ram'an kissing his companion only recently. He, too, had a little vengeance to exact.

"Agreed."

Ram'an swallowed and leaned closer to Eryn. "Why do I have the feeling that I have just been declared fair game?"

She followed his gaze, taking in the two men sitting at the opposite end of the low table and smiling faintly, but with a determined spark in their eyes.

"Because you are a very perceptive man, I would say. But you can always stay out of the next game," she suggested.

He sighed resignedly and shook his head. "No, it is not really what I feel free to do. I would look like a coward and, even worse, they would just wait for the next opportunity to get back at me."

"Face up to your doom then, oh brave one," she chuckled. "Under those circumstances I don't really mind not being on a team with you next time, to be honest."

"When will the training start, Orrin?" Intrea enquired. "Two months is not a lot of time to prepare, after all."

"For six people it will start in three days, then they will help me train the rest of those who have shown an interest, in about three weeks," the warrior explained. "The time will suffice for the things I consider most useful. There will be no hand-to-hand combat, just magical strikes and shielding, and almost everybody here is aware of the basics already. I shall leave it to each participant to do a little extra work when it comes to stamina and speed, as outrunning your opponents is on occasion just as necessary as hitting them."

"Why did I have to do so much sword fighting and unarmed combat training if in your opinion people here can do without it?" Eryn complained.

"Firstly, you are strong enough to defeat almost everybody even without honing your skills in magical fighting more than you have already. And secondly, sword fighting is a prerequisite for being a member in the Order. There is no getting out of that. Well," he amended with a pointed look at her belly, "at least not permanently. Also there is the little matter of being able to defend yourself against non-magicians without employing magic." He turned back to Intrea. "The rules for the next game will be slightly different to last time, though. With improved skills comes a new challenge."

She clapped her hands eagerly. "Nothing you and I will not manage, I am sure of it!"

Junar sent her a concerned look, but remained silent.

Vran'el took Junar's hand and squeezed it. "Intrea, dear, stop flirting with Junar's companion."

Intrea smiled apologetically. "Sorry, dear. I have no intentions of leading him into temptation, I am just being playful."

"Not that you would stand a chance against her, mind you," Vran'el smiled.

She nodded and winked. "I know. Otherwise flirting would be much too dangerous. Deep down I am a shy girl, after all."

Eryn snorted at that, earning herself a raised brow from Intrea. If the evening continued like this, it might even be enjoyable, she thought.

CHAPTER 19

Drawing Lesson

"What is going on here?" Vern whispered in horror when he saw the crowd in front of the building where he was supposed to be giving his first drawing lesson.

"I have no idea," Eryn replied, equally surprised at the commotion. "That must be at least two hundred people here. How many people do you have on your list?"

"Fifteen, I think."

"They are here to witness the change," Ram'an's voice said from behind them.

Both turned.

"So are you, obviously," she commented dryly.

"Of course. I am known to be friends with Vern, so people expect me to provide first-hand impressions when they ask me."

"Yes, I know what that is like," Vern snorted and gave her a pointed look.

She rolled her eyes. "Come on, now, you are not still angry at me for not summoning you before I knocked out Lord Tyront, are you? That was ages ago!"

"And yet you instantly knew what I was referring to. I take that as a sign of a guilty conscience," the boy said, snidely. However, his expression became serious as his gaze returned to the people that had assembled. "That does put me under a little bit of pressure. They have all come to watch my lesson? How am I supposed to teach like this?"

Ram'an shrugged. "That is the downside of being a local celebrity, my young friend. Are you ready? I think you are due to start in only a few minutes."

266

They spotted Intrea, who waved excitedly while coming closer. "There you are! Come on, we are all waiting for you inside." She looked around. "Is this not amazing? They are all here to witness your first lesson! This is a great way to whip up interest in the new academy." She kissed Ram'an, Eryn and Vern on the cheek and then took the boy's hand to drag him along into the building.

Eryn looked around, impressed. It was clearly an old building, but that was hardly something artists would object to. Quite the opposite - it lent the place character. There was some restoration work to be done, but nothing that was urgent or rendered the building unusable.

"We have switched the room we intended to use for today on account of all the observers," Intrea explained. "Now we will be in the largest space we have. Those who have not registered as participants will have to stand, though. We do not have nearly enough seats for all of them." She turned and winked at Ram'an. "Even the mighty Head of House Arbil, I am afraid."

"Not a problem for me, I expect no special treatment," the said Head replied.

Vern just nodded, clearly not especially comfortable. The prospect of having an audience so huge did nothing to calm his fretting.

They followed Intrea into a large hall where several people were arranging benches in neat rows.

Vern hesitated and looked concerned. "What are they doing?"

"Preparing the room for the lesson," Intrea replied, confused by the question. "Why? Is this not to your liking?"

"But they won't have any space for drawing!" he objected agitatedly and stepped forward hurriedly to stop them from what they were doing. "No, this is not good at all! I am not giving a speech here; I am teaching!" he called out, no further trace of his nervousness visible when he started pointing in different directions and indicating the distances he wanted between the seats and the rows.

"Now look who is taking control," Ram'an smiled.

"That is how we know it from Elwoi's lessons," Intrea shrugged helplessly. "We assumed this is what it is supposed to look like. Did he really say that he wanted people to *draw*? During his lesson?" she went on to ask, incredulous.

"Of course I want you to draw!" Vern huffed behind her. "I don't see any drawing materials here. Are people bringing them themselves or will the Academy provide them?"

Intrea swallowed and blinked rapidly several times. "We did not expect... well... Would you excuse me for a moment? I think I need to fetch a few supplies..." And off she went in haste.

"Elwoi is obviously not one to appreciate it if his students are distracted from his words of wisdom," Ram'an chuckled.

Vern shook his head. "No, that he isn't. He always tells them to practise at home. He does not take well to people doing anything other than hanging on his every word. I attended one of his lectures once, and that was not a pleasant experience. I made the mistake of interrupting him to ask a question and was almost kicked out of the room. I think only my status as ignorant barbarian back then made him exercise any leniency on me."

"They might be a bit overwhelmed by your new, unexpected teaching style at the beginning," Eryn warned him. "You might want to take that into consideration. They could react somewhat surprised when you ask them to pick up pen and paper."

"I know," the boy nodded. "But that can't be helped. I have no intention of talking for an hour and hope something sticks."

They watched a number of people filing into the hall, some of them seeking space along the front rows of chairs, others staying at the back.

"I had better guide the participants to where they are supposed to be sitting," Vern sighed and strode off.

"Wait!" Eryn called after him. "I am one of them! That means you might just as well start with me!"

He nodded and indicated a seat on the second row. "I'll have you in the middle. Make sure to ask questions to demonstrate to the others that doing so is welcome, will you?"

She nodded. "I can do that, yes."

Ram'an retreated to the back of the room to where the other spectators were assembling, then winked at her.

Vern positioned himself in front of the podium that had been put there for his use, ignoring it completely. He obviously wanted to demonstrate to his audience that he had no intention of talking down to them.

A few minutes later Intrea hurried towards him, her arms filled with numerous pens and notepads. Vern instructed her to distribute the drawing materials and put them in the places that had been prepared for the students. When she was done, Vern cleared his throat and raised his voice.

"We are about to start our lesson. I would thus ask those of you who are planning to participate to join me and take a seat up front. The others I would kindly ask to keep the noise to the level that still enables me to be heard by my students."

Several people detached themselves from the crowd in the back and came forward to sit on the benches where Intrea had distributed the drawing materials. The spectators at the back had calmed down so that only occasional whispering was audible.

Eryn surreptitiously scrutinised her fellow participants. They were a mix of men and women of different age and appearance. Apart from Intrea she didn't know a single one of them. But then she was very well acquainted with the teacher, which they were not.

Once all of them were seated, Vern took a deep breath and began to speak, "Welcome to this, our first drawing lesson. My name is Vern, though I think you probably all know who I am." He paused and exhaled, lifting his arms and letting them drop again as if at a loss how to continue. The seconds stretched on, then he sighed. "You know, this is my first drawing lesson," he said with candour. "I have been thinking about how to do this, have talked to people with more teaching experience than myself and I have prepared something I hope you will profit from. I know the kind of lessons you are used to, but I have to tell you that this is not my favourite format. It feels a lot like the history lessons I had back home."

Eryn saw a few smiles around her. They seemed to warm to his honest approach.

"The lessons I enjoyed most at home myself and also here when I attend the healing classes at the clinic are those which allow me to utilise what I just learned. And that is also what I am going to be doing with you. If anything is unclear, please ask. If I am too fast, slow me down. If something is too difficult, let me know. Clear enough?" He let his gaze wander over the faces in front of him, waiting for their hesitant nods before clapping his hands together. "Excellent! Then let's start, shall we?"

He picked up a pen and held it up for all of them to see. "We will start with something that you are all familiar with - a straightforward tool to handle. For drawing a precise instrument such as a pen is useful. Even if you normally prefer to work with a brush or something of that nature, you will see that, especially in the beginning, an instrument with a stiff, pointed tip is useful. The first thing we are going to try will probably seem ridiculously basic to you, but I hope you will come to understand why we need to do it. Having only a single colour at your disposal makes it necessary to put extra emphasis on distinguishing between dark and light shades to create a realistic picture. This means our first exercise will consist of working with different kinds of shades. There are darker and lighter ones - consisting of dots, cross-hatches, circles, stripes, waves and so on. After this we will move on to basic forms and after that we will combine the forms with the shades and create our first simple drawings. Are there any questions?"

The students looked at each other, then indicated negatively with their heads.

Vern nodded, satisfied. "Very well. Then let's start with how to position your paper in front of you so that your perspective is not distorted and how to hold your pen in a way that affords maximum flexibility for drawing and yet gives you the stability you need."

He quickly looked at Eryn and smiled in relief when she nodded her approval. So far he had done well enough. He had given them an idea what to expect and chosen his first exercises in a way to avoid scaring them off by making them sound too complex. She actually looked forward to trying what he had just presented. It had sounded interesting. She had rather expected to be there for his benefit alone, to help him overcome his nerves instead of actually profiting from the lesson herself. She watched him position the paper in front of him and then listened to his explanations on how to adapt the placement depending on one's preference for sitting and standing.

"Can I forego the standing positions?" Eryn called out, noticing how the people around her looked aghast despite Vern's earlier invitation to approach him with questions. "I am rather keen on sitting as much as possible currently, you know." She stroked her swollen abdomen to demonstrate.

"Well, whatever keeps the expectant Aren woman happy. We wouldn't want the building to collapse on top of us, would we?" Vern retorted with a grin, causing the students to relax immediately, aware that interruptions would indeed not trigger the reaction they had experienced from Elwoi.

* * *

Vern dropped onto the cushions of the teahouse Ram'an had insisted on bringing them to after the lesson. Intrea had accompanied them and sank down elegantly right beside him. Ram'an took Eryn's hand to assist her in sitting down.

"You were simply amazing!" Intrea called out and widened her eyes in astonishment. "Honestly, that was the first time in my life I have ever actually enjoyed being taught art! And really, I am not saying this simply to make you feel better. I have been listening to lectures, reading theoretical concepts and other resources for more than a decade now, and I would never have thought that learning about art could be even remotely enjoyable!" She flipped the pages of her notepad and looked once more through the drawings they had done during the lesson. "I cannot believe I did all this!" She leaned over to Eryn, stretching out her hand. "Let me see yours!"

Eryn was more coy and hugged her own sketches close. "I am afraid I did not exactly excel at it," she replied. She was, in fact, quite satisfied with her efforts, but when she had taken a peek at what the others had accomplished, she fairly soon realised that a certain ability was certainly helpful, in addition to mastering the techniques. An ability she clearly did not have.

"Nonsense! You did absolutely fine," Vern assured her. "Don't compare your outcome with those of the others, but with what you were able to sketch before. You were the only non-artist there, in any case. If you had been able to keep up with them as easily as that, I would have been really amazed. Also we would have had to question the accuracy of Ram'an's test as it should have identified you as an extraordinarily gifted artist."

Ram'an nodded at her notepad. "May I?"

She kept her grip. "No."

She cursed and tried to hold on to it as he mercilessly pried her fingers loose. "Why did you even ask me if you choose to ignore my answer? I hate it when people do that! It is like you made up your mind already and just wanted to give me the illusion of choice!"

Ram'an pretended to ponder her words for a few moments, before he gave the pad a final tug, freeing it from her grip. "That is a pretty accurate summary, yes. Now let me see what you have managed."

He inspected the different exercises on shading and her geometric forms, moving on to her first attempts at combining them. Then he flipped another page, perusing her sketches of a water glass, a human hand and several rather sorry drawings of leaves and blossoms.

"Not too bad, Theá. Nothing a little practice would not take care of. And as Vern told you, a beginner's efforts can hardly match those of trained artists." He handed over the drawings to Intrea without bothering to ask Eryn if she was alright with it.

"Why do you sometimes call her Theá but Eryn at other times?" Vern enquired curiously. "She doesn't like being called by her old name, but you still do so. Why?"

Ram'an smiled. "At the beginning it was my way of trying to make her see that she did not belong with the Kingdom, but with us here, with me. But after a while it turned into a kind of intimate way of addressing her. And Eryn still is the name Ved'al gave to her to keep us from finding her. I have no particularly fond associations with it. I just use it sometimes to accommodate her. But not always. If I feel like it, I satisfy myself by calling her Theá. It is the more beautiful name anyway, and one more befitting."

"That's a matter of opinion," Eryn rolled her eyes, then snatched Intrea's notepad to have a look at the drawings in it. As she had expected, they were far more polished compared to her own efforts. She stared at the outline of the hand, marvelling at the realistic effect her shading had given. Intrea definitely had no problem putting Vern's instructions into practice. Sighing, she flipped the page closed again and handed the pad back.

"Intrea is right, my lad. Your lesson was extremely well done. Your teaching style is very natural, it feels as if it's no effort at all for you to pass on your knowledge."

He huffed. "No effort? How I wish! I spent several hours a night for about a week preparing for these lessons. I mean, I had no idea how to explain the things that seem natural and reasonable to me. I talked to artists, asked them to draw something for me and only then worked out where to start, where the problems really lie."

"That you were well-prepared does not make your success any less remarkable," Ram'an said calmly. "Quite the opposite. It shows commitment to your task and that you are not willing to let fate or chance determine whether you are successful or not."

Vern beamed at the compliment.

"This all reminds me of how I have quite a few evenings of preparation ahead myself," the lawyer sighed. "Many of the business agreements with the Houses are in dire need of re-negotiation. Most of them are on the verge of expiring and need to be renewed while others I will be more than glad to get rid of."

"Negotiations?" Vern asked casually. Eryn grinned broadly, not fooled by his seemingly little more than polite interest.

"Yes," Ram'an nodded. "Terms on quotas, storage, reselling, raw materials, finished products, distribution, prices and all those no doubt immensely fascinating details a young man of your age finds utterly tiresome."

"I wouldn't say that," Vern replied slowly, clearly searching for words to add something else.

Eryn took pity on him. "Ram'an, Vern is very interested in acquiring some basic business skills. Would you consider letting him accompany you to your negotiations? Just for educational purposes? He won't be a bother, I promise." She winked at Vern.

Ram'an shrugged. "Sure, I have no objections to that. If you really consider this to be an entertaining pastime, be my guest." He was intrigued by the gleam that had entered Vern's eyes. "You are a strange young man, you know."

The boy snorted. "If I had a gold piece for every time somebody told me that, I would be rather wealthy."

"You *are* rather wealthy," Eryn commented dryly. "I remember Enric paying you rather handsomely for that painting I snagged from you to prevent you from burning it. I would say that five hundred gold slips is quite a fortune for a lad your age."

Intrea's eyes bulged. "He really paid you such a sum even though the painting already belonged to her?"

"Honourable Enric," Ram'an murmured wryly.

"He is," Intrea agreed with a sideways glance at the lawyer. "Still jealous of him, Ram'an? Time to get yourself a nice woman and start working on providing heirs for your House, I would say."

"A lofty task," he commented good-naturedly. "You have let yourself be snatched up by Vran'el, after all. So the good girls are all taken now."

Eryn raised a brow at that. Was he really flirting with Intrea?

The artist laughed. "You old charmer! Trust me, you would not be happy if you had to live with me. I think our current arrangement of spending the odd night together is fine the way it is."

"What?" Eryn exclaimed and almost dropped her cup. "You are doing *what*? Seriously?"

Intrea shrugged. "Do not tell me you are shocked about this. You are aware of the nature of your brother's and my relationship, and Ram'an is a grown man with needs. Though our last time together was quite a while ago, was it not? It was before you went to Anyueel and met Eryn. Now that you are no longer pursuing her we might get together again if you like."

Ram'an smiled and nodded. "It would be sheer pleasure."

"Stop that, you two!" Eryn hissed. "How can you just arrange for a... a... well, you know what you just arranged, in front of a growing teenager? Really now!"

"I do not have the impression that Vern is the problem here," the other woman smiled. "He is not a child any longer. How old are you, my lad? Sixteen?"

"Seventeen," he corrected her.

"Seventeen is more than old enough. He is very likely sexually active himself already," she shrugged.

That caused his face to blush a florid pink.

"Or maybe not," Ram'an chuckled. "Though I would not worry about that, my young friend. You are fast becoming renowned and exotic, which alone will make finding partners for pleasant pastimes easy enough for you."

Eryn exhaled slowly. "I really can't believe I am listening to this. Stop trying to push him into affairs! He has not even come of age yet! You will not be the ones to bear the consequences if he inadvertently gets a girl pregnant!"

"I *do* know how to avoid that!" Vern protested. "I am a trained healer, you know? And I worked on the prevention with you at the last Freedom Night, you remember?"

"Which is fine if you are doing it for somebody else, but there are occasions when you might be too caught up in the moment to act rationally," she contradicted.

"Eryn - stop mothering him! No matter how strong the urge is currently due to your emotional adaptations to bearing a baby," Intrea sighed. "You cannot keep him from having intimate relationships. And you should not; it is not healthy to deny oneself these elemental needs. Look at what it did to Ram'an. Well, before he started eating again and you healed away his wrinkles."

"Hey!" Ram'an protested. "I resent that! You might want to consider that there had been a few considerable changes in my life that were weighing upon me, not only the lack of sexual encounters."

"Stop!" Eryn hissed. "Why can't you people leave that topic where it belongs, in the bedroom?"

"Like the sounds that seem to escape your own bedroom at times?" Ram'an grinned, referring to what Vern had mentioned on a prior occasion.

"That has been taken care of," she replied stiffly.

Vern nodded. "True. I can't hear them anymore, but whenever I am in the garden in the evening, their window clearly discloses whether there are any nocturnal activities going on or not. They now close it when they are about to get heavy."

"Vern!" Eryn wailed and closed her eyes in exasperation. "I really admire how fast you are managing to adapt to this place, but if you don't stop talking about my love life, I am going to wallop you! Hard!"

"Sorry," he grinned apologetically.

"Why do you not drop by some time at my place, Vern?" Ram'an offered casually.

"For hearing more flagrant details about me?" Eryn remarked, sour-faced.

"To prepare for the negotiations he will be accompanying me at," the lawyer explained with a wink at the boy that belied his harmless answer.

"Oh yes, I'm sure," Eryn huffed.

"Alright, we will accommodate you and your fusty views and change the topic," Intrea sighed. "Pregnancy privileges. I recall that you are rather keen on having those at the moment. How are things going with your father right now? The family dinner last time was very harmonious, even though the two of you were rather wary around each other."

"Change of topic," Eryn hissed again.

"There is just no pleasing you," Intrea sighed with mock exasperation.

CHAPTER 20

Aiding House Arbil

Eryn was the only one to look up when Ram'an entered his study carrying a large tray with hot and cool drinks, baked goodies and fruit.

"Here. We need a larger quantity and a better price. But be careful of the quality. We are getting second choice now; don't let them trick you into accepting third choice," Enric said.

Vern just lifted a brow as if to say with a look what he didn't dare say with words: Who do you think you are talking to?

Enric seemed to get the message, though, judging from his fleeting smile.

"With the berries we can't really do anything at the moment. The agreement is still valid for another two years. But that's something to keep in mind for later. What we can work with are the fabrics. They are sold to every major tailoring shop and a few smaller ones as well. The price has not been adjusted in over ten years." Enric shook his head.

"What exactly are they doing?" Ram'an murmured beside Eryn.

"Saving your House. Judging from what I hear there are quite a number of rather disadvantageous arrangements in place with the other Houses," she replied.

Vern snorted. "That's an understatement if ever I heard one! Seriously, who does the negotiating in this family?"

"My cousin Alben. My father was very fond of him so he granted him a position of responsibility. Not to our advantage, as it turned out."

"You can say that again," Enric said and looked up. "He is either very bad at what he does or he is getting paid by the other Houses to agree to contracts that are unprofitable for your House. You might want to monitor his spending habits for a while. If they exceed his official income without his piling up debts, a little chat with him about family loyalty could be in order."

Ram'an nodded gravely, clearly not too thrilled with the idea, yet reluctant to contradict a man who was making such an effort to help him over the rough times.

"How good are your fabrics?" Vern enquired. "Do you have samples or anything?"

"They are the finest you can obtain," Ram'an said proudly. "Though House Landred does seem to suffer from the misapprehension that their products can compete with ours."

"Then Junar will surely be interested in having a look at them. She likes to try out new things. She basically had to rewrite the rules of tailoring to make Eryn look halfway female without a dress."

Ram'an nodded. "Then I will have a few bolts of fabric sent to her as a gift."

Vern shook his head. "No."

"No?"

"You will send to her a few free samples for her to peruse. She is a business owner. If she likes them, we will start negotiations with her. If she returns sporting fine fabrics from the Western Territories, soon every rich person in Anyueel will want to have them. Trust me," the boy explained. "All tailors and seamstresses will try to get in contact with you soon enough."

"But I am not sure we would be able to produce enough to satisfy these orders! We would have to increase our production, extend the flax and cotton plantations, increase the number of animals for the wool!"

Enric smiled. "Good. If the demand is high but the supply isn't, this will work wonders for the price."

Ram'an looked at Vern in astonishment. "You are very good at this, are you not? I bet you will be adopted by a House very soon."

Eryn smiled. "And there is only one logical choice, is there?"

Three voices spoke at the same time, "Aren," "Arbil," "Vel'kim".

The three magicians stared at each other.

Vern leaned back and started laughing loudly. "Not as obvious as you thought, eh, Eryn?"

"No," she admitted. "And I really wonder about that. He is a healer, and a very close friend of mine. Why would Houses Arbil and Aren even think they are the competition?"

"A healer he may be, but it is not the only thing he excels at," Enric explained with steepled fingers. "House Aren is a very rich and powerful House that could help him develop his potential no matter which path he decided to explore. Resources of whatever kind would never be an issue."

"Rich and powerful is not the main consideration, I am sure," Ram'an cut in. "Almost all the Houses can be called rich, even though

276

mine obviously is going through a bit of a rough patch right now. But our products are very good, and so are our connections. He is connected to your Houses already through his connection with you personally. I could offer him other valuable opportunities in addition to the ones you will hardly deny him merely because he joined another House than one of yours. And of course there is the matter of courtesy between Houses. Vern will assist in delivering my House from ruin, so I feel I should be granted the chance to make up for it by offering him an influential position and a place in my family."

Vern cleared his throat, "Excuse me? May I say something here?"

Eryn shook her head without looking at him. "No. You are the prize. The prize doesn't have a say in this. Unless you say that Vel'kim is the only possible choice for you. Then you may talk."

"Splendid," he murmured. "That freedom of choice you value so much for yourself is obviously not something you wish to extend to me as well."

"Not if you are making the wrong choice. Then you need a firm hand to guide you," she grinned.

"You are all aware that I am not planning to stay here in Takhan for more than a few months, aren't you? So whatever House should be granted the fine honour of adopting me into their circle would soon have to manage without me anyway. And let's not forget that I am part of a family already. My father is hardly going to be especially happy about me joining another family."

That seemed to relax the situation considerably.

"So it seems that the prize will continue to be out of our reach," Ram'an smiled.

"Yes," Eryn sighed, "that's what you get for granting the prize a vote. But just for your information: He is mine. I wouldn't have let him join any other House."

"Yours?" Enric enquired with a raised brow. "Not to my mind. Being his superior doesn't make him *yours*."

"Seems to have worked fine in your case," Ram'an pointed out.

"Yes," Eryn confirmed with a malicious smile. "And people keep pointing out that I show the typical characteristics of an Aren woman. Why, then, should I not indulge in their preference for much younger men as well? Malriel had an affair with the King, after all. She is almost twice as old as him, so the twelve years between Vern and me shouldn't matter at all."

"Oh dear," Vern said to himself. "Dark, bottomless pits are opening beneath us."

"Vern," Enric said with a humourless smile, "if you ever elect to join House Vel'kim, I will make you regret it."

Ram'an rubbed his hands. "Good. That eliminates one House, and I dare say Aren is not in the running either, because he would hardly join you now that you have threatened him like this. That makes me the victor, I think. Only in theory, of course."

277

"Can you even threaten me anymore?" Vern asked and turned to Enric with a thoughtful expression. "You are currently not a member of the Order which means no longer my superior, are you?"

Enric smiled. "True enough. But let me remind you once again that this is no more than a temporary situation. Whatever you think you can now say or do without fear of punishment might catch up with you later when I am back in Anyueel and the Order."

"Alright. It was just a rhetorical question, nothing more," Vern hurriedly assured him.

"Good. I am glad we cleared this *rhetorical* matter up. Now let's return to the mess here. There is still a stack of agreements to go through. Eryn, you look exhausted - lie down for a while and give my son some rest, will you? You are a distraction to our work here, anyway. Ram'an, I would appreciate your taking care of this."

Eryn was about to protest, but felt Ram'an take her hand and haul her up from her chair. "No, Theá, he is right. You are not used to the heat and your body has to deal with more strain than usual with the baby. Come and let me pamper you a little."

She sighed and eyed the plate of fruit greedily. "Can we take that with us?"

He chuckled. "Let them have it. I will get you another, bigger plate just for yourself."

$*$ $*$ $*$

Enric heard the entrance door closing and got up to stroll into the main room. That had to be Eryn. She was the only one not yet back.

So indeed it was that she emerged at the top of the stairs only little later, puffing and with hands holding her thighs.

"Is it possible that these stairs are getting steeper and steeper each time I climb them?" she wheezed.

"No, my love," he smiled and took her hand to gently pull her towards the seating cushions, "I rather think that the stairs are not really to blame here."

"How does Junar manage to climb them these days, I wonder?" she sighed and accepted a cool glass of water with a grateful smile before Enric sank down next to her.

"Willpower, I would imagine. Or stubbornness." He watched her lean back and observed how her breathing slowly returned to normal. "How was your day today?"

"Interesting. I had to heal three broken teeth today. A few boys got into a brawl and hurt each other pretty badly. Broken bones and teeth, bite lacerations, swollen eyes and lips, the whole array. Then I had lunch with Sarol and finally I learned from Vern how to proportion the human face and hands. I am getting better at this. The shading is still quite a challenge for me, as I have to consider the angle of the light all the time, but all in all they were clearly recognisable as human body parts."

Enric lifted a brow. "That is your accomplishment? I can make a recognisable face by using no more than two dots for the eyes, a straight line for the nose and a curved one for the mouth."

She glared at him. "Thank you for encouraging me like that."

"I am sorry," he apologised and kissed her forehead. "Do you have your drawings with you so I can have a peek at them?"

"Downstairs next to the towel bowl. I forgot to bring them with me when I tackled the task of climbing the stairs. Next time we are going to learn about drawing the different outlines and forms of noses, eyes, ears and mouths. That should help in making more individual faces." She sighed, the annoyance clear in her face. "Intrea did of course manage to shine again. By the way, she has invited us to a private gathering at her place in a few weeks. She says it is not like a dinner, but more like an evening at a music house with food, music, dancing and everything. I wonder if I am best to expect something like a ball."

He shook his head. "No, I heard about these occasions. They are a lot more casual than the balls we know. They are purely for enjoyment, no social obligations."

Pursing her lips, she nodded. "That doesn't sound halfway bad."

Enric remembered something and fished in his pocket, pulling out a small bird message cylinder. "From Pe'tala for you."

Eryn smiled and unrolled the small paper slip eagerly, letting her eyes dart along the minute script. She chuckled twice, then let the message sink again.

"Anything new?" Enric enquired curiously.

"People have started addressing her as *Lady* Pe'tala now. She is really annoyed about it and keeps telling people to stop, but they just don't listen. It's a lot like me and the name *Maltheá* around here. Oh, and Rolan has also been made a Lord." She looked at Enric when he whistled through his teeth and studied the paper slip thoughtfully.

"What?" she prompted.

"This is the first time a magician has been made a Lord without possessing above average strength and without being a member of the Magic Council. Don't you see what this means? It is the first step towards allocating power in the Order which does not depend on mere magical strength."

Eryn blinked, then nodded slowly when she realised that he was right. "And without any connection to the discipline of fighting," she said, incredulous.

He shook his head. "I never would have thought that they would actually make a change like that within such a short time." He looked at her. "This must have been a joint effort of both Tyront and the King. Tyront wouldn't have been able to do it without the King backing him up, and the King alone wouldn't have managed it without having Tyront on his side."

Eryn nodded slowly, then bit her lower lip. "What do *you* think about it all? I mean, you rose to power so quickly and so far up because of your magical strength. This revised approach to granting power in the Order might sooner or later lead to seeing the legitimacy of your position challenged."

He laughed at that. "That is not very likely. I have proven myself to be beyond reproach more than once in the past. My magical strength might be what got me the position, but it wouldn't have been enough to keep it."

She gulped, only now understanding that the insinuation that his powers were the only thing that qualified him for his rank of second in command was not a particularly flattering one. "I didn't mean to suggest..."

"It's alright, I know what you meant," he assured her and tousled her hair playfully.

"And how would they have been able to replace you, anyway? They could hardly have taken away your rank if you hadn't met their requirements, could they?" she frowned.

"Not officially, no. But Tyront would have resorted to delegating the more demanding and delicate tasks to somebody else and treating me as no more than a figurehead. He would have kept up appearances, but nothing more."

Then another thought hit her and her head jerked up. "But I haven't exactly done anything actually to earn *my* position, have I? This means that in time they might free me from..." She stopped when Enric shook his head indulgently.

"Not much chance for that, my love. Elevating Rolan to the rank of Lord is not something that is about to become an everyday occurrence for quite some time to come. He had to work hard for such a distinction and it might be years until it happens again to another. I strongly suspect that Vern is going to be the next candidate to be made Lord sooner or later. So the usual way of granting power in the Order still is magical strength for now. And until that changes I dare say you will have managed to convince the Order and the King that your rank is more than justified."

"I have no intention whatsoever of doing that!" she protested.

"Eryn," he sighed and cradled her face delicately between his palms, "you managed to discover this amazing barrier and little later how to penetrate it without even considering fighting a discipline worth spending time on. You introduced healing into the Kingdom and indirectly enabled us to establish friendly relations with a country we had not been in contact with for three hundred years. I honestly believe that there is nothing much you could do to make them think you are *not* fit for this high rank." He couldn't help smiling at her downcast expression. "And I bet there is not a single person apart from you who would show such a devastated reaction to a comment like that. Just think about everything you have managed to change in little over a year. I wonder what the Order will look like in twenty years if you keep making changes like that."

"A lot less focused on combat, if *I* have any say in it," she said quietly.

"Undoubtedly," he smiled.

"How about Vern's preparations for the negotiations on behalf of Ram'an?" she changed the topic, reluctant to talk about the Order any longer. "Ram'an's first reaction to Vern bringing you with him to look over the original agreements was not exactly enthusiastic."

Enric shrugged. "Of course not. Letting somebody who is not a member of his House see those documents is not without risk, and even more so when it comes to the Head of another House. But Ram'an is no fool; he knows that I, and thus House Aren, have more to gain once he quickly gets back on his feet than if his House perished. He can only benefit from my taking an interest in the negotiations. And even though I could accompany him when he meets his business partners, it would undermine his credibility considerably. Good thing we have Vern to send along."

"Vern..." she said slowly. "You know, his abilities were not valued so much back home, but here people are a lot more impressed by all the things he can do. I really wonder if he will want to return to being a mere healer in Anyueel. They offered him five hundred gold slips for a single painting here. He could live comfortably enough if he just painted and sold one or two per year! He doesn't even *have* to work if he prefers an idle artist's life."

She looked up when she heard his quiet laugh. "What is funny about that? I am really worried about losing him!"

"What makes you think that appreciation for talent and intelligence would stop him from working rather than encourage him to? You, of all people! You don't have to work either - your companion does happen to be loaded, if you remember."

He had a point there, she had to admit.

"Do you know what they said that day when you learned that you wouldn't be Head of Healers, after you and Vern had left the Council hall? I don't think I told you about it."

"No, what?" she enquired, curious.

"Lord Aldon stated that while it was not clear who was to be Head of Healers, he was in no doubt that we had just watched his successor leaving the hall as soon as he is old enough."

That made her smile. "That would surely entitle him to being appointed a Lord, if they deem the position of Head of Administration of the clinic important enough for it."

"Absolutely. Orrin would burst with pride."

"As well he should, with or without Vern being made Lord. Though that poor little sister of his has quite a sibling to try to equal."

He laid a hand on her belly, smiling when he felt a faint kick under his fingers. "I imagine our son also has a few expectations to live up to, with parents like that."

Eryn sighed. "If he wants to become a warrior, I am going to throw a fit."

"I wonder if he will even have that choice, or about where to live," Enric replied seriously. "He is, after Vran'el, the next in line to head House Vel'kim."

"Only as long as Pe'tala doesn't have any children," she corrected him. "I have great hopes of her performing her duty."

He just nodded. It was not quite that easy, he knew. Even if Pe'tala had children, there was no guarantee that she would return to Takhan again. And even in the case she did, Malriel would try to get her hands on her grandson. If Pe'tala provided an heir for House Vel'kim, then his own son would be available to take over House Aren one far away day. In theory, that is.

CHAPTER 21

The Fire

Eryn turned in her sleep, her dream switching from riding through knee-high grass to food scorching in the palace kitchen back in Anyueel, where she suddenly found herself the cook preparing dinner for two hundred ball guests, waving away billows of dark smoke coming from an oven that contained an enormous cake.

"Eryn!" a sharp voice commanded.

"I'm sorry," she murmured without opening her eyes, "I can fix this, I really can…"

She woke with a start when she felt herself being jerked into a sitting position, Enric's hands on her shoulders, his face unusually awake and alert for the night hour.

"Wake up, Eryn! We need to get out of here," his voice was instructing her in strident words. Only then did she realise that the tickly sensation in her throat had not been a mere impression in her sleep, but an aspect of reality her brain had wrapped the new dream around.

She started to cough and tried to locate the source of the smoke that had started to drift into their bedroom.

"Fire?" she asked, pressing her hands protectively onto her belly.

"Yes," he just replied and pulled her up into a standing position before dragging her along behind him towards the main room, where Urban was running up and down in confusion, whining pitifully. Here too, no sign of fire was visible apart from the smoke that was drifting towards the terrace door.

"Orrin!" Enric shouted loudly, enhancing his voice with magic to increase the volume enough to make Eryn cringe and press her palms

283

over her ears. He shouted twice more while ripping open the terrace door and taking her outside, whistling for the cat to follow them.

She sucked in the fresh air greedily, feeling heady after the first few gulps.

He waited until her steps were steady again, then pointed to a tree far enough away from the house for her to be out of danger. "Go there and wait! I mean it!" he added with a penetrating look and then sprinted back into the house without waiting for her reply.

Orrin stepped outside the corridor that led to his bedroom, carrying Junar in his arms.

"Out!" Enric barked and pointed towards the terrace door and out into the garden. "Where is Vern?"

"I don't know!" The warrior's head jerked towards the other corridor to Vern's room. The smoke seemed to be coming from there. His eyes widened and Enric could see the agony on his face while he stood frozen, torn between the urge for getting his companion and unborn child to safety or running for his son.

"Go!" Enric commanded. "I'll fetch him." He raced off towards the boy's room, blowing smoke out of his way with gusts of wind. He grabbed the door handle to push it open, but it wouldn't budge. He fuelled the muscles in his arm and shoulder with a surge of magic and gave a violent shove, making one part of the door and the frame splinter in the process.

Vern lay on the floor in front of the door unconscious, his night clothes rumpled, his feet unshod. Enric swiftly bent down to pick him up and haul him over his shoulder before running back to the main room and out through the terrace door, by which Orrin was poised to hurry back into the house. His eyes narrowed and his jaw clenched when he beheld the limp form over Enric's shoulder.

"Is he...?"

"I don't know," Enric just said and hurried on towards the tree under which Eryn and Junar were waiting. Junar clasped both hands over her mouth, her eyes brimming with tears. He was relieved to see that Eryn had managed to fight the initial panic he had glimpsed in her expression and had switched into healer mode when he stood in front of her. She calmly motioned for him to lay the boy down on the grass and stretched out her hand to let Enric help her sink to her knees. She then bent over Vern, placing her flat hand on his chest and closing her eyes.

Orrin was about to join her, his breathing laboured, sweat twinkling on his forehead despite the cold night air. Enric grabbed his shoulder to stop him.

"No. Don't disturb her." When the warrior started to push him aside, he strengthened his grip and urged, "Orrin, if there ever was one person in this world you could trust with your son's life, it is the one kneeling in front of him!"

The older man closed his eyes and let his head sink, his expression miserable.

"Take care of Junar," Enric instructed quietly. It would do him good to look after somebody instead of simply standing around and watching helplessly.

Eryn was still kneeling on the grass motionlessly, her hand remaining on Vern's chest. It was hard to see in the dark, but he did seem to be breathing.

After what felt like an eternity, but couldn't have been more than a few minutes, she opened her eyes again and searched Orrin's eyes, smiling up at him.

"He will be alright," she promised him. "He is no longer unconscious, but asleep. I would not wake him right now, he needs to rest a little." She didn't mention the alarming amount of poisonous substances in his blood due to breathing in of smoke, nor how a few minutes more might have done permanent damage to his brain or even cost him his life. All that mattered right now was that he was alive, and he would be well again.

Orrin leaned against the tree, exhaling in relief and almost sinking to his knees. He pressed Junar close and buried his face in her hair.

She saw Enric regarding her thoughtfully, aware that she had not shared all she knew. He very probably felt her agitation through the mind bond. She knew that it was not visible to an outsider.

Both of them turned back to the house. The columns of smoke rising from the terrace door and two open windows seemed almost white against the night sky. There was no telling where the fire had started merely from looking at it.

"We should take care of it," Eryn said determinedly and climbed back to her feet.

"We?" Enric's head spun around towards her as he stepped in her way when she made to return to the terrace. "*We* will do something, but that term does not include *you*!" He lifted his index finger in her face when she opened her mouth to challenge him. "If you dare to be difficult now I will tie you to that tree! You will not go into this burning house and put yourself and our child at risk!" He nodded towards Vern's recumbent form. "You will stay here and take care of Junar and Vern while Orrin and I look for the seat of the fire."

She sighed and nodded. It wouldn't make sense to argue with him, she knew. He wouldn't have let her return with him even if she hadn't been pregnant, but in this case she had to admit that he was right. The child had to come first.

"Orrin?" Enric called out sharply, aware that he had to take the lead to wrench the warrior out of the state of shock and disorientation he was currently struggling with. "Your family is safe now. They are with a healer. Come on, I need you to help me extinguish that fire. I will never hear the end of it if I return the residence to Malriel half burnt down," he remarked dryly, walking back towards the terrace door. Orrin kissed Junar on the forehead, hugged Eryn quickly and looked down at his son one last time before following him.

"Our best shot is somewhere in the direction of Vern's room," Enric explained. "The smoke was heavier there. We had better create an airtight shield that allows us to breathe in there without passing out. We need to remain in sight of each other at all times in case one of us needs the other's help. With the shield in place we will not be able to hear each other. When we see the fire, we will lock it inside another shield to collapse it through lack of air." He waited for Orrin to nod, then they both raised a barrier that enveloped each of them completely and provided a limited source of clean air before entering the house.

Both turned towards Vern's room, following the smoke that was becoming more and more dense with every step. Enric motioned towards a guest room at the end of the corridor right next to the boy's room. It seemed to be the source. Orrin stared at the broken wood for a moment when they passed Vern's room and his head swung around to Enric, who simply shook his head to indicate that this was not a good time, and moved on.

Enric carefully entered the uninhabited guestroom and looked around. It was inconvenient that he couldn't hear anything and the dark, billowing smoke stopped him seeing almost completely. It made finding the fire's source as good as impossible if he didn't want to wander around the room blindly until he stumbled upon it. He carefully stepped towards where he sensed there should be a window and found it after only a few moments. He reached through his barrier and opened it, watching how the smoke wafted out and away into the cool night air. Taking a deep breath that would enable him to hold his breath for several seconds, he then collapsed the shield around him and created a powerful gust of wind that pushed most of the smoke out the window, revealing a surprisingly small blaze in one corner of the room on an ornamental side table. Orrin quickly created a barrier around the fire, starving it of the oxygen it needed to burn. Then he stepped next to Enric, letting the airtight shield envelop him.

"Come on, we need to get out of here," the warrior instructed. "The fire is no danger now, but the smoke still is. My shield doesn't have enough fresh air left."

They turned and walked back the way they had come, stepping out onto the terrace. Orrin dropped the shield and turned to the younger man with a murderous expression. "Why was Vern's door damaged?"

"Later," Enric promised and nodded to the stairs that led down to the entrance door. "There is more smoke coming from the storage rooms. Same procedure as before," he said and raised another shield before he ventured back inside, crossed the main room and carefully descended the stairs.

Little later Orrin waved to him, indicating that he had found the room with a second blaze. This one, too, was extinguished moments later with the aid of a small shield.

Enric went to open the entrance door and let the smoke out, then returned and picked up what looked like a damp rag which gave off a pungent, unfamiliar smell. He looked around, found an undamaged earthenware pot and stuffed the rag in. Somebody needed to have a closer look at this.

"Where is Vern's cat?" Enric then asked.

Orrin frowned in annoyance, clearly eager to get back to his family. "That cat is not a major concern of mine right now, to be honest. It has probably fled."

"I don't want to explain to your son that we didn't check if his cat was around somewhere while we were in the house. Nor to Eryn, either." Enric turned holding the pot under his arm and walked back to Vern's bedroom. The air was starting to clear now. He looked around the room, behind a few chests, under the table and finally under the bed, where he spotted something that might or might not be the right size for an Anyueel street cat. It didn't move. He dropped down to the floor, reaching under the bed and pulling out the soft, immovable bundle. It wasn't breathing. He sent a quick surge of exploratory magic into the feline body, but there was no response. The heart wasn't beating, nor was there any other activity discernible.

He turned around, looking at Orrin, who was staring at the dead cat in his arms, and then back at the splintered wood.

"Somebody is going to pay for that," Orrin said softly, his voice resonant with repressed wrath.

Enric nodded slowly. "Yes," he agreed equally calmly. Judging from the dead animal in his arms and Eryn's emotions after she had finished healing Vern, the boy could easily have met with the same fate as his pet if he had been freed from this room only a short time later.

* * *

Eryn watched the two men returning and gave a gasp of relief. They were magicians, warriors, grown men with common sense, able to shield themselves against and react to whatever danger might be lurking in there, yet watching them walk into a burning building had still been deeply troubling.

Enric was carrying a bundle of some sort in his arms, placing it behind a couple of bushes and thus out of sight before he approached her with Orrin, who was carrying what looked like a dark, round pot under his arm.

"All the fires are taken care off. We will have to stay at the Vel'kim residence tonight. As long as there is smoke still in the house we can't stay here," Enric announced.

Eryn nodded with relief. It didn't exactly feel like a safe place right now in any case. Even the prospect of staying under the same roof as Valrad seemed more appealing than going back to the bed she had been roused from only a little while ago.

Orrin bent down to lift his son carefully into his arms and straightened up again, his features an expressionless, tense mask.

Enric spread both of his arms around Eryn's and Junar's waists to guide them through the garden beside the house so they didn't have to go through it on their way to the street. Urban followed them nervously, still occasionally letting loose a complaining whine that resonated eerily through the night air.

When Valrad opened his door several minutes later, his expression changed from sleepy to wide awake in a fraction of a second as he beheld the group in their sleeping attire.

"What has happened?" he asked and quickly turned to Orrin and the load he was carrying, laying a hand on the boy's forehead. He closed his eyes and opened them again a moment later, surprised. "He is asleep!"

Eryn nodded. "I have healed him already. There was a fire at the residence and he inhaled the fumes."

"A fire?" Valrad exclaimed and was about to say more, but Enric shook his head slightly, nodding at the two women at his side.

"May we stay the rest of the night at your place? Our house needs to be cleaned and aired before we can return. I would prefer to stay at your residence instead of the ambassadorial one for now." He knew that Kilan would have taken them in as well, but he counted on whoever had done this to be more careful when it came to trying anything like that when another House was involved.

"Of course! Do come in!" He stepped aside, then shouted, "Vran'el!"

"Could you have a look at Eryn and Junar? Just to be safe?" Enric requested while he ushered them up the stairs to the main room.

"I will, do not worry," the healer assured him and took Junar's hand before she could take a seat on the cushions. "No, my dear, you will not sit down here. As soon as I have made sure that everything is in order with you, you should lie down. You need to rest; it must all have been a terrible strain for you." Without waiting for her reply, he closed his eyes and sent a warm pulse of magic into her body. Less than a minute later he opened his eyes again and smiled at her. "Everything is fine with you and your daughter, Junar." He turned when a very rumpled looking Vran'el wearing nothing more than a pair of thin bright trousers wandered into the main room, rubbing his eyes when he encountered the sudden brightness and then blinking at the unexpected visitors.

"Vran, good. Please take Junar to one of the guest rooms and have Orrin put down Vern in an adjoining one, will you?"

"What happened?" he asked in confusion.

"Later, son." Valrad turned to Eryn when Vran'el led away Orrin and Junar. "Now to you, my girl. I assume you have taken a good look at yourself already, though healers treating themselves is something we discourage in situations like this." He held out his hand for her to take, knowing better than to take her assent for granted.

She swallowed. She had not done anything of that kind, considering that she had not been injured and had focussed her attention on Vern. With a sigh she obediently lifted her hand to place it into Valrad's and watched him close his fingers around hers before she felt the familiar warm sensation of magic entering through her skin.

"The two of you are fine as well," he exhaled in relief and held on to her hand. "Come with me. I will take you to your room for tonight."

Eryn raised a brow at him. "You are sending me to bed? I am a little too old for that."

"I just sent Junar to bed, and she is the more senior to you," he pointed out.

"Yes, but she is in her last month and can hardly stand upright without tiring after a few moments," she countered.

She felt Enric's arm move around her shoulders. "You should lie down. Take Urban with you. She is still nervous and skittish."

The cat was indeed prowling the room agitatedly, obviously not finding comfort in the familiar surroundings. She wasn't even interested in roaming the gardens right now.

Eryn regarded him for a moment, then nodded slowly. There was no doubt that Enric would talk to Valrad and Vran'el about the fire, and he didn't want her to be present when he did. That very likely meant that he was withholding information from her for her own good. How she hated that! Yet he wouldn't talk as long as she was with them, so she nodded dutifully and let Valrad guide her to a room that was suspiciously far away from the main room. Very probably to avoid any snippet of the conversation reaching her ears.

She let herself be tucked in by both men, ruffling the cat's fur as she sniffed the bed covers. Enric pressed a quick kiss onto Eryn's forehead, then Valrad briefly pressed his palm to her cheek before both of them left the room and closed the door.

Eryn listened until their steps sounded far enough away, then pushed aside the blanket, leaning down to Urban who was sitting on the floor next to the bed and sent her to sleep with a quick surge of magic. Then she swung her legs out of the bed and smiled with determined pluck. Enric had to be pretty preoccupied if he didn't question her lack of resistance and assumed that she was complying just like that.

Opening the door as quietly as she could, she checked the corridor carefully up and down and froze when she saw Orrin stepping out of one of the rooms to her left where either Junar or Vern had to be resting. He turned towards the main room, walking there with his usual determined stride.

She slipped out of the door as soon as he had rounded the corner and tiptoed after him, pressing against the wall that separated the corridor from the main room. She couldn't see anything, but she had come to listen, anyway.

A jingling of glass suggested that either Valrad or Vran'el were serving something to drink to their guests.

"Thank you," she heard Orrin murmur.

Eryn placed a shield around the area in her brain that sent out emotions through the mind bond. She didn't want to be discovered before she had learned what Enric so obviously wanted to keep from her.

"Now, talk," Valrad instructed, his voice sounding concerned.

"I woke when Urban started howling and scratching at the door," Enric began. "When I opened it, I smelled something burning and immediately woke Eryn. When we had taken care of Eryn and Junar, I returned to fetch Vern as there was no sign of him." He paused for a moment before he went on, his voice grave, "His door was locked. I had to open it forcefully."

For several seconds nobody said anything, then Vran'el asked, "Could he have locked himself in? I mean, he is a growing boy, after all. Privacy is all important to that age group."

"No," she heard Orrin reply with absolute certainty, "he doesn't do this normally, only when he is angry about something. Anyway, I never enter his room unbidden."

Eryn swallowed at the implication.

"So you think somebody must have locked him in," Valrad voiced her very thoughts. "Why? The boy is a magician, he could have freed himself with magic."

"Not in the state he probably was when he reached the door. I found him lying on the floor, collapsed," Enric replied. "When I returned to his room, I found his cat under the bed. It was dead."

Eryn clapped both hands over her mouth to stop herself from making a sound. So that had been the bundle Enric had carried out of the house to conceal it behind the bushes!

The men in the room had fallen silent and her own thoughts were racing. Vern had been locked inside his room during a fire. His cat was dead, and his own health status had not been exactly uncritical either. Somebody had wanted to kill him. The thought made her stomach clench and she felt dizzy. Leaning against the wall, she closed her eyes for a moment, trying to keep herself upright.

"I knew I shouldn't have trusted your uncharacteristic compliance when being sent to bed," Enric's voice rang out from directly in front of her.

She opened her eyes and looked at him, swallowing.

"You are getting better at shielding your emotions, but the shock just now was somewhat stronger than your shield could hold." He sighed and shook his head. "What am I going to do with you?"

She straightened and pushed past him to walk into the main room, where three displeased faces turned towards her.

"I will tell you what you are going to do. You will continue with that very intriguing conversation you were having just now. I have no intention of returning to that room you wanted to bundle me in out of the way. With what I have just heard I doubt that I would sleep very soundly, anyway." She took a seat between Vran'el and Orrin on the seating cushions.

"I don't think you should hear this right now, Eryn," her companion contradicted.

She turned to him angrily. "Don't treat me like a child, Enric! You and Tyront pushed me into this position of third in command, so you had better start sharing information with me. How am I ever to lead others if you think you have to cosset me from the big bad reality out there? In addition to that I am currently the highest-ranking Order magician present. You don't have any authority over me."

"She does have a point there," Vran'el agreed calmly. Even Orrin nodded, though reluctantly, clearly not too happy that reason had just overruled his own protective instinct.

"I am still not happy with this," Enric said.

"I am not asking you to be," Eryn shrugged. "What I am asking you, though, is to stop applying double standards. Somebody wanted to harm Vern. I am his superior which means that I am responsible for him. Don't make me write to Tyront to confirm that fact. You know as well as I that he will be on my side with it."

Enric looked discontent and pressed his lips together, but nodded once and then sat down.

"If Vern was locked inside his room," Vran'el ventured, "I assume that the fire was no chance event."

"No," Enric confirmed. "We found two burning rags drenched in some smelly liquid. The fire did not spread very far to the structure thanks to the stone construction of the house, but there was a lot of smoke, which has turned out to be every bit as dangerous."

"Do you still have these rags?" Valrad enquired and continued, when Enric nodded, "Then somebody needs to have a look at them. I recommend you contact the metal workers and see if they can identify what they were soaked in. They use different substances for etching and cleansing metal, many of them rather dangerous."

"You don't think this was Elwoi's doing, do you?" Eryn mused. "He is the only one I can currently think of who would benefit from Vern being... you know... out of the running."

Orrin's expression had darkened even further. "I intend to find out just that."

"No, you won't," Enric ordered him sharply. "We will inform the triarchy of this and see what they decide. You will stay out of it." He would undertake his own investigation, and Orrin would probably turn out to be more of a hindrance than a help with this.

"Pity you are no longer in a position to command me," the warrior shot back, unimpressed.

"But I am," Eryn growled. "And he is right. You stay away from Elwoi. That is an order!"

"We are talking about my son who was..." he began and started to rise, but Eryn sent him a furious glare.

"Not only *your* son, Orrin! Whoever did this endangered my own son as well, so don't play the desperate parent card here!" she snarled and watched with satisfaction how he sank back onto the cushions.

"Your cat warned you when she smelt the smoke," Vran'el then said thoughtfully. "So whoever managed to enter your house undetected, place both rags, ignite them and lock Vern in must have been a magician. It is common knowledge that you live with a huge wild cat, so not being able to shield from it would have been too dangerous for the intruder."

"That is not much help, I am afraid," Valrad sighed. "We have more than four hundred magicians residing in the city. This criterion does not exactly narrow down the number of suspects. And I imagine that whoever is behind this probably hired somebody else to take care of the execution of their plan."

"So we will inform the triarchy of this, then see if somebody can tell us what the rags where drenched in. What next?" Eryn asked.

"I will have the damage to the residence assessed and have it restored as quickly as possible. Then I will have to hire guards. I want you to avoid being alone - both during the day and at night. No more solitary walks through the city. We don't know if Vern really was the intended target or if it was an accidental or random act. I don't want to take any risk here," Enric explained.

"The repair work will take several days at least. I would be happy for you to stay here at our place for that time," Valrad offered. "You can post your guards here, though I would be surprised if another attempt like that were made. You have been served with a warning now, after all, and will take precautions."

"Thank you," Enric nodded. "I appreciate that offer and accept it gladly."

Eryn swallowed, but didn't object. Of course it was only logical staying here. That didn't mean that she had to like being stuck under the same roof as Valrad for the time being.

* * *

Eryn yawned and looked up from her book to the sleeping form of Vern on the bed in front of her. She had woken early despite the turbulent night and Enric had insisted that she stay at home for today, in Vran'el's tender care. Enric himself had left to get the paperwork he needed from his study at the Aren residence and to talk to the builder Valrad had recommended.

She thought back to the conversation they had had in the main room only a few hours ago. They had agreed not to inform Junar of their findings about the fire to avoid stressing her too much. The baby was overdue already, and additional strain would not do her any good.

Vern, however, needed to be informed, both of his cat's demise and the potential danger to his own life. Orrin had insisted on taking care of this himself, but Eryn had objected to that and found Enric on her side on that one. For a change. They had finally managed to convince the warrior that he was currently hardly in any frame of mind to deliver a message like that calmly and sympathetically. He had then given in, but at least wanted to be present when Vern heard about it.

She watched the boy moving slightly - a twitching hand, then he mumbled something unintelligible before he finally opened his eyes and stared up at the ceiling for some seconds. He slowly sat up and looked around, stopping when his gaze fell on Eryn.

"Eryn? Where are we?" Without waiting for her answer he jumped up and looked out the window. "These are the Vel'kim gardens! What are we doing here?"

She took a deep breath and got up from the chair, closing her book. "There was a fire. Come on, let's get you something to eat, then I will tell you the rest."

"A fire?" He stood still, his eyes narrowing as he was trying to remember. "There was smoke, but then somehow…"

"Come with me," she repeated, remembering the promise to Orrin that he could be there when she told Vern about everything. "Your father wants to see you; he is a bit worried."

"Is everybody alright? Has anybody been hurt?" he asked with widened eyes.

"Why don't we go to the main room and see…"

"You are evading my questions!" he complained, getting more agitated by the second. "Talk to me! Something is wrong, isn't it?" he demanded to know.

Eryn braced herself and walked out the door, safe in the knowledge that he would follow her. Follow her he did, begging and coercing her all the way to the main room, where Vran'el and Orrin were waiting for them. Orrin stood as soon as he beheld the both of them, and without a word pulled his son into a firm embrace.

Vern returned the embrace. "You are alright then," he sighed with relief. "How about Junar?"

His father nodded. "Junar is fine."

"Enric? And the cats?"

"He is alright," Eryn replied. At that moment Urban strolled in through the terrace door, walked lazily through the room and then pressed her head against Eryn's thigh.

"There you are," Vern cooed and bent down to scratch a brown, furry cheek. Then he looked around. "Where is Ram'an? I suppose he is hiding somewhere, isn't he? Judging from the last couple of times we took him to new surroundings, he doesn't adapt to strange places easily. I better see if I can make him come out and eat. Do you have any idea what room I be best to start looking in?"

"Vern," Eryn said carefully, "sit down with me for a moment, will you?"

He narrowed his eyes at her. "Where is my cat?" He swallowed at her sympathetic expression. "Eryn?" he asked quietly, "Where is Ram'an? Please tell me he is unharmed."

She took his hand between both of hers and looked him in the eyes. "I am so sorry, Vern. He is not. He did not survive. Enric found him in your room, under the bed. He had breathed in too much smoke."

The boy stared at her. "Ram'an is dead?" he whispered after a few moments, tears beading at the corners of his eyes.

She took his arm and led him to the seating cushions, gently coaxing him down and taking a seat next to him, waiting for him to say something.

He stared down at the floor, not bothering with wiping away the occasional tear that ran down his cheek. When Orrin took a seat at his other side, Vern closed his eyes and leaned back.

"He was just a street cat, right? Nothing that justifies mourning. Who is going to miss a mean creature like that? I mean, he was always peeing everywhere when he got upset. And scratching me deeply when I played with him. He always slept in my bed in a way that required me bending like a hook if I wanted to avoid having his claws sinking in me again..." He leaned forward again, burying his face in his hands, sobbing.

Eryn swallowed hard, fighting the moisture that built between her eyelids. As far as she was aware this was the first time he had ever lost a living thing he was close to. The fact that it was a cat didn't make much of a difference. It was a creature that had been close to him, that he had taken in and cared for, even shared a sleeping space with. It had been a friend, and now it was gone. It had died in a dark place alone and full of terror.

Orrin looked at his son, then to Eryn, at a loss how to react.

"We will get you another one," he murmured.

She cringed. That had been a colossally wrong thing to say.

Vern slowly let his hands drop and stared at his father. "What? Another one? *Another one*? You mean... just exchanging him like a broken dish?" He shook his head aghast and jumped up. "How can you say a thing like that? Seriously!" He stormed off, stopping only for a moment to look around, not sure how to find his way back to the room he had just come out of. Vran'el pointed him in the right direction without saying anything and then slowly walked towards the seating island.

"That did not go so well," he said, stating the obvious.

"No," Eryn confirmed and gave Orrin a dark look. "Somebody really messed that one up. Proposing to get him another pet? Really? What would you have told him if *I* had died last night? That you will find him a new tiresome friend?"

"It was a cat that died!" the warrior exclaimed in frustration, "Not *you*!"

"It was a living, feeling being he was very fond of!" she shot back. "You can't just replace it with something else!"

Orrin exhaled and closed his eyes for a moment. "Alright, I didn't handle this very well. And we didn't even get to tell him about the locked door and warn him to be extra careful."

"No," Eryn snapped at him, "because somebody made him run away!"

"Eryn," Vran'el sighed, "leave it be. He did not do it on purpose, he just wanted to cheer him up. Not very effectively, I admit, but he hardly intended to chase Vern off. So be a bit more sympathetic, please."

"Sure," she sighed. "Clumsiness is so much easier to deal with than malevolence..."

Orrin threw up his hands. "What do you want me to do then? You seem to be the expert in dealing with situations like this. Share your wisdom with me, then! What am I supposed to do, in your opinion?"

"Now we are talking," she smiled without humour. "You will follow him to his room, tell him that you are sorry for that heartless suggestion and that you understand that he is upset. Think of something nice to say about that vicious beast. And make it believable!"

"Did you just call the poor deceased cat a vicious beast?" Vran'el snorted. "That does not exactly seem in line with this commiseration you want Orrin to demonstrate, you know."

"Commiseration is something you show when the grieving person is around. I think I did well enough at that." She nodded towards the corridor where Vern had disappeared. "Now it's your turn."

Orrin rolled his eyes and slowly got up to follow his son. "All of a sudden she is diplomatic. Wonderful."

CHAPTER 22

A New Arrival

Enric stretched languidly and looked out the window. The view from the room Valrad had provided as his temporary working place was at the same time less pleasant and more distracting than that from Malriel's study. It looked out over the distant street and people passing by the entrance to the Vel'kim premises. Back at the Aren residence he had looked over lush gardens when he turned his head. It was amazing how quickly he had become used to living and working there, considering that he had spent thirteen years of his life in the same quarters. That was before he bought the two houses in Anyueel, following Eryn's bringing back the mountain cat from her herb gathering expedition.

He liked living in Takhan. The local habits regarding food, furnishing, clothes, music and even the climate appealed to him, as did the people and their customs. At least, those he had been exposed to so far. He thought about Anyueel and was surprised that there were not many things he really missed. Tyront, for once, despite the remaining tension between them when Enric had left. A few of his colleagues, among them Lord Poron with his relaxed view of the world that his advanced age and experience afforded.

He had brought along almost everybody and everything he treasured to Takhan. There wasn't really anything left at home he couldn't manage without. He considered the Order and his high rank, comparing it to the position he had here. Head of House and senator. Hardly less impressive than second in command of the Order, he mused, and he was subject neither to an immediate superior, nor to an all-powerful King. The idea of making this city his home was immensely appealing, but not one he could afford, that he knew. He would have to return to Anyueel soon enough, as Eryn was not as free from the Order's influence as he himself. For the first time he fully understood her resistance against being forced to remain a member. Potentially treacherous thoughts, and he knew he needed to keep them to himself. He would return to his former position in the Order and couldn't afford to have his loyalty questioned. The King and Tyront were aware enough of his eagerness to keep Eryn away from them for at least a while.

He returned his attention to the papers in front of him. Letters, lists and reports from his new shipping business in Bonhet. Thanks to the means of communication available to him, namely messenger birds and sending missives by ship, he was able to keep his businesses both in the Kingdom and the Western Territories running smoothly enough.

He let his breath go and pushed himself back from the small desk when he realised that he wasn't able to concentrate at all. His thoughts kept returning to Vern and the peril he had been in only recently. Eryn had admitted that only little longer in that room might well have cost him his life.

Vran'el had told him about how the boy had been informed about his cat's death, how hard it had hit him without even realising at that time about what risk he had faced himself. Orrin had told him about that, too, warning him about going anywhere alone from that moment. They had hired several guards, a few to discreetly keep watch over the house, some others to shadow Eryn, Junar and Vern at a safe distance, invisibly if possible.

According to Orrin, Vern had been more outraged than frightened by the idea that somebody could be after killing him. A surprisingly defiant attitude in the face of death from a boy with so little fondness for the defensive arts, he had to admit.

A knock sounded at the door and he called out permission to enter.

Vran'el poked his head in. "There is a messenger for you. He looks out of breath and it seems rather urgent. You had better come."

Enric got to his feet immediately. He went through a mental list of his people's whereabouts. Eryn was at the clinic, so was Vern. In addition, Junar had an appointment for a check there as well. Orrin was teaching magical combat methods. Theoretically the message could concern either of them.

The messenger stood in the main room, greedily gulping down a glass of water Vran'el had handed him.

"Enric of House Aren," the messenger panted, "your presence is requested at the Academy of Arts, there has been an urgent development!"

Academy of Arts? But Vern was supposed to be at the clinic, wasn't he?

"What kind of urgent development?" Enric asked while taking two stairs at once when he hurried towards the entrance door.

"Orrin, he is threatening Elwoi," the messenger called after him.

Enric cursed and increased his pace with the help of magic. So it was the *old* academy he needed to go to, not the new one as he had initially understood.

That bloody fool! It had been daft of him to rely on Orrin to exercise restraint, as he had been told, when an order had never in the past kept him from doing what he himself considered right and just. Eryn would have to deal with this. He was violating a direct order she had given him, after all. He wondered briefly if she would be up to disciplining Orrin for insubordination, but pushed the thought aside. There were more urgent matters to deal with right now. Like keeping an Order magician from murdering an artist he suspected of being after his son's life.

When Enric came into sight of the building, three people were standing in front of it and pointed at him when they spotted him, waving for him to hurry. That was clearly the welcoming committee.

When he was within hearing range, they shouted, "Come, quickly!" and preceded him into the building, running ahead of him to the room where he heard a voice that in his memory had always been very good at shouting. This time there was an underlying edge that resonated threateningly through the domed hall.

"Orrin!" he shouted angrily when he entered and saw the scene before him. There were chairs thrown backwards in a suspiciously regular pattern that had very probably been caused by a surge of magic. Several people who looked like artists with their flowing robes stood pressed against a faraway wall, motionless and wide-eyed, probably too afraid to move and at the same time unwilling to miss a single moment of the drama unfolding in front of them.

At the centre of the room Orrin was standing, a picture of bitter vengeance. He had seized Elwoi by the throat and was slowly lifting him up into the air. The artist's feet had already lost touch with the ground beneath; kicking about wildly, his hands frantically clawed at the warrior's strong hand to loosen the grip, but to no avail. Elwoi's face had already begun flushing purple.

Orrin didn't react to Enric's shout, but continued to lift the man a little higher.

Enric didn't hesitate but lifted his palm and directed a strike at his old combat teacher. The bolt hit its mark a moment later, delivering both the attacker and the victim to the ground, sliding them a few paces along the smooth and polished stone floor.

Orrin had landed on his back and groaned while Elwoi coughed violently and at the same time scrambled away from his blond attacker, backwards and on all fours. Enric couldn't help thinking of a retreating spider.

"Oh dear," he heard Vran'el's voice beside him. He hadn't even realised that the lawyer had been close behind him.

Enric slowly walked towards the recumbent warrior and looked down at him, arms folded. "Fool," he just said with considerably more control than he felt.

"You!" Elwoi gasped and pointed his index finger at Orrin from what he probably considered a safe distance. His other hand clutched at his throat. "I will have the Senate throw you in a dungeon! You will pay for this, you brute! I do not care how mighty and powerful your friends are, or whatever induced you to do a thing like this, you..."

Enric closed his eyes for a moment, then interrupted him. "What do you mean, *whatever induced him to do a thing like that?* He didn't tell you why he was here?"

"No!" the artist croaked and then coughed once again until his throat cooperated a little more. "That maniac just stormed in here, started hurling death threats and demands to own up to what I did and then started to choke me!"

"You idiot," Enric said, quietly enough for only Orrin to hear. "Telling him what you suspect him of is the least you could do before suffocating him. Where are your manners?" he added dryly. "Vran'el?" he then asked without taking his eyes off Orrin, "can you get me a golden belt for our friend here? I don't think he is fit to judge properly how to use his considerable powers right now."

"Certainly," Vran'el confirmed and turned to leave.

"May I have a word with you, Elwoi?" Enric then called out. "You at least deserve an explanation for the inexcusable behaviour you fell victim to just now."

"Nothing you say will stop me from having him punished for any of it," the artist hissed.

"That is not my intention. I agree - there must be consequences for him. We can't have people running rampant through the city and attacking others on a whim. Especially not magicians."

"Of course not," Elwoi rasped, clearly distrustful of Enric's concession. "Speak then! But let me first heal my throat, it is burning like fire." He closed his eyes for quite some time, seeming a lot calmer when he opened them again. His complexion had also returned to a healthier shade.

"I am listening," he announced grandly and folded his arms to demonstrate his readiness.

Enric positioned himself so that he could look at Elwoi and at the same time keep an eye on Orrin, who still lay on the floor, coping with the after effects of the powerful strike to his chest.

"I assume you are aware that Orrin and his family are residing with me at the Aren residence?" At Elwoi's nod he continued. "Two nights ago there was a fire which seemed aimed at poisoning the air rather than burning down the whole building."

The artist blinked in surprise, then asked, "Was anybody hurt?"

Enric appreciated the question, very much so. It certainly showed the right priorities. "Not apart from a cat. The point is, you see, that both Orrin's own and my companion are pregnant meaning the danger to them and our unborn children was not something we could take lightly."

Elwoi looked at him in confusion, then realisation dawned on him. "What? He surely does not suspect that I caused this fire, does he?"

"The thought has obviously occurred to him," Enric admitted. "There is more. When I went to get Vern from his room, I found his door locked and the boy unconscious on the floor, passed out from the toxic smoke. I got to him just in time. His cat in the same room was less fortunate. It did not survive."

The artist's eyes bulged. "Somebody wanted to kill the *boy*?" he whispered horrified, then his gaze dropped to his still recumbent attacker. "And he thinks it must be me because of my disagreement with his son? He assumes I wanted to kill him? To what avail? That would hardly reunite the artists, would it? Quite the opposite - it might start a riot." Shaking his head, he grabbed a nearby chair and sank down on it. "How terrible for all of you!" He looked back up at Enric. "I swear to you I did not have anything to do with any of it!"

"I didn't think so." He turned when he watched Vran'el re-enter the large hall, carrying a golden belt in one hand. "There is one request I have. I do not expect you to react very favourably to it and understand if you refuse. I understand that you are very probably not in an especially cooperative mood right now."

"What is it?" Elwoi asked warily.

"Would you be willing to answer a few questions under the influence of a lie filter? It will at least get Orrin off your trail."

The artist sighed, then nodded. "Of course, why not? It is probably the most convenient way to avoid being summoned before the Senate for questioning."

Enric smiled gratefully and nodded. "Excellent. Would you give me a moment? I dare say we will all be more relaxed after Orrin is relieved of his magic for the time being." He turned and walked towards Orrin, taking the golden belt from Vran'el's hand and bending down to fix it around the warrior's waist. "How are you doing?" he asked and grabbed the older man's forearm to pull him back to his feet.

"Woozy," he growled.

"Vran'el, be so good and have him lean against something solid and keep an eye on him while I am talking to Elwoi," Enric asked.

"Sure," the lawyer nodded. "Go and do your thing."

The mood in the large room seemed a lot more relaxed now that Orrin was no longer a danger to those around him. The artists had started whispering to each other.

Enric returned to where Elwoi was sitting and stretched out his hand for the other man to grip. When he had released a weak but steady stream of magic through his palm, he began.

"Thank you very much for agreeing to this, Elwoi. I greatly value your cooperation. Did you in any way participate in what happened at the Aren residence, which almost led to Vern's death?"

"I did not."

"Did you instruct somebody else to carry out this task for you or are you aware of anybody who might be responsible for this?"

"No to both."

"Has the thought of killing young Vern or having him killed by somebody else ever crossed your mind?"

"No," the artist replied coolly. "Never. The only punishment I visualised with regard to him were of giving him a good hiding."

"Anything else you would like to know to convince you of his innocence, Orrin?" Enric called to Orrin, who was leaning against a column with closed eyes. The warrior just shook his head.

Enric then nodded and released the other man's hand again. "Thank you. You are free to bring charges against him; I will not use my influence to have him cleared or spared punishment. Though I might intervene if I suspect your demands are out of proportion, I should add."

Elwoi looked over to the warrior thoughtfully, then rose from his seat and slowly walked over to him. He stopped in front of Orrin, waiting until the fighter had opened his eyes again. He looked beaten and exhausted.

"Sorry," Enric heard his old teacher murmur. "I don't know what else I can say right now, my head is empty. I was an idiot. I was obsessed with doing something, anything, and you seemed the only logical target." He shook his head. "Sorry," he repeated, then fell silent.

"You know," Elwoi pursed his lips, "I have two children myself, both daughters. I see how a father might overreact when fear and anger take over. I will refrain from pressing charges against you. I might have acted similarly in your place, though with less expertise in physically demonstrating my feelings." He narrowed his eyes. "I am sure, though, that all of us here in this city would feel better if a man with your considerable magical strength and knowledge of fighting exercised more restraint in the future."

Orrin blinked in surprise and clearly needed a few moments to comprehend what he had just heard. "Thank you, Elwoi. That... shows greatness of spirit."

The artist smiled faintly. "Good. Then you might spread the word. I could use a little complimentary gossip about myself after your son's admirers damaged my reputation." Thus he turned and walked away, head lifted high in the knowledge of a situation handled well.

Enric turned when Vran'el tapped him on the shoulder. "Look, there is another messenger. He, too, looks out of breath and comes towards us. I hope there is not another one in trouble."

"Enric of House Aren," the messenger panted and then beheld the warrior. "And Orrin, good. I have been looking for you."

"What is it?" Enric demanded impatiently.

"Eryn of House Vel'kim sends me. Junar has gone into labour."

Orrin's head snapped up.

Vran'el sighed and shook his head. "Oh my, it seems that this just now was the *uneventful* part of our day."

* * *

Eryn sat in the corridor, fuming. Vern was with her, but had taken to walking up and down instead of sitting.

Both turned when Orrin, Enric and Vran'el turned the corner and hurried towards them.

"Where is she?" the warrior demanded.

"In there," Eryn pointed to a door a few paces away, clearly irritated.

"What's the matter?" Enric wanted to know.

"They won't let us in!" she exclaimed, throwing up her hands. "I mean - we are both healers! I have been trying to get to her, but they say they discourage family and friends from working as healers during the birth. What piffle! If we were at home right now, *I* would be the one taking care of her!" She shot Orrin an annoyed look. "But they said to send *you* in as soon as you were here. Why ever is that supposed to be a good idea? I mean, you are not a healer and you will probably faint from all the blood and screaming!"

The warrior looked pale and swallowed. "Blood and screaming? And they want me in there?"

"Yes," Vern nodded gravely. "They do have rather different customs here when it comes to childbirth. The father is supposed to see the mother through the birth by holding her hand, letting her shout at him and be a pillar of strength."

Eryn snorted. "Go on in then, fighter. A little blood and screaming shouldn't make you flinch. It's basically your daily business."

Orrin shot her a devastating look before he went to the door and knocked tentatively. It opened moments later and he was pulled inside by an energetic arm.

Enric turned towards Vran'el. "Were you present at Obal's birth?"

"But of course. It is a mighty, empowering thing to witness a new life being brought into the world. Something you helped create." He smiled faintly. "Though I am not going to lie to you: It is not exactly a calm, relaxed or clean business."

"Nothing like pushing around papers in a tidy study," Eryn grinned.

Enric looked down at Eryn's swollen belly.

"Nervous, my friend?" the lawyer grinned. "I bet you are thinking about what is awaiting *you* in a few months in there." He nodded towards the room Orrin had just disappeared into.

The blond magician nodded slowly. "I admit that thought has crossed my mind, yes. It needs some getting used to."

"Do not worry, they cannot make you go in there if you do not want to. It is a custom, but there are fathers who prefer to stay outside and instead send in somebody who is better suited to help the mother through it all. And there are mothers, too, who prefer someone else than their companion to be with them. A sister, best friend or mother, for instance."

"Judging from your expression I think I will stick with someone else, as well," Eryn sighed.

"No," Enric quickly assured her, "I will be there with you. If Orrin can do it, I can do it."

Vran'el slapped him on the shoulder, laughing. "That is the spirit! Competition is a wonderful thing, is it not?" Then he turned to Eryn. "How does giving birth work in the Old Kingdom? Fathers do obviously not play such a great role in it."

She shook her head. "No, none at all in fact. Purely a female matter. The father more or less has his offspring delivered after the birth so he can examine it and see if it is a worthy addition to his family. If he does not consider it strong or healthy enough, he refuses to accept the child as his."

Vran'el stared at her in horror. "That is absolutely monstrous!"

Vern rolled his eyes. "It would be if it were true."

Eryn sniggered. "Oh dear, how can you be that gullible?"

"Nuisance," her brother muttered and turned to the boy. "You tell me about it."

He shrugged. "The part with it being a female domain was true. The fathers generally pace the room outside, on occasion other relatives keep him company. The child is then placed in his arms after the birth and he has to care of it for the next few hours so the mother can finally sleep and recover from the birth. That's when the relatives usually turn out to be useful by instructing the new father how to handle a baby correctly, bathing it and clothing it and how to hold it without letting the head hang back. Stuff like that."

"And idea how long this will take? Does it make sense to go and fetch us something to eat?" Enric asked.

Eryn nodded. "It always makes sense to get something to eat if you have a pregnant woman around. Her contractions were happening at fairly short intervals already when she finally realised what they meant. She first thought they were cramps. Convenient that she was at the clinic already. She has already lost her waters, so things are progressing the way they should."

"Finally," Vern sighed and leaned back. "She has not exactly been relaxed over these last few days. I think she didn't particularly enjoy being pregnant. And I can see why, to be honest. Constant cravings for food, swollen feet, carrying a heavy load around with you that fairly much takes away your ability to move like a human being..."

"Thank you so much," Eryn growled. "I think you had better stop right here."

The boy smiled apologetically. "Sorry. I was just trying to show compassion with Junar here."

"Better try to show some sympathy for me. Junar can't hear you right now, and I pose more of a risk to you than her."

Vern rose. "Why don't I go and get us something to eat?"

303

"That's what I am talking about," she nodded, satisfied. "Make sure to bring something sweet as well. But not just fruit. Something sinful. With that dark cream they make here." When Vern had slunk off, she turned to the two men. "Tell me something that distracts me from sitting here and waiting in a corridor. Something funny, if possible."

Enric looked at her brother, then back to her. "Well, there is something I could tell you. But I am not sure if you would consider it a funny story. Though looking back seeing Elwoi dangling from Orrin's outstretched hand does seem humorous."

She sucked in a shocked breath, her eyes wide. "What? Really?" Then she nodded slowly. "Tell me everything, every little detail. That should manage to distract me for a while. It doesn't happen to have anything to do with why Orrin is wearing a golden belt right now, does it?"

* * *

Enric was the only one awake when the door opened again after what had seemed like an eternity. Which was probably a valid term for a time span of seven hours if one spent them sitting on a modestly comfortable chair with an expectant, impatient woman close by.

Vran'el, Vern and Eryn were dozing peacefully in half-seated positions, propping themselves against handy walls, backrests and available shoulders.

He looked up at Orrin, who looked exhausted, pale, but happy. He smiled tiredly at Enric.

"It's a girl," he said in a failing, though clearly proud, voice.

The younger man shook his head and smirked. "I have known that for quite a while now, but thank you for the information. I assume it's over? I hear the sound of a crying infant from the room behind you. I assume that's your new daughter?"

"Yes," he replied and nodded.

"Is Junar alright?"

"She is, yes."

"You look done for. Are you going to pull through?"

"Yes."

Enric sighed. "Look, I understand that you have just gone through a very arduous and probably trying couple of hours, and I don't want to be difficult here - but you are not exactly contributing a lot to this conversation."

Eryn stirred next to him and lifted her head from his shoulder, opening her eyes to blink up at Orrin, still half-asleep. Then she jerked herself upright.

"Junar! Is it over?"

"Let me speed things up," Enric offered. "It's still a girl, Junar is fine and so is Orrin."

She frowned at him. "Of course it's still a girl. What a strange thing to say!" Then she slowly got to her feet. "Can I see them? Are they still in that room over there?"

"They have put Junar to sleep and have taken the baby away to be bathed and clothed," the warrior explained wearily.

Now Vern started to stir.

"Is it over?" he exclaimed.

Enric nodded towards Vran'el who was still quietly snoring next to Eryn. "Wake him, will you? Or we will have to go through this another two times."

Vran'el stretched when he was shaken awake by his sister and smiled at Orrin. "Ah yes, that is the look of a man who has just been part of a birth. An amazing experience, is it not? Yet the best part of all is when they tell you it is over."

"Definitely," Orrin confirmed emphatically and leaned against the wall behind him.

Eryn snorted. "If you think that was exhausting for *you*, try putting yourself in Junar's place. Imagine a head this size pushing through an opening this size, then..." She stopped and rolled her eyes when all four men grimaced as if on cue and turned their heads away from her with a pained exclamation. "Lucky for you the paternal part starts only after the painful work has been done. Otherwise humankind would have died out long ago."

"You will not hear me argue with you about that, sweetness," Vran'el smiled and rose to clap Orrin heartily on the shoulder. "Come on, my friend! This is a reason to celebrate! After they have showed us your daughter all cleaned up, we will have a few drinks properly to honour this new life you have so manfully created. With my sister's aid, that is," he added with a grin.

"Thank you for pointing that out," the older man sighed.

"Great," Eryn murmured. "That means I have to watch you boys getting drunk and see that I get you to bed before you pass out in the main room. Splendid, simply brilliant. Junar does all the work and you do all the celebration. Where is the justice, I ask you?"

Vran'el patted her head. "You are just envious because you cannot get drunk together with us. But when Pe'tala or Vern have a child one day, you can get as drunk as you like with us." He winked at Enric. "Enric can take over looking after your son then. He is free to indulge himself tonight, after all. And in a happy companionship, a couple should take turns when it comes to matters like that."

The door behind them opened once more and a young man stepped outside, holding in his arms a small pink-faced bundle wrapped in a soft, brown blanket. The little girl had her eyes closed in blissful sleep as if no less exhausted from the birth than her mother.

"Orrin? May I present to you your daughter?"

They stepped closer and watched the sturdy fighter carefully take the fragile load.

Eryn had to look twice when she saw the tiny head. "How is this possible?" she whispered and looked up at Enric. "The girl has brown hair!"

"Yes, that was quite a surprise," the healer who had brought the baby to them nodded. "Is it not amazing how quickly the first generation already shows visible signs of change after the removal of the barrier in your brains?"

"That's the reason for her hair colour?" Vern said in astonishment. "So Ram'an was right, the barrier really was the reason for the absence of different hair colouration back home! Incredible!"

"What is her name?" Vran'el asked and carefully touched a perfect little fist with his index finger.

Orrin sighed and looked at Eryn. "We have decided to call her Téa."

She blinked and stared at him, her mouth open but unable to say anything.

"Dear me," Vran'el marvelled, "she is truly speechless! I was not aware this was even possible with an Aren woman!"

"You named her after *me*?" she finally whispered, touched. Then she laughed. "Do you remember that one morning after you had learned about Junar's pregnancy? You stormed into your bedroom and told her that this child would never be named *Eryn* because you didn't want to challenge fate!" She leaned her head against his shoulder. "And now you have named her after me, anyway." She sighed. "You know, now I am almost sorry I have to discipline you for disobeying me by strangling that artist today, you bloody idiot."

CHAPTER 23

Punishing Orrin

"This is strange. I don't want to do this! He will just stand there, head lifted proudly, manfully enduring whatever I do to him. I will feel like a villain because I am dealing out punishment to him for trying to protect his son!" Eryn wrung her hands while pacing up and down the bedroom. "And this situation is incredibly stupid, anyway! Me discipline him? Seriously? I mean, he is twenty-five years older than I! It is like Obal disciplining *me* for something!"

Enric observed her restless movements from his comfortable position on the bed, understanding her dilemma well. "I know. I remember when I was elevated to my position and suddenly found myself forced to take corrective measures when it came to my former classmates and especially those who were my elders. But that is the price of power. Every now and again you need to use it to maintain the structure in the organisation that grants it to you."

She flashed him an irritated look. "That is your argument? Really? I would be delighted to step back from that position of power if only that bloody institution would let me! I don't see how anyone can ask me to value being made to uphold its structures. Especially this far away from the institution in question! Why can't *you* take care of this?" But of course she knew the answer to that one well enough. It was no more than an outburst of frustration, not a real question.

He smiled thinly, answering her nevertheless. "You keep pointing out to me that you are no longer subject to my command since my membership of the Order has been temporarily suspended. That means that you have to take care of the less agreeable tasks yourself as well, not simply relish the liberty of not having to follow my orders any longer."

"You don't have to look so damned pleased about it!"

"Small pleasures," he shrugged, then became serious again. "Look, it won't be too bad. He knew exactly what he was letting himself in for by disobeying that order. And it's not like he is the kind who is unwilling to face the consequences for his actions. He will accept your penalty willingly, safe in the knowledge that he incurred it while he aimed to protect Vern. And he has just become father to a healthy little girl, the very first female in our Kingdom to have magical abilities after a gap of centuries. Whatever you do to him will pale in comparison, really."

She groaned. "That makes it even worse! He has a little baby to take care of now, and I am disciplining him! I will look like the most heartless person ever!"

Enric sighed and stood. "Nonsense. You will look foolish if you don't react to his disobeying your order so blatantly. Orrin himself would be the first one to reprimand you for that. Now off you go and bestow on him what he deserves. By the way, what is it you are doing to him, if I may ask?"

She bit her lip. "I was about to shackle him in gold for a month. House arrest doesn't make sense as he is supposed to be training the magicians in magical combat. It means he will have to limit his efforts to explanations instead of demonstrations. That will make his work quite a bit more difficult I would think. Practical exercises do kind of benefit from demonstrations. Or is that too harsh?" She looked up at him uncertainly, then added quickly, "Not that I am asking you for guidance or anything, this is just out of curiosity."

"Of course not," he chuckled. "A mighty Order magician such as yourself would hardly look to an outsider like me for advice, would they?" He held on to her hand when she rolled her eyes and seemed about to run off. "No, I don't think this is too harsh. I think you picked an adequate punishment that is neither too cruel nor too lenient. Well done."

She exhaled in relief. "Alright. Then I suppose I will let him have the bad news when he returns here in the afternoon."

He raised his brow at her. "Not that I question your unerring judgement, but I strongly recommend doing this publicly. He has taken the day today off to be with Junar and the little one, but tomorrow you can go to his training and take care of it. It doesn't hurt if he spends the day today wondering what will be awaiting him."

She scowled. "Do I have to?"

"No," he shook his head. "You don't *have* to. I am just telling you what I would do in your place. You may just as easily choose a more... nuanced approach. I am sure nobody at home would accuse you of being too soft on Orrin on account of his being a friend of yours or that you are a woman..."

She sent him an unnerved look. "Alright, alright! I will do it the merciless, approved Order-way, then! Can't have my venerated colleagues back home sneering at my unwarranted compassion, can

I? Especially as it is so well known how much I appreciate their opinions!" She grabbed his hand. "And now let's go. We have to take care of getting Junar and the baby home. Sleepless times are about to befall us," she added with an expression of doom.

Enric shrugged and rubbed her belly affectionately. "Consider it a rehearsal. It's not as if we would have been able to escape them much longer than a few months anyway."

"I do so love it when some people see the silver lining everywhere," she muttered.

* * *

"You need to support her head more," Orrin insisted.

"Don't fuss," Eryn growled but adapted the position of her arm that held little Téa slightly. "I know how to hold a child!"

"I have seen you with children. They mostly try to stay out of our way for some reason. Makes you think..." the warrior said.

"I have delivered children myself back in the village where I used to live! That did entail holding them afterwards, so back off, will you?" She rolled her eyes. "Really now!"

Both of them looked down at the small, soft, warm human when she started wailing, her eyes squeezed shut, the little mouth wide open, affording a clear view of toothless gums and the tiny uvula.

"Look what you did," Orrin scolded her softly and took his daughter from her arms into his own.

"What *I* did?" Eryn shook her head disapprovingly. "It is probably just feeding time. Children cry every now and then; that doesn't mean that it has to be somebody's fault!"

"Says the woman who is yet to have her first child to the man now raising his second," he retorted dryly and turned towards the door to take his daughter to the main room where Junar was resting on the seating cushions.

"Incredible," Junar sighed and held out her arms to take the bundle, "I hear her cry and a moment later milk starts oozing from my breasts. Is that normal?"

"Completely. The frequency of the cries triggers the release of certain substances in the mother's body that signal the need for sustenance for the child thereby making the milk flow," Vern nodded earnestly and earned himself several surprised glances. "What?" he shrugged. "I have been reading things. And as I happen to be spending a lot of time at the clinic, there is ample opportunity for me to pester healers with questions about just about everything I can think of."

Junar unbuttoned the belt she was wearing to expose one breast and lay Téa against it, smiling when the tiny lips greedily closed around the food supply.

309

Eryn had to gulp in delight at the picture they made. It was one of blissful harmony, trusting intimacy and contentment. Would she be experiencing this in a similar way in a few months' time?

"I suppose we will have to wait a few years yet to see if she turns out to be a magician," Junar cooed. "I hope we won't first discover it when she throws a bolt after us or something."

Vern and Orrin both raised their eyebrows, and Eryn shook her head in confusion.

"Why?" she asked and looked at Orrin. "Didn't they tell you at the clinic? Even if there is no conscious access to magic in a child, you can still determine whether the area responsible in their brains is active or not."

Junar looked up, clearly surprised. "You can?"

Orrin nodded. "Yes, and they found out that she is definitely going to be a magician. I thought they had told you as well?"

The seamstress rolled her eyes. "Orrin, I don't know if you remember the birth, but I was pretty exhausted afterwards, all but collapsing from the strain. Whatever they might or might not have told me did not really stick, if you can forgive me such inattentiveness." She looked down at her daughter thoughtfully. "So you really are a magician." Her gaze found Eryn. "I suppose with your being the only other female with this ability you are going to be quite an important role model for her, then."

Orrin swallowed. "Fabulous."

"At least a warrior is not the only choice of profession she will have when she is fully grown," Junar sighed.

Eryn smiled. "Maybe she will follow in her brother's footsteps and do something useful. Such as becoming a healer. Wouldn't that be funny? The Head of Warrior's children both turning out healers?"

"Simply hilarious," Orrin deadpanned.

Junar's expression became worried. "She is the first girl to be born as a magician in the Kingdom for such a long time. What will that mean for her in the long run?"

Her companion replied, "That she will be a person of interest to quite a few people back home. And to the more traditionally inclined members of the Order she will represent a danger to the structures they have known and are trying to hold on to."

"Hardly more than I, I would think," Eryn snorted. "And so far the changes have happened regardless of their wishes."

Orrin turned to her and spoke calmly. "Some have, others have not. You know, those that did happen were in many cases a struggle. I remember Council meetings shortly after your arrival in Anyueel. We had several meetings only to discuss if venturing to get you to join the Order was a sensible course of action. Many were against it. That is why it took us so long until we first asked you to join us."

Eryn nodded slowly. "I see. I was rather wondering about that at the time. I mean, you trained me fighting but made no move to compel me to join you."

"We couldn't. The Council had to agree it first. But what we could do was to train you so you would meet the requirements for membership of the Order when the time came. When the King first feigned a wish of having children with you, Enric and Lord Tyront came under considerable pressure. They were not really at liberty to ask you to join us at that time, but would have done so nevertheless if there hadn't been that shield inside you. That was convenient, or they would have had to anger the Council."

She sighed. "Why am I even surprised that you are aware that the King had never really intended to procreate with me?"

He shrugged. "That was not hard to guess. Had he been interested in violating the law on having no magicians on the throne, he would very likely have approached Pe'tala for that purpose after her arrival."

Vern shook his head. "My father, the political analyst."

"A skill that will very likely come in handy when it comes to protecting Téa," Junar said calmly.

Eryn nodded and regarded the warrior thoughtfully. "Yes, you are right. I suppose if there is somebody fit to raise and protect that girl, it is him."

"But then I dare say that Téa will hardly remain the only girl with magical abilities being born to the Kingdom in the years to come," Orrin pointed out.

Vern nodded in agreement. "With that barrier removed, I would say that is likely, yes. And there are quite a few young magicians at home who have yet to start a family. I bet they will make sure that their and their companions' barriers are removed before." He pursed his lips. "I suppose that means that there are a few more changes to happen in the Order when there are more girls to join. I mean, we don't even have separate changing rooms for them for the combat lessons."

"That is a minor thing, I would think," Eryn smiled. "The trouble is rather that the boys will have to get used to being taught together with girls. And the teachers, too, will have to adapt to that."

"Well, in that case it's not too bad to have a woman among those responsible for making these changes happen," the boy grinned. "That means you will probably one day be worth all the upset you keep causing."

She narrowed her eyes. "I very much hope that sister of yours will turn out to be a lot stronger than you and treat you to a few evil pranks. Unfortunately I am too old and now also too important to be seen doing something like that to you."

They looked up when Enric entered the main room, returning from the temporary working place Valrad had set up for him.

"Done with your work for today?" Eryn asked and raised an eyebrow when he observed the breastfeeding that was going on with a certain interest. "I hope you are focussing that gaze on the child, not the mother, my friend," she warned him.

"Honestly, I can only tell you that the sight of a mother suckling her infant holds no particularly erotic appeal for me, my love. Especially when neither are even mine," he assured her with calculated subtlety. "And no, I am not yet done completely for today. But I thought you might be interested in hearing that we should be able to return to our residence tomorrow afternoon. The cleaning work will be done by then and the few patches that needed restoration owing to smoke blackening have already been taken care of. Repairing the door to Vern's room will probably need another week, but we will just assign him another room. There are more than enough empty guest rooms around, after all."

Eryn's relaxed mood changed to one of worry. This reminded her of the attempt on Vern's life; now there was one more person around to be protected. An utterly helpless person. She was about to ask Enric if there had been any news from the investigation the triarchy had ordered, but swallowed the impulse to bring this up in front of Junar.

Vern sighed in sadness and looked to the floor, his shoulders drooping. Eryn reached out for his hand and squeezed it. Mentioning his old room had obviously triggered the memory of his feline friend that had died in there. Maybe it was not such a bad thing that he didn't have to return to sleeping in the room.

At least the negotiations for the agreements for House Arbil would start in two days. She hoped that would distract him from losing the cat. A pity though, that he would be spending the time with the very man he had named the cat after, so that was bound to raise unpleasant memories every now and then.

"How are your preparations for your noble quest to aid House Arbil going on?" she asked.

"Well enough. I have a reasonably good overview now. We are meeting tomorrow to discuss a few last details, and the day after tomorrow we will see how cooperative the other Houses really are. The two that we will be talking to, that is."

"Only two?"

"For that day. There are two more scheduled for one week's time and three more a few days after that," Vern explained. "I am curious how this will work. I imagine they will hardly be as easily won over as our apothecaries back home."

"No, probably not," Enric agreed. "And you might want to keep in mind that House Arbil will want to part amiably with them even if there is no agreement. So you'd better make sure to treat them with respect."

"No problem. If they are nice, I fill follow suit. If they aren't - well, then they deserve no better."

Eryn shook her head and chuckled. "At least Ram'an is quite a bit stronger than you. If you are too aggressive for his tastes he can take you out easily."

"He is a lot more civilised than you, he wouldn't do anything like that," the boy commented.

No, probably not, Eryn agreed silently. It was not exactly his style.

"By the way, Intrea's gathering is in four days. I think we should go," Enric suggested. "We have already accepted her invitation and going out and having some fun will do us good."

"I will pass on that one," Junar smiled. "I am on a tight schedule with Téa here."

"That means we can also count out Orrin, I would think," Eryn grinned and turned to Vern. "Good for you, my lad. You can drink alcohol and have fun without your father's watchful eyes on you."

"That statement shows that I cannot count on you to look after him there," Orrin growled. "Good thing Enric will be there as well or I would have had to request Kilan to watch over him."

"Suits me fine," she laughed. "I have no intention of babysitting him there; he is a bit too old for that."

"What a preposterous thing for you to say," the warrior grinned. "The woman who stumbles from trouble to trouble thinks a teenage boy doesn't need to be supervised."

"Speaking of preposterous," she shot back with a malicious look at him. "Which of us was the one to end up wearing a golden belt on the day of his daughter's birth because he happened to think that choking a certain artist would be a splendid idea, no matter that the man was innocent?"

Orrin didn't reply to that but pressed his lips together and looked away. He was clearly more than aware that this had not been a feather in his cap.

* * *

"And? What news do you have?" She asked once she had closed the door to their bedroom behind her.

Enric paused and raised an eyebrow. "What makes you think there is some?"

"Oh, please!" she rolled her eyes and strolled towards him, folding her arms. "The great, mighty Head of House Aren has not been able to gather any new information on the fire in his residence after five days? Really?"

He smiled down at her, pleased at her faith in him. "Well, there might be a thing or two."

"As I currently am the highest-ranking Order magician in the Western Territories, you would be contributing to maintaining a friendly relationship between the Order and the Senate by sharing those things with me," she pointed out.

He pretended to think about that for a moment. "Would I now? Well, then it would be negligent of me not to make use of this chance. But then a relationship consists of give and take, does it not? What are you offering in return?"

313

She grinned. "What do you want, Aren? I suppose my carrying your child under my heart is of no consequence in this discussion and is not considered ample compensation?"

"None whatsoever," he confirmed. "You would be doing that no matter whether I shared my information with you or not. How about complete and total surrender?"

She shook her head in mock regret. "Not much chance for that, I am afraid. You may not be aware of that, but we Order magicians, well, we are a rather belligerent bunch. We spend our time training our combat skills so foreigners like you can't get the better of us."

He nodded seriously. "You know, I *have* heard something like that. I was even told that people in your country don't hunt their own meat but buy it. Barbaric!"

She laughed. "Incredible, isn't it?" Then she became serious again. "Now, are you going to tell me about the investigation or not?"

"Of course. The triarchy is not too thrilled about my own efforts at locating the culprits, but I think they are not yet sure what to expect of me and have therefore not yet put a stop to my endeavours. At the same time their own have not been that much more promising, either. At least judging from what they are telling me." He took a seat on the bed and began to take off his boots. "I first followed Valrad's advice to consult the metal workers and see if they could identify the substances that had been used to make the burning rags give off these poisonous fumes. They were very helpful, and it seems the liquid was a mix of several rather poisonous substances, and they couldn't identify all of them. It has turned out, however, that artists also use a number of the same chemicals for mixing, preserving and rehydrating their paints."

"So, back to suspecting the artists?"

"They were never really in the clear on account of Elwoi being innocent. There are quite a few more of them around, after all. Then there might also be a few Houses who are discontent with the developments in their art world."

"So basically everybody is under suspicion?" she frowned. "That does not exactly narrow things down."

He shook his head tiredly. "No, it doesn't. My hope is that we can identify how the smoking rags were put together and see who has connections with people who can do such a thing. That means looking into all occupations working with chemicals of some sort."

She sighed, resigned. "That means you have no actual lead to follow for now."

He shrugged. "Nothing too promising, I am sorry to say. I am trying to eliminate possibilities for now."

"That means we are going to have to rely on your guards to protect us for some time yet, it seems."

"Yes, there is no way around it, I am afraid. But I am paying them to be unobtrusive about it, so they should not cause any major changes in your daily routine. Have they been clumsy?"

"No, they are very surreptitious," she assured him. But that was not really the problem, was it? It was more the fact that they were in a situation where measures like employing guards were necessary.

*   *   *

Eryn exhaled and straightened her shoulders. She had to do this, there was no avoiding it. Neither Enric, Tyront nor Orrin himself would appreciate it if she shirked this duty. Though knowing that the warrior himself would also object to not being punished was particularly bizarre. She herself seemed to be the only one unnerved by any of it.

She walked towards the low building that had been put at Orrin's disposal for the lessons in magical combat. It was usually used for riding instruction from what he had told her, which made it spacious enough for his purposes. She wondered if the unfortunate people who wanted to learn how to ride a horse had been deprived of their lessons for now or if they had been offered another location for that.

Pushing aside thoughts that were more appealing than what she was about to do, she moved aside a heavy sliding door that led into the extensive space, adding a little magic to her muscles to avoid any overexertion.

She immediately saw Orrin shooting a bolt at a woman in her mid-twenties and give an appreciative nod when she dodged it with a swift move. Many heads turned as Eryn walked towards them on the sandy floor.

No need to feel bad about any of this, she reminded herself. He knew precisely what he was doing when he disobeyed that order, and he was more than willing to bear the consequences. She had reprimanded people in the past, shouted at them and occasionally insulted them, but this was the first time she had to issue an actual discipline. Dealing with Rolan or her healers had never made anything of this sort necessary so far. What a nuisance that the very first person to be disciplined by her was somebody rather close to her. Yet it couldn't be helped and at least it was no cruel punishment, but merely an annoying one.

She kept her eyes trained on Orrin's face as she approached him. His expression was calm but serious. He knew exactly why she had come.

"Lady Eryn," he said formally and bowed once she stopped in front of him.

"Lord Orrin," she nodded. "You disobeyed my order not to approach Elwoi and used force against him. I accept that you were guided by your strong feelings and the need to protect your family, but a man in your position and with such considerable magical powers and knowledge of fighting at his disposal must be able to keep himself under control." She saw the corner of his mouth twitching for a short moment. He knew that these words were not for him, but for their audience, and he obviously approved.

315

"As much as I regret having to take disciplinary measures, I know that you are aware that they are necessary," she went on and pulled a pair of golden manacles from her pockets. They were the broad ones from the game and would not only serve to block his powers, but were visible to all and thus noticeable as his chastisement. This was supposed to be a public punishment, after all.

Orrin nodded once and without hesitation lifted his wrists and allowed her to fasten them on and close the seam with magic to complete the block, making removing them impossible for him.

"You will wear these manacles for an entire month. As you have already noticed, they do not block your powers entirely, but diminish them considerably. This will enable you to take care of minor injuries and the like, but not enough for magical combat or noteworthy enhancement of your physical strength. You will thus have to continue your training without the advantage of being able to give demonstrations for a while. This will make teaching your students more difficult, but by no means impossible for a man with your resources," she explained, keeping her face bare of emotion.

"Well done," he whispered, low enough for only her to hear, and let his wrists sink again.

She stifled a groan and turned to walk back and out of the large hall. As if this situation wasn't absurd enough already. Now he had even complemented her on how she had delivered his disciplining. So much for appropriate behaviour between superior and subordinate.

CHAPTER 24

A Dance with Consequences

Eryn's head snapped up when she heard the entrance door. She quickly grabbed the book next to her on the seating cushions and pretended to read. Enric, seated across from her, smiled and shook his head at her pretence of nonchalance when underneath she was all but bursting with curiosity.

They had returned to the Aren residence only the day before and had found it almost completely restored to how it had been before. There was a faint smell of fresh paintwork which lingered, but nothing too strong. The odour would be gone completely in another day or two.

Vern appeared at the top of the stairs and greeted them wearily.

Eryn pretended to notice him only now, looking up from her book as though surprised to see him.

"Oh, hello. Back already?" she asked as if she had not been waiting eagerly for more than an hour now for his return.

"Obviously," Vern shrugged and took out a glass to fill it with equal amounts of water and juice.

"And? How did the negotiations go? Did you lay the foundations for House Arbil to return to its former glory?" she enquired with what was supposed to pass for polite interest.

Enric smiled and wondered if the boy could see through her and was just playing along to tease her, or if he was preoccupied enough not to notice that her casualness was no more than a pretence.

"I am not sure. I was a bit confused. They did seem immensely reluctant all the time, but in the end they did sign the agreement. Which was surprising for me, as I would have expected them to take

317

their time and go through it at a later time, deliberate and analyse it and only then get back to us." He rubbed his face. "It does seem a bit careless just to sign a contract then and there like that, if you ask me."

"That is one major difference here, culturally speaking," Enric explained. "I remember wondering about this when I was negotiating trade agreements with the Houses several months ago. They normally come to their negotiations very well-prepared meaning they have all the information they need with them. This enables them to take care of all the matters right there. You might also have noticed that they tend to bring quite a stack of documents and books with them to the meetings."

Vern nodded. "Oh, they did, yes. Previous agreements, books about trading law, quotas, climate conditions and so on. Whenever a question arose, they were able to check the answer in a matter of minutes."

"Exactly. They don't want these talks to stretch on for a longer time but have them taken care of quickly. That means they are normally willing to remain in that room until some consent has been reached or it is clear that there can be none. As compared to our own country, where negotiations often require several meetings, necessitating a lot more time. Both approaches have their advantages and downsides, I would say," Enric pointed out. "What did Ram'an think of the outcome? Was he satisfied?"

The boy nodded. "He said that he was very satisfied, yes. When I asked him about our negotiation partner's reluctance to commit to anything only then to agree finally and sign, he told me that this is a common way of behaving when negotiating. Strange, really," he sighed.

Enric smirked. "As opposed to our own approach of keeping our faces blank and not showing what we think or feel, you mean?"

Vern seemed to think it over for a few moments, then nodded. "Yes, I suppose."

"Amazing in what areas differences in culture become apparent, isn't it?" the Head of House Aren chuckled. "But this is a behaviour you can also see when you walk the streets in the mornings when the market traders are at work. Just watch them with their customers when they are haggling. They pretend to be insulted by every price that is suggested to them, yet would be utterly taken aback if you just paid the price they were asking, because it was no more than a starting point and much too high and unreasonable."

The boy stared at him. "Oh my, that's why they keep staring at me like that when I buy something! I am supposed to negotiate with them? For everything?"

"You are. Never ever accept the first price they ask of you." Enric grinned broadly. "I dare say you have become rather a sought-after customer to many vendors here if you just pay the first price they name. That probably means you have paid way too much for whatever you have bought here so far."

"Good thing he is a rich kid and can afford it," Eryn chuckled.

Vern let his head sink back into the cushions and grimaced. "So much for being considered a genius then. It seems I have been working on my second reputation as a complete pushover these last few weeks."

"Don't worry, my lad," she shrugged. "It's a matter of adaptation and needs time. And if you had made a complete fool of yourself, Ram'an wouldn't have taken you with him today."

"You know what?" Vern straightened again, a determined spark showing in his eyes. "I will go back there tomorrow morning and show those traders what negotiating means where I come from! Then we will see who walks away with the better bargain." He jumped up and disappeared in the corridor where his new bedroom was located.

"My, oh my. It seems somebody is about to become feared and dreaded by the local market traders," Eryn sighed.

Enric shrugged. "Let him. This is very good negotiation practice for him. If he can stave off claims that their families will have to suffer hunger and poverty because he is unwilling to pay more than warranted for a piece of merchandise, the Houses will not be serious adversaries for him afterwards. He is a fast learner, and House Arbil will profit considerably from it."

Eryn nodded slowly. "Well, as long as he doesn't try this at home... I am just trying to imagine the baker's face when Vern goes in and tries to undercut the price for the bread buns, claiming that his poor little sister will have to wear rags if he has to spend all his family's wealth on bread."

"I would imagine, since magicians are known to be rather well off, it wouldn't work very well," Enric laughed. "Don't worry. Let him experiment. And if people keep throwing things after him or hiding when he comes along, he at least knows that he has been doing reasonably well."

"I did that to you! And it was not meant as an indicator that you were on the right track!" she protested.

"Well, well, the messages we send..." he smiled when she flashed him a dark look.

*　*　*

Eryn admired the changes Intrea had made in the large main room at her family's residence. Dimmed lighting, numerous small tables that served as surfaces on which glasses and plates could be placed, many small seating arrangements for smaller and larger groups, and a single long row of tables against one wall that held cold food and beverages.

Vran'el strolled over to her. "Hello, sweetness. Where is Enric? Don't tell me you have come here without him?"

She snorted. "As if he would let me! He doesn't let me out of his sight if he can avoid it, especially since I carry his spawn."

"And yet you are standing here, unsupervised," he commented.

"He made me promise not to get into any trouble while he is gone before he followed the host to admire his collection of antique sabres. Really now, can you believe that? Just as if I am a child that stumbles from one disaster into the next if he didn't keep his eye on me every minute of the day."

"Well, to be completely honest, you do have a certain tendency to get into trouble," he pointed out.

"That's twaddle," she scowled at him.

"A bold claim, coming from you," a dry voice behind her said.

She turned to Ram'an with a raised brow. "An even bolder remark from you, considering that you were fairly much the main reason that I got into trouble here in the past," she shot back.

Vran'el nodded curtly to the newcomer. "Eryn, would you like something to drink? There is a good selection of fruit juices suitable for your condition."

"Yes, that would be lovely, thank you." She handed him her empty glass. "Not the green one - I don't like the look of those little things floating in there. And not the red on the left - that is too bitter. The yellow one smells fine, though. But a bit sweet. Maybe you could mix yellow with a bit of red? With a splash of water?"

Her brother rolled his eyes. "I should have known better than trying to be accommodating." He sauntered off towards the drinks tables at the back of the room.

"How are you doing, Theá? Is the child giving you any trouble? It should be moving around a little already if I am not mistaken."

She looked at him in surprise. "I wouldn't have pegged you for a man to have this kind of conversation with."

"And why not, if I may ask? I am a man of many interests, and as you know pregnant women have a very high status in our society. What would be more natural for a man of the world than to talk with and about them?"

It did sound reasonable when he phrased it like that, she had to admit.

"Well, then I will comply with my high status and graciously answer you. I am fine, but I suppose that magicians have fewer problems with that in general, especially healers."

He smiled. "From the health side of it, yes. But there is no chance of healing away a tendency to kick, so if the child inside you is very lively, there might still be long, sleepless nights in it for you."

She swallowed. That didn't sound too promising. Hopefully it would turn out to be a calm child. Unlikely, though, considering its origins.

"I could always send it to sleep if it bothered me, couldn't I?"

His frown expressed disapproval. "No, healers explicitly advise against that practice! It might become a regular thing, which would hamper the development of the child's cognitive abilities. I will take you to a friend of mine tomorrow after lunch. He is an expert in these matters and it seems there is still a thing or two for you to learn."

"I am having lunch with you tomorrow?" She raised an eyebrow. "Why do you never phrase your invitations as requests but always as demands?"

"A request, dearest, is what you make when you are willing to accept a No. I am not, so I adapt my wording accordingly."

"You are aware, that you are not Head of *my* House, aren't you? Just a little push to question your delusion that I have to do as you request."

He laughed. "I have no delusions of that kind, believe me. But I am pleasant company, meaning there is no sensible reason for you not to let me feed you. And I know the best locations in the city - I even happen to own a few of them."

"Dear me," she grinned. "What an advantage it is to have rich friends."

"Interesting words coming from a woman who stems from two of the richest families in the country and happens to be committed to a very wealthy man at that."

She shrugged. "As you imply, it's all other people's money, not mine. I get a retainer for my services from the Order, a rather generous one, but it doesn't qualify me as rich. And it has never been my goal in life to be rich, so being constantly surrounded by luxury often makes me feel uneasy. I work with people with very low incomes every day, after all. It does seem frivolous for few people to own so much when so many own next to nothing."

"Which is why you offer medical services for everyone, Theá," he said softly. "Here they were more or less limited to Houses which can pay the high prices. A matter that your father's House has taken great pains to alter."

"What can I say? I am my father's daughter." She noted with satisfaction that Ram'an was careful enough not to remark on that one.

"And your mother's, too. Though I can see that you want to neither admit it nor hear it."

He turned when a heavy hand landed on his shoulder. A young man who had seemingly had more than his share of wine grinned broadly at him and exclaimed, "Ram'an, my friend! I was hoping to catch you here tonight - we must talk about this matter with your House no longer selling fabrics to my tailors."

"We can talk about it, but not here. Come to my place tomorrow. Sober," Ram'an replied sharply and began to turn back to Eryn, when the man started to become agitated and raised his voice.

Ram'an's reply was something about the man's tailors not paying for the fabrics in time and making unreasonable claims, damaging the goods and then wanting them replaced. She looked up at another man who had come to stand next to her, and raised her brow questioningly when he smiled at her. He was in his mid-twenties and had bound his long, dark hair together in a ponytail that fell down his back.

"Good evening. May I ask you for the next dance?"

She heard the loud and drunken man still quibbling about fabrics with Ram'an behind her and Vran'el was still busy mixing her fruit drink.

"Sure, why not?"

"What? No! What are you thinking, Malthea?" Ram'an's voice snapped at her and she felt his hand on her arm pulling her back towards him.

"Why? What should I be thinking?" she replied in utter confusion. Had she just transgressed some custom by accepting an invitation to dance? She had done so countless times before, so what was the problem now?

He stared at her, incredulous. "That accepting intimate dances with total strangers might cause considerable trouble, for example?"

She blinked, then looked at him blankly in incomprehension. "But... there was no bell to signal it! How was I to know that it was one of those?" She turned back to the man, frowning. "What is the matter with you, asking strange and expectant women to dance that kind of dance with you? Really now! I decline!"

She heard Ram'an beside her sighing in desperation and the stranger in front of her regarded her. "You cannot decline after you already accepted." Then he extended his hand for her to take.

At this moment Vran'el returned with her glass and frowned. "What is the matter?" He looked at the man's outstretched hand. "Oh Eryn, you have not accepted this dance, have you? Did you not notice the silver light?"

"Silver light? I thought it was a bell chiming three times!" she exclaimed.

"But only in public places! In private abodes it is the silver light! With this noise level people would hardly ever notice a signal such as that! Did nobody tell you?"

"No! This is the first time I have attended a gathering like this!" She covered her face. "Listen," she told the man who still held out his hand. "I am not going to dance this dance with you! Come back for another one later, alright?"

"The invitation has been accepted," he insisted and looked annoyed.

"Where is Enric?" Ram'an interrupted urgently.

"I don't know! Gone somewhere to look at old weapons with Intrea's father," she replied and swallowed. "What am I to do now? Do I really have to dance with him?"

Ram'an closed his eyes for a moment. "No. There is one thing we can do. But I am not sure you will like it as an alternative." He took a deep breath, then looked at the man. "I claim this dance for myself."

Eryn drew in a sharp breath. "Doesn't this mean that..."

"That I have to dance it with you instead after claiming it. Provided you chose me over him as your partner." He looked at her tensely. "You have to decide quickly. The song is about to start."

Not good, not at all, she thought, her heart beating faster. Enric would not be happy with this, and neither was Ram'an, so it seemed. Vran'el did not appear too thrilled by the situation either.

"Yes or no?" the man demanded unnerved.

"No to *you*!" she shot back angrily.

"Which means Yes to me," Ram'an nodded and took her hand to lead her to the next room. "Get Enric," he whispered to Vran'el, who just nodded briefly and left without another word.

A few other couples had already assembled in the room where the musicians had set up their equipment. In contrast to herself and her reluctant partner they were smiling in anticipation of thrills to come.

"I am sorry," she said, and grimaced apologetically. "You were right. I can't seem to stay out of trouble. What will happen now?"

"That, my dear, is what we are about to find out. I have a very clear idea about what is going to happen to *me*," he said dryly. "About you... that remains to be seen. It depends how strongly you are attracted to me physically. The magic works with what is there."

"So if I am not attracted to you at all I won't feel any effect?" she asked carefully.

"Theá, my dear," he smiled in wry amusement, "you *will* feel an effect. There is at least a little attraction on your side, otherwise you would not have let me kiss you. Or at least not have experienced it as something pleasant."

Panic entered her eyes. "So we can assume that I am at least a little attracted to you and you have sent for Enric to observe us?"

"Not to watch. To be there for you afterwards."

"What if Enric turns up here during the dance? Can he claim the dance for himself and take over?"

"No, not when it has started already and you have agreed to dance it with me," he explained patiently and looked around to see if he could spot the blond head of hair somewhere. "He has only a few more seconds to make that claim - the music is about to start."

She felt the hairs on her forearms prickling when indeed a few seconds later the first notes of the song reached her ears. Looking up at Ram'an, she saw him take a deep breath before he stepped closer and took her fingers in his hand. The contact closed the connection, locked them together for as long as the music lasted.

Maybe she could fight it this time, her thoughts raced. With the wrong partner, how effective could the magic be? But who determined what a *wrong* partner was? The music itself? Music was not a thinking entity, but just something to trigger reactions, a human-made means of enjoyment, a tool.

She felt her heartbeat quicken when his hand came to lie on her hip and her hand mirrored the move. They slowly started turning, eyes locked, both facial expressions strained. Would imagining that he was somebody else, somebody she did not find at all attractive, even found repulsive, help? She tried to conjure up a picture of Loft. The King's advisor, with his plump figure, bald head and red face when he was angry, the high-pitched voice and the contemptuous sneer.

As soon as the image was complete, it dissolved instantly and was replaced by Ram'an, dark and handsome, jaw muscles tight, gaze intent. Was it her imagination or was there a pleasant odour that seemed to be originating from his flawless, tanned skin?

His touches started to send little sparks along her flesh. The evening he had kissed her re-emerged unbidden from her memory. How he had tasted, smelled. Warm, of sweet wine, exotic, scented soap... She tried to shake her head to clear it but couldn't. It was not a direction the music intended her to take. And thinking was becoming harder and harder by the moment. The music left no place for that, either.

* * *

Enric skidded to an abrupt halt, Vran'el not two steps behind him and almost bumping into him. He didn't even see the other couples, only Eryn and how she was moving in perfect harmony with Ram'an. Her face did not look relaxed but tense, and her partner's lips were pressed into a thin line. Both of them caught in the magic of a song neither of them had wanted to dance this way.

"What happens if I intervene? Stop the dance or take Ram'an's place?" Enric asked with balled fists, his voice a low grumble.

Vran'el looked at him in alarm. "You cannot! They need to finish it, the magic will not let them loose otherwise. And the shock of breaking might harm your child."

"What if I just knock out Ram'an and finish the dance with her, so she can end it?" he enquired urgently, watching how Ram'an's hand cupped her cheek and she leaned into the touch.

"She cannot finish it with *you*! They are bound to each other until the song is over! Honestly, if the Head of House Aren knocks out the Head of House Arbil in public, there will be trouble! Now stop these questions and just be there when it is over." He took a deep breath and then added, "One more thing. Ram'an is very attracted to her, that much is obvious and has been for quite some time. He will be under very great pressure after the dance is over."

Enric looked at him in alarm. "What are you trying to tell me? Out with it, man!"

"He will have to release some of the strain or he might lose control of himself. Think back to the first time you came here, the dance at the music house. What the first thing was you did after the music ended?"

He sucked in a quick breath when he remembered. "So he is going to kiss her? You mean, right here?"

"That is very likely, yes. Be prepared for it and do not intervene." Vran'el exhaled, looking at a loss to say anything to reassure Enric. "I do not like this, either. You know that my family is not too happy about Ram'an. But by taking it upon him to claim the dance for himself, he saved her from being touched by a stranger who would very likely not have shown any restraint. Ram'an sent for you immediately, so you may assume that his intentions were honourable."

"I know," Enric rasped. "But that doesn't make watching this any easier!"

They stood side by side, arms folded, their eyes glued to the dancing pair.

* * *

This was not supposed to be happening, she thought frantically. It had not been like this when he had kissed her that one time. No explosions, tension or innards tied in knots. Why were her muscles strung like a bow, her heartbeats so rapid and her thoughts telling her to grab him and be his for whatever he wanted to do with her?

She dreaded the end of the song and what it would bring.

Enric, she thought with a silent groan. How she hoped he wasn't watching this. But then that was not very likely, was it? Ram'an had sent for him before he had led her to the floor. And then he very was likely experiencing her distress through the mind bond. So he would be witnessing her reaction to another man, feeling a faint echo of it in his own head, being forced to stand by and do nothing except wait.

But the thoughts about Enric were soon driven away. The magic had no place for them, he was the wrong one to think about in the midst of the enchantment.

The music became slower and, beat by beat, decreased in volume, making them face each other with their fingers intertwined.

As soon as the last note had dwindled away, she felt his fingers burying themselves in her hair and only a moment later his mouth crushed upon hers. This time there was no gentle testing, but an immediate, bold claim that took her breath away for a moment. Her hands at his chest balled into fists, crumpling his tunic between her fingers as if to prevent him from withdrawing ever again. Explosions. The one word appeared in her head slowly, as if fighting its way through fog. It was like a forceful wave, violent, raw, uncontrolled.

She almost protested when he ended the kiss abruptly and instead leaned his forehead against hers, breathing heavily with closed eyes, still holding her close.

When he opened his eyes again, they seemed fierce, greedy - staring at her mouth as if only the very greatest effort kept him from taking possession of it again. He swallowed hard, took a step backwards, taking her hand firmly in his but breaking every other contact. His eyes searched and found Enric among the watchers and he urgently pressed Eryn's hand into his.

"Take her home. At once," he commanded hoarsely.

Enric nodded once and pulled her towards him to wrap an arm around her waist to guide her down the stairs to the exit of the residence and hold her upright when she repeatedly threatened to stumble.

* * *

She lay on her side, staring ahead out the window unseeingly, tears of shame, helplessness and regret slowly and silently trailing down her face until they soaked into the pillow against her cheek.

Enric had been gentle and attentive; not a word of accusation, reproach or reprimand had come over his lips. He had loved her with care, tenderness, unconditional understanding and she felt even worse for it. It couldn't have been a great pleasure for him to do it to release the desire another man had awakened.

Any sign of anger from him would have helped - something to give her the feeling that she got what she deserved. Yet there was nothing.

He had held her in his arms for a while, stroked her head, but when her tears had not ceased, he had risen from the bed and left. She felt alone, cold despite the warm evening breeze.

More than an hour had to have passed since he left her, when she heard his footsteps approaching. She closed her eyes, pretending to be asleep, hoping he had come back to sleep in the same bed with her instead of somewhere else.

But he didn't lie down, instead he crouched in front of her, gently touching her shoulder.

"Eryn? Come and put something on. Valrad is here."

She opened her eyes and stared at him in confusion. "What? Why? Has something happened?"

"No. I went and asked him to come here with me," he said soothingly. "Come."

That had been the reason why he had left her alone! To get her... uncle, not because he was angry at, disappointed with her or tired of her misery! The wave of relief was so powerful she felt her muscles almost going limp with the released tension.

He gently pulled down the blanket and took her hand to help her get up.

"Why?"

"To talk to you." He handed her a long-sleeved nightgown and waited until she had slipped into it before he linked his fingers with hers and led her outside into the main room where Valrad was sitting on the cushions.

"Eryn," he smiled. "Come and sit with me. You had quite an evening from what I was told." His expression turned serious. "From what Enric shared with me, it seems you are a little overwhelmed by the situation. I would like to help you put it into the right perspective."

Eryn sighed shakily and shook her head. "Valrad, I am flattered that you have come in the middle of the night, but there is nothing much you can do here."

He nodded thoughtfully. "Maybe you are right. But as your companion here woke and dragged me all the way here, you can at least let me make a futile attempt before sending me back home, my dear Eryn."

Now she felt guilty. He was right of course, indulging him at this point was the least she could do. She sat next to him on the cushions and felt Enric settle behind her so that she could lean against him.

"Now, my girl, what is it that troubles you so much that your tears cannot stop flowing?"

The words were there, but it was an immense strain to bring herself to utter them out loud, especially in front of Enric.

"The dance with Ram'an, it... had an effect on me."

Her father waited for more to come and raised his brow when she didn't go on. "But of course it had. That is what it was composed for, to cause this effect."

"You don't understand," she insisted. "It shouldn't have had quite that effect. I love Enric. Or at least I thought I did..." The tears were back and she felt them running down her cheeks, leaving wet trails on her skin.

Valrad leaned forward. "I would like to offer you some insights into the nature of magical music from a medical point of view. I think this should be some interesting knowledge for a healer."

Eryn straightened. That was a professional angle, she could deal with that. His voice had lost its edge of sympathy and taken on a more matter-of-fact quality.

Enric smiled faintly. That had been a bright move, he decided. She couldn't deal with pity or attempts at comfort very well, but she would listen to medical facts alright.

"Physical desire, you see," Valrad went on, "is something that is located in our brain and can be triggered through different means. There is physical stimulation, which we are able to control and direct and actively decide whether to permit or not. Then there is mental stimulation, which we can control only to a certain degree, as sometimes thoughts tend to turn up unbidden and may make us react whether we want them to or not. Mental or physical stimulation are often connected with emotions, which means that the same stimulus does not work with different persons. In one person a stimulus triggers a response, while in another it does not. This is a matter of preference. Emotions, however, are not always required for such a response, as you are surely aware. Otherwise we would never have sexual intercourse unless we are at least in love." He paused and waited for her to nod in agreement.

327

"And then we have in addition to these two a third way of stimulation to trigger lust: magic. Very powerful. And completely outside our control. There are a few prerequisites that need to be in place for it to work, though. Firstly, there must be magical abilities, and secondly, a certain degree of physical attraction." He looked at his daughter insistently. "Do you understand what I am telling you now?"

She looked away from him and out the tall windows. "You are telling me that I am attracted to Ram'an."

He rolled his eyes. "Of course you are, my dear girl. He is a very good looking chap, charming and very skilled at making people like him. Many women in this city are attracted to him, I would venture. But you would just as well be physically attracted to a number of other men in this city. As would Enric be to a number of women here, even though everyone can see how very taken he is with you. Eryn, we are talking about physical attraction here," he insisted. "It is not turned off completely and makes you deaf and blind to other compatible sex partners as soon as you develop an emotional attachment to the one person. You are just less eager to react to them. And the music pushes that eagerness without consideration for your feelings."

She looked at him thoughtfully, considering his words. She cleared her throat and then said slowly, "So the magic in the music also works if there is no emotional connection to the dancing partner whatsoever?"

She more felt than heard Enric chuckle behind her. "I distinctly remember one particular night when we were both wearing a mask. Unless you have the ability to form emotional attachments to masked strangers within minutes, you have already experienced yourself how well it works with purely physical attraction."

Of course, she thought and felt stupid for not thinking of it herself.

"Emotional attachment, however," Valrad added, "does increase the impact the magic has on you." He smiled. "The two of you demonstrated this quite effectively some time ago when you were in our city for the first time, when Ram'an had tried to dance with you. A very effective combination of magical strength, a firm attachment between you and a powerful song."

"That dance with Enric had a stronger effect on me than the one tonight," she said reflectively. "But the one with Ram'an was more powerful than the very first one I danced with Enric back home."

"The one where he was masked and anonymous to you?" Valrad asked to be sure.

"Yes. Am I to assume that I am more attracted to Ram'an now than I was then to Enric?" The very thought made her uneasy, enormously so.

"My dear girl, emotions are very powerful in our life and have an influence on everything we do. Of course you are more attracted to a man you find not only reasonably attractive but you see as a friend, than to someone who seemed to you like a complete stranger. The important fact is that the magic in the music is at *this* point more effective when you experience it with Enric than with Ram'an." He took her cool hands into his much larger warm ones. "You have not betrayed Enric in any way. Love, my dear child, is not the absence of physical attraction with regard to any other person around you, it is the conscious decision not to act on it."

"I let him kiss me," she said quietly, feeling that she *had* acted on it.

"The kiss after the dance is the first chance to release some of the tension that has built up inside us. Ram'an is a powerful user of magic, as you are yourself. Even if you had decided *not* to let him kiss you, there is nothing you could have done to stop him. Or should have done. There was pressure inside you as well that needed to get out, that is why you *wanted* to kiss *him* as well," her father explained patiently.

"So I am not a deplorable person and companion because I felt drawn to another man during that dance?" she ventured carefully, just to be really certain.

"No, girl, you would probably have to be a dead person not to," he replied wryly. "Which is a serious medical condition and much more problematic than possessing an active sex drive - something which is, as is natural in all animals and in ourselves, not primarily connected to emotions."

Enric exhaled in relief when he finally felt her relax against him.

Valrad smiled at them. "Any more questions or can I slip back to my bed now? I am an old man and need my beauty sleep."

"Why don't you stay here in one of the guest rooms? You can return after breakfast," Enric offered.

"No, I am a creature of habit, I am afraid. If my bed is too close to the window or the sun comes from the wrong direction in the morning, I am grumpy all day long. But it is kind of you to offer it." He got to his feet and nodded to them. "I shall bid you goodnight. Do not bother to get up, I will find my own way out."

"Thank you for coming here. I am very much indebted to you for doing so," Enric said sincerely.

"No problem, my friend. It warms my heart to see that you are taking good care of her, especially as she lives so very far away from here, somewhere I cannot normally be of much help if she needs a strong shoulder to lean on."

They heard his footsteps on the smooth stone floor fading with the distance and disappear completely after the door in the hallway was closed with a reassuring thud.

Eryn smiled and closed her eyes when she felt Enric's hand stroking her swollen belly and his lips pressing against her temple.

"I am glad you seem to feel better, my love."

"I do," she confirmed. "But I feel bad about Ram'an. You are not angry with him, are you? He didn't want to do it. He kept looking for you until the last moment so you could claim the dance from him."

"Yes, I know. Vran'el told me that he had sent for me immediately. I owe him greatly. And I admire his restraint in releasing you after the dance. That must have been an act requiring great willpower. I will visit him tomorrow to thank him properly."

"I will accompany you," she said and laid her hand on his.

"No, my love. I don't think that is a wise move. He is still attached to you, and now after finally giving you up he has found himself being closer to you than ever. This makes his deed even more admirable as he must have foreseen it when he claimed the dance. Let him work out how to handle this first before he has to face you again."

"My carelessness has hurt him," she sighed and shook her head at her own stupidity.

"I am not so sure about that," Enric said carefully. "The situation does seem rather strange to me. A man who has never met you before comes to you, an obviously pregnant woman, to ask her to join him in a magical seduction dance while your companion is looking at weapons, your brother is fetching you something to drink and your conversation partner is busy talking with somebody else and cannot intervene in time to warn you before you agree to it."

"What exactly are you saying? Somebody planned it all?" She frowned and thought hard. "So you think it was done in order to make Ram'an claim the dance while you were away? Why?"

"The last time he tried to dance with you," he mused, "I punched him in the face hard enough to send him flying over a table. I assume that a similar reaction was expected after I caught sight of you dancing and finally kissing. Today, however, the results of such an assault would have been quite different."

She nodded slowly. "Yes, indeed. Back then you were a foreigner, a stranger who was entitled to break the odd rule as it provided food for the gossips. And Ram'an was the member of a powerful House who tried to steal your companion. But now you are both Head of a House, and hitting him would have harmed House Aren, as your reputation would have suffered. And being hit by you would have been bad for House Arbil, as the Head of a House cannot be seen to be treated like that without defending himself. Defending himself would have opened a feud between your Houses. It would also have affected House Vel'kim, as they couldn't have been seen to continue business with House Arbil after such an incident." Her eyes began to glint with a new understanding when she turned her head to look at him. "Somebody tried to harness me to play out a little power game here, one that would have harmed our Houses! I want to know who!"

"So do I. I have sent a messenger to Vran'el at the party to find out the identity of the man who asked you to dance with him. As soon as we know who he is, we will have a nice cosy chat with him."

"Do you think this is somehow connected with the fire?" she asked and gulped hard. This would make this whole development a vendetta instead of a mere attempt at scaring or hurting them a single time. And it meant that Vern was very likely not the only target, nor probably even the primary one as she had suspected before.

"We can't rule it out," he replied carefully. "We will take care of this, my love. I will not rest until I have found out who is behind all this."

They shared a quiet smile that did not speak of joy, but of grim determination and a promise of seeking justice.

CHAPTER 25

Forgiving

Eryn sat in the canteen, staring at the table in front of her, eyes unseeing. The large room was empty but for her at this time of day, eerily so. It was early afternoon and the healers had either returned home after their shift or back to work after lunch.

She had been sitting in this way for more than one hour now, holding the same glass of water in her hands without drinking. She wasn't sure what had to be done now, but she knew that after yesterday night she couldn't keep hiding any longer. It was time to face up to the matter with Valrad, one way or the other.

She looked up when Iklan's prim assistant entered the canteen and came to her table, smiling.

"Maltheá? Iklan is now ready for you. His patient has left."

Eryn nodded and got up from the cushions, placing the glass on the table before her before following the woman out of the canteen, up the stairs and along the corridors that led to the healer's treatment room. She hadn't known that there was a shortcut when coming from the canteen. She had in the past always taken the long way round to his room. But then taking a shorter route would probably not have been too appealing in the past, considering that most of her visits had not been voluntarily. But this one was different.

"Eryn," the healer smiled when he beheld her and rose from the chair behind his desk. "Do come in. I was really pleased when you asked for an appointment with me. I am sorry you had to wait, but I am reluctant to reschedule prior appointments with patients if I can help it. Even for an important person such as yourself," he added with an apologetic smile.

She waved him off. "That's alright, I didn't mind waiting. And my request to see you was at very short notice, after all. I am grateful that you are seeing me at all today." She wondered briefly if his willingness to squeeze her in on the same day had something to do with trying to avoid angering Valrad. Probably.

She took a seat on his cushions on the floor without being asked. She knew he wouldn't take offence at that.

"Have you heard about yesterday? The gathering at House Feral?" she asked without an introduction.

Iklan picked up two fresh glasses and placed them on the table in front of her before he fetched a carafe of water.

"I assume we are talking about your dance with Ram'an of House Arbil?" he enquired carefully.

She nodded. Good. At least the gossips had saved her from needing to tell the whole story.

"Am I right in assuming that your acquiescence in this dance was unplanned?"

"You are, yes. But the dance is not what I have come to talk about. I admit it was a disconcerting experience to dance it with a man other than Enric, but I would rather like to talk about what happened afterwards." Then she frowned. "Wait, there is one matter that *does* interest me in connection with the dance. A lot. I dare say you will be able to enlighten me about it. Why is it not possible to change one's mind after accepting a seduction dance? This does hold quite a potential for trouble. At least in my case."

Iklan filled their glasses and handed her one before taking a sip.

"Agreeing to an invitation to a seduction dance equals the willingness to share something intimate, as you are surely aware. Such an invitation is not meant to be voiced carelessly, nor to be accepted without the intention to follow through with it." He regarded her thoughtfully. "I see that for somebody who has yet to acquaint herself with all our customs this is not always easy, that obeying these rules may indeed cause trouble when one is not aware of the consequences. But imagine a person who has gathered all his courage to ask for such a dance, been accepted and then only moments later is refused. It would be cruel."

"I wouldn't have refused the dance out of spite, but because I was not aware what I was agreeing to!" she protested.

"Yes, I know. But in our society that hardly ever matters as we locals are aware of the signals. In the past both men and women used the tactics of first accepting and subsequently refusing seduction dances to cause public humiliation. This more often than not resulted in violence. For this reason a law was passed several decades ago to prevent anything like that from happening. And then there is the matter that we do consider it a shame to step back from an agreement. I have heard that business and private relationships are not as tightly interwoven in the Old Kingdom as here, is that correct?"

Eryn nodded. "It is, yes. I suppose that makes things a lot easier at home. We do try to avoid binding ourselves to our business partners or superiors too tightly as personal feelings would only be in the way when it comes to protecting our own interests. This is not possible here from what I have seen."

"Indeed. A careless transgression of the rules of politeness at a music house may in the long run result in fragmenting the alliance of two Houses. Doing business with each other is a personal matter here, one of trust. If your companion had not made a trustworthy and honourable impression on us when he came here in his function as ambassador, there would not have been any trading agreements whatsoever," he explained. "So you see what harm a public insult can do here. And a personal, public humiliation such as pretending to grant a seduction dance only to step back from it again is something that weighs heavily on the person who voiced the invitation. It is a lot more painful than if the invitation had been rejected at the beginning. Hopes were raised that were then dashed again recklessly. And in accordance with the strong feelings this triggers, the retribution was often painful enough. It was a matter of showing to the watchers that this is not an acceptable treatment, especially when it came to members of the Houses who have to be careful of their actions to maintain their standing in society."

"So this law that a seduction dance once agreed has to be followed through is a means of ensuring that such an invitation is only accepted when there is no intention to ridicule the person who asks and thereby cause resentment and damage," she nodded. "I understand that. Yet the rule turned out to be quite dangerous for me."

"It is not impenetrable," Iklan smiled, "Hardly any of our laws are if one knows how to go about it. And as far as I know you profited from exceptions to the law both times you found yourself involuntarily accepting the dance, did you not?"

She thought for a moment, then raised her brows. "The possibility of having another person claim the dance?"

"Exactly. This enables the person who was invited to dance to correct any inadvertent mistakes in accepting it. Have I answered your question to your satisfaction?" he then enquired.

"You have, yes. Thank you."

"Good. Then I would be very interested in hearing what made you come to me today. You mentioned that it was something that happened after the dance, if I remember correctly?"

Eryn exhaled until there seemed to be no more air left in her chest to be squeezed out. She could do this. She had to.

"Yes." She shifted her position slightly so that she didn't face Iklan directly anymore. Maybe it was easier if she could pretend to just talk to herself. "The dance and my unexpected reaction to Ram'an have left me quite unsettled." That was putting it mildly, but she had no wish to share her feelings about that with him. "Enric was worried so he went and fetched Valrad in the middle of the night to have a talk to me. He came. And we talked. At first I didn't really want to listen to him, but what he said helped me. Quite a lot."

The healer smiled faintly. "And now you feel guilty because he showed you such unconditional kindness despite your refusal to talk to him about your changed family situation?"

She closed her eyes and nodded. Yes, that did summarise her sentiments pretty well.

"Do not worry about that, Eryn," Iklan said softly. "Valrad does not expect any compensation for it, I promise."

Her eyelids flipped open and she looked at him in confusion.

He chuckled quietly. "That did surprise you, eh? You expected me to try and persuade you to repay his kindness by making up with him, I suspect. It would have been a feather in my cap to make you go to him."

She bit her lip and he smiled at her guilty expression.

"I rather wonder that you came to me despite the unflattering impression you seem to have of me," he remarked mildly.

"I am sorry," she sighed and looked down. "You are right, of course. A part of me still seems to be convinced that you are more likely to be acting in Valrad's interest rather than mine."

"But the part that thought that I might not was obviously strong enough to make you come to me nevertheless. What is it you wish to do, Eryn? Forget what others might expect of you, what Valrad might be hoping, what Enric would do in your place. Think of why the current situation between the two of you does not seem to be right after last night," he urged her.

Kneading her fingers nervously, she let her wandering gaze range around the room as if looking for inspiration.

"I don't know! It's just... wrong somehow. If feels heartless and cold of me to push him away when he is being kind to me. You are right - I feel guilty about it. But that doesn't mean that I think I am not entitled to be angry at him any longer. I am confused and angry at myself because of it! And at him!" She lifted and then dropped her hands in helplessness.

He leaned back and pursed his lips, looking at the ceiling, obviously pondering something. "I think we should talk about the nature of forgiveness."

She groaned. "Don't you think trying to make me forgive him is a little premature given my current state of mind?"

"I have no intention of *making* you do anything, my dear Eryn," he reassured her. "I merely want to discuss with you the prerequisites for such a step and then you can decide where you stand and whether it is even something you would want to do at the moment."

She nodded reluctantly. "Very well, then. Tell me something about forgiveness." She wondered if it would be as revealing as his little lecture on safety before.

"Forgiveness, you see," he started, "is a very intimate process, probably comparable to true closeness in sexuality. We are talking about a process here, what is more, something that takes time and not a single step to be taken quickly and then is done with. And apart from time there is something else that is required for forgiving another person: courage."

She frowned, but didn't speak. Did that mean she was fainthearted because she was not yet ready to forgive Valrad?

"Forgiving requires lowering our inner defences, our barriers, as it were. We make ourselves vulnerable and at the same time give up our own impulse to harm the other person. There is always the risk of being hurt again, of finding that forgiving the other person was actually a mistake. That is why this process requires courage." He paused and waited to see if she wanted to comment on that, then went on when she just continued to look at him.

"The very first step is to address the source of the offence, to bring it out into the open to talk about the pain it has caused. Without admitting to the pain but instead denying or suppressing it, this process cannot begin. So the first question to ask yourself is: Are you ready to admit to your pain? Are you ready to share it with Valrad?" He lifted a hand when she opened her mouth. "No, do not answer *me*. Answer to yourself. Take your time. I am not the one you need to convince, my dear lady." He then went on, "As you are a healer colleague, I will use a healing metaphor here: An emotional injury needs to be treated, just like a physical one. But if you bandage it without cleaning it first, there will very likely be inflammation at the site of the injury. Merely covering it will not make it go away; it will just appear as if it were taken care of, but it was not. The same applies for painful situations. If you ignore what is underneath it all and just want to pretend that everything is in order without talking about it, it will continue to smoulder beneath the surface and one day break open with more than the initial potency." He leaned forward, looking at her emphatically. "That means every taboo will keep you from taking care of this properly, everything you refuse to address will hinder development between the two of you. It also means the question is not such a simple one if you are really ready to talk about it with your father. No half-measures here. You either do it properly, or take more time until you are ready to." He leaned back again and waited for her to speak.

She looked at him for a several moments, then pursed her lips. "Let's assume the answer to that question is *yes*. Let's pretend I am willing and ready to face him with all that entails. I am not saying I am yet, this is just a rhetorical question. What then?"

"Then you will grant him the opportunity to talk about his reasons. It is what he attempted last time when you were both here in this very room together, if you recall. He feels the need to share certain things with you, and facing him means that you give him permission to do just that and to listen earnestly to him. Only then will forgiveness be possible - when both parties have been completely open with each other, have made themselves equally vulnerable to each other." He chuckled. "Theoretically this ends the process, if there was not a considerable obstacle to overcome by this time."

Eryn lifted her brow in question.

"Vanity and moral superiority. Forgiving somebody else for something we feel was done to us changes our picture of ourselves as well."

She shook her head in confusion. "What?"

"Truly forgiving somebody forces us to give up our own moral high ground. It requires from then on meeting on the eye level instead of looking down on that person."

"I have never looked down on Valrad," she protested.

"Have you not? You have never even once been angry at him for acting carelessly, betraying his own brother and even his companion in the way he did, seemingly without any regard for anybody or anything but his own urges?" He smiled when he saw her react to that. "Ah yes, this clearly does sound familiar to you. Do not try to deny it. It would be to no avail. This is not about what I am thinking about you, but what you think about Valrad and how willing you are to alter that point of view." He smiled at her. "But there is also a considerable advantage for you in forgiving him; the wound will stop giving pain and start to heal, to return to our little metaphor from before."

She regarded him wearily. "I see. So that is the theory behind forgiveness. I had no idea it was so complex."

"Feelings generally are," he shrugged. "We just do not grant them such complexity as they occur spontaneously and without much effort on our side. Of course there remains one last step, one that cannot be undertaken by you, but by your father. He needs to ask you for your forgiveness. And unless you are willing to reply to that very intimate and crucial request in the affirmative, you had better keep your distance until you can."

* * *

Enric took the folded piece of paper the messenger handed him and then closed the door again. It was addressed to Eryn. He turned it around and raised both brows at the Vel'kim seal on the rear.

"Was that a messenger?" Eryn asked from the top of the stairs.

He nodded. So she had obviously expected this message. He climbed the stairs and handed it to her, watching her open and then skim it. She seemed to find some release and then looked up at him. There was determination, yet a certain amount of dread.

"I will visit Valrad at his residence. Do not wait up for me. I don't know how late I will be."

"Visit Valrad?" he enquired and blinked. "Now?"

"Yes. I asked him to see me, and this was the reply."

"Why?" he asked carefully.

"To talk to him. To clarify a few things. I had a meeting with Iklan today and, well, it opened my eyes for a thing or two."

Enric just nodded, hiding his surprise both by shielding his emotions and concentrating on his facial expression. "I see. Would you like me to accompany you?"

She smiled faintly and lifted her hand to his cheek. "No, Enric. I would very much like you to stay here and let me do this alone. I am a big girl, and there are things I need to take care of without you."

He turned his head to one side to kiss the palm against his face, then nodded. "Of course. But I don't much like the idea of your walking through the city alone. I would feel better if you would let me take you there and pick you up again. Is that acceptable to you?"

"It is, yes." She couldn't help but be amused at the very civilised way of conversing just now. A year ago he would very likely just have insisted on accompanying her, and she would have thrown a fit and also probably some tableware. Wasn't it nice to see that they had come such a long way together?

They descended the stairs as a pair and left the residence, walking briskly. She felt her conviction that this was the right action to take draining away little by little. Had she been too hasty in understanding that she was ready for this? Was Iklan right – would facing Valrad without being truly and utterly ready for this cause more harm?

No, she decided and lifted her chin. She could go through with this. She would take care of this. Tonight. This had been going on for more than two months now, it was time to act. She was ready for it. And she was strong enough. Or was she?

She sighed in relief when the Vel'kim residence came into view. At least it would now only be a few more minutes that she had to fight the impulse to turn around and walk back.

Enric could help by distracting her a bit.

"Did you see Ram'an today as you planned?" she asked.

He nodded. "I did, yes."

"And?" she prompted when he didn't volunteer any more information. "How is he doing? Was he as upset by the dance as you thought he would be?"

"Yes, I think he was," he confirmed slowly. "I fancy he will need a little time to get over it. He asked me to convey to you his wish to keep his distance to you for a while and he hopes you won't take this personally."

She slowed down her steps, feeling a lump in her chest. He was not really withdrawing from her, was he? But then the dance had not exactly left her unaffected, either. And as opposed to how Ram'an felt she was not in love with him. She wondered if he had felt the effect of the magical music even stronger than she had due to his emotional attachment. Recalling her own reaction to the dance, she could imagine that this would have been quite a strain for him do deal with it. Another thing came to her mind.

338

"Do you know if he... you know... after we left... I mean..." How could she even phrase this? But Enric seemed to understand.

"Intrea is a very considerate hostess, my love. And she was involved with Ram'an on numerous occasions in the past, from what I heard."

She swallowed and nodded. At least he had not been alone to endure the after effects of the magic, but had been with somebody who knew and liked him and didn't mind helping him deal with raw arousal kindled by a dance with another woman. Exactly how Enric had been with her.

"They were talking about meeting again not very long ago," she said lightly. "I suppose this was as good an occasion as any."

He squeezed her hand. "I believe it was not too much of a strain on her. Don't worry yourself."

"Is he very angry at me?" she asked with a grimace.

"No, my love. Not at all. He just needs some time."

They stopped at the gateway to the lane that led up the hill to the residence.

"Good luck." He bent forward to kiss her forehead. "Send a message when you want to return. Don't walk back alone in the dark," he insisted.

"I won't. I promise."

She turned and walked towards the entrance, cursing herself for asking after Ram'an. Now she had two things on her mind that were worrying her instead of one like before. Quite an accomplishment.

Valrad opened the door before she could lift her hand to knock, smiling as he beheld her.

"Do come in. I am glad to see that Enric brought you here. I thought a little too late that walking the streets alone right now is not a wise thing to do for you. But I am sure I can trust your companion to do his best to keep you safe." He handed her a moist towel and waited while she was wiping her face and arms with it.

"He insisted. He told me to send for him when I want to return."

"That will not be necessary. Vran'el or I will take you," he promised and preceded her up the stairs to the main room.

"What can I get you to drink, Eryn?" he asked when she had taken a seat on the cushions.

"The yellow fruit juice with a touch of water, if you have any."

"Of course." He chuckled. "We always have it on hand, it is Vran'el's favourite."

She accepted the glass and watched him sit down. He made sure not to sit too close to her, though also not too far away. He seemed a fraction nervous, she noted. Just like herself.

"You look better than last night. I am glad you seem to have recovered from your experience at House Feral and how it affected you," he said calmly.

She nodded stiffly. "I haven't thanked you for your help." Why did this feel so utterly absurd? It was like a very polite conversation between two strangers who were immensely careful not to say a wrong word for fear of causing offence.

"There is no need for that, I assure you." He looked at her thoughtfully. "You do know that I do not expect you to talk to me as some kind of compensation for coming to you last night, I hope?"

She nodded slowly. "I do, yes. Iklan told me that you wouldn't be expecting any service in return, as it were."

"You went to see Iklan today?" he asked with interest.

"I did, yes. I am surprised you don't know about it. I am told you are very well informed about whatever is going on at the clinic."

"I left early today to meet with a few people to review trading contracts. I would have learned about it tomorrow," he explained, then straightened. "You wrote that you wished to talk to me."

She swallowed and wished she could pace the room or do something else to get rid of the nervous energy that made sitting still so hard right now. "I do. And I have also come to listen to you."

He closed his eyes for a moment, then smiled. "I am glad. Please let me start with something I have been wanting to say to you for a while now. I have talked to Iklan, and he made me realise that my way of informing you of... well, of your origins was rather clumsy. I made a very difficult situation even worse by not doing this with any grace. I should not have let Malriel come here, no matter whether she insisted or not. Additionally, I should not have let you leave like that without going after you. I should have asked Iklan to come and guide us through this instead of trusting my own instincts to handle it properly. I am sorry about it."

She gulped, thinking back to the day of her arrival here and the distasteful revelation it had brought. Would it have changed much if she had learned about it in a different manner? She shook her head. "Don't worry about that, I don't see how Iklan's presence would have made this any better. And there was Pe'tala to come after me, after all. She was great. Really - I was glad she was there. And Malriel... I suppose you could say she deserved to witness my reaction to the whole thing." The start had not been too bad, she decided. He had apologised for a minor event, she had eased his mind about it. They had not yet started talking about what had brought her here, the matter that had been dividing them for the last two months, but this had been just a small step towards each other, a promising little accomplishment.

Iklan's words about being willing to talk about her pain came to her mind. He had insisted that it was unavoidable if she wanted to deal with this situation properly. She was so used to treating him coolly and distantly now that opening herself like that, changing her way of dealing with him so completely, was a scary prospect.

Would it help to talk about her pain in a cool and detached manner? Was that a contradiction in itself? Would it even seem believable?

She drew in a deep breath, then straightened and looked right at Valrad. She could do this. Shirking a challenge was not in her nature. What had Pe'tala said back then? *An Aren never shows fear, and a Vel'kim never shirks an unpleasant duty.*

"There are a few things I need to tell you. I am told there is no way around it, that I need to share them with you. I expect listening to them will not be any more pleasant for you than talking about them will be for me." Had that been too reserved?

"I am listening," he said calmly and leaned back. "I have been waiting for this for a while now and I am aware that this is not going to be easy for you or me. But we must take care of it, it is painful for each of us."

She exhaled slowly. "Iklan said that learning about you being my... father was the last of several big changes in my recent life. It was something that hit me so hard because it suddenly made me question everything I believed I knew about myself and who I was. It took me a while to realise that he was right." She looked down at her clenched fingers and consciously released them. Her hands felt clammy. "I felt safe in the knowledge of being Ved'al's daughter," she went on. "And he never gave me any cause to wish for this to be different. He was great, and when I lost him, I thought my world would come to an end. He was everything I had." She paused for a moment, then continued.

"Learning that this was not true made me question a lot. Who I really am, who I can still trust, what other errors in judgement I have made that I wasn't even aware of. And I was angry at being expected to give up Ved'al as my father. It felt... still feels like I am betraying him. First Malriel and you did this to him, and now even I turn away from him..." She pushed aside the stab of guilt.

She saw from the corner of her eye that he was beginning to lean forward to take her hand, but she shook her head.

"Please don't," she murmured. "Not yet. I need to finish this first."

She was glad Valrad didn't object or insist on comforting her but respected her wish to avoid physical closeness for now.

"I do love you, you know," she said calmly, staring at her fingernail. "Still. Despite everything that has happened. It's something I feel bad about, as if I am being disloyal to Ved'al. I have tried to keep the feeling capped, hoping that pushing you away would help." She fussed at the seam of her tunic with her fingernails. "It didn't help. I have provoked, insulted, ignored and spited you, but you didn't do anything in return that would have helped me to stop loving you." She smiled faintly. "How very inconsiderate of you."

"I had the impression that making you work with me and obliging you to see Iklan did not sit too well with you," he commented.

"No, it did not. But Pe'tala had warned me that you would sooner or later do something, that you would come for me if I stayed away from you. And you waited until after my exam for that."

She pushed a strand of hair behind her ear and wished she had brought Enric with her, just as he had offered. But then this would have appeared pathetic, wouldn't it? As if she wasn't able to deal with strong emotions without him. And yet having him squeeze her hand reassuringly would have been a great comfort right now.

"When I started spending time with Orrin, I came to realise after a few months that I was still in need of a father sometimes. And that the little things he did, like scolding me when I was careless, rewarding me for things he approved of, meant that he had taken on that role to a certain degree. It was hard for me to let him, to accept it. It may sound strange, considering that I was a prisoner at that time, but Vern and Orrin had somehow turned into family. That you insist on being my father now is somehow frightening. I have been alone almost half my life, and I am not sure how to handle it." Her voice had become slightly shrill towards the end. She took another deep, calming breath to regain her composure. "When I first came here, meeting Malriel was a shock, of course. But meeting you and Vran'el made it possible for me to deal with all that. Suddenly there was a family, a connection to my past, to Ved'al. Healers," she smiled at the memory of her joy when she had learned about this being more or less the family business. "Discovering that actually not Ved'al was my father but you were destroyed everything in a flash, made my world erupt once again. None of the revelations fitted the picture I had of you! You were trustworthy, loving, considerate, careful - not a man to betray his own brother so covertly. It was so painful to find the trust in you drained away. I was taught as a child not to trust people, that trust was dangerous. And it seemed like Ved'al had been right: trusting you had turned out to be a terrible mistake! Which meant that trusting my own judgement was not a sensible course of action either. That probably hurt the most, not trusting myself anymore." Her voice had become little more than a hoarse whisper. She took a sip from her juice, then looked at him for the first time since she had started speaking. There was a faint look of inner torment on his face and his lips where pressed together. His eyes rested on her, mirroring her own pain.

"I am so terribly sorry you had to go through this, my dear girl," he said softly, opening and closing his fingers as if to keep himself from reaching out for her.

She made herself smile, managing with effort to keep the moisture behind her lids at bay. "It's alright, I am working on it. If Iklan can be trusted, I am about to make a major leap." Enough of that for now, she decided. Opening to him like that had been hard and she needed a break, a change of the focus away from her.

"You offered to tell me about what happened when we met in Iklan's office two and a half weeks ago. I think I am ready to hear it now." Or as ready as she would ever be.

Valrad leaned forward to pick up his glass and took several gulps. He looked down at the floor for several moments as if to collect his thoughts and brace himself before he began speaking. "When Malriel was born, there were quite a number of Houses interested in a companionship agreement with the daughter of House Aren. Our House was the one to succeed. I was the older son, which meant that I was expected to take over the House one day. As Malriel, too, was the heiress of House Aren, it was the logical choice to intend Ved'al for her and not me." He stared into the distance, as if returning to a time several decades ago really had taken him back there. "Malriel was a beauty from the very beginning. And full of restless energy. So incredibly intelligent and always ahead of the others her own age. She was sixteen when I asked Ved'al if he was willing to give her up to me and take over the House one day in my stead. He was appalled and angry, and I realised only then that he, too, was in love with her and was not courting her merely out of duty. It took Ved'al and me a long time to get over this." Talking about the breach with his brother was obviously painful for him. His look of torment had deepened and his eyes held such sadness that it made her want to cry for both of them.

"How about Malriel? Was she in love with Ved'al?" Eryn asked and then bit her lip, wondering if asking questions was appropriate or if just letting him tell her about this in his own way would have been better. But then the main objective here was not for him to get it off his chest, but for her to learn about it, wasn't it?

"It is hard for me to speak for her, of course, but my impression was that she did indeed have feelings for him, yes." He smiled sadly. "He was dashing, daring and rebellious, while I was the calm, domestic, unexciting sort. It was hardly surprising that she found him more appealing. He was closer to her own nature and she was so young, too young to see that some of the things people have in common can lead to conflict instead of harmony. They committed to each other when Malriel was eighteen years old. The troubles began not long after. The matter of terminating pregnancies prematurely was raised, less than a year later they found themselves politically on different sides of this whole mess. They were both temperamental, so their fights were hard and bitter, increasing over time. Two years later their relationship was all but broken, but they decided to give it a last desperate try and have a child together." He chuckled, bitterness in his voice as he went on, "And after all, even if a commitment breaks apart, as long as there are offspring, it is in our society still considered a success. An heir for House Aren. That was more important than an intact commitment. I suspect that Malhora had been instrumental in convincing her daughter that this was the sensible course of action to salvage her relationship." He looked at Eryn, searching her face. "Malriel was so sad and too young to handle all this trouble on her own. These brown eyes... looking at you these last weeks reminded me a lot of her back then. The same sadness, this unwillingness to let anybody come close and see any weakness in you, burying everything within."

Eryn looked away uncomfortably. Hearing Malriel described like this - a young woman in distress, in more trouble than she could handle, having her compared to herself - felt unsettling. She was used to having her external appearance compared to Malriel, but not herself as a person, the things that determined who she was.

"I had started taking over a few areas of responsibility to ease myself into the position of Head of House," he went on, aware of the effect his last words had had on Eryn and eager to leave them behind. "And so had Malriel. This meant that we kept seeing each other fairly regularly at Senate meetings and also at the trade negotiations we both had taken on for our Houses. Of course I knew about the difficulties between her and Ved'al, and after a time we started to talk. At the beginning we met every once in a while at a teahouse, discussing matters that pertained to our Houses, but gradually our conversations started changing focus. First it was only a casual remark ever so often, then we dedicated the last few minutes of every meeting to private concerns. And somehow after a few months we started meeting without any official reason at all and just talked." He closed his eyes and shook his head slightly. "I realised that I was still in love with her - four years after I had asked my brother to let me have her. I am not sure whether Malriel was ever in love with me, but I know there was a connection between us that was more than mere physical attraction. She shared her grief with me, which is seen as a privilege when it comes to an Aren. I had not been aware that she and Ved'al had agreed to have a child when I took her to bed. I assumed that she used some protection herself and foolishly I did not take any measures. We met in secret over about three months, then she told me that she was pregnant. I asked her if it might be possible that I was the father, but she just laughed and told me not to be ridiculous. She seemed so convinced that I did not question her certainty about it. Anyway, we stopped seeing each other after that. We both knew that her main duty was now to try and make her commitment work, to transform her difficult relationship with Ved'al into a functioning family." His gaze found Eryn's, and he said solemnly, "I know it was wrong. There is no excuse for it. I was not strong enough to withstand her sadness, her beauty, the love I still felt for her despite her being my own brother's companion, despite being joined to another woman myself. I take full responsibility for everything." He smiled mournfully. "I am aware that you probably do not want to hear it, but looking at you today, I do not regret the outcome. The only thing I do regret is to see how much it pains you to understand that I am your father. It tears at my heart. I wish this were not such a burden to you. I wish you did not cringe every time somebody calls me your father."

Eryn blinked when he leaned towards her to finally take her hand between the two of his, kissing it and then pressing it against his heart. His hands felt cooler than usual, probably a reaction to the situation, the healer in her analysed without thinking.

344

"I am sorry for all the pain this has meant, that *I* have caused you. I want us to leave this behind us, to start something anew. I love you. Very much." He looked straight into her eyes, locking her gaze with his intense one. "Eryn, please forgive me."

She swallowed hard. That was not unexpected, of course. This was the process, wasn't it? Talking about the pain, listening to him and his reasons, and finally with him asking for her forgiveness. And yet it threatened to overwhelm her.

An intimate and crucial request, Iklan had termed it. She knew she was expected to accept it, she had to. And yet... Complying with his list was hardly enough of a reason if she didn't feel up to it, was it? Nobody could make her forgive him if she didn't want to, or couldn't. And nobody had the right to condemn her for not forgiving him.

Iklan's words about the necessity of giving up her moral high ground, to stop condemning him for his deeds as a young man almost thirty years ago, floated back to her. Was she ready to do that?

But then she owed it to him, didn't she? He had not condemned her when he had found out that she had, indirectly, caused his only brother's death, but instead stood with her, protected her, adopted her into his family. Just as one thoughtless deed in her own youth had not made her a bad person, following a forbidden path should not turn him into a villain.

She thought about how he had told her about the third level commitment bond in his garden, how he had agreed to adopting her in a flash to help her escape both Malriel and Ram'an, how he had taken all of them in after the fire. And how he had followed Enric back to the Aren residence only last night when she had felt miserable and guilty after that dance with Ram'an.

He was a good man, and in the short time they had known each other he had never really treated her as anyone other than his daughter, even before he knew about it.

Taking a deep breath, she nodded slowly, then leaned forward until her forehead rested against his. "Of course I do."

She could almost feel the relief that made him all but crumple. He cupped her neck with one hand and pressed a kiss on her forehead before he brushed away a tear that was running down her cheek.

"Finally," he sighed and closed his eyes for a moment, then pulled her towards him to envelop her in his arms and press her close, careful not to squeeze her belly.

She managed a small smile. "Iklan would have my head if I hadn't. He told me to keep my distance from you unless I was willing to forgive you."

"I am not really sure whether I should kick Iklan for telling you to keep your distance, or hug him for helping you to find your way to me, however risky his approach was," he chuckled.

"That depends. Can the relationship between your Houses take a good kick in its behind?" she smiled when he released her again.

"I think it might, yes. Though it might make my other colleagues rather reluctant to agree whenever I ask another one of them to do me a favour in the future." He took her empty glass and raised an eyebrow at her. "Will you spend a little more time with me or would you rather like me to take you home now? I surely do not have to tell you which option I prefer."

She leaned back and smiled. "You know, we currently have a baby at home that commands all the attention. I think I will stay a little longer and let you be nice to me. Are there any of Vran'el's favourite fruits left? I really could do with something sweet right now."

She watched him walk towards the kitchen, noticing that he suddenly seemed younger, his step lighter as if a great burden had been lifted from him. Which was basically what had happened. She wondered if there would be any visible changes in her own physique, if the relief of leaving this behind her would be as plain as in Valrad's case.

When he returned a few minutes later with a large, fruit-laden tray, she looked at him. "What now? How do we go on from here?"

He took her hand in his, holding it as if eager to make up for all that time he had not dared to touch her.

"I would like you to start speaking to me as *father*, my dear girl," he said gently and lifted a finger when she began to object. "In the long run I would very much like you to address me as such, but I see that this is a little much to ask of you right now, so let us say referring to me as your *father* when you talk to others is surely a more gradual way of getting you used to the idea. Would you do this for me, Eryn?"

She felt that this was a rather bold thing to demand of her.

"I will think it over," she said, noncommittally.

"You do that," he nodded, clearly satisfied that she had not rejected it on principle. "Is there anything I can do for you in return, my child?"

She couldn't help but smile at that. "Are we negotiating the terms of our father-daughter relationship here, Valrad?"

He thought for a moment, then nodded good-naturedly. "I rather think we are, yes. I suppose it is a frame of mind one cannot help getting into after representing a family's interest for such a long time. Negotiating on behalf of the family slowly turns into negotiating *with* the family after a while."

"So you are offering me something in return for speaking of you as my father when talking to others?"

"Indeed I am."

"Oh my," she sighed. "Had I known that I would find myself in a situation of negotiation, I would have brought Vern. Then you would probably have found yourself promising me all kinds of things with hardly any compensation."

"I will not take offence at your unflattering assessment of my negotiating skills but will attribute this confidence to Vern's prowess in that area," he quipped.

She felt a faint kick inside her and looked up. There was a little something that needed to be addressed.

"My son... I still intend to call him Vedric. And I hope this does not cause you any pain, but..."

"I understand," he assured her quickly and linked his fingers with hers. "I would not have asked you to do otherwise. If you are doing it out of respect for Ved'al instead of a wish to hurt me, I can accept this without a problem."

She nodded. Well, it had initially been her motivation to vex him, but that had changed now. "Good. Then I shall consider your assent in this matter compensation enough for the *father* thing."

"I am glad to hear it," he beamed.

"I am either dreaming or hallucinating," Vran'el's astonished voice came from behind them. He rounded the seating island and stared down at them, at their linked fingers and relaxed poses.

"Your sister and I have managed to find a way through our issues," Valrad explained to his son.

Eryn smiled. "We have. We seem to have entered into the negotiation stage now."

The lawyer shook his head, then laughed. "Have you now? What are you negotiating? Can I be of service here, perchance?"

"That depends on who you will be siding with in these talks." She raised her brow. "If it is not mine, you had better get out of here or keep your mouth shut."

"Sweetness, I have no intention of being on your or father's side here." He grinned broadly. "I am my own side. And my first demand is that we find a living arrangement for the three of you that will bring you to Takhan regularly for several months at a time."

Eryn stared at him, taken aback. "What? Are you cracked? This is a joke, of course?"

Her brother shook his head. "I am afraid it is not. I am the heir to the House, and you are about to provide us with my successor. We cannot have him growing up so far away from here without any regular contact, which will enable him to get to know his House. He needs to lead it one day, so he cannot start on growing into it too early."

She turned to Valrad and saw him smiling appreciatively at his son. Well, of course he wouldn't object to an idea such as that. He was probably more than glad that Vran'el had been the one to bring it up.

"I feel that I am at a slight disadvantage now, being outnumbered for once. And I am not even in a position to agree to a thing like that without Enric, anyway. You are aware that we are both supposed to be returning to the Order and being important pillars of Anyueel society, aren't you? What makes you think that having us travelling to and fro for months at a time is realistic?" She shook her head. "Really now."

"You are right, of course, sweetness," Vran'el nodded.

She lifted her brow. That was unexpectedly understanding of him.

"I am?" she ventured.

"Sure. We definitely need to have Enric here when we talk about this." He laughed when she groaned. "What do you think I meant?"

CHAPTER 26

Cornering Ram'an

Eryn balanced little Téa on her shoulder, walking up and down the main room at the Aren residence in an attempt to gently rock the baby to sleep. This was the first time Junar and Orrin had left her with her and Enric so they could have a little time together unburdened at a teahouse for two or three hours.

Junar had almost needed to drag out Orrin by his ear as he had, for some reason, been rather reluctant to leave his daughter in Eryn's care. Eryn herself was not thrilled about his lack of trust in her and had threatened to kick him where it hurt most if he didn't go out with his companion.

They had fed and bathed the baby and handed over a clean and tired girl before leaving.

Up to this point no problems had occurred. The tiny creature that still smelled faintly of the expensive soap Intrea had given them was being well-behaved and looked as if she was about to fall asleep any moment. By then her parents had been gone for no more than ten minutes.

Eryn shifted Téa from her shoulder into the crook of her elbow and scanned the small face, trying to determine for what surely was hundredth time which of her parents she resembled more. There were about as many different opinions as people about that. Orrin claimed the girl had his nose and chin, which Enric kept disputing. In his opinion the girl had been blessed with her mother's looks. Vern and Vran'el insisted Téa had Orrin's eyes, but that was pretty much it. And it was not like one could say a lot about her eyes apart from their general shape. They were still blue, as was normal at this age.

349

She let her index finger glide over the uncommonly full, fluffy hair with its unusual colour. She didn't remember ever before having touched something as soft and silky.

When she heard a quiet noise, she lifted her head and saw Enric leaning against the wall, watching her with a dreamy expression.

"You are not going all soft in the head because you can see me with a baby in my arms, are you?" she smiled.

He rolled his eyes and walked towards her. "I resent the term *soft in the head*," he murmured.

She shrugged. "Mushy, then. Soppy. Dewey-eyed."

He sighed and looked down at the bundle in her arms. "One might think that a man in my situation would be entitled to a little sentimentality."

"Suit yourself," she shrugged. "Where is Vern, by the way? I am used to him only gracing us with his presence every other evening, but I couldn't help noticing that he has been even more elusive than usually these last few days."

Enric kept his expression carefully blank. He had a reasonably good idea what Vern was up to currently, but he doubted that Eryn would value the young man's newly discovered pastime very much.

"He is a growing lad, going out and having fun is natural enough for him."

"As opposed to spending a quiet evening with us aged and tiresome folks?" she grinned.

"With the exception of yourself we are all of the generation above him, so I assume his idea of a good time is not necessarily in accordance with ours." He lifted his arms to take the child from her. "Give her to me for a bit, will you?"

"Practising for your son?" she smiled and laid the baby in his arm. She looked even smaller against his tall form.

"Not necessary, my love. I am a natural with children," he cooed and carefully stroked the patch of skin between her small arcs of brow with the tip of his finger. Only moments later Téa yawned, wrinkling her nose and showed off her toothless, pink gums.

Eryn blinked. She had rocked and swayed the child for several minutes to get her to fall asleep. He had done no more than taken her on his arm and touched her between the eyes, and she was on the verge of drifting off, just like that.

"Good," she grumbled. "You have just volunteered for putting your son to bed for two years after his birth."

He smiled at her vexed expression. "Not envious, are you?"

"Don't be ridiculous. The dubious talent to make children fall asleep by merely being close them is surely not desirable. Let's be glad you aren't a teacher. Imagine the lack of progress thanks to your sleep-inducing presence," she jibed.

He studied her for a moment. She seemed tense. "What's the matter, my love?" he asked mildly. "I am not really surprised that she didn't fall asleep while you were holding her. You radiate restlessness currently."

She gave him a pained look. "I sent Ram'an a message today, asking him to have lunch with me tomorrow. He declined. Very politely, of course. But very decisive."

"I told you he needs some time to get himself over this dance with you," Enric reminded her.

"I know, and I have left him in peace for more than a week now! I mean, how much longer does he need? And since when is shutting out friends a sensible way to deal with problems?"

He stared at her and slowly shook his head. "Seriously? Did I just really and honestly hear *you* say that?"

She folded her arms. "Well, I should know, shouldn't I? And it's not as if I haven't learned from my mistakes. But he was the most vocal among those pestering me into opening up, and now *he* is the one hiding! He should know better."

"You don't know if he is hiding from others as well. As far as we know he might only be keeping his distance from you for now," he pointed out.

She glared at him. "Thank you for that! Don't tell me you are seeing him?"

"Not since I went to him and thanked him for his intervention. How are things between you and Valrad going?" he changed the topic to something more agreeable. Téa had drifted off to sleep in the meantime, her lips twitching occasionally.

"Fine. We meet for lunch at the canteen every second day."

"I am glad you have managed to get this whole bundle of troubles behind you."

She nodded. "As am I. Working at the clinic is a lot less awkward now, and people have stopped being so careful around me."

"Have you acceded to Valrad's request?"

"You mean the one about referring to him as my father in my conversations with others? Partly so. I keep mixing things up and alternatingly speak of him as my father and then as Valrad. Once I accidentally spoke of my *uncle*."

"A good start, then." He looked down at the sleeping girl. "Give me a moment, will you? I had better put her to her bed."

She took a seat and gulped down a glass of water. She had to remind herself to drink more, especially during her pregnancy. It didn't take Enric long to return and he sank down beside her.

"I had an interesting chat with Vran'el yesterday," he told her.

"What about?"

"He wants us to return here regularly, basically splitting our life equally between Anyueel and Takhan."

"Oh no," she groaned. "He said something like that when I went to see Valr... my father, but I had kind of hoped he was joking!"

"I take it you are not in favour of it, then?"

"Don't tell me you are? Do you have any idea what Tyront and the King will do to us if we propose a thing like that to them? And then the Queen of Darkness at some point is going to return from her mission, which would mean that I would be forced to spend months at a time in the same city with her!"

"So Malriel is the only reason making you reject the idea as it stands?"

"It is a very powerful reason, as you are very well aware, I am sure! And how are we supposed to organise living in two different countries like that? What about our positions in the Order? Our work? How is our child supposed to be taught, having to be uprooted and moved that way? I don't see the two of us teaching him for hours each day because he is never long enough in one country to join any classes there."

Enric smiled thinly. "Let me assure you that I do not intend to take the King's or the Order's wishes into consideration here. And as both our Heads of Houses could insist on having us here regularly, I don't see how our influential superiors back home could deny us their permission to come. All in the interest of diplomacy, of course."

"The interest of diplomacy... I see. They have a permanent ambassador established here; they don't need us to take over any diplomatic duties. Kilan is doing well enough in his current function." She let her eyes dart across the room, seeking arguments against this ludicrous, this ridiculous proposition. "How about your businesses back home?"

"I seem to be doing a good job running them from here, even if I say so myself. Since I also have businesses here in Takhan, no matter where we would be staying, there would always be something too far away to be taken care of by myself at short notice. I would have to resort to paying trustworthy agents to act on my behalf on both sides of the sea as long as I am gone."

"You really want to try it, don't you?" she grimaced. "Why? I can see why Valrad and Vran'el would want us to, but what is the advantage in it for *us*?"

"I admit the idea holds quite some appeal. It would grant us more freedom. The King's hold over us would be a lot looser. Whenever we are here we are subject to nobody except our Heads of Houses."

"Which might not be a problem in case of my House, but in your case we are talking of the appalling Malriel of bloody House Aren! How is it possible that you fail to see the potential for trouble?"

"What makes you think that her ability to cause us trouble would be any less dangerous if we were staying in the Kingdom?" he countered. "That's where we were when she managed to have us sent to Takhan, after all."

"So you really want to push your son towards taking over House Vel'kim one day? What if he doesn't want to do so? I won't let you force him!"

He took in her angry frown and the hand she had placed protectively on her belly. "I wouldn't force him to do anything he does not wish to, I promise." She really seemed to think that she had to protect his own child from him. He suppressed his annoyance at that and continued in the same tone as before, "But neither would I wish to rule out this option entirely for him. No matter if he succeeds his uncle one day or not, it won't hurt him to get to know the House he belongs to and acquire some business skills when he gains an insight into keeping a House running."

"You made that decision already, didn't you?" She narrowed her eyes at him suspiciously.

"Of course not, my love," he conciliated her. "I wouldn't dare do any of this without you. I just wanted to air the idea, get a feeling for the advantages and disadvantages. There are still a few months ahead of us until we have to make a decision."

She regarded him worriedly. That was not the impression she was getting. Not at all.

* * *

Eryn smiled grimly when she spotted Ram'an among the senators who were leaving the Senate hall after the meeting concluded. He was talking to Uvel, Neval's father. She waited for him to reach the foot of the stairs, then detached herself from the shadowy wall she was leaning against and stepped in his way as if surprised to see him.

"Ram'an!" she smiled and saw his throat tighten at her approach. Unperturbed by this lack of enthusiasm, she took both his hands and pulled him close to kiss him on both cheeks, ignoring his tenseness.

Then she turned to Uvel, letting him kiss her hand.

"Eryn," the older man smiled at her. "What brings you to the Senate hall? The meeting is over, in case you had been wanting to listen to our doubtless fascinating discussions."

"I finished work earlier today, so I am here to pick up Enric."

She saw Ram'an raise an eyebrow at that. He was obviously not convinced of this really being her motive in coming.

"It is nice to bump into you here, Ram'an," she went on. "I was wondering if you have time for a cup of tea with me or whether you would like to join us for dinner tonight?" She waited for his reply, wondering if he would once more turn her down despite the witness. She had given him another week to deal with his issues, but when she had sent him another note yesterday, he declined just as carefully as before.

"I would love to accept your invitation, my dear Eryn," he smiled without much sincerity, "but unfortunately I am expected somewhere else later and cannot tell how long the appointment will take. I will come back to your offer at another time. Why do I not contact you when there is a convenient time slot opening up?"

She chuckled and raised her eyebrows at him to show him that she recognised the irony in the situation well enough. It was almost exactly how she had brushed him off when he had tried to invite her after her arrival in Takhan.

"Ram'an, my dearest Ram'an," she sighed, "I am afraid you have been rather negligent when it came to keeping up your social connections with Houses Aren and Vel'kim. I attribute this to your workload, of course. Let me tell you from a healing point of view that if you cannot even take the time for a dinner with friends or an hour at a teahouse, you are definitely working too much."

"How very considerate of you to point this out to me, Eryn," he replied with only a hint of reproach.

"Eryn?" she heard Enric's voice and looked up the stairs where he stood together with Valrad. They both walked on until they had reached her. "What are you doing here?"

Eryn smiled. "Picking you up, dearest." She had seen his quick glance at Ram'an, so he was well enough aware why she had come.

"Well, here I am," he remarked and took her arm to lead her away. "Good day to you, gentlemen."

She had not much choice but to let him take her with him.

"Very subtle," he commented when they were walking back to the Aren residence.

"You could have given me another minute or two, at least!" she protested. "I might have been able to corner him into accepting meeting me!"

"Really, Eryn?" he sighed and shook his head at her. "Are you that desperate? One would think you remembered his own attempts at making you meet him back then and how much they annoyed you. Why do you think that this approach might work on him when it didn't succeed with you?"

"Because he is more concerned with appearances than me? Because he is a Head of House and I am not? Because he is less stubborn than I am?" she ventured.

"Less stubborn? Look, we are talking about the man who refused to give up his claim on you despite your being bound to another man!" he rolled his eyes. "That shows a high degree of stubbornness in my book."

"So you are saying I am to wait for who knows however long for him to come to his senses?" she exclaimed. "That might need weeks, if not months! I finally managed to get along with both men I was avoiding here, and now he is ruining it again! I won't allow him!"

"I am not saying you should. What I am saying is that your strategy with sending him notes and trying to corner him will very likely not work. He is a politician, and a lawyer. Not letting himself be entrapped by others like that is part of his position."

"What would you do in my place, then?" she finally asked after pondering his words for a few moments.

"There is the possibility of coercing him to come to you, but that might require more time and effort than you would be willing to put in at the moment. The easiest and quickest way is probably to put pressure on him publicly so that he has no other choice than to oblige you," he smiled. "There is one considerable advantage you can use against him, after all: your pregnancy. We are in a country where treating a pregnant woman with anything but the utmost care is considered an affront."

"I thought that was what I just did?" she asked in confusion. "In my capacity of highly venerated, expectant woman, I invited him to have tea or dinner with me before a witness, and he declined anyway."

"Larger scale, my love. Not one witness, but many. And a situation where neither his rhetorical nor diplomatic skills could be of any use to him."

"Like what?" This was starting to sound interesting.

He thought for a moment. "Like an invitation to dance with you at a music house. If he accepts that, you have a suitable opportunity to talk to him. If he doesn't, well, there is always the strategy that worked so well with Malriel back home at the dinner."

"Crying?" she grimaced.

"Sure, why not? You are pregnant, that means you are entitled to behave irrationally, even though you are nominally this indomitable Aren woman. And him causing you to cry without doing something to comfort you would make him appear in a very bad light indeed."

She chewed her lip, weighing the merits of using the powerful weapon of her pregnancy in combination with tears to influence Ram'an against the embarrassment of once more crying in public.

"I don't like crying!" she whined.

He laughed. "I distinctly remember that you enjoyed yourself quite a lot that evening." He tapped his forehead. "I witnessed it first hand, don't forget."

"A little, maybe," she grinned. "Alright, I will give this idea of yours a try. I suppose I can ask Vran'el to let me know when Ram'an is at a music house for dinner and then go there. Will you accompany me? I might need a strong, intimidating man at my side to scold Ram'an for his lack of consideration in case he does not react quite as sympathetically as he is expected to."

"Of course. I do so enjoy your little performances, as you know."

* * *

Orrin returned from the bathroom after bathing his daughter, then handed her to Junar for one of her numerous daily feeds. Eryn marvelled at the routine they had established after less than a month.

The warrior was still wearing his shackles, which he had to for another two weeks before Eryn removed them. From what she had heard and seen he had adapted well enough to having next to no

355

magic at his disposal. It had required of him to change his approach to teaching, of course, and resort to explaining things in more detail instead of simply demonstrating them. It had very likely slowed him down a little, but she was confident that this was no major drawback for him.

There had been talk about his punishment as had been the idea of its public enforcement. But being punished by her had caused his reputation no harm. Rather the opposite. The stoic calm with which he had accepted the imposition of a magical block was discussed wide and far, and the incident of nearly strangling Elwoi gave Orrin an air of unpredictability that fitted nicely with the image of the fearsome warrior many people delighted in picturing him as.

His shirt was still damp from bathing his daughter and he smelled of baby soap. Dangerous warrior indeed, she couldn't help but thinking. She wondered how people would react to seeing him with his little girl, how it would affect his standing. Not unfavourably, she supposed. Being seen to be a devoted father was in this country hardly an indicator of unmanliness.

"Vern is out again, I assume? Or is he going to have dinner with us for a change?" she asked.

Junar shook her head and winced when Téa chomped down on her nipple hungrily. "He sent a message saying that he will be eating out and not to wait up for him. He has turned into quite the bohemian. There are times when I haven't seen him for days."

Eryn looked at Orrin with some concern on her face. "Doesn't this worry you at all? Who knows where he goes roving about? And with what sinister characters he might have hooked up with?"

"Sinister characters?" the warrior shot back. "What do you want me to do, order him back here every evening before it gets dark? He never ventured out to enjoy himself at home; I am glad he has met people he likes to spend time with. People his own age. It's good for him. And I know he returns here every now and then because the servants take away his dirty clothes in the mornings."

"I admire your lenience," Eryn stated, her tone making it clear that she did not appreciate it at all.

"Glad to hear it," Orrin grinned widely. "I can see that your motherly instincts seem to be awakening. Or is it plain enviousness because you aren't his only friend anymore?"

"Don't be ridiculous!" she huffed. Was he right? Was that the problem? No, she decided, hardly. Going out every now and then was one matter, but hardly ever returning to the residence except for a change of clothes was hardly appropriate for a boy his age.

"There is a guard following him, I assume?" she asked. "I imagine you would hardly be letting him run around without protection following the fire, would you?" She narrowed her eyes when he kept his face suspiciously free of emotions. "That means you know exactly where he is spending his time and who with. You just won't tell me because you enjoy watching me fret about it!" she complained. "Not nice! Don't trouble the expectant lady!"

Urban trotted in through the terrace door and stilled for a moment when she beheld Junar and the baby, before carefully approaching them with her nose testing the air.

She stopped behind them, leaning over the rear of the cushions to sniff Tea's head.

Junar giggled when the long whiskers tickled her throat and gently pushed the cat's head aside.

"I think she likes the smell of that soap. Maybe you should wash her with it every now and then," she suggested to Eryn.

"Wash a fully-grown mountain cat? Are you insane?"

Urban had in the meantime moved on to Orrin, smelling his hands to which some scent had also clung after he washed his daughter. He held out one hand and shook his head when the mountain cat started rubbing her nose and cheeks against his skin before wrapping both paws around his arm to keep him from withdrawing it.

"You do remember that I am more or less without magic here, don't you?" he addressed Eryn warily. "I would thus like it more if you stayed close by and helped me, in case your beast here shows more enthusiasm than I can deal with right now."

"Don't fear, warrior, I will protect you if need be," Eryn laughed.

As Enric entered the main room after finishing his work for the day, they heard a knock upon the entrance door.

"I'll take that - stay seated," he called and descended the stairs swiftly.

He returned only a few moments later, waving a piece of paper in his hand. "It's from Vran'el. Ram'an is having dinner at a music house. Get ready!"

She stood up quickly and hurried to her room to change into something a little less casual. Pawing through her chests she cursed when several of the more elegant tunics she slipped into felt too tight around her midriff. She finally found one that only just fit and hastened back into the main room where Enric was already waiting for her, dressed in his usual sartorial black.

"Where are you off to?" Orrin demanded, completely confused. "What about protecting me from your scented-soap-loving predator here?"

"Come on, Orrin!" Eryn rolled her eyes. "She recoils when you hit her on the nose with a cushion, as you know as well as I do. Stop fussing!"

Enric frowned and walked over to the warrior, bending down to remove his golden manacles.

"What are you doing?" Eryn complained. "He has to wear these things for a while yet!"

"Not while there is no other magician around and he is alone with his companion and child. We still haven't found out who started that fire. He will put them back on when we return," he explained.

She thought for a moment, then nodded. It was reasonable enough.

Wasting no time, they waved goodbye and left for the music house.

"Which music house is he at? The one where neither of our Houses has a permanent table?" she asked.

"No, fortunately not. This one keeps a table free for House Aren."

It took about twenty minutes to reach their destination. They heard some music interspersed with the soft sounds of muted voices and laughter from inside the building before they pushed aside the curtain in front of the entrance door and went inside.

Rich, spicy aromas from a dinner that had been served not long ago still lingered in the air, and Eryn inhaled greedily even though she had eaten fairly recently.

Flamboyant lanterns lent the colourful seating islands on the floor a cosy, intimate quality. The music house was well attended, with only a few tables empty - very likely those reserved for the members of certain Houses. Such as Enric's.

Enric led her to a table that was close to a window and also far enough away from the musicians to enjoy the music without letting its volume disrupt conversation. It was a good position, Eryn decided. Not in the centre of activity, but a little off to one side so one could also discuss semi-private matters without being easily overheard.

"That is the Aren table?" she asked him.

He pointed to a small crest discreetly carved into one table leg. The Aren emblem.

"Have you seen Ram'an?" she murmured and looked around.

"Yes. Four tables to your left," he nodded. "He has seen us as well and his expression is not too pleased from what I can tell."

"Then I had better approach him soon before he decides to leave to avoid dealing with me," she mused. She let her gaze glide along the tables, then to the dance floor.

She blinked when she discovered a familiar figure.

"Is that Vern dancing with that woman over there?"

Enric nodded slowly. This was not good. It was not an ideal evening for her to discover the secret of Vern's nocturnal whereabouts. "That's him, yes."

"Who is the woman with him? Do you know her?" She narrowed her eyes. "And is this a trick of the light or is that person quite a bit older than he is?"

"I don't know. I haven't seen her before. And she does seem a touch older than him, yes. What of it?"

"A touch? More like a *lot*!" She shook her head and continued watching them. "She must be around my age!"

"He was dancing with older women back home at the balls," he pointed out.

She pursed her lips. "But not quite like that, I imagine. Did you just see how she touched his cheek?"

"Why don't you ask him about her later? I would think that Ram'an should be your primary target tonight. We have been waiting for three days now for a chance like this. If you don't use it he might avoid going out from now on just to steer clear of you," he urged her.

"Alright, alright," she intoned and got up when the song ended. "I am on my way."

She took a few deep breaths, then started walking towards his table. From the change in his posture she recognised the exact moment when he became aware of her approach. He became immobile and kept his eyes trained on her.

She stopped in front of his table, smiling at the party of six that was with him. She didn't recognise most of them, only one of Vran'el's lawyer colleagues whom she had once met in passing.

"Good evening, Eryn," Ram'an smiled tensely. "What a pleasant coincidence to see you here tonight. I trust you are well?"

"Good evening to all of you," she replied and nodded at the men and women around him. "I am well, yes, thank you. I hope I am not disturbing you. I have come to ask you for the next dance."

His expression became apologetic. "I thank you very much for the kind offer, my dear, but you must excuse me tonight. I have been through a very long and exhausting day today. I fear that my performance would not do you justice right now. I am sure you understand this, Eryn."

Sure, she thought with malicious anticipation, she understood perfectly well. She made herself swallow audibly and made her voice sound high and slightly distressed, smiling unhappily and making herself react too joyful by far, as if she was overcompensating her disappointment rather clumsily.

"Of course!" she piped. "No problem at all, really..." She made sure to let them see the moisture at the corners of her eyes before turning away and letting her shoulders gently but nevertheless clearly visibly twitch with a quiet sob.

"Ram'an!" she heard a woman at his table hiss at him. "What is the matter with you?"

She hid her smile. Wasn't peer pressure a wonderful thing? And it worked just as well with adults as with adolescents and children.

"Eryn," she heard Ram'an behind her call out. His voice sounded resigned. She halted her retreat without turning around.

A moment later she felt his hand on her shoulder when he turned her back to him. He looked down at her, his expression all but pleased.

"You really have a talent for faking when you set your mind to it, I have to give it to you," he murmured quietly. "Come on, then. You win - a dance it is."

He took her hand in his and led her onto the dance floor. She passed Vern who was on his way back to a table and nodded at him once, noticing how his eyes widened once he recognised her.

They had to wait a few moments until the next song started. It was a non-magical one, so she had to concentrate on the steps Vran'el had taught her.

"A guileful, but simple manoeuvre to employ your tears so skilfully," he murmured. "I see that you are adapting rather well to how people treat pregnant women here. It surely does not leave much room for letting them walk away teary-eyed." He smiled faintly. "It is what you used to make Malriel leave Anyueel a week early, was it not? I imagine this would not have worked here without your being pregnant. People tend to be suspicious when an Aren woman starts crying for a minor reason such as that."

"Ram'an," she grimaced, "I am not doing this to torture you. I don't want things to be like that between us. Somehow it seems that peace between us is never of a long duration. Something always gets in the way. I don't want that."

"Theá," he sighed and she was surprised at herself for feeling relieved that he had right now used the name she dreaded. It was his way of addressing her intimately. "I see the irony in this situation. In the past I was the one to pursue you, and now when I am trying to stay back, you are the one who is not permitting me."

"What can I say? Since I don't have the advantage of being able to trap you within a shield, what with your being stronger than me, I need to resort to more subtle strategies." She became serious again. "Don't withdraw from me, Ram'an. Please. Staying here only started to become bearable when we got back on speaking terms. Did you know that you are the only one who I tolerate calling me by that blasted name of Theá?"

"I am?" he smiled wearily.

"Yes. When you say it, it's like an endearment, while in case of everyone else it makes me furious. I know that that dance must have been a terrible strain on you," she continued urgently, "but it was not exactly easy for me, either. I felt guilty for reacting to you the way I did when I was convinced that I love Enric."

He frowned. "This is a mere physical…"

"I know now," she interrupted him. "Valrad told me about how the enchantment works and he eased my mind a little. It pains me to see how helping me out there is making you suffer, how another careless choice of mine causes you problems when you were actually looking out for me." She looked up into his dark brown eyes that had lost their usual humorous glint and were now troubled.

"It is not your fault, Theá. You were not to know better. Enric told me he thinks this was a trap to make me and him have a go at each other." He shook his head slightly. "I am glad he exercised such restraint. I am not pushing you away because I am angry at you. I promise. I just need to recover a little. Since I have given up winning you for myself, since your return here I have found myself becoming closer to you than I ever managed before, even that time you were placed in my custody. I managed to pester you into letting me kiss you that evening. And I ended up dancing this dance with you as well. I would have given a lot for that opportunity when you came here the first time. But now it was a powerful reminder of my attachment to you and that it is still so strong. That kiss afterwards..." He trailed off and closed his eyes for a moment. "It keeps haunting me. It comes to my mind at the most inconvenient times, such as when I am supposed to be concentrating on negotiating agreements. I am glad Vern is there to help me, or I might have made things even worse for my House."

"I am so sorry, Ram'an," she said, now feeling miserable herself. "I am sorry I inflicted this on you. I want to help you get over this any way I can." Could she, even? Would seeing her, spending time with her make it even worse for him? How could she ask him to stop avoiding her to ease her own mind when it resulted in an increased burden for him?

"I care for you," she said slowly and avoided looking at his face, but focussed on his shoulder. "A great deal. And if spending time with me torments you, I will have to respect that and allow you the space you need. I see that it is not fair of me to ask you to have lunch or tea with me to set my mind at rest when you would suffer the more because of it." She took her hands off him and turned to leave the dance floor, but he quickly grabbed her and pulled her back.

"You have surely not just extorted me to dancing with you only to leave me standing alone on the dance floor for everyone to witness?" he sighed.

She gulped. Another thoughtless deed that would have harmed his reputation. "I am sorry. You are right, of course."

"Now you have gone all stiff and formal, dear Theá." He smiled down at her lopsidedly. "You know, it is strange. Now that you seem to have given up I suddenly feel more inclined to comply with your wishes."

Looking up, she slowly shook her head. "You are a strange creature, Ram'an."

"Certainly when it comes to you, Theá."

"What does that mean now? Are we friends again or do I have to make you eat that bracelet of yours, after all? If I could get it off, that is."

"We never ceased being friends. I just needed a little distance to recover from that evening. Or I thought I did."

"Does that mean the distance hasn't really helped?"

"Being with you right now feels better than being without you, so I dare say it did not," he admitted. "It is not as painful as I had expected. It seems thinking about you is worse than actually spending time in your presence."

She lifted a questioning eyebrow at him. "Does that mean the picture you have of me in your mind is a lot more alluring than the real me? Are you telling me that I can't really keep up with what your imagination has created? I find that a little insulting!" she complained.

"I assure you this is not what I..." he started, but was interrupted.

"Don't try to find pretty words and twist that unflattering statement into something like a compliment, you silver-tongued lawyer," she growled. "There is no way I am going to fall for that."

They danced in silence for a while, before he drew in a sharp breath when she trod on his toes.

"You did that on purpose," Ram'an stated. It was not a question.

"I did not. You know, I am not exactly proficient when it comes to dancing in general and especially not with your dances here. Neither have I been out that often in these last few weeks to practise any steps in them," she defended herself.

She saw a ponderous expression upon his face and followed his gaze. He was regarding Vern and the woman he was sitting with, the same one who had danced with him before.

"Do you know her?" she asked curiously.

He looked back down at her and a slow smile spread across his face. "Not very well but I know who she is, if that is what you are asking. I take it you are not acquainted with her?"

Narrowing her eyes, she took in his obvious amusement. "No, or I would hardly have asked you, would I? And this obviously delights you for some or other reason. Out with it!"

"Vern has not introduced her or told you about her?"

"I just told you that I don't know her, so this question is completely redundant!" she replied, her level of annoyance rising with each moment. "How is it possible that I came here to make you see the error of your ways and spend time with me again only to end up wanting to punch you?"

"Must be your bellicose nature, I suppose. I am a very peacefully inclined man myself." He grinned when she just lifted her brow. "Have lunch with me tomorrow, Theá."

"I have changed my mind. Go back to being evasive. I just realised that you are a lot less troublesome in my imagination than in person," she shot back.

"No, I am charming, and you know it. That is why you cannot resist me for long. Will you agree to have lunch with me if I tell you about that woman Vern is with?"

She pondered his offer for a moment, then nodded hesitantly. "Oh, very well. And this better be more than just her name."

"Of course. This is Alefer, she is a fellow artist and friend of Intrea. She is one of those who turned their back on Elwoi to join the new academy. This is how Vern knows her," he explained.

She turned her head towards them, watching Alefer laugh at something Vern had just said.

"She seems to enjoy spending time with him," she commented.

"I would think so, considering that they are having an affair," Ram'an said simply and grinned broadly when he saw her reaction. Her head snapped back to him, her mouth and eyes wide open.

"Him? Vern? My Vern? With that woman? But... she is old!" she whispered frantically.

"She is a year or two younger than you, Theá," he remarked.

"Which would still make her ten years his senior!" she hissed. "Is there no law against a thing like that here?"

"A law against two people enjoying a consenting and satisfying physical relationship? No, my dear, we do not make laws like that here," he chuckled. "Such things would not be received very favourably by the people."

"You know what I mean! He is seventeen! Not even of age!"

"Seventeen is mature enough for a young person to engage in that kind of thing. I was younger than that when I had my first experiences. And having a more mature woman share her expertise in that area with him is a great privilege that might prove an immense advantage for him in the years to come."

She glared at him. "Really? So am I to assume that you are speaking from experience here?"

"Yes," he replied.

"If you are about to tell me that you were one of those many lucky young men who enjoyed the privilege of having been initiated into the mysteries of sexuality by Malriel, I shall scream," she groaned.

"Malriel?" Ram'an grimaced and shook his head. "That would have been utterly inappropriate considering the circumstances. I was supposed to commit to her daughter one day, do not forget."

Eryn exhaled in relief, wondering briefly why this would have bothered her so much.

"How long has this been going on between the two of them? Do you know?"

"From what I understand they were seen to leave Intrea's gathering together late at night. So that would be a little over two weeks now."

She stared at him, open-mouthed, in disbelief. Her Vern, the boy who had begged her to teach him healing in secret, who had smuggled candles to her... he was now having an actual affair with a woman her own age! How was this possible? Why did this feel so wrong?

Ram'an took her hand and led her back to Enric's table after the music ended. She followed him as though entranced.

"What is the matter?" Enric asked and frowned at her bewildered expression.

"She has just heard about Vern and Alefer," Ram'an explained. "She does not seem to be very happy about that."

Enric looked serious. "You told her about it? Why?"

"It was in exchange for her having lunch with me tomorrow."

Eryn's head jerked up and she stared at her companion in dismay. "You knew about it all this time?" She slapped her palm against her forehead. "But of course you did! You have each of us followed by a guard, don't you? Of course you knew where he was spending his nights lately!"

The blond magician shook his head at the lawyer. "She has come here to reconcile with you. How did you manage to mess this up in a way that made bribing her to have lunch with you necessary? In such a short time, as well? Only a few minutes ago she would have jumped at the chance of spending time with you!"

"Mood swings owing to her pregnancy?" Ram'an suggested, then grinned. "If you will excuse me now, I need to return to my friends."

"Sure, just anger my companion and make off, why don't you?" Enric rasped, holding on to Eryn's hand when she was about to leave again.

"Wait, where are you off to? Not to confront Vern here, I hope?" he asked urgently.

She glowered down at him. "And why not? I am sure he will be excited at the chance to introduce her to me."

"If you must talk to him about this, I won't let you do it here. You would just embarrass us both. You wait here."

"Why? What are you doing?"

"I am letting Vern know that we would be delighted to have him spend the evening tomorrow with us for a change and have dinner together. There you will be able to scold him in the privacy of our residence without making him the laughing stock of the guests here."

She nodded reluctantly. "Fine. And I don't like that you keep calling Malriel's lair *our* residence!" she called after him sulkily, then folded her arms to wait for him as she had been told to.

CHAPTER 27

Vern's Affair

Eryn saw Ram'an waving his hand from his seat on the cushions of the teahouse. He got up when she came closer.

"Good day to you, Theá." He took her hands and kissed both her cheeks before helping her lower herself onto the cushions.

Eryn leaned back and wiped her forehead.

"Is it getting hotter or is it just me?" she sighed exhaustedly.

He chuckled. "I would guess that your advancing pregnancy might be making these temperatures particularly unpleasant for you. You should now be in your seventh month, is that right?"

She nodded. "Yes, though it rather feels like my tenth. I wonder how much rounder I am going to become. I remember teasing Junar when she complained about her limited mobility, so I can't even say anything at home or she will fling my rather insensitive words from then right back at me."

"Which would be entirely undeserved," he laughed and handed her a glass of water. "Are you hungry, my dear?"

"When am I ever not these days? I didn't know that teahouses served lunch."

"They do not normally. But I happen to own this own here, and I have asked them to fetch something for us. Actually, I find the teahouses a lot more pleasant than the eating places. They are rather full at this time of day, and this place here not only affords a charming view of the river, but also benefits from the lower temperatures beside the water," he explained and lifted a hand to indicate to the server that they were ready to be served now. "Have you managed to corner Vern yet?"

"No, he did not return home last night. Enric told him to make sure to be back tonight in time for dinner."

He screwed up his face. "I fancy he is not too eager to face you. But then he must have known that your hearing about his new friend was just a matter of time. Too many people know about it already, so it is hardly a secret."

She groaned. Why did this feel a lot like back at her first Freedom Night in the city, when everybody but herself seemed to be aware that she had spent the night with Enric? Why was she always the last to learn about anything?

"People like who?"

"The artists, of course. Very talkative bunch, that lot. And subsequently everybody close to them."

Her eyes narrowed. "Such as, let's say, their companions and others like them? That means Vran'el knew about it and didn't tell me! Damn him!"

"But then neither did your companion, did he?"

"No. Nor Orrin either. And it seems as though I am the only one who minds about it!" she complained.

"How old were you when you first went to be with a man, Theá?" he enquired with tentative curiosity.

"I don't see how this has anything to do with Vern," she huffed and folded her arms over her chest.

"Not an answer to my question."

"Seventeen," she grumbled.

"Pardon? I did not quite catch that."

"Seventeen!" she cried out. "So what? I was a lot more mature at that age!"

"Because you were providing for yourself, making a living?"

"Exactly!"

"Unlike Vern, who has not yet done a day's work so far, as your magicians in the Old Kingdom only start doing so at the age of twenty-one, do they not?"

She glared at him. "Stop it!" She hated it when people used logic on her when her gut feelings told her that this was not how things were supposed to be.

He sighed. "As you wish. I can see that the topic gets you a little riled. Did you hear about the message the Senate received?"

"No, I didn't. Is it from the Queen of Darkness, or from the King back home?"

"From Malriel," he grinned. "Do you address her like this to her face as well?"

"I haven't so far. What did she write? Will she be returning here in the near future so we can go back to Anyueel?"

"According to her, the negotiations seem to be going well at the moment, though she does not know how much longer they need. They appear to be particularly thorough and adjourn their meetings as soon as a minor detail becomes unclear, so it can be researched properly before the next occasion. So you may have to stay here for a while yet. So eager to return, still? I thought that after you had managed to reconcile with your father you would find staying here more pleasant."

"It's not that I find it unpleasant here as such, but the heat is currently a real trial for me. And the thought that there is somebody out there who is trying to harm us is not exactly reassuring, either. Especially with a baby in the house already and another one on the way."

Ram'an's expression became concerned. "Yes, that is a serious issue. Unfortunately, our efforts have not yet uncovered anything helpful."

She blinked. "*Our* efforts? I wasn't aware that you were participating in the investigations as well."

He gave her a measured look. "Somebody has been trying to manipulate us into acting in a way that might have caused considerable harm to our Houses. I do not care for what end, whether it was to take revenge on or damage yours, Enric's or my House. I do not like being the target of such actions either, nor a vehicle to be used for inflicting damage on others. I want these persons - whoever they are, and whatever their position - found and dealt with under our laws. We have to be sure this is taken care of so it does not escalate."

"Do you think that both incidents, the fire and the one at House Feral, are connected?"

"I cannot say for sure. There is always the chance they are, of course."

"And yet it could be a coincidence?"

He accepted the two bowls from the server and handed one to Eryn.

"I have heard people claim that they do not believe in coincidence. I admit that I tend to look for patterns as well, for connections, but assuming them to exist where there are none is as dangerous as ignoring them when they *do* exist. I am trying to keep both options open in my mind. Of course this also means that we have to look in different directions. If they should be connected, this means that Vern was not really the primary target back then, but probably no more than a convenient or random one. Otherwise they would have focussed on him the second time instead of on you and I."

She took it all in, nodding slowly. "And if these were two entirely different events, it would mean that the latter might just as well have been aimed at your House instead of House Aren. Or at you personally. Or even at House Vel'kim." She rubbed her face.

"I think so. Or it might have been retribution aimed at Orrin for some reason. Or aimed at causing you injury." He watched her staring at her food and sighed. "But we are breaking an important rule here: no difficult conversation topics while eating. I can see that this is affecting your appetite, and we cannot allow this in your current situation."

Eryn ate about half, then put the bowl aside, shaking her head when the server attempted to clear it away.

"No, please leave it here. I will finish it later. I eat smaller portions, but plenty of them."

The server smiled understandingly and disappeared again.

"So there is nothing that you or the triarchy have found out so far? Absolutely nothing?" she enquired.

"The trouble is that our only leads are the rags that were used to produce the poisonous smoke and that man who asked you to dance that evening. The enquiries as to the substances used points to the artists, but Elwoi was cleared of any suspicion by Enric himself, and all other members of both academies have been questioned under the effect of a lie filter. All to no avail. We think that this might have been a deliberate act to misdirect the investigations. Suspecting Elwoi was so very convenient, after all."

"And I assume the man who was at Intrea's gathering has not been found yet?"

"No, he has not. We are still looking for him, but as Vran'el, you and I are probably the only ones able to identify him, it is not that easy."

"I thought only invited guests could attend such an evening at a private residence?"

"Normally that would be the case, but then we do not usually place guards around the premises to avoid unwanted visitors. Sneaking into a residence at a social occasion is hardly a great challenge."

"This does not sound very promising at all. It basically means that we have to wait for another attempt at causing us harm and then hope that our enemy is considerate enough to leave more helpful clues behind," she frowned. "Maybe there is a way to provoke..."

"No!"

She looked up, startled at the sharp exclamation. Ram'an's features were set determinedly.

"You will certainly not do anything stupid that will put you in danger by trying to speed matters along! Do you hear me?"

"Well, I had not intended to..." she began and stopped when he moved closer to her, stretching out a hand towards her. "What are you doing?" she asked in confusion.

"I am making you promise that you will refrain from endangering yourself in order to catch whoever was behind the attacks. With a first level commitment bond."

She looked at him in dismay. "Really? You have so little trust in me?"

He nodded, the smile on his lips indulgent. "Yes. Go on." He beckoned with his hand for her to take it. "I am waiting."

She folded her arms demonstratively. "I don't have to do this, you know!"

"You are quite right, of course. I am leaving you with a choice, dear Theá: You either do this with me, or with Enric or Valrad. Really,

368

when I tell either of them what you just said they will undoubtedly insist on your making that promise under the influence of a bond."

"I didn't mean it! I was just thinking aloud!" she protested.

"Then the promise should not be a problem either, I would think." He narrowed his eyes at her. "Your refusal to do so makes me suspicious, Theá."

"I have no intention of endangering myself or my child! The only reason I am resisting is that I resent being pressured by you like this!" She grabbed his hand none too gently. "Come on, then - let's get this over with since you insist!"

She felt warm magic flowing from his palm into her hand.

"Do you promise not to consciously put yourself at risk?"

"I do," she growled and was about to withdraw her hand, but he held on to it.

"Do you in addition to this also promise to avoid any possible risk by taking whatever precautions are necessary to protect yourself?"

"I promise," she sighed and only then felt the stream of magic cease before Ram'an released her hand again and leaned back, clearly relieved.

"Bully," she snapped.

"Aren woman," he smiled and winked at her.

* * *

Vern sat on the cushions, holding his new sister on his arm and making soothing noises to her when she began softly whimpering.

"What's the trouble?" Enric asked and came closer.

"I can't say," the boy shrugged. "I checked her, she doesn't seem to be in pain or suffering from any ailments, all her bodily functions are normal, no digestive problems or anything like that. She was cleaned and fed, so she probably just wants attention."

"That's what I call a thorough check," the Head of House Aren chuckled and took a seat next to the two of them.

"Yes," Orrin remarked dryly, "one wonders how non-healers ever manage to raise children."

"With a lot more guesswork, I would think," Vern grinned, then looked around uneasily. "Where is Eryn? I would have expected her to be lurking behind the entrance door and seal it shut with a barrier as soon as I got here."

"With Valrad," her companion explained. "He insisted on her having another health check, and I assume that he has taken her to have tea with him afterwards. He makes sure to spend as much time with her as he can now that she no longer shies away from him. Who knows how long we will be staying here, after all? If Malriel's negotiations go well, we might be on our way back in a matter of weeks."

Vern's face clearly showed that this was not the desirable option from where he stood.

Enric didn't comment on that. It was not exactly unexpected, considering that the boy had here quite a lot more chances than back home, had people from two disciplines who admired him despite his youth, and had now also discovered the delights of being close to a woman. That was a lot to give up.

When they heard the entrance door, Vern swallowed. "That's her, then, I suppose."

"Valid assumption, considering that she is the only one not here," Orrin remarked.

Eryn arrived at the top of the stairs a few moments later, nodding with satisfaction when she saw that Vern really had followed Enric's instruction to at least have dinner with them tonight.

"Hello everyone," she said lightly and took a glass out of a low cupboard before letting Orrin help her sit down on the cushions. "Where is Junar?"

"It's her turn cooking dinner," the warrior informed her.

She raised both eyebrows. "Junar has to cook? Really? I wasn't aware that she joined the rota."

"She doesn't mind it," he shrugged. "Quite the opposite; she offered to do so herself. I think she needs a little time to herself every now and then and is glad when somebody else minds Téa for a while so she can do grownup things again."

Eryn pursed her lips. "I'll have you know that I have no intention whatsoever of taking on that duty in the near future. And very likely also not after I finally have this kid. Just to warn you. Unlike Junar, I am going to hold on to my pregnancy privileges for a while longer. Though we might have to rename them," she mused. "I like *motherhood privileges.*"

"Dangerous term," Enric remarked and lifted a brow. "You are going to be a mother for quite some time, after all."

She laughed. "That's why I like it! They can theoretically stretch on indefinitely!"

"Unlikely," Orrin muttered and rolled his eyes. "Junar?" he then called, "Do you need any help?"

"An extra pair of hands to carry things would be good. Or a couple of pairs," her voice came back from the kitchen.

"Well, boys, that was your cue," Eryn smiled. "Vern is excused, his hands are full."

Both men rose obediently to help carry in the food and tableware.

She studied Vern. He had focussed his attention on the baby, avoiding looking at her. He hadn't uttered a single word since she arrived. That meant he was uneasy. Good, she thought, that was justified. She would wait until they had finished their meal, then they would *talk.*

Junar leaned back contentedly. She had almost completely regained her figure in these few weeks following the birth and her movements were now a lot more elegant and light than before.

"Say," Eryn enquired, "can I have a look at the dresses you have been wearing since our arrival here? I am a bit taller than you, but the girth should be what I need now. I don't want to order new clothes that will be useless in a few weeks anyway."

Junar nodded. "Sure, I'll fetch them for you later. Lucky for you that I was very considerate of your needs when I made them and added a little extra to the bottom seams so we can adapt them to your height."

Eryn sighed blissfully. "You are my heroine!"

The seamstress laughed. "It obviously doesn't take a lot to make you worship me. Hold on to that frame of mind."

Vern was the only one who was not eating, waiting for the first of them to finish so he could hand over Téa.

"Why don't you just put her down on a cushion next to you and eat?" Eryn suggested.

"She starts complaining when I do that," he replied sheepishly.

"Oh dear," she sighed. "She is going to be one spoiled child! She has already taken command over her family as I can see."

Junar and Orrin just exchanged a knowing smile as if agreeing silently that they would soon enough see how she was doing with her own child.

Eryn put aside her half-finished bowl and raised her arms. "Give her to me, then. I need another hour or two before I can finish all that food, anyway."

Vern carefully placed the baby in her arms and then gobbled down his own food in no more than five minutes.

Junar didn't even ask, but refilled his bowl as soon as it was empty. She clearly had adapted well to living with a growing lad.

Eryn waited patiently until Vern had polished off his third helping. The last bowl he had emptied unusually slowly and she suspected that this had something to do with what he knew was expected of him afterwards.

He finally put aside his empty bowl, squared his shoulders and looked right at Eryn. "Alright, then. Let's have it," he grunted.

Eryn handed Téa over to Orrin next to her and folded her arms. "I heard about your affair when I was with Ram'an yesterday," she started without introduction. "With a much older woman. I don't approve."

He blinked and then looked at her belly thoughtfully as if judging how harsh he could afford to be with her in her current state.

"I was not aware that I needed your approval for my love life," he said, picking his words very carefully.

"You don't," she replied stiffly. "But I feel that as a close friend I am entitled to making my concerns known to you." She gave Orrin and Enric a brooding look. "It is a sentiment that hardly anyone seems to share, considering that I was the last one to know about this."

371

The boy swallowed, but kept the eye contact. "What are your concerns, may I ask?"

"Well, for one she is a grown woman, and you are not yet adult. That does not seem entirely proper to me. You do realise that she is about *my* age?"

He nodded. "Yes, that has not escaped my notice. I am fully aware of our age difference. Though considering that we are talking of about ten years here, and my father's companion is almost twenty years younger than he is, I don't really see the problem with it."

His voice was calm and he was obviously determined to talk about this in a mature fashion, she had to give him that. She would have preferred him to be irrational, emotional and less grown-up.

"Your father and Junar are both adults, very much so. You are seventeen. Older women sometimes tend to… take advantage of younger lovers, of their lack of experience, their trust and their eagerness to please. I would not wish you to find yourself in a situation that exceeds your ability to handle it."

"A situation such as what?" he asked gently.

"Well, falling in love with her only to find that you are no more than a diversion, an amusement for her. Or suddenly finding yourself the father of a child. She surely has different priorities for her life than you do for yours," Eryn said.

"I see," he said slowly. "So your concerns are mainly based on the fear that I might develop an unreciprocated attachment to her or be tricked into fathering her offspring, if I understand you correctly."

Why did the way he had rephrased it sound so much more sophisticated than her own wording? He probably had done this to unsettle her by making himself appear overly mature, but fancy words didn't have that effect on her.

"Well done, yes," she smiled without any humour.

"Then let me dispel your concerns by assuring you that my feelings for her are purely friendly and have so far not progressed into the realm of romance that you seem to consider so much of a threat to my happiness," he explained in a reasonable voice. "As for the other risk, I am, as you surely remember, quite capable of avoiding giving a woman an unplanned pregnancy. We spent an entire evening together to prevent just that on the last Freedom Night."

"What if she is slipping you some kind of potion, the way Malriel did with me to overpower your protective measure?" she threw at him.

He grimaced. "Not every woman acts on sinister motives the way your mother does. Some are just out to enjoy themselves. And not even Malriel ever tricked any of her lovers, did she?" He thought for a moment, then amended, "Well, apart from fooling Valrad into thinking that you were his niece, that is. But you know what I mean."

"What if she is just using you to bind you to her House? You are a local sensation and friends with three Heads of Houses, after all," she suggested.

He lifted his brow at that. "She isn't a member of any of the Houses."

Eryn frowned. She wasn't? That was a surprise. So far it seemed she had only ever been introduced to members of the Houses, and had even started wondering if the twelve families more or less made up the entire population of the city. How ironic that she couldn't even see the value in that right now. At least the boy was clearly not a snob.

"You might be breaking local laws with this!"

He spoke confidently. "I am not. I checked. All persons need to be at least sixteen years old to engage in legal sexual congress with another person. Anything else?" he asked politely.

She desperately searched for further arguments against this flippancy, this idiotic behaviour, but couldn't come up with anything. She looked at Orrin.

"And you are fine with this? Really? No objections from you? You don't see any problem in your son's affair with a much older woman who might have who knows what final plan for him?" she hissed, angry that there had been no solidarity whatsoever from him so far.

The warrior gave her a tired smile. "How do you think a teenage boy is going to react to his father forbidding him from seeing a lover? He would probably rush off and commit himself to her just to spite me. If you ask me, a lad old enough to work in a profession such as healing is certainly old enough to choose his bed partner without my oversight."

"You don't approve of his drinking alcohol, yet for this you think he is responsible enough?" She stared up at the ceiling as if the world around her had gone topsy-turvy.

"Alcohol becomes a trap if one isn't careful. This doesn't only apply to young people." He smiled. "I dimly remember warning you against it too, not only him. And while sex is a basic human urge, consuming alcohol is not," he pointed out.

Eryn shook her head at him disappointedly, then looked at Enric and Junar. "So neither of you is worried about this, not even a little bit? I am the only one seeing the danger here?"

"I am afraid so, my love," Enric replied.

"Look, Eryn," Vern pleaded and leaned forward, "I don't want to get into a fight about this with you. Really. You can't tell me who to take to bed, and I know you wouldn't appreciate anything like that coming from me, either. I know you think you need to look out for me, to protect me, but there is a thing or two I don't want you to protect me from. Even if this somehow ends up in trouble, it will have been worth the experience. Definitely."

She looked at him, taking in the stubble on his cheek that had grown since he had shaved in the morning. His hair was longer, he had not cut it for several months. The local clothes showed that he was taking after his father with the broad shoulders, even if he was nowhere as muscular as the warrior. His facial features had become slightly more angular, more defined than when she had first met him what now seemed like an eternity before. He was turning into a man, little by little. She knew it was wrong of her to fail to accept it. Even his father was doing better at this than she was. Was he right? Was it a wish to protect him that made her object to his lover? She remembered a remark from not long ago where she had been accused of just being jealous because she wasn't his only friend anymore. Was that true? Was his spending what seemed like every single night with that woman the real problem?

She swallowed hard and then nodded slowly. "So be it. I don't want us to fight about this, either. There is nothing I can do about anything anyway; I suppose that's the way it should be." She reached out for him, feeling guilty about the relief on his face when he took her hand to press a kiss to her palm. An affectionate, grown-up gesture a man would use with a woman he cared for. One he had never before used with her.

"Do come to have dinner here with us occasionally, will you?" she asked quietly, pushing aside the poignancy that had replaced anger. Now it was only a matter of time until he truly started living his own life. A life that would not include her to the same degree as it had before. "I miss you."

He smiled and squeezed her fingers. "I will. I promise. As you know, the prospect of food is one I find hard to resist." Then he moved across to sit down again next to her. "And now let me have a look at your son. It has been a while since I last checked his development inside you. I would say he should soon be done with development and enter the growing stage."

She nodded and smiled. Healer talk. Good. She could deal with that.

CHAPTER 28

An Unexpected Guest

The door opened almost immediately after Eryn knocked, and a broadly grinning Iklan took her hand and kissed it before linking his fingers with Enric for the formal greeting between men.

"Do come in!" he called out jovially, pointing to the seating cushions on the floor of his study with a flourish. He did not show any sign of unease when Urban trotted into his room after them, making herself comfortable under his desk.

"I am very pleased you could take the time, I really value it!" he beamed. "I do admit that I was a little worried whether you would still be willing to see me about the mind bond after you and I had a rather trying time together."

She looked at him curiously. "Were you? I can see how there had been a few less pleasant occasions, but all in all you really did help me, even though I didn't really appreciate it at the time. Or took your strange talking treatment seriously."

"And you do now?" he enquired with a smile.

"I would say I am open to the possibility that it might have its merits," she shrugged.

"This does not sound as if you are really convinced," Enric pointed out.

"I would first have to see if the effect it had on me was a stroke of luck or if there is a consistent rate of success with other patients as well. And since I don't know how exactly it works I cannot really say if I think the approach as such effective," she explained matter-of-factly.

"Understandable scepticism, my dear Eryn," Iklan conceded. "I would be more than happy to introduce you to its underlying principles or recommend books you can read. As for the success rate, as you are a fully certified healer, you have access to all patient files here and may look over my notes if you are interested." He nodded at her swollen belly. "Though I imagine there are more pressing issues that are going to keep you busy soon enough."

"There are, yes. But I would like to have a list of books I can use to take with me back to Anyueel."

"I will prepare one and give it to you the next time I see you at the canteen," he promised.

He ushered them to the seating cushions and asked them what they wanted to drink before joining them.

"I am very eager to hear about how you determined exactly how to shield your emotions from each other." He pulled a notepad towards him. "I have a few questions concerning the nature of the shield, its exact location, size, effectiveness, how long you generally keep it in place, how often you raise it and under which conditions. We have so far not been able to collect a lot of information on mind bonds here, as couples developing one generally consider it a curse. As far as I know every single one of those few mind bonds which are known to us have been removed only by dissolving the third level commitment bond. The Senate is very understanding when it comes to granting this under such circumstances. Would you like me to start with the things I know? It will not take very long, and then we can concentrate on the both of you."

"By all means," Eryn nodded. "Educate us."

"Do not expect too much, though. As I told you, we have not had much chance to explore this particular topic, as the mind bond generally causes people to get rid of it after a relatively short time."

"Have you found out which conditions may increase the likelihood of developing a mind bond?" Eryn asked.

"Nothing conclusive yet, only general assumptions. It might have to do with the degree of attachment between companions, their magical strength, character traits or willingness to open to each other. We do not know. Too few opportunities to do research on the topic have presented themselves so far." He rubbed his hands. "Although now I have the two of you here, and I am sure there are a few interesting things I will find out from you."

Eryn quickly cut in before he could begin interrogating them. There was something she wanted to know first. "You mentioned that dissolving the third level commitment bond also puts an end to the mind bond. How does that work?"

"It is rather straightforward. In order to dissolve it you need the same level of magic that was used to create the bond. That usually requires several persons. As soon as the commitment is lifted, it is a matter of days before the mind bond is gone as well. I am told it fades continually until there is nothing remaining," he explained.

"Is any of it painful?"

"Not as far as I know."

"What normally happens to the couples who got rid of the bond? Do they tend to remain together afterwards?"

"That very much depends on how long they had waited before dissolving the commitment. And how strongly sharing their emotions with each other affected them. One danger is of course that one of them realises that the other person's attachment is not quite as substantial as they had assumed or hoped. Such a finding tends to cause couples to split up, of course. If it is merely a matter of dealing with usual, but distracting emotions, then removing the mind bond enables some of them to continue their relationship and carry on happily together. Anything else you wish to ask at this point?"

Eryn shook her head, hiding her smile. He was clearly eager to start asking his own questions.

"Tell me about your shield, then. What effect does it have exactly?" Iklan leaned forward slightly, his pen hovering readily over his notepad.

She thought for a moment. "It significantly reduces the intensity of the emotions we receive from each other, meaning no more than an echo remains. This is a lot less distracting than feeling their full impact, as you may imagine. It also depends on their intensity. In case of very strong emotions, more feeling gets through the shield. We have not yet tried varying the intensity of the shield, but increasing its strength may also make it possible to block emotions entirely."

"Who does the shielding? You or Enric? Or both of you at the same time? Does the shield only prevent receiving emotions or does it also keep your own inside?" he asked while he scribbled on the paper before him.

"I do most of the shielding," Enric replied this time. "As I am the stronger magician, her shield cannot hold my emotions back. They are conveyed by magic, after all. My shield both keeps my emotions inside and also keeps me from receiving hers. When we both shield at the same time, we can stop the exchange almost completely."

"Where exactly do you locate the shield? I have a basic idea of the area you very likely cover, but I would like to verify this, if you do not mind."

Eryn lifted her hand for him to take. "Sure, no problem. Let me show you." She waited until she felt the warm, exploratory surge of magic from his hand before she closed her eyes and placed the mind shield around the area where she and Vern had found emotions to originate from.

Iklan opened his eyes again and nodded. "Yes, that is fairly much what I expected. I also had a good impression of the nature of your shield. It is more advanced than a simple barrier, I see. It needs to let all the fluids and impulses pass through but block the magic. I am impressed with how you managed to complete your work on the shield in such a short time. It is a real stroke of luck that an explorer had to deal with this for a change."

"Yes, luck," she grunted.

Iklan smiled. "I imagine it was not a pleasant situation to find yourselves in at the beginning. The tale of your fainting while being in bed together was discussed among the healers, of course. Many of us were thrilled when we heard that you had managed to deal with it. Quite a number of my colleagues have asked me to share my insights with them as soon as I managed to talk to you."

"I am glad to know that my bedroom antics kindled your professional interest," she said and rolled her eyes.

"Oh yes, they most certainly did," he confirmed cheerily, the sarcasm of Eryn's remark obviously over his head.

She looked at Enric, who smirked and shrugged as if to say *What did you expect?*

"How did you find out that you had developed a mind bond?" he went on to enquire.

"Seasickness," Enric replied. "We were on our way back to Anyueel, and Eryn reacts rather violently to the rocking and swaying while I seem to be immune to it. I started feeling sick as well and noticed that it was gone as soon as she was asleep. That was when I first suspected something. Vran'el had mentioned the chance briefly before the ceremony."

"How did you feel about this?"

The blond magician smiled quietly. "I thought it useful. Eryn did have a certain propensity for keeping secrets, and this made that a lot harder for her. Though I admit that it had its downside as well. Experiencing her pain each time she took a hit during her combat training sessions was really a distraction, especially when I was supposed to be concentrating on something or paying attention at a meeting."

The healer nodded. "I see. Normally people do not react that positively to the discovery of a mind bond. However, you seem to have been able to recognise its merits for yourself. Eryn, considering your expression I take it your attitude towards this development was not as... positive?"

"One could say that, yes," she said slowly. "I regarded it more as a curse than a blessing. Especially when considering... you know."

Iklan nodded in understanding. "Yes. I remember being told that sexuality is not something to be discussed as openly in the Old Kingdom, so I thank you for being so accommodating as to share this with me. I imagine Ambassador Sanaf's inability to adapt to this particular cultural difference must have been quite embarrassing for all of you."

"That is a fairly good summary of it, yes," Eryn sighed. "Though I imagine he accommodated the gossips quite nicely."

"And how do you regard the mind bond now that you have learned to handle it so well?"

"Less of a burden," she admitted. "It has turned out to be useful in getting to know each other better every now and then. But it certainly needs some getting used to, especially as I need to keep reminding myself that I am revealing more of my inner world to Enric than I would have otherwise. Also, I don't always remember to shield my emotions and thereby create worry for Enric. He comes running from wherever he is to save the damsel in distress, as it were."

"So you do not keep the shield in place all the time but raise it only when the occasion calls for it?"

"No, we don't," Enric confirmed. "Keeping a shield raised without connecting it to our life force does require concentration, after all. It would be too much of a distraction and drain on our energy. That would be too much effort considering that the need to shield arises only occasionally. Well, and in bed, obviously," he concluded.

"Obviously," Eryn repeated evenly with a glance at him. He had very likely only added that last comment to tease her.

They waited until Iklan had finished jotting on his pad and looked back up at them.

"There is one last question: Can you always distinguish between your own emotions and the ones you receive through the mind bond? How do you know which are your own? Do they... feel different?"

"Most of the time it is obvious from the context," Enric explained. "If there is for example a sense of amusement when I am not exposed to any influence which might provoke that, I know it isn't my emotion. The emotions we experience do not differ in their nature as far as I can tell. It's more the intensity that makes it clear whether they are hers or mine. Most of the time we experience situations differently, meaning I can tell if the level of amusement or anger I feel is adequate from my point of view and so where the feeling originates from."

Eryn nodded in agreement. That was how she experienced it, too.

"What are you going to do with this new-found knowledge now?" she asked and nodded at his pad.

Iklan pursed his lips and leaned back. "I have been considering contacting those couples who in the past dissolved their third level commitment bonds. At least those who still are in a companionship. I would very much like to attempt to convince them to give the mind bond another try and instruct them how to shield their emotions. I would of course have to ask the Head of the Clinic for his permission first. What I am proposing here is experimentation on human beings, after all. Yet it is such a remarkable topic that has for too long remained unexplored. I wonder what long-term effects there are, how the bond influences relationships over the years and decades. Whether it affects the next generation somehow." He looked at her rounded abdomen.

"How confident are you that you will secure this permission?" Enric asked with interest.

Iklan smiled roguishly. "I will admit I am very confident. I am convinced that I have a valued ally in Valrad for this proposal. Not only is his own daughter one of those few people to develop such a

379

bond, but she was also able to make revolutionary progress with it. That is something to be proud of for the Head of a healing House as it boosts the standing of House Vel'kim in rearing the unchallenged healing experts in our country."

Eryn laughed and shook her head. "So you will apply to Val... my father's vanity to get him to help you?"

The healer waggled his head. "Not exclusively, but primarily. There is still the matter of aiding the discipline of healing and the people profiting from our progress, of course," he winked at her.

"Of course," she chuckled.

*　*　*

They strolled back from the clinic to the Aren residence, hand in hand. The cat kept trotting ahead of them, then stopped to sniff around a house wall or frighten a passer-by before waiting for them to catch up with her, only to repeat the process.

"You look tired," Enric commented.

She nodded wearily. "I am. I am not sleeping so well these days. My back hurts. And my ankles are swollen. Everything seems to require so much more effort than before - minor things such as climbing stairs or getting dressed. Or even getting up from seating cushions. I know this is normal for the stage I am at, but it doesn't make enduring it any less testing. At least your son doesn't kick me at night right now. He is very considerate in that regard," she concluded dryly.

"Which would not make much of a difference, as you are not sleeping that well, anyway," he ventured.

"It would, honestly. I may not be sleeping well, but at least I am sleeping for an hour or two at a time."

"If we are lucky, he will be as uncomplicated after he has come into the world as he seems to be now. Téa has proved to be surprisingly well-behaved so far."

"Of course - she is content," Eryn sighed. "Junar focuses all her attention on the girl, as does Orrin once he is home in the afternoon. I wonder if this will change when we get back and both of them return to their regular work. I suppose Junar will not work as much as before, but she still has a business to look after. And as for the two of us..."

Enric squeezed her hand. "I will return to being mighty and powerful in the Order, and you want to resume with the healing work, I assume."

"Exactly. From where I stand there are not many other choices. Either we hire somebody to raise our son for us or I give up healing for many years ahead," she said, looking sullen. "Neither option is particularly appealing."

"We will find a way," he said confidently. "We may have to hire somebody, though not to raise our son but to assist us a few hours each week. You could work a few hours a day - say two or three. Or take over cosmetic corrections. You could fit in your appointments with the rich and vain for when they suit you."

She didn't reply but mulled his suggestion. Working only a little was better than not working at all. She would not lose the connection to her profession and her colleagues. But doing only cosmetic corrections for several years? It sounded utterly unappealing. Maybe she could make an arrangement with Junar, she mused. And there was also Enric. He had wanted that child, so he ought just as well to contribute something to raising it.

"You are aware that this is not only *my* son, of course," she said, smiling sweetly.

He looked down at her. "I am, naturally," he replied carefully.

"That means that you may also have to start thinking about adapting your work habits to include an infant. Most of what you are doing is pushing paper around, anyway. You can do that when the baby is asleep or at night."

She saw him tighten his neck and then nod hesitantly. It seemed that the idea of a man doing some actual child rearing as long as the child needed constant supervision and care was one he still needed to get used to. She smiled in spite of all the evidence. He would change his ways. She would make sure of that.

The residence came into view and she breathed a sigh of relief. The promise of shade and something to drink made her lengthen her pace slightly.

Enric opened the door for her to enter first and raised both eyebrows when she froze in mid-movement.

"What?" he asked.

"Shh," she said and lifted her finger to silence him.

He cocked his head to listen and heard an elderly, but assertive female voice talking.

"Who is that?" he asked quietly.

Eryn shook her head. "I don't know. The voice does sound slightly familiar, but I can't place it right now."

"Eryn?" she heard Junar's voice calling from above and then saw her appear at the top of the stairs. She seemed slightly tense and obviously relieved to see the two of them.

"Yes?" she replied, a feeling of dread slowly rising inside her.

"Why don't you hurry? We have a visitor who has been very eager for you to get home," she smiled with a waxen expression.

Eryn turned when Enric tapped her on the shoulder and indicated a collection of medium-sized chests and packages to one side of the entrance area. What kind of visitor travelled with that much luggage? One who intended to make an extended visit, common sense suggested.

Enric frowned and took Eryn's hand to help her up the stairs. This did not bode well.

When they entered the main room, both of them froze at the sight of the woman in what seemed to be her early sixties, her dark hair bound in a tight knot at the back of her head, her brown eyes scrutinising them. She somehow managed to make it seem as if she was the hostess instead of merely a visitor.

"Malhora," Eryn breathed and stared at her grandmother, one hand grabbing Enric's fingers more tightly, the other coming to lie across her belly.

"Maltheá," the other woman replied without emotion, a small, knowing smile playing around the corners of her mouth. It seemed she was more than satisfied with the reaction she had caused. Her gaze wandered across to Enric, starting at his head and wandering down to his feet in a leisurely fashion. "And the Head of my House. Enric of House Aren," she stated with a quiet satisfaction. She didn't even blink at the sight of the grown mountain cat that sauntered towards her to sniff the seam of her dress and then the hand that was fearlessly presented to her.

"Malhora," he nodded politely, remembering her well from the only time they had met before at the Aren estate during the hunting trip, when he had stepped between her, Malriel and Eryn to avoid violent escalation of the fight between them. She had stormed off angrily back then, while Eryn was carried unconscious over his shoulder and Malriel was left standing motionless due to his having taken control of her muscles. He wondered if she bore a grudge against him for the intervention back then. There had been a lot of injured Aren pride flying around that evening.

Not taking his eyes off the strangely familiar features that unmistakeable marked her as a close relative of Eryn and Malriel, he stepped towards Malriel's mother and took her hand to kiss it. "Welcome. Your visit is an unexpected pleasure."

"Is it now," the old woman sneered, then looked her granddaughter over. "You look healthy. Good. I take it the sweets you are known to stuff yourself with are not the only thing you are eating. But then I think as a healer your father must make sure to feed you with healthy food whenever you take a meal together. You have gained a little weight, but I trust you will get rid of it again soon enough, considering that this Order of yours sets such great score by fighting."

Enric hid a smile at Eryn's surprised reaction. She was clearly taken aback that this woman she knew to reside in the backcountry was so well-informed.

"Are you going to greet me properly this time or am I to assume that your companion is the one in charge of manners in your relationship?"

Eryn awoke from her stupor and obeyed, too perplexed to resist. At least Malhora did not insist on the more intimate greeting Malriel was so keen on.

Junar watched the scene from a safe distance, leaning against the wall next to the terrace door as if to make sure she was within reach of an exit.

"What brings you here?" Eryn finally asked. "Why didn't you send us a note that you intended to visit?"

"Because I wanted to make sure you were here," her grandmother retorted dryly.

"I saw luggage downstairs," the younger woman persisted. "I take it you intend to stay in the city for longer?"

"Well done. I see they do not praise you for nothing; you really are quite bright. Logical deductions are clearly your strong point," Malhora chuckled and went to fetch herself a glass from the low cupboard.

It was not lost on Enric how she wanted to demonstrate that she did not consider herself a mere guest in this house. He would have to be very careful here in case he needed to set her boundaries.

"Why are you here, Malhora?" Eryn repeated, becoming more impatient by the moment.

"I am here, Maltheá, to follow a tradition in our country you are plainly not yet aware of, or you would not be asking me this question. Let me educate you, child." She walked over to the seating cushions, taking a seat and looking up at both of them. "What is the matter with you? Are you going to just stand there or will you sit down so we can have a civilised conversation here?"

Eryn looked towards her companion as if to determine whether he had any intention of doing anything against this brazen intrusion into their living space. But Enric was intrigued by the brash woman who had just turned up and pulled Eryn with him as he began to sit down.

"When a woman is about to have her first child, her more experienced, and usually older, female relatives from the maternal side of the family aid her when it comes first to preparing herself for the birth and then caring for the new-born child afterwards. Under normal circumstances your mother would be here with you, but that is obviously not something she can accomplish. Trying to do so would probably have ended in mayhem anyway. Well, considering what we may describe as *normal* in this family nowadays."

Eryn slowly shook her head. "You have demonstrated that you know a lot of what is going on, so I am quite sure that it can't have escaped your notice that I ceased to be a member of our family some time ago." The mere idea of having this hideous woman staying with her for a few months made her hair stand on end.

"Nonsense," Malhora said with absolute conviction. "You may not belong to my House anymore, legally speaking, but family you are still part of. Or is there some written document somewhere, sealed and acknowledged by the Senate, stating that you are no longer my granddaughter?"

"Of course there isn't," Eryn huffed, "But that is fairly much implied, wouldn't you say?"

"I would definitely not say that or I would hardly have chosen to come here, would I now? Dealing with the immediate first, I would like it if you showed me which room I will be using for the present. Make it one with a view over the gardens."

Enric stared at her for several tense moments, then nodded slowly. "I take it the master bedroom is acceptable for you to stay in?" he then asked, making Eryn next to him draw in a sharp breath.

"It is, yes," Malhora nodded with satisfaction.

"I will send up your things in a moment," he promised.

Eryn gulped hard, grinding her teeth, wishing she had a moment alone with him to give him a proper telling off. What was he thinking? Had he taken leave of his senses?

"Listen, I am not sure that this is the best course of action," she said with as much restraint as she could muster. "I am touched by your generous offer, Malhora, but there is no need for..."

"I am glad that is settled, then," her grandmother continued, interrupting her as if she hadn't even noticed that someone was talking to her. "I would not have wanted the city to see a former Head of House Aren being treated with disregard by the current one."

Enric smiled thinly. "Of course not. There is reputation to be maintained, after all."

"And I would suggest an extra pair of hands with another child in the house soon will not be unwelcome, either," she nodded. "Especially as there is nobody else, considering that House Vel'kim is currently not exactly heavy with mature women closely related to the Head family."

He looked at her thoughtfully. "An extra pair of hands will doubtless be nice, though I am hoping that you will let us benefit from a bit more than your experience when it comes to caring for an infant," he said slowly.

Malhora leaned back and laughed heartily, though it sounded more like a cackle to Eryn's ears. "Seeing a chance to deal with the resistance you keep encountering, Order Lord?"

"It has crossed my mind, yes," he replied calmly, completely unperturbed that she was not only aware of his difficulties when it came to the more social aspects of leading the House, but also made fun of it.

"You are a smart one, I will give you that," she nodded. "We will talk after dinner. I am more alert at night, an age-related thing, I am afraid."

"Thank you," he replied and inclined his head before he got up to take care of her luggage.

Eryn stared after him, wondering what in the world had just happened before her. She looked over at Junar, who seemed equally disturbed at having this woman, who so obviously showed plenty of the less amiable Aren character traits, living with them.

They heard a high-pitched wailing from the corridor that led to Orrin's and Junar's bedroom.

"If you will excuse me," Junar said politely and pushed herself off the wall she had been leaning against.

"No," Malhora said plainly and forcefully.

"Pardon me?" The seamstress stared at her, taken aback.

"You will stay here. I will go myself." The old woman put aside her glass and stood with surprising agility and elegance. "This is what I have come here for, after all. And as far as I can see there is no female relative of yours around to advise you, either."

Both of them watched Malhora disappear, then looked at each other again.

"Can you believe that?" Eryn hissed.

Junar shook her head slowly. "Hardly. But you know what?"

"What?"

"I think I like her."

The healer groaned and let herself fall back into the cushions. "You can't like her! I forbid it! That is Malriel's mother, in case you didn't get it!"

"So what? Malriel is *your* mother, and I don't hold a grudge against you because of it," Junar said and shrugged. "I find that argument a bit hypocritical, coming from you."

"She is bossy, demanding, reckless and she thinks she is in charge here!"

"As do *you*!"

"Exactly!" Eryn wrung her hands. "Do you want two of that kind here? Really?"

They both fell silent when they heard steps coming closer, until Malhora reappeared with Téa on her arm.

"I approve of your choice of name," she stated majestically. "At least somebody uses it," she added with a sideways glance at her granddaughter. "I was the one to pick it for you, in case you were not aware."

"I was, thank you," Eryn growled. "The Queen of Darkness kindly informed me of that little detail. Would you like me to thank you for your efforts?"

"Queen of Darkness," the older woman repeated, rolling over the sounds. "At least it sounds grand, if not affectionate. But that is hardly your intention. What do you call me behind my back?"

She blinked at the unexpected question. "Nothing yet, but I am beginning to think that this should be rectified..."

"Good. Then getting yourself used to calling me Grandmother should not be too much of an effort for you," Malhora nodded and closed her eyes for a moment. "Téa is neither hungry, nor has she any other physical needs that need attending. For now a little attention will suffice." She sat down on the seating cushions again, not even considering handing the girl to Junar.

Junar stood for a few moments, looking rather baffled, but recovered quickly enough. She then slowly walked towards the seating cushions and sank down next to Eryn.

"Not worried about me causing harm to her, are you?" Malhora enquired gently but with a questioning look.

The seamstress shook her head. "You seem to know what you are doing, so no."

"I do. I was taking care of babies long before you were born."

"I am not going to call you *Grandmother*!" Eryn finally protested. "Why would I? I don't call Malriel *Mother*, either!"

"That should be business between you and her. How you address me is a matter between the two of us," Malhora declared, swinging little Téa in her arms with a tenderness that did not fit with her harsh tone. "And I do not see why you are resisting me in such a minor matter as this."

"You don't? Honestly? Could it be possible that you have forgotten how we met?"

"I recall that *joyful* occasion very well, my girl," she growled. "You were disrespectful and uppity, but I will be generous and put that aside for now. Consider yourself forgiven."

"Forgiven?" Eryn exclaimed just when Enric reappeared in the main room. "*I* am forgiven? You were impossible and unfriendly! Your first words to me were an insult from the start!"

"You had pretended to be Malriel! What a person delights in fooling an old woman without any reason or prior provocation, I ask you? Had you bothered to introduce yourself to me as would have been proper, our first and subsequently our second conversation would have been completely different," Malhora reprimanded her and glared daggers at her. "So, do I understand you correctly that the two great faults that make you refuse to address me with the title I am owed relate to my having the audacity to be Malriel's mother and having reacted angrily to being fooled by you back then?"

Eryn remained staring at her, suddenly at a loss for words. It did sound ridiculous and childish when it was phrased like that.

"Of course not!" she protested, refusing to let herself be made out as petty and unreasonable.

"Of course not *what*?" Malhora asked pointedly.

"Of course not, *Grandmother*," Eryn forced out from between tightened lips. She infused her legs with magic and all but jumped up from the cushions. "Now, if you would kindly excuse me, I need to go and bash my head against something solid. Repeatedly," she hissed and stormed off towards her bedroom.

Enric and Junar both stared after her, then focussed on Malhora. The old woman was smiling with satisfaction and chuckled at their astonishment.

"It is easy to tremble at the thought of mighty Malriel of House Aren, but people tend to forget that somebody raised her. That somebody was me. I dealt with adolescent Malriel, meaning I can deal with that one." She nodded in the direction her granddaughter had just fled.

"So it takes an Aren to be a match for an Aren?" Enric asked airily.

"House Aren has always bred for strength," the old woman explained matter-of-factly. "Magical and physical strength. And we raise our children to show strength of character in addition to those. Strength is what we understand, what we respect. We provide leaders, and those who want to lead *us* better demonstrate more strength than us, or we do not acknowledge their superiority, but claim their position for ourselves! Maltheá was not raised in this spirit, but there is an instinctive understanding, an appreciation for it, within her. No matter which pendant she is wearing now, that one is as much an Aren as Malriel and myself," she finished, lifting her chin proudly.

"She would not appreciate hearing that," Enric smiled.

"Of course not. She does not want to see that deep down her mother and herself are kindred spirits. The need to avoid showing weakness, you see, has led Malriel to handle approaching her own daughter as clumsily and stupidly as can be. Had Maltheá not been raised in a village in the middle of nowhere but instead in this very city, learning from an early age how to deal with the political system she was born into, she would resemble her mother even more. Malriel learned to shape her emotions as a prerequisite of survival, for being successful. Her daughter's character is more raw, more true to her nature," she concluded her explanation. "And now you will have to excuse me. I need to unpack my things and then have a look around the garden. I need to see whether some bushes of mine are still there or if Malriel had them chopped down in the meantime." She pressed little Téa into Enric's arms. "Here. The practice will do you good." With that she rose and went off to her room.

"How old is that woman?" Junar whispered.

"In her mid-seventies," Enric murmured.

"So she is older than Lord Poron?" Her eyes bulged and her head turned towards where Malhora had disappeared. "I really, really need to talk to Eryn about that magical rejuvenation programme…"

CHAPTER 29

Téa's Potential

Ram'an helped her sink down onto the cushions at the teahouse and then took a place next to her. It was late afternoon and thanks to the light breeze the heat was not as oppressive.

"Is it true, then? Malhora has moved into your residence?" he enquired curiously.

Eryn grimaced. "Unfortunately, yes. Though I seem to be the only one who minds about it. Junar is thrilled because the old minx helps her out with her daughter, and Orrin approves of whatever Junar is happy with. Enric obviously has a thing for Aren women, no matter which generation they are from. And Vern has not been home since yesterday, but is hardly around so much these days enough to object."

"I take it you are not getting along especially well?" Ram'an asked carefully. "But then the only other time you met before was not exactly harmonious, from what I recall."

"She treats me like a stubborn child, as though she has to teach me manners. She has made me call her *Grandmother*!" she complained.

"So I assume she does not consider your leaving her House a valid reason to call her by her name?"

"No, she says I might have left the House, but not the family, and that there is no official document stating that I am not her granddaughter anymore," she growled. "You don't happen to have any legal argument against this that I may throw at her at the next occasion, do you?"

He sniggered. "I am surely not going to provide you with verbal ammunition against Malhora of House Aren! If she were to hear about it, I am in for the chop."

"Coward! Is there even a tradition of older relatives helping out when a child is born, or has she made that up to make me put up with her presence here?"

"There are certainly a few Houses practicing that custom, yes," he nodded. "And Aren is known to be one of them."

"And why did nobody warn me?" she wailed. "Why didn't you say anything?"

He shrugged. "How was I to know that Malhora would even be willing to take over her daughter's duties after that bumpy start you both had? You are not a member of her House any longer, after all. Though she obviously chose to disregard this in favour of the fact that it is the family blood flowing in your veins."

"What about never shirking an unpleasant duty? I thought that was one of the virtues the House is known for? That means you should have been able to predict her coming here," she said and rolled her eyes.

"That is your other House, remember," he grinned. "House Vel'kim is known for it. Aren is a belligerent bunch that sets a high score by strength and breeding leaders. But try to see the positive aspects here. Malhora is a capable woman, and with two such small infants in one household you will come to appreciate her help, believe me."

"There are still about two months to go until then!"

"Two months you might use to get to know her a little," Ram'an suggested. "Did you know that she was tested for explorer a long time ago too? I looked it up today when I heard that she had come here. That should provide for some common ground for you both, I would think. And there is something else you might bond over: your difficulties with Malriel."

"Surely not! That would be tasteless. I am not on a campaign against the Queen of Darkness, I just want her to leave me and my family alone!"

"As you wish. I am just telling you that having Malhora on your side would be a clever thing to win. She may not be Head of House anymore, but she still has useful contacts; additionally, people are very careful not to get on her bad side."

Eryn rolled her eyes. "Yes, I know. Because she blew up that wine cellar who knows how long ago."

Ram'an pursed his lips. "It surely plays a role in how people perceived her back then - and still do - but let me tell you that neither has she become any less formidable with age. My uncle, Golir, told me that Aren women are intimidating as grandmothers, and that I fully believe. He should know, he is the grandson of one of Malriel's great-aunts."

"I expect my son will one day confirm this, considering who *his* grandmother will be," she snorted.

He laughed. "And I have no doubt whatsoever that one day you yourself will cause your grandchildren to cower in fear before *you*."

She leaned forward. "Can you tell me why people are so eager to have Aren women for companions? Is the chance to forge or maintain an advantageous alliance between the Houses worth spending a life mired in misery with a wayward, erratic, and dangerous woman?"

Ram'an shook his head at her. "Theá, are you really asking me this after falling in love with you shortly after I met you? Aren women may not be the easiest companions there are, but they generally are fierce, beautiful, strong and always know what they want. Look at Malriel. The fact that younger men are eager, and even privileged, to share a few moments of intimacy with her does not have much to do with her status or wealth."

"More with her ability to make herself appear much younger than she really is," Eryn grumbled.

"No, not that either. You saw her at the Senate several months ago when she had changed herself back to her authentic age, or at least one closer to it. Looking older has not caused her to lose any of her appeal. I have never seen a young woman radiate such self-confidence and determination. Making herself appear younger may have lost her a few wrinkles around the eyes, but not her charisma. What is more - and you may believe this or not - but heads also tend to turn when Malhora walks down a street, although we are talking about a different generation, of course."

"Thank you for pointing that last bit out," she huffed. "I am really starting to wonder about the unusual preferences for women the men in your country have..."

"How about Orrin? How does he get along with your grandmother?

She lifted a brow at him. "Why do you ask?"

"Because he is a man who is used to showing strength, considering his position in the Order and his profession. Malhora likewise. The question is now if they are both willing to respect each other's strengths, especially as they will be a part of the same household for quite a while."

"Malhora arrived only yesterday, so there haven't been many opportunities to watch them interact so far. But the dinner yesterday evening was civilised enough. He loves that she helps Junar with his daughter, and I think he is relieved to have somebody like her watching over me, too. Malhora keeps making provocative remarks both about Orrin and Enric, but they just smile at her."

"I have the impression you do not approve of this strategy?" Ram'an enquired carefully.

"No, I don't approve one bit! I think rather that they should set her boundaries instead of indulging her like that. This will only encourage her."

"My, my," he chuckled. "Having the two of you under one roof will certainly provide some entertainment. I imagine that will be an even greater motivation for Vern to spend time with his lover. Speaking of him, he mentioned that he talked to you about that very subject. He was not too thrilled at my having told you about it to bribe you, though."

"He did? When did you meet him?"

"Yesterday, we had lunch together."

She blinked. "You did?"

"Of course. I consider him a friend. And in addition to this he has turned into a valuable business contact. He has been doing very well at the negotiations, quite a talent. Especially as nobody expected him to be quite that good at it, considering he is not simply a healer and an artist, as well as his relative youth. Unfortunately, word has got around now, though. People know what to expect now when they see him sitting next to me. Not that it helps them too much," he added with a smug smile.

"What did he tell you about our talk?" she enquired.

"That it went better than he had been hoping, even though you seemed a little glum to him."

"Not glum, I think. More resigned," she sighed, feeling the heaviness of their talk return. "He seemed so grown-up all of a sudden. I didn't know that going to bed with a woman would have such an impact on the development of the lad. He always was more mature than most others his age, a bit too much for his own good - studious, reasonable, principled. But that evening there was something else, as if he had taken another important step towards leaving his childhood behind him. I don't know how to put better words to it."

"Do not bother, I know what you want to say. I am afraid you will have to find a way through this - there is no stopping it. Which is the way it should be. Imagine we were able to stop our young people's transition into adulthood out of sentimental reasons. Society would soon be stuck with a generation of immature, useless people." He looked at Eryn's rounded belly thoughtfully. "Speaking of generations, I will have to do something about providing my House with an heir within the next few years."

"Alright," she said slowly. "Which means what exactly? Looking for any leftover daughters in the Houses to join you in a commitment?"

He shook his head. "No, this is not where I intend to look. With the Houses, you see, the children would be members of the mother's House, which does not make sense in my situation."

"But there surely can be a way to negotiate something here? I mean, children have been adopted into their father's Houses before. Like myself, for example."

"True, but giving up the claim on its children is something a House does not agree to without sufficient compensation. And I am currently not in any position to offer that. A companion from outside a House will not help keep up alliances, but as I do have strong bonds with Aren and Vel'kim despite everything that has happened so far, this is very likely not necessary for the moment. I fancy I should make the need to provide an heir for my House my first priority."

She spoke with a sense of irony in her voice, "This does sound rather clinical, you know. Like some tidy business arrangement."

"And nothing much else will it be in my case, Theá," he sighed. "I cannot afford to wait for the time to fall in love. I am more inclined to make an arrangement rather like the one Intrea and Vran'el have. It works very well for them - both are happy and independent, free to follow their inclinations to their heart's content without causing offence."

"That is very... sensible and conscientious of you," she said slowly. It sounded detached and heartless, but if there was one person without any right to condemn him here, it was herself.

He smiled knowingly. "That is very diplomatic of you, Theá. But let us not worry about this now. Let us speak of more pleasant things."

She nodded and thought for a moment. "Junar and Orrin have gone to the clinic today to have the healers look at Tea's magic potential. It will be interesting to see how powerful our first magically gifted girl is going to be. I hope for her sake that she will not be too weak, she will have to stand up for herself against a number of boys in the years to come, after all."

"I would not expect this to be much of a concern with an older brother and Orrin as her father. Did you not tell me that Vern was virtually left in peace by the other boys due to his rather intimidating father?"

"Probably, yes," she admitted. "Anyway, how does determining magic potential in a baby work? Do you know about it or should I ask a healer instead?"

"I can probably answer this question to your satisfaction. It is a matter of examining the level of activity in the area of her brain which provides for magical abilities. The higher that activity is, the stronger the magical power will be when the child is fully grown. There might be slight deviations, but nothing unexpected. It is a very reliable way of predicting such powers. The magical strength grows with the child and reaches its peak around the age of twenty, so almost at the same time the Order does its testing."

She nodded slowly. "That does sound fairly simple. I imagine we will adopt this practice back home when I inform the Council about it."

"I would be surprised if they chose not to adopt it, considering how your ranks depend on magical strength. Being able to determine this at an early age would make awkward surprises like Enric less likely, after all," he said and winked at her.

"You really do have a talent for gathering facts about people, don't you?" she sighed.

"It was a matter of getting to know my enemy better. Of course I was trying to find out as much as I could about him. Not that he helped me much, though."

"The Order categorises magical strength. Do you do that as well?"

"Naturally. Without a referencing system, determining strength would be pointless. Ours is similar to the Order's, though we use numbers, and in contrast to your system a lower number signifies lower strength."

"What is the highest number you have?"

"Twelve. And there is currently only one magician in that category here, though I strongly suspect that we ought to make that two as long as Enric is residing here."

That had to be Golir, the triarch who had taken over guarding Enric back then, of course. "What category are you?"

"A solid eleven. Which would make you a medium-strength or low eleven, considering that our difference in strength is not that notable. I am looking forward to discovering what your son will turn out to be."

"He might not even be a magician," she pointed out. "Intrea's brother has not inherited the ability, so who is to say Vedric will?"

"There is a remote chance of that, of course, but in general the stronger the magical ability in the parents is, the more likely they are to pass it on to the next generation. Which significantly reduces the chances of your son being born without magic," he explained. "Would you prefer that outcome?"

"I don't really know. Being born with magical abilities caused me quite some trouble earlier."

"I see how it might. Yet there is magical healing, which clearly is an advantage for you, is it not?"

"There is that, of course," she conceded. "But being born a magician does limit one's choices somewhat, at least in my country."

He smiled. "I do not see your putting up with any restraints the Order or anybody else might impose on your son. There always remains the option of sending him to Takhan, do not forget. He is a member of a House. I know that Valrad and Vran'el would be thrilled about that."

"I bet they would," she scowled. "Vran'el is trying to make us establish a routine which would have us spending half of every year here. Can you believe such a thing?"

Ram'an thought for a moment, then nodded. "It would make sense, surely. Your son is next-in-line to take over Valrad's position following Vran'el. He should get to know the House. I would also not mind having you here regularly myself, Theá. Please do not look at me like that. You just told me about the limits Vedric might encounter in the Old Kingdom, so you must see that getting him to grow up here at least some of the time would extend his opportunities considerably."

"I know!" she groaned. "But the Queen of Darkness! Can you imagine I would choose to spend that much time in the same city as her? Sooner or later we would end up killing each other!"

Ram'an waved her off. "Nonsense. You might even manage to establish a truce between you."

She rolled her eyes. "I don't see that happening in the next half century. She is utterly evil!"

He regarded her thoughtfully. "What does Enric think about the idea?"

"He says it has its merits. Actually, I think he is seriously considering it. Though I think there will be quite a lot of resistance to overcome when he proposes this to the Order and the King."

The lawyer laughed. "Nothing he will not manage to sort out, I am sure."

She sent him a dark look. "How nice to see that you have joined the ranks of his devout admirers."

"Not admirers, not in any way. But I was overpowered by him, was I not? And when considering those who have defeated us, would we not rather see them as formidable opponents than people of average capability? It makes the fact of being defeated so much easier to bear."

* * *

Enric felt Eryn next to him on the cushions stiffen and looked up from his book. Malhora had just entered the main room and was heading in the direction of the seating cushions.

"I cancelled the order for these baked breads you have been stuffing yourself with," the old woman announced.

Eryn drew in a sharp breath and stared daggers at her. "You did *what*? How dare you, you meddlesome old..."

"Careful," Malhora barked sharply with a warning glance at her. "You may be with child, but I will not take cheek from you because of that. You need to eat proper food, not this sugar-laden stuff. You are not moving around nearly enough to use up all that excess energy. That not only makes you irritable but also helps you lay down excess fat."

The younger woman shot her a pointed look. "My being irritable has its source in a completely different reason, actually. It is the person looking at me right now! And I am not getting fat!" she hissed.

"Of course you are. Have you looked at your thighs in the mirror lately? Here. This is what you will from now on eat when you feel the need for something sweet." With this she lobbed an oval, dark-red piece of fruit at her granddaughter.

Enric shot out his hand reflexively without looking up from the book he had returned to and caught the heavy fruit before it struck his companion's shoulder.

"Not exactly the reaction I would have expected from somebody who has been trained in hand-to-hand combat," Malhora pronounced. "Let us hope they never send you to war, then."

"Why aren't you doing anything? She is more or less taking over here!" Eryn growled at Enric and grabbed the fruit from his hand, briefly considering hurling it back at her grandmother, but then deciding against it. It did smell rather appealing, after all.

"I bow to her expertise when it comes to babies," he shrugged. "I don't have much experience with them."

"What about *my* expertise? I am a bloody healer!"

"Which makes your eating habits even more of a disgrace," Malhora replied, her demeanour unfazed. "But I grant you that your cravings might at the moment be stronger than your rational thought processes," she continued generously. "Which makes those who still possess the ability useful to have around."

Enric looked up in relief when he heard the entrance door. That meant that Junar and Orrin were back from the clinic and he was no longer alone with the two Aren women. An excellent development.

Orrin appeared worried when he emerged from the stairway, his sleeping daughter resting against his broad chest.

"Bad news?" Malhora enquired sharply before Eryn could open her mouth to ask for herself.

"No," the warrior said slowly and shook his head. "Nothing, bad as such. Just... unexpected."

Junar entered the room behind him and looked at the expectant faces turned towards them. "She is going to be strong."

"How strong?" Enric asked with a frown.

"They say either a strong ten or weak eleven," the seamstress informed them. "I am not entirely sure what that means, though."

Enric blinked in surprise. Eryn swallowed and stared at the sleeping infant with its mouth slightly open. "Oh dear. Who would have thought so?"

"How strong are you?" Junar then enquired and nodded at Eryn.

"Ram'an says I am a medium-range eleven, Enric is very likely a twelve."

Enric nodded. "I am, yes. The interesting thing, though," he spoke and regarded Orrin thoughtfully, "is that Orrin is a nine. That makes Téa quite a bit stronger than he is. Which would make her number four in the Order one day, not counting Lord Poron any longer."

"How come you know that much about their categories and where we all fit in?" Eryn enquired.

He lifted an astonished eyebrow at her. "I am a warrior and a politician, and this is the kind of strategic information that is useful for both functions. Of course I have informed myself about it."

"How can it be possible that she is so strong?" Eryn then whispered.

"The healers at the clinic were also rather surprised at that. Her mother is no magician, after all. They wondered if it has something to do with the removal of the barrier in our brains," Orrin sighed and walked to the seating cushions. He sank down carefully to avoid waking his little girl.

Eryn frowned and looked at the baby critically. "But didn't Ram'an say that the barrier reduced the number of magicians in the Kingdom but somehow caused an increase of magical strength in those remaining?"

"That was no more than speculation, my love," Enric mused. "And we will very likely find out soon enough if it is wrong. There will be other magicians born back home, both male and female, in the next few years ahead. We will have to test them, or rather, *you* will."

"What if they are all that strong?" Eryn asked with an uneasy feeling.

Enric smiled without humour. "Then we will either be facing a rapid generation shuffle in the top Order ranks or we will have to reconsider our approach to legitimating leadership."

"I wasn't even aware that a child could be stronger than each of her parents," Eryn shook her head in confusion.

"Then you might try using that head of yours for a change," Malhora huffed impatiently. "You are stronger than Malriel and Valrad, after all."

Eryn bit her lip. That was true enough. She hadn't even thought about that part. Ved'al had been stronger than her, but Valrad was not. She turned to her companion. There was a good chance that he had read a book about that topic at some time. He had a habit of informing himself well on areas that might turn out to be useful, time had shown.

"How exactly does passing on magical abilities work? Do you have some idea?"

He looked up, trying to remember. "I recall reading that it is more or less a matter of chance how strong the child turns out exactly. It depends on several factors, including how strong the grandparents on both sides were, whether both parents are magicians and if the father or the mother is the stronger."

"So nothing that would help us to predict how strong our own son is going to be?"

"Not really, no. My parents were no magicians at all; in your case both are. You and I are rather powerful, so basically everything is possible," he shrugged. "But we will know in about three months. You had better write to Tyront about Téa. He will want to be informed about it." Though he would hardly be thrilled about the news, yet that couldn't be helped, he thought.

She sighed and nodded. "Alright, then I'd better despatch a bird to the King as well. That way he will not feel left out and I shall save his spy a little extra work."

"Very considerate of you," Enric murmured, "we will yet make an Order magician of you."

"If that was meant as a compliment, you failed to deliver it as such," she snapped.

"I am just teasing you, my love."

"Where is Vern when we need him? He would tell you not to provoke the expectant lady." She bit into the fruit Malhora had tossed at her a few minutes ago and pointed a finger towards her with narrowed eyes. "And I want my bread buns back! Don't mess with me on that account, or I shall hurt you, no matter how old and intimidating you are!"

* * *

"She needs to go," Eryn insisted when Enric had closed the door to their bedroom.

He chuckled. "Because she cut off your supply of sweet buns? Isn't that a little extreme?"

"The bread buns are just symbolic! They stand for her tendency to interfere where she has no right to, as well as how she disrupts our life after turning up here unbidden and unwanted! It's your House now, make her leave!" she demanded.

"I can't just toss her out like that, Eryn. I would make her my enemy that way. And she was right when she said that leading House Aren is not going as smoothly as it should. Many in the family don't accept me in the position, so having Malhora openly support me will help me considerably. What's more, she can hardly keep you from going to the baker's shop and scoffing your bread buns there, can she? So it's not like you are cut off from them completely. Also I know for sure that Ram'an keeps them on hand at a couple of his tea houses as well," he pointed out.

"So I am stuck with her? You just refuse to do your really, *really* pregnant companion a little favour like that?" she whined. "Why do I keep losing when it comes to your taking a stand against any Aren women, no matter which?"

"That is not true," he protested.

"It isn't? What about that one time during the hunting trip at the estate? I was the only one you knocked out!"

"That was a matter of politics. You were the logical choice, as either of the other two would very likely have made me pay dearly if I had knocked them out."

"Your reasons are of no consequence to me right now - the fact remains: I was the loser."

He sat down on the bed and wondered if there was a way to make her see reason and if he was still alert enough at this time of night to attempt it with any success. Probably not. But maybe some diversion would work for now.

"Not a loser, my love. The fact that you are the only one of the three of you with a devoted companion worshipping the ground beneath your feet would rather make you the winner, wouldn't it?"

"Worshipping the ground under my feet?" She rolled her eyes and struggled out of her tunic. "We have to work on how you demonstrate this fondness to me." She was about to pull her nightgown over her head, when her gaze landed on the image in the full-length mirror. She looked herself over, turned to one side to take in her profile, then back to scrutinise her hips and thighs critically.

"Am I really getting fat? Is the old nag right? I know that gaining weight during pregnancy is expected, so why does this even bother me? And why does Junar already just about fit into her old clothes again? This is so unfair!"

"Come to bed," he suggested, lifting the blanket invitingly. "And you are not getting fat. You are dazzling. Ravishing. Stunning."

She couldn't help but smile at that. "Am I? Then you should probably write a poem about me to give me proper praise. You composed one about Orrin, after all."

"True enough," he agreed. "And I didn't even like him back then. But I am not sure if my humble abilities in crafting lyrical rhymes should even attempt the colossal task of doing your magnificence justice."

"Don't tell me you have fallen prey to the vice of modesty all of a sudden?" she exclaimed in mock dismay.

"Can acknowledging one's own limits in the face of greatness truly be considered modesty? I think not," he grinned.

Eryn smirked and finally climbed into bed with him. "Good. Hang on to that attitude."

CHAPTER 30

Bonding

Eryn yawned loud and unashamed and then opened her eyes. The sun was already sneaking in around the edges of the curtains. Enric was not beside her - despite his insistence on their getting up together several weeks ago. So much for all that.

She got up carefully and pushed aside the curtains, letting in the morning light and averting her eyes from the sudden brilliance.

When she turned back to the bed, she found a piece of paper folded on Enric's pillow and picked it up. A slow smile spread on her face. It was a poem, written in Enric's neat, elegant hand.

Some may see you as unruly,
But I enjoy your spirit, truly.
A few may find your temper scary,
Not me, I've learned to be more wary.
Many know you just as fierce,
But I know more, I saw your tears.
Some may find your ventures daring,
I know you as kind and caring.

You brought to me variety,
Saved me from cold sobriety.
You keep me young and on my toes
With your ideas, triumphs, woes.
Each and every new disaster
I saw with fortitude you master.
No one beyond the sea or here
Can measure up to you, my dear.

The one thing for which now I strive
Is being with you all my life.

She stared down at the words of praise, then read them again. It was no rhapsody which focused on sparkling eyes, flowing hair or the dimple in her chin he loved. No poem that would just as well have fitted Malriel, but something personal about herself - her character, the things that really counted - that made her who she was and unique to him.

His words touched her, made her gulp back a flood of emotion as she felt moisture building between her eyelids. Good thing he wasn't here to watch her now, again being choked inside. How she hoped she would return to being less prone to weeping once the child was born, or he would have to add another paragraph about unstoppable lachrymal glands to his poem.

She refolded the paper carefully and put it in the little trinket box in which she kept the few pieces of jewellery she owned. How had he been able to write this, just like that? She had teased him about it only the night before, and the next morning he had presented her with a rhyme in her praise even before she had got up. Was it like in Vern's case, where the art seemed to ooze out of him whenever he permitted it to?

She slipped into one of Junar's dresses. True to her word, she had let out the seams so it fitted the way it should. The colours were brighter, more attuned to the seamstress's style than her own, but she could put up with that for a few weeks. And if Vran'el dared comment on the colours making her look pale, washed out or whatever else, she would just ignore or even hit him over the head. Whichever was the more satisfying at that point.

She strolled out into the main room, greeting Junar, who was refastening her shirtfront after having fed her daughter.

"Has Orrin left for his training? Today he will get rid of his manacles. And what's more important - is there any breakfast left?"

"No to the first; Orrin is out in the garden with your grandmother. And of course we left you something. Pregnancy privilege. People keep whispering that being Aren, pregnant and hungry is a deadly combination, after all," Junar smiled.

Eryn nodded and turned to get herself a bowl of fruit before returning to sit next to mother and child.

"You do look rather well rested, considering that you have a child who requires feeding every few hours," Eryn commented. "How often does she wake you at night?"

"Only once or twice. I feed her at night before I retire, and if I am lucky she cries only once in the early morning hours and then again after we have risen. Judging from what I hear from other mothers, she is very well-behaved for her age," the seamstress said proudly and pressed a gentle kiss onto her daughter's nose. "But you look a bit worn down. No wonder - I remember how restless my own nights were not so long ago. Please note how I avoid throwing your own words back at you. Out of consideration and solidarity."

"What can I say?" Eryn sighed and bit into another piece of fruit. "You are a role model."

"Good, you have finally decided to grace us with your presence," Malhora's voice bellowed from the terrace door through which she and Orrin had entered.

Eryn groaned. "Go away, old woman! Can't I even eat my breakfast in peace? Is that too much to ask? Come back when I have eaten."

Orrin exchanged a tell-tale look with his companion, then stepped next to Eryn, clearing his throat.

"I am glad you are up. I need to leave in a few minutes and unless I am mistaken, today means that four weeks of punishment are over." He lifted up his wrists with the golden manacles. "Would you mind?"

She gave a single nod of her head and lifted one hand to touch and then open first one shackle, followed by the other. She watched the warrior close his eyes and a faint smile appear on his lips. He was obviously enjoying the familiar sensation of having his full power flowing back, being at his disposal again.

"Thank you," he nodded and stepped towards Junar to kiss her and Téa on the head. "Goodbye, ladies. I see you in the evening." Thus he left, his steps noticeably lighter.

"Walk with me," Malhora instructed.

"What, now? I'm having breakfast, in case you hadn't noticed," Eryn wailed.

"The portion you have there is too large, anyway. Your stomach does not have that much space right now. You can finish it up later."

"Stop nagging about my eating habits! They are none of your business!"

Malhora merely ignored that remark and turned to walk out the terrace door again.

"Can you believe that bloody woman?" Eryn whispered angrily.

Junar chuckled. "Go and walk with her, Eryn. She means well."

The healer rolled her eyes, but put aside her half-full bowl to follow her grandmother out into the garden.

"Hurry, Maltheá! I am baking out here," Malhora complained.

"People here refer to me as *Eryn*," she replied stiffly and followed her grandmother down the stairs into the garden.

"That is for all you know, girl," Malhora snorted. "That is what they may call you to your face to humour you, but when they talk about you they sure enough use the name I gave you." There was more than a hint of satisfaction in that statement. "And I am told that Ram'an switches between your two names as he sees fit. I approve of the fact that you managed to re-establish a friendly relationship with him. House Arbil has always been a reliable ally. Not that he can afford angering us or House Vel'kim right now, anyway."

"I am glad to hear it," Eryn mumbled. "I do so depend on your approval when it comes to my friends."

"Shut up," Malhora commanded, but there was no real heat in it. "I do not have the patience to deal with your flippancy right now." She stopped in front of a row of bushes Eryn remembered from her first visit here. "What do you see?"

"Plants that were changed to combine the characteristics of two species into something new," the healer explained. "Malriel showed them to us and told us about the custom of each Aren generation adding something to the garden. The bushes were yours, weren't they?"

Her grandmother nodded, obviously content with that answer. "Quite right, they are mine. I worked on them for quite some time, experimented, discarded some, started anew and finally succeeded. We even managed to sell the seeds to another House and receive a share in the profits," she added proudly.

Yes, Eryn remembered dimly, that, too, had been mentioned by Malriel.

"Why did you bring me here?"

Malhora looked at her, studying her for a few moments before answering, "You are a bright one. You are intelligent, even though common sense is clearly not something that comes easily to you. You are not classic leader material, that is plain to see. And your test results confirm it."

Eryn breathed deeply and fought for patience. "You could have insulted me in the house instead of dragging me out here."

"Telling you that you are intelligent is hardly an insult, is it? Neither is stating that you are no born leader. I do not have the impression that leading is a great ambition of yours, so I do not see why you could be insulted. I brought you here to show you that we have something in common. I, too, am more interested in knowledge - both in understanding and increasing it. I was the Head of House Aren for a time, but not longer than I had to be. I was more than glad when Malriel turned out to be capable and eager enough to take over the responsibility; that was despite her youth. Having her take over enabled me to step back, advise her when required and to use my time differently."

Eryn listened attentively. That *was* interesting.

"So leading your House was for you obviously not the vocation it seems to be for Malriel," she suggested.

"Absolutely not, no. And even though we pride ourselves on our strength and aptitude in leadership, we do not only raise that kind who make natural leaders. Do not get me wrong, Maltheá, I was good at leading my House. I was trained to take over that responsibility from an early age onward, and I applied what I had learned, changing a few things, discarding others. Leading the House was to a certain degree... an experiment for me. I was careful not to put our wealth or the family's wellbeing at risk, but when the time came where I had the feeling that I was done with experimenting, I was relieved that my daughter was ready to take over." She smiled knowingly. "You are not the leading kind, either. Which does not mean that you are bad at it if you have to do it. Just that is not your choice if you are able to avoid it. However, your companion is good at it. Though he does not always enjoy it, he would rather lead than bow to others' commands."

"So, what is it you do, now that you live outside the city at this plantation?" Eryn enquired.

"Playing around with whatever strikes my fancy. I experiment with plants, try to create new cross-bred varieties, I devise and improve watering systems... Every now and then I invite experts from different specialities over for a day or two and discuss what news there is in their specific areas."

Eryn looked at Malhora with newly-kindled interest. She had rather been expecting her to spend her days reclining on cushions, terrorising her servants, but it seemed that she still was a useful and productive member of her House, putting her skills and inclinations to good use.

"Why don't you live here in the city, then? Wouldn't knowledge and the experts you meet be more readily available here?"

Malhora looked slightly horrified. "Myself and Malriel living in the same city is not advisable. Do not get me wrong - I love her. She is my daughter and I am satisfied with how she leads the House, takes care of it. Yet the past has shown us that we need to maintain a certain distance from each other with only occasional meetings in order to get along."

Eryn swallowed the comment that she herself would prefer not to need to meet Malriel at all.

"And people are so much more relaxed when there is only one of us around," the old woman continued with a quiet smile, then nodded at her granddaughter. "Many of them are curious about how the two of us are going to get along after the incident on the estate. You and I have more in common than either of us has with Malriel, and that is saying something. I would think that this should provide for some common ground."

The younger woman blinked. "Are you trying to make peace with me?"

Malhora rolled her eyes. "This sounds like I am preparing to die, so no. I am trying to see if I want you to be more than a family obligation."

"And? What is the current status of your deliberations?" Probably not a very favourable one, considering their interactions of these last two days.

"I am not yet sure. You are disrespectful, quick-tempered and impatient, but for an expectant Aren woman that is harmless enough," she mused. "You have learned how to use your brain properly, though not so much when it comes to dealing with people. But I attribute this to living in a village for such a long time."

"My fa... Ved'al has raised me to aid people, not to please them," she replied evenly.

"No need to correct yourself on my account, girl. Who is to say that you should not consider the man who raised you as a father?"

Eryn stared at Malhora. She of all people showing understanding for this?

"Well, for one, the man who considers himself my father now," she replied dryly.

"I would think that a woman with two fathers who loved her is a lucky one. Having Valrad insisting on being your father now does not make the man who raised you any less of a father. Quite the opposite, actually. Discarding Ved'al now after all he did to raise you would be ungrateful."

The younger woman managed a thin smile. "I agree. Yet people expect me to embrace the chance to exchange my dead father for a powerful, rich one who is still alive."

"Expectations," Malhora chuckled and shook her head. "If you limit yourself to following other people's expectations, you will end up being their slave. Only consider their wishes if they are useful to yourself. And I am sure Valrad himself would not want you to push aside his brother's memory just like that. He is not the kind to do that. He was the one to betray his brother, after all, not the other way round."

"I can't believe you are saying all this," Eryn sighed and shook her head. "Where were you two months ago when I was being eaten up by doubt and troubled without resolution?"

"Improving the fences to reduce the number of animals raiding the plantation at night," Malhora shrugged. Then she looked at Eryn's rounded belly. "Do not get me wrong, I am happy about the child you are about to have, but there is one matter that needs taking care of. What do you intend to do about Malriel?"

The healer shook her head in confusion. "I am afraid I fail to understand what exactly you are asking me here. What am I supposed to do about Malriel, apart from avoiding her?"

"She overstepped a boundary by slipping you that fertility potion. This cannot go unpunished."

Eryn's eyes widened with the intrigue. How was it possible that this woman knew about that? Had Malriel bragged about it? To her own mother, who she wasn't even on amiable terms with?

"What gives you that impression?" she asked carefully.

"I collect information and employ logical deduction. You made it clear that you did not want children last time we met, and yet only a few months later you become pregnant. Which happened to coincide with Malriel's visit to your home. And then I heard how you greeted her after you got off the ship. That lent itself to certain inferences," she concluded her explanation crisply. "Do not insult me by denying it. I shall repeat my question. What do you intend to do about her? This is not how an Aren lets herself be treated, especially not by another Aren. How are we to impress on people the need to show us respect if we do not even show it to each other?"

Eryn exhaled audibly. This was absurd! She was really being told by her grandmother to take measures against her mother? "Alright, no denying the obvious. I have no idea how to get back at her. I was considering accusing her publicly just to damage her reputation, but Enric was against it."

"As well he should be. This will harm your son more than your mother," Malriel frowned. "Keep thinking, then. And make it count."

Both their heads turned when they saw a man step out onto the terrace. Valrad. He did not look relaxed, more as if he was making himself take care of an unpleasant duty.

"Ah, yes," Malhora smiled maliciously. "There he is. I was wondering when he would turn up here. This is going to be amusing."

Valrad made himself smile and walked towards them, shoulders straight, his look cautious.

"Good morning to you," he said, kissing first his daughter on the forehead, then Malhora's hand.

"And a good morning to you, Valrad," the older woman replied politely. "What brings you here at this time of day? As far as I know there is no Senate meeting scheduled for today, so you should be at the clinic aiding the ill and infirm, I would think."

"I decided to take the day off and see you. It has been a while, after all."

Eryn remembered the Vel'kim reputation of never shirking an unpleasant duty and had to smile. He did not look relaxed, but grimly determined to deal with this.

"It has been, indeed," Malhora agreed. "Is this a purely social visit or are you here to tell me about how you broke the companionship agreement I made with your House by impregnating my daughter?" she then asked nonchalantly, causing him to close his eyes for a moment.

Eryn leaned against a tree immediately behind her, watching the scene with glee. There he was, the mighty Head of House Vel'kim, facing an old woman to whom he owed, theoretically speaking, nothing more than the respect her age commanded. And yet that did not seem to be enough when it came to an Aren. Especially not one that might feel she had been wronged in some way.

Valrad exhaled slowly. "I am sorry," he said sheepishly.

"Are you now. About what exactly?" Malhora pressed on mercilessly. "About the affair itself or that it was revealed? Let me tell you a little something in connection with this. I was aware of you and Malriel thirty years ago. If my daughter keeps meeting with a man other than her companion that becomes something to keep an eye on. I was even wondering for a time if that child really was Ved'al's, but she assured me that it was. Considering that you were a fully trained healer, and a good one too, I believed her. I would have expected you to have taken precautions, after all. An assumption that turned out to be too trusting by far," she added with a malicious smile.

Both Valrad and Eryn stared at the old woman, who was clearly enjoying herself.

"You knew?" he asked quietly with a frown. "Why did you not intervene? As you said, we were breaking the companionship agreement you had forged."

"Because I saw that she and Ved'al were in serious trouble. I doubted that there was any real chance for them to come to terms with it in the long run. I was hoping for the two of you to dissolve your respective companionships and commit to each other. Neither of you was a Head of House back then, and you could have stepped back and let your brother take over the position."

Valrad looked at her in astonishment, then slowly shook his head. "I would have. Without hesitation. I asked Ved'al to let me have her even before they became committed. But I doubt she would even have looked at me twice back then."

"She did quite a bit more than look at you a few years later," Malhora commented bitingly. "Bad luck for you that when you were finally both free, you had each taken over your Houses."

Eryn studied her father with a concerned look. Would he really have taken Malriel as his companion? Why did that chance seem so utterly out of the question to her? He was quietly powerful, wielding his authority only when he couldn't avoid it. A man with principles - well, usually. Somebody who rated family above everything else. A man who had given up running the clinic because he wanted to do work that really meant something for him: healing people.

And then there was Malriel, using her position and the authority it brought like a hammer. A devastating look here, a scowl of displeasure there, and the world hurried to make her happy again for fear of the consequences. A devious woman who had no scruples in stepping over others to achieve her goals, not even her only daughter.

How in the world could they ever have been happy with each other? What a thought!

"I can see your daughter is not too thrilled with the idea of her parents being reunited," her grandmother chuckled.

"No," Eryn admitted. "Not really. I don't see her making a man happy in the long run. She seems more the type for affairs than a grown-up commitment."

"Maltheá." Malhora shook her head indulgently. "Sharing a few nights of passion with a man and then exchanging him after a month or two is not something that makes intimacy possible. It is a mechanism for escaping it, of protecting herself. It is not a natural, healthy behaviour, only compensation for what she has not found so far - somebody to stand with her, who is not intimidated by her, who can stand his ground against her if need be without feeling threatened by her."

Eryn gulped at the implications. It sounded a lonely and vulnerable place to live, an area she would not have associated with Malriel of House Aren. It sounded strange, yet considering Malriel's past it might contain some grain of truth, she realised. She felt the resistance inside her that made attributing remotely human feelings and motives to the Queen of Darkness hard.

"Well," she heard Malhora saying, "at least her choice of lover back then broke only the companionship agreement, not the alliance between the Houses. A considerate transgression if ever there was one."

"As long as we don't lose sight of the silver lining here..." Eryn mumbled and rolled her eyes.

"You could have ended up with fathers much worse, my girl," her grandmother snorted. "It is even the same House, after all. And a good one, into the bargain."

Valrad visibly let go of most of his tension. The words were a clear signal that there were no hard feelings between Malhora of House Aren and himself.

"Thank you," he smiled and inclined his head. "And let me tell you how much I value your coming here to stay with my daughter. Despite her decision to join my House. I hope the two of you will come to see the good in each other the way both of you deserve."

"Coming from any other man that might have been a very cynical thing to say," Eryn smirked.

"Then I am glad that you know me so well," he retorted and winked at her.

CHAPTER 31

Incrimination

Eryn sat on the cushions in the main room, staring at her feet. Had they grown? Were her ankles thicker than last week?

Six more weeks, she groaned inwardly. Being heavy with child was not much fun in this climate. Well, it would probably not have been pure pleasure back home either, but the heat made everything worse, for sure. Lately every small movement seemed to cause rivulets of sweat to trickle down her spine.

"Brooding, sweetness?" Vran'el asked gently. "Not grumpy because you cannot participate in the game tonight, are you?"

"No," she sighed, "just eager to return to my former size again. I have seen women who seem to be thriving when they have a baby growing inside them. They claim they have never felt better in their lives, are more energetic, completely balanced and at ease with themselves and the world around them."

Her brother noted her obvious discomfort. "Which is not the kind of pregnant woman you are..."

"Really not. I shall be glad when the birth comes. I am all for sharing and everything, but I am really looking forward to having my body to myself again." Small things like climbing stairs without being out of breath or not feeling able to eat more than a few bites before her stomach refused to take in any more only to feel hungry again some minutes later seemed like pure luxury.

But Vran'el could at least provide a little diversion. He was already dressed in dark trousers and shirt, ready for the game that was about to start in less than two hours.

"So, I hear you are teamed up with Enric this time?" she enquired.

"I am, yes. There is a little score we both wish to settle," he smiled grimly.

"With Ram'an, I assume?"

"Yes. I am glad he did not manage to pair with Orrin, or it would have been quite a challenge. I trust that whoever he is going to be with will not pose much of a hurdle to Enric and me. Well, to Enric mostly," he added as an afterthought.

"Isn't taking revenge on a Head of House rather childish? Especially considering you are allies? I hope Enric will be gone from here sometime soon, but you are supposed to be taking over our House one day. Wouldn't it be nice *not* to have your ally holding a grudge against you?"

He shrugged and stretched lazily. "I am not Head of House yet, and father has not yet mentioned any plans to retire. That leaves me a few more years to fool around and have fun."

"I thought every member's actions reflect on the House's reputation, not only the Head's?" she pointed out.

"Basically, yes. But I am doing nothing that would be considered hostile. I am just going to take him out of the game, the way I am supposed to."

"Boys," she chuckled. "I suppose in the face of that kind of activity it is nigh on impossible to remain a grown-up."

"Is it? I seem to remember a few women enjoying themselves immensely last time. Intrea was disconcertingly enthusiastic about hunting me down with your companion, and you even made it up the stairs of the Senate hall," he countered. "I reject the implication that only men fall prey to the idea of running through the streets and shooting bolts at each other. Do not paint womenfolk as more mature than they are, sweetness."

"Alright, I stand corrected. Or in my present state, I should say *stoop* corrected. Which side are you going to play on? Is Enric still concerned about not being seen to invade the city instead of defending it?"

"He is, yes. So I am again on different sides from Intrea. Orrin cannot be on the same team as Enric, of course. Nobody would bother joining the opposing team. Speaking of opposing teams, I heard you and Malhora were seen out in public together without any breakable objects being thrown around or harsh words spoken. That means you have started warming to each other, I gather?"

She nodded. "Strangely enough, yes. She is just different enough from Malriel for that to happen. Though I try not to forget that I am still dealing with an experienced politician and an Aren woman here. Putting complete trust in her would probably be rash, but we are getting along well enough for now. And Enric really likes her help in a few matters concerning the House. It seems he has not yet managed to leave his Order style of leadership behind him, at least not to the degree that would please his new family here."

"Yes, I know. Word tends to get around. But then they know that Malriel will return again, so adapting to Enric would not really make sense, as many of them will surely see it."

"Probably. Do you know if Vern will be joining the game? I haven't seen him in ages. I think he is staying away from here because of Malhora. He does seem a touch frightened of her."

"He will join in, yes. I am told he is pairing up with Iklan this time. He is afraid of Malhora?" Vran'el grinned. "Splendid. I can use this to tease him."

"Oh no, please don't! I hardly ever see him these days, and if you tease him with something I told you this will certainly not improve his wish to visit."

He sighed theatrically. "Alright then, little sister. I will oblige you in this. Pregnancy privilege."

Enric walked in from the direction of their bedroom, lifting his hand to Vran'el in a casual greeting. He, too, was already dressed in the clothes he would be wearing for the game.

"Ready to defend the city against the aggressors, my friend?" the blond magician asked and walked over to the seating island to join them.

"We really are. Also, this time it will even be interesting to see who wins, since I assume that there are no... prior arrangements in place?" Vran'el asked carefully.

"No, victory will depend on nothing more than superior strategy and fighting skills tonight."

"Excellent. Though having Orrin as my opponent is bad news in this case."

Enric sighed and looked a little crestfallen. "You are aware that I am considered something of an expert in these areas as well, of course? I trust I will not prove too much of a liability," he added sarcastically.

"Do not tell me that I have injured your pride? Let me assure you that it is an honour and a privilege to fight beside you tonight. I am confident that we will be successful in completing our primary objective of defeating Ram'an. Winning the game would simply be an extra embellishment," Vran'el shrugged.

"Good. Losing is a realistic possibility this time. Orrin is determined not make this easy for us, now that he is assured that I shall not hold back to let the invaders win as they did last time."

"You are worried," Eryn said quietly, putting words to the sensation she was receiving through the mind bond. "Why?" She caught the quick glance at her round belly and narrowed her eyes. "Don't spare me on account of my being pregnant. If you don't inform me, I will worry all the time and wonder what is going on and how bad it has to be if you refuse to tell me."

He nodded slowly. "It is about the fire seven weeks ago."

Both Vel'kim siblings leaned forward.

"Finally something new!" Eryn breathed. "What is it?"

"Rags very similar to the ones used to produce the poisonous fumes in our house were found this morning. The same fabric, the same odour and thus very likely the same combination of substances."

"Where were they found?" Vran'el asked eagerly. "This might give us a useful lead on the culprit!"

Enric straightened and grimaced. "It is not that easy, I am afraid. They were found at the Arbil residence."

"What?" Vran'el exclaimed.

Eryn's eyes had widened, and she had clasped one hand over her mouth. The other had again come to lie across her abdomen in the gesture she had adopted over these last few months whenever she was distressed. Enric remembered noticing the same reflex with Junar.

"Wait," the dark-haired magician demanded. His demeanour had changed from one moment to the next. He had switched into professional mode, Enric was pleased to see. That meant they would now be discussing this without any unfounded accusations or wildcat theories.

"Who found the rags?" the lawyer asked.

"Ram'an."

"Where?"

"In one of the storage rooms."

"How do you know about this?"

Ah yes, Enric thought with a thin smile. He could depend on this man to put the right questions.

"Ram'an sent for me today and told me."

He saw Eryn exhale slowly. "So the chances of Ram'an being involved in this seem rather slim if he chose to tell you about it, don't you think?" she asked worriedly. "But then he might have done it just to make us believe exactly that..." She closed her eyes and tried to disentangle her feelings from the facts she had. The mere thought that Ram'an could be involved in this somehow was painful - it made her shiver, made her hair stand on end.

"Did he allow himself to be subjected to a lie filter?" Vran'el kept on asking.

"He did, yes. He offered it. Insisted, even. I questioned him and from what I could tell he was speaking the truth. We both think the rags must have been planted there to incriminate his House."

Eryn lifted a hand. "I don't understand this. If he told you under the influence of a lie filter, this would hardly incriminate him, would it?"

"Not him directly," her brother explained, "but his House. That he personally had no knowledge of any of this does not mean that nobody else in his House is somehow involved."

"And now? This doesn't help us at all, does it?"

"Not immediately, but it may eventually," Enric spoke. "This attempt at incriminating House Arbil shows us that both attempts -

the fire and the dance at Intrea's gathering - were very likely connected and not random single acts. And that they were aimed at dissolving the alliance between Houses Aren and Arbil, though the important question remains: which House is the primary target? But judging from this newest development, we do not seem to accommodate whoever is behind this. Our Houses are still allied."

"You think this would end if you are seen to be breaking up with House Arbil? Blame him for the fire?" Eryn asked thoughtfully.

"It has crossed my mind, yes," Enric confirmed calmly, curious to see if her thoughts would go along the same lines as his own.

"Then I suppose we might try giving the public that impression," she said slowly and thoughtfully. "It will prevent any other dangerous ventures to harm us and maybe gives us time to find out something, I hope. With a little luck our anonymous malefactor will become a little overconfident and with that careless."

Enric nodded with satisfaction. That had been his intention exactly. "Alright, my love. Let's do that. I dare say my and Vran's hunting Ram'an through the streets of Takhan will be a very helpful first public demonstration of crumbling alliances."

"Just one thing," Eryn frowned. "If he hadn't voluntarily decided to inform you of the rags himself, how would anybody have found out about this? I mean, wouldn't this have to be more public to work?"

"Ah yes, there is a little detail I failed to mention," Enric nodded. "The triarchy received an anonymous hint that searching the Arbil residence might shed light on the fire. They ordered a search to be carried out about one hour ago."

"Little detail indeed," Vran'el muttered. "You said Ram'an found them in the morning. So I assume he had them removed in the meantime? The searchers did not find anything?"

"Quite the contrary; he returned them to where he had found them for the searchers to happen upon them," Enric told him.

"That means you and Ram'an had already decided to play that little game even before I suggested it right now! Otherwise making this public would not have made any sense at all," she complained, folding her arms angrily. "What was this just now? A tiny test in political strategy to see if I could come up with a sensible course of action?"

Her companion smiled apologetically. "You rose to the challenge beautifully, my love, if that is any consolation."

"Hardly," she growled. "From where I am standing it was just patronising."

"Then I apologise." Enric took one of her hands and kissed her knuckles. "Will you come to the Senate hall at midnight to witness either my great triumph over Orrin or my utter defeat at his hands?"

She smiled darkly. "Oh yes, definitely. Just don't ask me which option is more appealing to me right now."

* * *

Eryn was waiting impatiently in front of the magical barrier that separated the playing area from the rest of the city. Malhora and Junar were standing beside her, Téa fast asleep in a sling across her mother's chest. Around sixty more people were standing about, awaiting the outcome of the game.

"How long until midnight?" Eryn asked impatiently.

"Half an hour," Junar informed her. "You know that a premature ending indicates that your companion has lost the game, of course?"

"He deserves to lose every now and then; I am told that's good for the character. And I need a bathroom! How long have we been standing around here now?"

"No more than ten minutes," the seamstress sighed. "Go and find yourself a bathroom, then. I definitely do not wish to watch you twisting and squirming for another half hour, not counting the announcement of the winners. Off you go!"

Eryn hesitated for a moment, then nodded and turned in the direction of a teahouse she spotted at the end of the street.

She hurried towards it and groaned after she had entered and spied the short queue in front of the room in question. To her surprise, all three people stepped aside for her immediately as if it was the most natural thing in the world. She briefly wondered if they had recognised her as the former Aren heiress, but then remembered that pregnant women were virtually worshipped here. Quite convenient.

When she returned, the waiting crowd was gone with only Malhora and Junar still standing there, looking a tad impatient.

"Hurry up!" Malhora commanded, "The game is over."

Too early - which meant Enric had lost, as he had not managed to defend the Senate hall until midnight. So she would see Orrin triumph over her companion. Which was fine. Losing would do the mighty Order Lord good, she decided. Well, former and future if not present Order lord.

She briefly remembered Kilan telling her during their first visit here many months ago that defeating Enric could hardly ever be more than a short pleasure as he would strike back and turn events to his favour quickly enough. That meant that one should probably make use of the opportunity and celebrate these occasions all the more, she decided. A pity she would only be doing it with juice instead of wine, though.

When they arrived at the Senate square, they saw Golir shaking Orrin's hand, Enric standing next to them, his arms folded.

Eryn didn't receive any sign of annoyance through the mind bond, so he was obviously not too concerned about losing this particular game. And he hadn't just lost against anyone, but Orrin - a master in both fighting and strategy. This was surely tolerable. And yet she was absolutely positive that Enric would be sure to win next time. There was the matter of pride, after all.

Ram'an stood a little off to one side, the manacles around his wrists showing black. Vran'el next to Enric caught her gaze briefly, looked at Ram'an and then winked at her with a telling expression. That surely meant that her brother had been instrumental in removing her former suitor from the game.

She saw Kilan and smiled at him when he gave her a little wave. He had again been on Enric's side. And thus lost once more. But he, too, seemed to be taking it well. But then it would hardly befit his status to be seen stamping his feet in rage or cursing like an unruly child.

Her gaze wandered back over to Orrin who looked... perfectly content. He was not the gloating type, but satisfaction was evident in his posture and the set of his mouth, which remained curved into a half-smile as if he was too modest to break into a full grin. Or didn't consider that beating Enric was worth displaying such a degree of complacency.

Junar next to her was smiling with evident pride. "My companion is better than yours," she sang and sniggered like a teenage girl, rocking her daughter in her arms, who was gurgling happily as if in support of her father.

"Seriously? That's how low we have sunk? Comparing the boys and seeing who is on top? You are aware that my companion is considerably stronger than yours, meaning he is going to resume his position as your companion's superior in the not too far future, aren't you?"

The seamstress shrugged such minor details aside. "A victory of a short duration, but a victory nevertheless."

Their gazes fell on Vern and the woman Eryn had seen dancing with him at the music house. He had an affectionate arm around her waist, chuckling about something she had said.

Eryn swallowed and watched the pair. She couldn't help a feeling of unease, but he had been right: his father's companion was rather younger than Orrin, so age difference alone was not the problem with his new consort. She would have to put up with it; there was no way around it. Either that or anger Vern considerably. And it was not as if she could do anything to thwart them, even if she had wanted to. She sighed when she thought about the two of them joining each other in a companionship, eventually having children. That would mean that he would stay here for good, wouldn't it?

But then all this might be a little premature. He was only seventeen years old, after all. Hardly ready and willing to settle down and have a family considering he was not fully a grown-up himself. She looked at the pattern of her thinking about him. She had real difficulties considering Vern as a more or less grown lad, and had now moved on to picturing him at the other extreme – a family man with a child on each arm, when he probably wanted nothing more than a little fun. She had been exactly his age when she had started discovering physical pleasures with others, and having a family had been the last thing on her mind then. Funny how things developed, she thought with a flicker of a smile, then touched her belly as she felt another kick.

Vern's gaze met hers and he said something to his lover before he strolled towards her with a lopsided grin.

"Hello, you," Eryn greeted him and nodded at his manacles. "It seems you made it to the end of the game. Whose side were you on this time, by the way?"

"Invaders. I wouldn't want to seem disloyal by opposing my own father. Not in a country where they take family bonds so seriously."

"That was probably prudent, especially considering your growing circle of admirers. You wouldn't want to sink in their estimation," she smiled.

He sighed theatrically. "What can I say? Fame can be a burden at times."

"Yet you bear it with fortitude. Well done," she laughed. "I see that Orrin is trying very hard to hold on to being modest."

Vern grinned broadly. "In vain. He is immensely satisfied with himself right now."

"Rightly so," Junar chimed in and waited impatiently for the official shoulder-patting to be over so she could approach her victorious warrior.

Eryn shot her a look. "I think I got the worst deal here. No matter what the outcome is, I still have to dwell under the same roof with both winner and loser. And in this case also with the winner's gloating companion," she sighed. "I am not even the right person for that. I don't begrudge Orrin his glorious victory! Quite the opposite; I think losing every now and then will be good for Enric ultimately. People can learn to grow with new experiences, after all."

"That's the kind of support every man would wish for," Enric's dry voice said from behind her. "You aren't still miffed about our conversation in the afternoon?"

"I am not," she huffed. "And even if I were it wouldn't be completely unjustified. Just saying." Then she grinned. "But be assured that I feel sorry about your defeat. Deeply sorry."

"Very credible," he sighed and shook his head. "At least you are content because you think I got what I deserved. A man has to make do with trifling achievements at times."

Vern snorted. "Especially with a grumpy companion in an advanced phase of her pregnancy."

"I may be pregnant, but I am still quite a bit stronger than you, my *friend*," she growled. Her gaze wandered over the crowd around them that had split up into numerous small groups discussing the goings on during the game or were imparting them to those who had come to hear news of the outcome.

She saw Ram'an standing together with a man she knew was his younger brother, and three women she hadn't seen before. He caught her gaze briefly, then looked away.

It took her a moment to remember that they were not supposed to interact in public for the time being. At least not in a way that implied that everything was going well between them. She felt a stab of regret about that. That also meant that they wouldn't be having lunch or dinner together any more nor meeting for the odd pot of tea.

After they had finally managed to turn that whole muddle between them into something resembling a beginning friendship, after first her being angry at him, then his avoiding her, now they had to pretend to resent each other even though they didn't. Whoever was behind this would get a proper kicking from her when they found him.

CHAPTER 32

News from up North

Eryn assumed a sceptical expression when the knock at the door came. She was holding on to her bowl of food. "That is definitely bad news, I know it. People disturbing meals never bring any glad tidings. Mark my words."

Orrin put aside his own bowl and got up to check who was at the door. He returned only a few moments later with a folded piece of paper addressed to the Head of House Aren.

Enric accepted it and read the few lines. His brow rose.

"What is it?" Eryn enquired nervously. "I bet I was right. It's bad news, isn't it?"

"I can't really say. It's a summons to a Senate meeting in half an hour. I would say that calling a meeting at such short notice and at such a late evening hour very likely means that there is a problem," he nodded, then looked up at her, his brow furrowed. "Golir has asked me to bring you along, too."

"Me?" She swallowed an overly large mouthful and grimaced as the lump painfully fought its way down her gullet. "And it doesn't say anything else? No hint?"

"Nothing whatsoever," Enric replied calmly. But he had a certain suspicion. The note had said, unlike as was usual, that this time the meeting wouldn't be public. No observers. That meant it was a delicate matter that was not yet supposed to become common knowledge for some reason. And the fact that Eryn was asked to attend as well probably had something to do with her being affected personally by it.

Combining these two trails of thought lead to one logical conclusion - the news had to be about Malriel. And it was probably not very cheering.

He wondered whether something might have happened to her. He fervently hoped not. But what whatever it was would very likely keep them from returning home for a while yet. Or make it necessary for him to send Eryn back to Anyueel to protect her and his son because war had been declared.

He pushed the thought aside. That would be the worst case and he would worry about it only if he had cause to.

He noticed Eryn regarding him with narrowed eyes. She managed to catch snippets of his emotions more easily now; they had become more attuned to each other in the months since the third level commitment bond. Which was a development he truly valued, but in situations like that it was a little inconvenient. He much preferred to be the one uncovering her secrets, not the other way round.

"Talk," she just said, a slightly menacing undertone in her voice.

"Just speculation," he shrugged. "I don't want to trouble you unnecessarily."

She breathed a sigh and continued eating. In her experience Enric had a tendency to be right with his suspicions. But he wouldn't share his thoughts, his lips were pressed together. Not into a thin line as when he was furious, but enough to convey his determination.

Junar watched them with a worried look on her face. "Would you like me or Orrin to accompany you to the Senate?"

"I am afraid this will not be possible," Enric declined her offer. "The public is barred from the meeting."

Malhora looked up sharply and rose abruptly, collecting the other empty bowls on the table to take them to the kitchen. "I will come." She smiled grimly at Enric's raised brow. "They can demand that I keep out of the Senate hall. But I doubt that any of them is brave enough to really try it. Most of them remember the time when I was a senator. Many of them not with much fondness."

She exchanged a long look with Enric, who then nodded slowly. Malhora was obviously as aware as he was of the likely nature of the news.

"Eat up, Maltheá," her grandmother ordered curtly. "We need to leave soon."

Eryn put aside her half-eaten meal. "Alright, I am full up anyway. But don't throw it away, I will finish that later," she added when Malhora had collected her bowl.

Enric helped her to her feet so she was able to use the bathroom and waited for her with a shawl for her shoulders when she returned.

Only minutes later they were on their way to the city centre. Eryn watched both of them walking next to her, both silent with concerned expressions. She had an uneasy feeling creeping up on her. Both of them worried, neither of them willing to share their thoughts with her...

She stopped when it struck her, causing Enric to turn to her when her hand slipped out of his grip.

"You think something happened to Malriel, don't you?" she accused them both.

"We don't know that," Enric replied evasively and shot Malhora a warning look when she said, "It is possible."

Eryn ground her teeth, trying to figure out why this bothered her, when Enric took her hand in his again to pull her along. Was it the thought of being stuck here with Enric in charge of House Aren or were her fears of a more personal nature?

She swallowed and decided to deal with this question in case the news really was about Malriel. No need to deal with this now. The reason for the Senate's summoning might be a completely different one, after all. It was just a stupid coincidence that her brain did not manage to come up with any other likely scenario at the moment.

When they turned the next corner the majestic Senate building with the domed roof came into view, more brightly lit than normal for this time of day.

Only one of the three double doors at the top of the stairs stood open, doubtless to make sure that only those authorised entered to participate in the meeting.

Eryn send a weak pulse of magic into her legs to make the stairs less of a challenge. She didn't want to enter the Senate hall out of breath.

Even though the meeting was due to start only in about ten minutes, almost all of the senators and the three triarchs had already arrived and were chattering amongst themselves.

As Malhora had predicted, there was no attempt to stop her from entering. Quite the opposite - she was treated with a reverence that made her granddaughter turn towards her and whisper, "You must have been a scary senator. Even those too young to have experienced you themselves must have heard about you. They are averting their eyes!"

The old woman smiled contentedly. "I was known to be a formidable opponent, yes."

They turned towards a familiar male figure who approached them with a serious expression. Valrad.

"Eryn, my dear girl, what are you doing here? The summons said this is for senators only," he frowned.

"Golir asked me to bring her," Enric explained.

Valrad's face turned bland in an instant. "I see."

Eryn swallowed. Immediate inexpressiveness was always a dead giveaway when worry or confusion would have been more natural reactions.

"So you, too, think this is going to be about Malriel," she said. "No need to spare my feelings..." She hesitated before she continued with a look at the people close enough to hear them, "...father."

Valrad briefly squeezed her shoulder before he returned to his seat next to Vran'el, who waved at her after sending her a questioning look.

The doors were closed once the last senator had arrived, and Enric preceded the two women to the front row seats that were reserved for Aren senators. A servant hurriedly brought a third chair from one of the unoccupied rows at the back.

When they were all seated, Torke'na got up from her seat between the two male triarchs and the hall felt silent immediately.

"Senators," she addressed them, then added as an afterthought with a sideways glance at the Aren table, "and guests. As you are indubitably aware with the short notice of the summons, there is important news we need to discuss. We have received word from Pirinkar. The news is disturbing." She paused, looked at Enric, Eryn and Malhora, then spoke, "The negotiations have stopped. Malriel has been locked up and proceedings are in progress against her."

Eryn gulped and stared at the woman on the pedestal. Malriel in prison? That was bad news, from whatever point of view. She turned to Enric.

His jaw muscles were tight, his brow furrowed, his eyes narrowed while he waited for Torke'na to go on.

"What are the charges against my daughter?" Malhora's clear voice demanded sharply.

This time Golir spoke. "She has been accused of forcing a man of an exalted religious community into bed with her."

The deathly silence following that statement was unsettling, as utter stillness in a room packed with people tended to be.

It was again Malhora's voice that rang out. "Malriel was never one to restrain herself when it came to bedding men, as you are all more than aware." She stood. "But whatever else you may say of Malriel of House Aren," her clear voice reflected from the smooth walls and the dome above them, "*stupid* she has never been. And neither has she ever had to worry about willing partners being at her disposal. Quite the opposite." She lifted her head and glared at the assembled senators as if to challenge them to contradict her. None did. "This is a tactic to stop the negotiations. They explored her most well-known weakness to accomplish this. She was tricked," she concluded, sounding absolutely certain.

Golir watched the old woman before he nodded calmly. "Yes, this is what I assumed. Now the question arises of what we are going to do about this. What we can do."

"Somebody needs to go there and investigate. And continue with the negotiations if somehow possible," Uvel of House Tokmar spoke up. "Whoever planned this is probably in favour of starting a war between our countries. We need to act quickly."

That started a wave of disturbed murmuring among the senators.

Eryn watched the goings-on around her mesmerised, still not sure how exactly she felt about the revelation. Malriel was obviously in danger. What would be the worst thing they could do to her? How serious an offence was non-consensual sexual intercourse considered there? Enough for a death sentence in case they found her guilty? She felt her stomach clenching at the thought.

Malriel had been neither considerate nor honourable in her dealings with her own daughter, had first tried to get her convicted and put under house arrest in Takhan and then impregnated her with an underhand and reprehensible trick.

Yet Eryn realised that death was not what she wished upon Malriel, however condemnable her conduct had been. It would deprive her of the chance of one day getting even with the Queen of Darkness, for once.

And there was some fear, she realised. Fear for Malriel. However undeserved that certainly was.

She felt Enric's fingers closing around her hand and squeeze it reassuringly.

Enric exhaled slowly, knowing that what she would not at all appreciate what he was about to do. But there seemed no other choice.

The mind bond communicated her fear, her shock, her regret all too clearly. She didn't hate her mother. Or at least not to a degree that overpowered the stronger feelings buried somewhere underneath.

Enric let go of Eryn's hand and slowly got to his feet. He didn't speak but just stood calmly and waited for the agitated discussions around him to settle to silence.

When they finally had, he raised his voice, "I will go."

Three simple words with an immense impact. Countless widened eyes stared at him. Only Malhora's were closed in what he assumed was from relief.

He felt Eryn's storm and avoided looking at her. A powerful stream of anger, apprehension, shock and dismay washed over him, strong enough that he was sure that she avoided shielding her emotions on purpose. She wanted him to feel what he was doing to her.

"No," her voice next to him stated surprisingly cool and calm, "I don't think that is a good idea."

Eryn pushed herself up from her chair and addressed the Senate without glancing at her companion, fighting for control to appear reasonable. They wouldn't listen to her if she seemed hysterical and emotional, and she needed them to halt this lunacy.

When all eyes were upon her, she continued, "I implore you to consider the implications of sending a foreigner to a land with which you are trying to avoid a war. A warrior who has hardly spent enough time in Takhan really to grasp your culture enough to represent you properly."

"She is right," another voice spoke up.

She looked over to Vran'el, relieved at his support. She briefly felt Enric's annoyance at her brother, but his next words made her gasp for breath.

"This is why I will accompany him. I know enough about our own laws and trade requirements to negotiate with our interest in mind. I am a senator, which makes me a proper representative of Takhan. Moreover, I have gained at least a superficial insight into the law system up north, which might turn out to be useful in helping Malriel out of her predicament."

Eryn stared at Valrad, willing him to intervene. His face was pale and he was forcing his lips together. He was obviously not happy about this. But he had chosen to remain silent for whatever reason.

Suddenly an odd sensation took hold of her, as if the floor under her feet had started moving. She felt Enric's hand on her arm to carefully lower her into her chair.

"Please take her home, will you?" she heard him say to Malhora, who nodded immediately and got up from her seat to do just that.

"No," Eryn shook her head and clung to the armrests, her knuckles white. She couldn't just leave, she had to stay and convince the Senate of the absurdity of this terrible idea of sending both her companion and her brother there, endangering them in this way. There had to be another, better method of accomplishing this. There had to be other people who could be despatched. People who were less close to her.

"Eryn, please," Enric begged her quietly. "We will talk about this at home. I promise."

She glared up at him. "No! You don't get to send me home like a child! I will have my say in this and then we will see if I still want to talk to you at all," she snarled.

"Her argument with him being a foreigner is not entirely unwarranted," Anfer of House Ulverd threw in. "This might look strange, even if he has one of us with him."

"Not just any one of us," Vran'el remarked, "but another senator and heir to a House. One Head of House, even though foreign, and an heir to another should sufficiently convey how seriously we take this matter."

"And in case something goes wrong you can always claim that the foreigner did not act in your best interest," Enric added. "You all know me, not only in my current function as Head of House, but you also had ample opportunity to observe me in my prior capacity as ambassador. You saw how I conducted negotiations, how I managed to adapt to a culture I had never before encountered and how I handled the difficulties that my companion and I had to face back then." His gaze darted across to Ram'an for a moment in case anybody was in confusion about the nature of the trouble to which he was referring.

"There is hardly any doubt that you would be qualified to go, Enric," Valrad now said, his voice strangely hollow. "The question is rather why you are so eager to. Malriel might be able to get out of her troubles on her own, they might clear her." He looked at his daughter. "And your companion is about to bring your child into the world in a few weeks."

Enric closed his eyes for a moment. The reproach in that last sentence had been more than plain. And it was the one matter that made offering to go such a trial for him. Yet it was for his companion and his son he was doing this.

"I will be back within a few weeks, I hope in time to stand by my companion when she gives birth to our son," he replied mildly. "I also know that she is in capable hands as long as I am away." Then he turned to the other senators. "I want to avoid war, for all of our sakes. I may not be a citizen of your country, but my companion has family here and I am in charge of protecting a House. In my opinion I can do that better by travelling to the place where I can take care of the threat directly instead of waiting for it to show itself here."

"Who will be in charge of House Aren while you are gone? As this mission might easily take longer than you anticipate you will have to nominate a temporary Head," Legara of House Finran enquired.

Eryn felt a cold shiver run through her at the words that remained unspoken, very pointedly so: that there had to be a name offered for another Head of House as there was the slim chance he might not return at all.

Enric turned to Malhora. "Would you be willing to take over this responsibility until I return, Malhora? I cannot think of anybody more able to lead the House."

The old woman gave him a regretful, but determined look. "I shall not. I gave up this function a long time ago and feel too old to bear the burden once more." She let her gaze rest on her granddaughter meaningfully before returning it to Enric.

He nodded slowly. "I understand." He turned to Legara. "In this case I leave Maltheá of House Vel'kim in charge of House Aren until my or Malriel's return."

Eryn's head whipped around and she stared at her companion, looking furious. She wouldn't have thought that this situation could become any worse. She opened her mouth to ask him if he had taken complete leave of his senses, but not a single syllable came out. Her throat was tight and dry. Even swallowing was a major effort, let alone talking.

Enric saw several of the senators nodding quietly. Malriel's daughter in charge of House Aren. That was the way it should have been anyway, so there was no objection there.

"I say we vote on this tonight. Our time is running out, we need to act quickly," Voreld of House Ordel proposed.

The three triarchs on their pedestal exchanged a few glances, then Torke'na nodded and stood. "Are there any other questions or objections that require discussing?" She looked at every single senator and nodded when none of them spoke up. "Then I call for a vote in favour of or against sending Enric of House Aren and Vran'el of House Vel'kim to Pirinkar to assist Malriel in clearing herself of the charges which were laid against her. Those of you in favour should now lift their arms."

Eryn closed her eyes. Please not, she begged fate, the stars or whatever forces might influence the outcome. When she forced herself to look at the men and women around her, she suppressed a sob when the number of raised arms showed a clear majority in favour of the idea without even counting them.

She saw that Valrad had folded both arms in front of himself, staring ahead. Ram'an's arm, however, was raised. He caught her eye and she could see the empathy in his eyes.

She jumped up so quickly the chair behind her tilted back and crashed to the floor. Turning around as quickly as her rounded belly permitted, she stormed out of the Senate hall, closely followed by her grandmother.

Enric let his breath out slowly, shielding himself from her emotions before raising his voice. "I thank the Senate for the trust it has placed in me and will do my best to prove worthy of it. I plan to leave in two days." Then he turned to face the triarchy. "There is one thing I require before my departure." He took a deep breath and felt everything inside him rebelling against the words he was about to utter. The effort of forcing them out was almost physically painful. Not in his worst nightmares had he dreamed of one day having to say them, especially after such a short time.

"I herewith request the dissolution of my third level commitment bond with Maltheá of House Vel'kim."

CHAPTER 33

Lifting the Bond

Enric sat on the cushions in the main room and stared ahead without his eyes seeing. It had to be close to midnight. Eryn was already in bed when he returned from the Senate meeting, which he had to admit he was glad about. It meant that he did not have to tell her about the commitment bond yet.

The triarchy had granted the dissolution without hesitation. Golir had thanked him for the great sacrifice he was willing to make to serve his Senate, and Enric saw that these had not been empty words. Golir knew how difficult it had been for him to get Eryn to agree to such a bond in the first place.

But of course the words - however sincerely they were meant - were hardly any consolation. Enric's hands felt cold and his stomach was a hard, solid knot.

He closed his eyes at the thought of losing the mind bond, this close connection he had termed a blessing and a gift, even if she had not been thrilled about it and had only come to tolerate it. He would miss the frequent stabs of anger that always made him wonder who she was feeling mad at, who had provoked her. Or waves of pleasure that made him look forward to meeting her in the evening so he could ask her about whatever lay behind.

Being alone in his head would ultimately be lonely. Even imagining it felt like a part of himself were to be removed, torn away, locked up out of reach.

He blinked. But then this was not necessary, was it? He wanted the bond dissolved to spare her the pain of being separated from him, which the bond would make a trial for her, as it would keep pulling them together without any chance of making it happen. And there

425

was the danger that they might torture him or otherwise cause him great pain in Pirinkar, should things go truly wrong up there. She would experience his physical pain, his desperation. It was something he wanted to spare her. Angering and hurting her now had to be worth the trouble to avoid possible agony later.

But *he* didn't have to give up the bond, did he? The bond could be removed from one person only. It had been done in Malriel's case. Eryn's father - well, uncle - had spent the rest of his life with an intact bond. He thought of what Valrad had said back then. That being out of the reach of his counterpart must have cost Ved'al some of his spirit, of his joy in life. Yet the man had obviously nevertheless managed to be a good father and a compassionate healer for several years.

That meant that he himself would be able to bear the strain of severance for a few weeks. In exchange for having Eryn's emotions with him. He nodded to himself.

He looked up when he heard the quiet knocking on the door. Good; he had been waiting for it for a while now.

He opened the door for Ram'an to enter and wordlessly turned to guide his visitor to his study.

Enric didn't sit but walked to the window to look out into the garden. It was a beautiful night with a brightly glowing, full moon that dipped the various trees, bushes and flowers in a soft, iridescent light. It was a night for a romantic walk, for stealing kisses, for promises of eternal devotion. Like the promise he had given to Eryn at the end of their first visit, the one he knew no other way to keep than by breaking their commitment.

He turned away from the appealing sight that seemed to mock his gloomy thoughts.

Ram'an broke the silence with his quiet words. "You wanted to see me?"

Enric straightened. "I did, yes. Thank you for coming at this time of night. But as you may imagine, I have to take care of many things and there is only little time before I leave here." He looked away from his visitor's face to avoid the sympathy he could read there before he went on, "I want you to take care of Eryn while I am gone. She will not take this well. You managed to be a friend to her before when she needed one and nobody else was able to get through to her. I shall depend on you to be there for her."

"I will," the Head of House Arbil replied without further comment, with a calm tone conveying the message that for him this was the most natural thing in the world.

Enric nodded once. "There is more. There is still the question of whoever is behind the fire and the dance at Intrea's gathering. I want you to find whoever was responsible for it and make sure that person is given appropriate punishment. Whatever financial resources you require for this will be made available."

He waited for Ram'an's nod before he broached the next subject. "There is the chance that I will not return," he said calmly, as if not talking about his own demise but rather of the rain over the ocean. He pushed a file on the desk towards Ram'an. "There are two ships at anchor in the harbour here in Takhan. I have sent for a third one, which should be here in two days. That is one ship for each House: Arbil, Aren and Vel'kim. Should there be a declaration of war and the city is about to be attacked I want you to take charge of the ships and make sure they all get to safety. Take them to Anyueel." His gaze dropped to the symbols on his wrists. They would be gone tomorrow. He let a finger glide over them, thinking back over how he and Eryn had discussed which ones to choose.

"In case I do not return, I want you to take care of Eryn. You once threatened to raise my son as your own." He lifted his head and stared into Ram'an's eyes. "I would like to take you up on this now. Should I die, my worldly goods shall go to Eryn. There are documents stored with Lord Tyront, containing a full list of all businesses under my ownership," he concluded, hearing his own words as if through dense fog. Was he really saying all this? Was he truly commissioning the man who was trying to take his companion from him only a year ago to raise his son and take control of his businesses?

He felt his knees buckling and straightened them with an effort. He couldn't afford to be weak. Not now.

Ram'an took a step towards him, and lifted his hand to Enric's neck, pulling his head closer until their foreheads touched.

"I will keep her safe for you, my friend. Use your energies to concentrate on your duty up there, and you need have no worries about Eryn. May your resolve bless you with success and ensure that you return to us safely."

Ram'an removed his hand again and both straightened, their faces looking resolved. "But I would advise you to focus your energy on achieving your goal rather than on taking steps for your failure. Though I see why you need to allow for both." He bowed. "I will see you tomorrow for the removal of the bond."

Enric nodded and watched him leaving, closing the study door carefully to avoid waking anyone.

The removal of the bond. This would probably turn out to be the worst day of his life. He fervently hoped so. He wouldn't have the strength to endure anything any more agonising.

In a sudden burst of anger and disgust at himself, he pounded his fist on the desk hard enough to leave a depression in the surface. Ram'an was right! He needed to look at himself in the light of future success and halt his self-pity. It was as if he was preparing himself for dying instead of avoiding a war.

No more of that. There was work he had to do.

* * *

Eryn lay in her bed despite the lateness of the hour. She had skipped breakfast and had sent Junar away when she tried to persuade her to at least have lunch with her and Orrin. She hadn't left the room apart from a few short trips to the bathroom. The baby was pressing on her bladder.

Enric had come by a few times and tried to talk to her, but she had just ignored him until he had left again to do whatever needed to be taken care of before his departure the following day.

She just stared at the ceiling, letting her thoughts course around the one topic that had kept her occupied since waking several hours ago: Enric's determination to go after Malriel.

She had been worried about Enric feeling drawn to her for some time now. Suave, sophisticated, confident Malriel with her penchant for younger men who had no difficulties whatsoever to make them desire her.

She had wondered idly if she should have picked up any feelings of that kind from the mind bond, but then Enric could have shielded himself. He managed to raise the shield in time more often than not if he wanted to keep something to himself. She could sometimes see it from the little tell-tale signs in his expression and posture when he was hiding his anger or agitation.

She wondered how his going away would affect them. Would the mind bond turn it all into a drawn-out torment for them both?

Words she had spoken to Junar a long ago came back to her. She had been standing in front of a mirror, getting ready for a ball. She had told Junar that she would survive it somehow if Enric decided to run off with another woman. That she was not the jealous type. And that she couldn't force him to stay with her if he didn't want to. Words said in another time, another place and, it seemed now, by another person.

She ignored the knocking at the door. They were probably trying to make her eat something. Once more. She knew that she had to eat, that her body needed sustenance, but the thought alone made her withdraw.

The door pushed open and Vran'el came in. His expression showed the extent of his worry.

"Sweetness, you need to get up now," he said gently.

He came closer when she didn't react and sat next to her. "Malhora says she will come herself and drag you to the main room by your ear if you do not get up from that bed right now," he added. "I do not know about you, maybe Aren women do not fear each other, but that threat sounded serious enough to me."

Eryn had no doubt that her grandmother had meant every word and would indeed turn up to put actions to her words. She slowly sat up, then motioned for her brother to hand her one of the few tunics that still fit along with a pair of baggy trousers to slip into.

"Why are you here? Don't tell me you are already saying your farewells," she asked coolly.

"There are a few people here to see you," he told her reluctantly.

She frowned. "Which people?"

He rose. "Come and see for yourself."

Her eyes narrowed. "Why do you look so grave? What is going on here?"

Shaking his head, he opened the door for her to leave first. She did so with another suspicious sideways glance at him and proceeded to the main room.

Several pairs of eyes turned towards her when she entered. Golir, Ram'an, Enric, Orrin and Valrad stood when they saw her, every single face expressing sorrow and empathy.

She came to an abrupt stop and looked at each of them in turn. "What is the meaning of this? What are you all doing here?"

Enric was the one to speak. His voice was low and soft, but his words froze her nevertheless.

"The triarchy has granted my request to release our third level bond, my love." He lifted his hands to placate. "This is just to make my absence easier to endure. The effects of the bond trying to pull us back to together would be almost unbearable. I don't want to burden you with such a thing."

Her eyes shot daggers at him and her fists balled. "You are about to leave me here - only a few weeks before I give birth to our son - with the responsibility of taking care of a bloody House, and now you start worrying about *burdening* me? How very considerate of you," she hissed. "Well, my friend, I have news for you: I don't agree to it." She folded her arms defiantly on her chest. "Making me suffer even more than your valiant rush to save Malriel does already will be *your* burden to bear."

Enric didn't look surprised, she noted. He had obviously been prepared for her refusal.

"No. This is the one thing I can do for you."

She cursed when she saw the shield around them he had raised to keep her from leaving the room.

"You are really doing this?" She shook her head in disbelief. "You are truly going to remove the bond against all my wishes?" Her eyes darted to Golir. "Don't just stand there! Do something! This can hardly be in accordance with your laws here! Vran'el, tell him!"

Golir sighed. "You are right, Maltheá. Removing a bond without both partners' consent is usually not something we perform. Only in the case there is a valid reason for it. Which clearly is what we have here."

"So you are helping him to leave me behind like this?" she whispered.

Enric shielded himself from her emotions when he felt his resolve weakening. He had to remind himself that not doing this to her now would make her suffer more later.

"I am not leaving you behind, my love," he said softly and made a step towards her. "I will be back as soon as I can. Then we will renew the bond."

Her eyes were brimming with tears as she shook her head and took a step back. Or tried to before the shield behind her stopped her. She looked at the faces around her. None of them would offer her help. Not even Orrin, who had never in the past let Enric's higher rank keep him from doing what was right.

She sobbed once and felt Enric's hand closing around her wrist and pulling her carefully to the seating arrangement.

"I won't cooperate," she whispered. They needed her, didn't they? It took at least as much magic to remove the bond as to forge it, if she remembered correctly. Of those five people she herself would not help them and Malriel was missing.

Now she realised why there were six of them here, all strong magicians. They had not counted on her enduring it voluntarily and made sure to have enough magic between them to balance Malriel's absence and her own refusal to comply.

Enric sat and made her sink down next to him before he put an arm around her shoulders. She tried to wriggle free, to create some space between them, but even at the best of times and without a rounded belly she wouldn't have stood a chance.

Valrad stepped closer and crouched in front of her. "Eryn, I am going to send you to sleep now. Otherwise your resistance might cause you harm. We are going to use a lot of magic and having you thrashing around would be too dangerous."

She stared at the hand he slowly lifted to her forehead and turned her head away.

"Make her drift off slowly, will you?" Enric requested.

The healer nodded once and then settled for sending the magic into her body through her hand.

Eryn almost immediately felt the effect of the warm stream of magic that feathered its way up her arm towards her head. Her limbs started getting heavier, her breathing slowed, her eyelids grew leaden and stared drooping.

Enric's hand turned her face towards him so he could look into her eyes. His voice was soft, his blue eyes intent. "Eryn, I love you, more than anything else. I want you to take good care of yourself and our son until I am back. It pains me to do this to you, but there is no other way. Really not."

His lips on hers were the last sensation she consciously took in before she sank into an enchanted sleep.

Enric looked up at the men around him, then nodded at Golir. "Alright, let's take care of this."

All five of them took their positions around him and Eryn and placed their palms on top of his. Golir directed the flow of magic where it was supposed to go and nodded at them after a few moments.

"It is done. She is free from the bond. Now for you, Enric."

"No. My bond will remain in place," he stated and shifted Eryn in his arms.

"What?" Vran'el exclaimed in horror. "What are you talking about?"

"Enric," Golir urged him, "I beg you to reconsider. You are aware of the effect this might have on you during your absence. This is why you wished to free your companion from the bond. We need you to be strong and able to focus on your goals when you go to Pirinkar. Having you suffer from the effects of the bond will not be of help to anyone."

Enric only looked more determined. "I understand your concerns, but for me, not knowing how Eryn is doing would be far worse. I need to sense that she is alright and healthy. Worrying about her would be an even more extreme distraction than being pulled back to her. I can handle this. I know I can do it."

"She won't be," Orrin stated with a glance at the sleeping figure.

"Pardon?" Enric asked with a frown.

"Alright and healthy. She won't be. You have just removed the magical commitment bond from her without her consent, leaving her behind while she is heavy with your child. In all honesty, I can only tell you that she will not be alright and healthy. And you will feel that. Is feeling how she suffers better than a lack of feeling, Enric?"

"Anything would be better than emptiness," he replied quietly. "And I can always shield myself from the feelings if there is a situation where I need to concentrate."

"Is this some misguided notion of penance?" Ram'an enquired, looking concerned. "Do you think you need to share in the pain you are causing her? This will not make it any easier on Eryn, you know."

"I know. And I am asking you not to tell her about it. She is not to be informed of my end of the bond being intact still. She wouldn't... like to know it," he ended with a sigh.

"You can bet she would not," her brother agreed and flashed him a solemn look. "And I understand why. This is not right, Enric. It is like spying on her emotions."

Enric got up from his seat, then bent down to lift his sleeping companion up. "I see your point, Vran. Unfortunately, there is nothing you can do about this. If I refuse to have the bond lifted, you can't do it. Without my cooperation there is not enough magic between you to do it." He narrowed his eyes at Golir. "And I don't think you would want to risk my willingness to travel up north by acting against my wishes right now."

The triarch held his stare unblinkingly, then nodded slowly. "Indeed we would not. But I do not consider this a wise course of action either."

"It is duly noted. Though this course is the one I have chosen."

Enric walked towards the bedroom he had shared with Eryn for a few months now and carefully laid her down on the bed. He had agreed with Valrad that he would send her to sleep long enough for him to be gone when she woke again. This was why he had wanted the last words she heard from him before his departure to be his declaration of love, and a promise to return.

When he turned back to leave the bedroom, he saw Vran'el leaning against the door frame with folded arms and a less than contented expression.

"Come on. There is still a lot to go through before we leave tomorrow," Vran'el remarked, then turned to walk ahead towards Malriel's study with determination.

Enric felt his will seeping away again. Now his travel companion was angry at him. This was certainly not the best opening for their joint mission.

* * *

Eryn slowly opened her eyes and let them wander from the ceiling to the window. Judging from the sun it had to be late afternoon. She felt ravenous.

It took several seconds for her sluggish thoughts to piece together her last waking moments. She cursed and swung her feet to the ground as energetically as her current condition allowed. She was wearing a nightgown, so the bastard had undressed her after she'd had the commitment bond forcefully removed.

She tore the door open and yelled his name. He had some listening to do, some abuse to endure and maybe, if she felt particularly generous afterwards, he might even find himself in a position of attempting an explanation.

"Enric!" she yelled once more when no reaction came, adding a little magic to make her voice carry further. Only then did it occur to her that little Téa might be asleep. Well, probably not anymore.

"Stop that," Malhora's voice called out from the main room. "He is gone. Come and sit down. You must eat something."

Eryn's breath hitched. Gone? Gone where? He surely hadn't left the city already, had he? She gulped hard and slowly walked towards the main room.

Malhora was sitting on the cushions, Téa in her arms.

"What do you mean by *gone*?" Eryn asked with an intense look.

"He left Takhan for Pirinkar a few hours ago," her grandmother explained, matter-of-factly.

"And you let me sleep through this?" Eryn exclaimed and gaped at her. "Why?"

"He wanted it this way," the old woman shrugged.

"And you didn't have the nerve to disobey him?" the younger woman snarled.

Malhora shrugged and swung the gurgling infant. "He was my Head of House. That entitled him to a certain degree of obedience on my part."

Eryn groaned and sank onto the cushions, slapping one palm against her forehead. "And now I am the Head of the House! I have no idea how to take care of a House! What am I supposed to do now? Why would anybody even listen to me? It's not as if being born to a family of leaders is an adequate qualification if one wasn't raised by them." She glared at her grandmother. "You refused when he asked you! Why would you do this to me? And why was everybody so eager to assist Enric in dissolving the bond when I told them that I was against it?" She struggled to get back to her feet again, her eyes glaring angrily. "Even Orrin assisted him! How could he? I am his superior, damn him!"

"Then I suppose you ordered him not to?"

"What?" Eryn blinked, and then shook her head. "No, I did not," she said sheepishly. "And I am sure it cannot have been necessary!"

"So he basically did not break any orders," Malhora stated calmly, her focus still on the infant on her arm.

"Whose side are you on? I would have thought that having an Aren woman treated like this is not good for the frightening reputation you have managed to cultivate for so long," she growled.

"Ah yes, I see. So you are considering yourself an Aren woman after all?" Malhora chuckled unperturbed. "Or only now, for argument's sake?"

"Really? That is what we are focussing on right now?" the younger woman barked.

"I am all for anger when dealing with heavy blows - it shows strength and is not as pathetic as self-pity, Maltheá. But you are making the girl nervous."

And indeed, Téa started voicing sounds of complaint a moment later.

"Thank you so much for granting me a little anger when my companion runs off after another woman! I suppose I am expected to make a building collapse or something now?" Eryn jibed.

Malhora looked up at her with an indulgent expression. "That is twaddle. He has no desire for Malriel."

"What do *you* know about Enric and his desires? You saw them together only once at your estate," Eryn huffed and folded her arms angrily. "I would think a man rushing off to save a woman in distress although he already has a pretty distressed one at his side does make some thing clear."

"Young fool," Malhora chuckled. "You have nothing to fear from Malriel. Well, not when it comes to your companion. In all other respects I would say it pays to be careful around her. This is nothing more than your feeling bloated and awkward in your current state. Now sit down and eat something," she commanded and nodded at the bowl of fruit on the table. "It is not much for now, but you have not eaten anything in two days. Orrin will be back soon. It is his turn to cook tonight."

Eryn frowned at the absurd feel of this situation. Enric had left the city to probably either aid or avoid a war by helping Malriel out of prison, and this woman talked to her about who was supposed to be providing dinner?

She rubbed her face wearily. "I need a bath."

"First you need to eat. Then you can take your bath. And then we must talk."

"I don't have to listen to you, old woman," Eryn snapped. "It's the other way round, in fact. I am your Head of House now, and I don't need you to tell me what to do when!"

Malhora shot her a look of pity. "Head of House indeed," she sighed as if this conversation was a trial of her patience. "If you do not sit down and eat something right this moment, Orrin and I will hold you down and feed you by force. The child inside you needs nourishment!"

Eryn sat down again sullenly, dimly remembering a similar conversation many months ago with Orrin when she had pointed out to him that he was bound to follow her orders. Just like her grandmother right now, he had refused and instead made her do what he had wanted her to. Which had back then been cleaning herself up, having a meal and then telling her why she and his son had returned to his parlour covered in dust, wooden splinters and dead spiders after drawing up the plans for the healers' building.

It seemed her authority was no more formidable now than it had been then. Or maybe she needed to pick more readily impressionable underlings to command to start with.

* * *

Enric watched his travelling companion from the corner of his eye. They had been on the road for more than six hours now and Vran'el had limited his conversation only to exchanges about directions and accommodation on the road. He was clearly still angry about the one-sided dissolution of the commitment and with it the mind bond. And Enric's decision not to inform Eryn of that.

Enric decided that they didn't have to make this journey any more unpleasant than necessary. The lawyer had definitely had enough time to sulk.

"Vran, talk to me," he sighed. "Four days on the road is a long time as it stands. Ignoring me is not going to make this any easier on either of us."

"This is not supposed to make it any easier on you, Enric. And for myself, I feel content with my righteous indignation, thank you very much," the dark-haired magician replied stiffly.

"I know you don't approve of how I handled this, but I did what I thought best. There is no changing it now, so being angry at me makes no sense at all. Quite the opposite. If we want to handle this muddle properly, we need to work together, be a team, Vran."

"I hear you. But then our work starts only after our arrival, so I can make use of the time until then by demonstrating my disapproval," Vran'el retorted stubbornly and kept staring straight ahead.

Enric swallowed an acid remark and readjusted the headdress he had donned to protect himself from the relentless desert sun.

He was rocked by occasional stabs of anger received through the mind bond from Eryn, and now Vran'el's accusing silence added to the torment. All this while he was riding through endless flat stretches that were only occasionally interrupted by a few particularly hardy plants, braving the scorching daytime sun only to look forward to enduring the frosty nights which followed. Just fabulous.

* * *

Eryn stared down at the sheets spread across Malriel's desk. They had once been stacked neatly, but that was before Malhora had her memorising the most important business lines of House Aren, the names of all major families connected to it and the nature and history of the alliances with other Houses.

She had tried to impress on her grandmother that diving into this all too deeply was useless since she was only filling in for a few weeks, but as opposed to all other people around her, Malhora of House Aren was not one to varnish unpleasant truths to spare the poor, expectant woman.

She had simply pointed out that there was a realistic chance that neither Enric nor Malriel would return from Pirinkar meaning she might be stuck in her position for decades.

When Eryn called her a heartless old crone, Malhora pointed at the stack of papers without speaking and then returned to the study at regular intervals to bring food and water, watching Eryn eat up before she would leave again.

At least this was a helpful distraction from missing Enric while at the same time being angry at and disappointed in him. She wondered if this was Malhora's true intention behind swamping her with tasks that occupied her mind.

When the door next opened, Eryn sighed. "I am full, I can't eat another bite. Go away."

"There is a message for you," her grandmother said and placed a small metal message bird tube on the paper she was currently poring over. "From Anyueel."

Eryn groaned and picked up the small container. It had the royal crest embossed on the lid. The King only ever wrote to her to demand a report, scold her or deny her something.

Eryn wondered briefly whether he had yet been informed of Enric's departure for Pirinkar and about her new position, but then thought that either Orrin or Kilan must surely have written home to impart the news to him and Tyront.

435

Reading the neat handwriting, she swallowed. The monarch had indeed been informed of everything, and he was not happy about it. Uncharacteristically, his words did not seem so much dismayed as worried. That was unusual. She hadn't thought that this emotion really was to be found anywhere in his repertoire.

He urged her to be careful and not to falter in her search for the culprit who had threatened them, even with the strain of both her advanced pregnancy and the burden of taking over her mother's House.

Her eyes reached his last sentences. *Open your eyes to the dangers of hunger for power and status, the fury at having it taken away, even if you yourself have never been bothered by those weaknesses. Remember what we talked about during our dance before your departure!*

Her heart was beating faster. This was a warning, and not one of those he normally gave her, which were more or less threats to comply with whatever he wanted her to do. This was something else. He knew who was behind this! Or he at least thought he did. But then he had in the past proved to be not only uncommonly well-informed but also able to put the pieces together correctly.

She let the message sink in, trying to calm down enough to think back to the ball several months ago. It had been such a long evening, continuous dancing for hours... She had spent only a few minutes with him back then.

And now she was supposed to remember what he had said to her back then? Did he think that just because he was the King his words would have lodged in her memory any better? That statements delivered by the glorious sovereign could not fail to stick to her mind for eternity? He was precisely the right person to talk of status and hunger for power, she thought sullenly.

"What is the matter?" Malhora enquired.

Eryn studied her grandmother for a few moments, thinking. She had to be very careful who to put trust in, but the chances that this very woman might betray her were slim. She was a former Head of House Aren and had given up the position willingly instead of being pushed aside by her ambitious daughter. And she had not taken the chance to reassume power when Enric had offered it to her.

Malhora would therefore hardly be harbouring any resentment against Eryn for being in power now, however reluctantly. Rather, she would be interested in finding out whoever was bold enough to play dangerous games with House Aren. A proud, energetic woman who would not approve of letting others get away after trying to harm her family.

"And?" Malhora smiled knowingly, "Did I pass muster?"

Undoubtedly her mind was as sharp as her tongue. Characteristics Eryn respected.

"My King has told me to be careful. I strongly suspect he knows who is behind the recent attacks. I wish he would just tell me instead of posing me riddles," she sniffed and dropped the paper slip on the desk.

"He would be foolish to have done so. Birds tend to be intercepted at times, and if he openly accuses an important member of society or somebody connected with them, this would not be received well." She nodded at the message. "May I?"

"By all means."

Malhora's eyes wandered over the few lines. "I assume that asking you if you remember the conversation he is referring to is fruitless?"

Eryn nodded, her brows furrowing in frustration.

Her grandmother pursed her lips. "That is unfortunate. It is not like any of his other words might narrow down the number of suspects. Quite the opposite. Finding people addicted to power is not hard in this city. The challenge is rather finding those who are not," she remarked dryly.

They both turned when another knock came. Junar walked in, her daughter slung across her chest with a colourful length of cloth.

"Bird from home," the seamstress announced.

Eryn blinked. "What, another one? Two in one morning?"

She unscrewed the lid and shook out another rolled up message.

"It's from Erbál," she said. When she had finished reading, she jerked her head up and looked at her friend. "Junar, I would like you to leave and close the door behind you. There is something I need to discuss with Mal... Grandmother," she said, correcting herself.

The seamstress nodded once and then retreated. She was no stranger to being sent away when confidential matters had to be taken care of. Not with a companion in the Magic Council.

When Junar had left, Eryn tossed the paper on the desk next to the first one. "He writes almost exactly the same thing as the King! He knows, too! Why in the world have those two people across the sea managed to work this out while I am at a complete loss!" she cried out and wrung her hands. "What am I missing?"

"What exactly does young Erbál write?" Malhora enquired patiently.

"He is less formal than the King. He tells me to open my damned eyes and finally start drawing logical conclusions. That I have almost all the information I need to pin it down to the right person and take proper care of things. He tells me not to forget that a kind deed towards one person may be a stroke of bad luck for another."

"That last bit sounds like a platitude," Malhora mused.

"Is there anything I can do to work this mess out even without understanding these cryptic messages from home? As far as I know, Enric's investigations have not really led anywhere useful so far. It has been a matter of eliminating options from what I understand." Eryn sighed and stretched tiredly. "It is a pity I can't openly talk to Ram'an at the moment. We still need to keep up the appearance of being on bad terms with each other. I really would have valued discussing this with him."

"Yes, a bright lad, that one. Malriel chose well when she signed the companionship agreement with his House."

The younger woman flashed her grandmother a withering look. "You are aware that this agreement has caused us quite a lot of trouble, aren't you? I find your referring to it in such an upbeat way rather tasteless."

"Tasteless?" the old woman chuckled. "You have not yet experienced me in one of my tasteless moods, honestly. What I said is no more than a simple statement of a truth. Expressing my approval of the man to a degree where I grant him being worthy of an Aren woman is more or less the highest praise I can give."

Frowning, Eryn regarded the woman for a few moments, then sighed. "Very well then, I grant you your own rather twisted way of paying compliments. Though I have to warn you that sentences containing the words *Malriel* and *companionship agreement* tend to set my nerves on edge."

"Anything in connection with your mother puts you on edge," Malhora stated. "Which is a fairly natural reaction for an Aren woman. We do have a tendency not to get on well with our mothers."

"Isn't that rather regrettable? It should tell you something about the values in such a family."

"It is a price we pay for the strength we uphold. Our mothers are our most formidable opponents, the ones we learn from the most. And," she smiled crookedly, "we compensate for this lack of closely-knit mother-daughter connections by learning to get on really well with our grandmothers."

Eryn couldn't help but laugh. "Then I am a model Aren woman, after all?"

"You are headstrong, demanding and do not take defeat well. I do not see that there was ever any doubt about your being as Aren as can be. Though you have gone further than most would by renouncing your own House to get out of your mother's grip. I am not too pleased about that, but Malriel risked more than she should have by accusing you. And then we got Enric instead, which was not exactly a bad deal."

Eryn put a hand on her belly and frowned. "How do we tend to get on with our sons in general? Equally problematic?"

"No, not normally. You surely know what they say about there being a special bond between mothers and sons. Sons of Aren women tend to rebel against their fathers, as they normally present the weaker target."

Eryn grimaced at that. Somehow the image of Enric being the weaker target did not fit, not at all.

CHAPTER 34

Travelling

Enric wiped his face with the cloth around his neck to get rid of the sand that seemed to find its way relentlessly into every gap. The heat was oppressive and his thoughts kept circulating around images of him taking a cold bath. Pure decadence in the middle of the desert and one he would refrain from putting words to when they reached their designated overnight location.

The quality of the light had started changing a little while before; the day was slowly nearing its end.

He cast a glance at Vran'el who seemed content enough on his horse, seemingly unperturbed by the scorching heat. Enric wondered why he was surprised at that. The lawyer was a native, after all, and this was certainly not his first time out in the desert.

Yet in the city he always looked like a work of art, something Vern might have created with his brushes and pens: every detail of his appearance impeccable, never a strand of hair out of place, his skin always flawless as if impervious to everyday things such as grime and sweat.

Enric suspected that he needed to spend a lot of time to achieve this visual perfection, but now wondered about that supposition. For sure, Vran'el no longer looked like the rich lawyer and heir he was, but neither did he appear ruffled, clammy from sweat or in any other way bothered by their less than comfortable way of travelling through the desert on horseback.

He just seemed to have adapted his city persona of quiet luxury to one more suited to his current surroundings. Less perfectly styled, but still a long way from appearing slouchy.

They had not spoken much in the last few hours and Enric had begun to worry that his travel companion would indeed continue to give him the cold shoulder for the rest of the journey. In surroundings as harsh as these a friendly word every now and then would have been at least some small comfort.

Vran'el stopped his mount and indicated the horizon at what looked like a number of pointed objects rising into the air.

"There. This is our destination for today. This tribe has agreed to shelter us for tonight upon Golir's request," he explained. "They are generally not happy about being asked for favours of this sort; their opinion of us city dwellers is not the most favourable one. They think we are feeble and have strayed from the path of our ancestors. Their worries are not about matters of state or anything of that sort, only about surviving out here, braving sand storms and reaching the next source of water in time. They prefer to be left in peace and do not want to be involved too much with the likes of us. This is just a warning not to expect very much enthusiasm from them. They will let us spend the night with them, sustain us, but they will not be at all unhappy to see us leave again tomorrow morning. Try not to be offended at that."

"I won't," Enric promised. "Anything I need to be careful about?"

"A thing or two. Do not look at their women too openly. It does not, like in the city, indicate polite interest but will be considered rude and imply that you are taking liberties because you wish to consort with them. They do not consider women equal out here - they are mostly relegated to looking after the children and taking care of indoor duties. They find the system we have in the city where a daughter secures the power to a House execrable. So do try to avoid mentioning that you have left your companion in charge of House Aren. As for the rest, just follow my lead. Do what I do, do not offer information voluntarily but only when asked."

Enric nodded slowly, wondering how people in the same country could differ so much in their lifestyles and values. They were only a day's ride from the city, after all. Yet it was like encountering a completely different culture.

Well, at least it would be a good exercise in adapting his behaviour. He would doubtlessly have to do just that when they reached their destination in Pirinkar.

They each took a long draught from their water pouches before setting in motion again. It was hard to judge distances in this monotony of sand with occasional patches of bleached and half-withered plants that braved the severe climate. It would probably take them another hour or two to reach the tents.

Enric healed away the pain in his lower back and set off again, looking forward to getting off the horse, eating something and retiring early.

He hoped he would have a chance to have a look at the little book Ram'an had sent them before their departure from Takhan.

*   *   *

Eryn stared at the draft contract before her, wondering how she was supposed to decide whether the conditions it contained were advantageous for House Aren or not.

Was ten percent of their revenue too much to give away for access to the distribution network for fruit? How much did the other Houses pay for that? Did it matter which kind of fruit it was?

She gave a weary sigh and leaned back in her chair. She would have to ask Malhora about that. Once again.

The knock at the door was a welcome distraction and she smiled when Vern came in, balancing a plate with fruit on his outspread palm.

"Hey there. Your grandmother says you are to eat this. She will be checking," he grinned and placed the food in front of her.

She chuckled and with two fingers picked up a yellow piece to pop it into her mouth. "I was wondering when the next load was due. Somehow I feel I spend the entire day consuming what she stuffs into me."

Vern shrugged. "She worries about you and wants to take good care of you."

"I know. Otherwise I wouldn't indulge that woman and her authoritative style." She looked at the paper in Vern's hand. "What do you have here? Another masterpiece I need to snatch away before those greedy healers start bidding horrendous prices for it?"

"You are one of those greedy healers," he reminded her good-naturedly and lifted the sheet for her to look at.

She saw it and drew in a sharp breath. It was a sketch of a man's face – one she recognised without a problem. He was the one who had attempted to dance the seduction dance with her at Intrea's gathering. They had given up trying to find him as only Vran'el, Ram'an and she had laid eyes on him. With her brother gone and herself and Ram'an both in charge of a House there was little hope for them to catch him by any means. Or so she had been thinking.

"How is this possible?" she gasped and stared at the picture.

The boy took a seat unbidden and smiled grimly. "Ram'an visited me at the academy today in the morning. He said he wanted to try something. Then he described the man's face as well as he could remember and asked me to draw it. It took us a good while and quite a number of failed attempts, but after countless corrections he was satisfied. And judging from your reaction just now the likeness is rather good."

She nodded slowly. "It is, really. So what does he want to do now? Display it everywhere and ask if there is somebody who has seen this man?"

"That's the plan, yes. He said to let you have a look at it first and perhaps make corrections if you remember anything different about the face. Then I am to sketch another one with shorter hair and one or two different beards in case he has changed his appearance in an attempt to remain incognito. Then Ram'an wants to show copies of the portrait to people who tend to be in contact with magicians a lot around here and see if they remember the face."

Eryn rubbed her face and sighed. "But there are at least four hundred magicians in the city! And I am only counting those resident here, not visitors."

Vern nodded. "True. But you can exclude the women and all men above and below a certain age. Ram'an says we are looking for a man in his thirties about his height but a little more heavily built than him. I would think that this should narrow it down considerably."

She nodded reluctantly. That did sound plausible, but was probably a lot more complicated than that. The man would surely try to remain hidden. If he found out that people were looking for him he might even leave the city to avoid capture. With him gone the chance to trace who was behind all this would be gone, too.

He smiled reassuringly at her doubtful expression. "Don't worry. I have a hunch that Ram'an knows what he is doing." Then he nodded at the picture in front of her. "So? Is there anything you want to change or can I make the variations and copies he needs?"

"No, that looks right to me. Go and do your thing." She handed the drawing back to him. "You really are a useful person to have around, my friend," she smiled appreciatively. "Could you send Malhora in when you see her? I need some help here."

Vern nodded. "Sure, no problem. She said something about bathing Téa, so I suppose you may have to wait a while." He thought for a moment, then added, "I like how she handles my sister. It makes her less fearsome."

*　*　*

Enric stretched out on the mat he had brought with him and unrolled on the carpeted floor of the small tent he and Vran'el had been allotted.

As Vran'el had expected, the welcome had not been a particularly warm one. They had been greeted, fed then all but shoved into their tent. Which was maybe not the warmest way of being treated, but it suited them both just fine, as retiring without having to make too much polite conversation was certainly less exhausting than watching their every word to avoid inadvertently insulting their hosts.

Enric pulled out the dark brown book Ram'an had given them. It was a diary he'd kept of his own journey up north more than five years ago. He had been permitted to accompany Golir, his uncle, when he had ventured up there on one of the few trips to discuss trade.

He opened it at the first page. It started with Ram'an's first impressions.

"He writes that they are obsessed with titles," Enric murmured.

"Are they now?" Vran'el smirked. "It should not be too hard for you to fit in, then, eh, My Lord?"

"I am afraid theirs exceeds even what my country views necessary in this regard. They insist on being addressed with their full name and title on every occasion. And from what I see here this may be a matter of memorising rather a lot in the case of some people. They use academic titles for everyday address, and then there is another one signifying one's standing in the family, then finally they add their professional function."

He pointed to a note in capital letters, twice underlined. It warned never to address anybody with a shortened version of the name they were introduced with without being explicitly invited to do so.

The lawyer winced. "This means we have to memorise all this information from every single person that is introduced to us?"

"It would seem so, yes," Enric confirmed and turned a few pages until he found what he had hoped would be there. "Here is an outline of the general system and the most important titles they use. They have three different academic titles, each signifying different levels of achievement. *Lam* is the most common one they grant after finishing studies of a discipline. Then there is *Etor*, which signifies high academic honours and finally *Gistor* which one may use only when achieving extraordinary accomplishments in one's field of expertise."

"Lam, Etor and Gistor," Vran'el repeated with closed eyes to memorise the titles. "Alright. I suppose my studies of the law for half a decade would qualify me to hold the title *Lam*. How about you? Will you stick with Lord?"

"I think I will, yes. I am not sure if they would consider my training programme a sufficient qualification for an academic title. It was a mix of several disciplines, fighting being among them. Lord will do fine for me." He looked back at the book. "So, next come the family titles. There is *Holm*, which is the one in charge of the family. Like a Head of House, I would assume. The second-most important one is *Reig*. That's the heir to the position of Holm. Most likely the oldest daughter or son. *Legen* is a child with no claim to leading the family unless there are special circumstances."

"Like the original heir dying under inexplicable circumstances?" Vran'el snorted.

"Probably." Enric looked up. "In your case that is fairly easy - you are clearly an heir to the leading position, thus a Reig. But for me... I was a Holm when I left, but am so no more. I am not sure if calling myself an heir to a position I have passed on to my companion is accurate."

"I dare say the point is less about accuracy than conveying one's importance. A Holm you are clearly not at the moment, as you are not in charge. Reig should do you fine. You still are Malriel's heir as soon as she is back in charge, after all. What did you say was the third thing they add to their names?"

"The profession."

Vran'el nodded. "That will be quite a mouthful in your case: Second in command of the Order of Magicians and senator in Takhan. I will make do with lawyer and senator."

Enric pursed his lips. "We were warned not to remind people of our magical abilities if we can avoid it. They distrust magic. So referring to the *Order of Magicians* might not be such a great idea, especially if they address me with the full collection of titles every time."

"Just the Order, then."

"Yes, I think that's for the best." The blond magician leaned back and closed the notebook. "So, that would make you Lam Vran'el, Reig of House Vel'kim, lawyer and senator in Takhan. And I would be Lord Enric, Reig of House Aren, second in command of the Order and senator in Takhan. Those are quite a mouthful. Modesty in communicating one's importance is clearly no virtue there but rather a sure way of being ignored."

"So it seems," Vran'el grimaced.

"Tell me about this place Pirinkar. I assume you have some general knowledge about it, even though the contact between the countries does not exactly appear to be a very close one."

The lawyer nodded. "Yes, there is a bit I can tell you. Though mostly superficial things, I am afraid."

"That's fine. Whatever information you can give me is more than I have right now."

Vran'el then told him about a country that was even more different from the Western Territories than the Old Kingdom.

They were on their way to a place where magic had little place in everyday life; it was a discipline limited to those pursuing religion, something that was practised to serve invisible deities, tolerated but only to a limited degree. And only in a certain few places, namely temples erected for that purpose.

This did not mean that there were no powerful wielders of magic in the city. Those rising to the top of the priest caste, as it was called, had considerable influence on a human, personal level as they were more or less in charge of people's relationships to the gods. And, what was doubtlessly also a major point in their favour was that they provided magical healing.

He had given this quite some thought to and discussed with Vran'el how they were to present themselves and behave in an environment where magic was looked upon as taint instead of something to be admired, nurtured and developed, as it was in their own countries. Also, those few who had managed to rise despite the disadvantage would hardly look kindly upon strangers from other lands with equal influence and strength.

Magic was the topic of contradictions in this place. On the one hand the priests were more influential if their magic was stronger, yet magicians were in general discouraged from procreating in order to limit the spread of their *defect*.

The discouragement seemed to be done by the politicians, though, as they probably feared losing their influence to the priests if there were too many of the latter. They also promoted progress of whatever kind, particularly in those fields where the priests were most influential.

Enric began to wonder - not for the first time - whether sending a magician to this place had not been a rather rash thing to do. Probably no more rash than sending two more to aid the first one would be.

Pirinkar society was characterised by a strong focus on technology of all kinds, as this was meant to reduce the dependence on magic. Vran'el told him that they delighted in inventing and developing machines, devices and appliances of all varieties, and had become very accomplished at it.

And as was to be expected, the priests were as averse to being replaced by technology as the non-magicians were to having to depend on magic. An everlasting dispute that bubbled under the surface.

Vran'el went on to explain that contact with Pirinkar had in these last two hundred years not exactly been close. The differences in values had been too huge to be overcome easily, yet not dangerous enough to trigger any major conflict.

The non-magicians had of course not been eager to mingle within a society where magic was acknowledged as a justification to political power. And there was always the danger that the priests could learn more than was advisable. It might have given them *ideas*.

The priests themselves had lacked the political influence to challenge this point of view successfully and had in time been led to envy and resent their magician colleagues from afar, instead of seeking contact with them.

There had been occasional diplomatic exchanges. When Ram'an was there, he had decided to keep his magical abilities under cover.

There was no permanent ambassador stationed in Kar - there just wouldn't have been enough work for one.

The climate was closer to what Enric was used to from Anyueel, though a little more sultry. The mountains, which were the natural border between Pirinkar and the Western Territories, prevented moist air from passing and hence clouds from forming over the desert. Which meant the clouds relinquished their loads of moisture and turned the southern part of the country into a lush, diverse jungle that became less dense and gave way to wide meadows and occasional woodlands the further north they travelled.

"I wish we'd had more time to prepare before coming here. I fancy I could have learned a thing or two from Ram'an about the social customs here," Enric muttered.

Vran'el shrugged. "I do not worry about that in your case. You managed well enough when you first came to Takhan. You had no clue about how to behave in our country then, either, yet you managed beautifully. You impressed us so much, in fact, that we even made you one of us," he smiled.

The blond magician grinned. Despite threatening to demonstrate his disapproval for the entirety of their journey, Vran'el had not followed through on the promise. To Enric's great relief he just wasn't the resentful type. Scorning a man he actually liked a lot, and who in addition was his only travel companion through what was fairly much unknown territory, did not come naturally to him. And would not have been too wise, either.

"Well, if you put it like that... And it's not as if we don't have experience in getting an Aren woman out of legal difficulties in a foreign country. We did it once, we will manage again."

The lawyer sighed. "I very much hope so. Unfortunately I am not on familiar ground there nor have any resources at my disposal such as libraries or amiable colleagues to ask for advice. I only have some rudimentary ideas about their current laws. If any of them is as accomplished in their ancient laws as Ram'an is with ours back home, thwarting any tricks of the kind he tried to use to bind Eryn to his House will be nigh impossible."

Enric nodded grimly. "Then let's hope that we can prove Malriel's innocence quickly and without getting tangled up in their legal procedures and laws too much. If Malhora is right and she really was tricked this can be resolved easily enough, I hope."

"That would certainly be preferable, yes."

Another thought occurred to Enric. "Do we know what their attitude towards your sexual orientation is?"

"No, we do not. But until we do I will keep this little preference to myself. We would not want it to cause us trouble in case they are as narrow-minded as..." He stopped, looking the other way as if he had just spotted an interesting detail on the tent wall.

"As my people?" Enric finished the sentence good-naturedly.

"I am sorry. I did not mean to insult you," Vran'el sighed.

"You didn't. I agree with you. I am in favour of a change of awareness back home as well and will actively promote it once I am back."

"I know. Yet it is a difference if *you* criticise your own country or if a foreigner who has never even been there does it," the lawyer sighed.

"Probably. But as long as it's only me hearing it you needn't worry, my friend. Guarding your every word in my presence is not necessary. Though we might want to be careful what is said without a soundproof barrier as long as we are in Kar," Enric warned.

"A sensible precaution, yes."

Neither of them spoke for some long moments before Vran'el asked carefully, "About Eryn... do you, you know, receive anything from her? Can you tell how she is doing?"

Enric nodded. This was the first time they had broached that topic. "There is anticipation and tension and has been all day long. She is preoccupied. I have asked Malhora to keep her busy and distract her from... you know."

He paused for a moment, wondering if he should mention the rest. But then he had just told the man that he didn't have to watch his words in his presence. This had to apply in both directions, or there could not be trust between them.

"Now at night she has time to lie down and there are no more distractions. I sense how she worries. Her pain. She feels lost, abandoned. And she is angry at me."

Vran'el simply nodded without commenting. Enric couldn't help feeling that Vran'el was very carefully refraining from pointing out that the last bit was certainly more than justified.

CHAPTER 35

A Lead

Kilan entered the study after Eryn had called him in.

She sighed wearily. "Hello."

The ambassador chuckled. "This is not a very enthusiastic reaction when you behold me."

"That's because you only ever come to me to pass on reprimands from Tyront and the King, or their demands to have me despatch reports," she grimaced.

"Believe me, I would much rather meet you in a teahouse for a pleasant conversation that does not involve mentioning either of them, but then you are aware that they both want to hear from you regularly. And ignore it at your own peril. As long as you don't change that, you will have to endure my delivering their messages," he shrugged without compassion.

"They are aware that I am busy, of course? I mean, House Aren doesn't run itself."

"Unfortunately for you, Eryn, they are both aware that you seemingly have enough time to write regularly to Vyril, Plia and Pe'tala, but not to them. I see why that might give them the impression that your personal friendships are a lot higher on your list of priorities than their business."

She nodded slowly and regarded him thoughtfully. "You write to both of them regularly, then?"

He raised an eyebrow. "I do, yes. In contrast to you I try to avoid having my position taken away from me."

She opened a drawer and took out her seal. "Here. From now on you will take care of that tiresome duty for me. This is an official order from a superior magician. Ah yes, and you will of course avoid mentioning our little arrangement to the delighted recipients of your letters."

Kilan stared at the seal in front of him, then back at her. "You are being serious, aren't you? You really are delegating this to *me*! Why?" He shook his head in annoyance. "Why not to Orrin? You are his superior, too!"

"Because he wouldn't do it. He would just laugh at me," she admitted. "I am still in the process of making him understand that I am authorised to command him. Unfortunately, he is immensely resistant to internalising that."

"What is to keep me from doing just the same?" he enquired carefully.

"What you have mentioned before: That you want to hang on to your position, *Ambassador*. Do try to remember what happened to the last ambassador who got on the wrong side of me, will you?"

Kilan gave a troubled sigh. "And what about the difference in our handwriting? Am I to attempt and copy yours?"

"That will not be necessary. Just have somebody else do the actual writing. It will look like I dictated the letters to an assistant or the like. Don't be too reverential, though. It wouldn't look like me. And remember to address Tyront without his title. We wouldn't want little giveaways such as that spoiling everything, would we?" she grinned broadly, feeling a lot more cheerful than only a few minutes before.

"Oh dear, no," Kilan grunted. "We would not want *that*."

* * *

Eryn lay in the dark, staring at the ceiling in her bedroom.

Her days were so occupied she hardly had a free minute. Malhora was relentless in that respect. Yet she would have been lost without the woman.

They had invited two members of House Partém over today in order to work on the draft contract for fruit distribution she was pondering over the other day. Malhora had just cast a quick look over it and snorted derisively. Then she had taken a pen, struck out a few paragraphs and added a few lines here and there.

She had warned her granddaughter that they were trying to see how far they could push with an inexperienced temporary Head. Malhora had offered her to remain with her during the talks provided she didn't fear appearing weak on account of asking for reinforcement. Eryn had accepted gladly; she was convinced that letting herself be taken advantage of would convey an impression of weakness rather more convincingly than having her grandmother at her side.

Judging from their visitors' reaction upon entering the study, facing two Aren women in negotiations did not come as a pleasant surprise.

449

She smiled at the memory. And wondered if they would have preferred to face Enric.

There she was again. Her thoughts kept returning to him, no matter how determined she was to think of something else.

She thought back to the meal Junar had cooked today. Again, she ended up asking herself if Enric would have liked it.

Her gaze wandered to the window through which she could see the moonlit garden. And the tree under which she had sat with Enric. Damn this!

He was everywhere, in every place they had been together, every dish she ate, every odour or sound around her. In every kick their son in her womb dealt her.

It was fairly easy to keep her conflicted feelings at bay during the day when so much had to be taken care of. But at night... It was as if all the thoughts she had pushed aside, wrestled into submission to get out of her way returned now there was no more diversion, as if taking revenge on having been ignored, by reappearing with more insistence.

She had hinted to Malhora that she would like a little help with falling asleep, but the old woman had just barked one single word at her: nonsense.

So much for that, then. Vern had explained to her that sending an unborn child to sleep with magic was frowned upon as it was simply too dangerous. There was the matter of getting the measure of force right, for one. An impulse too strong might cause damage.

And there was the danger of the mother getting used to the practice of simply silencing the child like that whenever it caused a restless night or other troubles. A child spending too much time asleep in the womb would not develop its mental capacities the way it ought. External influences, however attenuated they were, helped along that development greatly. Voices and other sounds such as music caused first associations and even enabled the baby to recognise familiar tunes and people after the birth.

As sending the mother to sleep with magic was not possible without the child being affected as well, she had resigned herself to enduring the nights. And their unpleasant restlessness.

She looked concerned when she heard steps in the corridor moving in her direction. The pace sounded urgent. A moment later came a careful knock.

Eryn opened the door a moment later, looking at Orrin who was clearly surprised at her quick reaction.

"You don't look as though I just woke you. Still problems falling asleep?"

"Yes. What's the matter?"

A fierce smile played around the warrior's lips, his eyes hard. "They have found that man who asked you to dance the seduction dance. He is currently being held at the Arbil residence. Ram'an is questioning him as we speak."

She felt how a shiver of delighted anticipation ran through her. Finally!

"I'll be ready in a moment."

She was about to turn back to get dressed, but Orrin's hand reached out for her arm.

"Ready for what? You are surely not going over there! I will go instead. I was simply informing you since you are the Head of House and my superior. Now go back to bed and try to sleep. I will report to you tomorrow."

Eryn stared at him, wondering if he had received a blow to the head or something.

"You really think that I will let you go there where a man is being kept, someone who might be involved in endangering your own son, and stay here myself so I can go to bed?" she asked slowly and inclined her head in incredulity. "I will go to the Arbil residence *myself* and *you* will go back to bed."

He blinked, then folded his arms. "No."

"Orrin! This is me giving you a direct order! And even if you wanted, you couldn't keep me from going. I am stronger than you, if you remember."

"And this," he pointed at himself with his thumb, "is me refusing your order. I will go there, you can depend on it."

They stared at each other silently for several seconds, before the warrior relented. "Alright, I'll let you come."

"No," she corrected him with an icy smile, "I'll let *you* come. And if I see you using an inadequate level of force, I will take you out."

He narrowed his eyes. "What is an inadequate level of force in your opinion, if I may ask?"

"You will realise it in that last waking moment when I raise my palm, just before you collapse." With this she turned and closed the door in his face to get dressed.

*   *   *

Ram'an opened the door and stepped aside for them both to enter. He didn't bother with offering them the customary damp towel. The temperatures at night caused people to feel chilled rather than sweaty.

"Where is he?" Orrin barked without a greeting.

Eryn gave him a warning look, then turned to Ram'an and let him take her hands and kiss her on the forehead.

"We will have to keep Orrin under control," the Head of House Arbil stated calmly. "Using force against a detainee is frowned upon here and will not aid us in presenting the matter to the Senate, no matter whether he was involved or not."

"How did you track him down?" Eryn asked eagerly while they were ascending the stairs to the main room.

"I had several copies of Vern's sketches made. I was afraid that he would leave the city if he learned of our efforts, so I wanted to have this taken care of within a very short time. An hour maybe, the shorter the better. I sent out fifty people to go to certain... well, let us just say *less respectable* locations as well as a few other socially accepted ones to make enquiries."

Eryn smiled. That had been smart. She herself had also been worried about giving the man a premature warning. Ram'an had taken care of it all very effectively. She would make sure to cover the expenses that hiring such a great number of people surely meant. House Arbil could not be expected to pay for that, especially in their current predicament.

Ram'an preceded them to his study and entered first. Two men stood in the centre of the room, between them on a chair was perched the man who had approached her at the dance. The one they had almost given up finding before Ram'an's idea of having Vern draw the face proved a success.

Eryn recognised one of the two guards as Ram'an's younger brother. He smiled faintly and nodded to her. They had never been formally introduced but of course he was aware who she was. She resembled Mariel too much to be mistaken for anybody else.

"What have you found out so far?" she asked Ram'an without taking her eyes off the suspect.

"Two things. He was hired by somebody from the Houses. And the idea was to punish you personally by harming what is dear to you."

Her eyes widened. Her *personally*? Not House Aren?

"Why?"

"I have not yet found that out. But I seriously doubt that he is aware of it. He is no more than a... let us call him a provider of services, someone people prefer not to be associated with, shall we?"

She stared down at the man in dismay. He looked back at her, a slight smugness showing in the angle of his jaw, she couldn't help but notice. He had grown a beard since they had last met. Good thing Ram'an had thought of that.

"So we don't know which House hired him?" she growled.

"I do not think it was a House as such, simply a member of one," Ram'an explained.

"So he caused the fire at the Aren residence? Or rather the poisonous fumes?"

"He did, yes. He also tried to incriminate my House of the act."

"You almost killed my son," Orrin said, surprisingly calmly. "You should be glad of your guards here. If it were just you and me in here, I would make you pay for what you did, the lives you risked. Dearly."

That finally seemed to cause their captive some discomfort. Orrin was known throughout the city, after all.

Eryn stepped towards the seated man and snatched his wrist, letting magic flow into him.

"What do you know about your..." What was somebody called who hired people like him? Customer? Principal? Employer? Contractee? "...client?" she decided.

She watched the truth block do its work when he reluctantly shared what information he had.

"Not much. Anonymity is a way of avoiding unnecessary trouble. For both parties."

Damn! So he really didn't know. That was a big hurdle to their investigation.

"Can you describe your client?" she then tried.

"Not really. We always made sure to meet in darkened locations in different parts of the city."

"Did you meet with a man or a woman?"

"A man."

"Can you tell how old he was?"

"Older. Forties, fifties. Something like that."

Eryn wondered if this was even a useful piece of information. Many magicians here knew how to change their outward appearance when it came to age.

"What did his voice sound like?"

"I do not know. We always whispered."

"Do you have any suspicion which House he might be from?"

"No."

She thought of what else she might ask him. There had to be something he knew that would help them. Unfortunately, he would hardly be likely to volunteer any information, not even the truth block could force him.

"What exactly did your client commission you to do?" Orrin asked next to her. He had his arms folded. His hands were balled into fists as if he found it a genuine trial not reaching out and doing something unpleasant to the culprit.

"To cause her pain."

"Why?" Ram'an now asked.

"Revenge," the man shrugged.

"For what?" Eryn demanded, leaning forward in keen anticipation.

"I do not know. I think it was about something you took away from him to bestow on somebody else."

Her breath hitched when a certain line from a message from Anyueel came to her mind. One kind deed to one person might be a stroke of bad luck from another, Erbál had written.

She closed her eyes. And the King had warned her about the dangers of hunger for power and status. There was one man to whom both applied. She had taken away his status to have it granted to another man instead.

How could she have been so very short-sighted and stupid?

"May I have a word with the two of you?" she said with considerably more calm than she felt, nodding to Ram'an and Orrin. "Outside?"

Both exchanged a glance with each other and followed her out into the corridor and then into the main room.

"I can't believe how blind I have been," she murmured and shook her head at herself. "I should be publicly flogged. Good thing stupidity is not against the law," she added bitterly.

"Talk!" Orrin barked, his gaze intent. "You know who paid him, don't you? Out with it!"

Ram'an, too, was looking tense and waited for her to share her insight with them.

"I have no proof. It is just a suspicion," she warned, somehow feeling awkward accusing somebody without any evidence as such.

"Don't make me shake it out of you!" the warrior rasped, his tested patience wearing even thinner.

"A man I took something away from. Somebody who happens to reside in this city, who returned here only a few weeks after we came to Takhan."

Ram'an's eyes widened when he realised who she was hinting at. "Sanaf of House Finran! You think this is his doing because he lost his position as ambassador!"

Orrin blinked, then frowned in incomprehension. "All that for a job he has lost?"

The Head of House Arbil breathed slowly. "Not just any job, Orrin. It had been his only chance at distinguishing himself. He was never a particularly bright, strong or diligent man. He was given tasks that did not require any particular skill in his House, nor was he ever much respected or important before. Then, as luck would have it, he was the only available member of the suitable House to be sent to Anyueel, and all of a sudden he had everything. Until Eryn made sure his incompetence had consequences."

Eryn closed her eyes when suddenly the conversation at the ball the King had referred to in his message came back to her. He had warned her to keep an eye on Sanaf and she had replied that they would hardly be moving in the same circles. Careless, he had termed her. He should have called her an idiot instead. Maybe the warning would have stayed with her if it had been wrapped in a proper insult.

"But," Orrin ventured, clearly not managing to fit Sanaf to the image of the villain they were looking for, "that man was a complete dolt. How would he have come up with a thing like that? I mean, that man doesn't even manage to get through a dinner evening without making clumsy insults. I don't see him plotting some evil deeds that require anything more outlandish than throwing a stone through a window."

Ram'an smiled without humour. "What makes you think that he has to be the one doing the thinking? There are more nimble brains than his available for hire for such tasks. And we happen to have one of them detained in my study right now."

"But his House is allied with Aren, isn't it? He surely was aware that there would be consequences for his House if this were ever found out," Orrin argued.

"Overconfidence at never being found out and a desire to see Eryn suffer for costing him the only chance of distinguishing himself in the world may have been stronger than considering the consequences for his House. Or he simply did not care." Ram'an leaned forward and looked at Eryn. "Whether he truly was behind it or not, we cannot afford to ignore the possibility. Act, Head of House Aren! And soon, too!"

She nodded and raked her fingers through her hair, making a ruffle of the ponytail hanging down her back. "But how? What can I do without endangering the alliance with House Finran if Sanaf turns out to be innocent? Legara is not a great fan of mine as it is! Nor did Enric endear himself to her exactly when he ignored her warning and voted in favour of the new academy for the artists. What would you do in my place?"

"It is a good thing you are considering the implications your actions might have on the alliances between the Houses. One option would be to seek a private appointment with Legara and talk to her about your suspicion," Ram'an suggested.

Eryn nodded. "Alright, that sounds sensible. Will she see reason?"

Ram'an immediately shook his head. "No, I am sure she will not," he stated with utter confidence. "Accusing a member of her House will be like a personal insult to her. She has always had a tendency towards ignoring wrongdoing when it comes to people associated with her. Turning a blind eye to their misdeeds is so much easier than making them answer for them."

"Why are you even suggesting it, then?" Eryn hissed. "Do you have any other, more workable ideas or are you just after driving me into paralysis?"

"I am helping you see your options here. You are the one to ultimately decide which course to take. One way forward is dealing with this in private, but as I told you, I do not expect Legara to react sensibly to this. The other option might be to inform the Senate of your suspicion and ask them to summon Sanaf before them to subject him to a lie filter and question him."

"The Senate would agree to that?"

"If enough senators are in favour of it, they would." He smiled thinly. "And I do not think that accomplishing such a thing would be too hard. Houses Vel'kim and Arbil will be on your side, and we will make sure our allies vote in favour of interrogation as well. That would be Houses Turbar, Ordel and Ulverd from my side and Feral and Tokmar that will almost certainly vote with Valrad. Partém is allied with both of our Houses, so you can count them in as well. With Aren we have seven Houses out of twelve. Unless the triarchs all vote against it - which is rather unlikely as Abrak is friends with your mother and Golir and Torke'na are both solid thinkers - this should not be a problem."

Eryn exhaled slowly. "Alright, a public accusation it is, then. What if it turns out that Sanaf is, against all our expectations, not to blame for the acts?"

Ram'an shrugged. "Then you will need to apologise to him and Legara, of course."

The Head of House Aren rolled her eyes and scowled. "Of course."

She hoped the imbecile could be proven guilty. Apologising to him would be a real test of her standards. And put her acting skills up for examination.

"The King and Erbál have sent me messages hinting at him. They are aware of the offender, I have no doubt about it. Why did those two idiots in Anyueel only write so late? Why didn't they share their great insights with Enric sooner?" Eryn questioned.

Orrin shrugged. "The question is how long they themselves have been aware of it. Maybe they reached their conclusion only a short while before. Or they trusted Enric to find out about this in time and did not want to anger him by implying that he wasn't able to handle this unassisted. Only now that Enric left here without having the matter resolved might they have realised that they had to warn you."

"So they could have avoided helping us to spare Enric's pride?" She ground her teeth in exasperation, then continued more thoughtfully, "I can't help feeling that this solution is too simple. If Sanaf really is the one behind it all, why did Enric never reach such an obvious conclusion? He is a master strategist, after all."

Ram'an leaped to his defence. "That he may be. Yet we must also allow him to be only human. None of us previously considered the chance that you might be the target. We were sure that the target had to be either House Aren or the alliance between Aren and Arbil. And leading House Aren was clearly more of a challenge than he had anticipated. Then there were two expectant women he had to protect, his new position as senator to grow into and probably most significantly he had a withdrawn and sorrowful companion on his hands to worry about." Ram'an raised his brow. "I would like to think we can forgive the master strategist one lapse. It is not as if anybody else made that connection before, is it?"

* * *

"Eryn, I am worried about you," Junar announced. She sounded as if she had needed to put all her courage together for this statement.

Eryn looked up from Valrad's message, which had arrived only a few minutes before. Junar was not the only one who was feeling that way.

Her father had been trying to make it seem like a casual enquiry about her general state of mind and body, but the concern behind his words was evident.

She sighed and decided to make herself appear as calm and relaxed as possible when she would meet him later when the Senate convened. He was currently worrying over all three of his children. Pe'tala was too far away for his liking, Vran'el was travelling into what might turn out to be enemy lands and she herself was rounded with child and had been left to fend for herself by her companion. In addition she was burdened with leading a House.

She returned to the here-and-now. "I am sorry to hear that. Would you like to sit?"

Junar sighed and gave her a pained look. "You are using your Head-of-House tone on me. Don't!"

Eryn raised both eyebrows. Was she? She wasn't even aware that she had such a tone. It seemed she had needed no more than a few days to adapt to her temporary position.

"Forgive me. I didn't intend to use any particular tone with you."

The seamstress looked exasperated. "You are doing it again. It is this quiet resignation for dealing with whatever vexatious affair you need to listen to, this faux patience. It is just not you!"

"And this is what you have come to tell me? This is what is troubling you?" Eryn enquired, wondering if she should throw in a little tantrum just to ease her friend's mind and disperse her concerns about what she deemed *faux patience*.

"No," Junar frowned and remained standing. "I came to tell you that you are overdoing it. Since you took over the House you have sat here for around ten hours each day without lying down, without sitting out in the garden or at least relaxing a little. We have to all but force you to take meals with us before you return here. You can't go on like this, Eryn. This is neither good for you, nor for your baby. You need to be more considerate about both of you."

"I appreciate your concern, Junar. I really do. Honestly, I am fine. And so is my son; I check on him every day. The thing is that there is something I really need to take care of today and I am confident that in a short time things are going to be less tense around here."

"This has something to do with the Senate meeting today, doesn't it? People are whispering, but nobody knows any particulars. They say you are about to accuse somebody today. Is this true? You know who is behind all this?" Junar searched her eyes.

"I have a suspicion, but I have no concrete proof for now. So please don't push me. The meeting today is public, so you can come to the Senate hall to satisfy your curiosity."

The seamstress nodded grimly and folded her arms. "I will. Depend on it."

* * *

Malhora released her granddaughter's arm when they arrived at the foot of the stairs in front of the Senate hall.

"You must be seen to be walking in without assistance."

A wisp of a smile played around Eryn's lips when she replied, "Never showing any weakness, eh?"

"That is it."

Both women set in motion and climbed the steep stairs to enter the Senate hall through the wide open double doors. Eryn lifted her chin when she entered, meeting Legara's hostile stare full on.

"Do not look away," Malhora whispered at her side. "Wait until *she* does." Then she nodded with apparent satisfaction when Legara turned away after almost a minute. "Good. Never underestimate the power of a good stare. You will not be able to outstare me for a while yet, but I see that there is definite potential there."

"I had no intention of trying to."

"Do not shy back from a formidable opponent, Theá. As long as you are willing to pay the price, defeat is a useful way to learn, to move on, to develop. To grow."

The younger woman chuckled. "How does that fit with the invincible Aren reputation you all are so careful to maintain?"

Malhora shrugged. "We make our victories public and keep the defeats private. Simple, but effective."

Eryn nodded. It would remain to be seen whether this hearing would fall into the first category or the second.

She smiled when Valrad approached them and pulled her into a careful embrace after studying her too pale face for some moments. To her relief he decided not to comment.

"Don't show too much affection," she said lightly. "It makes me look *human*."

"If your own father cannot put his arms around you without making you seem weak, you might want to rethink your concept of strength," he grumbled but freed her again. "I assume this also means that I cannot take your arm to accompany you to your seat?"

"You may walk next to me, but avoid supporting me. I can't afford to look fragile today."

He chuckled. "You never do. Even when you are." Then he sent Malhora a reproachful look that didn't need words to convey the meaning behind.

"You do not worry, boy. I shall take good care of her," the old woman remarked without rancour, putting her own staring abilities to good use.

Eryn stifled a grin at hearing a man in his mid-fifties referred to as *boy*. But then it was always a matter of who did the referring, wasn't it? For a woman old enough to be his mother it was not such an absurd term of address. Especially when she wanted to put him in his place.

"Who will check that he is telling the truth?" she went on to ask, breaking the tension between the two of them. "Myself?"

"No," Malhora shook her head. "And neither would we wish for that. It would just give rise to accusations of manipulation and wrongful testimony. To which we would have to respond accordingly.

No; somebody whose conduct and neutrality is beyond reproach will take care of this. I assume that one of the triarchs will offer. Not, Abrak, though - he is too closely connected with House Aren and has never bothered to hide it, the fool. It will eventually cost him his seat in the triarchy, you mark my words."

Eryn nodded and took a seat, watching the steady stream of watchers entering the hall and searching for advantageous spots to observe the proceedings from. So, word had spread that something interesting was about to happen today. No particulars had been circulated, though, as the senators were bound to keep them confidential until the meeting.

She let her gaze wander over her colleagues. Neval's father, Uvel of House Tokmar nodded once at her. She nodded back with a tiny smile. He had been a great help back when she had been forced to defend herself against Malriel's accusation of having been responsible for Ved'al's death.

Intrea's father, the Head of House Feral, also inclined his head when their gazes met. He had been expected to vote in her favour a year ago, but accepted a bribe to change his mind. Eryn had once teased him about it. Who would have thought that they would find themselves as fellow Heads of Houses one day?

Eryn got to her feet together with the other senators when the triarchs entered the hall and climbed onto their pedestal. They sat and so did the senators.

"Let us start with the item that has brought us here," Torke'na raised her voice. "The Senate has voted in favour of questioning Sanaf of House Finran in connection with the misfortunes that have befallen House Aren lately."

Legara, Head of House Finran rose stiffly, looking cool and proud. "I ask for permission to speak."

"Granted," Torke'na nodded.

"I would very much like to know," Legara growled with narrowed eyes, "how the *Head of House Aren*," she all but spat the words, "arrived at the conclusion that a member of my House was to blame for any of her problems. If I may be so bold as to ask this of you, Maltheá: Where is your evidence? Or is this something you do not bother about in that country of yours?"

All eyes swivelled to Eryn, who looked at the older woman for a while, idly remembering that she was a cousin of Malriel's. That made her, what, an aunt or a second cousin or something? Well, it was certainly not the first family connection in this country that had brought her more trouble than joy.

"I have not yet moved on to pinning blame on anybody, Legara," she answered softly, with a thin smile. "This is about conducting investigations, as you must be aware. Investigations as such are characterised by the search for evidence, and do not depend on its being available in the first instance. Providing evidence would only apply to an accusation and subsequent proceedings," she continued in a voice that contained only a slight undertone of didacticism. "For now I have not been granted anything but help in my search for the person trying to harm the House I am in charge of. Sanaf might be able to help me in achieving this. I have not levelled any accusations concerning any alleged involvement of a member of your House."

She had, in fact, been immensely careful to avoid exactly that. Ram'an had emphatically warned her against it and Eryn was glad she had heeded his advice. Not doing so would have subjected her to great inconvenience when trying to explain that it was a mere hunch on her side that had made her accuse somebody without solid proof.

Legara shot her a last devastating look, then sat down and avoided any further eye contact.

Torke'na raised her voice. "Sanaf of House Finran, enter."

Guards opened the double doors to the left of the triarchy and Sanaf walked in, trying to look confident, but his squared shoulders and angled chin did not manage to hide that he was nervous. His eyes darted along the rows of tables, taking in the senators, then the observers, then locked onto Eryn for a short moment before fleeting away.

Eryn wondered if he was aware exactly why he had been summoned. But according to how Ram'an had described her, Legara would surely have told him, despite the fact that she had been supposed to be keeping her mouth shut about it.

"Ask who will apply the lie filter," her grandmother murmured low enough for only her to hear.

"Who will be verifying the answers?" Eryn called out without asking for permission to speak as Legara had done earlier.

"I will," Golir replied calmly and looked down at her.

She nodded once. "Good. I approve."

The triarch lifted an eyebrow at her audacious statement and she cursed herself for that show of boisterousness.

But his mouth was curled into a barely discernible smile. "I am glad to hear it. It would have pained me no end not to have been considered trustworthy by the Head of House Aren."

"Keep your mouth shut now - no more witty or challenging remarks to that man," Malhora hissed. But Eryn didn't need such a command.

"Sanaf, you have been summoned before the Senate to aid Maltheá of House Vel'kim, Head of House Aren in her search for the truth," Torke'na announced. "You will answer her questions truthfully, being at the same time subjected to a lie filter. As you have heard, Golir shall be the one to apply it. Do you have any objections as to his impartiality in this matter?"

Sanaf had started sweating. Eryn saw his forehead glistening with a thin line of perspiration running down his temple, cheek and then throat, finally to be caught upon the collar of his yellow shirt.

"I have of course no doubts regarding Golir's impartiality," he assured the triarchy hurriedly. "Though I admit that I am not comfortable with being treated like a criminal. Which is exactly what applying a lie filter implies," he argued.

Golir rose and slowly descended the few steps until he stood before the former ambassador to Anyueel.

"As Maltheá has just explained to your Head of House, this is not about accusing you of anything. Maltheá requested you be summoned before the Senate as she believes that you may be in a position to aid her in her investigations. The lie filter is also for your own benefit, as it will leave no doubt that your statements are true," he explained and then added dryly, "Only if you have no knowledge that would lead to incriminating yourself, that is."

At this point Sanaf appeared to become even more unnerved. Perhaps he had thought that he could somehow wriggle out of having the lie filter applied, Eryn wondered, and watched him throw a pleading look in the direction of Legara.

If that wasn't a display of a guilty conscience...

His Head of House seemed to reach a similar conclusion. Her eyes narrowed and there was a slight furrowing on her forehead now.

Eryn's attention returned to Golir when he gripped Sanaf's forearm and pushed up the sleeve to enable direct skin contact. Had the imbecile started shaking or was she imagining it?

"Maltheá, please ask your questions," Golir instructed calmly.

She nodded and took a deep breath, looking right into Sanaf's wide eyes. "Sanaf, you are aware of the troubles House Aren had to face in the last few months, I assume?"

"Ah... yes, yes, I am," he stammered.

"Do you know who set the fire at the Aren residence?" she asked and held her breath.

"No, I do not," Sanaf's slightly whiny voice imparted.

She blinked. What? How was this possible? She pressed her lips together and stared at him. Was he truly innocent? But then how did his nervousness fit into the picture? What was she missing here?

Asking him if he knew who had ordered the fire to be set there was futile, then? But on the other hand, what did she have to lose? Things were going awry already.

Careful to avoid any direct accusation, she cleared her throat and then rephrased the question, "Do you know who ordered the fire to be laid at the Aren Residence?"

Sanaf shook his head vehemently. "I do not, no!" he emphasised.

"Are you aware of who it was that attempted to take Vern's life?" she asked with forced calm. Something was going rather wrong here.

"I am not!"

Even Golir looked a little surprised when he nodded. "He is speaking the truth."

"Did you arrange for me to dance the seduction dance with Ram'an of House Arbil at the gathering at the Feral Residence?" she ventured, one last desperate shot.

"No." Sanaf seemed to have gained more confidence now - still agitated, but noticeably calmer as if a burden had been taken from his shoulders.

"We were wrong," Eryn whispered, devastated. "It wasn't him."

Malhora didn't reply but just stared at Sanaf with pursed lips and a calculating expression.

"Maltheá, would you allow me to make an enquiry or two? I do not wish to impose myself on you, of course."

She looked up towards Ram'an's somewhat tense face across the hall and nodded. "Go ahead."

"Sanaf, did you order someone to harm House Aren in general or Maltheá of House Vel'kim in particular?"

Eryn's eyes widened as she watched the man trying to form words with his lips, while his mouth was unable to release them. He was attempting to lie!

"Answer the question please!" Ram'an thundered and made half of those present flinch at the unexpected show of temper from a man known for his quiet intellect and relaxed manner.

"I... I..." he stuttered and then tried to rip his arm out of Golir's grip. The triarch merely raised an eyebrow at him and strengthened it.

"Did you pay whoever was behind the fire at the Aren Residence and thus endanger the life of two pregnant women and a young man who was barely able to make it out there alive?" Ram'an barked and caused Sanaf to sink to his knees.

"She took everything away from me," the man then gasped, staring at the floor with a glassy expression.

"I would suggest we have located the man who was behind the incidents," the lawyer then announced with emphasis. Then he turned to Legara. "This is an accusation, in case you were wondering," he added acidly.

"You!" a sharp shout like the crack of a whip came from the ranks of the observers. Eryn's head snapped to its source.

Orrin was standing between his son and Junar who had their daughter slung across her chest. His hand was outstretched accusingly, his finger jabbing directly at Sanaf. His posture was as tense as a drawn bowstring, ready to release at the smallest provocation. Or even without any at all.

The people around him had taken a few hasty steps away. They knew a magician on the verge of violence when they saw one. And Orrin had built quite a reputation here, even before throttling the artist he had suspected of trying to harm his son.

Now he was really facing the man who was to blame for it and it was evident that nobody had much hope of the warrior showing more restraint when his wrath would this time find the right target.

Orrin moved menacingly slowly, the way Urban stalked when she was hunting. His eyes were fixed on the man standing before the pedestal, his fingers flexing as if in eager anticipation of clutching the culprit's throat between them.

"Maltheá!"

She blinked and snapped out of the strange trance of horrifying fascination which Orrin's reaction had put her under, and looked at Golir.

"Stop him! Now! If you do not, I shall have to. This would not look good and will cause unnecessary tensions and paperwork," he hissed at her.

Eryn held on to the table to pulled herself to her feet as quickly as she could manage.

"Lord Orrin!" she bellowed, hoping that using the title would remind him of how he was supposed to be behaving. It proved to be in vain - he ignored her, still focussed on Sanaf and drawing closer.

She cursed and quickly moved forward, positioning herself between him and his - for want of another word - prey. Sending him to the floor with a bolt seemed terribly inappropriate right here.

"Get out of my way," he growled like something not quite human without even looking at her.

"Get a grip on yourself right now! That is an order!" she snarled back.

"We have gone beyond orders now," he rasped, his gaze becoming more feverish. "He endangered my family."

Eryn nodded slowly and sighed in resignation. Then she lifted her hand, placed her fingers around his throat and sent him to the ground unconscious with a surge of magic and a greater wave of regret.

She really, really hated it when *she* had to be the sensible one around the place.

*　*　*

Eryn let herself sink deeply into the cushions at her back in the Aren main room. It was over. They had pinpointed the one responsible for these aggressive acts. That meant she could stop the investigations, release the guards who had been keeping an eye on all members of the household for so many weeks now and finally begin to feel safe again.

Malhora returned from Orrin's bedroom where she had deposited the lifeless figure. Eryn had to give a wide grin at the picture of the woman who appeared to be in her early sixties lifting the unconscious warrior as if he weighed nothing, then slinging him over her shoulder like a bundle of clothes.

Vern had very cautiously tried to offer carrying his father, but Malhora had just glared at him and told him to get out of her way unless he wanted end up on her other shoulder.

Eryn tried to stay behind and talk to Ram'an, thank him and above all ask him why Sanaf had managed to lie convincingly to her but not *him*, but he had just kissed her forehead, pressed her close for a moment and told her to lie down and relax. He promised to come by later after he had made sure that everyone here was aware of the legal consequences that Sanaf had to face now.

She had nodded, so very relieved that all of this was over, that she did no longer have to pretend to resent Ram'an that she had not even got around to properly hating and abusing Sanaf for his despicable deeds. She would take an hour out for that tomorrow. Or two. Wasn't being organised a handy thing?

She felt how her limbs started feeling slightly heavier, pleasantly so. All the tension, the exhaustion of the last few days and the hours at night when she had tried to sleep but was kept awake either by her unborn child or the mix of feelings when she thought of Enric, were exacting their toll now.

She fought the heaviness that had now also reached her brain for several moments longer, wondering whether falling asleep in the middle of the afternoon after everything that had just happened wasn't rather unusual. Then she decided she didn't care in the least about appearances and gave in to welcome slumber that claimed her almost instantly.

*   *   *

She stirred when the smell of food fought its way into her consciousness. Only the silence following her movements made her realise that there had been low murmuring before and she opened her eyes.

The voices had come from the terrace where everybody had moved, clearly to avoid disturbing her.

"Good evening, my dear," Ram'an smiled at her and walked towards her to pull her to her feet, careful not to tread on the mountain cat that lay sprawled on the floor between the cushions and the low table. "Your timing is impeccable. Malhora has just finished cooking and is about to serve dinner. Come and join us."

He took her hand in his and led her to the terrace where Junar, Vern, Valrad and Orrin were all sitting in the shade.

Her father stood up to press her close and kiss her on the temple. "I cannot tell you how glad I am that this is over now. One less thing to worry about."

Yes, which left only her brother and her companion and who knows what trouble they might get into, she thought, but kept quiet.

She looked down at Orrin, who raised his brow at her. "You clasped my throat and knocked me out cold." There was no real accusation in his tone, it was more a simple statement of fact.

"True. You disobeyed my order," she replied and waited for him to comment on that.

He pursed his lips and then nodded with a lopsided smile. "I suppose I did. Does this mean we are even now?"

"I haven't decided on that yet. But let me put it like this: If I think we are not, we won't need to involve the Order. I'll just have you take care of menial tasks for me. Such as rubbing my feet when they give me trouble."

The warrior sighed. "I know for a fact that you can do that much quicker with a bit of magic. But then it wouldn't be as satisfying for you, would it?"

"You said it!" she grinned and allowed Ram'an to assist her sitting down on the cushions.

When he had taken a seat right beside her, she took his hand between the two of hers and squeezed it. "I haven't thanked you yet, my friend. Without you I would have messed the whole thing up. Completely." She shook her head. "And now tell me why he was able to lie to me, but not to *you*. I asked him the same things!"

The lawyer smiled. "You did. But you were too specific. The trouble with it was that he was not involved in the planning to such a degree. The ideas were not his, nor did he participate in carrying them out. He just provided the money to have somebody else take care of the problem in a way that would leave him fairly removed from it."

His earlier words about there being brains for hire to do such thinking that were more capable than Sanaf's came back to her.

"So he did this on purpose?"

"If you mean that he avoided learning about any particulars so he could bluff through a lie filter, then yes. But he is not the first criminal to attempt this; I have had my share of questioning such miscreants in the past. His sweating and fidgeting around only to look so relieved when you were asking him your questions was a dead giveaway that something was not right there," Ram'an concluded.

"What will happen to him now? Will there be a trial or something similar?" she enquired then. "I assume now even Legara has to admit that he must be punished."

"The triarchy has decided to let Legara, as his Head of House, handle the issue," Valrad spoke. "I had a few words with her before I left the Senate hall. I hope she is smart enough to realise that she needs to make her punishment of him appropriate, or she will have at least three Houses angry at her. Her connections with House Arbil were never very close, but having Aren and Vel'kim against her would be more than she can afford."

Eryn sighed. Politics again. Well, this time they at least were aiding her own interests. It was probably all about knowing the right people. And in her case currently *being* one of the right people.

Malhora joined them carrying a large, steaming bowl in her hands which she placed down in the centre of the table. Then she sat down and leaned back, making no movement whatsoever to serve the food.

"I cooked it, somebody else serves it. I do not care about what is polite. I am too old for that," she said with obvious satisfaction. Then her gaze fell on Orrin and she grinned broadly. "Warrior. I see you are back on your feet. Did anybody tell you that I carried you back here over my shoulder?"

Orrin's eyes widened and his mouth dropped open. His head snapped to Vern and he grimaced. "How could you let that happen?"

The boy bit his lip and sent his father an apologetic look. "I am sorry. I tried. But you know what? She is intimidating, and not just a little."

Malhora winked at her granddaughter. "You see? That is how you do it."

CHAPTER 36

A Peculiar Aren

Vran'el pointed to a spot of green, without a word. Enric narrowed his eyes. This was supposed to be the oasis they were heading for? The promised relief from the sun, where they would finally enjoy the luxury of fresh water instead of the lukewarm contents of their pouches? The lawyer's words had somehow painted a picture of something different. He had imagined - had been hoping for - something a little... well, *larger* than what appeared to be no more than a cluster of fifteen trees.

They had been riding through what Vran'el had called a light sand storm. Enric could feel the fine grains everywhere, be it between his toes, under his arms or in his mouth. There even seemed to be some between his eyes and eyelids judging from that slight scratching sensation. His body did not seem to be able or willing to spare the tear fluid for flushing out the foreign objects and restoring his vision completely.

His only consolation right now was that this was the third and thereby last night they would need to spend in the desert. He was sick of the barren wasteland around them, which provided minimal distraction for the eyes and thus the mind. And after many arduous hours on the back of a horse under the sun his thoughts had slowed down enough to appreciate every external stimulus that helped him out of this dullness.

Somehow he had envisioned the promised patch of green rather differently, and wondered whether Vran'el had exaggerated or if he himself had rebuilt the words into something different. He scolded himself for being ungrateful. Even if it was no more than a small patch with a few tall trees it was definitely superior to their surroundings over these last three days. Yet there was this thing about disappointed expectations: they kept grumbling about in the background, sulking.

The sun had already started setting, but they would reach the oasis in time to be able to shelter from the gritty wind by nightfall, within whatever tents were set up to house them this time.

Enric was missing the comfort he had enjoyed for the last few months. The most recent time he had been forced to spend a night in less welcoming surroundings than a mansion with all imaginable luxury provided had been on the ship on their way to Takhan.

He was becoming spoiled, he mused. Pampered by his lifestyle in the last one and a half decades that he had spent wallowing in luxury.

Eryn would probably find that amusing. She had lived in a small cottage, provided for herself and had even gone on that blasted excursion with the herb gatherers, not especially perturbed by the fact that she'd had to sleep on the hard, cold ground, wash herself with cold water or eat only simple fare.

Eryn. He sighed. He felt the commitment bond pulling at him like a long leash, urging him to return to where he was supposed to be: at her side. He was certain it had been the right decision to free her from the bond. Even if she had not been in her seventh month of pregnancy and burdened with having to take care of a House he wouldn't have wanted her do endure it.

"You look glum. Are you thinking of my sister again?" Vran'el's brows furrowed. "There is nothing wrong with her, is there?"

Enric shook his head. "No, not that I can tell. It's just the bond."

The lawyer raised his brow at him. "No commiseration from my side. It was your decision to leave your side of the bond intact. I advised you against it."

The blond magician gave a single, slow nod - deciding that it was better to keep his mouth shut. He didn't want to start an argument. He simply lacked the energy. And what exactly had he expected? Surely no sympathy.

They rode on in silence, guiding their horses towards the trees. As they came nearer Enric blinked in confusion when he spotted another patch of green much further away at the edge of the horizon.

"What's that? Another oasis?"

Vran'el chuckled. "No, my friend. This is the same one. I told you that it is rather large, did I not?"

Only then did Enric realise that there was a connection that curved between the two spots, bending far enough back to be almost out of sight.

"One long, thin stretch of green?"

"Yes, it is shaped like a half moon. Curiously narrow but surprisingly extended. Our hosts for tonight are located a little further towards the centre, where the vegetation is broader. A very prolific strip of land, yet far too remote for my tastes. I was only ever here once before, as a boy with Pe'tala and father."

"Why would he bring you out here?"

"To show us rich city children that life was not as carefree and uncomplicated for everyone. That people out here had to worry about finding water, braving sandstorms and erecting shelters. It was certainly an education. Riding through the sandstorms was no pleasure back then," Vran'el said, shivering as he remembered.

"I didn't find that one a few hours ago very pleasant, either," Enric commented.

"That was hardly even a sandstorm. I am talking about real storms that force you to brave them by covering yourself and your mount with a shield - or some other means if you are not a magician - because otherwise the sand would scour your skin away."

Enric swallowed. That really did not sound very appealing. "Why are there never any sandstorms in Takhan? Is it the location of the city? Too remote from these forsaken and sandy parts of your country?"

"Yes and no. It is not exactly desert around Takhan but more steppe, which extends into the desert as you have seen. But every now and again there are major sandstorms. We have to protect the city with a large shield in such cases."

"What?"

Vran'el laughed at his baffled expression. "Come on, Order Lord, do not tell me that the principle of raising large shields is new to you?"

"Large, yes. But big enough to encompass an entire city? I cannot imagine any single magician could do it, not even mighty Golir. So I assume that many of you have to work together to create that."

"We do. There are about thirty of us to take care of this if the need arises. Everybody covers a patch as large as their powers permit."

"I haven't seen anything like that since I arrived in Takhan. I assume there hasn't been a storm in that time?"

"No, there has been none. If there had, we would very likely have asked you to assist us as your considerable strength would have made a few of the others surplus. You, Ram'an, Eryn and Golir could probably shield half the city on your own."

Enric shifted uncomfortably in the saddle. "Why didn't we shield when we were riding through that weak sandstorm before?"

Vran'el shrugged. "It takes too much energy, which you should better save for keeping yourself strong and upright despite the heat. Or healing yourself should that be necessary. Wasting force to be more comfortable is not sensible in a hostile environment such as this where you might need every bit of magic if there is an emergency."

They were now riding along a treeline interspersed with thorny-looking bushes, grateful for the shade.

"What kind of trees are these?"

"The usual type you will find in such spots. They can manage the heat, need only little water and have deep roots that reach the ground water, which is of course closer to the surface here. When we reach our destination you will also find various kinds of fruit trees the inhabitants planted," Vran'el explained. After a few more minutes he pointed at a collection of low stone structures and bright tents. "Here we are. And it seems they are expecting us. You see that man in front of the large tent? Unless I am very much mistaken this is Ganel, the chieftain."

"Chieftain? How many people live here? An entire tribe?"

"Not as such, no. He is a successful trader and has a large family. *Chieftain* is more or less the nickname he likes to introduce himself with. It is something of a joke surrounding his numerous offspring. That tends to happen with six companions."

Enric's head whirled around and he gaped at Vran'el. "*What*?"

"I see the concept of more than one companion catches you a little off balance, my otherwise unshakable friend," the other man laughed. "It is not a common practice in the cities any longer, though out here in the open where not always a healer is available when required, many children may die before they reach their third birthday. Having more than one companion is a way of ensuring that the tribes to not die out. Which is not really any danger with Ganel, from what I have heard. As far as I know he has thirty-two children now. If he goes on like this, he may start his own tribe soon enough."

"Thirty-two children," Enric whispered, staring at the man they would soon be close enough to greet. Time to remember his manners, he decided, and schooled his expression into one of polite interest.

"Ganel, I greet you and thank you for the hospitality you bestow on us. It is a great pleasure to see you again after all these years. It has been a long time," Vran'el smiled and dismounted to offer his hand for the formal greeting.

Ganel had to be in his late fifties, but with a man who had spent much of his life in the desert it was hard to guess. He might be a decade younger with a very weathered face.

He was dressed in a long, bright yellow kaftan with a matching headdress not unlike Enric's own. The magician's eyes immediately dropped to his hips around which he was wearing a belt. There was a long sword attached to it, its blade curved.

"Vran'el! A long time indeed!" Ganel boomed and ignored the younger man's hand to pull him into a hearty embrace instead, laughing in delight. "It must be fifteen years at least since I last saw you! You have grown into a man!" He then turned to Enric who had also dismounted in the meantime. "And you are the yellow-haired one that claimed Malriel's little girl for himself when she should have been bound to House Arbil instead." It came as no accusation as such - simply a statement of a fact. There was no resentment, just curiosity. Rather open curiosity judging from that overt survey from blue eyes that seemed like pools of clear water in his weathered face.

"Enric of House Aren," he introduced himself and offered his hand for the formal greeting.

Ganel accepted it and chuckled. "Of course. Malriel cannot have anybody but an Aren defeat her, can she?"

"You are acquainted with Malriel?" Enric enquired.

The older man grinned broadly and revealed his rows of glinting teeth, many of them white, several golden.

"Acquainted? Definitely. I am one of many cousins. My full name is Ganel of House Aren, if you must know. But let us go inside. It is rather more pleasant as long as the sun has not set and I assume that you two would like some refreshment before your baths."

Enric felt his knees weakening at the mere thought of a refreshing, cleansing bath, washing away the dirt and sweat, getting rid of the gritty sensation that marked his every move.

They entered a large tent with colourful, expensive-looking carpets woven in a multitude of patterns and even pictures covering every bit of the ground within. Additional carpets hung on the tent walls, bathing the surprisingly spacious interior into a dim light that was a relief to eyes that had been peering at glaring surfaces all day long.

Enric noted the equally elegant cushions on the ground. They looked incredibly inviting, yet he was reluctant to take a seat with his dusty, sandy clothes.

"Do sit down, please," Ganel waved at them and added with a look at Enric, "Do not worry about the sand on your clothes. When you live out here you learn to see it as something inevitable."

Both magicians nevertheless started patting their baggy clothes to remove at least the heavier coatings of sand before they sank down on the cushions.

Vran'el sighed contentedly before he accepted a tall glass with had seemed unthinkable decadence only an hour ago: cool, clear water.

"I cannot tell you how good it feels to sit on something that does not shake me around with every step. If I have never to mount a horse again in my life it will still be too soon," he said, and grimaced.

"Then I suppose this is the wrong time for pointing out that you will have to do just that tomorrow morning?" Enric smiled and closed his eyes when the sensation of the fresh, cold liquid spread throughout his mouth. Never in his life had water tasted sweeter. It was amazing how precious simple things such as a glass of cool water became somewhere like this, when in the past it was nothing he would have wasted a moment's thought on.

He would bring his son out here once he was old enough, he decided. To show him that life was not a walk along Kingsway for those not born into wealth or had chosen to give it up for whatever reason. Just as Valrad had done with his children. Eryn would surely appreciate that and maybe even decide to accompany them. He smiled at the thought. She would be interested in analysing the sparse vegetation, collecting the desert plants.

He pushed the thoughts aside when the dull ache of longing became stronger. He wondered how much of it truly was the bond that was pulling him back.

"You seem preoccupied, Enric of House Aren."

Enric looked up guiltily when their host's voice made him realise that he had been gazing into the distance instead of participating in the conversation. That was not a very polite way of repaying the man for his hospitality, especially in a place like that where hospitality refused could easily spell death.

"I apologise," he said quickly. "I will admit my thoughts were back in Takhan."

"With your companion, I imagine. Malriel told me that she was about to become a grandmother. So it is your family you are thinking of, I assume." Ganel leaned back and scrutinised him. "Has little Theá given birth yet?"

"No, she still has several weeks left. I hope to be back from Pirinkar before our son is born." Enric wondered how *little Theá* would react to being referred to as such.

"Ah, the wonder of birth. I have experienced it first-hand with most of my children. Only as an onlooker, of course," he added with a smile. "It first seems like inhuman torment, completely unacceptable pain for someone so close to your heart to endure. But then, when the tiny creature is cradled in your arms, yelling out loudly as if protesting about how they have been ripped from the enclosed and cosy surroundings of the womb, you know that watching the suffering was worth it." He chuckled. "Well, until they are old enough to talk that is, then all you hear are demands all day long. Then you wonder if the real suffering is not only just beginning. I think Malriel told me that she left you in charge of House Aren for the period of her absence. Who is taking care of that duty now? Not little Theá?"

"Yes, her alone. Malhora had no wish to do so and I assumed that Malriel's daughter would surely be an acceptable substitute for the members of House Aren."

"Malhora," said Ganel, looking pensive. "I recall the time she was Head of House. She was not cruel in any particular way, but after blowing up that wine cellar people became particularly careful around her and rather avoided making demands or even requests in any way which might be perceived as disrespectful. Oh, she did keep us all on our toes alright."

Enric lifted both eyebrows. "So Malriel was easier to deal with?"

"You could say that, yes. Or it is simply a matter of age. I have known Malriel since she was a little girl, so I did not grow up being cowered by her. She is more approachable; her way of wielding her power is more subtle, not like an ever-present warning as it is in Malhora's case. I would be interested to see what kind of Head of House Malthea will turn out to be. But then I assume this will only be a temporary condition as you surely intend to return. And take Malriel with you."

"That's the overall idea, yes," Enric nodded.

When both had finished their glasses of water, Ganel stood. "Now come. I am sure you are eager to rid yourselves of all the dust and sand. I know that city people tend to be more modest and are not comfortable with bathing in the stream, so I will have some tubs filled if you prefer."

"No need to on my account," Vran'el chimed in at once.

Enric nodded in quick agreement. Dipping his tired, sweaty, dusty carcass in a cool, clean flowing stream... the image of a tub could not compete with that. Not in any way.

"As you wish. I will take you to the spot we use for bathing here. Your horses are being taken care of as we speak and your belongings are in the tent that was prepared for you. If you leave your clothes next to the water, we will take care of them and have them ready for you to pack before you are ready to leave."

Both magicians nodded, their eyes fixed on the glinting blue surface that had come into view between the trees. A low, narrow waterfall fed water into it. It looked like a scene from a fantastic dream.

Ganel told them to take as much time as the needed, then he left them alone. Vran'el all but jumped out of his clothes, diving into the pool that was even large enough to swim a few strokes in.

Enric undressed more slowly, shaking his head at such boisterous behaviour. They didn't even know how deep the water was. Vran'el could easily have struck his head on the bottom.

But the lawyer re-emerged from under the surface only a few seconds later, an expression of pure rapture on his face.

"Come in, Order Lord! No need to be squeamish. You are not afraid of being naked in my presence, are you?"

Enric gave a faint smile and dropped his garments before carefully climbing into the water. "Hardly. I am bigger and stronger than you. If I feel that you are about to take liberties, I will just push your head under water for a while."

Vran'el chuckled. "Then I better hold myself back from doing so." His expression became serious. "I think Neval is concerned about just that. He was not happy to see me ride off with you."

"He is really not jealous of me, is he?"

"Well, I think it is easy for him not to be jealous when he sees you around Eryn, but the idea of the two of us alone in the great, wide outdoors does not sit well with him."

Enric narrowed his eyes. "You are not in love with me or anything of that kind, are you? I have always seen your flirtation with me as a kind of friendly banter you play to amuse yourself."

The lawyer laughed, a bark of honest amusement. "Please, stop right here! Do not give me the speech in which you tell me that you love me like a brother, but there can never be anything more between us, I beg you! I promise you, there is no need for it. If it makes you feel any better, I will repeat this under the influence of a lie filter."

The blond magician chuckled. "No, thank you. Considering the trouble stealing the companion of an Aren woman would mean for you

- especially as we are talking about your own sister here - I am inclined to believe you."

Vran'el nodded, satisfied. "Good. I would not want you to feel uncomfortable in my presence, Enric. Ever. You are a formidable man I do not mind having around, but my heart belongs to Neval."

Enric nodded and started cleaning himself. What an awkward conversation. But considering the time they would have to spend together in solitude it was a good thing that they had talked about that. This was probably why Vran'el had mentioned it.

"So you are saying you don't find me appealing?" he then asked casually, grinning when Vran'el rolled his eyes and groaned.

"There is no pleasing you, is there? First you are worried about me secretly craving you, then you are offended because I do not?"

"What can I say, my friend? I am an Aren, am I not? We are known to be hard to accommodate, unless I am very much mistaken."

* * *

Enric awoke with a headache and looked around. He had fallen asleep in the huge tent they had been welcomed to the evening before. Vran'el lay on the cushions to his left, his face buried in the fabric, one arm hanging limply onto the carpeted floor.

"Vran?" he croaked, his throat feeling raw, as if he had gargled with sand. When the other man didn't react, he lifted his incredibly heavy arm to pat a lifeless shoulder.

The dark-haired man made an indistinct sound and turned his head to one side.

"Vran'el, wake up," Enric implored with more emphasis, shaking the shoulder now.

"Go away," came a tortured moan from the recumbent figure.

"We need to get ready. Come on!" Enric climbed to his feet unsteadily and it took the tent a few moments to stop swaying. Or himself, however one wanted to look at it.

When Vran'el finally managed to lift his head a fraction from the cushions, leaving a slightly reddened imprint of the fabric on his cheek, the curtains that covered the entrance were flung aside with vigour. Both men groaned pitifully and averted their eyes from the sudden brightness.

Ganel marched in, clapping his hands loudly, took one look at his guests and then laughed out loud in obvious delight. And glee.

"City men! No stomach for a little nightcap! Big, strong fellows like yourself cannot compete with an old man such as myself?"

"Nightcap indeed," Vran'el murmured. "How many bottles did we empty last night?"

"Only one, my young friend. Only one," Ganel said innocently.

"It doesn't happen to be this one, does it?" Enric enquired and carefully bent down to lift a colourful glass bottle with one hand. It was about as long as his entire arm. "Where I come from, this would equal four bottles. At least."

The older man shrugged. "Still only one bottle, though, is it not? Now come and get yourselves ready for your morning meal. I would recommend a quick dip in the water. That does tend to help along the process of sobering up. I have brought your bundles from the other tent and these are your clothes from yesterday. They have been washed and dried; you can put them on after your bath. Off you go!"

He tossed their bundles at them. Enric managed to catch it without any conscious input from his brain. Nothing more than ingrained habit and honed reflexes enabled him to pluck the projectile out of the air and avoid a collision with his shoulder.

Vran'el, whose skills were not exactly well-trained when it came to dexterity, was hit full in the chest, causing him to release an inarticulate sound when he was thrust back into the cushions after he had managed the strenuous climb to his feet.

Enric sniggered, but quickly lifted his arm to shield his eyes when Ganel left and let in more sunlight through the parting curtains.

"You are not laughing at me, are you, Order Lord?" Vran'el snapped.

"Why does it sound like an insult when you call me that?"

"Because it is meant as one. For whenever you are stuffy or act superior."

"How nice. It's like your sister calling me *Lordling*."

Vran'el frowned and stretched out his hand to let Enric pull him back onto his feet. "I thought she calls you *Bastard* when she is displeased?"

"She used to call me both, but since she has been made a Lady of said Order herself she's been sticking with *Bastard*."

The lawyer thought for a moment. "Do you think Ganel is a magician? Being of House Aren, there is a good chance of that. We could ask him to heal away the after effects of our overindulgence."

Enric looked unsettled at the thought. "I don't think that is a wise idea. If he is anything like your father, he will not do it, even if he is able to. Moreover, asking him for it will just make us appear weak and helpless, as though we are unwilling to bear the consequences of what we have brought upon ourselves."

"So we are going to spend the entire day on swaying horses, sick and with a headache, but congratulating ourselves on our endurance and ability to suffer?"

"Exactly. Display no weaknesses. That is something you might as well get used to. We surely cannot afford to in Pirinkar. Now come on. He is right; cold water will help us at least a little."

They made their way to the pool, asking for directions twice when their unsteady memory and even more unsteady feet led them repeatedly astray. Walking through what appeared to be a little village, they marvelled at the bustle around them. Mostly women and children were carrying things around, plucking fruit from trees, mending fabrics and hurrying in and out of tents *and* stone buildings.

"Why do they have tents *and* solid buildings? Why not only buildings? Wouldn't they provide better protection from the elements?" Enric asked.

"Do you have any idea how hard building material is to come by here? They thus use it in structures for the purpose of storing food, walls to keep off the worst when there is a sandstorm and similar. Like the one behind Ganel's tent. And if you look inside, it is rather dark and uncomfortable inside these stone buildings. If you add too many windows, you might just as well stay outside. So it is rather gloomy. The tents are more spacious, much lighter, they can be erected fairly easily and moved if need be."

They reached the pool and both undressed rather clumsily before slipping into the cold water. What had been utter refreshment the evening before was now little more than a shock that seemed to freeze them to their bones.

Vran'el shuddered, wrapping his arms around his still undipped torso. "That does surely help in waking a man up. Probably even a dead one. It was not this cold yesterday, was it?"

Enric took a deep breath and disappeared completely into the water. The chill almost squeezed the air from his lungs.

He straightened again right next to Vran'el, shaking his head and flinging a rain of icy droplets onto the other man.

"Hey! Stop that, you idiot!"

Enric simply grabbed his neck and pushed him under the water, letting him writhe and kick for a few seconds before releasing him.

"Gaaaah!" Vran'el spluttered when he was able to breathe again. He climbed out of the water to don his clothes hurriedly, without bothering to dry himself first. "Arens!" he cursed. "They are everywhere! And each and every one causes me trouble! First Eryn and Malriel with their proceedings, now Malriel managing to get herself imprisoned, that charming cousin of hers who got me drunk, and if all this were not enough, now there is *you*! You were not even born an Aren, yet you have adapted to their troublesome ways seamlessly. Congratulations!"

Enric smiled up at him, making a few leisurely swimming strokes just to annoy the other man.

Vran'el narrowed his eyes, bent down to pick up the second bundle of clothes and strolled away, whistling to himself.

"Hey!" Enric called after him after he had disappeared between the trees. "That's just childish! Come back here, at once! Don't leave me here like that!" He waited for a few moments, but the lawyer didn't return. "Vran'el?" he ventured once again, his voice more pleading and less demanding now. No reaction.

Enric closed his eyes. Superb. As if a headache and a queasy stomach were not enough of a bad start to the day today. Being marooned naked in bitterly cold water without clothes nearby was certainly adding to the charm of this trying morning.

*   *   *

The two men rode on silently, a self-satisfied grin fixed across Vran'el's face, a sulky expression on Enric's.

Enric imagined that his dash from the pond to the tent would provide fodder for gossip and chatter among the inhabitants of the oasis for some time to come. It certainly seemed to have provided entertainment. He had increased his speed through magic and knew that his audience couldn't have seen much of him. But enough to see that the figure rushing past them had not been wearing any clothes.

It had taken Ganel several minutes to recover from the sight of Enric more or less diving through the curtains into his tent, grabbing the first available pillow to cover his groin and glaring at Vran'el with a look that promised retribution. As well as probably a serious helping of agony in the not too distant future.

The older man was laughing so hard that tears ran down his cheeks freely while he slapped his thighs repeatedly and finally sank back into the cushions, happily spent from his outburst of merriment.

Ganel continued to snigger from time to time while they were eating some kind of mashed grain or fruit, which he had insisted would keep them sated for quite a long time and give them the energy they needed for the last few hours until they reached the mountains that had appeared on the horizon the day before.

Now as they rode along, Enric looked ahead at the looming massif. He remembered that this was not only the natural border between the two countries, but also the barrier that kept the clouds away from the desert and thus made people on this side so dependent on groundwater.

The craggy mountains looked impressive, there was no denying that. The colour was a red-brown slightly darker than the yellow sand their horses were plodding through.

After about two hours of riding, the first bushes of dry grass started to break up the monotonous ground and became more frequent the further north they rode.

What a harsh, inhospitable region, he thought, not for the first time. Why would anyone choose to live out here instead of the city?

But then Ganel had supplied an explanation for that yesterday evening, he dimly remembered. He was even one of very few people who had left the city he grew up in to escape the politics, games, rules and what he called repression.

Enric had to admit that there were certainly not many people who would take the effort of making their way to his remote little spot out here to impose their will on him.

He had fairly much assembled his own little paradise here. He had told them that he had never much been one for marital fidelity. A single woman was just never enough for him. He had been in a companionship in the city which was dissolved when he had followed his tendency towards... diversity. The free and wild life out here, even though considerably rougher and more demanding in some ways while simpler in others, appealed to him a great deal more. And the freedom to take as many companions as he wanted.

Enric wondered how he himself would like a life like this and discarded that option almost immediately. Not that it would have been a realistic choice for him, anyway. There were the Order and House Aren with their claims to him. Neither of them would like it if he were swallowed up by the desert so as to escape them.

Tyront himself would probably come here personally to drag him back to Anyueel by the ear. Closely followed by Malriel, who would be content to send the magician ahead as she herself was not strong enough to force her adopted son to do anything if he didn't agree to it. This thought made him smile.

"Are you in a better mood again?" Vran'el asked carefully.

"I am working on it," Enric replied. "Is your head still hurting?"

"Terribly," the lawyer grimaced.

Enric smiled broadly. "You know, that lifts my mood wonderfully."

The other man sighed. "We are behaving like children. Is that what being free of the confines of civilisation has done to us men? We play pranks to each other and delight in each other's discomforts?"

"I wouldn't say that we are any less susceptible to rediscovering the delights of our childhood in the city. Think back to the Game and how well-received it was. That led me to believe that we still want to do these things but do not dare admit to it. But if we can justify it as a means of improving fighting skills, suddenly running through the city, hiding from each other and shooting bolts becomes socially acceptable."

"Bold thoughts," Vran'el sighed gloomily. "Your own head is back to normal then, I gather?"

"Fairly much, yes."

"Which probably means that you have healed away all the other wayward effects from our last evening?"

"Exactly that, yes," Enric confirmed cheerfully.

"So I further assume that there is little chance of your helping me out after I took away your clothes and forced you to dash naked through a rather large number of women and children?" Vran'el enquired without much hope.

"Right again, my friend." Wasn't it nice, Enric mused, how quickly moods could change?

CHAPTER 37

The Stain

"I want you to call me Eryn instead of Maltheá," Eryn said while she was strolling along the street with her grandmother, enjoying the evening atmosphere with people milling about or relaxing in teahouses.

It was an hour after dinner when she had felt the urge to leave the house, move around a little. She had initially hoped to do that alone but of course there had been little chance of that. Orrin had simply ruled it out then and there. He had not yet really come to grasp with the idea of him not being in a situation to order his own superior around. She wondered if that would ever change.

One day she would find herself in her seventies, probably still taking cheek from a grey-haired or maybe bald-headed version of Orrin in his mid-nineties.

Knocking him out in the Senate hall had not really helped remind him who was in charge. She wondered what it would take to do so.

Malhora's amused voice pulled her back to the here and now. "Now, is that a fact, my girl?"

"It is a request. Not an unreasonable one, I feel. I bowed to your wish to be addressed as Grandmother, which means that accommodating me through this one small change should be bearable for you, I would think."

"The thing is, Maltheá, that I really *am* your grandmother, while that name Ved'al gave you is not your true one. After renouncing my House, your name is the only official and obvious sign that you actually belong to us. To me."

Eryn blinked. That had very likely been the most affectionate words she had ever heard from Malhora.

"I won't stop belonging to you, Grandmother, whatever you call me," she said quietly.

They walked on aimlessly for a while, watching how the tents sheltering the teahouses were removed once sunlight had almost vanished from the sky. Lanterns around them were lit and blankets were put outside on the seating cushions so that guests wouldn't freeze in the chills of evening.

Eryn turned left, for no other reason but that she had never before walked in that direction. Aimlessly strolling through the city was certainly a lot less dangerous with somebody who had spent several decades here and knew her way around than on her own.

"Where are we going?" Malhora frowned.

"Nowhere particular. Just where my fancy takes us."

"So I am following you around like that cat of yours?" she huffed and nodded to Urban, who was trotting behind them, sniffing at objects that seemed to offer interesting smells to her actively twitching nose. Sometimes she extended her attentions to passers-by, who in the majority of cases were unperturbed. Eryn did see two of them raise shields to protect themselves, though. Almost everybody in the city knew of Urban by now. And that she was rather harmless. At least as long as Enric or Eryn were around.

"You insisted on accompanying me. You are free to return home anytime."

"While you carry my great-grandchild through streets you have never been along before? Definitely not. The area you are aiming for is not the most salubrious one. Are you sure this is where you want to head for?"

Not the most salubrious one? As in *poorer districts*? That remark sparked her interest further rather than discouraged her.

"Sure, why not? I can probably say I have been invited to pretty much every grand residence in the city, seen every important and impressively ornate building representing some or other cultural or political value. I always move around in the same parts of the city. I rather think it's time to extend my knowledge of this place to include what you do not normally offer your visitors." She lifted her head. "And considering the fact that I am now also a bloody politician, I should probably see where not only the powerful people live."

"I do not have a good feeling about this," Malhora pointed out.

"We are both powerful magicians, what's to happen to us? Come on. And I am still hoping to persuade you to call me *Eryn*."

"Yet I fail to hear you offering me anything in return," Malhora said plainly.

"I really have to do an exchange with you? Where is your concern for my happiness? Aren't grandmothers supposed to indulge and spoil their grandchildren?"

The old woman snorted inelegantly. "Not in this family, child."

"Obviously not. I have no idea what to offer you in exchange. Is there anything you want in particular?"

Malhora pursed her lips. "There is something I might consider appropriate compensation. You will not like it, though. At least not to begin with."

"I am listening."

"I want you to address Malriel as *Mother* as soon as she returns here."

"Do *what*?" Eryn exclaimed explosively, making a number of heads swivel in their direction. Being close to two women of the Aren family who seemed to be in some kind of disagreement was not exactly known to be beneficial for one's health.

"You are joking, of course? Why ever would I agree to anything like that? You may not have noticed this living on that remote estate of yours far away in the middle of nowhere, but I left your House to sever all connections with Malriel!"

"Calm down, girl. You are making people skittish. Come on, walk on with me. What I am proposing is you addressing Malriel with the same unnerved tone every time you call her *Mother* - just as she does with me. It drives me insane and I want to give her back some of her own medicine. This is my offer - take it or leave it."

Eryn narrowed her eyes. "It really bothers you that much?"

"Yes, it does."

The younger woman walked on, thinking. If Malhora was that annoyed by being addressed that way, there might be a good chance that Malriel herself would not be too happy about it, either.

"I call her *Mother* in an exasperated manner and from now on you address me with what I consider my real name? Eryn?"

"You have my word," Malhora announced solemnly and offered up her outstretched palm to her granddaughter.

Eryn reached out and they interlocked their fingers, considering each other thoughtfully for a few moments before they released each other's hands again.

Urban nuzzled her head against Eryn's belly and offered her cheek for scratching.

"She doesn't like arguments," Eryn murmured. "They make her jumpy."

"I imagine that her life must be a very hard one, then," Malhora remarked dryly. "I have noticed you tend to be involved in quite a lot of arguments."

Eryn shrugged. There wasn't really a lot she could say to that. Sadly, it was true enough.

"But you need not worry about that, child. Avoiding a conflict is never the lesser evil. Only those too cowardly to deal with problems need to resort to that. We Arens take care of what is before us. Always have," she added proudly. "What is more, we like to remind others that we are not to be trifled with."

"By causing buildings to collapse?"

"If need be, yes. And why not? It has always proved a reliable way of reminding people that they should not make us angry if they can help. Or are willing to bear the consequences. I have been trying to convince your mother that she needs to show people what provoking her would earn them, but she thinks she is too modern for this kind of flagrant demonstration. Old-fashioned, barbaric and brazen she calls it."

The younger woman frowned in disbelief. "Are you telling me that repeatedly collapsing our own home and whatever other useful buildings were to hand was not a matter of losing control but merely a planned warning to keep people on their toes?"

"In a few cases that is exactly what happened, yes. And as Malriel has said she has no intention of continuing this fine and so very effective little family tradition, I am setting my hopes on *you*."

"Me?" Eryn grimaced. "I don't know. I am not even an Aren anymore - officially speaking."

"You look like Malriel and you are the Head of House Aren. This is official enough for most people, I would think. I am not expecting you to target the next available building and lay waste to it. Just consider what I said. Maybe there is a situation one day where you might demonstrate just a little more force than you would normally. Nothing extreme, something that can be repaired easily if you are averse to causing damage. Of course you will have to make sure not to injure anybody. That would come back to taint us. People need to respect and maybe fear us a little, but we cannot be despised for hurting innocent people."

"Why don't *you* do it, then? You seem to have a fairly clear idea of what needs to be done."

"I do not need to prove that I am somebody to be treated with great care anymore. You cannot have failed to see how people here regard me despite the fact that I do not wield any executive power anymore. It is time for the next generation to remind the country that not only the old Arens are formidable people."

"Will you stop pestering me if I promise to think about it?" Eryn sighed.

"For now, yes."

They continued their walk and Eryn noted the change in their surroundings with curiosity. The streets as well as the buildings seemed to become more decrepit with every corner they turned.

She had been wondering where all the poor people - the ones without access or connections to the Houses - lived. And why they were never visible in the better-off parts of the city. She had even begun wondering if it were possible that there were no poor people remaining in this place, that everybody owned enough to afford a decent abode and enough to eat.

Ingenuous ideas, she now realised. The children here looked more hollow-cheeked than those she normally saw. They were wearing clothes that looked so worn they had very likely already been passed on from several others.

Eryn thought back to Plia and what she looked like when they first met in that side alley where she was being attacked with stones by a bunch of children.

These children didn't look worse than she had back then - better even, if she looked more closely. Yet seeing them here, after she had for these last months only been in contact with the well-fed, well-dressed and well-scrubbed offspring of the upper classes, the difference seemed so much greater than at home where one saw them everywhere. In Anyueel, at least, poor people and their children were not confined to a part of the city as if they were shut away, limited to an area where they would not insult the sensibilities of wealthier citizens.

She pressed her lips together and walked on, dreading what else she would discover here.

The buildings were in various states of decay - gaping holes in walls, lopsided roofs, broken windows, crumbling stucco. As well as this, the smell - of unwashed people and refuse piling up without being burned or buried - kept getting worse.

Her fingers were curled into fists as she walked on with a look of grim determination.

Those belonging to the rich Houses, with their residences in all the wealthier areas of the city, the extensive gardens that served little other purpose than showing off wealth in a climate such as this, had to know that this part of the city existed.

When she was about to turn the next corner, she felt Malhora's hand around her upper arm.

"It is time to return. It is getting late. You should not walk too far in your condition," the old woman said calmly.

Eryn's eyes narrowed. "Why do you seem nervous all of a sudden? What's around this corner?"

"Nothing much. More grime, desolation and hopelessness I would think. Take a look yourself."

The younger woman did. Another alley like the ones they had walked along, timid yet resentful eyes bearing down on them all the time. Was Malhora worried about being attacked? It hardly seemed she was.

Eryn walked on and then turned another corner. She froze in horror.

* * *

Enric flinched. That had been a powerful stab of disdain, anger, disbelief and a maelstrom of other sensations. He felt Vran'el's hand on his arm.

"What is the matter? Eryn?"

He nodded, desperately trying to determine if there was fear among the cluster of impressions. No, there was none. He indulged in a moment of relief that she seemed not in any danger.

"Is she hurt? What is going on? Talk to me!" Vran'el urged him worriedly.

"No, there is no pain. At least no physical pain. She is… saddened by something." That was putting it extremely mildly but he didn't want to worry her brother even further.

"Are you sure?"

"Yes. Sad and angry. Probably a fight with Malhora," he shrugged, willing himself to believe it.

"Can you ride still or shall we take a break?"

"No, let's move on. It's getting dark and we'd better find a well-protected spot to spend the night in."

Vran'el nodded and rode ahead on the rocky path.

They had left the desert behind them several hours ago and were now crossing the mountains. The path was surprisingly easy to ride on considering how little traffic it saw. This was thanks to the infrequent contact between the countries on either side.

They heard a distant howl and swallowed. Whatever that was, it sounded hungry.

Enric then pointed up to a mountain ledge not far above them. "That looks good. There should be enough space for us and the horses below that."

Vran'el was about to nod when both their heads whipped around to a man in the middle of the road, blocking their way.

He had the reddest beard and hair Enric had ever seen, looked sturdy, confident and as if he was up to no good.

When he spoke, the words coming out of his mouth were strange and incomprehensible and sounded as if every single one of them was formed with the tip of the tongue and the teeth. Lips did not seem to play any major role in modulating what was probably the native language to Pirinkar.

Enric cleared his throat. "I am afraid I do not understand you," he said very slowly.

The red-headed man nodded once, then pronounced a single word in their language. It was strangely altered by his peculiar way of voicing it, but to the keen listener still decipherable.

The word was *Ambush*.

* * *

Eryn kept staring at the wide opening in front of her, mouth open in astonishment.

It was a collection of shanty huts, put together with whatever random materials had been ransacked. She saw old towels and pieces of ripped fabric fixed to crude structures, which provided at least some protection against the elements. Broken pottery, stones and bundles of dried grass had been used to construct thin walls that looked unstable enough that the next strong gust of wind might make them topple. Hardly any fires were visible anywhere. People probably couldn't afford to burn anything to gain the luxury of light. Or warmth.

She turned her head as if in trance to focus her gaze on Malhora, who had gripped her arm, attempting to pull her back the way they had come.

Eryn ripped her arm free from her grip and wandered into the sea of makeshift shacks. There had to be several hundred of them. It was like another town nestled against Takhan, a town consisting of the outcasts from the city - those not wanted, not needed or simply forgotten.

Mesmerised, she stared at the faces drawn tight with misery that scrutinised her briefly before they disappeared behind whatever makeshift shelter they had ventured out from before.

She hardly noticed the smell that was even more pungent here, or Malhora's quiet curses behind her.

People cowered in fear before her, as if afraid that she was here to punish them for something, make their life even more of a misery than it was already. What would these people still be afraid of? What did they have left to lose?

Their lives. Their loved ones.

She stopped next to a very young woman. Hardly an adult, she pressed three infants against her frail body. Eryn could see the bones in their shoulders and felt the moisture that had been building behind her lids increase.

She realised that she had placed both her hands on her belly protectively. Her eyes met those of the young mother, and there was a moment that seemed to extend into eternity. A moment that spoke so clearly of hunger, illnesses, thirst, feeling bitterly cold, and a desperation as if she had used actual words to communicate those torments. And there was a plea. A beseeching plea not to harm her or her starving children.

Eryn's breathing became laboured and she searched with clumsy, shaking fingers for her pockets to pull out the three gold slips she had with her. She held the money out to the woman who just stared at her wide-eyed, frozen.

Eryn bent down, grabbed the woman's wrist and pressed the gold into her palm before whirling on her heel and stomping back the way she had come from. She felt something inside her clench, wondering with this strange detachment she experienced in stressful situations if it maybe was her stomach.

Malhora jumped out of her way with surprising agility, then hurried after her.

"Eryn?"

The younger woman stopped once they reached the first proper buildings of the city, breathing heavily. She was cold, her fingers felt as impossibly chilly as if she had dipped them into a mountain stream. She didn't feel the warm evening air. There was just... coldness.

Malhora grabbed her shoulders, looking uncharacteristically worried. "You have gone completely white. Come with me."

Eryn let herself be pulled forwards, not seeing where she was going, just following the hand that gripped hers tightly.

"So many children," she murmured, slowly shaking her head as if still not believing what she had just seen with her own yes.

They walked on for a several more minutes. As though through a haze Eryn realised that their surroundings had changed back to the clean, bright, well-maintained inner districts that should have been a familiar and welcoming sight, but instead suddenly appeared ugly in their opulence. She looked at the blankets at the cushion islands that were there to keep the patrons warm and cosy. All this while on the edge of the city children were freezing in the same air.

She stopped abruptly, freeing her hand from Malhora's grip. The numbness and pain inside her made way for something else, something she welcomed like a lost friend, something she could use, something almost comforting in its familiarity: fury.

"There were children," she growled, scowling at Malhora as if she alone was to blame for it, challenging her to justify this abomination.

"It is true. Many of those living there are children," Malhora nodded. She stood straight and waited patiently for whatever else was to come, to be thrown at her.

Eryn closed her eyes and shook her head. "I would be lying if I said that back home in Anyueel children are treated the way they should be, must be, deserve to be." She paused and opened her eyes again. "But they at least have a sturdy roof over their heads and have a place to sleep. I freely admit that they are not always well-fed, or properly clothed. But this..." She pointed back the way they had come from. She felt how her rage made her muscles clench and she started shaking.

"The children are well-fed, clothed and educated in your city now from what I hear," Malhora said calmly.

Eryn stared at her. What?

"You took care of that, did you not? At least that is what my sources tell me." There was a challenge in her eyes.

"Me? I did nothing! It is Enric's money that pays for it, and other people's time and efforts that make it all possible! What can I do here? I have nothing to my name, I am a stranger here, nothing more than a gossip sensation, a cause for amusement and entertainment whenever something happens to me! I can't..."

"That is *not* how we start sentences in House Aren," Malhora interrupted her icily.

"That is your primary concern right now?" Eryn hissed, balling her fists. "How I phrase my frustration because it is supposed to be in accordance with the Aren rules of bloody invincibility?"

She felt the old woman's palm smack against her forehead ungently.

"No, you stupid girl! We do not bother with *I cannot* because it is a principle we reject, a concept we have decided never fully to grasp." Malhora lifted her chin. "There is nothing an Aren woman cannot do! You are the Head of a powerful, rich House! What exactly is your excuse for inaction, Eryn?"

"I have no money!" Eryn cried out, throwing her hands up in exasperation. Wasn't this obvious? What did this woman want from her?

She noted how people from three different teahouses had turned towards them, but she ignored them.

"Utter nonsense."

"What? No, that's *not* nonsense! You would hardly have me spend the fortune of House Aren, a House I do not even belong to, for charity causes, would you? I have no right to lay my hand on that gold, and you know that better than anyone," Eryn barked. "Neither will I touch my companion's money. I had no share in earning it, and spending his money when he is already supporting an orphanage in Anyueel is out of the question."

Malhora looked at her with a faint smile. The first word that came to Eryn's mind to describe it was... *wicked*.

"You have not had a chance to pay your mother back for her involvement in extending your family yet, unless I am mistaken."

Had the old woman lost complete control of her senses now?

"No, I have not. Her being far, far away makes that a little difficult presently. And to be completely honest, that issue is not exactly a priority of mine at this very moment," she said in her best talking-to-infants voice.

"Do not address me as if I am not right in the head. Come on. It is time to give you a little tour through your current home. Or rather, under it." With that she marched off, evidently confident that her granddaughter would follow.

Eryn stared at Malhora's retreating back for another few moments, wondering what all that was supposed to mean. Then she followed, determined to find out.

* * *

Enric scanned the scene and nudged one of the seven recumbent figures around them with his foot.

"They are all out," he then announced. "You can drop the shield now."

Vran'el obeyed and let the barrier disappear. Red-beard and his six bandit friends lay spread-eagled over the hard ground, unconscious.

After the man Enric guessed was their leader had stopped them from riding on, the others had emerged from behind various rocks beside the trail and other hideouts. They held long, menacing swords, which resembled Enric's own weapon. The very one he had left behind as he didn't want to appear to be an invading force but something closer to a diplomat. The attackers brandished their weapons as if they knew precisely how to use them. And were more than willing to.

Enric had swiftly instructed Vran'el to raise a weak shield to halt the men's approach and then shot strong bolts right through it, taking out one astonished assailant after the other. Luckily, his assumption that they were no magicians proved accurate. It was based on the fact that they carried weapons meant for close combat and on what he had read about Pirinkar's efforts at keeping magicians limited to the confines of the temples rather than letting them roam the land unsupervised.

"And now? What do we do with them? Leave them lying here on the ground?" the lawyer asked. "I would very much prefer to tie them up together and take them to Kar with us, but I see that this would slow us down too much. Also, I would probably not want try to sleep with any of them around me then."

"Yes, taking them with us is not something we are at liberty to do. However, I am reluctant to leave them here like this as well. They will either be eaten by something - which would be cruel - or nothing will happen to them until they come to - which means that they will get away with ambushing us unscathed," Enric pondered. "Can you think of any punishment we can subject them to here without sentencing them to death?"

"We could take their clothes away."

"It seems you have found a new favourite pastime," Enric snorted.

"Very funny, Order Lord. I was just thinking that this would clearly cause them considerable inconvenience out here. Any better ideas yourself, then?"

Enric thought for a while, then shrugged. "Alright. Let's take their clothes. And they must have mounts somewhere. We will look for those and take them, too. And any weapons, of course."

"How long will they remain knocked out? Is there a chance we can spend a peaceful night under that ledge up there or do we have to deepen their sleep first?"

"I think the latter. I only used relatively weak bolts to avoid permanent damage."

"How very considerate of you. Then let us hurry up. We should drag them behind that rock over there, then deepen the sleep and slice their clothes off," the lawyer instructed. "And then I need something to eat and a few hours of sleep. Which means that you are going to take the first watch."

Enric sighed, but nodded. "Alright. And I am not sure if I am very happy with you in command."

"Funny - I imagine that is something my sister might say to *you* every now and then. Good thing I am not in your Order."

"I agree," Enric harrumphed. "One rebellious Vel'kim in the Order and another one staying very close to it is probably the limit of what we can take right now. I am just glad you don't have any more sisters. Otherwise we would probably ask you to strengthen that barrier between our countries again, this time for *our* protection instead of yours."

Vran'el clasped an unconscious bandit under his arms and pulled him away from the path. "Very nice. Who was it again who thought it was a good idea to let you go to Pirinkar to represent our country and save us from a war?"

*   *   *

Eryn's brow rose when Malhora did not approach the main entrance to the residence, but walked around one side of the house, beckoning for her granddaughter to follow and pressing her index finger against her lips to indicate silence.

They stood before an unobtrusive door, which she had noticed before while taking walks in the garden. She had assumed it was the entrance to a cellar for storage. Malhora fished a key from an inside pocket and inserted it into the lock, turning it with no sound.

Surprisingly, the door swung open without noise, and Eryn wondered if somebody made sure to oil it extra carefully. Malhora lit a lamp she got from next to the door and Eryn saw her suspicions confirmed. This clearly was a root cellar. It was half-filled with various boxes and bags of vegetables she knew from the market and had cooked herself every now and then.

The old woman closed the door again and then turned to a stack of heavy sacks.

"What are you doing? Do you need any help? You didn't bring me here to tidy up, did you?"

Her grandmother ignored her and dragged the sacks with hardly any effort away from the wall they were leaning against. Magic truly was a practical thing to have at one's command.

Eryn widened her eyes as she watched Malhora slide aside a small panel, otherwise indistinguishable from any other part of the wall, to reveal another lock. Malhora inserted the key once again and a section of the wall swung open, revealing utter darkness beyond.

"What is this?" the younger woman whispered.

Malhora picked up the lamp and walked ahead down what turned out to be more steps that led to a narrow corridor. Eryn carefully felt ahead with her toes for every step for fear of slipping and falling. She gripped the slim handrail to one side tightly.

"Where are you taking me?" she asked once more, again not receiving an answer. She remembered her grandmother's words about taking revenge on Malriel.

"If you want me to kill her and bury her down here, let me tell you that I won't do it. If you want to get rid of her, do your dirty work yourself. Which doesn't mean that I won't support you in it," she added as an afterthought. "I wouldn't tell anyone about it. I mean, family needs to stick together, right?"

"Be quiet," Malhora said softly without turning. They walked on in silence until little later the corridor opened up into something like a cavern. It looked like several rooms could be accessed from here. Six, to be precise. They were all secured with the aid of heavy metal doors with impressive looking locks.

"Please tell me this is not some kind of family crypt and we are about to dance around naked to resurrect some long-forgotten ancestors?" Eryn whispered and looked around uneasily.

Malhora slowly turned to her and shook her head, frowning. "Sometimes I really wonder what is going on inside that head of yours. What exactly do you barbarians from across the sea think we do here?"

Eryn grimaced. "Sorry. Just sometimes my imagination runs a bit free... So, what is this place really?"

"This, my dear girl," explained Malhora in a low voice, "is where the wealth of House Aren rests." She lit two more lamps in the cavern leaving one hanging on the wall while handing the other one to her granddaughter.

"This vault contains valuable family heirlooms. Some of them beyond value, but most of them merely indecently expensive." She inserted her key into the first lock and turned it. It responded with a soft clunk and Malhora pulled open the door, nodding to Eryn. "Look inside."

Eryn did so cautiously, lifting the lamp in front of her. There were several large cupboards arranged along the three walls. She picked one door randomly and opened it. It was packed tightly with books, at least one hundred of them. She gingerly touched the back of one binding, quickly removing her hand when it crackled dryly at the contact from her finger. They looked, smelled and felt old, immensely old. Not daring to pull one out to look at the title for fear of damaging it, she closed the doors again carefully and moved along to the next cupboard, looking now at weapons crafted from different materials and in different styles. They looked impossibly expensive with precious stone inlays and curly engravings. The last cupboard contained a vast number of documents, assorted pieces of jewellery, delicate-looking musical instruments and strange old contraptions that might have been used for some or other craft at one time.

"Very impressive," Eryn said dutifully. Certainly, these items were delightful to look at, but she did not exactly see what about them was supposed to be so very important that she had to be dragged down here when she would prefer to curse and hurl things about to give vent to her rage at the discovery of so many hungry children.

"Come on," Malhora instructed and closed the first vault door once Eryn had stepped out again. Then she opened the second one. It was larger than the first and packed tightly with what had to be about forty dark, sturdy chests, similar to the ones she stored her clothes in.

"Listen, Grandmother, I appreciate that..."

"Just look inside one," Malhora interrupted her. "Pick any you like. It does not make a difference which."

Eryn obeyed and bent down to lift one unlocked lid and drew in a sharp breath when the light of her lamp was reflected brightly by so many gold slips she didn't even feel able to hazard a very rough guess at their number.

"That's... that's gold! A lot!" she exclaimed and looked at her grandmother wide-eyed. "How much is in there?"

"This chest contains five thousand gold slips."

The younger woman slowly lifted her gaze to the other chests around her, feeling her breath hitch. "How much gold is in here?"

"Two hundred thousand gold slips. This represents the entire amount of Gold House Aren owns. Not counting our estates and other material objects, of course."

"Of course..." Eryn whispered, still staring at the chests. Then she turned towards the door. "Why are you showing me this? I told you that I won't touch Aren gold, no matter how outrageous the amount you possess obviously is."

"Come with me. There is one more I want you to see."

"Alright. Why answer my questions when you can order me around instead?" Eryn grumbled but did as she was told.

"The three vaults on the other side are not important for now. There we store the things other Houses asked us to keep safe for them," Malhora explained and then unlocked the last of the three doors at that side of the cavern. "This here is the vault belonging to the Head of House Aren." She stepped aside and let Eryn enter. It was about as large as the first one with the cupboards inside.

Ten chests of the same design and volume as those in the vault next door stood against the walls. Eryn slowly turned back to her grandmother.

"This belongs to Malriel, does it not?"

"It belongs to the Head of House Aren, as I told you. He or she is entitled to save it or use it for whichever purpose they see appropriate," Malhora explained.

Eryn quickly counted the chests. Ten. "So these are Malriel's private savings? Fifty thousand gold slips?"

"Not Malriel's anymore as long as they are in the Head's vault," she pointed out with a glint in her eyes. "But the amount should be correct, yes."

"So you are saying..." Eryn ventured, hardly daring to put words to it herself.

"I am not saying anything, child. But I would very much like to hear what you have to say. And you had better not start with the words *I am not able*."

* * *

Eryn groaned softly when a hesitant knock at her bedroom door awoke her much too early. She had repaired to bed long after midnight and had for a change been so exhausted that neither gloomy thoughts about Enric nor the baby had managed to prevent her falling asleep mere minutes after lying down.

"What? This better be important or I will kick you, whoever you are!"

The door opened and Orrin stepped in. He looked worried and came closer to sit on her bed, looking down at her.

"Eryn, what exactly were you doing yesterday evening?" he asked patiently. "I was under the impression that you wanted nothing more than take a stroll. I didn't think that you would manage to do anything stupid with your grandmother around, but it seems I underestimated you."

She glared at him, shifting the cushion behind her so she could sit up. "What makes you think I did something stupid?"

"The number of people who are demanding to talk to you immediately to ask you what you think you are doing and to stop it unless you want more trouble than you can handle."

He shook his head when a slow smile spread over her face. "Why do I think that Enric being out of reach is not a good thing?"

"Because you think I am lost without big, strong Enric and that I can't handle things on my own. Now get out of my way, I should dress and talk to the mob. From what I can hear you let them into the house?"

"Be careful, Eryn," the warrior warned her. "There are quite a few Heads of Houses among them. While some of them appear to be more curious than angry, others are obviously quite offended."

She laughed and swung her legs out of bed. "*You* are reminding me to be diplomatic? That doesn't seem very apt somehow, considering how you nearly choked the life out of poor Elwoi and were about to do something similar to Sanaf the other day. Tell them that I will be with them in a few moments."

Orrin nodded reluctantly and left the room so she could dress.

Eryn took her time; it wouldn't do to rush. She would keep them waiting for a few minutes. They had come to her home unannounced and uninvited, they didn't deserve any particularly friendly treatment - quite the opposite. She anticipated this exchange being anything but amiable.

The door opened again, this time without any knock. Malhora stepped inside and smiled grimly.

"Take your time, girl. The Head of House Aren does not hurry without good reason. Having them show up here like this does certainly not qualify as one."

"I had not intended to," the younger woman said and grinned back. Was it wrong to look forward to the confrontation? Probably. But then she was determined to make the best of every opportunity to enjoy herself that came up. She would not drop back into that hole she had all but plummeted into after her arrival in Takhan when she had learned about her true connection to Valrad.

"Will you be with me out there?"

Malhora indicated the negative. "Not if we can avoid it. I will be in the kitchen. Should I hear you struggling, I will join you and support you. But only then. You should be seen to be able to handle this on your own, if possible."

Ah, yes: showing strength, being an Aren. Eryn sighed and slipped into one of Junar's tunics. It was a bit too tight around her breasts, but there was little else that currently fit.

"Any helpful suggestions before I go out there?"

"Nothing much. Just remember that they are wrong and you are right."

Eryn sneered. "That is my default view of the world anyway."

Malhora nodded approvingly and patted her on the back. "That is my girl."

* * *

Several minutes later all eyes darted to the corridor Eryn had stepped out of. The numerous voices stopped their buzzing chatter instantly.

She let her gaze wander through the room, taking in the faces. Legara, Head of House Finran. Belkim, Head of House Turbar. Anfer, Head of House Ulverd. There were a few others she knew to be senators of Houses, but no Heads.

Valrad and Ram'an were present also, but she suspected that they wanted to have an eye on her and make sure nothing went wrong here. If they had a problem with what she had done they would hardly turn up at her house as part of an angry crowd. They would have tried to talk to her in private.

"A good day to all of you," Eryn announced without any particular warmth. "I welcome you to my house, yet I would ask you to send word ahead the next time you intend to visit. I had a long night and could have used a few more hours of sleep."

"Yes, we know about your *long night*," Legara huffed, her arms folded. "We are the ones bearing the consequences, after all. Which is what brings us all here, as you might imagine."

"The consequences," Eryn repeated thoughtfully, walking towards the seating cushions and gratefully accepting Valrad's hand when he helped her sit. "Which dire consequences would those be, pray tell?"

"You know *exactly* which ones I am talking about," Legara growled. "When our servants went to the markets today there was basically nothing left to be purchased! And all that thanks to the new Head of House Aren, we were informed, who saw fit to awaken all the traders in the middle of the night so as to purchase their goods and have them sent to the shanties."

493

Eryn regarded her coldly. "So this is why you are so agitated? Are you hungry, Legara?"

"As a matter of fact, I am! There was no breakfast and neither is there anything available for making lunch with! If we are very lucky we will manage to get enough goods here from the plantations so we can at least scrape together something for dinner! What were you thinking, Maltheá? I know you are new to your current..."

"Shut up."

That one, quietly spoken command did indeed astonish her into silence.

"I see why you are agitated," Eryn began and made sure to look into as many eyes as possible. "Let me tell you something of my evening yesterday. I went out to have a pleasant stroll through this beautiful, very clean city of yours. Imagine my surprise when I went further north than I had ventured before."

She saw some realisation dawning on a few of them as to what had led Eryn to act the way she did.

"So you saw the shanty dwellings for the first time?" a senator asked. "I can see how this might have been a bit of a shock for somebody who has not grown up here, but..."

"I did see them," she cut him short. "It gave me a very nasty shock which also made me very angry. I returned to my residence here, to the luxury I am obviously entitled to due to being born into the right family. Just as every single person in this room. And then I had to remember the children I saw. Arms as thin as sticks, timid, hungry waifs. And I couldn't bear the thought of lying down in my overly large, soft, warm bed while they were squeezed into little more than rude shacks, cold and starving."

She saw several tell-tale glances at her rounded belly and gave them time to reach the conclusion that opposing a pregnant woman when it came to feeding starving children might not be the most reasonable course of action. Especially when the woman in question was Aren by birth, if not by choice, and they happened to be standing in her very own main room without invitation.

"You have come here to air your frustrations, your discontent at being deprived of food for less than a day," she went on. "Not a single one of you - nor your children - is in any danger of suffering any lasting damage from missing your meals, yet you have turned up here to challenge what you no doubt consider some great injustice. I suppose none of you has thought of going out into these marvellously extensive gardens you all possess and plucking a piece of fruit from one of your trees there or collecting a few berries for breakfast, have you? That is because the food in your gardens is for decoration while others are dying from lack of it. Oh, I forgot that you are not used to preparing your own breakfasts, are you? That's work for your servants."

Belkim, Head of House Turbar, lifted his hands in placation. "Now, Maltheá. We understand that your current condition makes you more

494

susceptible to the suffering of children. Also of course you are known to have a weak spot for them, considering your support for orphaned children in Anyueel. Furthermore, you have not been here long enough to fully understand how our society..."

"How your society works?" she interrupted him sharply. "Oh, you are quite wrong there, I have a fairly clear picture of how it works. Ourselves, the privileged ones – privileged through birth, not achievement, mind you – have nearly everything and those who had the bad luck of being born in the shanties are destined to go hungry, boil in the daytime, freeze at night and die from illnesses, injuries and malnourishment. But as long as the rich do not see their possessions or lifestyle endangered, they have no reason to act upon any of it."

"Does this mean you aim to go on like this, buying up all the food and having it sent to the shanties?" a young senator asked with a concerned look on his face, clearly not happy about the lost meals he was already seeing as part of his own future.

"Malriel will skin you alive when she returns and sees how you are spending the Aren fortune," Legara growled. "I even wonder that Malhora permits you to do this."

"Malhora is not the Head of House Aren, I am," Eryn snapped back. "We don't even know if Malriel will ever return. I might be in this position for some while yet." She suppressed a smile at Legara's expression. "Moreover, I have not touched the Aren fortune, nor do I intend to. Not that this is any of your business, mind you. Yet I feel generous since you expressed such concern for my House's prosperity. So I will share a little something with you: the Head of House Aren has her own savings. Let me tell you that they represent a considerable sum. I could probably go on feeding the poor in the city for *years*."

"You have touched Malriel's savings?" Legara whispered in shock. "Her personal savings? What she put aside for decades to buy an estate when she retires?"

Eryn rolled her eyes. "I clearly see your priorities here, Legara. While the idea of depriving House Aren of their hard-earned money seemed to cause nothing more than a little indignation, the thought of spending gold that belongs to one single person is obviously an outrage. Interesting priorities. But I was told that as long as the gold is being held in the place designated for the Head's use, I am entitled to use it as I see fit."

"Maybe we could find a way to deal with what you obviously see as more pressing that leaves the Houses a few bites to eat as well?" Ram'an's amused voice proposed.

"By all means, Arbil, I am all ears," Eryn purred. "Share your ideas, if you have any. We can't allow the Houses to starve, can we?"

"As our plantations are the ones providing the food you enjoy buying and giving away to the poor, I dare say feeding the Houses might make sense to some degree," he replied good-naturedly. "You asked for my ideas though. I really do have a suggestion or two and

495

would be happy to discuss them with you personally before taking them before the Senate. They concern the disposal of surplus food, a tax exemption for donated goods and related things."

Eryn blinked once and worked hard to hide her surprise. She had made the same mistake she tended to make with Orrin. Every time the warrior said something she considered uncommonly intelligent she was taken aback, because her brain simply refused to unify the terms *fighter* and *bright* in the same person. And with Ram'an it was not much different. Here the opposing characteristics seemed to be *modest* and *brilliant*.

She really needed to work on her stereotypes and get rid of the idea that a fighter had to be stupid and a brilliant person arrogant. Though after spending some time with Sarol not drifting back to that perception was definitely a challenge.

"I would be delighted to discuss this with you and see if your ideas align with what I hope to accomplish," she acknowledged gracefully.

"Thank you, Eryn," Ram'an smiled and bowed.

"Is there anything else you wish to discuss? I have to say that I am rather hungry myself and intend to take a stroll through the garden and collect my breakfast personally."

She watched the Heads of Houses and senators exchanging doubtful glances. They had just been dismissed, that much was clear. Had they achieved what they had come to? They had told her that they did not agree with her actions, hadn't they? And that they would not like it at all if she continued this way.

Yet when it came to her reaction, appraising the situation was less simple. She had not exactly seemed contrite nor had she promised never to do it again. Actually, the opposite was the case. She had come right back with attacks and arguments that would make anybody who contradicted her seem greedy and heartless. But then fighting with a very obviously pregnant woman was not right at all, was it? And then she was an Aren. One never knew what an angry Aren might do if pushed.

They slowly moved towards the stairs that led to the exit, avoiding eye contact with each other.

"We shall talk about this at the next Senate meeting," Legara announced by way of summary.

"Yes, we shall. Ram'an just said that, didn't he?" Eryn replied in an exasperated voice that earned the Head of House Finran a few indulgent smiles.

Malhora returned from the kitchen when everyone but Valrad and Ram'an had departed the house.

"Well done, Eryn. We will yet make a Head of House of you." The old woman put a bowl with sliced fruit in front of her. "I took the liberty of raiding the garden for your breakfast. We cannot have you going hungry. Eat up and feed your son."

Eryn looked up to her father. "Anything you would like to say to this muddle? You were very quiet just now."

Valrad sat next to her and took her hand to squeeze it. "I did not come here to join the others, but you."

She leaned her head against his shoulder for a moment. "I know. You made that fairly clear to everyone present when you were standing behind me after you helped me sit." She then looked at Ram'an, who had taken a seat on her other side. "And you. When did you come up with these ideas?"

"I locked myself in my study for two hours after I learned that there was no food available in any of the markets and the reason for that. I knew that I would need something tangible to pacify either your visitors or, well - you."

Eryn leaned forward to kiss his cheek and lean her forehead against his for a moment. "Thank you. I mean it. I am glad you are on my side." Then she sunk back again and shook her head tiredly. "Why has nobody ever done anything to change how people have to live in these shanty settlements? You obviously all know about it, so why does nobody care?"

Ram'an and Valrad stared at each other for a while, before the latter ventured, "We grew up knowing that there were people who had more and others who had less. It has always been the way the world works."

Ram'an sighed. "I suppose sometimes it takes a fresh perspective, somebody who has not grown up accepting things the way we have."

Eryn pressed her lips together. She didn't want to accuse them or make them feel bad about themselves. Or about her. Yet she couldn't help asking herself how it was possible that people could be raised to believe that it was perfectly acceptable to have children starving on what was basically their doorstep.

Ved'al had been raised here, and he had taught her that watching others go without food and shelter was not something to shrug off or accept as part of how the world was meant to be.

She imagined him at her side at this very moment, fighting together with her the injustice he had taught her to reject. But that was nonsense, of course. If Ved'al were still alive, they would have incarcerated or even killed him had they managed to take him back to the Western Territories.

She missed him, almost painfully so. She hadn't felt that particular stab in a while. He might not have been the one to father her, but he had definitely been a kindred spirit.

CHAPTER 38

Charitable Outreaches

Eryn let the message sink and shook her head in disbelief before handing the sheet of paper to Malhora to read.

They were sitting on the terrace while the setting sun was bathing their surroundings in a gentle orange glow.

"I need to react to that somehow, don't I? Or am I supposed to let her do this because of the alliance between our Houses? I have started to wonder what kind of ally Legara really is, though. Surely not the supportive kind," Eryn growled.

The old woman nodded and smiled when Junar joined them after having bathed her daughter.

"What do you need to react to?" the seamstress enquired. "Or is this all secret House business I am not supposed to know about?"

"House business it is, but not exactly secret," Eryn sighed and grimaced when she felt another kick from her inside. "Legara has made Sanaf's punishment public knowledge."

"I take it you don't agree with that? What's the trouble? Too lax or too harsh?"

"You tell me. She declares that she is going to send him away from the city to manage one of their estates somewhere for the next five years. For the first three years his wages will be taken from him and invested in the public good."

Junar stared at her in dismay. "What? That's all? A position on a bloody *estate* where he can spend his days pointing his fingers and have others do his bidding? You can't mean it!"

"Unfortunately, it's true. And now I have to decide whether to swallow the insult in favour of preserving what's left of the alliance between the Houses following Malriel's departure, or I have to speak up at the next Senate meeting. Which happens to be tomorrow." Eryn turned to Malhora. "I assume there is a rule that allows me as the

498

wronged party to object to the punishment given to the culprit if I don't agree with it for some reason?"

"There is," the old woman nodded. "It is something I recommend you make use of. The alliance with House Finran as it is now is more of a burden than an asset anyway. We obviously cannot rely on them any longer. Ram'an will be on your side. His House was to be incriminated wrongly, after all. He will not be any happier about this than you."

Eryn let her head fall back and moaned. "As if this damned meeting tomorrow won't be heated enough with what I am going to propose there. Now I have to deal with that annoying creature as well."

"Nobody ever said that being Head of House was easy," Malhora shrugged unimpressed. "And I suspect that Legara is trying to see how far she can go when dealing with you. She never had a chance against Malriel and probably hopes to have it easier with you."

"But I thought Malriel and her were friends?" Eryn frowned.

"They are now. Legara worked out quite swiftly that she was no match for your mother. We have a saying here: If you cannot beat your opponents, attempt to join them."

"A friendship of convenience? Why would Malriel want that? What about the proud Arens? Or do they just avoid being defeated by falling for insincere offers of friendship?"

Her grandmother sighed. "My girl, there is the principle of having others vote with you. A House's current strength depends very much on its allies. Legara was not only convenient, but also easy to win over. They have known each other since they were girls, and being the only two female Heads of Houses at that age was another connection. But Malriel is not stupid. I am telling you in all honesty that she knows well enough how far she can trust Legara."

"So it won't even annoy her when she returns and sees that I challenged her cousin?"

"No, I imagine she will not even be particularly surprised at it," Malhora shrugged, then smiled. "I am sorry, but not provoking your mother through going against Legara is a downside you will have to accept."

* * *

Vran'el was about to push up his sleeves, but stopped and scoffed when Enric admonished him, "You know well enough that we are not supposed to expose our skin here in this part of Pirinkar. This is where that strange, sleep-inducing insect species breed is endemic to. We were warned repeatedly to avoid getting bitten."

The lawyer sighed in defeat and tugged the sleeves back down.

"I feel like I am melting inside my clothes. How is this possible? It is a lot hotter in the desert, but I have never in my life sweated as profusely as here in this place! Should riding in the shade of these trees not be cool and pleasant?"

"No, not with the humidity here. The heat in the desert is the dry kind. This is damp heat."

"Obviously," Vran'el snorted. "This is completely topsy-turvy. I mean, one side of the mountain range there is nothing, just sand and nearly no vegetation at all. And here, only a few hours further north we are surrounded by this sultry abundance. Incredible." He lifted a finger when Enric opened his mouth to speak. "Please, if you were about to, do not offer me a lecture on the mountains being high enough to stop the moist air from entering the desert and forming clouds that release their water on this side. You may have read plenty of books, but we here also try to educate our children thoroughly."

"What a strange thing to say to a citizen of a country you consider barbaric and backward," Enric chuckled.

"Well, we probably have changed our perception slightly after meeting a few of you. Even if you had not managed to open our minds to the chance that your Kingdom might be a little less... underdeveloped than we had thought, Vern would have changed that for sure. Gifted boy if ever I met one."

Enric pulled out Ram'an's notebook and turned a few pages. "We should soon get clear of this forest. Ram'an writes that it did not take them more than half a day to cross it, and we already have a few hours behind us."

"Good. Never in my life would I have thought that I would be cursing an overabundance of water one day. Here it even permeates the air. My clothes must be at least twice as heavy as before I put them on."

"Stop complaining, Vran. It could be worse, really. It could be freezing."

"That would not be worse at all! We could put on clothes against the cold, but we cannot take anything off for fear of falling prey to those insects."

Enric didn't reply to that. Vran'el obviously needed to air his frustration about the unfamiliar weather conditions, and he didn't mind listening to it if it helped him.

He felt a faint stab of annoyance through the mind bond and smiled. It was no intense emotion that worried him, more like her usual dissatisfaction at minor things that were not working out the way she had planned them.

During the day she was doing remarkably well when it came to dealing with her feelings, but at night he sensed how lost and lonely she felt, how abandoned. It tore at his heart and last night he had for the first time shielded against the emotions or they would have kept him awake even longer, and he needed his sleep and strength to take care of the task ahead of him as quickly as possible. And to return home to her.

* * *

Eryn grimaced when her lower back gave her a twinge in complaint, and applied a little bit of soothing magic to make the pain go away. The baby was growing well, but the load was a strain to carry around all day for her body. She wondered if she would even be able to walk around unaided in another month.

Ram'an looked up from his breakfast bowl. "Is everything alright, Theá, dear? You look displeased."

"Not displeased as such. It's a mix of apprehension, dread, anticipation and excitement."

"A little contrary," he commented.

Orrin and Vern finished their breakfast at the same time and both bent forward to place their empty bowls on the low table.

"You had better lay these papers aside for now and get on with your breakfast," the warrior instructed. "We need to leave here in less than half an hour and you are not even dressed yet. Well, not properly for a Senate meeting," he amended with another look at her attire.

"Pregnancy privilege," she just shrugged but put the papers aside. "And I tend to dribble when I eat a lot these days, so dressing properly before breakfast is futile in my case."

"What do you think how the Senate will react to your plans?" Vern asked curiously.

"Let me put it this way: it certainly is an advantage that I am pregnant, otherwise some of them might be tempted to kick me out the door and down the stairs."

"That bad?" the boy grimaced.

"I am not counting on much support, to be honest. But Ram'an tells me that I don't really need it. As I am utilising what are technically my own funds for a purpose that is not against the law, there is little they can do to stop me. And then there are at least two Heads of Houses on my side, so I won't be completely alone." She smiled at Ram'an. "It's good to have powerful friends who like to indulge me." She put aside her bowl and let Orrin pull her to her feet.

"If you would excuse me now, gentlemen, I had better get myself properly attired."

When she returned to the main room little later, the men had already cleared away the remainders of the breakfast and were standing by the stairs, chatting amongst themselves while waiting for her. Ram'an had collected her notes and returned them to the file they had put together and that she would take to the meeting with her.

"Is Junar still asleep?"

"Yes. Téa had a restless night, and from what I remember Junar returned to bed only in the early morning hours," Orrin explained.

"And Malhora? I would have expected her to be here bustling around, warning me not to disgrace the family by showing any weakness or similar. She is not normally the type to sleep in. At least from what I have seen since she arrived here."

"That she isn't," the warrior confirmed. "She left the house before you got up and warned me to make sure to get you to the Senate in time."

"Where has she gone, then?"

"She mumbled something about scaring a few people by turning up early." He shook his head. "The women in this family are indeed rather... special," he concluded carefully.

"Right," Eryn smirked. "And don't you forget it."

"How could I? We currently live under the same roof."

They stepped out into the refreshing morning air and moved on towards the city centre, the streets around them bustling with activity.

When they had reached the Senate building, Eryn looked up at the stairs. Was it only her or did they seem steeper every time she came here?

Vern and Orrin both offered her an arm, but she declined and instead infused her leg muscles with a little magic.

"That's sweet of you both, but the almighty Aren Head can't be seen being led into the hall like a geriatric. You remember? Invincible warrior queen with frightening temper? Hanging on to your arms would destroy that image completely. And Malhora would give me an earful."

"Warrior queen?" Vern chuckled and shook his head. "I'll keep that in mind."

The hall was about as full as on the day when she'd had Sanaf questioned. People knew that something was probably about to happen and wanted to be there to watch. They knew it had something to do with the poor and that woman who was familiar by sight due to her resemblance to Malriel, but a lot stranger in her behaviour.

Malhora had already taken her seat on one of the two chairs reserved for the Aren senators and nodded at her granddaughter.

"You certainly have an audience. We will see if this works out in your favour," the old woman stated without any greeting.

Orrin and Vern had found a spot among the observers that afforded them a good view. The seats for visitors were all taken.

She turned when she heard Valrad's voice behind her.

"Good morning, Eryn. How are you doing? You look tired."

"I had a few rather long nights, but I hope that after today the worst will be over." She thought for a moment. "Or is only about to start. We will see."

Her father squeezed her hand and returned to his seat when the three triarchs entered the hall and marched on to their seats on the pedestal. Both the senators and the people in the back fell silent a few moments later.

Torke'na was again the one to rise and speak. Eryn wondered briefly if she was the official spokesperson of the three or if it was just a practice that had established itself in the course of time, then returned to concentrating on her words.

"A good morning to all of you. You were all informed of the punishment Legara of House Finran has seen fit to set for Sanaf of House Finran, after he owned up here before the Senate to purposely endangering five people, among them two expectant women and a young man who barely survived after having been locked in his room. He furthermore was shown to have paid for House Arbil to be incriminated wrongly so as to disrupt a long-standing alliance between the two Houses." Her gaze wandered to Eryn for a short but telling moment before gliding over the other senators. "Is there any objection to the sanctions Legara considers appropriate for these offences? Namely that of sending Sanaf to one of the Finran estates and having him take over the administration for five years, and in addition denying payment of his wages for the first three years instead to be submitted as additions to the taxes House Finran pays?"

Eryn felt a surge of triumph go through her. The triarch was clearly anything but satisfied with this penalty and was not afraid to communicate it, even though she was not in a position to object to it as she was not among the wronged parties in this case. She felt Malhora's nudge at her side and cleared her throat.

It would be wrong to say that all eyes were suddenly focussed on her. They had been shortly after Torke'na had commenced speaking. Even if she had decided against speaking up and accepting the ridiculous sentence for Sanaf, she would have had to rethink that decision right now, when everybody expected her to do what Arens were known to be good at: getting back at those who insulted them.

"I object to what Legara obviously considers appropriate measures," Eryn said calmly.

"So do I," Ram'an spoke up from the other side of the room, equally composed.

Not a single face showed any sign of surprise, she noted. Not even Legara's.

"What about the measures in particular do you question?" Torke'na enquired, a hint of satisfaction in her narrowed eyes.

"The brevity of the term for both the confiscation of his wages and his exclusion from the city. And the level of hardship of the duty she intends to assign to him. Or rather, the lack of any rigour."

"Ram'an, what are your objections?"

"I fully agree with Maltheá and have nothing else to add."

Torke'na nodded once, then addressed all representatives of the Houses. "Does the Senate acknowledge these objections as just and reasonable? Show of hands."

Eryn watched as most senators raised their hand without hesitation. Even House Roal, which was a known adversary of House Aren, agreed.

"This is a clear majority and the punishment of Sanaf of House Finran will thus be subjected to some... amendment," Torke'na stated, back to her usual unflappable demeanour. "Malthea, I assume you have suggestions pertaining to this?"

"I do." She wondered briefly if she was expected to get up from her chair from this, but then decided against it. She had not been asked to do so and taking the trouble unprompted would show a degree of reverence that would spoil rather than aid her efforts. She was not making a request, but a demand here.

"Appointing the culprit to a position of power over others is not my understanding of punishment. I therefore demand a more humble position for the offender, one that does not consist of tasks to be taken care of from behind a comfortable desk, but of carrying out actual manual labour on the estate. My second objection concerns the duration of five years. I demand ten years instead, both for his confinement to the duties and the confiscation of his wages for use toward the common good. My third and last objection is about the location of the punishment. I do not agree with sending him to a Finran estate as I believe that he will be treated with more clemency than I feel is warranted. This brings me to my last demand that will not only ensure that his time away from the city is anything but a holiday but also compensate House Aren for the damage the man inflicted. I want Sanaf of House Finran to work at one of the Aren estates, namely that which Malhora is in charge of."

The reactions were mixed, both among the senators and the observers, she noted. Some grimaced in sympathy for Sanaf, others smirked gleefully, a few whispered and nodded, while Legara visibly clenched her teeth and tightened her lips across her teeth until they were no more than a thin, almost white line.

Torke'na's gaze rested on a very content-looking Malhora for a moment before it switched to Ram'an. "Do you concur with these suggestions, Head of House Arbil? You are within your rights to wish for one part of the sentence to be carried out on one of your own estates."

Ram'an smiled and shook his head, looking at Malhora. "I agree with Malthea's demands and have nothing to add. I am confident that Malhora is the person best suited to supervise the punishment."

That statement caused quite a few hands hastily covering mouths to obscure smiles, with a clearing of throats and nervous coughs that very likely saw birth as chuckles.

The triarch nodded and then turned to the other senators. "Does the Senate agree with the punishment Malthea of House Vel'kim, Head of House Aren and Ram'an, Head of House Arbil demand? Do you declare the measures they propose as just and reasonable?"

Eryn felt how her muscles let go of part of their tension at the sight of what was clearly more than half the senators raising their hands. Even those Houses allied with Finran were discontented with how Legara spurned those she was supposed to be connected with.

Torke'na nodded. "Then it is hereby officially granted. Legara, you will inform Sanaf of the terms of his sentence. As the Senate has voted in favour of it, his only chance to lodge an objection is through appeal to the triarchy."

"Although I would tell him not to trouble himself with that, if I were you. To be perfectly frank, it would be a waste of his time and ours," Golir added with a thin smile.

Legara nodded stiffly. "When will he be sent away?"

"Tomorrow. Tell him to be ready to be escorted from his home in the morning," Torke'na replied, then wrote something on a sheet of paper in front of her before raising her head again. "I was informed that there is another matter the Senate wishes to address." She looked down at Eryn. "It concerns certain, hmm... charitable efforts House Aren seems to be embracing lately."

Eryn nodded and rose, lifting herself with the help of the armrests of her chair. "I ask for permission to step before the Senate."

"Permission granted."

She walked towards the centre of the semicircle, taking her time, letting them take in the sight of her and looking at them in return. The first item about Sanaf's punishment had not affected them directly, this latest item would.

"As most of you are aware by now, my discovery of the shanty settlements in the north and northeast of the city two days ago were an unpleasant shock for me. My reaction to beholding underfed and freezing children was one I would say is the natural one: feeding them."

It became silent in the large hall, everybody wanted to hear what would come next. Her voice was calm, her words paced. This was not about accusing people, but presenting to them a scheme that she hoped would make up for at least a part of their own negligence in the past. Accusing them directly would make them oppose her, and this she wanted to avoid.

"My actions, however, have caused a certain disquiet among many of you. I do not wish to apologise for those actions. I rather consider them a way to shake us all from our slumber, make us aware that there is a problem, even if the wealthy among us have been raised to dismiss it as simply one of those things that are just the natural order," she went on, careful to include herself. She needed to convey an impression of them being on the same side.

"I am eager to avoid such disagreements in the future. Neither do I wish to deprive your families of food, as you will certainly be relieved to hear." A few smiles. "However, let me make clear to you that witnessing this outrageous situation of children who go hungry through no fault of their own is not anything I can continue to live with." She lifted her chin. "It is a disgrace for any society to treat its children this way."

"So you are about to bestow upon all the poor children the exact privileges your own son is entitled to?" Legara snapped back, arms folded. "How else do you intend to reach that state of equality that seems to be your driving concern? I suspect that the boy growing inside you will grow up enjoying rather a lot of luxury himself. Or am I mistaken about that?"

Splendid, Eryn thought and returned to her breathing exercises to stay calm, now Legara had taken the first chance at revenge: sabotaging the launch of her project. But that couldn't be helped now. She hoped people here would identify it as nothing more than Legara's need to get back at her.

"I am not talking about equality here, Legara," she replied without rancour, "That would obviously be a huge step from fighting for survival. What I am talking about is covering basic needs such as food, clothing and - unless we want to watch another generation of criminals grow up at our doorstep - education." She glared at Legara. "Of course my son will grow up in luxury; all doors will be open for him, both on this and the other side of the sea that separates our two countries. Yet this does not mean that I consider seeing the suffering of others, who simply happened to be born to the wrong – meaning impoverished – parents an adequate price to pay for it."

"What do you propose to do about it, then? Just for argument's sake," a senator of House Uvel asked indulgently. "If you wish to use up all your gold through sending food to the shanties, this is your decision entirely. But we would certainly have to increase the food supply for the city."

Yes, she thought grimly, feeling the bile rising in her throat. It's acceptable for others to go hungry, but not you, is it?

"Sending food there may for now avoid the imminent danger of starvation, but hardly the problems with cold and the lack of education. Most of you have heard about the efforts in Anyueel we have made to give homeless children a refuge. This is what I want to do here as well."

"And who is to pay for this refuge, if I may ask? Both for the building and the running costs of such an establishment?" asked another senator, with a deeply suspicious frown as if he feared for his precious tax money being used on such a scheme.

"For the establishment of such a place *I* will be the one to pay." She waited for the murmuring to die down again. She heard the words *Malriel's savings* uttered several times. "The day to day costs of keeping it running will be borne by House Aren for as long as they can afford." She half turned and looked up to the three triarchs. "In exchange for the tax relief I hope to negotiate for my House." She saw Golir raise his brow before she turned back to her audience.

"So what exactly do you intend to do, clear the shanties and build proper houses there?" a female voice from among the senators asked.

"No," she replied and felt like she was arguing against a wall, "this is not what I intend. I have already bought a building for that purpose. Yesterday, to be precise."

She saw how Enkil, the Head of House Feral started to gasp for air. He had been the former proprietor.

"What?" he exclaimed. "You cannot really expect to do this! It is in the middle of the trading district!"

Eryn felt fury rising inside her and swallowed to keep the angry words inside. They had been expecting to keep the problem out of sight, away from their precious, clean surroundings that were only meant to be enjoyed for those of means.

Legara now rose from her seat, palms flat on the surface of the table in front of her. "You are not really planning on bringing these young criminals into the heart of the city?"

"Young criminals? I wasn't aware that being poor was viewed as a crime here," Eryn snapped back, feeling her patience wearing thin quickly. She wondered how long concentrated breathing would work to keep her below boiling point.

"They are thieves, they sell forbidden substances, can be hired as goons and thugs for all manner of crimes!" Legara exclaimed agitatedly.

"Like the goon Sanaf hired to take revenge on me for his own incompetence? I don't see that the moral standing of *some* Houses is in any great danger here." Eryn's saw the words hit their mark like the tails of a whiplash.

"How dare you! You do not even qualify as one of us!" Legara had gone pale, her hands tightened into fists.

"Which is my fault, of course, isn't it? Because being taken away from here by my... by Ved'al was something I could have avoided easily, couldn't I? Claiming that I was but five years old at that time would be a feeble excuse for sure! Just like saying that a hungry person who makes use of whatever means is available to feed themselves is a victim of circumstances rather than free choice, isn't it?" Eryn was breathing somewhat heavily now, her voice had become shriller and she felt the hairs on her arms standing up. That preposterous, arrogant idiot, how dare *she,* of all people? She felt her fingertips begin to tingle with an unfamiliar urge to slap this woman full across her face, cause her physical pain, and then revel in it afterwards.

"They would come in contact with our own children, be there when we are on our way to work or meet friends! Whatever justification you give for their crimes, criminals they still are!" Legara had taken to screaming her replies.

"So is that bloody member of your House who almost killed my friend!" Eryn rasped back, feeling how something had clenched within. "How dare you - of all people - accuse others of criminal behaviour! You yourself were protecting a member of your House after all he did! You were sheltering a known criminal in your own ranks! I say shame on you and pity on those who are subjected to your flawed leadership!" She felt as if rage was radiating off her in simmering, almost tangible waves of energy.

She didn't notice the commotion around her when people's attention switched to the high domed ceiling and the dust that seemed to be falling from there.

"I want to see how long you are able to hold on to your moral high ground, to be a law-abiding citizen in a city that offered nothing to you when you were hungry and freezing cold! I want to see you when the question most pressing is one of survival, when adhering to the so noble principles of the rich and powerful is a lethal luxury you simply cannot afford! You maintain your own wealth by taking more than you are eligible for, stealing from those who have nothing!"

She sensed more than saw Golir leaping up from his seat before he barked, "Maltheá!"

Only then did she realise, in her ember-hot rage, what was happening around her. People had sprung up from their seats and were hurrying towards the three exits while the air was thick with ochre coloured dust.

Her eyes flicked up to the domed ceiling. It was crumbling. Pieces broke away and fell down only to stop in mid-air. She stared at the levitating pieces of plaster, then realised that there had to be a shield in place to protect the people in the hall. Golir's.

Had she done that? Her throat tightened. Had she just endangered a large room full of people because she had lost control of her fury? Her wide, panicked eyes snapped to Malhora, who was watching the roof crumble with the air of an interested, but uninvolved, bystander. As if not just the very roof over her head was in the process of collapsing in on itself. She seemed like an unreal point of calm among people around her who were panicking towards the nearest opening.

Malhora's gaze fell on her granddaughter and she smiled faintly. Only moments later her expression grew serious and she got up to walk towards her granddaughter to take her arm.

Eryn turned her head as if in trance when she felt another hand on her second arm. Valrad.

"Come, Eryn. Time to go."

"Go? Where?" she whispered, lost. All coherent thought seemed to have abandoned her, as if the after effects of her rage and the enormity of what she had just unintentionally unleashed were too much for her over-taxed brain.

"To the clinic, my girl," Valrad explained with the quiet seriousness of a medical professional who knew that losing the grip on himself was unhelpful to both of them. "Your waters just broke."

Slowly, she looked down at the puddle of clear, slightly pink liquid around her feet.

"That... it's too soon! I have six more weeks to go!" she exclaimed.

"No, you do not. You only have a few more hours left," Valrad corrected her patiently and started walking, his arm now around her shoulders, easing her forwards.

New panic kindled itself and almost choked her. This was too early! And she was not prepared sufficiently for it! There was so much she had wanted to read beforehand, procedures she had intended to familiarise herself with...

"I haven't got through all my books yet!" she wailed.

Valrad rubbed her shoulder reassuringly. "That is alright, my girl. Our colleagues at the clinic have."

They had descended the steps about halfway when they heard behind them the deafening rumble of a cupola weighing several tons being eased into a controlled collapse.

* * *

Enric whistled through his teeth when the city of Kar, the capital to the country of Pirinkar, came into view after they had passed the woods. There were still about two more hours' ride ahead, so they had ample opportunity to take in the impressive sight.

Exactly as in Takhan, there was no wall to protect the city from would-be attackers. Here, however, a wall was not necessary since there was a large lake following the city's limits that served as a natural barrier.

Nonetheless, that made poisoning the water supply for the entire city very straightforward, the strategist in Enric concluded without further thought. He pushed away the gruesome notion and returned to taking in the details that could be perceived from a distance.

The buildings did not appear as varied in size or shape as in Anyueel, nor as uniformly coloured as in Takhan. He caught glimpses of blue, red, yellow, different shades of brown, green and grey - like a garden comprised of buildings.

He thought back to what he had read about this place and what little Vran'el had been able to tell him. He suddenly stopped his horse and closed his eyes.

"What?" Vran'el gripped his arm. "Say something!"

"Anger," Enric blurted out and quickly raised a mind shield to block out this incredibly violent flood of emotion. He couldn't remember ever having received something that intense from her previously. "And a lot of it."

Had it been fear, he would have turned his horse around in that very moment and returned to Takhan at once. *Fear* of such an intensity could have meant only one thing: an imminent danger of death.

Her brother nodded cautiously. "Alright, anger is not so bad, is it? It means that she is not the one in trouble, but most likely causing serious difficulties for somebody else."

Enric exhaled once he had dulled the sensation. He couldn't shield it entirely - the barrier just raised the threshold but did not interrupt the connection completely when emotions were that powerful.

"Better now? Would you like to take a break?"

"No, it's alright, let's move on. It's a lot easier to manage now. I can feel how the rage is becoming less intense with every moment."

He gasped when a brief sensation of panic reached him. What was going on back in Takhan? Was nobody with her to take care of her? Why else would she be that afraid?

He forced himself to ride on. His gaze was no longer on the impressive sight of Kar, but on the ground, concentrating on the emotions he was receiving.

A few minutes later the panic became weaker as well and he felt profound relief. Whatever had bothered her that much seemed to be over at this time.

Yet only a moment later a sensation of searing agony, like a stab with a knife, took his breath away, making even crying out impossible. It was agonising and powerful enough to make him topple over, causing him to slip out of his saddle and land hard on the trail of packed dirt.